Following the Eagle

ISBN-10: 1-4196-7021-2

ISBN-13: 978-1-4196-7021-3

LCCN: 2008901938

Cover design by Tom Butsch

Interior formatting design by
Rend Graphics 2007
www.rendgraphics.com

Published by:
BookSurge Publishing.
www.booksurge.com

To order additional copies, please visit:
www.amazon.com

For my mother, Grace
and in memory of my father, Carl
and my good friend, Scott Weldin

Acknowledgements

I am grateful to everyone whose time, expertise and encouragement helped in the creation of this book.

In the course of my research travels I was fortunate to make the acquaintance of any number of knowledgeable, friendly people, including Park Rangers George Elmore, Pete Bethke, Tony Cyphers, and George Butler at Fort Larned, Kansas, Evelyn Cox at the Old Cahawba Historical Site, Katie Mulkerne at the Bragg-Mitchell house in Mobile, Alabama, Barbara Dey at the Colorado Historical Society, Sandra Lowry at the Fort Laramie Library, Warren Newman of the Cody Firearms Museum/Buffalo Bill Historical Center, and the rangers at Chickamauga/Chattanooga National Military Park. Locally, I couldn't have done it without assistance from research librarian Sara Barnicle who provided not only the information I requested, but other fascinating tidbits.

My thanks to Mr. Albert White Hat, Sr. at Sinte Gleska University who corrected my attempts at translation and supplied the Lakota for Ethan's story of the eagle, which was adapted from "How the Sioux Came to Be" (*American Indian Myths & Legends*, Richard Erdoes and Alfonso Ortiz). And to Dr. Lawrence & Betty Hart, at the Cheyenne Cultural Center for introducing me to Lenora Hart who provided not only translations to Southern Cheyenne, but much appreciated insight and advice. Any errors in translation are my own, and for them, I apologize.

Many thanks to my readers, Martin Benson, Margaret Brewer, Heather Gray, Steve Guest, Caitlin Guyan, Lyn Ianuzzi, Kathy Jenkins, Janet Mebust and Rosalind Wagner for their astute comments and criticisms. To Vicky Bijur and Alyson Hagy who took time to read, comment and advise, and to David Rambo for pointing me toward publication.

Most especially, I would like to thank Monique L'Heureux for tirelessly reading and re-reading my manuscript, for her constructive comments and ruthless editing. And above all, my husband, Ted Carlsson for his companionship on my travels and his unending support. You are always there for me.

While many of the historical events, people and places described in this book are based on fact, and despite a concerted effort to make the reader believe otherwise, it remains a work of fiction.

Characters
* denotes fictional character

Ethan Fraser*
Joshua Fraser* – his half-brother
Sarah Fraser* (Pine Leaf) – his mother
James Fraser* – his father
Kate Fraser* – his sister
Alice Fraser* – his sister-in-law
Peter Scott* – friend of Josh, suitor to Alice

Georgia / Alabama / Tennessee
Braxton Bragg – CSA, Commander of the Army of Tennessee; fought at Perryville, Stones River, Chickamauga, Chattanooga
General Leonidas Polk – CSA, second in command to General Bragg at Perryville; urged Bragg's replacement after Stones River; removed from command, ordered court-martialed by Bragg after Chickamauga; reinstated by Jefferson Davis, killed during the Atlanta campaign June 14, 1864, at Pine Mountain, Georgia; Episcopal bishop
Captain Howard Henderson – CSA, commandant at Cahaba Prison; Methodist minister
Sergeant Shunk* – CSA, guard at Cahaba Prison
Rat-Face* – CSA, guard at Cahaba Prison
The Harelip* – CSA, guard at Cahaba Prison

Sergeant Thomas Murray* – USA, 36th Illinois, J Company
Corporal Zachariah Fisk* – USA, 36th Illinois, J Company
Private Fergus Connolly* – USA, 36th Illinois, J Company
Private Frank Myers* – USA, 36th Illinois, A Company
General Joseph Jones Reynolds – USA, Chief of Staff of the Army of the Cumberland at Chattanooga
Captain Sanford C. Kellogg – USA, aide and nephew to General Thomas
Captain Frederick Johnson* – USA, lawyer
General John Converse Starkweather – USA, fought at Perryville, Stones River, Chickamauga (wounded) and Chattanooga; lawyer
Archie Gilles* – southern merchant and Union sympathizer
Rebecca Gilles* – his daughter

Mobile
Elizabeth Magrath* – a wealthy widow
Isaac* – Elizabeth's butler, house servant
Hannah* – Elizabeth's maid, house servant
Josiah* – Elizabeth's stable hand, handyman
Hattie* – Elizabeth's cook
Rose* – her daughter

Kansas/Colorado Territory
Henri Broulat* – mixed-blood Cheyenne; Indian trader
Micah Broulat* – his son, mixed-blood Cheyenne
Feathered Bear* – Micah's uncle

Wind Woman* – Micah's aunt; first wife of Feathered Bear
Plum Moon Woman* – Micah's aunt; second wife of Feathered Bear
Singing Bird* – Micah's cousin; daughter of Feathered Bear and Plum Moon Woman
Tall Grass Woman* – Micah's widowed sister-in-law
Girl Who Laughs* – her daughter
Red Hand* – Cheyenne warrior
Two Bulls* – Cheyenne warrior
Black Coyote* – Cheyenne warrior
Black Kettle – Cheyenne chief; friend of the whites; to Washington in 1863; negotiator for peace
Lone Bear (called One Eye by the whites) – one of Black Kettle's sub-chiefs
Starving Bear (called Lean Bear by the whites) – Cheyenne chief; friend of the whites; to Washington in 1863
William Bent – trader, established Bent's Fort in 1833 with his brother, Charles and Ceran St. Vrain; married Owl Woman, daughter of Gray Thunder, keeper of the Medicine Arrows; friend of and negotiator for the Cheyenne
George Bent – mixed-blood son of William Bent and Owl Woman
Julia Bent – his sister
Robert Bent – his brother
Charley Bent – his half-brother; son of William Bent and Yellow Woman
Edmond Guerrier – mixed-blood Cheyenne; married to Julia Bent
John Simpson Smith (called Blackfoot by the Cheyenne) – Indian trader, interpreter
Jack Smith – his son; mixed-blood Cheyenne

Nancy Jane Morton – captured by the Cheyenne near Plum Creek Station, August 8, 1864
Laura Roper – captured by Cheyenne and Arapaho at the Little Blue River settlement, August 8, 1864
Colonel John Chivington – moved to Denver in 1860 as presiding elder of the First Methodist Episcopal church; appointed commanding colonel of the military district of Colorado in 1862
Major Edward Wynkoop – appointed captain of Company A when the Colorado First Regiment was formed; promoted to major when Chivington was appointed colonel
Major Scott Anthony – a cousin of Susan B. Anthony, became commander at Fort Larned in August 1864

Washington, D.C.
Edmund Stedman – pardon clerk to Attorney General Edward Bates

Idaho Territory (Wyoming, Montana)
Black Wolf* – Pine Leaf's older brother
Brings the Buffalo* – Ethan's aunt; Black Wolf's first wife
Chases As She Walks* – Ethan's aunt; Black Wolf's second wife
Moccasin Woman* – Ethan's aunt; Black Wolf's third wife following the death of his brother, Bone Necklace
Spotted Horse* – Ethan's cousin; son of Black Wolf and Brings the Buffalo
Standing Elk* – Ethan's cousin; son of Black Wolf and Chases As She Walks
Fat Bear* – Ethan's cousin; son of Black Wolf and Chases As She Walks
Long Face* – Ethan's cousin; son of Black Wolf and Chases As She Walks

Bone Necklace* – Ethan's cousin; son of Bone Necklace and Moccasin Woman
Kicking Bird* – Ethan's cousin; son of Bone Necklace and Moccasin Woman

W. G. Bullock – sutler at Fort Laramie

Lieutenant Henry Bretney – in command Company G, 11th Ohio Volunteer Cavalry
Lieutenant Caspar Collins – second in command Company G, 11th Ohio Volunteer Cavalry; son of Colonel William Collins
Lieutenant James Hanna – Company L, 11th Ohio Volunteer Cavalry
Sergeant Hervey Merwin – Company G, 11th Ohio Volunteer Cavalry, in charge of the howitzer
Private John Friend – Company G, 11th Ohio Volunteer Cavalry; telegraph operator

Colonel Thomas Moonlight – 11th Kansas Volunteer Cavalry; arrived Fort Laramie April 9, 1865; command suspended by General Connor after "a series of blunders" in dealing with the Indians
Corporal Henry Grimm – Company K, 11th Kansas Volunteer Cavalry
Major Martin Anderson – 11th Kansas Volunteer Cavalry, arrived at Platte Bridge Station from Fort Laramie July 16, 1865; ordered Lieutenant Bretney and all his men except four in charge of the howitzer to relocate to Sweetwater Station
Lieutenant William Drew – Company I, 11th Kansas Volunteer Cavalry
Lieutenant George Walker – Company I, 11th Kansas Volunteer Cavalry
Captain James Greer – Company I, 11th Kansas Volunteer Cavalry

Captain A. Smith Lybe – 6th U.S. Infantry

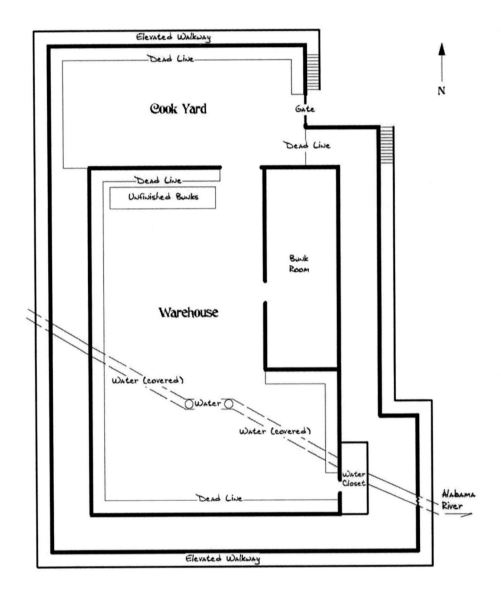

Cahaba Federal Prison

Based on drawings by D.T. Chandler, Ass. Adj. & Inspector General, Cahaba
in a report to Colonel R.H. Chilton, Ass. Adj. & Inspector General, Richmond

and by

Jesse Hawes, prisoner at Cahaba, from memory, following his release

PART 1
SEPTEMBER 1863 – MARCH 1864

SEPTEMBER

1

The smell of damp earth and rotting leaves greeted him as consciousness slowly returned. The pounding in his skull was excruciating. He drew a halting breath against it, then moaned as nausea gripped him and bile burned the back of his throat. When his stomach settled, he shifted slightly, turning his face out of the dirt, hungering for a breath of fresh air. The resulting explosion of pain nearly caused him to black out again.

As the throbbing in his head began to ease, he became aware of protests from other parts of his body. His left thigh hurt, and a dull ache emanated from his shoulders. He tried moving his arms, but met with resistance. *What the...?* he thought dully, then realized his hands were tied behind him. He lay without moving, waiting for his head to clear. When memory returned, it came in a rush.

Stupid! After all these months, he'd walked right into them.

He had come riding up from the south early that morning, pushing his tired mount hard, just as he had all the way from Macon. The sun was barely brushing the treetops when the first scattered pops of musketry reached him. The gunfire increased, joined by the boom of artillery and the shrieking whistle of flying shells, building to a roar as the battle ahead intensified.

Topping a ridge, he saw gunsmoke wafting above the trees in the wide valley separating him from Missionary Ridge. *Too late*, he thought, kicking his horse into a headlong gallop. With a battle raging, the papers he carried were of little value—none, unless he could get through to the Union lines quickly.

The movement of Confederate troops south of Chickamauga Creek brought him up sharply, blocking his westward course and forcing him to retreat. Abandoning the road for the relative safety of the woods, he picked his way through dense underbrush, around soggy bottoms and over fallen trees, further hampered by fingers of dense fog that snaked out from the creek.

Approaching Thedford Ford, he nearly collided with a company of infantry, their movements ghostly in the mist. Doubling back, he found a wooded area between cleared fields where the trees grew thick to the edge of the creek. He urged his reluctant horse down the steep bank, riding through belly-deep water until he found a way up the other side. Beyond the untamed strip bordering the creek, the forest ended. The fog lifted on a breath of wind, and for a moment, there was sunlight and all around him open fields.

He retrieved his haversack and let the horse go, thinking he would stand a better chance of getting back to Union lines on foot. He tried going west, then north, but all around him enemy troops were on the move.

The day warmed; the last remnants of fog dissipated. Sunlight filtered through the autumn canopy, catching the haze of gunsmoke in dancing, shifting beams. Keeping to the woods as much as possible, he avoided open fields and the few scattered farmhouses, skirting the ever-changing boundaries of the battle and dodging gray and butternut-clad troops. In places, where livestock had been allowed to roam free, and the forest was grazed clear of underbrush, he found the going relatively easy. In others, thick tangles of vegetation slowed him down, stopping him a couple of times, and forcing him to backtrack.

As the day wore on, the layer of smoke beneath the forest canopy thickened, diffusing the light and cutting visibility by half. More than once, he ducked from movement, only to discover that light and shadow were playing tricks on him.

He had given up, was heading south, retreating from what appeared to be the entire Confederate army, when they spotted him. Their approach masked by the cacophony of battle, a battery of artillery was almost upon him when he stepped from a tangle of vegetation onto the road north of Dalton Ford. He froze, squinting through the haze, trying to make out the color of their uniforms. When he saw who they were, he scrambled back toward the cover of the thicket, but his hesitation cost him. They were on him in an instant.

Thinking back, he knew it had been a mistake to run. *Like admitting guilt.* Even so, he might have made it if they hadn't got in a lucky shot.

The wound to his left thigh hadn't stopped him, but it had slowed him down. He'd put up a fight, but it hadn't done much good. *More harm than good*, he thought ruefully, considering how much of him hurt. He tried shifting his left leg. The resulting stab of pain momentarily rivaled the fireworks in his head.

"Hey, you. You awake?"

The voice, coming from close at hand, startled him. He opened his eyes. *Too bright!* Pinwheels of pain exploded in his head. He screwed his eyes shut, willing it to stop.

"Hey, you. I seen ya move." Fingers jabbed his shoulder. "Wake up."

He opened his eyes, mere slits this time. *Maybe not so bright.* Cautiously, he opened them wider. A few seconds, and a pair of feet came into focus... legs

4

...hands on knees. It came to him that someone was squatting beside him. A face dipped down close to his. It too, came into focus. *A kid!* he realized with a start.

"Hey, you. You awake?" The boy peered closely at him. "What was ya doin' runnin' away back there? Y'all a deserter? The lieutenant says mayhaps yo' a deserter." Getting no response, the boy shifted nervously on his haunches. "You speak English?"

The man on the ground drew breath, tried to speak. Something between a cough and a croak was all he could manage. His mouth was bone dry. He ran his tongue over his lips, tasted blood. Drawing another breath, he cleared his throat. It was a mistake. Until then, he hadn't thought the pain in his head could get any worse.

When the worst of it subsided, he moved his tongue inside his mouth, trying to work up some spit. He didn't have much luck, but he managed a faint whisper. "Water... ?"

The boy eyed him uncertainly. "I dunno..." he said, slowly. "They said I 'uz to take care. Said not to git too close."

"You're... close now."

There was a flurry of movement as the boy fell backward, skittering away across the ground. He came to his knees, armed with an ancient musket.

"Won't hurt you... " The effort of trying to talk was making the man nauseous; making him want to cough. He swallowed dryly. "My canteen?"

When the boy didn't budge, he gave up and closed his eyes. He was drifting at the outer edge of consciousness when the boy's voice, coming from a long way off, brought him back.

"Hey, you. Ya ain't daid, is ya?"

With supreme effort, he opened his eyes. The boy had closed the distance between them by half. Crouched low, he balanced the musket across his knees.

"No." The word came softly on a breath of air.

"So, if'n I was to ge'cha some water... mayhaps ya won't die?"

"Try not," he murmured, wishing the boy would stop tormenting him, would bring him water.

The boy stood up and stepped from sight. He returned almost immediately, dangling the familiar canteen by its strap. "I gots it." Getting no response, he swung the canteen closer. "Hey, you. Injun. Wha'cha want me to do wit' it?"

A good question. He was lying flat on his face in the dirt. As much as he dreaded the prospect, he was going to have to move if he wanted to drink. "Help me... sit?"

The boy took a hasty step back, slipping the cloth strap of the canteen over his shoulder and hefting the musket.

"Promise... won't hurt you."

The boy chewed his lip apprehensively and shuffled closer. "Wha'cha want me to do?"

You're making this hard, kid. The man ran a dry tongue over drier lips and forced out the words. "Lean me... against something."

The boy shifted from one foot to the other, weighing his orders against the prospect of being left alone as the shadows deepened—alone in the dark with a corpse. He said, "If'n I puts this here gun down, ya ain't gonna jump me, is ya?"

"Uh-uh."

The boy stood undecided for several moments. Then he stepped closer and hunkered down, cradling the musket. "Ya swear?"

"Swear."

The boy considered him a moment longer before laying the musket on the ground.

The next few minutes were excruciating. The man drifted in and out of consciousness as the boy rolled him onto his side, pulled his legs around, and propped him against a fallen tree. That accomplished, the boy retrieved his musket and squatted with it across his knees, waiting for his captive to recover.

The ordeal had cost the man his vision. When it returned, he saw that they were in a tiny clearing, trees and undergrowth pressing in all around. His legs were roughly bound at the ankles, and someone had tied a strip of cloth around his left thigh. It was stained with blood, none of it fresh. *Doesn't look too bad*, he thought with relief. *Lucky.*

"Hey, you. Ya want this here water?"

The man looked up. He started to nod, but a burst of pain stopped him. "Yes."

His prisoner's change in position made the boy nervous. He came as close as he dared, and leaning on the musket for support, stretched out an arm and tilted the canteen against the man's lips.

More water went down his front than into his mouth, but the portion that made it in tasted good. His thirst sated, the man looked to where the boy had retreated at the far side of the clearing. He was a scrawny runt of a thing, barely as tall as the musket he was holding. The ragged gray coat he wore was too big, hanging past his knees, and turned back at the cuffs to expose tiny hands. An unruly lock of straight, mouse-brown hair hung between his eyes. The aggression and fear in those eyes belied the cherubic look of the rest of his face.

"Thanks," the man said, wishing the boy would relax, wishing he'd point the musket somewhere else. "What's your name?"

"Seth," came the cautious reply.

The man's lips twitched, a sad, fleeting smile. "Seth," he repeated. "I had a brother named Seth. He was killed in the fighting." He blinked against a sudden burning in his eyes. His brothers had been raring to go the day they'd left the family farm to fight the Rebels. He'd wanted desperately to go with them, but everyone said he was too young. The look in his mother's eyes kept him from arguing. Six months later, word had come that Seth was dead, killed in Arkansas at a place called Pea Ridge. Another six months, and he'd run away, joining his three remaining brothers with the 36th Illinois, Sheridan's 11th Division, at Louisville, Kentucky.

"What's yo' name?"

Seth's voice jolted him back to the present.

"Hey, you! I said, what's yo' name?"

The man studied Seth, deciding what to tell him. He figured the truth probably wouldn't hurt. "Ethan," he muttered, remembering belatedly to mask his northern accent. "M' name's Ethan."

"You a deserter?"

"No."

"A Yank?"

"Uh-uh."

"Then why'd you run?"

Ethan lifted one shoulder in a shrug.

"I ain't got no use fo' Yanks," Seth announced. He pointed a thumb at his chest, his voice quivering with false bravado. "I's a loader fo' the cannon. Hepin' drive them Yanks back north where they belongs." Sounding less sure of himself, he added, "But t'day, the lieutenant, he says they's too many trees fo' cannon, so's he tol' me to wait here wit' you."

At the mention of cannon, Ethan gave his full attention to the thump of artillery that persisted to the north and west. Even as daylight waned, the battle

7

continued to rage. Frustration welled up, and he jerked angrily at his bonds. His head and leg exploded in agony. He moaned and sagged against the tree.

Seth leapt backward, leveling the musket at Ethan's chest and pulling back the flint. "Hey! Don'chu go doin' that again, or I's gonna shoot!"

"Calm down, Seth," Ethan muttered. "I ain't gonna hur'cha none." He glowered until the boy lowered the musket, then closed his eyes.

I should never have gone to Macon! He'd been saddled up, ready to ride north, when Price demanded he go south instead. Sitting bound against the tree, Ethan cursed him. But for the wasted trip to Macon, the papers he carried would be safe in Union hands. And maybe, once they'd been delivered, he would have obtained permission to see his brothers. He hadn't seen them since spring, when as far as they were concerned, he'd simply vanished.

He had gone into his first battle at Perryville naively confident that it would be the stuff of legends, glorious and heroic. Nothing had prepared him for the sheer horror of it; for the sights and sounds and smells of it; for the large number of hideously maimed, for the indiscriminate slaughter. His shocked senses had shut down, instinct had taken over, and he had fought, desperate only to survive. When the fighting ended, he had collapsed on his hands and knees among the dead, and vomited. His eldest brother, Duncan, had found him, still trembling, and helped him from the field.

Mortified by his display of weakness, and unwilling to have his brothers think him a coward, he'd fought again twelve weeks later at Stones River, then silently thanked God when winter closed in, and Rosecrans' army settled into inactivity. Desperate to find an honorable way out of the fighting, he'd listened to rumors that circulated of men working as spies for the Union. He'd made inquiries, and early one March morning, presented himself at General George Thomas' headquarters and volunteered.

He had been assigned as courier to a spy, a man he knew only as Price. For the next six months he'd traveled throughout Georgia and Alabama, and on one occasion, east into the Carolinas. He returned north periodically, slipping through both armies' picket lines to relay the intelligence Price gathered before turning south again, headed for their next rendezvous.

Initially, he'd been in awe of Price. Poised, rakishly handsome, accustomed to money and all that came with it, Price had swept him under his wing. It hadn't taken long for Ethan to figure out that beneath the smooth charm and genial smile, lurked a ruthless soul and a cunning mind. When Price realized Ethan was no longer dazzled, could no longer be manipulated, he let the mask drop and distanced himself from his courier, cutting interaction between them to a minimum.

Ethan had been perfectly happy with the arrangement. Immersing himself in the South, he'd learned all he could about it. He had pored over maps of Georgia and Alabama, memorizing them and coming to know their back ways better than most who lived there.

And in the South, he'd made another discovery. All his life he had suffered taunts of "Injun" and "half-breed." Now he found he could make the dark skin, hair and eyes inherited from his mother work to his advantage. He let his hair grow, took to wearing shabby clothes, and affected the subservient posture slaves assumed around their masters. To his delight, many whites ignored him. Assuming he wasn't clever, wasn't educated, they talked openly in front of him. What Ethan saw and heard, he remembered. Unbeknownst to Price, he used it to supplement the often-meager reports he carried back to the generals in the North.

Life as a courier appealed to him. He'd thrived on it. And he was good at it. *Until today.*

The thought stopped him. Today he'd gotten careless. *No*, he decided. *Not careless. Just plain exhausted.* There had been the long, added miles from Atlanta to Macon, followed by a nerve-wracking wait for an operative who never showed. Minutes had stretched into hours until half a day had been wasted. All the while, he'd been plagued by knowing that time was critical for the information he already carried. In the end, he'd made the gut-wrenching decision to disobey Price's orders and begun the long ride north to Chattanooga. *Only to get here too late.*

There isn't much I can do about it now, Ethan told himself. *Except avoid getting hung.*

He'd been warned, when he volunteered, that the penalty for spying was death. And here he was, out of uniform, caught behind enemy lines. Caught while trying to run. *If I'm lucky, the Rebs won't find the papers.* If they didn't, he was almost certain he could convince them he was a Southerner, a civilian—convince them to let him go. But if they found them, he wasn't at all sure he'd be able to convince them he was just a courier. As a courier, he figured he'd wind up in an enemy prison camp. *But as a spy...* Ethan shivered. *Better not to think about it.*

Another shiver ran through him, and he opened his eyes. The last of the light was fading. Deep in the woods, the little clearing had grown quite dark.

Ethan could barely distinguish Seth where he huddled against the undergrowth several feet away.

As the temperature dropped, the cloud of smoke that had hung in the air all day began to settle, filling Ethan's nose and throat with the acrid smell of burnt gunpowder. Without thinking, he coughed, re-igniting the agony in his head. He caught his breath, waiting for it to ease.

It's going to be a long night, he thought when the worst of it passed. *Cold, too, without a fire.* "It's cold," he said to the huddled form.

"A bit," Seth muttered through chattering teeth.

"How 'bout a fire?"

"Dunno. Dunno if'n I should."

Ethan rolled his eyes heavenward. *Not quick, this one.* He tried to sound encouraging. "Think on it, Seth. We got no way a' knowin' when someone'll come fetch us. Could be we'll be here all night. It'll get mighty cold without a fire, don'cha think?"

"Guess," came the reluctant reply.

"I'd help if I could. Do it m'self even. But since I cain't, it's up to you." Getting no response, he tried another tack. "Whadda ya think, Seth? It'll help ya to see me better. Help ya to keep an eye on me."

That did it. There was movement on the far side of the clearing, followed by the sounds of Seth blundering about in the underbrush. He reappeared and dropped an armful of branches near Ethan's feet. Repeating the process several times, he knelt beside the pile, pulled his knapsack to him, and dug through it. A match flared, suddenly bright against the darkness. The flame steadied, and Seth held it to a pile of twigs and dead leaves. As the fire took hold, he piled on larger pieces of wood.

Within minutes, Seth was squatting beside a cozy fire, hands held out to warm them. Some of the heat reached Ethan, enough to ward off the chill, but as the front of him warmed, he became aware of the intense cold at his back. His hands were numb with it, his neck stiff. And, he realized, his stomach was cramped with hunger.

"Don't s'pose ya got anythin' to eat?" he asked hopefully.

The boy shook his head. "Naa. What I had, I et while I 'uz waitin' fo' you to wake up."

Ethan swallowed his disappointment. He'd downed the last of his provisions just before sun-up and had nothing since. The hours ahead looked bleak.

They sat for what seemed a very long time, Seth disappearing periodically and returning with wood to keep the little fire going. Ethan had resigned himself to being there all the night when the sound of muffled voices and plodding hooves reached them. They both tensed, looking toward the sound.

Seth grabbed his musket. "See?" he hissed, springing to his feet. "I tol' ya we shouldn'a lit no fire! What if them's Yanks?" Before the words were out of his mouth, he melted into the darkness.

There was crashing in the underbrush, and four men appeared at the edge of the light. Ethan looked down the barrels of four muskets.

"Seth, boy! Where are ya?"

"I's here, suh." Twigs snapped, and Seth stepped into the clearing.

"Good job, son. Now let's be a-goin'." The man bent his head toward Ethan. "Get him."

They hoisted him up without untying him. One man grabbed his legs; the other two grasped him under each arm. They carried him backward, twisting and bumping through the thicket, rekindling the agony in his head and leg. As his vision blurred, Ethan glimpsed Seth following along behind. Then the leader kicked dirt over the fire, taking the light.

They slung him on his belly over the back of the horse. Seth was put up behind him, and they set off. Blood rushed to his head, lending renewed force to his headache. A moan escaped him. With every step the horse took, the pounding intensified. By the time they arrived at their destination, he had been unconscious for some time.

2

He woke suddenly, wet, cold, and sputtering. The man who'd emptied the bucket of icy water over him stepped back. Others moved to fill the gap.

Ethan blinked water from his eyes. He started to shake his head, but a white-hot burst at the base of his skull stopped him. He caught his breath in a gasp, then blinked again and tried to focus.

He was in a narrow, slope-roofed lean-to, the air heavy with the odor of cow. A single lantern hung from the low rafters, illuminating gray uniforms pressed in around him. Ethan noted stars on collars. Major was the lowest rank among them.

Looking down, he saw he'd been propped on a chair, wrists bound in front of him. A rope lashed about his chest and arms held him in place. He had been stripped to his longhandles, his haversack, boots, clothing, and the contents of his pockets strewn in the muck at his feet.

His eyes came to rest on his right leg. Panic shot through him. His longhandles had been ripped open from the ankle to above his knee, exposing bare calf where the documents had been.

The man standing directly before him cleared his throat. Ethan looked up into a cadaverous, bearded face. Bright, piercing eyes regarded him from beneath bristling gray brows.

"Why don't you tell me about these?" the general said, holding up a familiar batch of wrinkled papers.

Ethan couldn't speak, couldn't drag his eyes from the papers.

"You speak English, boy?" a voice from the shadows demanded. "Answer General Bragg when he talks to you."

Ethan's heart thudded in recognition at the name. He tried to keep it from his eyes as he raised them to General Bragg's face. The general's expression was unforgiving, his eyes unkind.

Dumb Indian, Ethan decided, wishing his head didn't hurt so much, wishing he had all his wits about him. *It's my only chance.* He shivered, from fear as much as from cold, and shifted his gaze from General Bragg to the big white-haired general at his side.

"He give 'em to me to carry, suh," he said, mimicking Seth's accent and offering what he hoped was an ingenuous smile.

"Who?" General Bragg asked.

Ethan looked at the papers. He lifted one shoulder; let it fall. "A white man. He give me money. Said if'n I took 'em where he said, the man there 'ud gimme mo'."

"What was his name?"

"Suh, I..." Ethan looked frantically at the ring of faces. "I dunno," he offered hesitantly.

"Do you know what's in these?"

"Nosuh," Ethan mumbled. "Cain't read."

"Speak up, boy. And look at me. Where were you told to deliver them?"

Ethan raised his eyes, but only as far as the gold wreaths and stars on the general's collar. "Umm... It were a general, suh. Like yo'sef." He wrinkled his brow in concentration before adding tentatively, "General Rose, I think it was." Raising triumphant eyes to the general's face, he added, "Yessuh! Tha's it! General Rose at Chatt'nooga!"

General Bragg's stare was unwavering. Ethan was forced to look away. He scanned the shadowed faces behind the general nervously before letting his eyes drop back to the papers.

"Maybe if'n I was to give 'em to you, suh," he suggested hopefully. "Stead a' General Rose. Maybe you'd gimme the money, 'stead a' him?"

General Bragg snorted in disgust. Shaking the papers in Ethan's face, he said, "I have the papers, boy. No need to pay fo' them." He jammed them into the hands of the major standing nearest him. "Hang him!" To the others: "Come! We have matters to discuss."

There was movement in the crowded lean-to. Slowly it began to empty.

Ethan's stomach churned. He couldn't catch his breath. Despite being wet and half-frozen, he'd broken out in a cold sweat. He had been so certain his deception would work.

They're going to hang me…!

Through a haze of terror, he realized someone was standing in front of him. He looked up.

"General Polk, sir," a voice urged from the open end of the lean-to.

"In a moment."

Trapped under intense scrutiny, Ethan's eyes wavered, then slid away.

Long seconds passed before the white-haired general turned to leave. As he passed the guard, he said, "He's to be kept here until I return. Dry him off, and get him dressed. And fo' God's sake, give him somethin' to eat."

The next few hours would have been almost tolerable if Ethan hadn't known he was about to die. Two guards helped him into his clothes and provided a meal of beans, cornpone and weak goober coffee. Ethan's appetite had vanished, but he forced himself to eat. When he finished, his captors once again tied him to the chair. One draped a blanket over him and dimmed the lantern. Without a word, they stepped out into the night.

Left alone, Ethan squinted into the shadows, seeking a means of escape. Nothing presented itself, and despite his struggles, the knots held firm. *I'll fight them*, he vowed, jerking angrily at his bonds. *When they come for me, I'll fight! Make them work to kill me.*

The notion lasted only until it occurred to him that it might be better to go quietly, to die with as much dignity as he could muster. He prayed that when the time came, his body wouldn't betray him, that he would find the courage to make his final walk unassisted.

This is it, he thought, resigned at last. Somehow, despite the warnings, he'd never imagined being captured, much less hung. He'd always assumed death, if it found him, would take him quickly, unexpectedly, somewhere in the open. *But not like this...*

He despaired at never seeing his family again, and briefly considered telling his captors the truth. Telling them his name, at least, so that one day his parents might learn what had become of him. The thought of his mother waiting, never knowing, was almost more than he could bear.

There had always been a special bond between them. He was her firstborn, her solace, her link to her past during the first difficult years in Illinois. Separated from her people, she sang to him in the language of the Lakota, teaching him the legends of her forefathers even as she struggled to learn the ways of the whites. Her husband's other young sons kept their distance during those early years, and mother and son clung to one another for comfort.

His father, James Fraser, was the sixth of nine children, the son of Scottish immigrants who had settled in the farmlands of central Illinois. Wracked by grief following his wife's death during childbirth, James left his four young sons in the care of a married sister and headed west. He got only as far as the eastern foothills of the Rocky Mountains before the early onset of winter in the high country stopped him. He took refuge at the American Fur Company's new, whitewashed adobe fort. Situated on a grassy plain above the Laramie River, the company called it Fort John. It was better known as Fort Laramie.

As the days lengthened, and winter gave way to spring, James watched the transformation from brown to green, captivated by the towering mountains, the endless skies, and the vast prairies of the land that would one day become Wyoming. In July, when John C. Fremont's scientific expedition passed through, he joined them, traveling west, along the North Platte to the Sweetwater, through the South Pass, and into the towering mountains of the Wind River, before returning overland with Charles Lambert and the main party while Fremont and six others attempted to navigate the Platte. When Fremont's party returned to the States in the fall, James remained behind.

He headed west again the following spring, this time in the company of a pair of trappers. They angled south, then west, trapping their way across the mountains at the southern edge of the Great Divide Basin. When the days grew short, and nighttime temperatures dipped, they headed up the Seeds-ke-dee to Jim Bridger's newly erected fort. James returned to Fort Laramie the following summer, fully intending to continue east, when his life took a sudden, unexpected turn.

Indians were a common sight at the fort. Mainly Cheyenne, Arapaho and Sioux, they came to trade and were known to camp along the river for days, or even weeks at a time. James traded with them on occasion, but idle curiosity aside, had little to do with them.

Late one afternoon, as he was unsaddling his horse, he sensed he was being watched. He turned to look into the eyes of the most beautiful girl he had ever seen. She looked away quickly, but James couldn't take his eyes off her. When the group she was with left the fort, he followed.

As he entered the Sioux camp, a group of young bucks hemmed him in, swaggering and yelling. He was on the verge of retreat when a gray-haired man intervened. The young men backed off, eyeing him and muttering. Confronted by the question in the old man's eyes, James was tongue-tied; the few words he knew in their language deserted him. He pointed in the direction the girl had gone. An amused smile came to the old man's lips, and he beckoned James to follow.

Her name was Wazi Ápe, Pine Leaf, and their courtship lasted through the final days of summer and into the fall. When the Lakota moved north for the autumn hunt, and then to the headwaters of the Belle Fourche River to spend the winter, James went with them.

One day in early spring, he delivered three of his best horses to the lodge of Pine Leaf's parents. An hour passed, and when no one emerged to claim them, he delivered a fourth, then retreated a short distance to watch. Before long, Pine Leaf's father stepped from the lodge, followed by Pine Leaf herself. She smiled shyly at James before turning to untie one of the horses.

The following day was spent dancing and feasting. As the afternoon waned, they were paraded through the village behind the medicine man. By the time they reached the lodge her family had erected for them, James and Pine Leaf were man and wife.

With the coming of summer, more whites than ever before streamed west. The grasslands the Lakota relied upon to feed their vast pony herds were grazed bare by the white men's livestock. The trees they used for wood and shelter were felled and fed into emigrant campfires. The deer, antelope, and buffalo they depended on for food, clothing and shelter were slaughtered or migrated elsewhere. As each new train of white-covered wagons appeared over the horizon, life for the Lakota grew a bit more precarious.

When James learned Pine Leaf was pregnant, he began thinking seriously of home. He suggested a return to the safety and security of a farm in Illinois, but she resisted. By the time their son was born in early September, James was more determined than ever to return to the States. Concerned for the future of his new family, and missing his other children, he pressed Pine Leaf to agree.

Winter that year was brutal. In the spring, on the heels of a horrifying, bloody raid by the Pawnee, Pine Leaf allowed herself to be persuaded. Giving her no time to change her mind, James Fraser packed up his little family and headed east.

Initially, everything in Illinois was frightening to Pine Leaf. For the first two years, she immersed herself in the care of her child, at times retreating even from James, and visibly alarmed by his four noisy, robust sons.

A third year passed, and Pine Leaf was baptized Sarah. The son she called Two Moons, for the sliver of new moon reflected in the still waters of a beaver pond on the night of his birth, was baptized Ethan. Seven months prior to the birth of their second child, James and Sarah were married in a small church ceremony. The arrival of their daughter was the catalyst that brought the family together: James, his beloved Sarah, Duncan, the twins James, Jr. and Joshua, Seth, Ethan, and the baby, Kathryn.

Alone, bound to the chair, Ethan concentrated on the image of his mother's face. Hoping to touch her across the miles, he willed her to know that one day they would be together. Whether in the white man's hereafter or the Lakota's, he would find her. He begged her not to worry, not to mourn.

"Wake up, son. Look at me."

Ethan started, shot through by a chill of terror. *No!* his brain screamed. *No, please! I'm not ready yet!* Heart slamming against his ribs, he raised panicked eyes to the stern face of General Polk.

The general considered him thoughtfully before speaking. "I find myself on the horns of a dilemma here, son. I can't decide how much a' yo' story I should give credence to. General Bragg has decided yo' a spy, and I have to tell you, there's somethin' about you that makes me wonder if yo' as innocent in all this as you'd like us to believe."

He paused, watching Ethan closely. Ethan stared back, silently begging for his life.

General Polk sighed and gave a ponderous shake of his head. "Lord knows what might have happened had General Rosecrans come into possession of those papers you were carryin'. But the fact that you were still blunderin' about in the woods long after they ceased to be of value leads me to believe there might be some of truth in what you've told us."

The general wagged his head and turned away. He took two steps and stopped, his back to Ethan, hands clasped behind him. Only the nervous tapping of one thumb betrayed his agitation.

Nighttime sounds of an army at rest drifted into the shed, but Ethan failed to notice. He sat with his eyes glued to the general's back, scarcely daring to breathe. A drop of sweat inched down his side; his heart thudded uncomfortably in his chest.

General Polk blew a long breath through pursed lips and turned to Ethan. "It troubles me that General Bragg has so precipitously ordered you hung, without benefit of a tribunal. Whatever the truth is, I find I can't, in good conscience, agree with him." Sharing a look with a captain who waited at the open end of the shed, he added, "It might be best if you were to disappear into one of the camps where the Yankee prisoners are bein' held. I shall instruct my men to deliver you there, after which you will be transferred wherever the Provost Marshal sees fit, to be incarcerated until yo' release can be negotiated. As things now stand, I wouldn't count on that happenin' until the last shot has been fired in this cursed bloody war."

Turning to his aide he said, "See to it, will you, Captain? I'm off to bed."

Ethan released the breath he'd been holding. His head dropped to his chest and he sagged against his bonds, weak with relief. He could barely stand when two men came for him.

The nearest holding area was half a mile south of General Bragg's Thedford Ford headquarters, occupying one corner of a fallow field, adjacent to a tiny rough-planked farmhouse. Armed guards surrounded the Union prisoners huddled around dozens of fires.

One of Ethan's escorts turned as he was leaving and pressed the blanket into his hands. Ethan accepted it gratefully. The night was clear and cold; the fires nearest him packed several deep with sleeping men. He hadn't the strength to walk, so he wrapped the blanket him and collapsed where he stood. For the first time in forty-eight hours, he slept.

* * *

The discovery of the papers strapped to Ethan's leg had interrupted a meeting between General Braxton Bragg, commander of the Confederate Army of Tennessee, and his major subordinates. When the meeting reconvened, General Bragg announced a new command structure, dividing his army into two wings. He placed General Polk in command of the right wing, and General James Longstreet, expected to arrive shortly from Virginia, in command of the left. General Polk's orders were to launch the initial assault at dawn, sending his units into battle in succession from right to left. Once Polk's attack began, Longstreet would begin his own assault from the left.

When the meeting ended, General Polk returned to the cow shed to deal with the Indian boy. He then retired to the comfort of his headquarters, a farmhouse several miles south of Chickamauga Creek, and far from the front lines. From there, he dispatched couriers to his subordinates with details of the attack. Not all the couriers reached their destinations, and as General Polk slept, communication along the Confederate line disintegrated.

General Longstreet arrived at Bragg's headquarters at eleven o'clock that night, having narrowly avoided capture when his party stumbled across a Union picket line. General Bragg roused himself long enough to place Longstreet in command of five newly arrived brigades from the Army of Northern Virginia and three more on loan from General Polk. Supplying him with a crudely drawn map, Bragg returned to bed. Longstreet rested briefly, then set out before it was light to inspect his lines and prepare for battle.

3

The woods were thick with fog and lingering gunsmoke when the sun rose pale and diffused on Sunday morning. Random shots broke out along the lines as men from both sides took potshots at one another. The day brightened, but General Polk failed to launch his attack. When it became clear that Polk had failed him, General Bragg moved General Breckinridge to his far right with orders to begin the assault.

By mid-morning, a full-scale battle was under way. Bragg's Confederate forces were assaulting the Union line under General Thomas on the Union left, when General Rosecrans received a report that a gap had opened on his right. Unable to see his forces through trees and smoke, Rosecrans ordered General Wood's division to fill the alleged gap. In doing so, he unwittingly created a very real gap nearly half a mile wide. General Longstreet, with eleven thousand men under his command, and ten thousand more in the immediate vicinity, swept through, driving the entire right wing of the Union army into retreat.

It took time for the sounds of battle to penetrate, and even then, Ethan clung to sleep. The sun climbed higher, burning through the last of the mist, and the noise built until he could no longer ignore it. With a groan, he rolled onto his back. His head throbbed, and cold-stiffened muscles protested the beating he'd taken the day before. He tried opening his eyes, but the day was too bright. He closed them and lay still, mustering the strength to move.

Eventually, he pushed himself into a sitting position. Movement made his headache worse. He leaned forward, sitting cross-legged with his hands supporting his head. After what seemed an eternity, the pain began to ease. Ethan raised his head and squinted into the light, deciding it was bearable. He probed his head gently with his fingertips, finding two wounds that were swollen and tender to the touch. The same was true of his leg.

Slowly, carefully, he pushed himself to his feet. For several seconds, the world spun; then it began to right itself. He was standing with all his weight on his right leg, gingerly testing his left, when he heard his name called.

"Fraser? Ethan Fraser? That you?"

Ethan turned to see a familiar figure striding toward him. "Thomas," he said, offering a guarded smile.

Eight years Ethan's senior, Thomas Murray was a crony of the twins. He was a big man, taller than Ethan by a couple of inches, and a good deal heavier. Where Ethan was slender and long-limbed, Thomas' neck, chest and arms were thick with muscle. Blue eyes beamed from a ruddy face crowned by a tousle of curly blond hair, and there was a good-natured grin on his lips.

Ethan noted the stripes on his sleeves. "Sergeant. Sorry."

"Thomas'll do," the other man said, waving off his rank. He clapped Ethan on the shoulder, dropping his hand when Ethan stiffened and winced. Leaning in, he took a closer look at Ethan's bloodshot eyes, the bruised smudges beneath them, the split lip.

"You even lay a hand on the other fellow?"

Ethan smiled ruefully. "I did, but there were too many."

"What the devil are you doing here? I almost didn't recognize you with all the hair. But then I said to myself, 'Ain't many has his kind a' looks.' And here you are in this shithole of a place looking like you were on the losing end of an argument." Thomas' grin broadened. When Ethan failed to respond, his look turned serious. "What *are* you doing here?"

"I... uh... " Ethan hesitated, uncertain what to answer. "I was..."

Seeing Ethan's discomfort, and mistaking the reason for it, Thomas interrupted. "No matter. It's good seeing you. Good to see a familiar face." He waved a hand toward one corner of the field. "I've laid claim to a spot over yonder. I'm with a couple of boys from the 24th Illinois. We got us a place by a fire, and the coffee's hot." Grasping Ethan's arm, he said, "Come on."

"Wait." Ethan pulled back, stopping him. "What about my brothers?"

"Last I knew, the Thirty-sixth wasn't in the fighting. Not yesterday morning, at any rate. Last I saw, they were all doing fine."

Ethan looked down, but not before Thomas saw his relief. When Ethan looked up, his brows were drawn together in confusion. "If the Thirty-sixth wasn't in the fighting, what are you doing here?"

Thomas looked briefly at the ground, then squinted at him. "I was carrying a dispatch. Got turned around in the fog and stumbled into a Reb picket line." He shrugged. "Guess this is where the war ends for me."

Ethan nodded grimly. "For both of us."

They wended their way through the huddled groups of men, Thomas supporting Ethan as he limped along. When they reached the corner of the field, Thomas nodded toward a man lying on the ground, a bloody bandage encasing his right foot.

"This here's Colm O'Donnell. And that's Caleb Pender. Boys, this is Ethan Fraser."

Caleb was an emaciated young man with straight, straw-colored hair that brushed the shoulders of his coat. He slouched against a pile of rocks, long, bony legs stretched out before him. He scowled at Ethan, studying him with rheumy eyes. He started to speak and was overcome by a fit of coughing.

Colm was heavier, his thick black hair cut short, with a neatly trimmed beard and mustache. His blue eyes were dulled with pain, but he attempted a smile. "Hallo, Ethan," he muttered, his voice tinged with a soft Irish brogue.

Thomas squatted beside him, waving flies off the bandage. "The Rebs sent a steward around last evening, but he didn't do much. I'm betting Colm here's gonna need to have this foot taken off." He gave Colm's shoulder a squeeze and pushed himself to his feet. "Settle in. I'll see if I can't get someone to look after him."

Ethan tossed his blanket on the ground and lay down next to Colm. As time passed, and the sun warmed him, he dozed.

He was jostled awake when a pair of slaves lifted Colm onto a litter. The steward, offering assurances that when the battle ended, Colm would be exchanged with the rest of the wounded, watched as the litter was hoisted, then followed it away.

Late in the day, the influx of Federal prisoners increased dramatically. With them came word that most of Rosecrans' army, including Rosecrans himself, had been chased from the field. Night fell, and the firing ceased. The only sounds were the murmur of men's voices and the cries of the wounded. The last prisoners to filter in brought news that the entire Union army had fled, leaving the field, and the victory, to the Rebels.

4

Ethan spent the next day sleeping in the sun while Thomas roamed the camp. He returned bearing three potatoes and a hunk of salt pork to supplement their meager provisions.

They were rousted from sleep the following morning, just as it was getting light. Ethan's headache had subsided, but pain shot through his leg when he put weight on it. Caleb's condition had worsened, and Thomas had to coax him to his feet. They were herded toward the eastern boundary of the field, the mass of prisoners narrowing into a ragged column as they shuffled between ranks of Confederate guards.

"Where're we headed?" Thomas asked.

"Richmond," came the brusque reply.

"Richmond." Thomas looked at Ethan. "Any idea how far off Richmond is?"

"A ways. Six hundred miles, maybe more."

"Jeez!" Caleb cried. "They ain't gonna make us walk six hunnert miles, are they?" He was overcome by a fit of coughing, and Thomas supported him until it passed. When he was able, Caleb looked at him with desperate eyes and wheezed, "I cain't make it no six hunnert miles!"

"There's a rail line east of here," Ethan offered. "Chances are, that's where they're taking us."

Caleb's brow lowered, and he looked at Ethan with suspicion.

The straggling line of prisoners trudged east. Thomas supported Caleb, but after the first quarter mile, he began to falter. Ethan took his arm, prepared to shoulder some of his weight, but Caleb shook him off. Too ill to take offense, Ethan let him be.

Their progress was slow, the sun well past its zenith by the time they reached the rail depot at Tunnel Hill. Thomas and Ethan exchanged looks when they emerged from the woods and saw the scene spread before them. The fields around the depot had been turned into a vast holding area for the nearly five thousand Federal prisoners awaiting transport to Richmond. They waited in groups, sitting or lying on the ground, with the greatest activity centered around an aging steam engine at the head of a long line of freight cars.

"Who'd have thought there'd be so many?" Thomas muttered.

Ethan's eyes swept the sea of men in blue. "Do you think any of my brothers are here? Or someone who knows what happened to them?"

"Hard telling. We'll get Caleb settled and ask around." Thomas looked at Ethan, noting the pinched look around his eyes, and added, "If you're up to it. If not, I'll see what I can find out."

"I'll go."

"You sure?"

The look Ethan gave him put an end to the discussion.

They saw Caleb settled and began wending their way through the camp. Thomas watched with mounting concern as Ethan limped beside him, his eyes glazed with pain. They had been searching for over an hour when Ethan stopped suddenly, and swayed. Reaching out blindly with one hand, he pressed the other to his eyes. Thomas grabbed his arm, then seized him around the chest to keep him from falling.

"My head... I... Everything's blurred."

Ethan's legs buckled, and Thomas lowered him to the ground. Ethan rolled onto his side and brought his knees up. He lay with his eyes closed, his breath coming in short, shallow gasps. Thomas watched him for several moments, then settled beside him.

After a time, Ethan's breathing steadied, and he relaxed. Thomas laid a hand on his arm. "Stay put. I'm gonna fill my canteen and see if I can't find us something to eat." Getting no response, Thomas gave his arm a squeeze and got to his feet.

He returned a short time later to find Ethan exactly as he'd left him. The only food he'd been able to procure was a portion of stale cornbread, bought at an exorbitant price off one of the guards. "Here," he said, squatting. "Eat some of this. Maybe it'll help."

Ethan's eyelids fluttered. "Can't," he mumbled. "Please... leave me alone."

"All right," Thomas replied, stuffing half the cornbread into his mouth and stowing the rest in his haversack. "I'll hang onto it for you."

The setting sun silhouetted the trees atop the western ridges when he touched Ethan's arm again. "C'mon Ethan. We gotta get back. Caleb's been on his own way too long."

Ethan muttered, but didn't move. Thomas heaved a sigh and pushed himself to his feet. Placing his hands under Ethan's arms, he pulled him to his knees. Ethan moaned and sagged sideways. Thomas hauled him to his feet. Pulling one of Ethan's arms across his shoulders and grasping him firmly about the waist, Thomas half-carried him back to where they'd left Caleb.

Caleb's condition worsened markedly during the night. He burned with fever, his breath coming in shuddering gasps. Thomas sat with him through much of the following day, dripping water between parched lips and rewetting the handkerchief he'd laid across his forehead. The shadows were beginning to lengthen when he turned to Ethan.

"We need more water."

Ethan was lying on his back, one arm thrown over his face. He lowered it, looked at Thomas, then slowly sat up. "Go. I'll look after him."

Thomas stood, scooping up the canteens. Ethan moved to the spot he'd vacated. Caleb's face was flushed with fever, and he shivered violently, his clothes soaked with sweat. His lips were cracked, and his throat clicked dryly as he struggled for breath.

Ethan looked at Thomas in alarm. "Shouldn't we do something? Find someone to look after him?"

Thomas shook his head as he turned away. "It's too late. I'll be back as quick as I can."

Ethan sat with Caleb until after dark, the vise around his head slowly tightening. He wasn't aware Thomas had returned until he spoke.

"I'll do that."

Ethan held up the handkerchief, and when Thomas took it, crawled back to his blanket.

"I got some food. You should eat."

Ethan ignored him. Wrapping the blanket around him, he closed his eyes, hoping for sleep.

Soon after daybreak, another train arrived, spewing great hissing clouds of steam as it clanked to a stop before the depot. Ethan woke to find Thomas stretched on the ground beside him. As he watched, Thomas came awake, looked at Caleb, and abruptly sat up. He put an ear to Caleb's mouth, then sat back on his heels. He saw Ethan looking and shook his head.

Guards moved through the camp, prodding men to their feet, and herding them toward the boxcars. Thomas rifled through Caleb's pockets, taking his pocketknife, watch, and a few coins. Ethan, who had lost everything at General Bragg's headquarters, grabbed Caleb's haversack, canteen and blanket as the guards closed in. Leaving Caleb's body next to the fire, they joined the throng of men shuffling toward the train.

They were loaded forty to a car, cramped and uncomfortable, enveloped by the stink of cattle. The sun beat down on the closed, crowded cars, and still the train didn't move. The stench became unbearable as human waste accumulated in the buckets at either end of the cars. Men grew ill, and a few, already weakened by wounds or illness, died.

Thomas laid claim to a place where Ethan could lean against a wall and catch an occasional whiff of air as it wafted through the cracks. Even so, in the heat and the fetid air, Ethan's headache grew steadily worse. He hunched forward miserably, knees pulled up, arms cradling his head.

At last, the whistle sounded. The car lurched, then began to roll. Groans of relief went up as fresh air flowed between the slats.

The hundred-mile trip south to Atlanta took a little over thirteen hours. When in motion, the aging steam engine failed to gather much speed, and there were countless delays as the train stopped for water, or was forced onto sidings to allow northbound trains transporting more important shipments to pass. At each stop, citizens turned out to gawk and jeer at the captive Yankee soldiers. A few of the more enterprising sold breads, cakes, nuts and rye coffee to any prisoner with money or something to trade. Thomas, with no other outlet for his energy, passed the time bargaining.

The train lumbered into Atlanta just before dawn. Down the line, bolts were thrown, doors rumbled open, and the prisoners staggered out, hobbling on cramped muscles and sucking in grateful lungfuls of clean, crisp air.

Thomas roused Ethan and helped him to his feet. Once outside, he revived somewhat, but Thomas kept hold of his arm, steadying him as they were marched away from the tracks.

"You gotta eat," he insisted. "Not eating's probably making your headaches worse and it's definitely making you weak."

"I try. It's just... the headaches. They make me nauseous. The air in the car... the heat. It made everything worse."

"Well, you gotta eat," Thomas said, rummaging in his haversack. "Try this."

Ethan took a bite of stale cake, surprised to find that it stirred his appetite. As the column of prisoners trudged along, he devoured everything Thomas offered. He was stuffing boiled peanuts into his mouth when they were brought to a halt outside the high walls of a prison stockade.

Guards moved among them like predators, systematically searching, stripping them of their belongings. Haversacks, blankets, canteens, money, watches and knives were confiscated— boots and coats, as well, if they were deemed in good enough condition. When Thomas realized what was happening, he stuffed the last of his money into the waistband of his britches. The guards failed to find it, but just about everything else he owned was rooted out and taken.

When the guards were satisfied they had everything of value, a sergeant, accompanied by another man bearing a ledger, passed through the ranks, recording prisoners' names and unit numbers. Thomas glanced sideways when Ethan identified himself as a private with the 36th Illinois, but refrained from comment.

The count complete, the gates were thrown open, and the prisoners were herded inside. The ground in every direction was strewn with Union soldiers. A few sat or moved about, but the majority slept.

Thomas and Ethan wound their way among them, searching for a place to settle. There was no room beneath the meager shelters, and men were packed several deep around the fires, so they settled for a patch of open ground near the center of the yard. Thomas was still grumbling as they lowered themselves to the ground.

"I understand stealing money and watches, things with value, but stealing the boots off men's feet. It's... it's..." He groped for a word to describe his outrage.

"Thomas?" A man propped himself on his elbows and peered bleary-eyed at them. "Fraser?" he added, blue eyes widening. "What the devil you doing here?"

Thomas and Ethan gaped. He was a small man, lean and dark-haired, with a full beard and corporal's stripes on his sleeves. "Zach?" they chorused, and the men around him began to stir.

"Fergus!" Ethan blurted, recognizing the lanky red-haired Irishman who sat up next to Zach.

"Sweet Mother of God, is that yourself, Ethan?" Fergus grinned and stuck out a hand. "What are you doing here?"

"How long you been here?" Thomas asked.

"We were on the first train outta Tunnel Hill on..." Zach sat up, fingering his beard. "Let's see... musta been Tuesday night. Got here yesterday." He glanced at the men around him. "You all know each other? This here's Frank," he said, gesturing to an older man in a private's uniform, lanky and sharp-featured with humorless brown eyes and narrow lips. His straight brown hair was thinning on top and hung raggedly over his collar. "I don't reckon you ever met him, or Horst here. They're with A Company."

Frank shook Thomas' outstretched hand, but ignored Ethan's. Ethan eyed him warily before returning the nodded greeting of the fair-haired Austrian at his side.

"Frank, Horst. Ethan here's Lieutenant Fraser's little bro—" Zach broke off, his expression stricken.

Ethan's heart seized. "What?" he demanded.

"Guess you ain't heard." Zach's voice caught. "Duncan got himself killed Sunday." Tilting his head toward the Irishman, he added, "Fergus here was with him when he got hit. Tell him, Fergus."

"Piece of shrapnel took the top his head right off," Fergus muttered, only briefly meeting Ethan's eyes. "Lad never knew what hit him."

Ethan looked away, jaw clenched, blinking back tears. When he felt he could control his voice, he turned to Fergus. "Jamie and Josh. What about them?"

Fergus eyed him miserably and shook his head. "Jamie was hit right off when Sheridan brought us up. Gut shot. Tore him up bad, so it did. Last I saw, Josh was dragging him back up the hill. I don't know what happened after that 'cause our line collapsed and the Rebs overran us."

Fergus looked to Zach, and Zach shook his head. "He was hit bad," he muttered. "A man don't survive a wound like that."

Ethan heard Thomas moan, felt him grip his shoulder. *First Seth, now Duncan and Jamie.* He gasped for air, feeling as if he was drowning. Suddenly, all he wanted was to get away. Shaking off Thomas' hand, he lurched to his feet. Careening into other prisoners, stepping on them, stumbling over them, he struck out blindly across the yard.

A split second, and Thomas was up and after him. The guards near the gate were raising their weapons when he tackled Ethan and pulled him to the ground. The men around them scattered.

"Let go!" Ethan bellowed, arms and legs flailing. "Let go, dammit!"

Thomas held on gamely. He straddled Ethan, and after several attempts, succeeded in pinning his arms to the ground. Ethan continued to kick and buck under him, but his strength was no match for Thomas'. He quit struggling and lay tensed, his breath coming hard as tears seeped from beneath closed lids.

Thomas waited until he thought Ethan ready to listen. "Think, Ethan. Your parents have lost three sons. You and Josh and Kate are all they have left. Josh is still in the fighting, so anything could happen. You owe it to your parents to survive, to get back to them alive."

Ethan didn't respond, but the fight went out of him. He opened his eyes, and seeing his own grief reflected in Thomas' face, was instantly contrite. "Sorry. I... it was a shock, hearing it like that." Embarrassed by his loss of control, he repeated, "I'm sorry. I could've got us both killed."

Thomas let go of Ethan's wrists and pushed himself to his feet. Reaching down, he grasped Ethan's hand and pulled him up. He would have turned back toward the others, but Ethan didn't move. He stared at the ground, hands wedged deep in the pockets of his coat, shoulders hunched.

"All right if we walk some? I need time before I have to face them."

"Sure." Thomas waved a hand. "Lead on."

They moved slowly, threading their way past huddled groups of men. It was impossible to walk side by side, so Thomas trailed behind. They were beginning their second circuit of the yard when Thomas realized Ethan had spoken.

"What?" he asked, leaning forward. "Did you say something?"

Ethan raised his voice and repeated, "Duncan has a wife and kids. What'll happen to them?" He stopped where Thomas could come up beside him. "And my mother..." Ethan's eyes watered. He swallowed and looked away. "Duncan was her favorite. He was the one who reached out to her. I was just a baby, so I don't remember, but Ma told me how he'd do things for her. She never saw him, but she knew it was him."

Ethan prodded the ground with the toe of his boot. "I don't know how much you know about my family, but when Ma and I came to live in Illinois, she didn't speak much English. She didn't know anything but Lakota ways. Duncan was almost nine, the twins were seven and Seth was... I don't know, six, I guess. It was hardest on Duncan because he remembered his real ma. He told me at first he resented her. Because she wasn't his ma, and because she didn't dress or act like anyone else's. He took a lot of ribbing on account of her. They all did. Ma said she was afraid to talk to them because she didn't have the right words."

Ethan looked up, eyes fixing in the distance. "Duncan said after a while, he got curious. He'd watch her when she wasn't looking, and it didn't take long to figure out she was more scared than he was. So he started doing things for her. Like making sure there was always wood stacked by the stove and cleaning up after the rest of us. And he started sticking up for her at school. I didn't know what it was about at the time, but I remember him coming home bloody. At first he was angry and wouldn't let Ma near him, but after a while, he started letting her tend to him.

"He started looking out for me, too. Up 'til then, I'd been pretty isolated. They were so much older, and Ma only talked to me in Lakota, so I hadn't but a few words of English. Duncan took to carrying me around on his shoulders, taking me with him wherever he went, and talking. It was him taught me English. And Seth. He followed Duncan's lead and started helping Ma and playing with me. What they did made a big difference to both of us. The twins helped out when they thought of it, but..." Ethan shrugged and looked at Thomas. "You know how they are. All they ever needed was each other." His eyes filled. "I don't know how Josh'll manage without Jamie."

It was Thomas' turn to look away. "Neither do I." He cleared his throat. "Neither do I," he repeated with a slow shake of his head.

They stood where they were, lost in thought, united by grief.

Eventually, Ethan sighed. "I'm ready, if you are."

Thomas responded with a grim nod.

Together they trudged back across the yard.

OCTOBER

5

They were held in Atlanta for nearly a week, awaiting a train that would carry them east. The large number of men crowded within the walls discouraged unnecessary movement, so they spent much of their time talking or sleeping. The only distraction came once each day when slaves with wooden buckets passed among them doling out rations— hard bread or a cracker and a hunk of boiled meat. There was no consistency to the slaves' schedule; they would arrive late in the evening and again, early the following morning. Then as many as thirty hours might pass before they reappeared. The weak grew weaker and morale plummeted.

Ethan's leg began to mend, but the intensity of his headaches fluctuated. Most of the time, they were nothing more than a dull, steady ache that he was learning to live with, but occasionally, they were incapacitating. When the pain grew unbearable, he was reduced to lying huddled on the ground, eyes closed, waiting for it to pass.

Two days after their arrival, a train bearing another load of prisoners arrived from Chickamauga. The population of the stockade swelled to the point of bursting. Relief came late in the day when men were called forward by company and herded out through the gate.

Three days passed, and early one evening, another list was read. Last to be summoned were the five men from the 36th Illinois. They attached themselves to the end of the long column of men headed for the depot. Last to board, they squeezed into the boxcar ahead of the caboose. When the door closed, Thomas and Ethan were pressed against it.

The car was cleaner than the one they'd previously occupied, and until the buckets began to fill, the air easier to breathe. When it finally began, long after dark, the trip was similar to the one six days earlier. The train trundled east at a leisurely pace, passing fallow fields, dense pine and hardwood forests, and the flickering lights of farms and hamlets. After sun-up, the townsfolk turned out at each stop to stare and hurl insults—all but the pie-sellers who remained determinedly friendly as they hawked their wares. Thomas put his money to good use, and their meager diet of the last few days was quickly supplemented.

Toward evening, the train pulled into a town that Fergus, one eye to a crack, announced as Crawfordville. They waited on a siding for over an hour. Thomas made his final purchases of the day and handed food to Ethan, ordering him to eat.

Dusk was settling when a shudder ran through the train, and it began to inch forward. It didn't go far before stopping, this time to take on water. Guards walked along the line, slamming bolts and rolling open doors. Reeking buckets were passed from the ends of each car, and a man from each was delegated to empty them. A guard beckoned Thomas, and he jumped down, walking back and forth to the edge of the woods until all the buckets were empty. He was handing the last of them to Zach when there was a shout further up the line, followed by the crack of a gunshot. A burst of shots followed.

Thomas froze, looking toward the commotion. Guards ran past him. One pushed Thomas, forcing him into the car before rolling the door closed and giving the bolt a shove.

A chorus of voices rose from the gloom, wanting to know what had happened.

"One of the men," Thomas said, looking stunned. "They shot him."

Questions came from throughout the car: "Why?" "Did he run?" "Was he trying to escape?"

Thomas shook his head. "After the first shot, I saw him standing at the edge of the woods. He'd dropped his buckets and was backing away. That's when they all started shooting." He peered through the darkness at the faces nearest him. "He had his hands up, and they shot him."

Voices rose in fear and indignation. As the initial shock wore off, protests sank to a murmur. By the time they heard the guards returning, a gloomy silence had settled over the car.

Eventually, the whistle sounded, and the train lurched into motion. As it did, the door at Thomas' back shifted. He looked at Ethan. Ethan's brows shot up, and he gave a slight nod.

Fergus leaned in. "Ye feel that?"

"Yes," Ethan whispered.

Thomas twisted, slipping fingers into the crack and hauling on the door to see if it would move. It did.

Ethan was on his knees beside him. "We have to go before they discover it."

"It'll be risky. There are guards everywhere."

"We'll never get a better chance. We have to try." When Thomas continued to stare through the opening, Ethan persisted. "Who's to say Richmond won't be worse than Atlanta? And what about the man they shot? It could be one of us next time." He seized Thomas' arm. "We have to go. Now! Before the next town."

"I'm with you," Thomas muttered, squinting at the darkened landscape. "I'm just not sure how to go about it. When I got off, there were two guards on the back platform of the caboose. If they ride back there, the lanterns'll show them everything along the tracks." He paused before adding, "I guess we find a place where we can roll into cover."

"Look for a place," Fergus whispered.

"Open it wider," Zach urged.

Thomas moved the door several inches.

"What's goin' on?" Frank demanded.

A murmur spread through the car as men spied the opening. They began edging toward it, crowding one another until one of them shoved Thomas.

He rounded on them in a fury. "Back off, dammit! You'll get your turn, all of you, but not if you push me out and alert the guards. Now back off!"

The opportunity that presented itself was better than any they could have hoped for. The train slowed to a crawl as it topped a small rise. Before it could gather speed again, the men from the Thirty-sixth dropped off and rolled into the underbrush.

"Now what?" Zach asked as they scrambled to their feet, staring after the receding red lanterns.

"We stay south of the tracks, parallel them 'til morning, then find a place to hole up for the day." Ethan's words came in a rush as he pushed his way through the undergrowth. "Come on!" he urged, glancing back.

The other men shared a look, then hurried to catch up. Moments later, gunshots split the night air, followed immediately by the frantic screeching of the train whistle.

"Damn," Thomas muttered.

"They'll be after us now," Ethan said, quickening his pace.

The darkness that had aided their escape proved a hindrance as they pushed through untamed forest. Vines and roots tripped them; branches tore at their clothes and faces. Horst fell hard at one point, bruising a knee and cursing in German. The others stumbled, caught themselves, and hurried on.

After several tortuous miles, they staggered out of the woods onto a narrow lane. Without hesitation, Ethan turned west.

"Wait!" Zach panted. He pulled to a stop, supporting himself with his hands on his thighs. The others straggled to a halt around him. "Rest a minute. We need to figure out what to do."

"We haven't gone far enough." Barely breaking stride, Ethan flung the words over his shoulder. "They'll be after us. We need to keep moving."

"You got any idea where you're going?"

Ethan stopped. Turning to face them, he said, "I told you. We stay south of the tracks 'til morning, then find a place to hide. If they don't catch us, we head out again tomorrow night."

"That's it?" Zach demanded. "None of us have a say?"

"Come on, Ethan," Thomas implored. "Let's talk about it."

"There's no time for talk. We need to put as much distance between us and them as we can. Now!" Ethan turned and started away.

"To hell with him," Frank growled. "Who needs him?"

Thomas spoke over him. "Ethan, stop! Wait a minute!"

Ethan stopped, but didn't turn around. He waited impatiently for Thomas to come to him.

"What's wrong with you?" Thomas demanded. "We're in this together. Why can't we talk?"

Ethan rounded on him. "Because talk's a waste of time! Instead of standing here, we should be getting away. But if you want to talk, fine. Go ahead and talk. I, for one, don't intend to be anywhere near here when the Rebs come looking."

With that, he was off. Thomas looked from his retreating form to the others. A nod from Fergus, and they set out after him. The remaining three exchanged looks. Horst shrugged and started walking. Frank swore under his breath. Zach looked at him, then followed Horst. With no choice left to him, Frank trailed along behind.

Over level ground, aided by the faint light of a crescent moon, Ethan lengthened his stride. The others hastened to keep up. He kept to the road until it intersected a stream, then turned south, pushing his way through the undergrowth for fifty yards before grasping an overhanging branch. He tugged at it, and satisfied it would bear his weight, slid down the steep bank into the water.

Thomas looked down at him. "Ethan! What the—"

"Dogs," Ethan hissed. "Once they figure out we're gone, they're bound to come after us with dogs. We need to throw them off our scent." Standing knee-deep in the cold water, he waited. As they continued to hesitate, a look of irritation crossed his face. "We need to keep moving. If you're coming, do it in the water, not where the dogs can follow you."

The five men on the bank looked at one another. When no one offered a better suggestion, they took hold of the branch and slid, one by one, into the water. When they were all assembled, Ethan doubled back, heading upstream.

The going was difficult. Nerves frayed and tempers flared. After an hour, Frank had had enough. Hurrying to catch up, he grabbed Ethan by the arm and yanked him around, demanding they go ashore. Ethan refused.

"You ain't the ranking officer here," Frank snarled, jerking a thumb at Thomas. "He is."

"I don't care. I'm sticking to the creek."

"We're done listening to you, breed."

Ethan flushed with anger. He pulled free of Frank's grasp and splashed away.

"I'll see to it yer brought up on charges!"

"Go ahead," Ethan flung back at him. "*If* you make it back."

Zach stepped across his path. "Frank's right," he said, jabbing a finger into Ethan's chest. "You show up outta nowhere and start giving orders." He looked at the shadowed faces of the other men. "I don't know about you, but I've had enough."

"Damn right," Frank muttered.

"No one's giving orders," Ethan said, making an effort to his control his temper. "I know what I intend to do. If anyone wants to stick with me, fine. Otherwise, I'll go it alone." He looked at Thomas. "Now, please, if you'll let me by?"

Tense seconds passed before Thomas ordered Zach to step aside. Zach bit back protest, moving just enough for Ethan to brush past. They watched as darkness swallowed him.

"Now what?" Fergus asked.

"We get outta the damn water." Frank headed for the bank, looking for a place to climb out. Zach started after him.

"But what about za dogs? What if he is right about za dogs?"

Thomas looked at Horst. "He's right," he said, after a moment. "I don't think leaving the creek's a good idea just yet."

"Everything Ethan's said sounds right to me," Fergus said, starting upstream. "I'll be going after him, so I will."

"I also," Horst informed them.

Thomas turned to Zach. "Ethan's the only one with a plan. Until someone comes up with a better one, I'm sticking with him."

The three of them waded past Zach and Frank, Fergus holding Zach's eyes with his own. Zach threw up his hands and followed.

Still grasping an overhanging branch, Frank watched them go. They were little more than shadows in the darkness when he cursed, slapped the branch away, and splashed after them.

As the night wore on, clouds obscured the moon, making the going even more treacherous. Adding to their misery, just before sunrise, a light rain began to fall. Ethan kept to the creek until the sky began to gray, then led them ashore at a bend in the stream where three large, flat slabs of limestone protruded like steps from the bank.

"Fan out," he told them, standing on the highest rock. "Head off into the woods for a few hundred yards in different directions, then double back, keeping to the same path you went in on. We'll meet here. After that, we'll head upstream a ways and find a place to spend the day." His eyes traveled the sullen faces arrayed before him. His shoulders rose and fell in a weary shrug. "It's the best I know to do."

Frank turned to Thomas. "You ain't gonna let the likes a' him keep telling us what to do, are you?"

Thomas looked at Ethan. He was staring at the ground, arms crossed, shoulders hunched against the rain. He looked at Frank. "Do what he says." Frank opened his mouth to argue, and Thomas' voice hardened. "Do it, Frank."

Frank looked to the others for support, but they were already spreading out among the trees. Casting Ethan a look filled with loathing, he thrashed into the underbrush.

Thomas was first to return. He trod carefully, coming close to Ethan before stopping to observe him. He was seated on the highest rock, knees pulled up, his head resting on crossed arms. Thomas took a deliberate step, snapping a twig underfoot.

Ethan looked up. His eyes, in that first unguarded moment, revealed just how much he was suffering. He tried to hide it as Thomas came to stand beside him.

"Your head?"

"Mmhmm..."

Ethan put down a hand, preparing to stand. Thomas grabbed him by the arm and hauled him to his feet.

"We need to go further in the creek."

"You're sure?"

"I am."

Thomas shrugged deeper into his coat and stared gloomily at the rain pitting the sluggish brown water.

"Come or not," Ethan said softly. "It's up to you." Without waiting for a response, he stepped down the rocks into the creek.

Thomas looked around. Fergus and Horst were visible among the trees, Zach in and out of sight beyond them. There was no sign of Frank.

"Ethan..." Fergus protested, emerging from the woods. He looked at Thomas, then shook his head in resignation, and waded into the water. Horst followed without a word.

"What the... ?" Zach came to a stop beside Thomas.

"Not much further." When Zach still hesitated, Thomas added irritably, "Just do it."

They were making their way upstream when Thomas spotted Frank. He was back from the bank, following them among the trees.

"Get back there, Frank!" he shouted, pointing toward the rocks. "Go back and get in the water!"

Ethan swung around, furious. "Get outta here, Frank! I'm fed up with arguing. This is the first place the dogs'll pick up our scent if they keep after us. Up there, they'll follow you. If they find you, they find us. So go on! Get outta here! Don't lead them to the rest of us." He turned and splashed upstream. Everyone but Thomas waded after him.

"You can't have it both ways, Frank. Either get back in the water or head out on your own."

Frank scowled. Thomas glared at him. The other four were disappearing around a bend when Frank cursed and stalked back to the rocks.

The going was easier in daylight. After interminable hours spent floundering through darkness, it seemed only a short time before Ethan waded to the western edge of the stream and scrambled up the bank. The rain turned to mist as they made their way across a fallow field and into the woods beyond. When they were well hidden, Ethan stopped. Without a word, he sank to the ground and rolled onto his side. The others looked at one another, then dropped down around him.

Midway through the afternoon, Thomas woke to the faint baying of hounds. He bolted upright, jostling Ethan. Ethan stirred and moaned, then heard the dogs and came fully awake. The sound grew louder, rousing the others. They sat up, looking at one another in alarm. Ethan pushed himself to his feet and walked to the edge of the woods, staring across the sunlit field in the direction of the creek. The others came to stand with him. For too long, the hounds seemed to be getting closer. Then, miraculously, the baying began to recede. Before long, it faded all together, leaving only the twitter of birds and the rustle of dying leaves.

"We fooled them, Ethan!" Fergus exclaimed, grinning and clapping him on the back.

Ethan shook his head. "I don't think so." Leaning one shoulder against the trunk of a tree, he continued to stare across the field. "My guess is they're down where we first got in the creek. The way it curves, we didn't come all that far. They'll probably follow it south a ways, running the dogs along the banks. When they don't find any sign of us, they'll come back." He looked at Thomas. "I'm hoping they stop before they get to the rocks. If not, maybe our scent fanning out and stopping will confuse the dogs enough that they'll give up."

"And if it doesn't?" Zach demanded.

Ethan shrugged and looked toward the creek. "We go to Richmond, I guess."

Frank cursed under his breath and stalked away. He was back within seconds. "Yer so all-fired smart. Why don'chu do something?"

"Like get us outta here," Zach added, shoulder to shoulder with Frank.

Ethan pushed himself upright, eyeing the two of them silently before shifting his gaze to the others. "If we panic now, and run, it won't solve a thing. Just take them a little longer to hunt us down, is all." He ran his eyes over them before adding, "You're all in uniform. Showing yourselves in daylight would be a mistake." He looked at Frank and Zach. "Run if you want. Only give us your word you won't let on about the rest of us when they catch you."

Frank thrust his face into Ethan's. "What makes you so all-fired sure we'll get caught?"

"Chances are you will."

Frank snorted contemptuously.   "An' *yer* gonna see to it we don't?" Grabbing a handful of Ethan's coat, he shoved him backward against the tree. "Just who do you think you are, breed?"

"That's enough, Frank!"

Thomas spoke sharply. Frank's grip relaxed enough that Ethan pulled free. He took several steps away as Frank turned accusing eyes on Thomas.

"What I'd like to know is why yer in such an all-fired hurry to put yer faith in the likes a' him. What's he know that we don't?"

"He's done all right by us so far," Fergus put in.

"All right?" Frank scoffed. "There's hounds almost on top of us an' yer saying he's done all right?" He flung a hand at Ethan. "Even he says they'll be back."

"I sink maybe we do what he say. We wait; see what happen."

"You!" Frank sneered, turning on the Austrian. "Whadda you know?"

Horst shrugged. "Not so much about zis. So I listen to him."

Frank's angry gaze took in each of them in turn. "What're *you* gonna do?" he asked when his eyes settled on Zach.

Zach hesitated, and in the silence they heard it again. This time, the baying grew louder until it seemed the dogs would burst from the trees along the creek at any moment.

Thomas went to stand with Ethan. "Where are they?" he asked softly.

"At the rocks." Ethan shook his head. "I was hoping they wouldn't follow us that far." A note of desperation crept into his voice when he added, "I don't know what to do if they keep after us."

Thomas took him by the arm, turning him away from the others. "You did the best you could. Better'n any of us would have done. If you hadn't kept us moving, we'd be back on the train by now."

Ethan looked across the field. As he did, the baying began to falter. It turned to a sporadic series of yips, then died away completely. The men from the Thirty-sixth strained to hear, staring toward the creek.

"I think we lost 'em," Thomas muttered.

No one could believe it. They stayed where they were, watching and listening.

"I think we did it," Thomas repeated at last. "I think we lost 'em."

Ethan nodded. Thomas clapped him on the shoulder, and Fergus let out a muffled whoop. Horst caught Ethan's eye and grinned.

"You did good, Fraser."

Ethan turned warily, looking from Zach's face to his extended right hand.

"Thanks," Zach muttered as they shook.

They made their way back to where they'd slept, their mood celebratory as they pulled the last of the food from their pockets and clustered together to eat. Ethan moved off by himself, sitting with his back against the trunk of aged oak. He dug in his pockets for his few remaining peanuts and ate them slowly, cracking them and tossing away the shells.

Thomas wandered over and sat down next to him. They didn't speak until Ethan popped the last peanut in his mouth and brushed the debris from his coat. Pushing himself to his feet, he said, "We need food. I'll see what I can find."

"I'll go with you."

Thomas started to rise, but Ethan laid a hand on his shoulder.

"It's best if I go alone. Best if only one shows himself."

"But—"

"I'm not in uniform. I'll go."

Ethan turned away before Thomas could protest. Half a dozen quick strides, and he vanished into the underbrush.

6

The thicket wasn't particularly deep, and Ethan reached the far side in a matter of minutes. He stopped while still in the cover of the trees and looked across the dried, broken stalks that were all that remained of a cornfield. A hedgerow marked the far boundary, and beyond it, slaves with hoes and shovels worked the adjoining field.

Keeping a wary eye on them, he crossed the cornfield and crouched in the cover of the hedge, not far from where two slaves stood talking. Ethan craned his neck, studying the field's occupants. Failing to spot a white overseer, he crept along the hedge.

As he came opposite the two men, one of them turned and walked away. Waiting until he was out of earshot, Ethan raised his voice and commanded, "Come here. I want to talk to you."

The remaining slave spun around, startled. Seeing no one, he took a cautious step toward the hedge.

"Can I trust you?" Ethan asked, straightening enough for the man to see him.

The man stared, clearly puzzled. "Yessuh," came the guarded reply.

"Where's the overseer?"

"Ober there." The man pointed.

"Which one?"

"The man I 'uz jes' talkin' to."

"The overseer is a Negro?" Ethan confirmed.

"Yessuh."

"Good. Now tell me, would you say you're a friend to the Yankees?"

The man's eyes widened. "I never met no Yankee afo'."

"If I was to tell you I'm a Yankee soldier, would that be all right with you?"

The man grinned and took a step closer. "Why, yessuh."

"I need food. Is that something you could help me with?"

"We's diggin' sweet taters. You want somma them, Massa?"

"Yes. Enough for six of us."

"Theys six ob you?" The man's eyes darted over the field behind Ethan. "I bes' call Abel. I 'spects he can 'range sumptin'."

"Wait! Who's Abel?"

"He the obaseer."

"You trust him not to tell anyone there are Yankees nearby?"

"Why, yessuh."

"All right." Ethan nodded dismissively. "Go fetch him."

"Yessuh," the man said, and hurried away.

Ethan hunkered down to wait, annoyed at having revealed too much. *Exactly what I told Frank not to do.* He shook his head. *Too late to take it back now.*

He heard the men returning and rose to meet them.

"I's Abel, Massa," the older man said, clutching his hat to his chest. He was powerfully built, with skin like coal and hair the color of smoke. "Sam say you a Yankee sojur. That the troot, suh?"

"It is. I need food if you can spare it."

"And they's six ob you?" Abel wagged his head. "We got nuttin' here to feed that many, I kin tell you that. But you welcome to somma these sweet taters. After it git dark, if'n you was to follow that road aroun' to the gate, I kin see you has mo'." He turned to the other man. "Fetch a gunnysack, Sam, and bring somma them taters."

Sam departed, leaving Ethan and Abel to eye one another over the hedge.

"You fo' sure a Yankee sojur?"

"I am."

"You been fightin' in the war?"

"Yes."

"It the troot the Yankees gonna set us free?"

Ethan nodded. "It's true."

"That's mo' than I can imagine, bein' free." For a moment, the older man's eyes lingered in the distance. He cleared his throat and looked at Ethan. "What else you Massas need?"

Ethan thought quickly. "Anything you can spare. A knife, matches, a bucket—"

Sam's return interrupted him. He hoisted the heavy bag over the hedge as Abel said, "Come aroun' to the gate after dark."

"I'll be there."

Ethan shouldered the gunnysack and made his way back across the cornfield. At the edge of the woods, he stopped and looked back. The two men were still watching him. Too late he realized his mistake. Two weeks since he'd been hit in the head, and still his thinking was muddled. He skirted the tree line and continued to walk long after the men were gone from sight, hoping to mislead them in the event they betrayed him.

His companions started nervously when he appeared from the opposite direction and dumped the sack of potatoes in their midst.

"That's all for now," he said wearily. "I think I've arranged for more later." Looking up at the cloudless sky, he added, "It's probably safe to light a fire, if anyone has matches. Keep it small, and no flame after dark."

"There he goes," Frank muttered. "Givin' orders again."

Thomas ignored him, watching Ethan lower himself to the ground at the foot of the oak and roll onto his side. Going to stand next to him, he asked, "There anything I can do for you?"

"No." Then, as an afterthought, "Thanks."

Thomas shook his head and went to gather wood. Fergus produced a match safe and went through several matches before finding one that would light. They clustered around it, shielding the tiny flame with their bodies, waiting for the tinder to catch.

Once the fire established, they laid the potatoes in a ring around it, turning them periodically with sticks. Hunger compelled them to pull some from the fire long before they were done. Ignoring singed fingers, they pulled back the skins and consumed them nearly raw.

The edge had gone from his hunger before Thomas realized Ethan hadn't joined them.

"Hey!" Frank protested as Thomas grabbed a stick and speared three of the blackened potatoes.

Thomas tilted his head in Ethan's direction. "For him."

Frank turned to look. They all did.

"How you sink he knows what he knows?" Horst asked.

"No idea," Thomas replied, spearing a potato for himself.

They ate in silence until all the potatoes but three were gone. The last of the light was fading when Thomas reluctantly kicked dirt over the fire, knocking down the flames. They remained huddled around it as night fell, drawing warmth from the embers.

At the edge of the clearing, Ethan shifted and jerked awake. He sat up quickly, then moaned, cradling his head in his hands. When the pain was bearable, he looked toward the shadowy figures ringing the fire. "How long has it been dark?" he asked crossly, pushing himself to his feet. "Why didn't you wake me?"

"You didn't say anything about waking you," Thomas said, rising to meet him. "I figured you needed some rest." He gestured toward the potatoes. "We saved—"

"To hell with them," Ethan interrupted. "I'm supposed to meet someone. How long has it been dark?"

"Not long. Half an hour or so."

Ethan pulled his coat more tightly about him and buttoned it to the throat. "I need one of you to come with me. The rest of you wait here. If we're not back in an hour, or if you see or hear anything suspicious, move on without us." He squatted next to the fire, and picking up a stick, began drawing lines in the dirt. "We're here. This is the creek we followed. This is where we jumped from the train. Head west 'til you're south of Madison, here, then angle north. Keep away from Atlanta, here, up towards Lawrenceville. Then head for Canton, then Kennesaw, then Rome. After that, keep to the mountains. It'll be rough going, but if you keep heading northwest, you're bound to run across a Union picket line. Somewhere around here, I'd think." He made a final mark in the dirt and rose, tossing the stick aside. "Who's coming with me?"

They stared at him, speechless. Thomas was the first to recover. "Me. I'll go."

Ethan gave a curt nod and strode past him into the trees. Thomas shared a baffled look with the others before hurrying after him.

He caught up with Ethan at the edge of the cornfield, grabbing his arm and forcing him around. "All right," he said, peering at Ethan's face in the darkness. "It's time you told me what the hell's going on. How do you know to draw a map like that?"

Ethan tried to pull away. Thomas' fingers dug into his arm.

"Now's not the time. We're late."

"Late for what?" Thomas demanded. "Who do you know around here?"

"Down the road a piece. I think I've arranged for some food."

Suddenly, inexplicably, Ethan relaxed. Thomas had been ready to force a confrontation; to beat information from him if necessary, but Ethan's sudden lack of resistance rattled him. His grip loosened, and Ethan pulled away.

They'd reached the far side of the cornfield when Thomas tried again. "Look, I'm sorry I didn't wake you. It looked to me like your head hurt, and always before—"

"You can't baby me, Thomas. Not if I'm going to get us through this."

"What do you mean?" Thomas demanded, irritated all over again. "Why is it up to you?" When Ethan didn't respond, he repeated, "Why? What the hell's going on, Ethan?"

"Keep your voice down!"

Thomas glared at him, and they continued on in uneasy silence. They had traversed the second field, and were trudging along a narrow lane, when Ethan spoke.

"When we get down here a ways, there's supposed to be a gate. I want you to hang back, out of sight, where you can see what's going on. If everything's all right, I'll give a whistle. But if it's a trap, get away as quick as you can. Get back to the others, and head north the way I showed you."

"And leave you behind? No."

Ethan stopped abruptly, grabbing Thomas by the arm. "You will," he hissed. "To get enough food, I told the overseer there are six of us, so if there are men waiting, there'll be a lot of them." He took a breath before adding, "Please, Thomas. Do as I ask. If you have any doubts, leave me."

Unwilling to agree, Thomas said nothing.

"I can take care of myself." Ethan squeezed his arm. "Promise me, or we turn back. We leave without food."

Seconds stretched before Thomas gave a slight shake of his head, blowing air through pursed lips in frustration. "All right. I promise."

"Good."

Ethan released him, and they continued along the lane until it curved out of sight behind a clump of bushes. Thomas followed as Ethan moved into their shadow and crept around the bend. A large two-story farmhouse came into view, light glowing from curtained windows. Closer stood the slave quarters. Cooking fires glimmered, and they could see people moving about. Standing in dim silhouette against the light from the fires was a pair of stone gateposts.

Ethan surveyed the darkness. Seeing nothing out of the ordinary, he whispered, "I'm going over by the gate. If you see or hear anything you don't like, get out fast." He touched Thomas' arm. "I have your word?"

"Yes," came the reluctant reply.

Ethan stepped into the road and walked toward the gateposts, eyes searching, muscles tensed. He reached the nearest post without incident. Slipping into its shadow, he hunkered down to wait.

Twenty minutes passed before he heard voices. Rising cautiously, he watched several dark figures approach. As they drew closer, a voice he recognized called softly, "You there, Massa?"

He made out the shapes of three men and two women. At the sight of the women, he relaxed. "I'm here," he said, stepping from the shadows.

"We brung the food, Massa, an' some s'plies you asked fo'." Abel peered into the shadows behind Ethan. "Where the udder Massas? They too much fo' jus' you an' me to carry."

Ethan gave a low whistle. Thomas emerged from the bushes and came to join them.

The women handed Ethan two large, covered baskets. Thomas collected a tin pail and a bulging pair of gunnysacks from the men. With Abel accompanying them, they headed back toward the thicket.

They had been gone the better part of an hour, and the waiting men were on their feet, pacing and anxious. Abel produced and lit a covered lantern before unloading a feast. There was a pail of stew made with chicken broth and vegetables. Another pail contained milk. One basket was packed with cornpone and biscuits; the other held boiled ears of corn. There was a jug of molasses. It was their first decent meal in two weeks, and they downed the food hungrily.

When he could eat no more, Ethan looked at Abel. "I know this means doing without. I want you to know we're grateful."

The others licked their fingers, murmuring agreement.

44

Abel's grin showed in the light from the lantern. "Lor' bress you, Massas. We happy to hep." He indicated the two unopened gunnysacks. "They the things you asked fo'. They ain't much, but we wants you suhs to have them."

He loaded the used plates and utensils into the baskets and got to his feet. "They anything else I kin do fo' you, Massas?"

"You've done enough," Ethan said, rising with him. "We're in your debt, Abel. Thank you."

Zach snuffed the lantern and handed it to Abel.

"It's time we were going," Ethan said as the old man blended into the darkness. This time, he got no argument.

He struck out west, across fields and through woods until they came to another track. They had been following it for several hours when suddenly, he stopped. The others came to a halt around him, and in the stillness, heard it, too. As one, they flung themselves into brush bordering the lane, lying hidden as a troop of armed horsemen trotted past, saddle leather creaking and bit chains jangling. When they were gone, Ethan stepped back into the lane.

"Who were they?" Fergus asked, coming to stand beside him.

"Hard telling. Not regular cavalry, that's for sure. Whoever they are, we need to stay clear of them."

They continued along the track until it intersected a major roadway. Crossing over, they plunged into the woods beyond. An hour later, they came to a stream. Ethan hesitated, then slid down the bank into the water.

"You sure this is necessary?" Thomas grumbled.

"You sure it's not?" came the weary reply.

A moment's indecision, and they waded in after him. Ethan kept to the creek for more than a mile before leading them out on the opposite bank and angling through the woods. Light was beginning to streak the eastern sky when they came to another, larger stream. There were groans and muttered curses as Ethan waded in.

The sun had been up for some time when Ethan scrambled up the western bank into a stretch of untamed forest. When they were well hidden, he sat down, pulling wet boots from blistered feet. The others did the same. Horst rummaged through the sacks Abel had left, finding a hunk of salt-pork, a sack of cornmeal, sweet potatoes, ears of corn, a spoon, a tin cup, a wooden bucket, a knife, a tin of matches, two moth-eaten wool blankets, and a ragged quilt.

"Enough for two days, maybe sree," he announced, setting aside a portion of food to be cooked and stowing the rest.

"Good," Thomas said, turning to Ethan. "That means you won't have to..." The words died on his lips. Ethan was curled on the ground, head resting on one arm, already asleep. Taking the quilt from Horst, Thomas laid it over him.

Ethan woke at mid-day to the sound of voices. He crept toward the stream, lying hidden in the undergrowth as two Negro boys with cane poles stopped on the opposite bank. He worried they would settle in to fish, but after a short conversation, they moved on. He waited until he no longer heard voices before rejoining Thomas under the quilt.

It was late afternoon when they woke. They ate the corn and salt pork Horst prepared, and the last of the cornpone. Their boots were dry, but the leather had stiffened, and it was painful to pull them on.

"I ain't going nowhere like this," Frank announced.

Fergus cast Ethan an imploring look. "We can scarcely walk. We need to stay here tonight."

Ethan was hobbling in circles, trying to reshape his boots to his feet. "We need to keep moving."

"Ethan..."

"We need to keep moving, Thomas. We're less than twenty miles from where we jumped."

"Twenty miles?" Zach protested. "We walked a hell of a lot further than that."

"Not in a straight line. Now are you with me or—"

"You been leadin' us in circles, breed?"

Blisters forgotten, Frank was on his feet, face thrust into Ethan's. Ethan gave him a look of disgust and turned away.

"Don't turn yer back on me!"

Frank grabbed Ethan's arm and yanked him around. Ethan kept coming. His fist connected with enough force to send Frank sprawling onto his back. He pushed himself up on one elbow, hand to his jaw, his expression stunned. With an angry growl, he staggered to his feet and would have thrown himself at Ethan, but Zach and Fergus seized his arms.

Ethan struggled in Horst's grasp, glaring angrily at Frank.

"I'll ge'chu, you bastard!" Frank snarled. "See if I don't!"

Still furious, Ethan forced himself to relax. A nod from Thomas, and Horst released him. Ethan bent to collect his hat, slapped it against his leg and jammed it on his head. Without a word, he headed off into the trees.

"Ethan! Wait!"

Fergus released Frank and hobbled after him. Horst stuffed the blankets into one sack, Zach scooped up the other. Thomas kicked dirt over the fire. No one spared Frank a glance as they hurried past.

Ethan struck out northwest, skirting farmhouses and following tracks wherever he could, pushing through dense forest until it opened onto to a river. Moonlight rippled silver across a swath of inky blackness, the distant shore a ragged shadow beneath starlit sky.

"Where are we?" Thomas asked, limping to a stop beside him.

"Oconee River," Ethan said, staring across. "Twenty-five, thirty miles from where we jumped."

"How do we get across?"

"Ferry. There's bound to be some along here. All we have to do is find the right one."

"What do you mean?"

"One that's run by a Negro. No whites around." A moment passed before he asked, "How are your feet?"

"Worse since we've been walking, but I'll live."

"How are the others?"

"Same, I reckon."

"Where's Frank?"

Thomas tilted his head. "Back a ways. The soles are coming off his boots."

"Will he be able to keep up?"

"He got a choice?"

Ethan continued to gaze across the river. "It's important that we get across before morning. You think they're up to it?"

Thomas shrugged. "You earned their trust when you fooled the dogs. More'n likely they'll do what you say." He looked sideways at Ethan. "But if you want my advice, you might try talking to them some. Being so tight-lipped's making everyone nervous."

Ethan was silent for several moments. "That go for you, too, Thomas?"

"Yeah," he admitted. "It does."

"Sorry you feel that way." Stung by his unexpected betrayal, Ethan snapped, "I'm not used to traveling in a pack, let alone having to answer for every move I make."

Thomas rounded on him. "Just what *are* you used to, Ethan? You show up outta nowhere, tell the Rebs you're with the Thirty-sixth." He snorted. "You haven't been with the Thirty-sixth in months. Hell, you're not even in uniform. It's time you told me what the devil's going on."

Ethan stood silent, eyeing the dark water. When he spoke again, his tone was more civil. "Sorry. I'm used to traveling alone. Looking out for so many is wearing." He offered Thomas a brittle smile. "I'll make an effort to consult you more often."

Thomas would have forced the issue, but Fergus spoke up behind them. "Where are we?"

"Oconee River," Thomas muttered, glowering at Ethan.

"Mein Gott!" Horst muttered. "How we do zis now?"

When Frank caught up, they turned north. Before long, they glimpsed light through the trees. Ethan went ahead to investigate, returning almost immediately.

"There's a rowboat in the bushes up ahead. The oars are leaned up against the house, but there's a dog. One of you will have to distract it while I get them. The boat's small, so two of us'll have swim." He scanned their faces. "I'll volunteer. Or we can keep going and look for another way across. It's up to you, but we need to be on the other side by sun-up."

"I'll swim," Fergus volunteered.

Zach said, "I'll distract the dog."

They carried the rowboat to the river and floated it. Finding it free of leaks, Ethan and Zach went to fetch the oars. Zach circled away from the river before showing himself. The dog leapt up, barking, and gave chase as he darted into the woods. Ethan had no sooner laid hands the oars than the door to the shack slammed open. He pulled back into the shadows as an elderly white man, clad in longhandles and armed with a shotgun, stepped outside. Waiting until the man's back was turned, Ethan lifted the oars and slipped away.

Back at the river, he and Fergus stripped off their clothes. Zach appeared, limping badly and gasping for breath. Hands reached out to him, and he fell into the boat. It was a tight fit, and the little craft rode low in the water. Following a hurried discussion, they agreed to risk it. With Thomas manning the oars, they set out.

For as long as Ethan and Fergus could touch bottom, they helped steady the little boat. Then they dropped into the main channel, the current caught the bow and swung it around sharply. Thomas strained against the oars, and the two swimmers kicked, but the heavily laden craft swept downstream faster than it moved across. Fergus had just announced he'd touched bottom, when they swung around a bend.

"Everyone down!" Zach hissed, startled by the sight of a large number of fires among the trees on the western shore.

Thomas looked over his shoulder, cursed, and released the oars. The boat rocked dangerously as the four men shifted, crouching low. Fergus and Ethan hugged the sides. They could see uniformed men around the fires and tents among the trees. Voices carried, and fingers of firelight stretched across the water, threatening to expose them.

When the light receded, Thomas shifted back into position and grabbed the oars. The current had carried them back to the middle of the channel, and he strained to angle the boat toward the shore. Ethan and Fergus resumed kicking, but the long minutes of inactivity had left them both chilled. It seemed a long time before Fergus said, "I've touched bottom."

Seconds later, Ethan felt it, too. The current slowed among the shallows, and Horst, then Zach stepped out to help pull the boat ashore. Frank pulled out the blankets, and the four who'd been in the boat toweled down the two who'd been in the water, rubbing warmth back into them.

The eastern sky was turning from black to gray when they came upon an abandoned barn, and Ethan called a halt for the day. The walls were weathered gray, barely standing, and much of roof had caved in. Previous occupants had built fires in the area open to the sky, so they gathered wood and did the same, drying the blankets, and heating the last of the pork and sweet potatoes. Horst added water to the cornmeal, shaped it into patties, and placed them on the hot rocks next to the flames.

While breakfast cooked, Thomas went in search of Ethan. He found him sitting in the sun, his back against the wall of the barn. He was gazing across the overgrown field they'd just crossed, but as Thomas, approached, his eyes closed. Thomas ignored the attempt at evasion and settled next to him.

"How's the head?"

After a moment, Ethan's eyes opened. He turned to look at Thomas, the pain behind them evident. "Hurts. It's worst in the mornings."

"What can I do to help?"

"Nothing."

"Back at the river, you said being responsible wears on you. Why's it up to you?"

"I know this country." Ethan leaned his head back and closed his eyes. "I know the people. I know how to survive here, and I think I can get us back without getting caught."

The flatness of his voice and the tightening around his mouth communicated his pain and reluctance to talk, but having got this much out of him, Thomas wasn't about to give up.

"All right. Now you've started. Tell me why."

Ethan sat silent for so long that Thomas felt certain he was being ignored. Then Ethan's eyes opened. He turned to Thomas, his look one of tired resignation.

"Because I was a spy. Or to be more accurate, a courier to a spy. I've spent most of the last six months here in Georgia."

Thomas stared at him, slack-jawed. "But... But I thought you'd deserted. That's what we all thought. Why in God's name didn't you tell anyone?"

"There wasn't time." Sick at heart, Ethan looked away. "So Duncan and Jamie died thinking I'd deserted?"

"That's what we all thought."

Ethan closed his eyes. "Please, Thomas. I need to be alone."

He didn't join them for breakfast, and a word from Thomas saw he wasn't disturbed. He set aside Ethan's portion, and when the others had stretched out around the fire, took the quilt and laid it over Ethan. Ethan gave no indication that he noticed, and Thomas, assuming he slept, went back inside.

He woke with a start several hours later. Pushing aside the quilt that had been laid over him, he sat up. Ethan's food was untouched, and there was no sign of him. Thomas hastened to the door, then walked the perimeter of the barn before setting out along the rutted track that led to the road. He'd no sooner reached it than the sound of voices sent him diving for cover.

The cart was a small one, drawn by a skinny mule and driven by a Negro. Half a dozen slaves, women and men, were crowded into the back. One of the men looked directly at Thomas. He caught his breath, certain he'd been spotted. The man laughed and turned to one of the women, and the cart disappeared around a bend. Adrenalin pumping, Thomas made a beeline back to the barn.

Zach rolled over when he came in, eyeing him sleepily. In no mood for conversation, Thomas went to sit where Ethan had been sitting—outside, against the barn, out of sight of the road.

Daylight was fading, the last of the light rimming the clouds in the western sky, when Zach and Frank came to squat beside him.

"Any idea what's going on?" Zach asked.

"What do you mean?"

"Where the hell is he?"

"How should I know, Frank? He probably went looking for food."

"I gotta tell ya, that boy makes me nervous. The way he keeps to himself, not telling us what's going on. You an' Fergus say you know him, but I don't I trust him. Not one little bit."

"He's gotten us this far, hasn't he?" Thomas retorted, trying to hide his dislike for the man. He directed a level gaze at Zach. "Right here, right now, there's no one I'd trust more than Ethan to get us home."

"You talked to him?"

"Yeah."

"He told you where he was when folks said he'd deserted?"

Thomas nodded, but the look in his eyes kept Zach from pressing.

Oblivious, Frank demanded, "Well? Arn'chu gonna tell us?"

"It's none of your business, Frank."

Frank's face flushed with anger. He slapped a hand against the side of the barn and stood up. Casting Thomas a withering look, he walked away.

Zach watched him go, then settled next to Thomas. He picked up a twig and began doodling in the dirt. Eventually, he said, "What Ethan said, you believe him?"

"Absolutely. I trust him with my life."

"All right, then." Zach flicked the twig away and leaned back against the barn.

They sat in silence as the last of the blue gave way to darkness. Neither was aware Ethan had returned until he tossed a gunnysack on the ground beside them.

"This is all I could get," he announced, voice thick with exhaustion. "I've been to every farm in walking distance, and they all have white overseers. None of the slaves have food to spare. I came across a patch of potatoes and dug these myself. It's too late for a fire, so we'll save them for morning. Right now, we need to get going."

Thomas and Zach clambered to their feet.

"We'll go just as soon as you eat."

Zach stepped between Thomas and Ethan, hefted the gunnysack and walked into the barn.

Thomas couldn't see Ethan's expression, but he turned after a moment, and followed Zach. Thomas went after him to make sure he ate.

Ethan swallowed the last bite of cold pork and looked up to find all eyes watching him. A look of irritation crossed his face. He started for the door, then stopped. After several seconds, he turned to face them.

"When I went out today, I discovered that the river carried us further south than I'd thought—a lot further than I'd hoped. I told you before that it was best to angle up east of Atlanta, but we're far enough south now that I figure it's best to go up past it on the west. If we do that, we'll pass near a town called McDonough. There's someone there who might be willing to help—give us food, clothes maybe, so you can get rid of the uniforms." He hesitated, watching their faces before adding, "That's what I aim to do. You're welcome join me."

Zach's eyes met Thomas'. Thomas looked at Ethan.

"We're with you."

Everyone but Frank murmured assent. Frank stared at Ethan, eyes narrowed with suspicion. Ethan failed to notice. He was looking at Thomas, who favored him with a quick smile and a nod before scooping up one of the gunnysacks and walking with him to the door. The others followed, Frank bringing up the rear.

7

It took three more long nights of walking to reach McDonough, Georgia. Thomas watched Ethan anxiously, aware that by this time he was functioning on willpower alone. Even so, he led them unerringly through each night, and each morning left to go in search of food. Thomas tried reasoning with him, tried to get him to rest before setting out, but Ethan had found that the slaves on many of the farms and plantations received their daily allotment of food in the morning. He insisted that, if he waited, there would be none left. As it was, he obtained only small portions of bread and meat from the few slaves willing to share. Supplemented by sweet potatoes they dug, and the few hard-kernelled ears of corn scavenged from fields they passed through at night, they had barely enough food to survive.

In the red hills outside McDonough, Ethan once again took up a stick. In the first gray light of dawn, he drew a map, providing detailed instructions for how they should precede in the event he failed to return. Sunlight was grazing the treetops when he threw a sack containing a balled up blanket over his shoulder and headed into town.

He hadn't been entirely truthful in saying he knew someone in McDonough. More accurately, he knew *of* someone who might be willing to help. Archibald Gilles was a wealthy merchant and Union sympathizer who lived on a quiet street near the center of town. His house often doubled as a safe house for Union spies. Ethan had never met Archie Gilles—Price had seen to that—but he had glimpsed him on more than one occasion when the house had been their meeting place.

He trudged across the town square, noting that the hands on the clock tower above city hall stood at a few minutes past seven, and turned down a gently sloping street that curved beneath a spreading canopy of scarlet oak. He scanned the houses as he went, until he found the one he was looking for. Like its neighbors, it was set back from the road, secluded on a large plot of land. Ethan went along the graveled drive, turned before he reached the stables, and pushed through the wrought iron gate that opened into the walled courtyard between the rear of the house and its outbuildings.

Sunlight filtered through overhanging branches, dappling the brick walkway. A pair of kittens scampered across his path and disappeared into the shrubbery. From the nearest building, the one housing the kitchen and scullery, came the reedy voice of a child singing. Ethan walked to the open door of the scullery and rapped on the jamb.

A pigtailed Negro girl of eight or nine turned from scrubbing a counter and looked at him. When he asked to see Mr. Gilles, she darted past him, across the courtyard and up the back steps to the house. She returned almost immediately, staring from behind the skirt of a young woman, pretty and plump, who bustled out the back door and down the steps to meet him. She wore an apron and carried an empty pitcher in one hand, the other pushing back an abundance of blond curls escaping from under her ruffled cap. Ethan recognized her as a relative of Mr. Gilles—a daughter, he thought.

"Mornin', miss," he said, removing his hat. "I was hoping I might speak to Mr. Gilles."

The young woman eyed him critically. "I've seen you befo', haven't I?"

"Yes, miss," he replied, suddenly self-conscious.

"I remember. You've been here with Mr. Price." The young woman smiled, her blue eyes warming in recognition. "My father isn't in, but I expect him shortly. Why don't we find a place fo' you to wait?"

Ethan nodded, acutely aware of his shabby clothes and how he must look.

Miss Gilles led him up the steep flight of stairs outside the kitchen. At the top, four doors fronted on a narrow gallery. She pushed the first one open and stood aside.

"Why don't you wait here? I'm fixin' to put breakfast on the table. Can I interest you in some?"

The aromas emanating from the kitchen had overwhelmed his senses the moment he'd stepped into the courtyard. "Yes, miss," he said, stepping past her into the room. "Thank you."

Miss Gilles smiled, her round cheeks dimpling. "I'll have Agnes bring water fo' you to wash. Make yo'self to home, and I'll send up breakfast as soon as it's ready." She departed, pulling the door closed behind her.

Ethan looked around the tiny, cell-like room. *Slave quarters.* A pair of narrow, plank beds took up most of the floor space, a rickety wooden table and cane-bottomed chair against the wall between them. Ethan dropped the sack and sank down on the chair, suddenly too exhausted to stand.

He was nodding off when a tap at the door roused him. Hoisting himself up, he pulled it open. Agnes stood on the gallery, weighed down by a tray containing a pitcher, washbasin, soap and towel. Ethan relieved her of it and turned to set it on the table. Behind him, the door clicked shut. He poured steaming water into the basin and stripped to the waist. Taking his time, he savored the luxury of soap and the feel of hot water against his skin.

Another knock came as he was toweling his hair. Before he could react, Miss Gilles pushed the door open. Her fair skin flushed scarlet when she saw his state of undress. Ethan turned away, stuffing his arms into his longhandles and grabbing his shirt from the chair. When he turned back, Agnes had removed

54

the washbasin and was replacing it with a tray of food. Miss Gilles watched him from the doorway. Her cheeks colored prettily when their eyes met.

"Enjoy yo' breakfast. I'll tell my father yo' here just as soon as he comes in."

The door had no sooner closed than Ethan spun the chair to face the table. There were biscuits with gravy, scrambled eggs, fried ham, grits and coffee. Real coffee. She'd given him large portions of everything, and he ate until he hurt. When he couldn't swallow another bite, he leaned back and looked longingly at the bed. Knowing it was a mistake he moved to sit on the cornhusk-filled tick. Within minutes, he was stretched out, sound asleep.

When Archie Gilles rapped on the door half an hour later, he got no response. Looking into the room, he cleared his throat loudly. Then he called a greeting. When that failed, he stepped over to the bed and shook Ethan by the shoulder. Ethan barely stirred. Recognizing the sleep of absolute exhaustion, Archie went in search of his daughter. Instructing her to send for him when their guest awoke, he left to attend to business.

***

Thomas slept fitfully. He kept half-waking, expecting to find Ethan returned. By noon, he was wide-awake and worried. He walked to where the woods ended at the edge of a fallow field and stared across it to the road. After a while, he returned to camp. He was too edgy to sleep, so he puttered about, adding wood to the fire and gathering more. Eventually, he wandered back to the edge of the field and sat down, his back against the rough bark of a southern pine.

Where is he? he wondered. *What's gone wrong?* Over the past couple weeks he'd developed a grudging respect for Ethan. It wasn't that he'd disliked him when he was with the Thirty-sixth—in fact, he'd barely known him. In five months, he figured they'd exchanged half a dozen words. Ethan was young and quiet and kept to himself, and Thomas had preferred the rowdier company of the twins. Truth be told, he'd paid Ethan scant attention until just before Perryville.

It was Ethan's first battle, and his brothers had had no idea what to expect. Duncan had fretted, and the twins had worried that they'd be stuck looking out for him. Their fears had proved unfounded. Ethan had demonstrated the same single-minded determination in battle that had driven Thomas to distraction halfway across Georgia.

Thinking back on it, knowing Ethan as he did now, Thomas couldn't believe their willingness to believe he'd deserted. But Duncan had been convinced, and his certainty had persuaded them all.

Well, he didn't desert then, and he won't desert us now. Not intentionally. Thomas stood up, scanning the road, and then began to walk. Skirting the field, he paralleled the road until he neared the outskirts of McDonough. There was no way to go further without being seen, so he settled in to wait. Hours passed with no sign of Ethan. Eventually, he retraced his steps.

His companions were gathered around the fire when he returned. They looked up, expectation replaced by uncertainty when they saw he was alone.

"Where is he?" Fergus asked.

"I don't know," Thomas said, sinking down next to the fire.

"What do you mean?" Frank demanded. "You telling us he's been gone all day?"

"That's right."

"What do you think happened?" Zach asked.

"I don't know. Something's kept him."

Frank snorted. "What makes you so all-fired sure he didn't just up an' leave us?"

Thomas scowled, but before he could respond, Fergus intervened. "What if he doesn't come back?"

Thomas blew out a long breath and shook his head. "We do what he said. Wait until dark, and if he doesn't show up, go without him."

"Shouldn't we look for him?"

"I already looked. I went as close to town as I dared. There's no sign of him."

"Thomas is right," Zach put in. "If he ain't back by dark, we go without him."

"He's up and left us," Frank declared. "He don't tell us anything, an' now it turns out he's got friends in these parts. I'm betting he's with 'em now, having a good laugh at our expense. Next thing you know, there'll be hounds after us." He shook his head and muttered, "Damn red niggers. Ain't no trusting any of 'em."

Thomas leaned forward, muscles tensed. "What did you say?" he asked softly.

An ugly smile twisted Frank's features. "Red nigger. We're fools to trust him."

Thomas made a sound deep in his throat and lunged across the fire. He landed on top of Frank, knocking him backward and hammering down blows until Fergus and Horst dragged him off.

Thomas fought their hold on him. "You son of a bitch! Get outta my sight, or so help me, I'll kill you!"

"Get him out of here!" Fergus screamed at Zach.

Zach hesitated.

"Get him away!"

Zach grabbed Frank under the arms and hauled him to his feet. Blood gushed from his nose and a cut over one eye. Frank pulled away from Zach. Casting a scathing look at Thomas, he slunk off into the woods.

Thomas quit struggling. Fergus and Horst exchanged a look behind his back and let go. Thomas jerked free and stormed across the clearing.

"Bastard's on his own! I never want to lay eyes on him again!" He rounded on the other three, jabbing a finger to punctuate his words. "Never! He finds his own way back!"

He turned away, then swung back and demanded, "How could he say that?" Getting no response, he took a menacing step toward them. "How? After all Ethan's done?"

For a moment, no one spoke. Then Fergus said, "It was uncalled-for, so it was. But we can't leave him. If he was to get caught, I don't know as I'd trust him not to talk out of spite."

Zach squatted next to the fire. Picking up a twig, he subjected it to intense scrutiny before looking at Thomas. "Frank's a whole lot older than us. Nearly forty. He don't like taking orders from a boy that don't even shave."

"Is that how you feel, Zach?" Thomas looked from him to the others. "Fergus? Horst?"

Zach answered for all of them. "You gotta understand, Thomas. Ethan keeping to himself the way he does, it makes us nervous. But he's got us this far. If he shows up, we'll follow him the rest of the way. Won't we, boys?"

"Aye, we will."

"We will," Horst echoed.

Zach tossed the twig into the fire and stood up. "I'll go find Frank. See if I can't talk some sense into him." He looked at Thomas. "You'll accept it, won't you? If he apologizes? No sense having you two at each other's throats."

Thomas regarded him for a long moment. "See what he has to say. I'll go watch for Ethan."

The sun had set, the last of the day's pale light lingering in the western sky, when Thomas heard them approaching. He got to his feet as Zach and Fergus came into view among the trees. Fergus caught Thomas' eye as he came close and gave a slight nod. They stopped, waiting for Frank to join them. He trailed to a stop, looking everywhere but at Thomas. In the gathering gloom, Thomas could see his eye was swollen shut.

Frank shifted from one foot to the other before blurting out, "There weren't no call for what I said. I apologize."

Thomas could see that the words cost him. Pushing animosity aside, he said, "We're under a lot of strain here, Frank. Sorry for the damage to your face."

"Tain't nothin'." Frank looked to Zach for approval, then turned back toward camp.

When he was gone, Fergus asked, "No sign of himself?"

Thomas shook his head.

They looked across the field. Nothing moved in the deepening twilight.

"We best go back. Eat what's left of the food and decide what to do." Zach turned and started away through the trees.

Fergus watched Thomas stare into the shadows. "He ain't coming, lad. Standing here won't make it happen." He touched Thomas' arm. "Let's be going."

Thomas turned abruptly, slamming a balled fist into the trunk of the nearest tree. Shaking his head in frustration, he set off after Zach.

The meal was a somber affair. Tension remained between Thomas and Frank, and the apparent loss of Ethan weighed heavily on them all.

Zach eventually broke the silence. "It's time we got started."

The others looked at him, then at each other.

"There's no choice," Thomas said. "We go without him."

"Do ye think we might wait a wee bit longer?" Fergus asked.

There was a murmur of agreement.

Thomas looked up. "When the moon comes even with that bright star there, we go."

***

It was dark when Ethan woke. Several moments passed before he remembered where he was. He sat up in alarm, instantly light-headed, and braced himself for the onset of a headache. The dizziness passed, but the pain didn't come. He pushed aside the blanket that had been laid over him and swung his legs over the side of the bed. The breakfast tray was gone, replaced by a lamp with the flame turned down low. He waited, but the headache failed to materialize. Pushing himself to his feet, he stepped to the door and opened it.

Light peeked from shuttered windows at the back of the house, casting linear patterns across the darkened courtyard. Ethan stepped out onto the gallery and looked over the rail. Light spilled from the open doorways below, and he could hear the murmur of voices. He went down the stairs and stopped outside the kitchen.

Miss Gilles stood with her back to him, hands on hips, lecturing a trio of Negro women. Their eyes moved to him, and she broke off in mid-sentence. She turned and saw him, and the beginnings of a blush crept into her cheeks.

"Yo' awake, then? You musta been awfully tired. Can I get you anything?"

"Your father... ?"

"In the parlor." Miss Gilles started toward the door. "Why don't you wait upstairs while I fetch him?"

Ethan nodded and withdrew. He went back and turned up the lamp, then sat on the edge of the bed to wait.

It wasn't long before Archie Gilles appeared. Ethan had no idea what Mrs. Gilles looked like, but it was obvious their daughter had inherited a good deal from her father. He was a beefy man with an assortment of chins and a head crowned with an unruly mass of reddish-blond curls. He entered the room, filling it.

"It's good to see you again," he said, pumping Ethan's hand. His smile revealed deep dimples inadequately disguised by a pair of bushy muttonchops. "Rebecca reminds me that you were here with Mr. Price. I'm embarrassed to say, I can't remember yo' name."

"We never actually met, sir. I'm Ethan Fraser."

Ethan gestured toward the chair and waited while Archie lowered himself onto it. It squeaked mightily as it took his weight. Ethan perched on the edge of the bed.

"So tell me, son, when can we expect Mr. Price?"

"I'm afraid I don't know, sir. I haven't seen him in nearly a month. I'm here on another matter."

"I see," Archie Gilles muttered, drawing out the words.

"I was captured by the Rebs a couple weeks back and escaped. I'm trying to get back north." Ethan looked at the floor, then at Archie. "I was wondering if you might be willing to help."

Archie wagged his head and chuckled, the multitude of chins quivering. "They only had you two weeks and you got away?" He guffawed loudly and slapped his thigh. "So tell me, son, what I can do fo' you?"

"I was hoping for some food and clothes." Remembering the condition of Frank's boots, he added, "And a pair of boots, if it wouldn't be too much trouble."

"I'll be more'n happy to do what I can. I'll arrange fo' a horse, as well."

The offer was tempting. Very tempting. He could take the horse and be back behind Union lines in a matter of days instead of weeks. *It would be so easy.* Seconds passed while Ethan considered it. Then conscience got the better of him. There was Thomas to think of. And Fergus. All of them. *But even so...*

"Thank you, sir," he said. "You're very generous. But, before you commit, I should tell you the rest."

Archie's smile wavered.

"There are five men with me. Anything you do, I'd have to ask you to do for them, too."

The smile broadened. "Well I'll be! Why don't you come in to supper and tell me about it?" Archie's face reddened as he pushed himself to his feet.

Ethan rose with him, recalling a glimpse he'd once had of an elegant room with high ceilings, carved moldings, and candlelight glinting off crystal chandeliers. "It's late, sir. I hadn't counted on falling asleep, and I told them I'd be back by now."

"I take it yo' friends are somewhere close by? Somewhere you could go and come back?"

"Yes, sir. I could."

Ethan shrugged into his coat and stooped to pick up the gunnysack. Archie took him by the arm and steered him through the door.

"Get yo'self back here as quick as you can," he said as they crossed the courtyard. "I'll have things ready fo' you."

"Yes, sir. Thank you."

The words were no sooner out of his mouth than the gate clicked closed between them.

The crescent moon was high above the rooftops, but Ethan didn't dare hurry through town. The moment the last house was behind him, he broke into a run, sprinting along the road in the direction he'd told the others to take. When he figured he'd gone far enough, he turned into a field and doubled back, picking his way over uneven ground, watching for any sign of them. He had crossed one rutted field, was entering another, when he saw movement. He sank to the ground and waited. When he was certain, he gave a low whistle. The five forms froze.

Thomas was the first to move. Recognizing the whistle, he came stumbling across the field, the others scrambling in his wake. He let out a low whoop when he came close, scooping Ethan into a bear hug and slapping him on the back.

"Where have you been? Lord A' mighty, we thought we'd lost you!" He stepped back, then leaned in and sniffed. "Maybe we shouldn't have worried. Just who is this friend of yours?"

Ethan looked at him in confusion. "What do you mean?"

"You smell good. Like soap. Kinda flowery to boot."

Fergus leaned in and sniffed. "Aye. All clean-like."

"Oh." Ethan looked away, self-conscious. "I was given soap and water, so I used it. You could do with some yourselves."

There was muffled laughter, and Ethan noticed Frank. He was hanging back further than usual, and something about him didn't look right.

"What took ye so long?" Fergus asked, seeking to distract him.

Ethan was still staring at Frank. "I fell asleep." He looked at Fergus and shrugged apologetically. "No one woke me. Sorry."

"But you saw your friend?" Zach asked.

"I did, and he's gathering some things. I need to go back for them." He paused before adding, "You mind waiting?"

"Any idea how long?"

"I don't know. A few hours. We'll lose half the night, but I think it'll be worth it."

"You sure this isn't some kind of trap?"

"I'm not sure of anything, Thomas, but I've had dealings with him before. I wouldn't have gone if I didn't think I could trust him."

"I don't like it. You're taking a chance going back into town."

"I don't see as I have a choice. We need food, and you'll be a whole lot better off without the uniforms."

"All right," Thomas agreed reluctantly. "Where do you want us to wait?"

Ethan led them back the way he'd come. Leaving them in a wooded area outside of town, he returned to the house without incident. The gate opened before he touched it, and Agnes led him across the courtyard and into the kitchen. Rebecca Gilles was there, busily supervising the loading of food into three canvas bags.

"My father asked you to wait here," she said, crossing the room to meet him. Their eyes met and she blushed. "I kept supper warm fo' you."

"Thanks," he said, smiling. "I appreciate it."

Her color deepened, and she turned away abruptly. Ethan watched her go, baffled by her behavior. He had little experience with women and no understanding of the affect his good looks had on them. With a shake of his head, he went to sit at the table.

He'd been in the kitchen three times before. Price saw to it that he wasn't allowed inside any of the homes they visited, so he had passed many hours in Southern kitchens. This one was big and comfortable with a large iron cook stove, wide wooden countertops, and tall cupboards. In a way, it reminded him of home. Ethan counted back. *A little over sixteen months.* It felt like years.

Agnes broke in on his thoughts, placing utensils and another heaping plate of food before him. Ethan thanked her and settled in to enjoy thick slices of ham, baked beans, hominy, and cornbread with butter and molasses. When he'd eaten all he could, he leaned back, watching the activity in the kitchen. It wasn't long before Archie came in, accompanied by a short, balding black man.

"I see 'Becca's takin' good care of you," he said, settling in a chair opposite Ethan. "I've got a cart and mule outside, loaded with everything I could lay my hands on in such short notice." He inclined his head toward the man who stood by the stove, sipping coffee. "Calvin here will drive out with you. The cart and mule are yours, if you want them. If not, Calvin'll bring them back, along with anything you can't carry."

"I don't know how to thank you, sir. I'm in your debt."

"Pish," Archie said, waving off his thanks. "Jus' get back safe, and help win the war. Puttin' an end to it'll be thanks enough." He grunted as he pushed himself to his feet. "Now, let's ge'chu on yo' way."

Ethan and Calvin collected the bags and walked with him across the courtyard. Rebecca followed. One hand on the gate, Archie turned to Ethan.

"We'll say good-bye here." He stuck out a hand. "Good luck to you, son. Give my regards to Mr. Price."

"Yes, sir. I will. And thanks again. I hope to repay you one day." Looking past Archie he added, "You, too, Rebecca. You've been very kind."

It was too dark to see her blush, but Ethan was certain she had.

Calvin drove the cart with Ethan sitting beside him. More than once, he looked back at its contents thinking there was more than they could possibly carry on foot. But taking the cart worried him. On foot, they moved relatively quietly, free to cut across fields and through woods—places a cart couldn't go. And in the cart, six men of fighting age were bound to attract attention. No, tempting as it was, Ethan decided they'd be better off without it.

He directed Calvin off the road, into the cover of the trees, and gave the same low whistle as before. The men emerged from the shadows and dug through what he'd brought, shedding their uniforms and replacing them with what fit. Ethan appropriated a wool vest and replaced his worn coat with a longer, heavier one. He tossed the pair of boots to Frank and watched as he tried them on. Frank grumbled about them not fitting properly, but when everything they were leaving was back in the cart, the boots were still on his feet.

<h1 style="text-align:center">8</h1>

It took two full nights and a portion of another to reach the Chattahoochee. They followed it north, looking for a way to cross. Whenever a light appeared through the trees, Ethan went ahead to investigate.

Returning from his third such foray, he announced, "There's a ferry about half a mile upriver. I'm told a white man runs it, but there's only a Negro there at night. I'll go see if he's by himself. If he is, I'll get him to take us across."

The moon was directly overhead when they spotted the ferry stanchion, looming gray against the dark forest ahead of them. Ethan went to take a look.

The sound of voices reached him as he approached the ferryman's shack. He crept up to it, sidled onto the rickety covered porch, and peered through the window. Illuminated in the glow of a lantern, he saw two men, one black, the other white. They slouched in their chairs, a jug of whiskey on the plank floor between them. Ethan drew back from the window, and stepped off the porch.

"Wha'cha doin' sneakin' 'round here?"

Ethan whirled find a scrawny white man standing next to the shack, doing up the buttons on his britches. The man swayed and took a step toward him.

"I said, wha'cha doin'?"

Something glinted in the moonlight, and the man went into a crouch. He took another step, and Ethan saw the knife. He moved quickly, aiming a kick that sent the knife soaring. Before he could regain his balance, the man lunged at him. Ethan hit the ground hard. His assailant rose above him, bringing down both fists in a savage blow to his kidneys. Grunting in pain, Ethan twisted under him. Bringing up both knees, he kicked the man away. He sprawled across the ground, and Ethan dived on top of him. He was straddling the man, hands tightening on his throat, when something cold touched the back of his neck.

There was a metallic click, and a voice behind him drawled, "Now whadda we got here?"

Ethan sat back slowly, hands held away from his sides. The man he'd been fighting scooted from between his legs and staggered to his feet. Casting a spiteful look at Ethan, he headed off to search for his knife.

"Henry, boy, fetch us a piece a' rope," the man at Ethan's back said. "An' bring the lantern." He prodded Ethan with the muzzle of the shotgun. "Stand up real easy-like, an' put yo' hands behind yo' back."

Ethan had no choice but to obey. Henry returned, and his hands were bound behind him.

Another prod and the man said, "Now turn aroun'. Hol' up the lantern, Henry."

Ethan turned. The shotgun's owner, a burly white man with bad teeth and a scruffy beard peered at him and grinned. "Hey, Clem! Looks like we got us a Injun boy."

Clem came up behind Ethan, pressing the tip of the knife to the skin below his right ear. "Wha'cha doin' sneakin' aroun' here, boy?"

Ethan felt hot breath on his neck; smelled whiskey.

"You lookin' to steal somethin'?"

"Nosuh." Ethan winced as the knife broke the skin. "I 'uz lookin' to cross the river, is all."

The man holding the shotgun snorted. His face turned mean and he rammed the barrel into Ethan's stomach, doubling him over.

"Yo' lyin', Injun," he snarled. "You 'uz after somethin'."

Ethan gasped for air, tried to straighten.

The man's eyes narrowed. "Now what'd a boy like you be lookin' fo'?"

"Our likker?" Clem suggested helpfully.

The owner of the shotgun jabbed Ethan again. "That it, boy? You after our likker?"

"Nosuh," Ethan gasped. "I swear I 'uz jus' lookin' to cross the river."

Clem grunted in disbelief and stepped onto the porch, upending a wooden crate and sitting on it. He flipped the knife, embedding it in the floor, pulled it out and flipped it again. Henry took a nervous step back; the hand holding the lantern trembled. The man with the shotgun sat down on the edge of the porch. He laid the gun across his knees, finger idly stroking the trigger guard.

Clem continued to flip the knife. "Wha'cha think we oughta do wit' him, Eugene?"

Eugene considered Ethan for several moments before saying, "Fetch the jug, Henry, while me and Clem here ponders it."

The Negro set the lantern in the dirt and went inside the shack. Returning, he handed the clay jug to Eugene. Eugene hooked it over one arm and took a swig. Exhaling with noisy satisfaction, he looked at Ethan. "You want somma this here rot-gut, boy?"

Ethan hesitated, unsure what the safest answer might be. "Nosuh," he said truthfully.

Eugene passed the jug to Clem, who took a long swallow. Wiping his mouth on the sleeve of his coat, he passed it back to Eugene.

Eugene took another swig, staring thoughtfully at Ethan. "I'm thinkin' maybe yo' right, Clem. This boy *was* lookin' to steal our likker." He smiled, eyes like flint. "Wanna drink, boy?"

Assuming the outcome would be the same whatever he answered, Ethan shook his head. "Nosuh."

Eugene patted the porch next to him. "Why don'chu si'chersef down?" When Ethan hesitated, he raised the shotgun. "Now, Injun."

Ethan lowered himself to the porch.

Eugene hefted the jug. "Give the boy a drink, Henry."

Henry wiped nervous hands down his overalls and took it. Clem grabbed a handful of Ethan's hair and pulled his head back.

Eugene said, "Open up, boy. You wanted our likker, now yo' gonna git some."

Ethan felt the knife prick flesh at the base of his skull. He took a breath and opened his mouth. Henry tipped the jug, and a flood of fiery liquid poured into his mouth and up his nose. He spewed it out, coughing, his eyes flooding with tears. The two white men whooped with laughter as he choked and gasped for air.

"That was a tad too much, Henry," Eugene wheezed. "Yo' gonna drown him. Jus' dribble it in easy-like, so's he kin enjoy it proper."

Ethan felt the prick of the knife; Clem forced his head back. Henry raised the jug. Ethan braced himself, but this time, only a trickle of whiskey dribbled into his mouth. He concentrated on swallowing a little at a time. Its heat seared his insides, made his eyes water, but he managed to get it down without choking.

They kept forcing him to drink, passing the jug between them. After a while, Ethan didn't notice the burning as much. Voices ran together, and his vision blurred. When Eugene ordered him to stand up, the words slipped right by him.

Eugene prodded him with the shotgun. "I said, git up, Injun. Now!"

Ethan struggled to his feet. Standing made everything worse. Shapes shifted around him, doubling and tripling as he tried to focus.

"Start walkin', boy."

Ethan took a cautious step, then another hasty one to catch himself. The world tilted crazily. Voices and laughter rang in his ears, and the shotgun prodded him.

"Keep a-goin', boy. Yo' doin' jus' fine."

His legs threatened to buckle under him. Ethan concentrated on placing one foot in front of the other. His tormentors roared with laughter, shouting taunts as he veered wildly, trying not to fall. A toe caught, and he sprawled face-first in the dirt. There were gales of laughter, and he was hauled to his knees.

"Git up, you sumbitch!"

Shapes swirled around him. His muscles refused to respond. A sharp kick to the buttocks would have toppled him, but the hand grasping his arm kept him from falling.

"Git up, damn you!"

Ethan struggled to his feet, so dizzy he could barely stand.

"C'mon, Injun. Git yo'sef back to the porch."

Somehow he arrived. He stood there stupidly, not knowing what to do next. He was grabbed by the arm and spun around. He sat down hard, his shoulder slamming into one of the posts supporting the roof. He sagged against it.

His head was forced back. He heard the command, felt the tip of the knife. He opened his mouth, and more whiskey dribbled in. When the grip on his hair loosened, he slumped forward. Closing his eyes made the spinning worse. He opened them again, feeling sick.

His head was forced back. Ethan saw faces looming, heard shouting. Without warning, he was backhanded across the face. He tried to turn away and was hit again. He let his mouth fall open.

* * *

He's been gone way too long. Thomas searched the sky for the same star he'd selected three nights earlier. *If he isn't back by the time the moon comes even with it, I'll go looking for him.*

When the time came, he told the others to wait and moved cautiously through the woods. He hadn't gone far when he saw a glimmer of light. As he crept closer, he heard voices. Illuminated in the light from a lantern, he saw Ethan slouched on the edge of a sagging porch, his head hanging loosely against his chest. A man crouched behind him. Another sat next to him, cradling a shotgun. A Negro stood before them, a clay jug in his hands. The fixed smile on the Negro's face told Thomas he wasn't enjoying himself.

The man sitting next to Ethan spoke. The other man grasped a handful Ethan's hair and pulled his head back. The man with the shotgun spoke again. When Ethan didn't respond, the man leapt to his feet. Shoving the colored man aside, he backhanded Ethan across the face. Ethan tried to twist away, but his movements were sluggish. The man hit him again, and Ethan's mouth sagged open. A barked order, and the Negro stepped forward, pouring liquid from the jug into Ethan's mouth. Ethan choked and pitched forward, toppling off the porch. It was then Thomas saw his hands were tied behind him.

The white men laughed as Ethan lay choking. The Negro stepped back, lips frozen in a grin. The man with the shotgun prodded Ethan with the barrel, yelling at him to get up. When Ethan didn't move, the second man stepped down from the porch and kicked him. Ethan struggled briefly, then lay still. The man yelled an obscenity and kicked him again. Grabbing Ethan beneath his armpits, he pulled him to his knees. The other man took a step, swinging his leg in an arc that lifted Ethan off the ground and sent him sprawling. The two men went to stand over him. One of them prodded Ethan with a toe, but he didn't move. The men looked at one another and shrugged. They retrieved the jug, and with a few parting words to the Negro, disappeared into the shack.

The Negro stood for a time without moving. Then he walked to where Ethan lay. Crouching, he rolled him unto his stomach and untied his hands. Then he grasped him by the ankles and dragged him into the woods.

Thomas found him there, facedown in his own vomit, still retching. He knelt beside him, supporting him until the heaving stopped. Ethan was unconscious by the time Thomas scooped him up and started back downriver.

9

The day was half gone when Ethan stirred. He tried to sit and fell back with a groan. His head pounded, his stomach churned, his mouth was bone dry and tasted awful. Every part of him ached. He heard Thomas say, "Welcome back," and squinted into the light.

"Wha'... what happened?"

"You ran into some trouble at the ferry. Remember?"

"Ohhh... Yeah." Ethan opened his eyes and looked around. "How'd I get here?"

"I came for you. Carried you back."

"Don't remember..."

"I bet you don't. From the smell, I'd say you'd drunk enough to kill half a dozen men."

Ethan moaned. He rolled onto his side and retched miserably.

Thomas waited until he lay back. "You need to drink some water. Just as soon you can keep it down. And try to eat something. It'll make you feel better."

Ethan tried to sit up. Pain knifed through his ribs. He gasped and lay back.

Thomas reached over and pulled back the quilt. Ethan gasped again as cold air hit bare skin.

"Where are my clothes?"

"We had to wash them." Thomas ran the tips of his fingers over the angry bruising along Ethan's ribs, eliciting a wince. "You're black and blue where they kicked you," he said, restoring the quilt. "I don't think anything's broken." He handed Ethan a cup. "Drink."

Ethan took a few sips. The water hit his empty stomach hard. Despite his thirst, he couldn't swallow more. The corn patty Thomas handed him tasted good though. He ate most of it before closing his eyes.

He was asleep, Thomas dozing beside him, when the others began to stir. They huddled around the fire as daylight waned, talking in whispers and casting anxious looks at Ethan. Frank finally blurted what all of them were thinking.

"What if he ain't fit to go on?"

"We wait until he is," Fergus replied querulously.

"We can't stay here. It ain't safe." Frank caught Zach's eye. "We gotta keep moving. Get across the river and head north. He said we're halfway there."

"Frank's right," Zach agreed. "This close to the ferry, someone's bound to stumble on us. If Ethan can't go on tonight, we should split up. Anyone who wants can stay. The rest go on."

Across the camp, Thomas stirred and sat up. The men around the fire looked at him. Thomas looked at Ethan, then stood and stretched. Nodding a greeting to the watching men, he wandered off into the bushes.

"We'll wait for him to wake up. See how he's feeling. Then we'll decide what to do," Fergus said, putting an end to the discussion.

Ethan woke a short time later. His head ached, his mouth tasted rotten and was dry as cotton, but the nausea had passed. He drank from the cup Thomas handed him, dressed, and walked to the fire.

"How are ye?" Fergus asked, rising to greet him.

Ethan responded with an embarrassed shrug. "All right, I guess. Hungry. Sore."

"You able to go on tonight?" Frank asked.

A look of irritation crossed Ethan's face. "Why wouldn't I?"

"What's the plan?"

"How the hell do I know, Zach? I just woke up." Ethan caught himself and looked away, staring into the deepening shadows among the trees. "We go back to the ferry," he said more evenly. "If the Negro's by himself, we get him to take us across."

"You plan on being the one that goes?"

"Yes." Seeing the expression on Thomas's face, he asked, "Why not?"

"You're not going without someone to back you up. From now on, wherever you go, someone goes with you. Even if all they do is hang back out of sight while you do the talking."

Ethan bit back a retort and stared into the fire. "You're right," he agreed, at last. "We'll all go once it's dark."

They found Henry alone, and when he saw Ethan, instantly contrite. He led them to a flatboat made of rough-hewn lumber, attached to a wire cable strung between log stanchions on either bank. When they were aboard, he manned the pole and pushed off. The raft floated at an angle to the current, drifting across the river of its own accord.

A cloud passed over the moon, leaving the river in inky darkness. No one saw the floating log until it was too late. Frank yelled a warning, but Thomas was caught off balance. The impact sent him tumbling into the river. He resurfaced several yards downstream, sputtering and slapping the water as everyone yelled at him to swim for shore.

"I can't swim!" Thomas' voice came in a shriek as he vanished beneath the surface.

Without a word, Ethan dived in after him. He was a strong swimmer, and with the current aiding him, was almost on top of Thomas when he resurfaced.

"Thomas!"

Ethan reached out, but Thomas was quicker. He grabbed Ethan and pulled him close. Seized by the blind panic of a drowning man, he tried to climb up him, forcing him under. Ethan's first reaction was to struggle. Realizing it was useless, he pushed himself deeper. Ethan's lungs were near bursting when Thomas finally let go, knocking him about the head and shoulders as he clawed his way to the surface.

Ethan resurfaced, sucked in air, located Thomas and dived. He flailed about blindly until his hand brushed fabric. He grabbed a handful, then a leg, causing Thomas to kick violently. Buffeted by Thomas' attempts to break free, Ethan worked his way behind him and climbed, hand over hand, up his body.

Thomas was very nearly spent, but he twisted in Ethan's grasp, trying to grab hold of him. Ethan surfaced gasping for air. Thomas reached back and seized a handful of Ethan's hair. Kicking hard to keep them both afloat, fighting not only Thomas, but the drag on his own wet clothing, Ethan threw an arm around Thomas' neck. Seizing his wrist with his other hand, he tightened it like a vice. Thomas let go of his hair and began clawing at his arm.

"Thomas!" Ethan gasped. "Relax! Relax, or we both drown."

Thomas continued to tug at his arm. Ethan jerked it tighter, increasing the pressure on Thomas' airway. "Stop fighting or we drown!"

Thomas' hands hesitated, then dropped away.

"Listen!" Ethan panted. "You need to trust me. I'm going to let go of your neck. I want you lay back against me and I'll pull you to shore. If you fight, we won't make it. You hear me?"

"Yes." The word came in a strangled gasp.

Ethan slid his arm diagonally across Thomas' chest, grasping him below the armpit. With Thomas lying against him, he began the long swim to the western bank.

As the initial rush of adrenaline wore off, Ethan became aware of how much he hurt. Every breath, every stroke, sent pain searing through his ribs. Closing his mind to it, he swam.

His foot struck something, jarring him from his stupor. When it happened again, he realized he'd kicked the bottom. A few more strokes, and he let go of Thomas and struggled to stand. Thomas floundered, then staggered up beside him. Clinging to one another for support, they stumbled out of the Chattahoochee and collapsed on dry land.

They lay where they'd fallen, exhausted and shivering. The moon broke free of the clouds and was halfway across the sky by the time Thomas coughed, then vomited up the water he'd swallowed. Eventually, he pushed himself into a sitting position and shook Ethan's shoulder.

"Ethan, wake up. We're gonna freeze if we don't build a fire."

Ethan groaned and rolled onto his back. He looked at Thomas. "You all right?"

Thomas shrugged and looked away, embarrassed. "Fine." A moment, and he added, "Sorry for how I acted out there."

"Don't worry about it."

"I could have drowned us both. I'm sorry."

Ethan sat up, wincing and clutching his ribs. "I didn't know you couldn't swim."

Thomas shrugged again. "Never learned. You saved my life. Thanks."

"I owed you, Thomas. You've looked out for me since Chickamauga Creek." Ethan offered him a weary smile. "I still owe you."

"No you don't." Thomas staggered to his feet and held out a hand. "How 'bout a fire?"

"Yeah." Ethan grasped his hand and was pulled to his feet.

They collected kindling and found a sheltered place among the trees. The matches in Thomas' oilskin pouch had faired badly, and he went through most of them before finding one that lit. A good deal of coaxing was required before the tiny flame took hold. They added wood and huddled close as the fire established, hands outstretched, wet clothing steaming. Ethan was staring straight ahead, mesmerized by the flames, when Thomas spoke.

"What happened last night?"

"Hmmm?" Ethan looked blankly at him, and Thomas repeated the question.

"Oh... One of them came at me with a knife. I fought him off, but the other one had a gun." He stared into the flames, his voice turning harsh as he continued. "They called me names. Accused me of trying to steal from them." Ethan picked up a stick and jammed it into the fire. The flames leapt higher, spinning sparks into the night sky.

Thomas said nothing, waiting for him to calm down. When he figured enough time had passed, he asked, "Then what?"

Ethan had known prejudice all his life. He had learned early on to hold others at a distance, to keep his feelings from showing and temper his reaction to what was said, but a lifetime of resentment hovered just beneath the surface. It erupted with his answer.

"What do you think happened, Thomas?" Ethan glared angrily at him. "They called me names, forced me to drink, made me do tricks for them. *Great* entertainment, a drunken Indian." He threw the stick into the fire and scrambled to his feet, walking away into the darkness.

Thomas let him be for several minutes before changing the subject. "What do we do next? Look for the others?"

At first, there was no response. Then Ethan made his way back into the light. Crouching in the warmth of the fire, he picked up another stick and toyed with it before answering. "I don't know. We need to figure out where we are. There's no telling how far the river carried us. My guess is it's far enough that we'll never catch them if they keep moving."

"You think they will?"

"I'm betting Fergus'll wait a while—maybe even look for us. But when we don't show up, Frank'll pester them into going." Thomas looked up, and Ethan caught his eye. "I know what he's said to my face, Thomas. I can imagine what he's said behind my back. All he's wanted from the start is to be rid of me. Now's his chance." A smile crept over Ethan's face. He cocked an eyebrow at Thomas. "You gave him that black eye, didn't you? 'Cause of something he said."

Thomas grinned. "He made me so mad I couldn't see straight."

Still smiling, Ethan looked into the flames. "You're a good friend, Thomas," he said softly. "Thanks."

A comfortable silence settled between them.

The fire was dying when Thomas spoke again. "What do you think we should do?"

"You want to keep going for a while?" Ethan looked at the moon. "What time do you think it is? Around midnight?" He looked at Thomas, who nodded. "Five hours 'til dawn. We could figure out where we are, put a few miles behind us."

They headed due north, making their way through dense forest until they stumbled upon a road that angled northwest. It was deserted at that hour, and they made good time. Skirting a tiny settlement, they kept going until they came to a larger one.

"This has to be Carrollton," Ethan muttered, recalling details of maps he'd studied. "If it is, and we stay on this road, it'll take us up to Rome, then into Tennessee."

Thomas shook his head in amazement. "I don't know how you do it—keep all that stuff in your head. I read something and ten minutes later, it's gone."

Ethan shrugged. "'Bookish,' Pa says. He was always catching me reading when I was supposed to be doing something else." He smiled wistfully. "For a couple years, after I'd learned to read, and while Seth was still in school, we'd trade off. He'd do my chores, and I'd read his lessons. Then I'd tell him what he needed to know. I guess that put me in the habit of remembering." He tilted his head back and looked at the sky. "I'd say we have another hour before daybreak. You want to keep going?"

"Might as well."

The eastern sky was beginning to lighten when the sound of approaching horsemen sent them scrambling for cover. With the coming of day, traffic on the road increased. They moved deeper into the woods, tired and hungry and looking for a place to rest.

They slept briefly before setting out again, desperate to find food. They had little success. Darkness was falling when they very nearly stumbled into a Confederate picket line. Unnerved, Ethan veered west, into the mountains of Alabama.

10

Ethan half-woke to a snuffing sound and hot, smelly breath on his face. He jerked, coming fully awake, and the startled hound leapt backward, barking. Two more joined it. Thomas bolted upright, and together, they leapt to their feet.

A pair of armed men emerged from the woods ahead of them, so they turned and ran back the way they'd come, the excited dogs bounding at their heels. Ethan sprinted ahead, but Thomas wasn't as quick. He had only gone a few steps when a dog became entangled in his feet. Arms pinwheeling, he struggled to maintain his balance, then tumbled to the ground.

The two men had broken into a run. They were on Thomas before he could recover, guns aimed at his chest. Thomas lay back in surrender. One of the men raised his musket and squeezed off a shot. The ball whistled past Ethan, thudding into the trunk of a hickory several yards ahead. Caught in the open with no place to hide, Ethan pulled to a stop. Panting, clutching his bruised ribs with one hand, he raised the other and turned to face their captors.

One of the men was tall and lean, the other stout and a head shorter. Both had a goodly amount of gray in their hair and whiskers. The taller of the two finished tamping a new load into his musket and motioned Ethan to join them. The other kept his weapon trained on Thomas.

"Wha'cha runnin' from, son?" he asked conversationally.

Without stopping to think, Thomas answered. "We were asleep. The dogs startled us."

Both men grew instantly more alert. The shorter man prodded Thomas with the barrel of his musket. "You ain't from aroun' these parts, are ya, son?"

Too late realizing his mistake, Thomas chose not to reply.

Ethan came within hearing as the man said, "Sounds like ya'll hail from up north a ways. That right, son?"

Not knowing what to say, Thomas looked to Ethan.

"How 'bout you, boy?" the tall man asked. "You a Yankee, too?"

Alone, Ethan was certain he could have talked his way out of it. But with Thomas, especially now that he'd opened his mouth, there was little he could do. *Even so*, he figured, *it's worth a try*.

"Nosuh," he answered, slipping easily into the subservient attitude that had served him so well in the past.

The man's eyes narrowed. "Where ya'll from, boy?"

"Geo'gia, suh."

"Don't see many of his kind here 'bouts," the shorter man mused.

His companion shook his head, staring hard at Ethan.

"My Pa's white," Ethan rushed to tell them. "I been livin' wit' his kin over Henry County way fo' nigh on ten year."

"What brings you to these parts, boy?" the tall man asked.

"We's headin' west. Out Califo'nai way."

The bearded man looked pointedly at Thomas. "Yo' friend, here. Who's he?"

Thomas' eyes sought Ethan's, begging help.

"Cousin."

The tall man snorted. His companion grinned.

"Tell me if'n I got this right, boy. Ya'll 'spect us to believe yo' a half-breed from Geo'gia, an' this here yella-haired fella's yo' Yankee cousin? An' all yo' doin' is passin' through on yo' way to Califo'nee?"

To hear him say it, it sounded far-fetched, even to Ethan. He had little of hope of being believed, but nevertheless, he nodded. "Yessuh."

The tall man peered closely at him. "Why'd you run, boy?"

Ethan looked at the dogs panting at his feet. "Dawgs," he muttered. "I's asceared of 'em."

The short man nudged Thomas with the barrel of his musket. "Wha'cha doin' in Alabama, son?"

"I... uh..." Thomas looked at Ethan.

"Don't look like he knows the story as good as you," the tall man observed. His eyes hardened as he looked at Ethan. To his partner, he said, "I reckon we should take these two into Gadsden. Let them tell their story to the marshal."

They were taken to a shack belonging to one of the men and loaded into a mule-drawn cart. The bearded man handled the reins; his friend faced backward, musket ready.

It was late in the day when they reached Gadsden. The sky was leaden, the air heavy with the scent of rain, when the cart pulled to a stop before the jail. People stopped and stared as the two elderly men herded their prisoners inside.

"We got us a couple fellas the dogs sceared up down along the river," the tall man announced to the white-haired man seated behind the desk. "The yella-haired fella talks like he hails from up north. T'other says he's from over Geo'gia way. They ran when the dogs flushed 'em, so we figured to bring 'em in to you, Marshal."

The marshal studied Thomas and Ethan, taking in their exhaustion, their soiled and rumpled clothing. "You boys got anything to say fo' yo'selves?"

Neither of them did. Contemplating them a moment longer, the marshal picked up a ring of keys and headed for the room's other door. "We'll lock you up. Le'cha think on it a spell."

The door led to a room housing two cells, one on either side of a narrow walkway. The marshal opened the barred door to his right and stood aside for

Thomas and Ethan to enter. Turning the key in the lock, he gave them a long look before turning back to the office.

The cell was small, a plank bed and a bucket its only furnishings. Gray light filtered through a barred window high on the wall, fusing with the sickly glow of the single lantern that hung from a hook between the cells. The small, pot-bellied stove beneath it was the sole source of heat. In the other cell, a man snored.

Ethan stepped over to the bunk and sat down. Thomas dropped down beside him.

"That was some act you put on," he muttered, eyeing the man in the other cell. "Sorry I couldn't think fast enough to help out." He paused before asking, "What do we do now?"

Ethan clasped one drawn-up knee and slouched against the wall. "Wait, I guess."

"For what?"

"I don't have any brilliant ideas, if that's what you're asking. If one comes to me, you'll be the first to know. In the meantime, they only suspect you're a Yank. And when you get down to it, all we did was run from some dogs. If you keep quiet, maybe the marshal'll let us go."

"You think so?"

"No. Not really." Ethan patted the thin mattress. "Meanwhile, we've got shelter from the rain, and maybe he'll feed us. If you'll move over, I could do with some sleep."

The commotion created by the arrival of another prisoner woke them after dark. The man was drunk and angry. He cursed the marshal as he was led in, hands secured behind him. The marshal released him into the cell opposite and turned to Thomas and Ethan.

"You two got anything to say fo' yo'selves?"

Met with silent, sleepy stares, he shrugged and walked from the room.

Marshal Andrews was an easygoing, methodical man who dealt with all but the most pressing requirements of his office in a slow, deliberate manner. He had his suspicions about the two boys back in the cell. That they were on the run was obvious, based on their appearance and refusal to talk. From their age, he figured it must be one army or the other. He decided he'd wait until morning, then mosey over to the railhead to see if there were any troops passing through. If not, he'd feed them and let them sleep in his jail until he found someone to take them off his hands.

That night, the skies opened. The deluge continued throughout the morning. When it tapered off in mid-afternoon, the marshal made his way to the depot. Finding no troops encamped there, he left a message with the stationmaster and trudged back through the mud to his office. Three days passed before he received a response.

Monday morning dawned gray and overcast, the skies threatening to open again at any time. Despite the meager efforts of the stove, the jail was cold and damp. The snoring man had been released to his agitated wife late the first evening. The other man had raged about his cell, cursing and muttering until he finally nodded off. He had awakened the following morning, docile as a lamb, and been released. Thomas and Ethan had been alone ever since, and the long hours of confinement were beginning to wear on them.

Thomas sat on the bunk, wrapped in one of the blankets the marshal had provided, watching Ethan as he paced the cell. When Thomas pointed out, somewhat irritably, that Ethan was going to wear holes in his boots, if not the floor, Ethan snapped at him to leave him be. A few more circuits, and he stopped, his back to Thomas, forearms resting on the crosspiece of the door, hands dangling through the bars. He was still there when the door to the office opened, and the marshal walked in. Behind him was a Confederate officer.

Ethan's heart sank. He backed away from the door, glancing over his shoulder at Thomas, who stared at the officer in dismay. The marshal let the lieutenant into the cell and pushed the door shut, holding it with his hand.

The lieutenant was a good-looking man in his mid-twenties. His uniform was immaculate, his grooming impeccable. He eyed Thomas and Ethan with disdain. When he spoke, his quiet, cultured voice belied the threat of his words.

"The marshal here tells me you boys don't have much to say fo' yo'selves. You want to tell me who you are, or shall I have you hung as deserters?"

Ethan stared at the floor and quickly made up his mind. He had faced death anonymously once before and wasn't about to do it again. Squaring his shoulders, he met the lieutenant's gaze.

"Private Ethan Fraser. 36th Illinois."

Thomas' initial disbelief turned to outrage. He surged to his feet and crossed to Ethan in a single stride, fists clenched. The marshal and the lieutenant barked at him to stop.

Ethan made no move to defend himself. Thomas glared at him before scowling first at the lieutenant, then the marshal. With a snort of disgust, he turned his back, and stood clenching and unclenching his fists.

At last, he blew out a long, frustrated breath. "Sergeant Thomas Murray," he muttered through clenched teeth. "36th Illinois."

One corner of the lieutenant's mouth turned up at the relative ease of the confession. The smile vanished when he turned to Ethan. "Would either of you care to tell me what yo' doin' in Alabama? Am I to understand, since yo' out of uniform, that you were sent here as spies?"

"No, sir," Ethan said. "We were captured in Georgia last month and escaped. We were trying to get back to Tennessee."

The lieutenant studied him intently before asking, "Why should I believe you? If you've been spyin', I'd expect you to lie."

"It's the truth," Thomas muttered. He whirled to face them. "Damn you, Ethan!" He dragged his eyes from Ethan to the lieutenant. "We were captured at Chickamauga Creek on the nineteenth of September and put on a train bound for Richmond. We escaped three weeks ago." He shot Ethan an accusing look. "That's how long it's taken us to get this far."

The lieutenant looked back and forth between them, evaluating. Turning smartly, he stepped to the door of the cell. The marshal pulled it open, then locked it behind him. As they left the room, the lieutenant said, "I'll ask you to keep them another night, Marshal. Someone'll be around to fetch them in the mo'nin'."

Ethan looked at Thomas, who glared at him before flopping onto the bunk. He lay on his back, staring up at the ceiling. Ethan considered him briefly before moving to the far corner of the cell. He sank to the floor and sat with his knees pulled up, back pressed against the wall. Forearms resting on his knees, hands dangling, he waited.

"So it was all for nothing."

Ethan tilted his head back and sighed. "I guess it was." After a time, he added, "I had to tell him. You know that, don't you? There was no other choice."

Thomas rolled up on one elbow and looked at him. "Wasn't there?"

Ethan shook his head slowly, eyes on the ceiling. "It was tell the truth, or risk being hung. I couldn't go through that again. Especially when there's no reason for it." He looked at Thomas. "I couldn't see any other way. Sorry."

Thomas continued to glower, even as his anger faded. "You're right," he said at last. He rolled onto his back, and a lengthy silence ensued.

"We were so close," he said, eventually. "Another week, and we'd have been back behind our own lines."

"I know, Thomas. Believe me, I know."

"And now what? Do you think he believed us, or will they take us out of here tomorrow and hang us?"

Ethan lifted his hands, let them drop, a shrug of sorts. "I don't know. To tell the truth, I'm not sure what I want him to believe. The thought of spending months, years maybe, in a Reb prison..." He blew air between pursed lips and left the sentence unfinished.

Rain was sheeting down when the door opened the next morning. Thomas and Ethan rose apprehensively as the marshal entered, followed by a gray-clad sergeant and two privates carrying chains. The marshal unlocked the door, and the men crowded into the cell.

"Hold out yo' hands."

"Why—?" Thomas began.

"Lieutenant's orders," the sergeant snapped. "Says ya'll are escaped prisoners, and he's bound to see it don't happen again. Now, hold out yo' hands."

Manacles snapped closed around their wrists, and they were ordered to stand close together. A single length of chain was draped across their shoulders and secured around their necks with padlocks. They were herded out into the rain and turned toward the depot. Ashamed at being treated like common criminals, they bowed their heads, grateful the weather kept all but a few curious onlookers indoors.

A line of boxcars waited on the tracks. They were taken to one where the door stood open and ordered inside. The door rolled closed behind them; the bolt banged into place. Thomas and Ethan squinted into the gloom.

The car was an improvement over others they'd inhabited. It had been used to transport mail or other supplies, and no animal had ever been inside. The floor near the door was drenched, so they moved away from it, toward the cast iron stove at one end of the car. It was cold to the touch, and though there was coal in the bin beside it, they had no means to light it. They huddled together, resigned to wait.

Thomas broke the silence, lifting the length of chain between them and letting it drop. "I guess the lieutenant believed our story. Where do you think we're headed?"

Ethan shook his head. "No idea. The only rail line I know of runs south to Selma. From there, they could put us on the river, send us anywhere."

"But prison, that's for sure."

Ethan nodded. "They've seen to it we wouldn't get far, even if we did escape."

There was nothing left to say. Cold and dejected, they sat listening to the drumming of the rain on the roof.

Eventually, they heard voices. The bolt screeched as it was drawn, and the door rumbled open. The barrel of a shotgun appeared, closely followed by a boy's face. Water ran in rivulets from his cap, and he squinted past it, searching the shadows until he spotted them. A second boy's face appeared. He trained a musket on Thomas and Ethan while the first boy handed his weapon, a lantern, and two knapsacks into the car, then climbed aboard. Retrieving the shotgun, he waited while the second boy climbed in and lit the lantern. They collected their belongings and moved cautiously along the car, guns ready. Behind them, the door rolled closed, and the bolt slammed home.

They were young, fourteen or fifteen at most, skinny and rawboned. One was a head taller, red hair sticking straw-like from beneath his forage cap, his face and hands a mass of freckles. The other boy's hair was brown, curling softly over his forehead and around his ears. His eyes were large and dark, his face angelic.

The redhead kept his shotgun trained on Thomas and Ethan. The other boy squatted before the stove. When it was lit, he unrolled an oilcloth and blanket. Both boys sat, the redhead never taking his eyes from his prisoners, his finger hovering over the trigger. No one spoke. The whistle sounded; the car jerked and began to roll.

As the chill dissipated, the dark-haired boy dug in his knapsack and came up with a handful of crackers. He looked questioningly at the other boy.

The redhead nodded and gripped the shotgun tighter. "Luke here's gonna slide some crackers over yo' way. Don't neither a' you move 'til I say."

Luke got to his knees and stretched out a hand, laying four crackers on the planked floor between them. When he pulled back, the redhead gestured with the shotgun.

"You. Injun. Move over slow and git 'em."

Ethan eased forward, watching the boy's finger tremble against the trigger. Placing both hands over the crackers, he pulled them to him. Still eyeing the shotgun, he sat back and handed two to Thomas.

"Thanks," Thomas said, inclining his head toward their guards. He took a bite. The cracker was stale and hard, and he wasn't sure he could get it down without water. He chewed until he worked up enough spit to force it down. "Where are we headed?"

"Cahaba," the redhead replied.

Thomas looked at Ethan.

"About ten miles south of Selma." Ethan looked at the redhead. "Why there?"

"They's a prison. It's where yo' headed."

Ethan's brow furrowed. "I've never heard of a prison at Cahaba."

"It's new. A depot prison, they calls it. Y'all go there 'til they decides where to send ya."

"How long'll it take to get there?" Thomas asked.

"Dunno."

Thomas had more questions, but the redhead had apparently decided he'd said enough. They stared at each other across the swaying car, lulled by the clatter of the wheels. As the heat from the stove warmed them, they dozed.

11

As the train trundled south, four exhausted, hungry men stumbled across a Union picket line southeast of Bridgeport, Alabama. They identified themselves as members of the 36th Illinois, escaped after capture at Chickamauga Creek. Passed through the lines with instructions to report to the officer in charge, they told and retold their story. They were greeted as heroes, given a hearty meal and assigned quarters, informed that they would remain in Bridgeport until the siege at Chattanooga was lifted.

In Chattanooga, the spy named Price put his departure on hold when he heard that General Ulysses S. Grant had placed General George Thomas in command of the Army of the Cumberland, replacing General Rosecrans, and that Grant himself was due in the city within the week.

Price had traveled north from Atlanta a week after the battle at Chickamauga Creek to find General Bragg's Army of Tennessee firmly in control of Lookout Mountain, Missionary Ridge and Orchard Knob, the high ground surrounding Chattanooga. The city, hemmed in by mountains and backed up against the

Tennessee River, was virtually cut off, the only supply route a tortuous one of more than sixty miles from Bridgeport, through the Sequatchie Valley and over rugged Walden's Ridge.

Price had passed easily through the Confederate lines, and on the afternoon of October twelfth, entered the city. He found it much changed from previous visits. The once bustling commercial town of spreading shade trees and well-maintained residences had been laid to ruin. Houses stood open and abandoned, ransacked by both armies for food and valuables. Some of the town's finest homes had been burned to the ground to make way for fortifications and give unrestricted views of enemy positions. Many of the trees had been cut for firewood, and horses and mules grazed at will, decimating lawns and gardens.

Going directly to the Kindrick house, the house General Thomas had taken as his headquarters, Price relayed a modicum of information to a lowly captain on general's staff, then announced his intention to remain in Chattanooga for at least a week. His plans changed quickly when he discovered the extent of deprivation in the beleaguered city. He was packed, ready to leave when news of Grant's imminent arrival reached him.

General Grant arrived late in the evening on the twenty-third of October, wet, hungry and covered with mud after an arduous journey over treacherous mountain roads. He found the situation in Chattanooga desperate. Since the start of the rainy season, the time it took supply wagons to reach the city from Bridgeport had doubled. The strain of pulling heavily laden wagons through the mud had left thousands of mules and horses dead along the trail. The few that remained could carry only the lightest of loads. Soldiers were reduced to quarreling over scraps and stealing corn meant for the mules. Trapped in Chattanooga, men and animals were starving.

General Grant's most pressing concern was the lifting of the blockade. He gathered his generals to devise a solution. While they were meeting, a lieutenant assigned to General Sheridan's staff observed a civilian lingering outside the room and confronted him. Tall, impeccably dressed, with receding sandy hair and a thin mustache, the man introduced himself and handed the lieutenant an envelope, requesting it be delivered to General Thomas.

The following morning, the lieutenant once again spotted the man who'd introduced himself as Price. He was deep in conversation with a young private, a relation to someone on General Thomas' staff, who was serving as a messenger.

Price appeared to be flattering the young man who, reticent at first, soon began to speak freely.

When he felt the conversation had gone on long enough, Lieutenant Joshua Fraser stepped into view and walked toward them. Seeing his approach, Price put a hasty end to the conversation and departed. The young man looked anxiously between them before scurrying away. Josh let him go, but assigned a man to follow Price. Late that night, the man reported that the private had spent the evening in Price's company, sharing a bottle of brandy, relaxed and loquacious.

Price spent the next morning in and around army headquarters, chatting with anyone who cared to pass the time. That afternoon, he returned to his lodgings, gathered his belongings and headed out of town. Alerted by the man who'd been tailing him, Josh ordered him stopped.

As darkness fell, the operation to relieve the Union forces in Chattanooga got underway. Dubbed the "Cracker Line Operation," its aim was to open a supply route from Bridgeport, through Wauhatchie, and into Chattanooga. General Joseph Hooker's force, moving north from Bridgeport, crossed the Tennessee River and joined forces with troops under the command of General William Hazen, who had slipped out of Chattanooga. Taking the Confederate brigade at Wauhatchie by surprise, they drove the Rebels out. General Hooker continued north to Chattanooga, leaving a division at Wauhatchie with orders to protect the line of communication to the south, as well as the road to the west.

At three o'clock in the morning on 27 October, fifteen hundred handpicked men left Chattanooga and drifted downstream under cover of darkness, securing Brown's Ferry and the heights overlooking it. A pontoon bridge was floated into place, and on October twenty-eighth, the supply line from Bridgeport to Chattanooga was cut from sixty miles to thirty.

* * *

It was dark when the train pulled into Selma. Thomas and Ethan were taken to a three-story brick building near the station and turned over to the provost marshal. Their bonds were removed, their names and ranks entered into a logbook, and they were searched.

This time, the guards discovered the last of Thomas' money. Ethan held his breath as a guard fingered the fabric of his coat. He threw Thomas a look of relief when the man left without taking it, but Thomas failed to notice. He stared straight ahead, lips compressed, his jaw tight with anger.

No one spoke as they climbed the stairs to the third floor. Their guards released them into an empty room that smelled of unwashed bodies and human waste, and left them, taking the lantern.

Thomas waited until he could make out Ethan's form in the faint glow from a boarded-up window, and turned on him. "This is what you got us, giving in to that lieutenant!"

The pain that had pulsed behind Ethan's eyes all day spiked up a notch. "No, Thomas," he said softly. "This is what you got when you stumbled into that Reb picket line. Same as me when I got caught."

"But if you'd kept your mouth shut in Gadsden, maybe we wouldn't be here now. Maybe they'd have let us go."

Ethan gave a faint shrug. "I doubt it." The sudden return of his headaches distressed him, and he snapped, "If you hadn't opened your mouth, if you'd left it to me, I'd have got us out of it. It's *your* fault we're here, not mine." He walked to the corner furthest from the waste bucket and curled onto the floor, his back to Thomas.

Thomas stood for a moment, then walked to where he lay. "Head hurt?"

Getting no reply, he let out a long sigh, and settled next to him.

He woke to bright sunlight streaming past the boards barring the window. Squinting into it, he saw Ethan pulling at one of them, testing its strength.

"This one's loose," he said, demonstrating as Thomas came to stand beside him. "But it's the only one. The rest are nailed down tight. We need something to pry them off."

Thomas peered between the boards and shook his head. "It's a long way down, Ethan. And there are people on the streets. We wouldn't get far."

Ethan slammed a balled fist against the boards in frustration. "I know. I just never imagined how much I'd hate being locked up."

Thomas continued to stare through the crack. "Sorry for last night," he said softly.

Ethan glanced sideways at him. "Yeah," he said after a moment. "Me, too."

Breakfast, when it came, was two fingers of bacon and a cup of water each. When the guards came again, it was to announce that the boat from Montgomery was due shortly. The chains were restored, drawing hecklers as they were marched through the streets to the wharf.

Once they were on the water, Ethan's spirits soared. The air was crisp and clear after the rain, the sky a cloudless sapphire blue. The Alabama River sparkled in the sunlight, dense forest crowding in on either side, the autumn colors a vibrant contrast to the dark green of the pines. Blue-gray moss trailed from among crimson oak leaves, the hickories had turned golden-bronze, and willow branches drooped low, scattering pale yellow across the water.

They steamed past an occasional boy or old man lounging on the bank, line dangling in the slow-moving current. And once, as they rounded a bend and passed close to a house, the happy shouts of children at play rang across the water.

It'd be easy to forget where we're headed, Ethan thought, remembering the times he'd traveled freely through the same country. *Easy except for the chains.*

The steamer covered the ten miles to Cahaba all too quickly, slowing as it passed the spit of land where the Cahaba River emptied into the Alabama. The forest between the two rivers tailed off, revealing a magnificent pillared house situated among oaks and cedars high on the western bank. Moments later, the town wharf came into view, and on the bank above it, a massive structure of another kind; a wooden stockade where armed guards patrolled walkways set high on the outsides of the walls. Ethan and Thomas shared a look, knowing it was where they were headed.

Their guards led them up the steep ramp from the wharf, but to their surprise, failed to turn toward the stockade. They continued into town, along sidewalks shaded by ancient, moss-draped oaks, chinaberry and mulberry, and past an Artesian well where water rose from the ground, sparkling like diamonds as it cascaded into a concrete basin. Lettering on windows advertised dry goods, groceries, tailoring, millinery, jewelry and the services of doctors and lawyers. The homes they glimpsed were set back from the streets, each on an acre or more of land, surrounded by gardens and groves of trees. Some were painted white with long galleries and green shutters. Others were red brick, palatial two and three-story mansions with tapering white columns and sunlight glinting off a multitude of mullioned windows.

The citizenry of Cahaba was rapidly becoming inured to the sight of Union prisoners in their midst, so their presence provoked little reaction as they were shepherded through the streets to the office of the prison commander. They were shown to an anteroom where their names and ranks were logged once more, and they were asked to turn over anything of value for safekeeping.

"Anything ya'll hand over now'll be returned when you leave," the sergeant in charge told them. Placing his pen on the desk next to the logbook, he leaned back, steepling his fingers before him. "But anything my boys find when they search you will be confiscated."

"We've already been searched," Thomas told him irritably. "Twice. There's nothing left to hand over."

"Have it yo' way." The sergeant nodded to the guards flanking them.

The search was thorough. *Too thorough*, Ethan thought, choking back protest as the man's hands moved from his clothing and began to probe his person.

As Thomas had predicted, the search turned up nothing. They were marched back the way they'd come, this time to the gates of the prison.

12

The Federal Prison at Cahaba was a former corn and cotton warehouse situated high above the Alabama River. The thick walls of the warehouse were red brick and stood fourteen feet high. There had once been a roof, but time and the elements had taken their toll, leaving much of the interior open to the sky. The sections still intact, at the front and rear of the warehouse, were badly damaged, and provided only minimal protection from sun and rain.

The floor was hard-packed dirt, and the water supply, for drinking, washing and cooking, came from an artesian well located several hundred feet outside the prison. The water rose from the ground and ran along an open ditch, under the wall of the stockade, and through the warehouse before emptying into the river. Before reaching the prison, the water channel was essentially an open sewer, a repository for anything the citizens of Cahaba chose to dump into it.

The stockade walls had been added when the warehouse was converted for use as a prison. The walkway, accessed by two sets of stairs, one along the eastern wall, the other next to the gate, afforded the guards an excellent view of both the yard and the interior of the warehouse.

As Thomas and Ethan came to a halt outside the gate, a lanky, unkempt man in a sergeant's uniform descended the stairs and strolled to meet them. His face was unremarkable, long and narrow, thin lips fringed by a stringy ginger mustache and tobacco-stained beard. In contrast, his eyes were a startling shade of blue. He gave Thomas a cursory glance, then the blue eyes narrowed as they came to rest on Ethan. Ethan met his gaze briefly, then looked away.

The sergeant's lips twisted into a grin. "Welcome to Cahaba, boys. I hear you tried to escape. Well, we ain't had no one escape from here yet, and you two ain't about to be the first." His eyes flicked briefly to Thomas before settling on Ethan. "We got us a list a' rules here. You boys 'bide by 'em, an' you an' me'll git along jus' fine." He reeled them off quickly, by rote:

"Roll call every mornin' at 7:30. Rations after, cooked in the yard.

-Roll call and rations at 5:00 p.m.

-Lights out at nine o'clock.

-Durin' the day, yo' free to move about the yard. At night, yo' to stay in the warehouse.

-Any prisoner crossin' the dead-line'll be shot without warnin'.

-Any prisoner stoppin' in the doorway to the warehouse'll be shot without warnin'.

-No prisoner to leave the prison without permission. Any attemptin' it'll be shot without warnin'.

-Any prisoner attemptin' to escape'll be shot without warnin'.

-Prisoners are to obey all orders given by the guards, an' be quick about it. No backtalk. Any prisoner failin' to obey'll have his food ration cut by half.

-No visitors allowed to enter the prison or talk to a prisoner without permission of the commandant. Conversations between a prisoner and a visitor are to be held in the presence of the commandant.

-No letters or packages are to be sent in or out without permission. Letters are to be one page, and don't be sealin' 'em. They's gonna get read befo' they's sent."

The sergeant glanced at Thomas, then looked hard at Ethan. "You boys got that?"

They nodded. "Yes, sir."

Another guard had come through the gates during the recitation. At a signal from the sergeant, he dropped the chains he carried and knelt behind Thomas. Thomas' face suffused with anger as leg irons were secured about his ankles. The sergeant's eyes locked into his, cutting off any objection.

Still staring at the ground, Ethan bit his lip as his legs were shackled. He had expected the chains to be removed when they got to the prison, not more added.

He looked up, relief plain on his face when the sergeant said, "You kin unlock their hands now. An' take off'n that chain from aroun' their necks."

One of the guards, the old man who had escorted them from the commandant's office, produced the keys. When the chains were removed, the sergeant jerked his head. "Take the yella-haired fella over there fo' a bit. I wanna talk to this boy alone."

For a moment, Thomas looked as if he might argue. The sergeant's eyes dared him, and the old man laid a hand firmly on his arm. Casting Ethan an apologetic look, Thomas allowed himself to be led away.

The sergeant waited until they were out of earshot. "You ain't white, are ya boy?"

"Half," Ethan replied. The sergeant's eyes narrowed dangerously, and he quickly added, "Sir."

"What's t'other half? Some kinda Injun?"

"Yes, sir."

The man's upper lip curled in disgust, exposing tobacco-stained teeth. "A breed *an'* a Yank. Cain't say as I care much fo' that. Worse'n a nigger in my book. Least niggers knows their place. Not like you red bastards."

Anger flared; Ethan fought to keep it from showing.

The sergeant eyed him, scowling, then spat. A long stream of tobacco juice spattered across Ethan's boots. "Watch yo'sef, boy. Watch yo'self *real* careful-like an' don't do nuttin' what brings you to my notice. Nuttin'. You unnerstan'?"

Too furious to speak, Ethan nodded.

The sergeant moved quickly. Ethan took a startled step back. The chain pulled taut, throwing him off balance. He would have fallen if the other man hadn't grabbed the front of his coat.

The sergeant pulled him close, his voice low and threatening. "Answer me with respec', boy."

"Yes, sir," Ethan stammered, sudden fear tingeing his anger.

"White boys I might make allowances fo', but not the likes a' you. You mind yo'sef in my prison. Hear?"

"Yes, sir," Ethan said, hating the tremor that came to his voice. "Yes, sir," he repeated firmly. "I understand the rules. I'll abide by them and won't cause you any trouble, sir."

The sergeant released him and took a step back, the sneer returning to his lips. "See to it ya don't, boy." He started away, tossing parting words over his shoulder. "See to it ya don't."

Ethan watched him mount the steps, heart racing, his stomach in knots.

"What was that about?" Thomas asked, joining him.

Ethan shook his head, eyes still on the sergeant. "Nothing, I hope."

The white-haired guard pressed a hand to Thomas' back, urging him toward the gate. Ethan took a step and stumbled. Catching himself, he shuffled after Thomas, trying to adapt to the restriction and weight of the chains.

The prison yard was forty-five feet across and thirty-five feet deep. The noses of two large artillery pieces poked through the north wall, and armed guards were stationed at intervals around the perimeter. Bedraggled groups of prisoners loitered around cooking fires and passed in and out through the doorway to the warehouse. Heads turned as the gate swung open. Cries of "Fresh fish!" went up, and the prisoners surged to meet them.

One of the leaders, a short, wiry man with thick black hair and a full mustache, stuck out a hand. "Welcome to Cahaba, boys. Hugh Eldridge, 6th Missouri. Captured at Neosho, Missouri the first week in October."

"Thomas Murray, 36th Illinois. Captured at Chickamauga Creek, Georgia, a month ago." Thomas offered him a lopsided grin and gestured toward the leg irons. "And again last week in Alabama. This here's Ethan Fraser."

Hugh nodded a greeting as more men crowded around, shouting questions, wanting to know where they were from, where they'd been captured, and pleading for news of home and the war. Ethan took a half-step back, preferring to let Thomas be the center of attention. Thomas provided answers as best he could and told them about the escape from the train. Encouraged by shouts of approval, he regaled them with the tale of the trek across Georgia. Ethan listened skeptically as, in the telling, it became more adventure than ordeal.

As the questions, and Thomas' answers, grew repetitive, interest waned. Men were beginning to wander away when Hugh spoke.

"It ain't too bad here, boys. Rations are passable, a quarter-pound of meat and a quart of cornmeal two times a day. The meat ain't what I'd call fresh, but it don't smell too bad neither. They grind the corn together with cob and husk, but if you pick it out there's nothin' left, so you learn to like it." He offered them a grim smile adding, "The worst part's the rats. They're big as cats and crawl over you at night."

"You been treated all right?" Ethan asked, his mind still on the sergeant at the gate.

Hugh shrugged. "Well enough. The commandant's a decent man, and fair. Goes by the name of Henderson. You meet him?"

"No," Thomas said. Ethan shook his head.

"The only time there's problems is when he's away. He's an agent for the prisoner exchange, and every once in a while, he goes to Vicksburg. When he's gone, the lieutenant in command of the military post takes over. He don't keep a close eye on things the way Henderson does. The guards know it, and some take advantage. Last time Henderson was gone they stole damn near everything they could lay their hands on."

"None of them's worth much," another man grumbled. "If they was decent soldiers, they'd be fighting the war, not tending to us."

"Most of them are real young or real old," another man put in. "Some ain't too smart, neither. Others just plain got a mean streak."

"That's true," Hugh allowed. "But, most of them are decent enough. Friendly even." He paused, eyeing Ethan. "You some kinda mixed blood?"

Thomas said, "He's half Sioux Indian."

A murmur spread among the men still listening. Ethan ignored the looks, shut his ears to the comments, and listened to Hugh.

"Well then, I should warn you about one of the guards. A sergeant name of Shunk. He's a mean one, and some of the guards are in cahoots with him. They're real hard on folks that ain't white."

"There was a man here a few weeks back," a slender, bespectacled young man put in. "A Turk. He had dark skin like yours, and Shunk and his boys made his life a living hell while Henderson was gone. You best watch yourself."

"As long as Henderson's around, Shunk won't do much," Hugh interjected. "Just keep an eye out. Do what the guards say, and keep clear of the dead-lines."

"Dead-lines?" Thomas asked.

Hugh pointed to the rows of posts set several feet inside the stockade fence and running parallel to it. "The dead-line. There's another inside the warehouse. A couple of guards have been known to take potshots at anyone standing too close. And Shunk likes to walk just outside it, using his whip on anyone he can reach. And another thing: Don't stop in the doorway to the warehouse. Don't even hesitate. The rule is no stopping, and just about any of the guards'll take a shot at you if you do."

"We heard prisoners don't stay here long," Thomas said. "Any idea when they'll move us?"

Hugh shrugged. "There ain't any logic to it, near as I can tell. Some get moved after a few days, but there's boys got here before us, that are still here."

"Has anyone thought about escape?"

Hugh glanced at Ethan's leg irons. "Looks like they don't plan on you going anywhere."

"They can't leave these on forever. I plan on getting out just as soon as they take them off."

Hugh heard the conviction in Ethan's voice, acknowledging it with a brief dip of his head before glancing around. Most of the prisoners had wandered off, but a few still listened. He indicated the two men flanking him, introducing the young man with the spectacles as Jacob Sutherland, and the other, a gangly youth with a cowlick and buckteeth, as Simon Liddell, both with the 6th Missouri.

"Come with us," Hugh said, starting toward the warehouse. Thomas and Ethan shared a look and shuffled after him.

"You were asking about escape," Hugh said, when they were out of hearing. "We've been thinking to give it a try before they move us further south."

They stepped past the guard at the doorway, into a vast open room, several times larger than the yard. The dead-line paralleled the walls, with guards posted at intervals behind it. A row of unfinished bunks stood to the right of the door, built from rough-cut lumber and overhung by a decaying section of roof. Further along, a doorway on their left revealed a room where bunks tiered five high lined the walls. Smoke permeated the air, shifting through shafts of sunlight that filtered through holes in the roof and a row of narrow windows high on the eastern wall.

As they moved further into the warehouse, an odor like rotten eggs reached them. The stench grew stronger as they approached a ditch running diagonally across the center of the room.

"Sulfur," Hugh remarked, coming to a stop and looking down at the water. "It makes men sick. Me, I only drink it boiled and flavored with the stuff we call coffee. Still, there's times when it gives me the runs."

He inclined his head toward a doorway at the back of the warehouse. "That's the water closet over yonder. We've been thinking about going out through there. See how the water flows from here and goes under the wall? It runs under the water closet, then out through the stockade fence and down to the river.

There's a plank floor in the water closet, set up off the ground. We figure we could pull up a couple planks, or part of the seat, and squeeze out under the wall with the water." He shrugged. "Only problem's finding a way to do it without the guards noticing."

The sun had sunk low as they talked. Prisoners were beginning to drift in from the yard. A group of guards entered, herding the stragglers before them, and starting a general migration toward the south end of the warehouse.

"Roll call," Hugh said.

When the count was complete, Hugh invited Thomas and Ethan to join their mess. Jacob did the cooking, placing the five portions of meat at the center of an iron kettle and leaving it to cook. He set a portion of the cornmeal aside before mixing the rest with water and forming it into patties, placing them in the kettle around the meat. When the meat was cooked, he removed it from the pot and sopped up the juice with the corn patties. The remainder of the cornmeal was sprinkled into the pot and left to brown. Once they'd eaten, he used it to make coffee.

The air grew cold quickly after the sun went down, and the men huddled around the fires for warmth. Some talked, others had cards or dice and gambled. One of the prisoners began to sing, and more voices joined in. Another read aloud from the bible. All too soon, the guards yelled for lights out. The prisoners pushed themselves to their feet and filed into the bunkroom.

"You're welcome to roost with us," Hugh said.

"Roost?" Thomas asked.

"Like chickens," Simon told him, indicating the tiered bunks.

Stout posts were set at seven-foot intervals, supporting a framework over which rough planks had been secured. The tiers were thirty inches apart, and the men slept close together, feet against the wall, heads toward the center of the room. A fireplace on the north wall produced little heat, leaving the room cold and drafty. Thomas and Ethan had no blankets, and there were none to spare. They climbed up to the third tier and huddled together for warmth.

When the prisoners were all inside, guards filed through the room, extinguishing the lanterns. One of them, a tall man with close-set eyes, a long nose and stringy black hair, came to a stop before Ethan. Ethan propped himself on one elbow and looked at him. Seconds passed while the man studied him. Then he hacked and spit. The viscous glob hit Ethan full in the face. Furious, he would have sprung at the guard, but Thomas flung out a hand, grabbing a fistful of coat. Ethan struggled until common sense prevailed. Glaring angrily at the guard, he lowered himself to the bunk. The guard's lips lifted in a humorless grin, and he moved on.

"This is going to be rough," Ethan muttered, wiping his face on his sleeve. "Thanks for stopping me."

"Don't let them get to you," Thomas said. "Things'll work out. You'll see."

Neither of them slept much that night, kept awake in part by the cold, but mainly by rats that sniffed at them and ran back and forth across their bodies. When their fellow prisoners began to stir soon after daybreak, Thomas and Ethan shared an exhausted look and climbed down from their perch.

The day had dawned sunny and mild. At roll call, prisoners were assigned to details for work both inside and outside the prison. A detail left under guard to gather wood; others were sent to work at the hospital or at various jobs in town where their pre-war skills could be put to use. Hugh had been a carriage-maker and spent many of his days working outside the prison, as did Simon, who knew carpentry. Once it was learned that Thomas had carpentry skills, he and Simon were often sent to work together. Some of the remaining men were issued rakes and a wheelbarrow and set about cleaning the prison; others walked circuits around the yard. A trio of men tossed a baseball; other groups rolled dice, played cards, read or talked. A few simply sat, staring into space.

Their first morning at Cahaba, Thomas shuffled over to a group of men gathered around one of the cooking fires and joined easily in their conversation. He motioned Ethan to join him, but Ethan waved him off and wandered into the warehouse, looking with interest at men hunched over books. He was curious to know where they got them, was wondering who to ask, when he spotted Jacob lounging in the sun at the far end of the room. Ignoring the stares, and the smattering of comment generated by his passage, he walked the length of the warehouse to join him.

Jacob looked up at the sound of the chain and smiled. Ethan hunkered down next to him.

"Where'd you get the book?"

Jacob closed the volume he'd been reading and held it out. Ethan took it, running his fingers over the rich leather of the cover and the gold-embossed title on the spine: *David Copperfield.* He opened the book, fanning the pages slowly as he listened.

"There's a woman lives just outside the prison, a Mrs. Gardner. She has a library full of books and she lends them to us."

Ethan looked up, intrigued. "But how does she know when you want one? And how do you get it from her?"

"Some of the guards, if you give them a note, they'll take it to her. She sends a book. Just be sure to ask the right one. There's some 'ud sooner shoot you than fetch a book."

"Who do I ask? And how do I write a note? I don't have anything to write with."

"Ask the old guard, the one with the white hair and the limp. Or there's another one, kinda stocky, with gray hair and a mustache. If I see either of them, I'll point them out. There's others, but until you figure out who's who, they're the best ones to ask. They'll give you pencil and paper." Jacob held out a hand for the book.

Ethan handed it back. "Have you seen either of them today?" he asked hopefully.

"Can't say as I have, but then I haven't been looking." Jacob pushed his spectacles up on his nose and craned his neck. "Don't see them in here. Let's go look in the yard."

As they walked through the warehouse, Jacob elaborated. "Mrs. Gardner's got a daughter name of Belle. She's eleven. She passes us vegetables through a hole in the fence. I've had a couple ears of corn and some potatoes since we've been here. Some of the boys have had cabbage and carrots and such."

"How do you reach them across the dead-line?"

"Belle knows the guards. She waits 'til one of the friendly ones is on duty along the fence near her house, then passes them through. The guards hand them to us, or let us step over the line if we're quick about it."

They had come out into the yard. Jacob shaded his eyes and scanned the guards along the fence.

"There," he said, pointing to the old man who'd brought them to the prison the day before. "In the corner over yonder. Be sure to keep back from the dead-line. Get his attention, and let him come to you." He turned, and with his book under one arm, headed back to his place in the sun.

Ethan went to the old man and made his request. The guard dug in his knapsack and came up with a scrap of paper and a pencil. Ethan wrote a brief note and handed them back.

Knowing a book was on its way made him restless. He looked enviously at the men walking the perimeter, thinking there was nothing he'd like more than to stretch his legs, but the shackles wouldn't allow it. Thomas was still among the men gathered around the fire. If anything, the crowd around him had grown larger. Ethan wandered back into the warehouse and settled near Jacob. The sun's warmth made him drowsy, and he rolled down onto his side and closed his eyes.

He hadn't been asleep long when pain shot through his left hand. Ethan pulled it to him and struggled to his knees. A guard was strolling away along the dead-line. He looked over his shoulder and grinned. Enraged, Ethan would have gone after him, but he was grabbed from behind.

"One of Shunk's boys," Jacob said, keeping a tight hold on him. "I didn't see him 'til it was too late. Sorry."

Ethan flexed his fingers. Movement hurt, but no bones appeared to be broken. A nasty-looking weal was rising across the back of his hand where the guard's heel had gouged it.

"You all right?" Jacob asked.

Ethan nodded. The guard was standing with the rat-faced man who'd spit on him the night before. Rat-Face saw Ethan looking, and his upper lip lifted in a sneer.

"Sorry I didn't see him sooner," Jacob repeated, releasing Ethan. "I'll try to keep a better eye out." He hesitated before adding, "Maybe you should stick close to your friend. If you know what I mean?"

Ethan saw his concern, and nodded. Jacob smiled awkwardly and returned to his book. Afraid to risk falling asleep, Ethan left him and made his way to where Thomas still held court, entertaining the men with some preposterous tale. Ethan sat down near him, half listening, half daydreaming. He was miles away when someone touched his shoulder. He whirled, prepared to defend himself.

"Whoa, son!" the white-haired guard said. "Dint mean to startle ya none. I jus' wanted to give ya this."

It was a worn volume of *Ivanhoe* by Sir Walter Scott. Ethan thanked him and opened the book. He sat spellbound until Thomas said, "Come on, Ethan. Roll call."

Ethan closed the book reluctantly and followed him into the warehouse. After supper, he opened it again, and in the light from one of the fires, read until lights out.

The commandant, Captain Henderson, was present at roll call the next morning. He was a short, dark-haired man, clean-shaven but for a luxurious, drooping mustache. Attended by the sergeant who'd met them at the gate, he passed along the rows of prisoners, making small talk, and pausing periodically for lengthier exchanges.

The captain's brows drew together as he approached Thomas and Ethan "Sergeant Shunk, why are these men chained?"

"They're the ones sent down from Gadsden, suh," Shunk reminded him. "The ones that escaped."

"Ah, yes." Captain Henderson turned to contemplate Thomas and Ethan. The muscles in his jaw worked, but his eyes were merely thoughtful. "Leave them on fo' a week, Sergeant. If there are no problems, see they're removed."

"Yes, suh."

Ethan glanced at Shunk, found the man watching him, and looked away.

The commandant started to move on, then turned back. "If there's anything I can do fo' you, let me know. I make it a point to be available."

Thomas seized the opportunity. "There is one thing, sir. We could use blankets."

"Two blankets. See to it, will you, Sergeant?"

That night, Thomas was issued a blanket, but Ethan was not. They bundled together under one, and it not only kept them warmer, it provided an extra layer of separation from the rats. Overcome by exhaustion, they slept.

At roll call the next morning, Captain Henderson was nowhere to be seen. Sergeant Shunk took advantage of his absence, assigning Ethan to clean the water closet each morning until further notice. Hiding his resentment, Ethan did as he was told.

The guard assigned to watch him was the same man who'd searched him the day they arrived. He was short with a high, balding forehead, a badly healed broken nose, and a misshapen upper lip. He rarely spoke, but his milky blue eyes followed Ethan's every move. Ethan found his mute attention unnerving and couldn't wait to be away from him. Each day, as soon as it was allowed, he joined Jacob in the sun. He read compulsively, requesting a second book as soon as he finished the first. He consumed Dickens' *A Tale of Two Cities*, then embarked on a wordy tome entitled *Harold, the Last of the Saxon Kings* by Edward George Earle Bulwer-Lytton.

On the day he began the third book, the breeze cooled perceptibly, and the sky grew overcast. By lights out, it had begun to drizzle, turning to a steady rain by morning. The prisoners hunched miserably during roll call, then dispersed to seek shelter wherever they could find it.

The bunkroom provided the best protection from the weather. The walls cut the chill wind and allowed a small amount of heat from the fire to accumulate. Despite water sluicing through holes in the roof, portions of the room remained relatively dry. Ethan went there as soon as the harelip allowed it.

Thomas was gone, sent to work in town, so Ethan collected the blanket and his book, and looked around for a dry place to spend the day. The weak gray light from the windows was all but lost in the smoke-clogged air, but he figured if he climbed high enough, he'd have enough light to read by. Encumbered by the leg irons, he hauled himself up to top tier of bunks and found a dry place to settle. He opened the book to where he'd left off and sat plowing through the meticulous detail of *Harold, the Last of the Saxon Kings* until the words on the page began to blur. Bracing his head against the heel of one hand, Ethan squeezed his eyes shut. After several minutes, he opened them and looked around. His vision had cleared, but he knew if he kept reading, the headache that threatened would grow worse. He set the book aside, leaned against the wall, and closed his eyes.

Shouts of "Roll call!" roused him hours later. Coughing in the smoke-laden air, he sat up. His head didn't feel much better, but it wasn't any worse. Ethan scooted to the edge of the bunk and lowered himself to the ground, aware that the room was nearly empty.

He grabbed the blanket and book, set them on the bunk he shared with Thomas, then headed for the door, reaching it at the same time as another man. They very nearly collided, but Ethan squeezed through first.

"Outta my way, breed."

The other prisoner shoved him, the chain tripped him and he fell. Ethan rolled onto his side, lashed out with both feet, and connected with the side of a knee. The man went down with a howl of pain. Ethan was on all fours, scrambling through the mud toward him, when a guard grabbed him from behind, yanking him back.

"Enough a' that! Hear?"

Ethan was too angry to think about consequences. He twisted free, would have thrown himself at the other prisoner, but a second guard stepped between them. Ethan looked down the barrel of a musket and stopped. Sinking back on his heels, he brought up both hands in surrender.

The other man lay in the mud, clutching his knee and moaning. More guards ran toward them. At the other end of the warehouse, prisoners and guards assembled for roll call turned to stare.

Guards clustered around the downed man. Another dragged Ethan to his feet. With a guard firmly in possession of each arm, he was hustled toward the officers at the far end of the room. Oblivious to the stares of the other prisoners, he strained to see who was in charge. His heart sank when he saw Shunk.

It wasn't until they drew closer that he spotted the mustache. Hope rose. With Captain Henderson present, he stood a chance of fair treatment. As the guards brought him to a halt before the two officers, help came from an unexpected source.

"Emory pushed him, suh," one of them said. "Knocked him down comin' through the door."

Captain Henderson glanced briefly at the guard. Then his eyes bored into Ethan's. "Is that what happened?"

"Yes, sir."

"You give him cause?"

"No, sir. I don't think so. We were in a hurry and bumped into each other."

Henderson looked past Ethan to where the other prisoner still lay on the ground, guards clustered around him. "I take it Private Emory's injured?"

"It's his leg, suh, where this one kicked him. Don' know any more'n 'at."

The captain's eyes shifted to Ethan. "A mighty strong reaction to bein' pushed, wouldn't you say, Private Fraser?"

"Yes, sir. I'm sorry."

"Half rations tonight. See it doesn't happen again."

Relief surged through Ethan. "Yes, sir."

He turned away, failing to notice the flush of outrage that suffused Shunk's face and neck.

13

The next morning, the last Friday in October, Ethan woke to find his headache gone and his stomach rumbling with hunger. He tugged the collar of his coat up around his ears and followed Thomas out into the rain.

Sergeant Shunk was waiting beneath an overhanging portion of roof, wearing a wide-brimmed hat and an oilcloth cape. He stood under shelter while his men proceeded through the count, interrupting frequently to question or comment. The prisoners were still lined up, wet and shivering, long after they'd normally been issued their rations. When the count was at last complete, it was to a collective sigh of relief.

"Private Fraser. Step forward."

Ethan's heart rose in his throat. He threw Thomas a panicked look, but there was nothing Thomas could do. He looked back helplessly.

"Now, Private!"

Ethan took a halting step forward. Steeling himself, he shuffled past the lines of shivering men, toward the shelter of the roof where Shunk and his henchmen waited. He came to a stop before them, eyes lowered, staring at the sergeant's muddy boots.

For the longest time, no one spoke. The only sound was the hiss and splatter of falling rain. Ethan realized his nails were biting into the palms of his hands and willed himself to relax.

Shunk spoke at last, raising his voice to the assembled prisoners. "Dismissed!" Under his breath, he added, "All bu'chu, Injun."

Prodded by the guards, the prisoners began moving toward the far end of the warehouse. Ethan stood where he was, hunched against the rain, feeling their eyes on his back.

"Fraser," Shunk mused when they were alone. " Now that's an intrestin' name fo' an Injun."

The comment wasn't at all what Ethan expected. He looked up.

Shunk moved quickly, lashing him across the face with the whip he'd held concealed in the folds of his cape. "Answer me when I talk to you!"

Ethan staggered back, gasping in shock and pain. He raised both hands to protect himself, then clenched them into fists. He took a step forward before noticing the look of savage anticipation on Shunk's face. Forcing his hands to his sides, he choked out the words, "Yes, sir."

Shunk crowded in close. "Yessuh what, boy?"

Ethan fought to keep pain and indignation from his voice. "Yes, sir, I am to answer when you speak to me, and yes, sir, Fraser is an interesting name for an Indian."

"Look at me, boy." Shunk placed the butt of the whip under Ethan's chin, forcing his head up.

Ethan raised his eyes slowly. The intensity of the hatred in the other man's eyes sent chills of fear radiating through him. He wanted to look away, but the pressure of the whip kept him from moving. Focusing on the sergeant's mustache, he waited.

"Tell me, boy. How'd a piece 'a shit Yankee half-breed like you wind up with a name like Fraser?"

Ethan kept his eyes on the mustache. "It's my father's name, sir."

"Yo' father, huh? What'd he do, take himself a squaw? Find him some fat, stinkin', red bitch squaw and mount her like a dog? That's how they like it, isn't it, boy? Being mounted like bitches? That where you come from, boy?" Shunk's voice rose until it was nearly a shriek.

Blood pounded in Ethan's ears. He was light-headed—from anger or hunger, he wasn't sure which—but at the moment, nothing mattered but keeping his wits about him and his answers civil. "Yes, sir," he replied softly.

"Yo' ma's a bitch. Don't that make you her pup, boy?"

Ethan's eyes wavered. He swallowed before answering. "Yes, sir. I suppose it does."

Shunk lowered the whip. Ethan's eyes followed it.

"So why're you sleepin' inside? Sleepin' with white boys? No one ever teach you yo' place, breed?"

"I... No, sir."

"No, suh, what?"

"No one ever..."

Shunk's voice rose shrilly. "Ever what, boy?"

It was all Ethan could do to answer him. His voice was little more than a whisper as he forced out the words. "...taught me my place, sir."

"Speak up, boy! I cain't hear you!"

The whip snapped across Ethan's chest. He flinched, but stood his ground. Raising his voice a fraction, he repeated, "No one ever taught me my place, sir."

The sergeant's lips screwed into a contemptuous sneer. "That's what I thought. It's high time someone did. Kept you away from decent folks. Kept you from attackin' 'em." He made a clicking sound and rapped the whip against his leg. "Come wit' me, boy. We got a place fo' the likes a' you."

Rat-Face and another guard grabbed Ethan by the arms. They hurried him past the curious stares of other prisoners, out the door of the warehouse, across the dead-line, and down the narrow passage between the warehouse and the eastern wall of the stockade. They came to a halt behind the water closet, where the wall of the stockade jutted out several feet. Shunk stood aside, and the guards gave Ethan a shove. His foot caught on the sergeant's outstretched boot, and he sprawled up to his elbows in the water flowing from beneath the water closet. One of the guards laughed.

Ethan pushed himself out of the ditch and turned, sitting in the mud. Shunk was watching him, a look of cruel satisfaction on his face.

"This suits you better, breed. Now here's the rule. Yo' not to leave this place. You go past this here corner, or the corner of the warehouse back yonder, an' yo' gonna git shot. They's a man up on the wall 'ud like nothing more than to put a bullet in you." Shunk turned to Rat-Face. "Give him his rations."

The man grinned, tossing something that splashed into the mud next to Ethan's knee. Chuckling and glancing back over their shoulders, the three guards sauntered toward the front of the warehouse. It wasn't until they disappeared around the corner that Ethan looked down. Lying in the mud was a bone.

He sat where he was, angry tears streaming unheeded down his face, mixing with mud and rain and blood. All his life, he'd been the target of taunts and insults, but never had a verbal attack been so devastatingly calculated. The sheer maliciousness of it left him shaken to his core. *And there's nothing I can do to stop him,* he thought, shuddering against a cold rush of fear. *Nothing. I'm completely at his mercy.*

A drop of rain slid down the back of his neck, chilling him further. Ethan pushed himself to his feet and looked around. Moving away from the water closet, he stopped several feet shy of the stockade wall and hunkered down to wash mud and excrement from his hands. When he'd done the best he could, he stood up. Pressing icy fingers into his armpits, he surveyed his surroundings.

The area where the guards had left him was long and narrow, and there was little to offer protection from the rain. The only place that looked promising was the corner where the wall of the water closet intersected the wall of the warehouse. The water closet had been built as a lean-to addition and there, in the corner, the overhanging portions of the two roofs converged.

Ethan turned his eyes to the line of the stockade fence. The sheltered corner was very close to the boundary he'd been told not to cross. He hesitated uncertainly, but as water continued to stream down his neck, he decided to risk it.

He edged toward shelter, expecting the crack of a gunshot at any moment. It never came. He wedged himself into the corner, squatting with his back pressed against the walls. The roof protected him more than he'd thought it would. Not that it mattered much; his hair was plastered to his head, his clothing soaked. He was wet to the skin everywhere except where Archie Gilles' wool vest protected him.

Not knowing what else to do, Ethan crouched in the corner for hours. Early in the afternoon, the rain tapered off, then stopped. With an involuntary shudder, he struggled to his feet. His muscles were cramped and stiff with cold. He leaned against the building, shifting his weight from one foot to the other until slowly, painfully, blood began to circulate. When he felt his legs would support him, he pushed away from the corner and hobbled out into the open.

He wandered the confined space between the fence and the ditch, swinging his arms and stomping his feet in an effort to get warm. As he paced, he studied the place where the water passed through the stockade wall. It wasn't part of the wall at all, but a row of saplings set close together allowing the water to flow out around them. He thought of Hugh's plan for escape and shuffled over for a closer look.

A shot rang out. Splinters flew as the ball tore into one of the saplings close to his face. Ethan sprang backward, toppling into the mud as the chain tripped him. Rolling onto his side, he looked in the direction the shot had come from. A guard grinned down at him, tamping another load into his musket. Ethan waited, heart racing, fully expecting the man to take aim and fire again. Instead, the guard cradled the loaded musket. Ethan scrambled to his feet. Keeping a wary eye on him, he sidled back to his corner.

The afternoon crept by. The clouds lifted, but the sun refused to poke through. Ethan ventured out periodically in futile attempts to get warm. Always, he returned to crouch shivering in the corner. Once he tried sitting, but the cold and wet soaked up from the ground chilling him further, and he returned to his haunches.

As the gray afternoon light began to fade, Ethan sensed he wasn't alone. He looked up to find the harelip standing several yards away, staring at him with pale, dead eyes. Ethan shifted uncomfortably and looked away. He glanced over from time to time to find the man still watching him. It wasn't until shouts went up for roll call that the guard finally turned and walked away.

A short time later, the smell of cooking meat drifted back to him, reminding him that he'd missed the morning meal and had little to eat the night before. His stomach had long since ceased to rumble, but it came alive at the smell of food, cramped with hunger. Ethan leaned his head against the wall of the warehouse and fought back tears. He had never felt so desperately alone.

He ventured out once more, briefly, as twilight deepened. The cold and damp had begun to penetrate the wool vest, and he returned to the corner shivering worse than before. He looked up, and his heart sank when he saw stars. Without clouds, the night would be even colder.

It wasn't until he heard the call for lights out that he gave up all hope of being allowed back inside. Huddling down as tightly as he could, he pulled the wet collar of his coat up over his ears and burrowed his mouth and nose down inside. He pushed numbed fingers into his armpits, all the while knowing there was little he could do to preserve the dwindling amount of heat left in his body. By morning, he would be dead, or close to it.

His thought of his family, longing for them, picturing them as he'd last seen them—Kate, the tomboy; Seth, awkward and kind; the twins, so different physically, yet thinking and acting as one; and Duncan, who'd always looked out for him, and whose serious demeanor masked a wicked sense of humor. He stifled a sob when he thought of Duncan and wondered how his parents were bearing up under the loss of three sons.

Four.

The thought came without warning. Ethan roused himself, shaking off sleep, determined to fight it as long as he could.

He very nearly lost the battle. His eyelids drooped and the shivering all but stopped. He was lingering at the outer edge of consciousness when a sound, somewhere close at hand, penetrated his awareness. Slowly it dawned on him that someone was speaking. The voice continued, and Ethan fought his way back. Opening his eyes, he stared into the darkness. He thought he saw movement near the fence, but couldn't be certain. He remained absolutely still, watching and waiting.

The whisper came again. "Son? You there, son?"

He must have groaned because the speaker materialized before him. A warm hand pressed against his cheek. Someone grasped his shoulder, shaking him.

"Son? You awake?"

Strong hands grasped his arms, hauling him up.

"Yo' gonna hafta hep us, son. Come on, git yo' feet under ya."

Mustering all that remained of his strength, Ethan stood. The shivering renewed itself, and he leaned against the wall, a man on either arm supporting him.

"Come wit' us, son. Time to ge'chu inside."

Ethan hesitated, his fogged brain trying to decide if it was a trick, wondering if he should resist. Either way, he realized, the outcome would be the same. He took a tentative step. His legs gave way beneath him, but the men on either side kept him from falling, taking his weight as he staggered from the corner. At the imaginary boundary of his prison, Ethan braced himself, afraid to take another step. Choice was taken from him as he was lifted across.

"Come wit' us, son," the man in the lead whispered.

Aided by his unknown rescuers, Ethan stumbled the length of the warehouse and into the yard. It seemed to him that the chain made an ungodly racket, and he couldn't understand why no guards came running. They passed into the warehouse, and he was guided toward the remains of one of the fires. As they neared it, light caught the white hair of one of his rescuers. He had no sooner recognized the old guard than he vanished into the darkness. Ethan looked after him as the other guards lowered him to the ground beside the fire.

A cup of steaming liquid was pressed into his hands. He clutched it, confused because he couldn't feel its heat. Then the warmth began to penetrate. Within seconds, his hands ached so badly that he nearly dropped the cup. One of the guards steadied it, pressing it to his lips. Ethan took a sip. *Coffee.* Not the real thing, but hot. It burned all the way down, radiating warmth. The shivering compounded itself. He shuddered violently, convulsively, would have dropped the cup if a guard hadn't taken it from him. When the worst of it passed, the guard placed the cup in his hands. This time Ethan drank greedily, teeth chattering against the tin. When it was empty, the cup was taken from him. He wanted more, but the white-haired guard had returned.

"I set yo' supper aside," he said, handing Ethan a greasy lump of fried cornmeal. "Eat up, son. Yo' gonna need yo' strength."

The cornmeal was gone in a few quick bites, swallowed almost without chewing. Ethan looked hopefully at the old man, who handed him his portion of meat. It was burned black on the outside, raw on the inside, but at that moment, it was the best he had ever tasted. A few quick bites, and it was gone, too. As he swallowed the last of it, Ethan's stomach began to growl ravenously.

"Is there more?" he asked, looking from one guard to another. "Please."

The old man shook his head. "That's' all they is, son. Now let's get you warm."

One of the guards brought an armload of wood and built up the fire. Another draped a blanket over Ethan's shoulders. Ethan stretched his hands to the flames. The heat pricked his skin, and steam rose from his wet clothing. He leaned forward, closing his eyes and feeling the glow on his face. He inhaled the warmth, savoring it as it flowed through him. Chills ran through his body as the worst of the cold left him.

The guards let him sit for much of the night, feeding the fire to keep it going. Ethan soaked in the heat as if he would never get enough. He was half-dozing when the old man shook him.

"Time to go, son."

Dread tightened in his chest. "No. Please..."

"Sorry, son. We gots to ge'chu outta here."

The old man stood waiting. Ethan looked from him to the fire and reluctantly pushed himself to his feet. He shivered as he left its warmth, realizing he was still chilled. Pulling his coat tightly around him, he followed the guard toward the door.

He couldn't believe his good fortune when the old man turned into the bunkroom. Men stirred and muttered at the noise the chain made as they passed. The guard stopped when they came to the bunk where Thomas lay sleeping. Pressing the blanket into Ethan's hands, he said, "Git yo'sef some rest befo' roll call."

Ethan watched him limp away before climbing onto the bunk. Despite his attempts to keep it quiet, the chain scraped and rattled across the wood. The men nearest him shifted restlessly.

Thomas, his voice thick with sleep, muttered, "Wha... ?" Coming wider awake, he pushed up on one elbow and peered through the darkness. "Ethan? Ethan! Is that you?"

"Yes. Move over. Give me some room."

Thomas scooted closer to Simon, and Ethan snuggled in next to him.

Thomas grasped his arm. "I thought they'd killed you!" he said, his voice raw with emotion. He drew a breath, but his voice cracked when he added, "Jacob told me they heard a shot. When you didn't come back we... I thought you were dead."

"It was a warning, is all."

Thomas struggled for words. "I thought you were dead," was all he could say.

"I'm all right," Ethan assured him. "I got cold, but I'm all right now."

Thomas squeezed his arm. "I'm glad you're back."

"So am I." Ethan pulled the blanket more snugly about him and stared into the darkness. *But this isn't the end of it.*

He lay awake long after Thomas began to snore, thinking about what had happened. The old guard's kindness had not only saved his life, it proved he wasn't alone. The more he thought about it, the more determined he became to resist Shunk. To do whatever it took to survive.

He woke to Thomas shaking him.

"Ethan! Roll call. Let's go."

Ethan pushed back the blanket, rolled onto his stomach and looked up. The expression on Thomas' face stopped him cold.

"What the hell did they do to you?"

"What?" Ethan said, not understanding.

"You're covered in mud, and there's a gash across your face, clear from your nose to your ear."

Ethan touched the tips of his fingers to the raw wound on his cheek. "Shunk had a whip," he said briefly.

Thomas was looking at him in such consternation that Ethan forced a smile. "It's nothing. Come on, we need to get going." He swiveled his feet over the edge of the bunk and jumped to the ground.

Thomas turned to walk away, and it was then Ethan saw his leg irons had been removed. Resentment welled up. Then he remembered the vow he'd made the night before. Telling himself he would do well not to expect anything to be fair, he drew himself up and shuffled after Thomas.

Shunk was absent from roll call. The count was completed quickly, and the prisoners milled in the yard while breakfast cooked, welcoming the return of the sun.

Ethan stayed behind to wash, a concerned Thomas standing close by. He cleaned his face, hair and hands, but there was little he could do about his clothes. He settled for picking off pieces of dried mud. Giving one pant leg a final brush, he straightened—and locked eyes with Rat-Face. The guard was lounging against the wall several yards away. One corner of his mouth curled unpleasantly, and he raised a hand, slowly drawing a finger across his throat.

Thomas saw Ethan's expression and turned to see what he was looking at. One look at the menace on the guard's face, and he grasped Ethan by the arm.

"Let's get outta here."

Ethan stared at the guard a moment longer before allowing himself to be led away.

He devoured the food Jacob prepared, then returned to the bunkroom to fetch his book. It wasn't where he'd left it, and the blanket the old man had given him was gone.

"Wha'cha lookin' fo', boy?"

The voice, coming from very close behind him, caused him to start. Ethan drew a steadying breath and turned to face the harelip. Pale eyes bored into his.

"I can't find my book."

"Likes a' you ain't 'lowed books no mo'."

Ethan's heart sank. "I see," he said, keeping his face empty. "I guess I'll go back outside then." Unable to stop himself, he added insolently, "It's where I belong, isn't it?"

The corners of the harelip's mouth turned up, more a grimace than a smile, and his eyes came alive in a way that made Ethan's skin crawl. The look was gone in an instant, and Ethan edged past him, headed for the door.

He spied Thomas sitting in the sun near the south end of the warehouse, part of a group that included Hugh, Simon and Jacob. Ethan walked the length of the room and lowered himself next to them. The ground was still damp, but the sun had begun to warm it, and the thick walls offered protection from the breeze.

"I was sorry to see Shunk come after you," Hugh said. "You all right?"

"Yeah. Fine. Thanks." Ethan acknowledged them briefly before looking away. He wanted to stop to the conversation before it began. He couldn't bear the thought of sharing his humiliation with anyone, not even Thomas.

"Henderson musta left town," Hugh continued. "You best keep an eye out."

"I will."

"What did they do to you?" Jacob asked.

Ethan shrugged. "Left me out in the rain a while." He offered them a perfunctory smile. "I'm fine. Thanks for asking."

"You oughtta get that cheek looked after," Hugh persisted. "Talk to the guards about goin' to the hospital."

"No! I'm all right." The last thing Ethan wanted was to call attention to himself. He put an end to the discussion by rolling down onto his side and closing his eyes.

There was a brief, uneasy silence before conversation gradually resumed, drifting back to the usual topics: speculation on the status of the war, the possibility of exchange, when and where they would be moved. Ethan half-listened, but before long, exhaustion and the sun's warmth won out.

When Hugh was sure Ethan was sleeping soundly, he leaned closed to Thomas. Keeping his voice low, he said, "After watching Shunk with the Turk, I guarantee you what went on yesterday ain't gonna stop as long as Henderson's away. If you don't mind my saying, you best stick close to him."

"I will," Thomas said, looking from Ethan to Hugh. "But there's not much I can do if they take him like they did yesterday."

"True enough," Hugh agreed. "But there'll be things we can put a stop to. Far as I'm concerned, Shunk and his boys spring from the bottom of the dung heap. They'll torment him like a cat with a mouse." He glanced down before looking directly at Thomas. "My gut tells me they won't bat an eye at killing him if they get tired of the game."

The sun was sinking low, the interior of the warehouse in shadow, when Ethan shivered and sat up. Everyone but Thomas had moved several feet away and built up one of the fires. They made room when Ethan and Thomas joined them.

The evening passed quietly. At the call for lights out, the five of them walked toward the bunkroom together. Ethan tensed when he saw Rat-Face standing next to the door.

The others had seen him, too. Thomas moved between Ethan and the guard, while the other three stepped protectively around him. As they approached the door, Rat-Face stepped across it, blocking their way.

"Stand aside," he ordered, pressing the muzzle of his musket to Thomas' chest. Thomas stayed where he was. Rat-Face pulled back the flint.

"Do as he says, Thomas." Ethan pressed a hand to Thomas' back.

Thomas refused to budge. Ethan pushed past Simon, and the barrel of the musket swiveled his way.

Eyes fixed on Ethan, Rat-Face stepped clear of the door. "All right, the rest a' you keep a-goin'."

Thomas started to protest.

"Go!" Rat-Face barked.

Hugh took Thomas by the arm and urged him through. Jacob, Simon, and the men who'd backed up behind them, followed.

Ethan stood with Rat-Face until the last of the prisoners were inside. When they were alone, Rat-Face gestured with the musket, tilting his head toward the row of unfinished bunks. "Move on down to the far end, Injun."

The muzzle at his back, Ethan walked along the row of bunks. Coming to a stop just shy of the dead-line, he waited. Rat-Face tapped the bottom tier with his toe.

"From now on, this is where you sleep."

He waited while Ethan lowered himself to the bunk, then crouched beside him. "You ain't to move befo' sunup. One foot on the ground an' yo' gonna get shot. Hear?"

"Yes, sir."

Rat-Face pushed himself to his feet. Casting a final contemptuous look at Ethan, he strolled away along the dead-line.

The night was clear and cold. Ethan had no blanket, and there were no bodies to help keep him warm. He pulled his coat tightly around him and curled into a ball, grateful it wasn't raining.

He was half-asleep when a blow to his back stunned him awake. Ethan rolled over, prepared to defend himself, but there was no one in sight. He twisted to look behind him. A guard he couldn't identify was walking away along the dead-line.

Ethan shivered and pulled the collar of his coat up over his ears before curling up again. It wasn't long before he was hit again. Each time he dozed off, another blow jarred him awake.

NOVEMBER

14

Ethan woke bruised and exhausted to a clear, cloudless day. He crawled stiffly from the bunk, comforted by the thought that, with Thomas at his side, he could pass the day sleeping in the sun.

Shunk thwarted that notion by sending Thomas and Simon away for three days, to work on a plantation across the river. Hugh was sent into town, and Ethan was assigned, a detail of one, to clean the prison. He was given a rake and a wheelbarrow and ordered to spend the day collecting rubbish and hauling it away. Several prisoners volunteered to help, but the harelip turned them away. It wasn't until evening roll call ended that Ethan was finally allowed to rest.

He fell asleep after dinner, next to a fire, between Hugh and Jacob. Hugh had to shake him awake at lights out. Ethan trudged to his bunk and crawled onto it. Still warm, he was instantly asleep.

It wasn't long before he was hit. The torment continued throughout the night, and the next morning, he was once again assigned to clean the prison.

By the third morning, it was all he could do to drag himself from his bunk. Relief flooded through him when he saw Shunk was absent from roll call. After breakfast, he joined Jacob in the sun and slipped quickly into a deep, exhausted sleep.

Thomas and Simon returned early in the afternoon, their spirits buoyed by having been away, even for such a short time. Thomas' grin faded when he saw Ethan. The gash across his cheek had scabbed over, and most of the swelling was gone, but there were dark smudges beneath his eyes, and his skin stretched tight over the bones of his face. For the first time, Thomas realized how much weight he'd lost. There wasn't an ounce of spare flesh on him.

"He all right?" he asked, squatting next to Jacob.

Jacob pushed his spectacles up on his nose and looked at Ethan. "Tired, I guess. He's been sleeping like that all day."

"They still making him sleep outside?"

Jacob nodded.

"He can't be getting much rest," Thomas said, settling next to Ethan. "It's too cold."

Jacob nodded again and returned to his book.

Twice during the afternoon Thomas looked up to find a guard watching them. The first time, it was the rat-faced guard. He sneered when he saw Thomas looking and walked away. Later, it was the scrawny man with pale eyes and distorted features. He stared at Ethan, oblivious to everything around him. Something in his expression pricked the hairs on Thomas' neck. He wanted to yell at him to move on, but didn't dare. The guard watched Ethan for a long time before turning away.

The monotony of life at Cahaba was broken late in the day by the arrival of more than a hundred new prisoners. Cries of "Fresh fish!" went up as they were released into the yard, and men swarmed to meet them. With their arrival, the population of the prison doubled. That night, the bunkroom was filled to capacity. Ethan alone remained outside.

A thick blanket of white fog, chill and damp, veiled the first light of day. Ethan rolled onto his stomach and looked around, then rose stiffly and headed for the water closet. He passed a couple of men headed in the opposite direction, but aside from them, and the guards leaning ghostly against the walls, the prison slept.

He was halfway back to his bunk when he realized someone was standing beside it. Peering through the mist, he tried to make out who it was. As he drew closer, he recognized the harelip. Ethan slowed his pace, eyeing him warily.

He sensed movement as he passed the door to the bunkroom and darted a glance in that direction. Rat-Face stepped out, and Ethan turned to face him. Rat-Face lifted his musket, pointing it loosely at Ethan's mid-section. Ethan looked over his shoulder and saw that the harelip was moving toward them. Rat-Face took a step forward. Ethan took a step back.

The harelip kept coming, and Rat-Face edged forward, herding Ethan toward the door of the warehouse. Ethan looked around in desperation. There was no guard in the doorway, and the guard stations nearest him were mysteriously empty. The only guards were at the far end of the warehouse, two hundred feet away, and all but lost in the fog.

They're going to trap me in the doorway, Ethan thought, feeling a rush of panic.

He reached the dead-line and stopped. The harelip closed the gap to his right. Rat-Face took a final step, bringing the musket up and nudging Ethan in the chest. A split-second, and Ethan made his decision. He spun around and threw himself through the doorway. A gunshot exploded over his head. He rolled and came up kneeling, facing the door, hands held out from his sides, palms up.

Rat-Face lurched through the doorway, his face distorted with fury. The harelip emerged close behind him. Guards shouted, and footsteps pounded along the tops of the walls. Keeping his hands away from his sides, Ethan rocked back on his heels and got to his feet.

The guard pressed the muzzle of the musket to Ethan's throat. "You r'member the rules, don'cha, breed? Anyone caught tryin' to escape gits shot. You r'member that, don'cha?"

Breathing hard, Ethan jerked a nod. The harelip appeared beside Rat-Face, and Ethan ventured a glance in his direction. The man's teeth were bared in a vicious smile, his eyes wild with excitement. A jerk of the musket brought Ethan's eyes back to Rat-Face.

"Yo' not answerin' me, boy. What'sa matter? Cat go'cher tongue?"

He let out a harsh laugh and forced Ethan back a step. The harelip quivered in anticipation.

Prisoners, roused by the shot, burst from the warehouse, quickly filling the space behind the two guards. Seeing Ethan's eyes focus behind him, Rat-Face let the musket drop and looked around. Up on the wall, a guard yelled for the prisoners to back off, but men continued to pile through the door, pushing the leaders forward. A guard fired a shot into the dirt. The men in front leapt back, and the prisoners dispersed into the fog.

"This 'un 'uz tryin' to escape," Rat-Face shouted for the guards on the wall to hear. "He run when we tried to stop him." To Ethan he said, "Git yo'sef back inside, breed."

Rat-Face stepped aside and gestured with the musket. Reluctant to turn his back on him, Ethan hesitated. At that moment, Thomas came barreling through the door, elbowing his way past men who continued to stream from the warehouse. Catching sight of Ethan, he stopped, the panic on his face changing to relief, then to uncertainty when Ethan's eyes met his. For an instant Thomas recognized fear, combined with desperation and entreaty. Then Rat-Face grasped Ethan roughly by the arm, turning him away. More guards rushed into the yard, driving a wedge between them, and forcing Thomas away from the door.

Rat-Face pushed Ethan ahead of him, back into the warehouse. He shoved him along the row of bunks, all the way to the end, before releasing him. He waited for Ethan to turn, then backhanded him across the face with all his might.

Ethan never saw the blow coming. The force of it sent him crashing into the bunks. He toppled sideways, grasping at air. At the last instant, he managed to grab the corner post and keep from falling across the dead-line.

Rat-Face moved in close behind him, his voice low and threatening. "Don'chu ever run from me again. Hear?"

"Yes, sir." Ethan's voice shook as he pushed himself upright, easing clear of the dead-line. He turned to face the guard, half-expecting to be struck again. The blow didn't come. Instead, Rat-Face leaned in until their noses were almost touching.

"What'd you say, boy? I didn't hear you."

"Yes, sir," Ethan repeated hoarsely, resisting the urge to wipe away blood gushing from his nose.

Rat-Face took a step back, fists clenched, glaring furiously at Ethan.

Ethan struggled to keep fear from showing, even as his heart raced out of control. He wanted nothing more than to back off, to avoid further confrontation, but he was certain it would be a mistake—that any move away would be interpreted as weakness.

Time seemed to stretch until the standoff was broken by the return of the harelip. The shackles he carried clanked together, and Ethan took advantage of the opportunity to look his way. Rat-Face glowered a moment longer before he, too, looked at the harelip. Ethan turned his eyes to the ground and waited.

Rat-Face grabbed the shackles and turned to Ethan. "Hold out yo' left arm."

Ethan did as he was told, and a manacle was locked about his wrist. Rat-Face looped the chain around the corner post and secured it with the other manacle.

"Now, git down on yo' bunk, boy."

Ethan started to sit on the second tier, since that was where the chain was fastened, but Rat-Face put a hand on his shoulder, forcing him lower.

"I said *yo'* bunk, breed."

Ethan squatted and slid onto the bottom bunk. The chain made it impossible for him to lie on his stomach, and when he rolled onto his back, his arm was pulled up tight, stretching his shoulder in its socket. The edges of the manacle bit painfully into his wrist.

Rat-Face jerked the chain, eliciting a wince that brought a smile to his face. "Now you stay put 'til the sarg gits here. We'll see no one bothers ya."

Rat-face moved away. Ethan stared at the planks above him, avoiding the curious stares of the other prisoners. By the time Shunk strolled into the warehouse, his shoulder had cramped, and his hand was numb with cold.

The sergeant came to stand close to Ethan's head. He surveyed him briefly, then reached down with the tip of his whip and tapped him on the cheek. "Look at me, boy."

Ethan tilted his head back obediently and looked up. Shunk stared down at him without speaking. Then he turned and walked to where the rest of the prisoners waited in the mist, at the far end of the warehouse.

Shunk returned an hour later and stood rapping his whip against his thigh. Ethan stared at the bunk above him, watching the movement of the whip out of the corner of his eye. After what seemed an eternity, Shunk smacked the whip against the wood next to Ethan's head.

"Git up."

Ethan rolled to his right and got an elbow under him. Setting his jaw against the pain that knifed through his left shoulder, he swung his feet around and sat up, his chained left arm pulled awkwardly across his body. He pushed himself to his feet and stood before Shunk, eyes downcast.

"My men tell me you tried to escape."

"Yes, sir."

Shunk's brows shot upward in surprise. "Yo' admittin' it?"

"No, sir," Ethan replied, knowing it was a mistake. "I agree it's probably what they told you."

Shunk's face turned purple with rage. The whip came down hard, catching Ethan's left shoulder and slashing across his chest. Ethan was expecting it, but even so, he flinched. Jaw clenched, he stood his ground. His defiance only served to fuel Shunk's rage. He lashed out again, and this time the whip caught Ethan a stinging blow across the side of his neck.

At that, he yielded, turning into the bunks and bringing his right arm up to protect his face. The whip came down again and again, lashing him across the back and shoulders, across the buttocks and the backs of his legs. His clothing offered some protection, but the sting of the whip brought tears to his eyes. He clenched his jaw harder, determined not to cry out.

Shunk's rage was soon spent. The ferocity of his blows diminished, the pace of them slowed. Eventually, they stopped. Panting with exertion, his face contorted with hate, Shunk grabbed his prisoner by the arm and spun him around. The boy's eyes were bright with unshed tears, but his face betrayed nothing.

"You!" Shunk panted, shaking the whip in Ethan's face. "You are to be chained to this bunk until I order you released! You git nuttin' to eat fo' three days, an' half-rations after that. You talk to no one, and no one talks to you. You hear me?"

Ethan drew a shallow breath. Eyes glued to the glob of brown spittle at the corner of Shunk's mouth, he whispered, "Yes, sir."

Shunk turned on his heel and strode from the room. Ethan watched him go, then ventured a look at the other two guards. Rat-Face's mouth twisted into sneer when their eyes met. He sauntered over, stopping directly in front of Ethan. Ethan looked at the ground. Rat-Face smirked as he leaned down and unlocked the chain from the post. Squatting, he re-attached it to the bottom tier of bunks, then motioned for Ethan to lie down. Ethan did as he was told, grateful the episode was ending.

A line of guards prevented the prisoners from entering the warehouse after rations had been distributed. Thomas and Hugh left Jacob to cook breakfast and lingered as close to the doorway as they dared. Noise in the yard kept them from hearing what that went on inside, but when Shunk stormed out, the look on his face confirmed that Ethan hadn't fared well. Shunk spoke briefly to the guards, issuing an abrupt string of commands, then strode across the yard and disappeared through the gate. Following a brief, hushed discussion, all but two of the guards followed him. The two went into the warehouse. Thomas and Hugh exchanged a look and went in after them.

Rat-Face stood with one shoulder against the bunks. The harelip squatted beside him, eyes fixed on Ethan's face. When Rat-Face saw Thomas and Hugh, he pushed himself upright and walked toward them.

"Git out," he commanded.

Hugh stopped, but Thomas took another step, eyes riveted on Ethan. He was lying on his back, so still that, for a moment, Thomas was certain he was dead. His face and clothes were smeared with blood, and a gash on the back of his right hand oozed red.

"Ethan?" Thomas said, oblivious to everything but the prone figure on the bunk.

Rat-Face swung the musket off his shoulder. "I said, git, Murray! Now! Git out, or I'll cut yo' rations."

"Is he... ?" Thomas asked, his eyes never leaving Ethan's face.

"That's it, Murray, half rations. Now git befo' I chain you up, too."

Ethan's eyes opened. He swiveled his head to look at Thomas. "Go," he mouthed silently. And when Thomas hesitated, "Please."

Thomas let out the breath he'd been holding and took a step back. Hugh grasped him by the arm, and the two of them backed down before Rat-Face's advance. He followed them until they stepped into the yard.

Distraught, Thomas turned to Hugh. "Now what?"

Hugh pressed his lips together and shook his head. "There's no way to get near him. We'll have to wait. Come eat while you still can." He took Thomas by the elbow and steered him back to where Jason and Simon waited by one of the fires.

15

Eight days passed before Shunk allowed Ethan to be released. A bucket was provided for him to relieve himself, and he remained chained in the corner the entire time. He was bruised and sore, but ultimately, suffered more from cold, hunger and thirst than any lasting effects of the whipping.

He was starved for three days, but each day after that, one of Shunk's men appeared with a cup of coffee, a lump of fried cornmeal and a piece of meat half the size of his usual allotment. Selected specifically for him, it was comprised mainly of fat or gristle, and was often rancid or wormy. Ethan was so hungry he barely noticed. He inhaled every morsel he was given, and only pride kept him from begging for more. The old guard, and several others, tried to compensate by sneaking him coffee and scraps whenever they could.

No prisoners were allowed near him, and only a handful of guards spoke to him. The few times his gaze strayed, Ethan invariably made eye contact with someone who looked back in sympathy. Each time, self-pity welled up, and Ethan had to remind himself there was no room for weakness. He trained himself to avoid eye contact, to shut out everything that went on around him.

As the days passed, he grew steadily weaker. More and more time was spent dozing. Occasionally, he awakened with a start to find the harelip crouched close beside him. The look in the man's eyes was of such savage fascination that it made his skin crawl. Each time, he resisted the urge to slide as far away as the chain would allow. He forced himself to lie where he was, eyes averted, waiting through the long minutes until the guard departed.

At dawn on Ethan's ninth day in isolation, Rat-Face appeared beside his bunk. Without speaking, he unlocked the manacle that held the chain around the post. The sound roused Ethan, but only barely. His head rolled toward it, but his eyes remained closed. Rat-Face gave the chain a savage jerk. Ethan yelped in pain, and the guard's mouth twisted into a grin. He hauled upward on the chain, forcing Ethan from the bunk.

Ethan got both feet on the ground, but when he tried to stand, his legs failed to support him. He fell to his knees.

"Git up," Rat-Face commanded, tugging on the chain.

Ethan sat back on his heels and reached around with his right hand, feeling for the edge of the bunk. Using it to push himself up, he staggered to his feet. Too lightheaded and weak to stand on his own, he clung to the bunk for support.

"Look at me."

Ethan looked up, then quickly away, but not before Rat-Face caught the flicker of defiance in his eyes. He stared at Ethan with undisguised hatred. Grabbing him by the arm, he removed the manacle from his wrist. Without a word, he turned and walked away.

Ethan held his injured arm to him, watching him go. It wasn't until the guard stepped out into the yard that he looked down and examined his left hand and wrist. The cuff had cut deeply; the newest wound was bleeding freely, while older sores oozed with infection.

Steadying himself against the bunk, Ethan looked around, searching for a trap. Seeing none, he let go of the bunk, swayed, and grabbed it again. Suddenly, there were men all around him. Hands reached out, and voices offered help. At first he rebuffed them. Then he heard a familiar voice above all the others.

Panic surged through Thomas when he emerged from the water closet and saw the knot of men in Ethan's corner. He hurried the length of the warehouse, prompting warning shouts from two of the guards. When he caught sight of Ethan, he grinned in relief and pushed his way to him.

"Ethan! Are you all right?"

Ethan looked at him, and Thomas' step faltered. He was painfully thin. His hair was matted; his face and clothes stained with dried blood. The bones in his face stood out sharply, and there were dark hollows around his eyes. But it was the look in those eyes that troubled Thomas most. Ethan had attempted a smile, but it hadn't carried past his lips. His eyes remained distant and wary.

"Are you all right?" Thomas repeated.

"All right," Ethan replied, his voice hoarse with disuse. "Hungry. Weak." Half-lifting his injured arm, he added, "And this. It needs washing."

Thomas moved to his side. "Here, let me help you."

The other prisoners parted to let them through. Thomas supported Ethan through the warehouse to one of the barrels sunk into the ditch.

Ethan had the strength to do nothing more than bathe the wrist and splash water onto his face. Drying it on the sleeve of his coat, he once again surveyed the room. "Where is everyone?"

Thomas looked around. "What do you mean?"

"Hugh. Jacob…"

"They were transferred out."

"When?"

"The day after Shunk locked you up."

Ethan nodded briefly and looked away, a closed expression settling over his face. Thomas watched him anxiously, dismayed at the change he saw in him.

Ethan received his rations, eyeing the food ravenously as Thomas helped him to one of the fires. He sank down next to it, accepting the coffee one of the men handed him, and gulping it down quickly, despite its heat. He watched intently as Thomas prepared the meal. The meat had barely begun to brown when he could contain himself no longer. Snatching his portion from the kettle, he consumed it greedily, followed by one of the half-cooked corn patties.

Thomas saw his eyes linger covetously on the other men's rations. Then the same closed expression settled over his face, and he looked away.

Thomas used a sharpened stick to skewer his portion of meat. "Here" he said. "Take this."

At first, there was no response. Then awareness came into Ethan's eyes. He focused on the meat, eyeing it hungrily. He looked at Thomas. "I can't. It's yours."

"I've had plenty to eat." Thomas jiggled the stick at him. "Here. Take it."

Ethan looked at the meat. After a moment, he reached out and took it. When Thomas handed him his corn patty, Ethan accepted it without comment. Both were gone in seconds.

Before he could withdraw again, Thomas said, "You need to be careful, Ethan. This isn't over. It won't be until we're out of here." He leaned in close, his voice low with intensity. "You need to promise you'll never go anywhere by yourself. Nowhere. Not ever. Promise me, Ethan."

The raw emotion behind his words got Ethan's full attention. "I promise," he said softly. He favored Thomas with a brief, hollow smile before wrapping his arms about drawn-up knees and retreating back into himself.

16

The first rays of the sun were streaking the western wall of the warehouse when Ethan bolted awake. He pushed up on his elbows, searching for the source of his unease. Guards leaned wearily at their posts. Others paced atop the wall. The only sounds were the snores of sleeping men and the early morning twitter of birds.

A half-felt presence sent fear prickling along his spine. Ethan rolled onto his side and looked behind him—directly into the pale, soulless eyes of the harelip.

The guard was crouched beside him, one elbow resting on the edge of the bunk, fingers dangling inches from Ethan's leg. Instinctively, Ethan pulled it away. The expression on the harelip's face didn't alter. He continued to stare, holding Ethan's gaze for several moments before his eyes slid slowly along the length of his body.

"What do you want?" Ethan demanded, his voice strained, nerves on edge.

The man's eyes moved back to Ethan's face. The deformed lips twisted into a smile, but the pale eyes remained empty. He said nothing.

Ethan resisted the urge to slide further away. He lowered his gaze, staring unseeing at the pattern of bloodstains on the planks, waiting for the man to leave. It seemed to take forever, but at last he did, pushing himself to his feet with a little grunt and ambling away along the dead-line.

Ethan watched him go. He didn't move until the guard reached the far end of the warehouse. Then he lowered himself onto his back, realizing as he did so, that his bladder was achingly full. *Too much coffee yesterday.* He rolled toward the bucket. It was gone.

The harelip had begun a conversation with another guard. They stood only a few feet from the door to the water closet. A couple of early risers came and went as the conversation dragged on.

At last, the harelip started back through the warehouse. He appeared to be headed for the yard, but instead, turned into the bunkroom. Ethan waited. Minutes crept by with no sign of him. Keeping a wary eye on the door, Ethan sat up, lifting the chain to keep it from dragging, and swung his feet to the ground. He stood with effort, clutching the bunk for support. At first he was light-headed, but it passed, and he headed for the bunkroom to fetch Thomas, the previous day's promise fresh in his mind.

He stopped just outside and ventured a peek into the room. The harelip stood at the far end, near the fireplace, deep in conversation with Rat-Face. Ethan looked in the other direction, toward the bunk where Thomas now slept. Only a couple of steps, three or four at most, and he could reach out and shake him awake. Fearing what would happen if the guards caught him in the room, he hesitated. Following a brief debate with himself, he decided not to risk it.

The morning air was brisk, the sky overhead a brilliant shade of blue, wisps of scattered cloud suffused with pink by the rising sun. The guards stationed around the perimeter of the warehouse paid him scant attention as he passed. Ethan nodded in response to a mumbled greeting from another prisoner, stood aside to let a man out, then stepped through the door to the water closet.

It was a long, narrow room, the plank floor a step up from the dirt floor of the warehouse. An enclosed wooden seat, built to accommodate six men at a time, ran the length of the wall opposite the door. Despite a six-inch air gap beneath the eaves, an ungodly stench permeated the room. From habit, Ethan breathed through his mouth.

He had emptied his bladder, was doing up the buttons on his britches, when a board near the door squeaked. Ethan glanced over his shoulder and froze.

"Hands behind yo' back, breed," Rat-Face said, grinning. He swung the musket off his shoulder and pointed it at Ethan.

Ethan backed away, down the length of the room. Rat-Face sauntered after him until Ethan was brought up short, hands and back pressed against the wall.

"I said, hands behind yo' back," Rat-Face snarled. "Now turn aroun'." The barrel of the musket centered on Ethan's chest. Rat-Face pulled back the flint.

Ethan defied him for as long as he dared. Then he turned to face the wall. The musket dug into his ribs, and he put his hands behind him. Rat-Face bound his wrists, pulling the rope tight and causing it to bite into the open sores. Ethan pressed his forehead against the wall, determined to bear it in silence.

An odd, strangled moan came from behind them. Rat-Face grabbed Ethan by the arm and spun him around, stepping aside to give him an unobstructed view of the room. The harelip was standing just inside the door. He stared at Ethan with wild, excited eyes, his tongue flicking over the misshapen upper lip.

Ethan took a step back, watching in mounting horror as the harelip slowly advanced, the fingers of one hand undoing the buttons of his fly. He came to a stop several feet from Ethan, exposing himself, fully erect.

With a cry of protest, Ethan lunged sideways, but he was weak and the guard's grip was like iron. Rat-Face yanked him back, spinning him around and flinging him to the floor. Ethan landed hard, his shoulder crashing into the base of the seat. He tried to roll away, but Rat-Face was on him, seizing him by the collar and pulling him to his knees. Grabbing a fistful of Ethan's hair, he forced his head back. Ethan stared into the mad eyes of the harelip.

"Like a dawg," the harelip panted.

Ethan scrambled to get away. Rat-Face jerked him back.

"NOOOOOOO—!"

Rat-Face forced a rag into Ethan's mouth, cutting off his scream.

"Like a dawg," the harelip repeated. The pink tip of his tongue darted over his lips.

Ethan screamed through the gag, bucking and lunging against the guard's hold on him. Rat-Face laughed, holding him easily. He wrenched Ethan around, pushed him against the seat, and forced his head over one of the holes. Ethan resisted, and his forehead was slammed into the rim. Rat-Face placed a knee between Ethan's shoulder blades and pressed down. Ethan lashed out with his feet, but the harelip was standing on the chain.

A hand slid under his coat, fumbling with his braces. He bucked against it, and Rat-Face pressed down harder. A second hand grasped his waistband, and his pants were yanked down, the buttons he'd fastened rattling across the floor. When the seat of his longhandles was ripped down, Ethan's struggles grew even more frantic. Twisting and squirming, he fought with all the strength left in him. The harelip gave an excited laugh and grasped him firmly by the hips. Ethan felt pressure, then pain more appalling than any he'd ever imagined. He screamed through the gag, and tears blinded him as the harelip pounded against him.

He had no idea how long it lasted, but eventually his head was pulled free of the hole. He was dragged back onto his knees, and the hand in his hair forced his head around.

The harelip leered down at him. "Yo' mine now, purdy boy," he said, reaching out a hand.

Ethan cringed, eyes closed, as the harelip caressed his cheek.

"You know yo' place now, breed?"

Choking on a sob, Ethan swiveled frightened eyes toward the sound of the new voice.

Shunk was standing behind the harelip, a small, cruel smile on his lips. "Keep in mind what happened here, boy. Keep yo' mouth shut an' do exactly as yo' told. Maybe we kin see this don't happen too often. You hear me?"

A moan escaped Ethan. He jerked a nod.

Shunk gazed with satisfaction at his tear-stained face, then spit, the thick glob catching Ethan on the gash below his left eye. Ethan let out a strangled cry and shrank away. Shunk nodded to Rat-Face. The guard gave Ethan a shove that sent him facedown on the floor. Bending over, he untied his hands.

Footsteps thudded the length of the room. Then it was quiet. When he was certain they were gone, Ethan reached up a numbed hand and pulled the rag from his mouth. He sucked in air, his breath coming in great gasping sobs. For several minutes, he could do nothing more than lie where they'd left him and cry. Eventually, he pushed himself up on one hip, and leaning heavily against the seat, used the rag to wipe the tears from his face. He wiped again, unable to stem their flow.

He was unaware that another man stepped into the water closet and stopped abruptly upon seeing him. Appalled, the man backed out and hurried to the bunkroom. He thought he knew where the Indian kid's friend slept, but when he got to the bunk, its snoring occupant was dark-haired. He examined the occupants of nearby bunks, then walked the room, searching. The light from the windows was dim, and twice he shook the wrong fair-haired man awake.

As he passed the door a second time, he glimpsed telltale yellow curls peaking from beneath a blanket. He pulled it back to make sure. Thomas muttered in protest and grabbed at the blanket. The man shook him by the shoulder, and Thomas came partially awake, looking at him in sleepy confusion.

"Your friend," the man whispered. "The Injun kid. Somethin' bad's happened. You better come quick."

Thomas gazed stupidly at him. Then he registered what the man was saying and came instantly awake. Throwing off the blanket, he scrambled out of bed and looked across at Ethan's empty bunk.

"Where?" he demanded. "What happened?"

"In the water closet," the man replied, looking embarrassed. "You better see for yerself."

Thomas hurried the length of the warehouse, moving as quickly as he dared. Even so, one of the guards shouted a warning, forcing him to slow his pace.

Tears slowed as hysteria wore off. His breath still coming in hiccupping gasps, Ethan wiped his face again. There was shout from the warehouse, and he cast a panicked glance toward the door. No one yet, but it wouldn't be long. Ethan pushed himself to his knees and dropped the rag into the hole. Using the seat for support, he staggered to his feet. He pulled up his britches, and with shaking fingers, did up the remaining buttons. He had barely finished when someone burst into the room behind him. Ethan whirled to see Thomas, followed closely by another man.

Thomas stopped dead when he saw Ethan. His eyes, in the moment before they dropped away, were red-rimmed with crying and wide with shock and fear.

"Ethan?" And then, not wanting to know the answer, "What happened here?"

Ethan's only response was a slight shake of his head. He didn't look up.

"Ethan?" Thomas repeated, walking toward him.

Ethan attempted to shoulder past. Thomas grabbed him by the arm.

"Ethan, tell me what happened."

"Please." Ethan's voice came in a strangled whisper. "Let me go."

Thomas released him and stepped aside.

Ethan hobbled to the door and made his way slowly through the warehouse. He knew the guards were watching, and he was sure some, if not all, knew exactly what had happened. Men were beginning to emerge from the bunkroom, and he could feel their eyes on him. It took every ounce of courage left in him to make the long walk back to his corner.

Thomas followed Ethan to the door and watched him go. He scanned the faces of the guards, looking for Ethan's two principal tormentors, Rat-Face and the harelip. Neither was in sight, but several of the guards watched Ethan's progress with interest. A pair of them sniggered and exchanged crude gestures.

Thomas rounded on the man who'd awakened him. "What happened?" he demanded. "What did you see?"

The man was a head shorter than Thomas, and of a much slighter build. He backed down before Thomas' wrath.

"He was sittin' on the floor, britches down around his knees, sobbin' like a baby. I backed straight out and come to find you." He eyed Thomas anxiously before adding, "I didn't see nothin' else. Honest."

The man's distress penetrated, and Thomas relented. "Thanks," he said, extending a hand.

After a brief hesitation, the man shook it.

Thomas found Ethan curled on his bunk, his back to the room. He squatted next to him, touching his shoulder as he said his name. Ethan gasped and flung himself away. The fear in his eyes turned to shame when he saw who was.

"Ethan," Thomas repeated softly.

Ethan looked away, tears spilling over and sliding down his cheeks.

"Ethan, what happened in there?"

Ethan refused to look at him.

"Tell me who did it."

Ethan gave a slight shake of his head. "Please, Thomas," he pleaded, his voice breaking. "Leave me alone."

"I'll just sit here, keep you company 'til roll call." Thomas turned and lowered himself to the ground. Leaning against the bunk, he stared across the room. More men were awake now, a steady stream of them in and out of the water closet. He shook his head. *Why'd he go in there by himself? Why didn't he wake me? Or wait? All he had to do was wait another fifteen, twenty minutes and there'd have been too many men around.*

When Thomas turned his back, Ethan moved out of the corner and resumed the same fetal position as before, fighting the urge to cry, and gripped by shame and horror. He tried to block out what had happened, sought refuge in sleep, but his mind defeated him, reliving it in every ghastly detail.

Thomas sat listening to his tortured breathing until shouts went up for roll call. Pushing himself to his feet, he looked at Ethan. "Roll call."

Ethan gave no indication that he heard.

"Ethan, we need to go." Then, more forcefully: "Now, Ethan."

Ethan slowly unbent his legs and rolled onto his stomach. After a moment, he brought his legs around and put his feet on the ground. He stood with effort, but when Thomas tried to help him, he pulled away. With Thomas trailing, he made his way to the far end of the warehouse.

Shunk proceeded quickly through the roll call. Ethan received his rations and followed Thomas to one of the fires. He sank down beside it, hugging himself tightly, and staring at the ground while Thomas cooked. He made no response to Thomas' efforts to draw him out, and when the food was ready, accepted his portion without comment, eating slowly and mechanically.

A far cry from yesterday, Thomas thought.

Ethan forced down the last bite and hunched back into himself, staring at the fire. Several times he looked on the verge of speaking; each time he swallowed and hugged himself more tightly, his eyes brimming with tears.

Thomas kept Ethan with him the rest of the day. Despite his efforts, Ethan remained withdrawn. A couple of times, Thomas snagged his attention momentarily, but always he withdrew without responding. There was no sign of Shunk or any of his men until just before sunset.

They were sitting next to one of the fires inside the warehouse when Thomas saw Rat-Face step through the doorway and stop, eyes searching. The guard moved slowly through the warehouse, scanning the huddled groups of men. When his eyes lit on Ethan, his step quickened.

Thomas heard the sharp intake of breath and knew Ethan had seen him. He reached to lay a hand on Ethan's arm, but Ethan was already scrambling to his feet. Panicked eyes fixed on the guard, he began backing away. Thomas rose and stepped between them.

"Stand aside, Murray."

Thomas stood his ground. Heads turned and conversations died; several guards stepped away from their posts. Thomas backed up until he stood directly in front of Ethan.

"I said, git away from him."

"What do you want?" Thomas' eyes flicked from Rat-Face to the approaching guards.

Rat-Face held up a key. "I come to take off them leg irons. Now step aside."

The other guards were close now. Assured that none were Shunk's men, Thomas did as he was told. Ethan took a half step after him.

"You! Breed! Stay put!"

Ethan froze, frightened eyes darting from Thomas to the guard's face to the key.

Rat-Face moved in, a mocking grin on his face. Going down on one knee, he unlocked first one ankle iron, then the other. Grabbing the chain, he pushed himself to his feet and pressed his mouth close to Ethan's ear. "Sleep inside t'night, hear?"

Unable to speak, Ethan nodded. Rat-Face favored him with a final contemptuous sneer and walked away. The guards wandered back to their posts, and conversation slowly resumed.

"Ethan," Thomas said softly. "Ethan!"

Ethan's head turned. His eyes focused, and Thomas tilted his head toward the fire.

"He's gone. Come sit down."

Ethan gave a slight nod. He took a step and stumbled, would have fallen if Thomas hadn't flung out a hand to steady him. Awkward without the weight of the chain, Ethan walked to the fire and sank down next to Thomas, close enough that Thomas felt the shudder that ran through him.

17

Captain Henderson was present at roll call that evening. As was his custom, the commandant walked among the prisoners, exchanging words. When he came to Ethan, he stopped, leaning forward in the failing light to study the healing gash on his cheek.

"What happened here, son?"

"Nothing, sir," Ethan whispered, eyes to the ground.

Captain Henderson examined him more closely, noting the bruised knot on his forehead and the stains that looked to be blood on his clothing. "Look at me, son," he commanded.

Ethan glanced up. Their eyes met only for a second, but it was enough for Captain Henderson to see he was scared.

"Tell me how you came to have those marks on yo' face, Private."

"It's nothing, sir," Ethan repeated softly. "An accident."

The commandant considered him thoughtfully before moving on.

Midway through the following morning, a guard approached Thomas and Ethan.

"You," he said, pointing a finger at Ethan. "Commandant wants to see you."

Ethan looked at Thomas in panic. "I... Not alone. Thomas, please..."

Thomas looked at the guard, seeing what he took for sympathy on the man's face. "Go with him," he said.

Ethan looked at him in desperation.

"Go," Thomas said firmly. "You'll be all right."

Ethan got to his feet, stumbling and catching himself as he took his first step. Thomas watched him stagger away, still weak and unused to walking without leg irons. Ethan turned at the gate and looked back. Thomas nodded encouragement as the guard took him by the arm and propelled him through.

Captain Henderson rose from behind his desk when Ethan was ushered into the room. Indicating a pair of armchairs, he said "Come in, Private Fraser. Sit."

Ethan took a halting step and stopped, taking in the upholstered seats. "Sir. I can't. I'm…" He gestured toward his clothes.

The commandant smiled. "Please, son. Sit. I insist."

Ethan hesitated a moment longer before lowering himself onto one of the chairs. Captain Henderson angled the other chair closer and leaned back comfortably, observing Ethan before he spoke.

"I want to ask you again, here in the privacy of my office, how you came to have that gash across yo' cheek."

Ethan's eyes flitted to his face, then away. He opened his mouth, on the verge of repeating that it had been an accident, but the words wouldn't come. He didn't dare tell the truth, and he didn't know what else to say. His shoulders drooped, and he responded with a resigned shake of his head.

"I assure you that whatever you tell me won't leave this room. Now that I see you in daylight, I see you have other injuries, as well. I can only imagine what yo' clothes must be hidin'." Captain Henderson paused, watching as Ethan slid his left hand over his right, hiding the wound left by Shunk's whip. "Considered along with the fact that you look like you've been starved, I'm led to believe you were mistreated while I was away. I would appreciate you tellin' me who did it."

There was a long silence while Ethan thought about it. When he raised his eyes to reply Captain Henderson saw the fear in them.

"I can't." Ethan's voice was an agonized whisper. "They told me…" His eyes watered. He bit his lip and looked away.

"Was it Sergeant Shunk?" the captain asked. "I'm told he's mighty fond of that little whip of his."

Ethan's eyes darted to him, then to the floor.

"Why don't you tell me what happened?" Captain Henderson leaned forward, his tone gently encouraging. "I can see someone's scared you, but you have my word that there will be no retaliation. Whoever did this will not be allowed near you again." When Ethan said nothing, he added, "You need to understand, I can't keep that promise unless you tell me who was involved."

Ethan raised searching eyes to the commandant's face. He saw only kindness and concern. And there was something else, something calm and reassuring that invited confession. Ethan opened his mouth, but couldn't bring himself to speak. Shaking his head, he looked away.

Captain Henderson said nothing, waiting patiently as the silence lengthened.

Slowly, awkwardly, Ethan began to talk, groping for words, stumbling over them, ashamed of what he felt an increasing need to reveal. As he went on, the words came faster, tumbling over each other in his haste to get them out. He was breathless when he finished, his face streaked with tears.

Captain Henderson sat back, stunned to silence. He had long known Shunk for a bully, but nothing had prepared him for what he'd just heard. Reaching a trembling hand to his pocket, he pulled out a clean white handkerchief. "Here, son. Take this."

Ethan stared at the handkerchief. After a moment, he took it.

The commandant pushed himself to his feet and came to stand beside him. "I cannot tell you how sorry I am for what happened to you in my prison, Private Fraser. Nothin' I can say or do will make it up to you, but I assure you that Sergeant Shunk and his men will be severely punished." He paused before adding, "I'll leave you to compose yo'self while I deal with matters. Make yo'self comfortable until I return."

The door closed behind him, and Ethan drew a long, shuddering breath. He used the handkerchief to wipe his face and blow his nose, then leaned back in the chair and closed his eyes. For the first time since he'd arrived at Cahaba, he dared to hope he was safe.

Four days later, on the eighteenth of November, a list of names was read at morning roll call. Thomas and Ethan were among the prisoners who filed out through the gates of the stockade and down the steep ramp to the wharf where the gleaming white steamer *St. Nicholas* waited. They were herded aboard, sequestered on the boiler deck amid piles of baggage and crates of clucking chickens and squealing pigs. Smoke billowed from the two tall black smokestacks, the whistle shrieked, lines were cast off, and the steamer set off downriver. Within minutes, the dark stockade high on the bank disappeared behind the trees.

Thomas was relieved to see the change that came over Ethan as they steamed south. For the first time since their escape, nothing was demanded of him, and he could relax. They lazed together on the deck, watching the countryside slip by. Much of it was familiar to Ethan, and slowly he began to talk, sharing tidbits he remembered from maps and books, embellishing them with recollections of things he'd seen and heard when passing through the same country before.

After that, the need to talk about anything not related to Cahaba seemed to take hold of him. He told Thomas, in exacting detail, everything that had happened during the months he'd spent behind enemy lines. Thomas was delighted by his sudden willingness to talk. He listened as Ethan supplied answers to questions he'd been dying to ask for nearly two months.

The Alabama River widened as it merged with the Mobile River. Pine and hardwood forest gave way to swamps and cypress, and finally, to spits of sand supporting nothing more than reeds and grasses. The steamer threaded its way past heavy pilings driven into the river to prevent attack from the north and into the upper reaches of Mobile Bay. The sun sank low beyond the city, a pale yellow-white orb tinting the western clouds lavender and rimming them with gold. Overhead, high wisps of pink and white streaked pale sky, the pink intensifying as the sun dipped below the horizon, then fading slowly to gray. As dusk settled, lights from the city twinkled across the water.

As the sky darkened, so did Ethan's mood. He stood at the rail, overcome with dread at the thought of another Confederate prison. It wasn't until the steamer bumped against the wharf that he abruptly broke his silence. Staring unseeing at the slaves hauling on the ropes, he said, "If something happens to me, you'll see that my parents know why I left the Thirty-sixth, won't you, Thomas? Make sure they know I didn't desert?"

The request caught Thomas by surprise. He looked at Ethan, but his hair had fallen forward, masking his face. Making an effort to sound cheerful, he replied, "Nothing bad's going to happen, Ethan. You'll be able to tell them yourself in a month or two when this is all over."

Ethan turned despairing eyes on him. "Please, Thomas. Promise you'll tell them. So they'll know the truth."

Suddenly, the reason for Ethan's willingness to talk became clear. All along, he'd been leading up to this one request. Thomas so was shaken by Ethan's conviction that he wouldn't live to see his family again that he had no idea what to reply. In the end, he simply said, "I promise."

18

The Union prisoners were held on board the *St. Nicholas* until morning. Weak sunlight filtered through haze, and the damp air hung heavy as they stepped from the gangway onto the wharf, already teeming with men, draft animals and wagons. Despite the restrictions imposed by the Union blockade, the quay at Mobile bustled with activity. A number of steamboats were berthed along its length, many in the process of loading or unloading. Others, their tall smokestacks belching smoke, plied the bay where several tall-masted ships floated at anchor, their sails furled.

The guards herded the rag-tag line of prisoners across the broad expanse of wharf, angling past mountainous piles of baled cotton, around stacked crates and barrels, toward the row of warehouses abutting the city. A heavy freight wagon was drawn up before one of them, a slave high on the driver's seat holding the team of six mules steady while three others clambered over a load of wooden casks, securing them with ropes.

As the first prisoners drew abreast of the wagon, one of slaves stumbled, his shoulder striking an unsecured cask. The empty cask teetered, then fell, barely missing the driver as it glanced off the wagon box. It hit the wharf with a resounding crash, splintered wood flying. One of the mules leapt sideways, braying in panic, a shard dangling from its flank. The others took up its fright and began lunging wildly. The driver yelled and dragged on the reins. The load shifted, another slave went down, and barrels cascaded onto the wharf.

Guards and prisoners leapt to avoid the rolling, shattering mass. Men were crushed against the wall of the warehouse as others pressed against them. Some sprang for cover behind bales of cotton; others scattered, running away along the wharf. Guards who were not directly involved looked toward the commotion, then set about rounding them up.

In the ensuing confusion, Ethan found himself separated from Thomas and not far from a gap between two of the warehouses. A glance around assured no one was looking, and he edged toward it. Another glance, another step and he slipped into the opening.

It was a narrow alleyway, wide enough to accommodate a walkway and the staircase leading to the second floor of one of the buildings. At the far end was the brick back of another building. Ethan scurried toward it, hoping for a way out. He found the walls only inches apart, and looked around frantically, searching for a place to hide. Spying a door recessed into a shallow alcove, he dived into it.

The commotion on the wharf continued for some time. Overseers cursed the slaves, and guards shouted as they attempted to reassemble and count prisoners. At one point, there was a disturbance in the alley, and Ethan was certain he would be discovered. He pressed flat against the door as another prisoner was hauled from beneath the stairs and shoved back toward the wharf.

The noise gradually quieted. Ethan was considering sticking his head out for a quick peek when, without warning, the bolt behind him was thrown, and the door swung inward. He grunted in surprise and grabbed the doorjamb. Launching himself, he was already fleeing when a woman's voice stopped him.

"They've gone, but you might be safer in here until we decide what to do with you."

Ethan whirled to face her. Dark curls framed a heart-shaped face. Blue-gray eyes crinkled at the corners as she smiled. She wrinkled her nose and pulled a handkerchief from her sleeve. "I'm sorry," she said from behind the scented, lace-trimmed square. "Your odor is really quite strong."

Ethan could only stare, too stunned to speak.

"Well, sir. Won't you come in?"

He regarded her warily. Weighing his options, he decided to risk it. He took a tentative step, and the woman moved aside. Ethan edged past her, into the room.

He found himself in a cavernous warehouse. Wooden columns stretched to a network of interconnected beams overhead, the light from windows high on the walls above casting an angular web of shadows across the room. Enormous mounds of baled cotton took up most of the floor space. The area near the front was lined with rows of mostly empty shelves, and the rest of the room was piled with crates and barrels labeled "Magrath Trading Company."

The door clicked closed, and Ethan spun around. The woman slid the bolt home and turned to face him. She was still holding the handkerchief over her nose and mouth. The corners of her eyes creased. Ethan realized she was smiling.

"Do you have a name?" she asked.

She was pretty—*very pretty*, he thought—petite, with flawless porcelain skin. Ethan shifted from one foot to the other, uncomfortably aware how he must look. "Yes—" He cleared his throat and tried again. "Yes, ma'am. Ethan Fraser."

"Well, Ethan Fraser, I'm Elizabeth Magrath." Her eyes twinkled and she added, "I'd offer you my hand, but perhaps we'd best wait until you've washed." She motioned toward the far side of the warehouse. "Wait over there, next to those bales against the wall. I'm afraid it's the best I have to offer until I decide what's to be done with you." Lines of doubt wrinkled her brow. "You will be able to make yourself comfortable on the floor?"

If she only knew. "Yes, ma'am."

She smiled. "I'd appreciate it if you'd call me Elizabeth. Ma'am makes me feel like an old spinster schoolmarm."

"Yes ma'a... Yes. I will," Ethan replied, more ill at ease by the moment.

Somewhere beyond the shelves, a bell tinkled. Elizabeth glanced toward the sound. Lowering her voice, she said, "I have to leave you now. If anyone comes in, please be quiet and stay out of sight." With that she turned and vanished among the shelves, trailing a scent of lilac.

Ethan watched the place where she'd disappeared, then cast a nervous look around before hurrying across the room. He found a concealed spot between the wall and the stacked bales of cotton and wedged himself into it. Lowering himself to the floor, he strained to identify the muted sounds coming from the front of the building, certain that at any moment, he would hear the tromp of boots as guards came to fetch him. The murmur of voices reached him, and periodically, the tinkle of the bell. At one point, a door opened and someone came into the warehouse. Ethan listened anxiously as crates were shifted and someone rummaged through their contents. Eventually, the door opened and closed, and there was silence.

It seemed a very long time before Elizabeth returned. She called his name softly, and he pulled himself to his feet. She smiled when she saw him, and came to meet him.

"I've sent for Isaac," she announced. "He should be here directly." She held out an armload of clothes and a gunnysack. "Change into these and put the clothes you're wearing in the sack. When Isaac gets here, you will go with him to my home where you will be cared for until my return. Does that meet with your approval?"

"Yes, ma'a... er. Yes," Ethan stammered. As an afterthought, he added "Thank you."

The bell tinkled, and Elizabeth moved to look down one of the aisles. A door at the front of the warehouse opened and closed.

"Isaac, back here, please."

Footsteps thudded along the plank floor, and a black man emerged from between the shelves. He was tall and loose-limbed with a powdering of gray in his hair. He cast a dubious glance at Ethan before looking to Elizabeth.

She smiled a greeting, then looked at Ethan. "Change your clothes. When you've finished, go with Isaac." She took Isaac aside and spoke with him before departing.

Under Isaac's watchful eye, Ethan changed into the clothes she'd provided. They were worn and patched, but clean, and like the clothes he'd been wearing, hung loosely on his wasted frame.

"Better," Isaac grunted. "Come wit' me."

Ethan followed him along a row of shelves, toward the front of the warehouse. Isaac stopped, rummaged through one of the boxes, and came up with a wide-brimmed hat.

"Put this on," he said. "An' tuck you hair up unner it."

Ethan leaned over, twisted his hair into a knot on top of his head, and placed the hat over it.

"It gonna haf'ta do," Isaac said with a dubious shake of his head. "Lez go."

They went through a door that led directly into an office. There was no one about, and Ethan followed Isaac to a tall desk heaped with parcels.

"Hold out you arms." Isaac stacked on bundles until they reached Ethan's chin. Collecting his own hat from the counter, he scooped up the remaining parcels. "Come wit' me," he said. "An' keep you head down." He held the door for Ethan and followed him outside.

The freight wagon was gone, but two slaves still worked to clean up the litter of broken casks. A smaller wagon, drawn by a single horse, stood before the warehouse. Isaac placed his parcels in the back and indicated Ethan should do the same.

"Keep you head down," he ordered when Ethan set his parcels down and looked around. "Ain't no sense lettin' folks git a look at you. Now git up nexta me."

Isaac flicked the reins over the horse's back, turning it through the bustle along the wharf. Ethan cast a final look at the *St. Nicholas* before Isaac turned the wagon onto a street that led away from the water.

The tenor of noise and activity altered subtly as they entered the city. The street they passed along was cobbled with blocks of charred wood and populated by an array of wagons, carriages, carts, and animals. Pedestrians bustled along wide sidewalks, traversing the open sewage ditches on either side of the street over a random series of ramps. Multi-storied buildings rose above them, some with second and third floor verandas that extended out over the sidewalks, bordered with intricate wrought iron grillwork. Ethan gazed about until a muttered command from Isaac reminded him to keep his head down.

They passed the tall iron fence surrounding Bienville Square, where citizens loitered on sun-dappled walkways beneath the spreading boughs of live oaks. Beyond the square, the businesses resumed, intermingled with elegant townhouses, jalousie windows propped open, their galleries graced with more of the lacey iron grillwork.

Isaac angled the wagon onto another street, one that paralleled two sets of trolley tracks. As the distances between the houses increased, he urged the horse into a trot, passing a mule-drawn trolley headed in the opposite direction. Ethan watched it pass before looking questioningly look at Isaac.

"We goin' to the Hill."

"The hill?"

"Spring Hill. Where Miz 'Lizbet lib."

Ethan nodded, content to wait and see. Several minutes passed before he ventured another question. "What's the white stuff on the road?"

"They oyster shells. They keeps the mud down when it rain."

They passed through a line of earthen breastworks, the land beyond cleared of vegetation. Stumps were all that remained of the forest that had once ringed the city. The scattered houses they passed stood naked and exposed.

Beyond a second line of breastworks, the trees resumed—cedar, magnolia, gingko, pecan and oak lining the road and dotting the wide lawns of elegant homes set so far back that Ethan caught only glimpses of them at the end of long drives.

Isaac turned the wagon through a pair of elaborate gateposts that opened onto a curving drive, canopied by live oaks dripping with Spanish moss. Beyond the trees, a white gazebo stood on a broad expanse of lawn, overhung by the branches of another ancient oak. Ethan glimpsed portions of buildings through the trees, but it wasn't until they rounded the final bend that he got his first look at the house.

It was a stately, two-storied mansion with a gabled roof and a massive entrance portico supported by four white, fluted columns. The front door was carved mahogany, the transom and sidelights, etched and leaded glass. A veranda ran across the center of the second story beneath the portico roof, a pair of mullioned doors opening onto it. Like all the windows, they were framed by a pair of tall, dark green shutters.

Isaac turned the wagon around a circular bed at the center of the drive, thick with azalea, japonica and gardenia, and continued around the corner of the house, past a flat-roofed, single-story wing topped by a railed parapet. Ahead, a tall hedge masked all but the upper windows of the carriage house. It was painted the same white as the main house, with three pairs of wide green doors opening onto the brick carriage yard and a row of green-trimmed dormer windows above.

One pair of doors stood open, and at Isaac's direction, Ethan climbed down from the wagon and followed him inside. He blinked, eyes adjusting to the dimness, and found himself in a barn large enough to accommodate four or five carriages. At the moment, only a single small buggy stood near its center. To his right, box stalls lined the walls front and back, and beyond them, a pair of doors opened into the paddock.

Three horses looked over the doors of their stalls, ears pricked with interest. A young Negro appeared at the open door of another stall, rake in hand. He nodded a greeting to Isaac before turning curious eyes on Ethan.

"This here's, Josiah. He take care a' Miz 'Lizbet's horses and do the heavy work aroun' here." And to Josiah: "This here's Mista Ethan. Miz 'Lizbet say no one to know he here."

Josiah nodded understanding and went to unhitch the horse.

Isaac told Ethan to wait, leaving him at the foot of the steep staircase that ran along the back wall of the carriage barn. He reappeared moments later, followed by a tall, light-skinned Negro woman. She moved with an easy, long-limbed grace, and though her hair was streaked with gray and there were lines around her eyes and mouth, it was obvious she had once been a great beauty. She had a narrow nose and high cheekbones, and her dark eyes, when Ethan looked into them, were flecked with gold.

"I's Hannah," she said, looking him over appraisingly. "Miz 'Lizbet say you need a baff an' she right about that. You bes' come wit' me." She looked to Josiah, who was leading the horse to its stall. "Come help Isaac wit' the water."

Isaac opened the door at the foot of the stairs, and they followed him outside. Directly ahead stood a large stone fireplace, a pair of steaming black pots suspended from an iron framework over the flames. Using squares of quilted fabric to protect their hands, Isaac and Josiah lifted the pots by their handles and carried them into a lean-to built against the back wall of the carriage house. They emerged moments later, pots empty, and Hannah motioned for Ethan to go inside.

The room was tiny, built of rough-cut lumber, but an attempt had been made to make it homey. A rag rug covered the floor, and curtains made of brightly colored fabric framed the single window. A folded towel had been placed on the wooden bench beneath the window, and in the center of the room stood a large tin bathtub, steaming water reaching halfway to its rim.

"Call Isaac if'n you needs mo' hot water. An' make good use a' that lye soap. Ain't no sense bringin' critters into the house."

Hannah stepped out and closed the door. Ethan stepped over to the tub and stuck a hand in. The water was warm—*very warm*—and there was soap and a cloth on a tray attached to the rim. He shed his clothes and stepped in, sighing as he eased himself down. It had been so long since he'd been truly warm that he'd forgotten how good it felt. He leaned back, resting his head against the rim of the tub, and let the heat work its way to his bones.

His body jerked, and his eyes opened. Shaking his head to clear it, Ethan pushed himself upright and reached for the soap. He lathered his face and hair and slid under the water. He stayed there as long as he could, holding his breath while the heat permeated his face and scalp. He had just resurfaced when the door opened, and Isaac came in.

"Hannah say, see what fit," he said placing a pile of clothes and a pair of ankle boots on the bench. Stooping to pick up the clothes Ethan had discarded, he eyed the cuts and bruises covering his body, the numerous places where scratched fleabites had become infected. "Hannah'll fix sumptin' fo' them sores. You need mo' hot water?"

"No. Thank you."

Isaac left, and Ethan began scrubbing the rest of his body. The lye soap burned the open sores, but that didn't bother him nearly as much as the bones protruding from beneath his skin. Even muscle had wasted away.

The water was filthy when he finished, but he leaned back, relaxing in its lingering warmth. When it began to cool, he pushed himself up and padded to the bench. The clothes Hannah had left for him were worn, but clean. He held them up, inspecting them, and selected what fit best.

Isaac was waiting when he emerged from the lean-to. He led Ethan back into the carriage barn and up the stairs. The door at the top opened into a large, open room, its peaked ceiling sloping low along the walls. Light and air came from six dormer windows, three at the front, offering a glimpse onto the drive, and three at the back. The room was pleasantly furnished with an assortment of rugs and worn, comfortable furniture.

There was a large stone fireplace centered on the wall adjacent to the door. Hannah bent over a pot suspended from one of the hooks, ladling its contents into a bowl. The room was filled with the smells of cooking, and Ethan's stomach came alive, rumbling with hunger.

"Close the do'," Hannah said straightening. "An' come have sumptin' to eat."

Ethan promptly did as he was told.

Hannah placed the steaming bowl and a loaf of bread at one end of the long wooden table before the front windows and motioned Ethan to a chair. Isaac took two cups from the mantle and filled them with coffee. He placed one in front of Ethan and carried the other to the far end of the table, where he sat, taking occasional sips, and watching Ethan closely.

The gumbo was like nothing Ethan had ever tasted, thick with vegetables and chunks of seafood. The bread was fresh-baked, and the coffee was the real thing, not one of the adulterated versions he'd grown accustomed to. After the first bite, he was certain there couldn't possibly be enough, but his stomach wasn't used to large portions, and he was achingly full long before the bowl was empty. He pushed it aside and looked up to find Hannah watching him from the doorway at the far end of the room.

"If you finished, come wit' me."

With Isaac tagging watchfully behind, Ethan followed her along a narrow hallway with five closed doors on either side. Hannah stopped before the last door on the left and pushed it open, standing aside for him to enter.

Ethan stepped into a narrow room with a steeply sloping ceiling and a single dormer window. A plank bed stood against the wall to his right, a small table with a basin and pitcher, on the wall to his left. Ethan stepped over to the bed and ran his hand over the worn quilt. Aside from the lumpy mattress at Archie Gilles' place, he hadn't slept in a real bed in months. Suddenly, his legs would no longer support him. He turned and sat down abruptly.

Hannah had been watching from the doorway, Isaac looking over her shoulder. She hurried to kneel before Ethan, unlacing his boots and pulling them off. She helped him out of his coat and pulled back the quilt. Taking him by the arm, she guided him to the head of the bed. He slipped under the covers, and she tucked them in around him. He was asleep before she left the room.

19

Ethan slept for the better part of two days. At times, he was on the verge of waking, but the effort required was more than he could manage. The cocoon he inhabited was so warm and soft and dry that he couldn't bring himself to leave it. At some point during the second day, he was aware of a hand pressed to his cheek. Later, there were footsteps, and a lantern, much too bright, was held close to his face. When the footsteps receded, the scent of lilac lingered.

He opened his eyes the following morning, just as it was getting light. The smell of frying bacon filled the room, and though his stomach rumbled noisily, he lacked the will to move.

When he could no longer ignore it, he pushed the covers aside and sat up. Swinging his feet over the side of the bed, he saw that a chair had been brought into the room. A neat pile of clean clothes lay on the seat, and a towel hung over the back. Ethan stood and stepped over to the table. A straight razor lay next to the basin, a strop on the wall beside it. Ethan ran his fingers over the smooth skin along his jaw, and leaned down to look into the small, discolored mirror that hung on the wall above the basin. A stranger stared back, strained and wary. Protruding bones hollowed his eyes, and an angry scar ran across his left cheek. Ethan poured warm water from the pitcher into the basin and washed his hands and face. He didn't look in the mirror again.

He changed into fresh clothes and ventured into the hall, walking softly toward the sound of voices. At the door to the common room, he hesitated. Isaac, Josiah and two young boys were seated at the table. Hannah was at the fire.

"Lawdy," she exclaimed when she turned and saw him. "Look who's alive."

The others turned to stare. Isaac grunted a greeting. Josiah, his mouth full, nodded. Hannah indicated that Ethan should take the same chair he'd occupied before. He was no sooner seated than she set a heaping plate of food before him.

"This here's Ben an' Moses," she said, introducing the boys.

They murmured greetings and pushed back their chairs. Josiah followed them out the door, their footsteps clattering down the stairs.

Hannah collected all the plates but Ethan's and set them on a tray next to the fire. Then she went out, leaving Ethan alone with Isaac.

Ethan ate greedily, but again, there was more food than his stomach would tolerate. He forced down as much as he could and looked up to find Isaac watching him.

"Miz 'Lizbet say they's rules," Isaac announced. "You not to go anywhere 'cept out back to the privy. If'n folks comes callin', you to stay hidden 'til they's gone. Unnerstan'?"

Ethan nodded. "I understand."

Isaac held Ethan's eyes and said firmly, "Miz 'Lizbet a fine woman. She takin' a big risk bringin' you here. You make trouble, you cause anything bad to happen, an' I gonna see you pays. Unnerstan'?"

Ethan nodded again. "You have my word I won't do anything to bring her to harm. Just tell me what to do and I'll do it."

Isaac studied him a moment longer. Deciding he was satisfied with Ethan's sincerity, he pushed his chair back and stood up. He added Ethan's dishes to the pile on the tray, and taking it with him, walked out the door.

As his footsteps receded down the stairs, Ethan got up and wandered the room, examining the few objects in it before stopping to gaze out one of the front windows. To his left, he could see a portion of the paddock that abutted the carriage yard. Two horses, a bay and a dappled gray, stood head to tail, tails swishing. As he watched, the bay's head came up, ears pricked, and Josiah came into view. The gray turned, and he offered them both something from his pocket before clipping a rope to the gray's halter and leading it back the way he'd come.

Ethan watched them out of sight, then looked to the carriage yard directly below him. It was rectangular, surrounded by a brick wall four feet high. A wide pair of iron gates opened onto the drive, and to his right, a matching single gate led to the large open courtyard behind the main house. It was paved with the same red brick as the carriage yard and shaded by a single massive oak. There was a water pump near the base of the oak, and beyond it, a white, single-story building that Ethan assumed housed the kitchen and scullery. Two doors opened onto the courtyard, flanked by a pair of windows.

One of the doors opened, and a girl stepped out carrying a wicker basket heaped with laundry. She hadn't gone far when a light-skinned Negro woman appeared in the doorway and called after her. The girl turned, and the woman tossed a towel onto the pile. It puzzled Ethan to see a Negro woman giving orders to a white girl, but that appeared to be what was happening. The woman went back inside, and the girl went on her way, vanishing toward the rear of the property.

From his vantage point, Ethan could see over the hedge that bordered the carriage yard, to the back of the main house. A door and four tall windows opened onto a wide, covered gallery that ran the width of the ground floor, jogging to include the single-story wing. An ornate triple window was centered above the door, flanked on either side, by four windows. The roof of the single-story wing had two pairs of French doors opening onto it and was landscaped with clusters of potted plants. As Ethan watched, the pair of doors nearest the front of the house opened. He caught a glimpse of Hannah before she retreated into the room, lace curtains fluttering in her wake.

Noise in the yard below captured Ethan's attention, and he looked down as Josiah led the gray, now hitched to the buggy, into the carriage yard. Isaac emerged from the back door of the main house and crossed the courtyard to join him. Following a brief exchange, he climbed onto the buggy seat, took up the reins, and headed along the drive toward the front of the house. Before long, he reappeared, Elizabeth on the seat next to him.

Ethan turned from the window and settled on the worn, cushioned sofa. He had grown used to long hours of doing nothing, and if this was to be a prison of sorts, he figured he'd do just fine. In the quiet warmth of the room, he dozed.

Over the next few days, a pattern developed. The more Ethan slept, the more he needed sleep. When he was awake, he was hungry. Hannah brought food up from the kitchen, and Ethan would eat as many as six small meals a day. By the end of the first week, he was having difficulty buttoning his britches, so Hannah brought him another pair. Before long, he needed an even larger size.

* * *

In Chattanooga, General Ulysses S. Grant chaffed at the delay in ending the siege. During the first half of November, more than sixty thousand men under the commands of Generals William T. Sherman and Joseph Hooker had poured over the "cracker line" to Chattanooga.

In contrast, General Bragg's Confederate Army was seriously depleted. After the battle at Chickamauga Creek, Bragg had gone back to feuding with his generals. Polk, Hindeman and Hill had all been replaced. When Longstreet got involved, Bragg responded by sending him to take Knoxville. As Grant prepared to attack, Bragg was down to just two corps, having sent nearly a third of his army away.

By November twenty-first, Grant was determined to wait no longer. His first plan of attack stalled when rain prevented Sherman from moving out, but then Bragg ordered two more divisions away to support Longstreet in Knoxville, and word spread that the enemy might, in fact, be withdrawing. On November twenty-third, General Thomas, with twenty thousand men mustered from the Army of the Cumberland, was sent to make a strong reconnaissance of Orchard Knob, the Confederate forward position in the middle of their line on Missionary Ridge. The thin line of Rebels holding the ridge proved no match for the men in blue. Following a brief pitched battle, Federal forces took possession of the hill.

General Grant moved his headquarters to Orchard Knob, and from there, ordered simultaneous advances by Sherman and Hooker's armies. Sherman's divisions crossed the Tennessee River and attacked the Confederate north flank, taking the north end of Missionary Ridge. To the south, General Hooker's army advanced on Lookout Mountain. Heavily outnumbered, the Confederates battled for the high ground throughout the day, repulsing wave after wave of Union troops that scrambled up the steep mountain slopes in dense fog. Under cover of darkness, the Rebels withdrew to the southern end of Missionary Ridge. On the morning of November twenty-fifth, men from the 8th Kentucky scaled the last cliffs to the top of Lookout Mountain and planted the Stars and Stripes where it was visible to the Union troops in the valley below.

Bragg's forces were left with but a single position to defend, the three-mile front slope of Missionary Ridge. At dawn, General Sherman attacked from the north. He was repeatedly driven back. General Thomas' troops advanced to the base of Missionary Ridge with orders to drive back the men in the rifle pits.

Bragg had split his forces, leaving half at the bottom with orders to fire a volley when the enemy came within two hundred yards, then withdraw up the hill. Consistent with his usual lack of communication, large numbers of men knew nothing of the plan. When Thomas' army advanced, they stayed and fought. Many of them died. The rest, vastly outnumbered, retreated up the hill.

Lieutenant Josh Fraser, caught in the murderous hail of bullets raining down from above, realized he could not hold his position as ordered. He had either to fall back, or charge up the hill. Driven by fear, adrenaline, and an overwhelming need to avenge his brothers' deaths, Josh bellowed for his men to advance. All around him, other companies did the same. They reached the top, swarming unchecked over the crest as the enemy's lines crumbled. As Josh's men fought their way through the few Rebels still standing their ground, there was a sudden flurry of movement ahead. A shout went up as a group of officers wheeled their horses and fled before the advancing blue tide.

"It's Bragg hisself!" someone shouted, and others took up the call. Men in blue charged after the fleeing horsemen.

Above the din, Josh heard his name called and turned to see a lieutenant from another company standing atop a captured Napoleon, waving his hat and gesturing. Shouting to his men to follow, Josh led them along the ridge to where an entire battery of enemy artillery had been overrun and captured. Josh's men threw their shoulders against the big guns and wrestled them around. A cheer went up as the first volley was fired into the retreating ranks of the Confederate Army.

The enemy was in full retreat when a shot echoed from high in the trees. The bullet smacked into Josh's left shoulder, spinning him to the ground. The shot was answered ten-fold by his men, and the body of a lone sniper fell from the branches where he had been stranded.

One of Josh's sergeants rushed to his side, tearing open his clothing to expose the wound. Through pain, Josh's eyes asked the question. The sergeant assured him the wound wasn't life threatening. What he didn't say was that Josh would bleed to death if they didn't get him off the ridge quickly. Josh offered a weak smile as his men prepared to lift him. Long before they got him off the hill, and into the care of the surgeons, he was unconscious from pain and loss of blood.

Atop Missionary Ridge, some of the Confederate forces held out until after dark, but then they too retreated toward Dalton, Georgia to wait out the winter. General Grant and his armies were left to celebrate Thanksgiving in Chattanooga, freed from siege.

Three days after the collapse of his army at Missionary Ridge, General Bragg asked to be relieved of command. He returned to Richmond to serve as military adviser to Jefferson Davis while General J. E. Johnston took command of the Army of Tennessee.

DECEMBER

20

During the first ten days Ethan lived above the carriage barn, he glimpsed Elizabeth several times, but she never came up and he rarely went out. At first, he was content to do nothing, but as the days passed, and his strength began to return, he grew restless.

"Is there some chore that needs doing? Anything I can do to help out?" he asked one morning when everyone but Hannah and Isaac had gone.

Isaac shook his head without looking up from his plate.

"Isaac," Hannah said pointedly.

Isaac looked up, still chewing, and considered Ethan. "Could be they some wood what needs splittin'."

"Show me what you want done, and I'll do it."

"Splittin' wood Josiah's job," Isaac said, eyeing him uncertainly. He looked at Hannah, then at Ethan. "But if'n that what you want, then come wit' me."

They went downstairs, and while Isaac collected the ax, Ethan found a piece of twine to tie back his hair. Behind the carriage barn, a gentle slope led to the woods that covered the rear of the property. Several logs had been dragged in, some already cut into sections, ready for splitting.

"You sho' you wanna do this?" Isaac asked.

Ethan held out a hand for the ax. Isaac eyed him a moment longer, then left him to it.

Splitting logs proved harder than Ethan expected. Just a few swings of the ax left him winded and shaking. He removed his coat and slowed his pace, stopping often to rest. It took most of the morning, but he stuck with it until a quarter of the logs had been split.

When he no longer had the strength to swing the ax, Ethan set it aside and stacked the split wood. Upending one of the remaining logs, he sat down, enjoying the fresh air and the warmth of the sun on his back. Birds twittered, and a rabbit emerged from the undergrowth, making its way in timid hops. It stopped near the woodpile, nose twitching, then sat up on its hind legs and looked at Ethan. Without warning, it leapt straight into the air, twisting as it went, and with a flash of white tail, vanished into the undergrowth. For the first time in weeks, Ethan laughed.

He heard Hannah call his name, and turned to see her standing at the back door of the carriage house. Waving in response, he stood up. It was hard to leave the sunshine, but hunger won out.

He finished his solitary meal, and was wondering what to do for the rest of the day, when footsteps thudded up the stairs. Terror shot through him. Ethan looked around, searching for a place to hide. He was halfway across the room when the door behind him opened. He whirled to face it.

Isaac saw the panic on Ethan's face and stopped short. After a moment, he said, "Hannah say you gots to have anudder baff."

Ethan's expression changed from relief to puzzlement.

"Miz 'Lizbet want you at the big house tonight."

"Why... ?"

"She dint say. She say bring you over after supper, an' Hannah say you need anudder baff."

Ethan took a lingering bath, heat soaking into aching muscles. He put on the clean clothes that had been set out for him, then climbed the stairs to the living quarters where he spent the remainder of the afternoon alternately dozing and looking out the window.

Late in the day, he saw Isaac leave in the buggy. Sometime later, he returned with Elizabeth. Ethan watched as lamps were lit and shades drawn in the main house. He speculated on what each room must be, was wondering what it would be like to go inside, when Hannah emerged from the kitchen with his supper. Ethan rose and lit the lamp before meeting her at the top of the stairs and taking the tray.

When he finished eating, Ethan dimmed the lamp and returned to the rocking chair he'd drawn up before the window. He hadn't been there long when the back door of the house opened, catching Hannah in light. He watched her shadowy figure cross the courtyard and listened as she climbed the stairs. She came into the room, a suit of clothes over one arm, a pair of shiny black shoes dangling from her hand.

"Get yousef dressed, Mista Ethan. Isaac gonna come fo' you after a bit."

Ethan took the clothes and carried them to his room. He laid them out on the bed and examined them—black trousers and a dark red satin vest, braces, a black frock coat and a white, starched shirt, more elegant than anything he'd ever worn. There was also a thin strip of black fabric that he figured must be a tie. Ethan used it to tie back his hair, leaving the shirt open at the neck.

He was donning the coat when Isaac arrived. He looked Ethan up and down, then walked over and pulled at the coat, adjusting it, and flicking away imaginary lint. He fastened the top button of the shirt and stepped back, subjecting Ethan to further examination. At last, he grunted in what Ethan took to be approval, and muttered, "Come wit' me."

They crossed the courtyard and ascended the steps to the gallery. The back door opened into a passageway, brightly lit by a trio of kerosene wall brackets. A steep set of stairs marched up the wall to the left; to the right, was a good-sized pantry. Isaac continued straight-ahead and pulled open a door.

They emerged in the front foyer beneath a sweeping flight of stairs, curving upward on their right to a landing above, before continuing their arcing climb on the left. The polished mahogany railing curved around on the floor above until it came back over the railing at the foot of the stairs, completing the circle. Ethan looked up, past the sparkling light from the crystal gasolier, to the carved plaster ceiling thirty feet above. Pivoting, he took in the tall triple window, bordered in beveled glass, that ran the width of the landing.

Isaac cleared his throat, and Ethan turned to follow him. A door near the foot of the stairs gave a glimpse into an elegant dining room. Soft light glowed through the door opposite, revealing a parlor. They passed beneath a mahogany-molded arch, burnished wood glowing softly in the reflected light from a pair of oil lamps set on either side of a tall pier mirror. Isaac stopped before a closed door on the right and knocked softly. At a murmured response, he turned the knob and stepped inside.

"Mista Ethan here, Miz 'Lizbet."

Isaac stood aside, and Ethan took a cautious step into the room. An elegant pair of rosewood settees upholstered in pale, blue-striped satin faced one another across a gold Florentine tea table before the fire. Armchairs covered in blue and cream fabric were placed at intervals around the room, and a rosewood piano occupied the space between the two front windows. A cream-colored rug bordered in shades of blue covered all but the edges of the parquet floor, and the walls were papered in a blue and cream floral print. The carved marble fireplace and all the moldings were white; a massive gilt-framed mirror above the mantle reflected glittering light from a pair of crystal oil lamps. Heavy damask drapes of pale blue framed tall windows masked by linen shades.

Elizabeth was seated on one of the settees. She rose as Ethan entered the room, and he caught his breath at the sight of her. She was much more beautiful than he remembered. The bodice of her gown left her neck and shoulders bare. A fall of black lace covered the tops of her arms, and continued in a V down to her waist. The bodice itself was a deep, lustrous blue, as was the full skirt, looped and beribboned with black lace and bows. Her hair was swept up, tendrils falling in soft, dark curls to her shoulders. She wore a thin gold chain around her neck, and something glittered expensively at the base of her throat.

Elizabeth's smile of greeting quickly turned pointed. Ethan realized he'd been staring. Embarrassed, he looked at the floor.

"Thank you, Isaac," Elizabeth said, her eyes never leaving Ethan's face. When the door closed, she said, "You've cleaned up quite well. I approve."

Ethan looked up, uncertain what to reply.

Elizabeth looked into his dark, guarded eyes and tried her most charming smile. One corner of his mouth twitched, but that was the extent of his response. She gestured to the settee opposite where she'd been sitting. "Won't you sit?"

Ethan crossed to where she'd indicated and waited until she was seated before lowering himself stiffly to the edge of the settee. It took him several moments to figure out what to do with his hands. In the end, he placed them on his knees.

Elizabeth watched his discomfort with amusement. When he looked at her, she said, "Relax, Mr. Fraser. I asked you here because I wanted to meet you again now that you've rested." An impish look came into her eyes and she added, "And bathed."

His expression didn't alter, and she immediately regretted having said it.

"That was rude. I apologize. Now please, sit back while we get to know one another." She arched her brows in silent command, and he slid back a few inches.

"That's better," she said, finding his wariness disconcerting. "Why don't you begin by telling me something about yourself? Where are you from?"

"Fulton County, Illinois, ma'am. My folks have a farm on the Spoon River south of Lewistown."

She arched an eyebrow in mock annoyance, her lips pouting prettily. The jewel at her throat twinkled where it caught the light. "Now, don't I remember asking you to call me Elizabeth?"

He recalled that she had. "Yes, ma'a... Yes."

"I'm sorry if it makes you uncomfortable, but ma'am makes me feel ancient, and Mrs. Magrath..." She smiled and shook her head. "After all these years, I still find myself looking around for James' mother. So, Elizabeth it will have to be."

"All right," he agreed. And after a brief hesitation, "Elizabeth."

"Good! And I shall call you Ethan." She smiled, hoping he would respond in kind. When he didn't, she pressed on. "Tell me how you came to be on my doorstep. I assume you were fighting for the Union when you were captured?"

Ethan nodded, preferring to avoid the truth. At her insistence, he told her of the stockade in Atlanta and the escape from the train. Omitting all but the most mundane details, he told of the journey that ended at Cahaba.

Occasionally Elizabeth interrupted with a question, but mostly she listened. When it came time to speak of Cahaba, Ethan described what he knew of Thomas' life there.

Elizabeth leaned forward as he talked. By the end, her eyes glistened with tears. "No wonder you were frightened and half-starved. What a terrible ordeal to have lived through."

Ethan offered her a brief, tight smile that didn't touch his eyes. "It was, but as you say, I did live through it. A lot of men didn't." He looked toward the fire. After a moment, he added, "Last I heard, three of my brothers had died in the fighting. Them and a lot of others I knew."

Elizabeth's heart went out to him. "I'm so sorry. It's small consolation, I know, but I understand what it's like to lose someone you love."

When Ethan didn't reply, she looked at her hands where they lay clasped in her lap. For more than a minute, the only sound in the room was the quiet hiss of the fire. A chunk of coal slid against the fender with a metallic clunk, and Ethan's eyes moved back to Elizabeth.

"What's been hardest is not knowing what happened to Thomas. After everything we went through, after all he did..." Ethan shook his head. "When I escaped, I abandoned him."

He had finally offered something without her having to prompt. Elizabeth wanted to encourage him, but at the same time, was afraid to offer more than she could deliver. She bit her lip, weighing the possibilities before speaking.

"Perhaps I can find out where he was taken, your Thomas. Once I know where he is, I might be able to help him in some small way." She paused, tapping a finger against her lips, then added, "I might even convince them to let me see him."

"You would do that?" Ethan asked, not certain he believed her. "Why?"

Elizabeth smiled, wishing he would lower his defenses. "I can't think of any reason why not. Through my husband, I am acquainted with any number of influential people. Let me think about it and ask a few questions. I'll let you know what I discover." She shifted, preparing to stand. "Now tell me, is there anything you need?"

At first, Ethan could think of nothing. As he rose, a thought struck him. "Something to read. A book. Do you have any books?"

Elizabeth laughed in delight. "You have no idea," she said. "Come with me."

He followed her out of the drawing room and into the parlor directly across the foyer. The room, adjacent to the parlor he'd glimpsed earlier, was lit by a single lamp, too dark to reveal much as he trailed her to a closed door at the far side of the room.

Elizabeth glanced over her shoulder. "Wait while I light some lamps and draw the shades."

She left him, closing the door behind her, and Ethan considered what he had seen of the house. He decided the door must lead to the single-story wing. As he thought it, Elizabeth pulled the door open with a flourish.

"Welcome to the library!"

Ethan stepped into the room and stopped short. The walls were lined floor to ceiling with polished mahogany shelves filled with books. Access to the upper shelves was by means of a ladder attached to a brass rail that ringed the room. The shelves alternated with a pair of tall windows on the wall opposite and pairs at each end of the room. Framed by dark green velvet curtains tied back with tasseled cords, their ivory shades were drawn against the night. A writing table stood near one of the front windows; burled walnut tables positioned before others supported softly glowing lamps and were flanked leather-upholstered wingchairs. A fireplace of black-veined green marble was centered on the wall nearest him, flanked by shelves. A sofa and chairs were arranged before it, set on carpet of greens, rust, gold and black. Beyond the fireplace, a door led to the other parlor. Ethan had never seen a room like it.

Elizabeth let him stare for several moments before recapturing his attention. "I have no idea what all is here. Most of these belonged to my husband." She gestured to a set of shelves next to the fireplace. "Those are mine, the ones I enjoy reading, but you're welcome to borrow anything you find that's of interest."

Ethan walked to the nearest set of shelves and began looking at titles. He wandered slowly, fingering embossed leather bindings, overwhelmed by what he saw. Occasionally he saw a title that was familiar, but most he had never heard of. There were volumes of history, geography, art, philosophy, and the sciences, in addition to novels and poetry. He saw titles in Latin, Italian and French. There was so much to choose from that he had no idea what to select.

Elizabeth solved the problem for him. Pulling a matched pair of volumes from one of the shelves, she held them out to him. "Here. You might try this. It's one of my favorites."

He took the books from her and read the title: *The Count of Monte Cristo* by Alexandre Dumas. Looking up, he smiled, his eyes coming alive for the first time.

Elizabeth's heart gave a lurch and her pulse quickened. She felt heat rising in her face and looked away.

Ethan failed to notice. "I've never read it," he said examining the books. "But I'd like to." He favored her with another smile. "Thank you."

Flustered, Elizabeth turned and walked away. When he had first entered the room that evening, she had been struck by his exceptional good looks, but nothing had prepared her for his smile. It lit up his face, softening his eyes and chasing away the haunted look. She drew a breath, endeavoring to keep her voice steady as she said, "I hope you enjoy it." Another breath, another moment, and she added, "There are plenty more if you find it doesn't appeal. I'll tell Isaac you're to be allowed in here whenever you wish."

She reached the door as she finished speaking, and now fully composed, turned to face him. "I think this has been quite enough for one evening, don't you? It's late and I need to leave the house early tomorrow." On impulse, she added, "I've enjoyed this evening. I hope you'll join me again soon."

He offered her that smile again, and her whole being tingled.

"I'd like that," he said softly.

She led him back to the drawing room and rang for Isaac. He appeared so quickly that she knew he'd been lurking just out of sight. Turning to Ethan, she said, "Enjoy the book. I look forward to hearing what you think of it." With that, she vanished into the foyer.

Ethan stared at the empty doorway until Isaac said gruffly, "Lez go."

Ethan was a long time falling asleep, his thoughts filled with all he'd seen, but returning time and again to the library. He had never imagined such a wealth of books could exist in someone's home. There were more volumes in that one room than in the entire lending library back home. Elizabeth's admission that she'd read so few surprised him. He couldn't understand owning them and not wanting to read them all.

Elizabeth... Ethan still wasn't sure why she'd wanted to see him. It was natural, he supposed, after the risk she'd taken, that she would want to know something about him, but the invitation to return puzzled him. It wasn't like they had anything in common. He was from a farm in Illinois, while she was a wealthy southern lady who lived in a fine house and knew important people. And besides, evenings alone with her couldn't be considered proper. *No,* he decided, *if she invites me back, I'll find a reason not to go.*

Then he remembered Thomas. Elizabeth's offer surprised him. He found it hard to believe she would actually do it. *Why should she?* He turned the question over in his mind without drawing any conclusion. *If she does, I'll be grateful. If not...* It would be wise not to expect too much.

Ethan was almost asleep when another thought struck him: *I never thanked her.* After all she'd done—offering him escape from the certainty of another prison, feeding and clothing him, providing him shelter—the least he should have done was thank her. Before he slept, he vowed to do it—the next time she invited him to the house.

* * *

In her large, comfortable bed, Elizabeth also lay awake. Never in her wildest dreams would she have expected someone to affect her the way Ethan had. *It's ridiculous,* she told herself. *Infatuation, nothing more. Why, I barely know him!*

She had only been half-watching the day the line of prisoners trudged across the wharf. As always, they were a pathetic-looking bunch, ragged clothes hanging from wasted bodies. As the war dragged on, each group seemed more pitiful than the last. It had crossed her mind to wonder what they were doing in Mobile. In the past, Union prisoners had been put on ships bound for prisons in the Carolinas and Virginia, but now that the Union blockade had virtually sealed Mobile Bay, there was nowhere for them to go.

She was turning away when the first cask crashed to the wharf. Ethan caught her eye immediately. She saw him notice the alley and watched as he disappeared from view. She stayed where she was as the guards struggled to restore order, listened to the ruckus in the alley as someone was hauled out. Pressing her face to the glass, she strained to see who it was. No copper skin; no long, ebony hair. She waited, but no one else went into or came out of the alley.

When they had gone, she left her office and walked quickly through the warehouse. Pressing an ear to the back door, she listened. It was impossible to tell if anyone was on the other side. Having no idea what she would do if she found him, she grasped the bolt and yanked, pulling the door open in the same motion.

He nearly fell in on top of her. He regained his balance, poised to flee, and without stopping to consider the consequences, she spoke. He whirled to face her, and it was then she saw his eyes—wild and frightened; more like a hunted animal than a human being. He was pitifully thin, infested with fleas and lice. And the smell! Tucked safely in her bed, Elizabeth wrinkled her nose at the memory.

She left him in the warehouse and spent the next few minutes formulating a plan and setting it in motion. She assumed that when the prisoners arrived wherever they were going, the guards would discover him missing and begin their search. The scene of the disturbance would be the logical place to begin, which meant she didn't have much time.

She sent the office boy to fetch Isaac, then sorted through the donated clothing in the warehouse, looking for what might fit him. She wrapped more clothing into parcels, and when Isaac arrived, gave him instructions and left him to see Ethan safely removed to the house.

She didn't see him again until the following night when Hannah, worried that he hadn't awakened and thinking something must be wrong, asked her to look in on him. With Isaac holding the lantern, she looked down at his face. The change in him was staggering. Dark, shining hair fanned across the pillow; thick lashes brushed his cheeks. Relaxed in slumber, his face had returned to child-like innocence.

He's beautiful! she thought, and found herself suddenly short of breath. The room felt overly warm. She dragged her eyes from him and hurried into the hall, assuring Hannah that he would be all right, and suggesting she open his door before cooking breakfast.

All that week and the next, Hannah reported that Ethan mostly slept, rising for brief periods to eat, before returning to bed. She had given him liniment for the sores Isaac said covered his body. By the beginning of the second week, Hannah told her, he was looking better and beginning to put on weight. Then this morning, when Hannah mentioned he was splitting wood, Elizabeth, overcome by curiosity, asked that he be brought to the house. She rummaged through her husband's clothes and found some that would fit. For herself, she selected her most elegant gown. She wasn't exactly sure why, but she felt it important to appear just a bit intimidating.

She knew why the moment he entered the room. He was taller than she remembered, still terribly thin, but no longer starved. His features combined to make him the most striking young man she had ever seen. He had tied his hair back from his face, accentuating fine high cheekbones; his copper skin was smooth and unblemished but for a fresh scar across the left side of his face. His eyes were dark, almost black, and unreadable until the two fleeting moments when he'd smiled. Then light came into them, changing them to a deep, warm brown, and smoothing the harsh lines of his face. Something in her stirred in a way she'd never experienced before.

Elizabeth had met her husband, James Magrath, when she was sixteen. He was thirty-four. His family had moved from New York to Mobile when he was a child and established the Magrath Trading Company. They dealt primarily in cotton, purchasing bales that came down the rivers to Mobile and selling them to the textile mills in the North and in Europe. The money was used to purchase goods, primarily from New York, which were then sold in the South.

The youngest of six children and the only son, James had been sent north to be educated. Upon graduation from Harvard, he returned to Mobile to run the company alongside his father. By twenty-five, he had assumed much of the day-to-day operation of the business. When he turned thirty, his father bestowed on him full ownership of the Magrath Trading Company. During his father's reign, the company had been successful. Under James' leadership, it prospered beyond all expectation.

James was on a business trip to New York when his banker, Elizabeth's father, introduced them. He was instantly enamored of her beauty and wit; she was charmed by his generosity and outrageous sense of humor. Discovering they shared a fondness for many of the same things, they quickly became friends. James took to traveling to New York more often than business required.

Eighteen months later, they were married, and Elizabeth came to live in Mobile. James had never divulged the full extent of his wealth, so she had no inkling of the grand lifestyle she was entering into until the carriage turned onto the drive. At first, she thought there'd been a mistake, but James laughed in delight and welcomed her to her new home.

James cut back on his travel, preferring to send others whenever he could. The two of them settled in happily together, balancing a hectic social life with quiet moments at home. Seven glorious years were blemished only by their inability to have children.

Then, in the fall of 1862, during one of James' increasingly rare business trips, an explosion ripped through the steamboat on which he was traveling. He was trapped inside and drowned when it sank. Elizabeth mourned him deeply, but after a month, unable to bear another day of the heartfelt, but cloying attention of her in-laws, she dressed and went into town.

Business had diminished as the war dragged on and the blockade strengthened, but there was still work to be done, and the two elderly men who remained as James' managers were eager for assistance. Increasingly, Elizabeth found herself drawn into the business. By the time the last men of fighting age left for the war, she had become an integral part of the operation.

Elizabeth settled happily into the daily routine at the warehouse, content to let her social life wane. Early on, she discovered there were many older men in Mobile who were overly interested in her money and far too earnest in their desire to relieve her of the responsibility of running a business. Their attentions annoyed her, and she began to avoid gatherings where she would have to be polite to them.

She continued to entertain friends and family at home, or join them for an occasional outing to the theatre or a concert, but her preference was for solitary evenings at home after a busy day. She was perfectly content to live alone with only her few remaining servants for company.

All that changed when Ethan smiled. Still wide-awake at half past one in the morning, Elizabeth found herself desperate to know more about him, eager to spend time with him. *That's ridiculous,* she told herself. *He's only a boy. An escaped Yankee prisoner.* How would she explain his presence, particularly to her in-laws, if she were to encourage him and he stayed? Before she slept, she convinced herself not to see him again. Before the week was out, she would send him on his way.

***

Huddled in the damp chill of the makeshift camp, Thomas lay awake, wondering, as he often did, what had become of Ethan. One moment, they'd been together; the next, there was pandemonium and he was gone. It was as if he'd vanished into thin air. Even when the guards restored order and they were on their way again, Thomas had been convinced he was still with them.

They were marched to a city square and lined up for roll call. Ethan's name was called to no response. It was called again. Following a hurried discussion, guards were dispatched to search for him.

The prisoners were herded past a crudely lettered sign that read, "Negroes for Sail and Good Feald Hands', into the stables where slaves were held for sale. There were expressions of horror and shouts of outrage when the men realized they were to be left there, but Thomas took no part in it. He found a corner where he could see the street and settled in to keep watch. Darkness fell with no sign of Ethan. He spent the night wondering if he'd been found and shot. Or, if against all odds, he'd managed to escape.

They were held in the squalor of the slave stables for two weeks before being transferred to a hastily erected camp on the outskirts of the city. Free to mingle, Thomas wandered the camp, questioning everyone he knew. No one remembered seeing Ethan after the first cask exploded. Thomas was on the verge of giving up when he spotted a familiar face. When Thomas asked, the man who'd fetched him to the water closet said he'd seen Ethan slip into a gap between two buildings. He'd followed, but a guard had seen him and dragged him out. There'd been no sign of Ethan in the alley, and as far as he knew, the guards hadn't found him. Thomas fell asleep that night hoping Ethan might, indeed, have escaped.

21

Immediately after breakfast, Ethan took the first volume of *The Count of Monte Cristo*, collected the ax, and went down the slope to the woodpile. He took it easy until his muscles loosened, then fell into a slow, steady rhythm, stopping frequently to rest. He was stacking the last of the split logs when Hannah called to him. Surprised at how quickly the morning had passed, he went up to eat, leaving his coat, with the book folded inside it, atop the woodpile.

He returned a short time later, and using the coat as a pillow, stretched out in the sun to read. There he remained, utterly absorbed, until the light began to fade. Closing the book with reluctance, he pushed himself to his feet.

He ate the meal Hannah brought up for him, then pulled the lamp closer and opened the book. Ben, Moses and Josiah came up a short time later and sat talking before the fire. Much later, Hannah and Isaac joined them. Ethan was still hunched over the book when they drifted off to bed.

The next few days passed in much the same way, until early one warm afternoon, when he finished the second volume. He wandered up the slope to the carriage barn, hoping to find Isaac. Instead, he met Josiah coming down the stairs. It was Sunday, Josiah informed him, and Isaac had driven Elizabeth to church, followed by dinner with her in-laws.

Josiah went on his way, whistling, leaving Ethan standing indecisively at the foot of the stairs. He not only wanted something to read, he wanted to explore the library, but with Isaac away, he wasn't sure it was allowed. In the end, the lure of books proved irresistible.

Ethan pushed through the gate and crossed the courtyard quickly, taking the three steps to the gallery in a single bound. At the door, he stopped and looked back. Assured that no one had seen him, he slipped inside.

Alone in the quiet elegance of the house, he felt like an intruder, nervous and out of place. He hurried through the back parlor and cracked open the door to the library. The room was empty. Stepping inside, he eased the door shut behind him.

By day, the room was even more impressive. Sunlight streamed through tall, mullioned windows, reflecting off polished wood and brass. Ethan stood motionless for several seconds before returning *The Count of Monte Cristo* to its place. He then began a slow circuit of the room, reading titles, removing books, and replacing them. He was so engrossed in what he was doing that he failed to hear Hannah come into the room.

She stopped in surprise at seeing him. "Afta'noon, Mista Ethan."

The book Ethan had been holding crashed to the floor. He spun to face her, his back pressed to the shelves.

Hannah saw the terror on his face. "I's sorry, Mista Ethan. I dint mean to scare you none."

"I... I was looking for a book," Ethan said, unable to control the tremor in his voice. "Elizabeth told me I could borrow her books."

"I knows, Mista Ethan." Hannah stepped back, laying a hand on the doorknob. "Stay as long as you wants. I kin come back later." She left, pulling the door closed behind her.

Heart pounding frantically, Ethan pushed away from the shelves. He bent to pick up the book, but his hands shook so badly that it took several fumbling attempts. Dropping it on the table nearest him, he sank onto a chair. Head bowed, hugging himself tightly, he waited for the panic to subside.

In the comfort and security of the preceding weeks, he'd tried to block out everything that had happened at Cahaba. At first, it had been easy because so much time had been spent in exhausted, dreamless sleep. But lately, as he'd begun to recover physically, he found it more and more difficult to keep the memories at bay. Several times recently, he'd bolted awake, drenched in sweat, his heart pounding in terror. And now, the same thing had happened in broad daylight. Hannah's unexpected appearance had panicked him beyond all reason.

Before Cahaba, there had been little that truly frightened him; he had been confident that he could handle just about anything. That was no longer true. All he wanted now was to be safe. The thought of one day being asked to leave, of being forced out into the world and risking capture again, terrified him.

Ethan sat for a long time, forcing himself to go back over everything that had happened at Cahaba. Reminding himself that he *had* been strong; that right up to the end, he'd defied them. Telling himself they would never have succeeded if he hadn't been so weak and exhausted.

But if Captain Henderson hadn't come back when he did... The thought, coming without warning, sent a shudder through him. For the first time, he understood what truly frightened him. That morning in the water closet, Shunk and his men had stripped him not only of his dignity, but of his faith in himself. They'd broken him, and they'd known it. Worse, he'd known it. From that day on, there would have been no stopping them.

Ethan could see the harelip's eyes; feel his fingers on his cheek. *"Yo' mine now, purdy boy."*

If Henderson hadn't come back... A sob welled up. Ethan closed his eyes against a sudden rush of tears, trying not to dwell on what might have happened. *It's over*, he told himself, repeating it to make it true. *It's over. It didn't happen again. I'm safe.*

He slumped in the chair, letting comforting stillness of the library envelop him. *I am safe*, he told himself, beginning to believing it. He looked around, taking reassurance from the quiet beauty of the room. *It's over. I'm safe.*

Shafts of late afternoon sunlight were slanting across the golden wood of the floor, dust motes dancing in the beams, when Ethan heaved himself from the chair and started toward the door. As he reached it, it swung inward. His breath caught, and he took a startled step back.

Elizabeth stepped into the room, a hand flying to her throat in surprise. She was first to regain her composure. "Ethan! You startled me. I didn't expect to find you here."

"I'm sorry," he blurted. "I was just leaving. I brought back the books." He took a tentative step toward her.

"Please. There's no need for you to go." Her brows drew together. "Wouldn't you like to borrow another while you're here?"

Flustered, Ethan looked toward the table where the volume he'd selected lay forgotten. Offering her a brief, self-effacing smile, he went to retrieve it.

He turned back to discover Elizabeth settling herself in one of the chairs that stood in the path of the sunlight. She picked up a small volume from the table beside her and leaned her head back, a contented smile on her face.

"I so enjoy this room in the late afternoon, especially in winter."

She said it so softly that Ethan wasn't sure the remark was meant for him. He paused uncertainly. When she added nothing more, he started for the door.

"You're welcome to stay," Elizabeth said quickly, sitting upright. "Don't let my being here drive you away." After a moment, she heard herself add, "I would enjoy your company."

Ethan stopped. He had been on the verge of leaving, but only because he felt he didn't belong. He turned to find her watching him.

Elizabeth had been unaware she was holding her breath. When Ethan nodded, accepting her invitation, she let it out in a rush. She could feel the heat rising in her face. Opening her book, she stared blindly at the page.

Ethan selected the chair opposite her and sat down. He glanced sideways, but she appeared engrossed in her book. He opened his before he remembered.

"I want... I need to thank you," he began awkwardly.

Elizabeth looked up. "You're welcome. As I said, please feel free to come here any time, borrow any book you like."

"No. No, that's not what I mean. I'm talking about... about the risk you took helping me escape. About you letting me stay. I..." Words failed him.

She tried to put him at ease. "Ethan, I'm happy to do it. Please, there's no need to thank me." When he looked at her, she smiled.

"But, I do," he insisted. "It's important that you... that you know how much this means to me. You have no idea... You don't know..." His fingers tightened on the book, and he looked down, groping for words.

When he raised his eyes, the look in them frightened her.

"There are things I haven't told you... Things I can't tell anyone. Because of who I am... the way I look... I was treated different from the other prisoners at Cahaba." His voice failed him, and he looked away. Taking a deep breath, he continued, "If... if that kind of thing had happened again in another prison, I... One way or another, I would have died. I'm certain of it."

Elizabeth shuddered at the flat note of finality in his voice. Despite the warmth of the sun on her shoulders, she felt chilled.

Ethan's eyes traveled back to her face. "You saved my life. That's why I need to thank you. That's why it's important for you to know how grateful I am."

Elizabeth stared at him, speechless. His words and the unspoken horror behind them left her with no idea how to respond.

Seeing her distress, the harshness faded from his face. He leaned back, resting his head against the back of the chair, his face tilted toward the ceiling. "I'm sorry," he said softly. "I didn't mean to say all that." He looked at her and forced a smile. "I just wanted to thank you. I apologize if I upset you." He sat forward, preparing to stand. "I think I should go now."

"No! Please don't." Elizabeth wanted to reach out to him, to touch him, but something warned against it. Instead, she said, "I understand. Or, rather, I don't. If it was so dreadful that you can't bring yourself to talk about it, how could I possibly understand? I'm pleased I was able to help when you needed it." She paused before adding, "You should know that I will to do all I can for you. Just as soon as you feel able, I'll see you have what you need to return home."

Ethan turned to face her. "I don't understand. Why are you willing to risk so much?"

She offered him a gentle smile. "I may look like a southern belle sitting here 'deep in the heart a' Dixie', but I was born and raised in New York City, and my sympathies have always been with the North. Helping you, seeing that you get home safely, is one of the few ways I have of fighting this war. Doing what I can for your friend Thomas will be another." A thought came to her, and she added, "Which reminds me. Can you describe him?"

Ethan leaned toward her. "Why? Have you found him? Where is he?"

"He was taken to a temporary camp outside the city." Elizabeth allowed herself a smug little smile. "Yesterday, I persuaded an acquaintance to escort me there."

Ethan looked at her in amazement. "How did you find it?"

"It wasn't difficult. Soon after you left the warehouse, some soldiers came looking for you. When you told me about Thomas, I asked people who work for me if there had been any mention of where the prisoners were taken." Elizabeth threw Ethan a wicked grin. "We're to contact them if we have news of you."

Ethan found himself smiling back. For a moment, something in Elizabeth's eyes held his. She dropped her gaze, and the moment passed.

Not understanding what he'd seen, Ethan said, "Who took you to the camp?"

Elizabeth continued to stare at her lap. "Before his death, my husband was a member of an organization called the Mobile Supply Association. Briefly, it is a group of wealthy men who have used their own money to purchase supplies and sell them, at cost, to the people of Mobile during the war. There are still shortages, but the efforts of the Association have kept prices relatively stable." She looked up. "I don't know how much you know about Mobile, but Union ships set up a blockade at the entrance to the bay at the beginning of the war. For a long time, there were a number of fast ships, sailing on the darkest of nights, that evaded the blockade and carried our cotton to Havana. Once there, it was traded for supplies, which were then smuggled back. Most of those ships are gone now—captured and sunk—so very little moves south out of the bay.

"Because of the blockade, and because the military has appropriated the railroad and river steamers for its own use, my husband's business shrinks a little more each month. Most of the cotton you saw on the quay and in the warehouse has been there since before the war. The piles are smaller now, as we've been able to ship some out, but these days I use the warehouse mainly as a storehouse for supplies—for the Association and a couple other relief organizations that distribute food and necessities to Mobile's poor, and to the families of men away at war. I work with them all, and it brings me into contact with a wide variety of people. A man I know is friendly with the commandant at the camp. I persuaded him, in the name of Christian charity, to drive me there so I could see conditions for myself."

Elizabeth looked away, but not before Ethan saw in her eyes what she'd witnessed. She drew a steadying breath, and continued. "I've convinced a number of fine, upstanding citizens that we are under moral obligation to render aid to those poor men, despite the fact that they are the enemy. I have tugged shamelessly at heartstrings, particularly the women's, reminding them that they would want the same done for their husbands and sons in northern prisons."

She looked at Ethan. "So I will be returning to the camp to help distribute whatever supplies the good people of Mobile provide. If I know what Thomas looks like, I hope to tell him you are safe and report his condition back to you."

Ethan stared at her in mute astonishment. Then he smiled in the way that made her heart flutter, and reached across the table.

Elizabeth looked down, seeing for the first time, the jagged scars that marred his wrist, a cruel contrast to the slender hand and long, graceful fingers. She started to ask about them, but quickly thought better of it. Instead, she placed her hand in his. The spark that surged through her was so powerful she was certain he must feel it, too.

Ethan started to speak, then stopped, puzzled by her expression. After a moment, he simply said, "Thank you. For everything." Giving her hand a quick squeeze, he withdrew his own.

The clock on the mantle chimed the half-hour. Elizabeth used it as an excuse to look away. It surprised her to see how much time had passed. Setting aside the book she'd been clutching, she got to her feet. Ethan rose with her.

"I had no idea it was so late," she said, not daring to meet his eyes. "If you'll excuse me, I need to change for supper." She moved past him, toward the door. When she reached it, she stopped, her back to him. "You haven't described Thomas yet. Why don't you join me so we can finish our conversation?" The words out, she looked to see his response.

A brief look of surprise was followed by a cautious smile. "Yes. I'd like that."

Elizabeth nodded and hurried from the room.

As she dressed, she worried that she'd given in to the urge to ask him to dine with her. She told herself that she shouldn't continue to see him. The feelings he stirred left her incapable of rational thought. For both their sakes, she needed to send him away as soon as possible. *Just as soon as I make good my promise to see Thomas,* she told herself.

Ethan went back to the carriage house and waited for Hannah to bring his clothes. It had been an unsettling afternoon, but he was looking forward to supper. It would be a pleasant change not to dine alone.

He sat across from Elizabeth at one end of a mahogany Chippendale table for twenty. Light from an array of white candles supported by a matched pair of Baroque silver candelabra glinted off imported bone china, fine crystal and a small fortune in sterling silver dinnerware.

Ethan had arrived in the dining room before her, taking in the portraits of James' parents on either side of the mantle, the gilded clock at its center, and the intricately stitched tapestries on the wall opposite. He had made his way across richly patterned carpet to examine an antique silver tea service on the sideboard and the collection of Chinese porcelain displayed in a matching breakfront of bird's eye maple.

When Elizabeth joined him, he greeted her with the quiet reserve she had come to expect, and held her chair before taking his own. Hannah arrived with the soup, and the meal proceeded uneventfully. Ethan described Thomas as he'd last seen him, after which Elizabeth steered the conversation to other topics, gently endeavoring to set him at ease. Ethan did his best to keep his mind on the conversation, mimicking her choice of utensil as each course was served.

When the meal ended, they drifted by unspoken agreement to Elizabeth's sitting room. Seated across from one another on the blue settees before the fire, Elizabeth told Ethan something of her upbringing. She was the youngest of five children and an afterthought, the next youngest being nine years her senior. Her father was in banking, her mother a wealthy socialite. They had left much of her upbringing to nannies until she was sent to boarding school in Boston.

She told Ethan about meeting and marrying James, how they had once had more than twenty servants and entertained lavishly, throwing open the house at least once each month for extravagant parties. The pocket doors between the parlors had been opened, the rugs removed, musicians ensconced on the gallery, and there had been food and drink and dancing until the wee hours. Then the war had come, and most of the servants, all of them freed slaves, had gone; some north to fight, others she knew not where. Finally, she told him of the disaster that had claimed James' life, and briefly, of her life since.

Ethan listened in silence. When Elizabeth asked, he told her a little about himself. She was intrigued by his parentage, but found him disinclined to talk about it. Bit by bit, coaxing and prodding, she got the story out of him.

"And you still speak Sioux?" she asked.

"Lakota," he corrected, eyeing her guardedly. After a moment, he nodded.

"Say something."

It was a language he spoke only with his mother, something private between them. He had no desire to share it with a stranger. "If you don't mind, I'd rather not."

Elizabeth persisted, playfully insisting. When Ethan saw she wouldn't easily be dissuaded, he gave in.

"This is the story of the eagle," he said, eyeing her apprehensively.

Elizabeth smiled, nodding encouragement.

Seeing no way out of it, he began: "Ehaŋni oyate eya maķoce waŋ ble ota ċa el wiċoti, ķeyapi. Yukaŋ mni el ṫaķu wakaŋ waŋ ouŋyaŋ ce he mni taŋ ṫaŋķa ķaġa, ķeyapi. Mni taŋ ķi le saŋm waŋķa u nahaŋ oyate ķi paha k'uŋ henana el napapi nahaŋ ṫaķu yuhapi k'uŋ hena iyuha oķaḣ iyaye. Ognaṡ Wakaŋ Ṫaŋķa ṫakul uŋ iyoķipi ṡni uŋ leċuŋ seċa, ķeyapi."

Ethan translated, adding the rest in English.

"It is said that, a long time ago when the people were living in a land of many lakes, a water monster caused a great flood. The waters rose higher and higher, driving people from their lodges and washing away their belongings. Maybe it was because the Great Spirit, Wakaŋ Ṫaŋķa, was angry with the people for some reason that he let this happen.

"The waters rose higher and higher until all but one hill was flooded. The people climbed the hill to save themselves, but winds came down from the north and swept the water over them. Waves smashed rocks and pinnacles down on them, killing everyone but one beautiful girl.

"As the water swept over the hill, a big spotted eagle, Wanbligleṡka, swooped down and allowed the girl to grab hold of his feet. With her hanging on, he flew to his home at the top of a tall tree on the highest pinnacle in the Black Hills. The girl lived, but she was very sad. Her family, all her people were gone, and the only way to rejoin them was for her to die, too.

"Wanbligleṡka told her, "If you die, there will be no more like you on the Earth. That cannot be. You must live." He kept the beautiful girl with him and made her his wife.

"She became pregnant and bore him twins, a boy and a girl. She was happy because now there would be people again. When the waters receded, Wanbligleṡka helped her and her children down from his rock and put them back on the earth, telling them, 'Be a great Nation—the Lakota Nation.'

"When the children grew up, they married and had children and a nation was born. We— The Lakota," he corrected hastily, "are descended from the eagle. They are the Eagle Nation."

"What a fascinating story!" Elizabeth exclaimed. "I've never heard anything like it. Do you know others?"

Ethan nodded.

"Will you tell me another sometime?"

Ethan studied her. Her interest seemed genuine. He could think of no reason to refuse, so once again he nodded.

As they said good night, Elizabeth, without thinking, offered him her hand. At first, Ethan was unsure what was expected. Then he took it, brushing the back of it lightly with his lips. He was mortified when Elizabeth snatched it from him and fled without a word. He saw himself out and climbed the stairs of the carriage house, wondering what he'd done wrong.

22

That night, Ethan dreamed of the harelip. The guard reached out, and when his fingers touched Ethan's cheek, Ethan struggled against him and screamed. And screamed. A hand touched his arm and he lashed out violently. Another voice, an unexpected voice, cried out in pain and surprise. Ethan woke abruptly, shaking and drenched in sweat.

Hannah rose to her knees from the floor where he'd knocked her. Moonlight slanted through the window, catching her as she put a hand to her cheek. Her eyes glistened with tears. Ethan stared at her in horror, then reached out a hand. Hannah recoiled. Stumbling to her feet, she ran from the room.

Moments later, he heard Isaac's voice raised in anger. A door crashed against a wall, and he heard Hannah pleading. Josiah joined in, and all three voices were raised as they came along the hall. Ethan braced himself for the inevitable confrontation. Before they reached his door, Hannah and Josiah prevailed. The voices receded.

The house quieted, and he lay back, too agitated to sleep. He was still awake when the others began to stir. He couldn't face them, so he stayed where he was. When they had gone, when the house was silent, he drifted off to sleep.

It was dark when he woke. At first, he was confused. Then he remembered the nightmare. And the shock and hurt on Hannah's face. Ethan dragged himself up and rolled out of bed. A glance out the window told him the evening was overcast, threatening rain.

He dressed and went along the hall to the main room. The food Hannah had brought up for him at mid-day was still on the table. Ethan picked at it, but had no desire to eat. He flopped into one of the chairs in front of the dead fire and sat staring into space, wishing he could take back what had happened and dreading the consequences.

He was still there when he heard Hannah's footsteps on the stairs. He turned as the door opened and watched her come into the room. In the darkness, she didn't see him. She placed something on the chair by the door and started toward him.

Not wanting to frighten her, he said softly, "I'm here, Hannah."

He heard a gasp, saw her step falter. Then she came on, seating herself on the chair opposite him and striking a match. She lit the lamp on the table between them and adjusted the wick. Replacing the glass, she looked at him. Her cheek was bruised, her right eye swollen.

"Oh my God, Hannah!" The words came in a horrified gasp. "I'm so sorry. I didn't mean to hurt you. It was a dream... Please... Hannah, I never meant to hurt you. "

"Some mighty bad things musta happened fo' you to have them kinda dreams." Her expression softened. "I knows you dint mean to hurt me none, Mista Ethan." She reached a hand across the table.

Ethan looked at it, then laid his hand in hers. Hannah covered it with her other hand and said, "Doan worry yousef none, Mista Ethan. I knows it warn't me you was hittin' at."

The gesture, and her willingness to forgive, brought a lump to Ethan's throat.

"You gots family, Mista Ethan?"

He nodded. "In Illinois."

"A mama an' papa an' brudders an' sisters, all waitin' fo' you to come home?"

Ethan nodded.

"That's good. I got no one, save Isaac. An' Miz 'Lizbet. My daddy got sold away befo' I was born. I lived wit' my mama fo' a time, but then I got sold away, too, to work in some white folks' kitchen. When I was older, they put me on the auction block buck-naked, an' sold me to a man what kep' me fo' his mistress. I bore him two babies, but the Missus, she done sold them away. When I got too old fo' his likin', he sold me to Mista James." Hannah smiled at the memory. "Mista James, he tol' me I's free. Tol' me I gots a home if'n I wants to work fo' him. After a time, Isaac asked me to marry him, but by then I 'uz too old fo' babies."

She sat silent for so long that Ethan stole a look at her. Her face was etched with such deep sadness that his heart went out to her.

Hannah sighed and gave a slight shake of her head. "So you see, Mista Ethan, they's lotsa times when I wunners about my babies. Wunners what become a' them. An' I wunners about my mama an' papa, too. Thinkin' on it make me sad. But they times when it make me angry, too, what white folks done to me an' mine. But then, I remember what's good in my life. I gots a home. I gots Isaac. An' mo' impo'tant, Mista James made me free. Cain't no one take that away from me." She gave Ethan's hand a squeeze and was rewarded with a fleeting smile.

"Now, I knows sumptin' bad happened befo' you come here. Maybe it hurt you pride; maybe it hurt you soul. Maybe somma both. So when I finds you sittin' alone in the dark, I wunners if you thinkin' 'bout them bad things. Thinkin' 'bout them bad men what done them to you. You think on it long enough an' one day, you gonna start to hate. When you starts to hate, you starts to destroy you own soul. You unnerstan' me, Mista Ethan?"

He looked at her. After a moment, he nodded.

"You young, Mista Ethan. You gots family what cares fo' you. You gots Miz 'Lizbet what cares fo' you mo' than you know. She a good woman, and she gonna see you gets back home." Hannah looked at their clasped hands. "Could be you think it ain't my place to say this, but I been watchin' you since you firs' come here and I knows you a good boy. This bad thing, you can't let it ruin you life. You gots to push it aside an' go on."

She looked up, smiling when their eyes met. "I gots to go now," she said, patting his hand. "I gots to help Hattie wit' the supper." She cocked a questioning brow at him. "You know Miz 'Lizbet 'spectin' you?"

Ethan didn't and it showed.

"You clothes is on the chair." Giving his hand a final squeeze, she stood up.

"Hannah, wait."

She turned back, a question on her face. Ethan rose and took her hand.

"Thank you, Hannah." Impulsively, he leaned in and kissed her gently on her bruised cheek. "For everything."

"Hurry now," Hannah told him, pleased and flustered. "Hurry, or you gonna be late!"

It was raining heavily by the time Ethan dressed. When it became obvious that Isaac wasn't coming to fetch him, he went downstairs and started across the darkened carriage barn, headed for the single door that stood partially ajar. As he approached it, Isaac stepped from the shadows, something long and thick in his hand.

Ethan's heart seized, and he fell back a step. Isaac raised his arms and opened an umbrella. Relief flooded through Ethan. He went to the older man and attempted to apologize. Isaac ignored him, turning his back and stepping out into the rain. Ethan was forced to scurry along beside him in order to keep dry.

Elizabeth was already seated when Ethan came into the dining room. He apologized for his tardiness and slipped into his seat.

"I hope you will forgive my behavior last night," she said, avoiding his eyes. "I suddenly felt unwell. Something I ate didn't agree with me."

A long moment passed before he realized what she meant. "Are you feeling better?"

"Yes..." Elizabeth said, distracted as Hannah came in with the soup tureen. "Hannah, please. I wish you would tell me what happened." And to Ethan: "Look at her. Something's happened, and she refuses to tell me about it."

Ethan looked at Hannah, then at his plate.

Hannah gave Elizabeth a quiet smile and began ladling soup into her bowl.

Elizabeth laid a restraining hand on hers. "Please, Hannah."

"I done tol' you, Miz 'Lizbet. Ain't nuttin' fo' you to concern yousef over."

Realizing she couldn't force an answer, Elizabeth removed her hand. Hannah finished serving and left the room.

Elizabeth watched her go. "She came in like that this morning. I've asked her repeatedly, begged her to tell me what happened, but she refuses. And she won't let me send for the doctor."

Ethan swallowed a spoonful of soup. He didn't look at Elizabeth. "If it was something she wanted you to know about, I'm sure she'd tell you."

Elizabeth's eyebrows arched in surprise. Irritated by his response, she ate her soup in silence.

Isaac fixed Ethan with an unwavering glare when he came with Hannah to serve the main course. Ethan looked briefly at him, then away.

Elizabeth observed it all. Waiting until Hannah and Isaac left the room, she rounded on him.

"So!" she said angrily. "It appears everyone but me knows what's going on. Including you, Ethan! I insist you tell me what happened." When Ethan didn't respond, she pounded a fist on the table. "Tell me!"

Ethan raised agonized eyes to her face. "I was dreaming. A nightmare. I have them sometimes. I must have cried out because Hannah came into my room. I hit her."

"Oh!" Elizabeth sat back, staring at him in dismay. "How could you?"

"It was a dream," Ethan said, desperate to make her understand. "She must have touched me, but I thought it was part of the dream. I apologized, explained what happened, and Hannah understands. She knows I didn't mean to hurt her." Ethan looked down, then miserably, at Elizabeth. "I'll never forgive myself. I'd give anything to take it back."

"Oh, Ethan," Elizabeth said softly. She leaned toward him. "I'm so sorry. I shouldn't have raised my voice. I just..." She gave a slight shake of her head. Her expression turned to one of concern. "I had no idea you had nightmares. What causes them?"

Ethan shook his head, refusing to meet her eyes.

It was obvious he wasn't going to answer, so she asked, "What about Isaac?"

Ethan shrugged. "I think he was ready to kill me last night, but Hannah and Josiah stopped him. I tried talking to him earlier, but he won't have any part of it."

"I see." Elizabeth picked up her fork and began to eat slowly, considering what she should do. Ethan had provided her with a perfect excuse to send him away. *Immediately. It would be best*, she thought, knowing it was what she should do.

Ethan pushed his food around his plate, too upset to eat. He had disrupted the entire household. Hannah was hurt, and he was responsible. Isaac hated him. Even Elizabeth was angry. As much as the prospect frightened him, he would have to leave.

A glance at Elizabeth confirmed it. She was staring at her plate, her mouth set in a grim line. Ethan was on the verge of blurting it out, when she looked up suddenly and announced, "There's no other solution. You can't stay in the carriage house, so you will have to move in here. There's a suitable bedroom at the back, away from the road. I'll have Hannah make it up for you. And tomorrow morning, I will have a talk with Isaac."

For a long moment, Ethan could only stare at her. Then he uttered a heartfelt, "Thank you."

Ethan never went back to his room above the carriage barn. That night, he accompanied Elizabeth and Hannah up the wide, curving front staircase. At the top, Elizabeth bid them good night and turned toward her room. Ethan followed Hannah the length of the hall in the opposite direction, into the biggest bedroom he'd ever seen. A high tester bed stood against the wall ahead of him, flanked by a pair of tall windows. Oil lamps glowed on tables at either side of the bed, and there was another on a writing table at the corner of the room. Still another stood on a table between a pair of wingchairs before the fire. A magnificent Persian rug in red, white, and gold covered the floor.

Hannah went to the chifforobe opposite the fireplace and pulled open a drawer. "They's a nightshirt here. An' clothes fo' you to put on in the mornin'." She gestured to the pitcher and basin atop the bureau. "They's hot water. An' I brung up the book you been readin'." She turned to him. "They anything else you need, Mista Ethan?"

Ethan smiled and shook his head. "Thanks, Hannah. For everything. Sleep well."

He washed while the water was hot, avoiding his reflection in the oval mirror above the bureau. It wasn't until he was drying his hands that he ventured a look. His face had filled out; the dark hollows beneath his eyes were gone. Leaning in, he ran his fingertips over the long, narrow scar on his cheek. At last, he screwed up the courage to look himself in the eye. His reflection stared back, older, more experienced than when he'd left home, but no longer frightened.

He loosened the ribbon that held his hair back and shook his head, watching his hair fall around his face. It surprised him to see how much it changed him. *No wonder people think I'm an Indian...* He toyed briefly with the idea of cutting it, but decided against it. He liked the way it looked, and there was no harm in leaving it for the time being.

He undressed slowly, examining himself in the mirror. The bruises were gone, the sores healed. There were scars from wounds he couldn't remember and a couple, including the one on his left thigh, from ones he did. He was still shockingly thin, ribs and hipbones protruded sharply, but he was gratified to see the return of muscle in his arms and chest.

He donned the long linen nightshirt Hannah had left for him, thinking it a far cry from the patched cotton garment he'd been supplied with at the carriage house. Smiling absently at this latest, unexpected twist his life had taken, he explored the room, stroking rich fabrics and running fingers over carved, polished wood. He climbed onto the high tester bed, but found he wasn't sleepy. Propping himself against four plump pillows, he read for half the night.

It was noon when he ventured downstairs. Apart from the steady drumming of rain, the house was silent. Ethan wandered through it, exploring on his own for the first time. He studied the portrait of James Magrath that hung next to the front door, finding him a pleasant-faced man, with laughing blue eyes. His dark hair was beginning to thin on top, something he'd apparently compensated for with a thick pair of muttonchops. They had the unfortunate effect of making him appear jowly.

Ethan went from the foyer to Elizabeth's sitting room, eyeing the costly knickknacks on display and scrutinizing the paintings on the walls. He ran a finger soundlessly over mother of pearl piano keys before walking across the hall to the front parlor. The pocket doors had been opened, the two rooms combined into one. The fringed, gold drapes had been tied back, but the light through the windows was dreary and gray. Even so, the room was breathtaking. Tiered crystal gasoliers hung from fifteen-foot ceilings at the center of each parlor, and there were matching sconces at intervals along the walls. Each room boasted a white Italian marble fireplace carved with intricate floral designs, and there were matching gilt-framed mirrors above the mantles. Persian rugs covered the hardwood floors; the furniture was the work of old world craftsmen. Paintings hung on the walls opposite the fireplaces, a portrait of Elizabeth prominent among them. She was seated in the gazebo, sunlight dappling the cream lace and pale blue of her dress and the clump of white roses behind her. A parasol lay open at her feet, a beribboned straw hat on the bench beside her, and one hand rested on the open book in her lap. Her dark hair was swept up, soft tendrils falling to bare shoulders, and though she did not smile, the painter had captured the laughter in her eyes.

Rumblings in his stomach reminded Ethan that he'd missed breakfast. He took a last look around before going into the foyer and through the door beneath the landing. Helping himself to an umbrella from a stand beside the back door, he stepped out onto the gallery. The air outside was cold, the rain pelting down. His trip across the courtyard was accomplished at a mad dash.

Hannah looked up, breaking off in mid-sentence, when he burst into the kitchen. She was seated near the center of the room, a pile of green beans and a bowl on the table in front of her. Another woman was stirring a pot atop a large iron cook stove. She looked at Ethan, then guiltily, at Hannah. For a moment, no one spoke.

"Have a seat, Mista Ethan." Hannah tilted her head toward the other woman. "This here's Hattie. Miz 'Lizbet's cook."

"Mista Ethan." Hattie glanced from him to Hannah, then turned back to the stove.

She was the woman he'd glimpsed from the carriage house window, young and light-skinned, pleasantly rounded with close-cropped hair, large dark eyes and full lips.

"Dinner almos' ready." Hannah informed him. "You welcome to eat here wit' us. O' I kin bring you food to the dinin' room."

The thought of eating alone in the dining room was daunting. Ethan threw Hannah a look of gratitude and pulled out a chair. "I'll eat here. No sense going out in the rain."

Hannah nodded and picked up a handful of beans. As she snapped and Hattie stirred, and the silence in the room lengthened, it quickly became apparent that he had been their topic of conversation. Ethan shifted uncomfortably and looked around.

The kitchen occupied half the building. Straight ahead, through a wide archway, were the long tables and sinks of the scullery. The walls of both rooms were whitewashed; the floors red stucco tile. There were windows on three sides. Rain coursing down obscured the main house and the carriage barn, but beyond the scullery, he glimpsed the long narrow building that housed the washhouse, additional servants' quarters and the privies.

The kitchen door opened, and Josiah and Isaac came in, stomping their feet and shaking water from their clothes. Ethan watched apprehensively as Isaac hung his coat on a peg beside the door.

He turned, eyeing Ethan before inclining his head in a slight nod. "Afta'noon, Mista Ethan."

"Afternoon, Isaac," Ethan said, relieved that Elizabeth's talk had apparently done some good.

The door opened again, this time to admit Ben and Moses. As they removed their coats, the girl Ethan had seen his first day emerged from the scullery. She was slender and pretty—about twelve, he guessed. She looked at him shyly when Hattie introduced her as her daughter, Rose.

Ethan nodded in wordless surprise as Rose hurried to help her mother carry food to the table. Up close, she still looked white. Her skin was lighter than his own, her eyes a dusky shade of blue. Dark hair hung in loose curls to her waist, tied back with a red satin ribbon. Nothing about her betrayed her Negro heritage.

During the meal, it fell to Hannah and Josiah to carry the bulk of the conversation. Isaac said little, and Ethan could tell from the occasional looks the older man threw him that he wasn't entirely forgiven. The others, uncomfortable in Ethan's presence, consumed their food in silence.

23

It remained rainy and cold for four days. Each morning, Hannah laid a fire in the library, and everyday after breakfast, Ethan retired there to read. Once, Elizabeth joined him for several hours, saying she needed to deal with correspondence. As the week wore on, she returned home earlier each day, and the two of them spent quiet afternoons together, talking and reading.

By week's end, the rain let up, the skies cleared, and the temperature rose. When Ethan raised the shades in his room on Friday morning, the sun was shining, and only a few lacey clouds traced the sky.

Hattie was the only one in the house when he came downstairs. He ate the breakfast she brought in for him, then wandered into the library. Rose was standing with her back to him, a feather duster dangling from one hand, gazing out the window.

"Mornin', Rose."

She started guiltily. He heard a mumbled, "Mo'nin', suh," as she set to work with the duster.

Ethan settled in his customary chair and picked up his book, his eyes following her. "You could pass, Rose," he said after a time. "You know that?"

Her back was to him, but he saw the duster hesitate.

"You ever think about it? When you get older, living as a white woman?"

Rose's shoulders rose and fell. The duster moved faster as she worked her way away from him. Ethan watched her, thinking how arbitrary life was. In a few short weeks, he'd gone from degradation and abuse to being addressed as sir by a servant whose skin was lighter than his own. He shook his head. If there was any logic to it, it escaped him.

Rose dusted her way to the far end of the room before darting a glance in his direction. Finding Ethan watching her, she turned and fled.

He sat a few moments longer before opening his book. The words failed to hold him, and before long, he set it aside. The room was stuffy, the heat from the fire oppressive, so he got up and went to one of the back windows. Turning the catch, he lifted the sash and was instantly enveloped by a mass of warm, sultry air. The thud of the ax reached him, but the carriage house blocked his view of the woodpile. Bored and restless, he left the library and wandered outside.

He came within sight of the woodpile to see Josiah, stripped to the waist, splitting the last of the cut logs. Sunlight glistened off sweat, rippling over muscle in his arms and back.

Josiah saw Ethan and lowered the ax. Wiping his brow on the back of one arm, he leaned on the handle and waited for Ethan to join him. "I got used to you doin' this," he said with a grin.

Ethan held out a hand for the ax.

Josiah pulled it away. "Devil'd be to pay if'n Isaac found you doin' my work."

"Please, Josiah. I've been cooped up in the house all week."

Josiah upended another log and swung the ax, embedding the blade in the wood before replying. "I tell you what. Isaac done took Miz 'Lizbet off somewhere, sayin' she won' be back 'til late. Say you was to finish splittin' these logs while I gets the saw? Then, if'n you wants, we can work." He lifted the log with the ax and brought it down hard. It fell away in two pieces. He handed the ax to Ethan and set off toward the carriage barn.

There were only a few pieces of wood remaining. Ethan shrugged out of his coat and had them split by the time Josiah returned carrying a long, two-handled blade. Together, they wrestled one of the tree trunks into place. Then they each grabbed a handle and lined up the cut. After the first cut, Ethan called a halt to remove his shirt. Using it to wipe the sweat from his face, he tossed it aside. Grinning a challenge to Josiah, he flexed his fingers and wrapped them around the handle. Once they established a rhythm, the saw whipped back and forth between them and sawdust flew.

When the entire log had been cut into sections, Josiah straightened and grinned. "You sho' better at this than Ben or Moses!"

"Let's cut another."

They worked until Ethan's hands began to blister, and he begged to stop. Anxious about Isaac's return, Josiah agreed.

Tired and dirty, but exhilarated, Ethan walked with him to the carriage barn, intending to walk through it to the house. The sound of hoofbeats stopped him as he stepped into the carriage yard. Striding to the wall, he peered through the hedge in time to see a sporty two-wheeled calash zipping up the drive beyond the gazebo. Elizabeth sat close beside the well-dressed man holding the reins. He said something, and she laughed, touching his arm as the calash spun out of sight.

The gesture provoked an unexpected stab of jealousy. Ethan rolled his shoulders, telling himself not to be ridiculous. Nevertheless, he waited, waited what seemed an extraordinarily long time, until the man reappeared alone, passing Isaac coming along the drive in Elizabeth's buggy, and disappeared through the gate.

Ethan went to the pump and washed off the worst of the dirt and sweat. Using his shirt as a towel, he put it back on and went inside, intending to slip up the back stairs. As he stepped into the passage, he heard Elizabeth's voice from the foyer.

"Where's Ethan, Rose? Have you seen him?"

Ethan hurried to the stairs. He had his hand on the railing, a foot on the bottom step, when the door opened and Elizabeth burst through.

"Ethan!" she exclaimed. "I've had the most amazing day! Come! Let me you about it."

Ethan gestured toward the top of the stairs. "I was going up to change..."

Elizabeth's eyes focused on bare skin beneath the unbuttoned shirt. Her heart gave a little leap. She looked up, found him watching her, and blushed. "Can't it wait?" When he didn't move, she said, "Please, Ethan. It's important. Come with me to the library."

Curious, puzzled by her behavior, Ethan nodded. He held the door to the foyer and followed her through the back parlor, buttoning his shirt and stuffing the tails into his britches as he went. He was shrugging into his coat when Elizabeth closed the door to the library and leaned against it. Ethan turned, a question on his face, and the news burst from her.

"I spoke with Thomas today!"

The question turned to disbelief. "Where? How is he?"

In truth, he had been gaunt and dirty, but Elizabeth said, "Much better now that he knows you're safe. He's been half-crazed with worry." She gestured to the nearest chairs. "Shall we sit? I'll tell you all about it."

For more than a week, since Ethan first mentioned Thomas, Elizabeth had spent many of her waking hours planning and organizing the trip to the camp. She had solicited contributions from wealthy friends, women's charitable organizations and churches—anyone she could charm or shame into making a donation. She'd spent her own money purchasing whatever food, clothing and blankets could be found for sale in Mobile. This morning, she and a group of women, escorted by the man who was friends with the commandant, had gone to the camp.

Initially, the commandant had been opposed to any form of contact between the women and the prisoners. He insisted that the donations be left at the camp for distribution by the guards. Elizabeth persisted, and in the end, the commandant relented, allowing the prisoners to file past the women who handed out the precious commodities while murmuring words of compassion.

Elizabeth's heart had been wrenched by the suffering in the men's faces and their pitiful expressions of gratitude. She had been so caught up in what she was doing that she nearly missed Thomas. She later thought, that had it not been for the yellow curls, he might have passed without her notice. As it was, he was already walking away when she realized who he was. Without thinking, she'd said, "Thomas?"

Thomas turned and looked blankly at her. As the women and guards gaped in astonishment, the lie she'd rehearsed came quickly to her lips. "Thomas Murray?" she asked, and he nodded.

Elizabeth looked at the women. "He's my cousin," she said, the boldness of what she was doing lending her voice just the right amount of breathless excitement. "We haven't seen each other since I moved to Mobile." Turning to the nearest guard she said, "Please, may I speak with him?"

"No one's allowed to talk to the prisoners, ma'am. Not without the commandant's permission."

"Oh, please!" Elizabeth cried, tears springing to her eyes. "Let me talk with him for just a few minutes."

A murmur of support went up from the ladies. The guard looked at them, realizing he was up against a situation he was ill equipped to handle. "Let me fetch the commandant, ma'am," he said, backing away.

He hurried off while everyone, guards, women and prisoners, waited. Elizabeth didn't dare look at Thomas for fear he would give her away. Instead, she merged into the circle of sympathetic women. Dabbing her eyes with her handkerchief, she murmured, "To see him like this after all these years," and "I don't know what I'll do if they won't let me talk to him," to a comforting chorus of platitudes.

The guard returned in short order, saying that she might, with the commandant's permission, have five minutes with the prisoner, but only under close supervision. He motioned to Thomas, ordering him away from the other prisoners. One of the women offered to accompany her, but Elizabeth declined. Drawing a deep breath, she walked to where Thomas waited. She was relieved to see he was grinning, even as his eyes questioned.

Elizabeth gave the guard a sweet, tearful, pointed smile and waited for him to move a short distance away. "Elizabeth," she murmured into the heavily scented handkerchief she'd brought for the occasion. "Take my hand."

Thomas had no idea what was happening, but he was delighted to oblige. "Elizabeth."

"Ethan is safe. He is well," she whispered.

Thomas' grip slackened perceptibly, and she said, "Keep talking loudly enough for the guard to hear."

It took Thomas a moment to react after the unexpected announcement, but then he blurted, "Elizabeth! I can't believe it's you!"

"You may release my hand," Elizabeth told him.

With great reluctance, Thomas did. Elizabeth turned away, wiping her eyes, and moved a few steps further from the guard. Thomas followed.

"Is he still in Mobile?" he asked leaning toward her solicitously.

"Yes. At my home. He slept for the first couple of weeks, but he's stronger now. When he's ready, I plan to give him what he needs to get home. At this point, his main concern is for you." She raised her voice and, for the guard's benefit, asked, "How are you, Thomas? And how is your dear mother?"

"I'm well," he told her. "As well as can be expected." In an undertone he added, "Better now that I know Ethan's safe. I've lost sleep worrying about him."

"There's no need to worry. He's rested and putting on weight. Physically, he's fine."

Elizabeth looked up, and Thomas saw the question in her eyes. He grappled with what to reply. After a moment, he said, "He was treated badly at Cahaba. Worse than the rest of us."

Elizabeth nodded. "He implied as much. I was hoping you could tell me more."

Thomas cast a surreptitious glance at the guard. "Now isn't the time. I know some of what went on, but not everything. And other things, it isn't my place to tell. If you're going to hear them, it'll have to be from Ethan."

Elizabeth smiled. "You've been a good friend to him, Thomas. He speaks fondly of you." The guard edged closer, and Elizabeth raised her voice. "Tell me what I can do to help. What do you need?" She directed a fetching smile at the guard, adding, "I'm sure arrangements can be made."

"Food. Always food. And clothes. I've been wearing these for months."

"I noticed." Elizabeth wrinkled her nose behind the handkerchief. Thomas saw the corners of her eyes crease as she smiled.

The guard cleared his throat.

Elizabeth raised her voice for his benefit. "I've missed you, Thomas. Now that I know you're here, I'll arrange to visit on a regular basis."

"I'd like that," Thomas told her, meaning it. He deposited a cousinly kiss to the cheek she presented and watched with unabashed admiration as she walked back to the waiting group of women. The guard nudged him, and he reluctantly turned away.

"So I told Thomas you are well, and he says you're not to worry," Elizabeth said, winding up the abbreviated version she'd told Ethan. "He's fine, all things considered. And the ladies are making plans to return. Now that they've seen conditions for themselves, they're determined to do all they can to help." Elizabeth bit her lip, and her eyes clouded. "I should have guessed what it would be like. I should have known from the state you were in when you arrived. But nothing prepared me for being in a place like that. It's so... so hopeless." Her voice caught as she added, "And the men—boys mostly—were so grateful." She dabbed at her eyes with the overused handkerchief. A thought came to her and she looked at Ethan, her expression faintly accusing. "You were trying to protect me, weren't you?"

One shoulder rose and fell. "It seemed best."

He looked so guilty that Elizabeth couldn't help smiling. "I spoke with the commandant and obtained permission to visit Thomas again. I intend to return once a week and take what I can." She paused, watching Ethan's face. "So there's no need for worry. I'll see he's looked after."

Ethan said nothing, struggling with a wide range of emotions—relief at hearing Thomas was well; gratitude to Elizabeth for finding him; dismay at the squalor she'd witnessed; delight at her courage and resourcefulness. In the end, he smiled. "Thank you." The smile grew and he added, "You're quite an actress, aren't you?"

She beamed. "Do you think so?"

"Without a doubt."

Elizabeth laughed.

Ethan looked as if he might join her, but instead his look turned serious. He rose and stood before her, holding out his hands. Elizabeth took them and came to her feet.

"Thank you, Elizabeth. I owe you so much. I don't know how I'll ever—"

Something in her expression stopped him. He stared wordlessly at her, baffled by what he thought he saw. A small smile formed at the corners of her mouth, and she stepped closer, laying her face and hands against his chest. Ethan stood motionless, his heart racing, unsure how to respond. He placed his hands on her shoulders, holding her tentatively for several seconds, before releasing her. He would have stepped back, but Elizabeth's arms came around him, holding him close. She tilted her head back and smiled, the look in her eyes leaving no room for doubt. Placing a hand behind his head, she pulled his face down to hers, kissing him once softly on the lips, then again with an urgency that took his breath away. Unable, unwilling to stop himself, Ethan returned her kisses with a mounting passion of his own.

Elizabeth moaned and pressed against him, bringing him sharply, to his senses. He pulled away and stumbled across the room, appalled by what he'd done. He'd learned the hard way when he was sixteen that women like her were beyond his reach. Now, like a fool, he'd overstepped his bounds.

I need to apologize, he thought, panicked. *I made a mistake. I misunderstood and made a mistake. It's not me she wants. Not like that...*

"Ethan?"

Struck by the plaintive note in her voice, Ethan half-turned to face her. Hurt and vulnerability were the last things he expected to see. *Not me,* his mind protested. *Not like that.*

"Ethan, I..." Elizabeth gestured helplessly, looking as if she might cry.

"I'm sorry," he said, offering her a tentative smile. "Please, Elizabeth. I'm sorry. I didn't mean to..." His words trailed off as relief flooded her face.

"Oh, Ethan!" Elizabeth came headlong across the room, throwing her arms about him and burying her face against his chest. "I thought for a moment you didn't want me."

Her words were muffled; Ethan couldn't believe he'd heard correctly. He held her timidly, but as she continued to press against him, he wrapped his arms more tightly about her. His reward was a contented sigh.

The sound emboldened him. He lowered his head, inhaling the fresh scent of her hair. Running a hand down her back, he marveled at how small she was. Always before, he'd thought her strong, imposing even. Now, in his arms, she seemed fragile. His hand half encircled her tiny waist, and her skin, where his fingers brushed her neck, was downy soft. He closed his eyes and held her to him, pushing reservations aside and savoring the moment.

Safe in his arms, Elizabeth's eyes filled with tears of relief. She had been so afraid, when he turned away, that he'd rejected her. She pressed her head against his damp shirt, listening to the hurried beating of his heart and inhaling the sweaty, masculine scent of him.

Ethan shifted, and Elizabeth looked up to see the question in his eyes.

"Are you sure... ?" he asked, unable to believe what was happening.

Elizabeth nodded, smiling through tears. Ethan searched her face, desperate to believe she meant it. Her look assured him. As he grew convinced, Ethan's expression softened. He kissed her on the forehead, then gently on the lips. She responded in kind, and they kissed slowly, softly as they came to know one another.

A tap on the door caused them to spring apart. Ethan walked quickly to the fireplace and stood with one elbow resting on the mantle, while Elizabeth sank onto the nearest chair and pinned back a loose strand of hair. "Yes," she said. "What is it?"

Isaac stuck his head in the door. "I come to light the lamps, Miz 'Lizbet."

Ethan and Elizabeth looked around, aware suddenly of how dark the room had become.

"Yes, Isaac. Please," Elizabeth said, getting to her feet. "We were just going up to change for supper."

With that she walked from the room, leaving Ethan to weather several long seconds of Isaac's scrutiny before he, too, bolted for the door.

An hour alone to think about what had transpired, and they were shy with one another at supper. It wasn't until later, when they retired behind the closed door of Elizabeth's sitting room, that they relaxed. They spent the evening together on one of the settees, Ethan's arm around Elizabeth's shoulders, her head nestled against him, kissing and talking. Later, they kissed again, longer and more deeply, before parting at the top of the stairs.

Ethan watched Elizabeth walk away, half-hoping she would motion him to follow. She reached the door to her room and turned back, bestowing on him the most enticing smile he had ever seen. Ethan's hopes soared. They were dashed immediately, when she closed the door firmly behind her.

Ethan was still staring at her door when he heard Hannah's footsteps on the back stairs. He turned and walked quickly along the hall to his own room.

He changed for bed, but found he wasn't the least bit sleepy. He wandered the room for a time before turning out the lamps and raising one of the shades. Leaning against the jamb, he gazed at the lighted windows of the kitchen and the carriage house beyond, marveling at how quickly things changed. A smile played across his lips as he relived the events of the evening, recalling Elizabeth's scent, her touch, and the myriad expressions that played across her face.

After a time, his thoughts drifted. For the first time since the night at Cahaba when he'd vowed to survive, he allowed himself to think of his family. To summon up the faces of his parents and yearn for them. To imagine what Kate must look like now that she was, what? Fourteen? To worry about Josh without Jamie. And, finally, to mourn—for Duncan, dead at twenty-six, for Jamie, who'd been twenty-four, and for Seth, killed two months shy of his twenty-second birthday.

As the last of the emotional barriers he'd erected came tumbling down, the pain of missing them became almost palpable. Ethan caught his breath and gripped the sash tightly as a torrent of emotions washed over him.

Elizabeth closed the door and leaned against it before crossing the room to ring for Hannah. A nightdress had been laid out, but she rejected it, selecting one that was more elaborate. Hannah raised questioning eyebrows when she saw the substitution, but Elizabeth pretended not to notice. Hannah, obligingly, said nothing. She helped Elizabeth out of her dress and unlaced her corset before Elizabeth bid her goodnight and finished dressing for bed by herself.

She took great care with her appearance, removing the pins from her hair and letting the long dark tresses cascade over her shoulders, brushing them until they shone. She washed her face, pinched color into her cheeks, and applied scent to her neck, her wrists, and after a moment's indecision, between her breasts.

Half an hour had passed by the time she climbed into bed. She opened a book, barely noticing what she read as the minutes ticked by. Twenty minutes later, she thought she heard a sound in the hallway and looked expectantly toward the door. When there was no tap, when it failed to open, she settled back, fighting down disappointment. Ten more minutes, and she could contain herself no longer. She went to the door and opened it, peering down the darkened hall toward Ethan's room.

Why doesn't he come? she wondered, pacing the room, glancing at the clock every few minutes, amazed by how slowly time was passing. Another creak from the hallway, and she was back in bed in an instant. This time, when the door failed to open, she went to it immediately. Still no one.

Maybe he isn't coming, she thought gloomily. She had been so certain that he would.

Moments later, realization struck. *Maybe he has no idea what's expected!* She had been so preoccupied with needing him, with wanting him, that it had never occurred to her he might be inexperienced. There had been the tentative nature of his first kiss. And he'd pulled away when she'd pressed against him. At first, she'd thought he was rejecting her, but now she remembered his expression when he turned to face her, and knew she must be right.

Elizabeth wandered the room, trying to decide what to do. Twice she went to the door and opened it. Twice, she closed it. Eventually, she stepped into the hallway. She hesitated before releasing the knob, then walked along the hall to Ethan's room. She had never imagined doing anything remotely like this, and the thought of seducing him both thrilled and terrified her.

What if I'm wrong? What if he knew what was expected and chose not to come? She turned and walked back to her room. When she got to the door, she stopped. *But if I'm right...*

Elizabeth retraced her steps. At the end of the hall, she paused, twisting her handkerchief into a damp knot, and summoning the courage to go in.

Utterly spent, Ethan let go of the window and groped his way to bed. He climbed into it and lay half-thinking, half-dreaming—caught between wakefulness and sleep. The muted click as the door opened brought him instantly awake. He pushed up on one elbow and waited, tense in the darkness.

Elizabeth stepped into the light from the open shade, and Ethan released the breath he'd been holding. He lay quietly, waiting to see what she would do.

Her hair hung loose over her shoulders and she wore a long white nightdress, trimmed with ribbons and lace. Frozen for a moment in the shaft of moonlight, she was more beautiful than he'd ever seen her.

"Ethan?" she whispered softly. "Are you awake?"

"Yes... ?"

Elizabeth stayed where she was a moment longer. Then she stepped out of the light and came toward him. He waited, watching her white form move through the darkness, then felt the mattress give as she climbed the steps and sat beside him.

"Ethan?" she repeated, her voice tinged with uncertainty.

His heart pounding wildly, Ethan touched her hand where it lay on the quilt beside him.

Elizabeth responded by leaning in and kissing him on the lips, once quickly, then again, more deeply.

Eventually, she pulled back, bringing up a hand to caress his cheek before running her fingers into his hair. "Ethan," she asked quietly, "have you never been with a woman?"

He hesitated, embarrassed, before giving a slight shake of his head. "No."

Elizabeth smiled. "Come then," she said softly. "I'll teach you."

24

There was movement in the bed beside him. Ethan jerked awake. For a panicked instant he didn't remember what it meant. Then he smiled and rolled over, propping his head on one hand to look at her.

Elizabeth lay on her back, her head turned slightly away from him, one pale arm exposed atop the covers. Ethan touched it, tracing the faint blue veins on the back of her hand with a finger. Elizabeth murmured in her sleep, and he leaned over and kissed her gently on the cheek. Her eyes fluttered open, and she smiled sleepily and pulled him to her.

It was noon when Elizabeth returned to her room and rang for Hannah. The shades had been raised, the bed made, so she knew Hannah had been there earlier. She sat at her dressing table and began brushing her hair, dreading what was sure to be Hannah's disapproval.

There was a tap at the door, and Hannah entered, catching Elizabeth's eye in the mirror before crossing the room to set the pitcher of water she was carrying on the bureau. In the silence that followed, Elizabeth turned to face her. To her amazement, Hannah smiled. She walked to Elizabeth, and taking the brush, gestured for her to turn around. Their eyes met in the mirror.

"I sho hopes you knows what you doin, Miz 'Lizbet."

"I do, Hannah." Elizabeth smiled. "He makes me very happy."

Hannah stopped brushing and looked at her. "He young, Miz 'Lizbet. One day, he bound to get restless. He ain't gonna be content trapped here in this house."

"But, Hannah, he won't be. The war will end, and he'll be able to go about openly."

Hannah studied Elizabeth's reflection before saying, "An' what Mista James' folks gonna say? What all you rich white friends gonna say? They gonna ask where he come from an' how long he been here. An' a whole lotta eyebrows gonna go up when they sees the color of his skin."

Elizabeth's eyes filled with tears. Hannah was right. She wasn't saying anything Elizabeth hadn't already considered. She responded, venting uncertainty with anger. "We'll just have to deal with that when the time comes, won't we, Hannah? I'll thank you not to mention it again."

Hannah shook her head and concentrated on arranging Elizabeth's hair. When the last pin was in place, she looked up to find Elizabeth watching her anxiously.

"He a good boy," Hannah said with a smile. "Good an' kind. If'n he makes you happy, then that's all what matters."

That night, Elizabeth left no doubt as to her wishes. After waiting what he thought was a reasonable amount of time, Ethan joined her in her bed.

The following day was Sunday. They rose early and bid one another a lingering farewell. Ethan watched from the window as Isaac handed Elizabeth into the buggy and drove her off to church, followed by her weekly dinner with James' parents. He remained at the window long after the buggy had gone, watching the road. Through the oaks lining the drive, he caught occasional glimpses of vehicles rolling past.

Suddenly, the house seemed suffocating; its walls confining. Ethan turned from the window and strode through the empty house to the back door. He hurried down the steps and across the courtyard—past the kitchen and the building housing the washroom and privies, past the kitchen garden, down the slope, and into the woods. Out of sight of the house, he veered left, away from the woodpile, toward a section of the grounds he had never visited before.

He knew, from looking out his bedroom window, that this side of the property was wilder, less cultivated than the other. There were gardens close to the house, but they gave way quickly to trees and shrubs that had been allowed to grow wild once the servants departed. Ethan made his way through the undergrowth, hoping to get close to the road.

It proved easier than he'd expected. He found a spot, inside a tangle of bushes, where he could view the road unobserved, and sat watching as the citizenry of The Hill passed by, dressed in their Sunday best. Despite the hardships imposed on them by war, they seemed cheerful, almost gay as they promenaded along the broad tree-lined road. People in carriages called greetings to one another and pulled to the side of the road to chat. Men and women on horseback rode by in pairs and in groups. Ethan overheard occasional snippets of conversation and strained to hear more, realizing suddenly how little he knew of what was going on in the world. As he thought it, three middle-aged men drew their horses to a halt in the shade of a nearby oak.

"But this'll be the third line of entrenchments the army's built inland since the spring of '62," a portly gentleman astride a bay mare protested. "The *third* in a year and a half. Every time a new chief engineer arrives, he finds a fault with what the man befo' him did and starts all over again. First it was Lienur, then Leadbetter, now it's von Seliaha callin' on us to lend him our slaves. I for one, fail to see the point in it. If the Yanks are goin' to attack Mobile, they'll come by sea, not by land. I say, better to put all our resources into stoppin' them at the mouth of the bay than wastin' time diggin' ditches an' destroyin' our gardens up here on The Hill."

"Now, Oliver," an older man chided. "You don't care what the army does, just as long as they keep you and yours from fallin' into Yankee hands. What you resent is bein' forced to give up yo' slaves to build the durned things."

"I do, sir, when it happens repeatedly," Oliver sniffed, his feathers ruffled. "I'm as patriotic as the next man, but I believe the army should decide on a course of action and stick to it. Surely both of you will admit that *three* sets of earthworks is excessive." He leveled a piercing gaze at first one man, then the other.

"It could be yo' right, Oliver," the third man agreed. "Only time'll tell. But you should know that I dined with General Maury last night, and he confirmed the rumors we've been hearin'. In his opinion, a Yankee attack on Mobile is imminent."

"And you believe him?" Oliver asked. "As I recall, he was convinced of the same thing last August and nothin' came of it."

"He seems certain this time. He's asked fo' experienced artillerymen to replace the infantrymen at the batteries—and this won't make you happy, Oliver—he's plannin' to ask fo' more slaves so the soldiers workin' on the defenses can return to their commands."

"And where does he think this attack will come from?" the other man asked as they moved on.

"I'm not sure he knows. He has von Seliaha at work improving fortifications up and down the bay and..."

They moved out of earshot. Ethan sank back, wondering if Federal forces really were planning to attack Mobile. Watching the seemingly carefree populace parade by, he found it hard to believe there was a war on; much less that attack was imminent. As if to confirm his thoughts, a band struck up not far away, breaking into the rousing strains of *Dixie*. Ethan half-listened, his mind wandering as the band moved on to other tunes.

Watching people move past him on the road made him long to move about freely—to go wherever he wanted, whenever he wanted. And he wanted desperately to see his family again. But even as he longed for them, the thought of making his way back through enemy lines was still too daunting, the fear of capture still too great. *Besides*, he reminded himself, *going back would mean leaving Elizabeth*. At the moment, that was something he had no desire to do.

The street had all but emptied, the music long since stopped, when Ethan roused himself and got to his feet. Looking around to be certain he was unobserved, he stepped from his hiding place and slipped silently back through the trees, taking care not to show himself until he was well behind the house. He was passing the door to the kitchen when Hattie called to him.

"Mista Ethan, suh! Miz 'Lizbet been askin' fo' you."

"Where is she?"

"In the liberry, last I knowed.

Elizabeth was standing before one of the front windows, her back to him, when he walked in. She turned, dropped the handkerchief she'd been twisting, and rushed to him across the room.

"I thought something bad had happened!" she cried, flinging herself into his embrace. "Or that you'd gone. I couldn't find you anywhere, and no one had seen you for hours."

Stricken by guilt, Ethan held her close. "I was outside. I could hear a band playing and lost track of time. I'm sorry," he said, nuzzling her hair. "I didn't mean to frighten you." He lifted her chin and smiled. When she smiled back, he kissed her.

During the next week, Elizabeth was gone from the house only as often as necessary to meet obligations and maintain appearances. When she was away, Ethan prowled the grounds, careful to watch for her buggy so he could be back inside before she had cause to worry. Their time together was spent talking, laughing or reading, but always touching. Each night, after a lingering kiss at the top of the stairs, Ethan would wait half an hour before joining her in her bed.

When she left for church the following Sunday, Ethan went to the library and sat at her writing desk. He searched the drawers until he found paper without her name or initials, and began a letter to his parents.

He assumed that mail leaving Mobile for the North would be opened and read, so he was careful not to say anything that would betray his whereabouts or lead authorities to Elizabeth. His first attempt revealed too much. The next was cold and stilted. Upon further consideration he settled for:

> *Dear Ma, Pa and Kate,*
> *I am writing to tell you I am safe and well. There has been no fighting as yet in Mobile, though people do suffer from the shortages of war. I hope you are well and that we will be together soon.*
> *With all my love,*

He signed his name, addressed an envelope, and went in search of Hannah. He found her in the dining room, setting the table for supper. She looked up and smiled when he walked in.

"Afternoon, Mista Ethan."

"Afternoon, Hannah. I've written a letter to my folks. To let them know I'm alive. I was wondering if you'd see it mailed?"

Hannah took the envelope. "Isaac kin take it when he drive Miz 'Lizbet to town in the mornin'."

Ethan thanked her, and would have left the room, but Hannah's next words stopped him.

"You take good care of her, Mista Ethan. See she doan come to no harm."

He turned to find Hannah's look grown stern.

"I would never do anything to hurt her, Hannah. I think you know that. Under normal circumstances, I'd swear to do everything in my power to protect her. But since she's the one protecting me, that would be presumptuous, don't you think?"

He raised an eyebrow, and in spite of herself, Hannah laughed. She had never suspected that this cocky, self-assured side of him existed. He grinned at her and left the room.

Tuesday morning at breakfast, Elizabeth announced her plan to visit Thomas. "To take him a Christmas package," she added.

Ethan looked at her in surprise. "When is it?"

"What?"

"Christmas."

"Friday. Didn't you know?"

Ethan shook his head. He finished his breakfast in silence, trying not to dwell on images of Christmases at home that came unbidden to his mind. Instead, he tried to imagine spending the holiday with Elizabeth and found he was looking forward to it.

He looked up to find Elizabeth's eyes on him, her expression troubled. His heart thudded in alarm. He kept it from his face as he asked, "Is something wrong?"

Elizabeth bit her lip. "There's something I haven't told you. I'll be leaving Thursday to spend Christmas with the Magraths. I won't return until Sunday evening." She looked down at the napkin she'd crumpled in her lap, then at him, desperate to explain. "It's something we did when James was alive, and I've continued to do it. I can't not go at this late date without causing concern."

Ethan nodded. "When will you see Thomas?" he asked, trying to deflect the hurt.

"I need to go to the warehouse this morning to meet with some people from the Military Aid Society," Elizabeth replied, watching him closely. "After that, I'll go to the camp. I should be home by early afternoon, and we can spend the rest of the day together."

"That'll be nice," Ethan told her, careful to keep his voice neutral and offering her a brief smile. He pushed back from the table and walked around to hold her chair. As they left the dining room he said, "Be sure to give Thomas my best. Tell him I think of him."

When Elizabeth was ready to leave, Ethan accompanied her to the front door and stood to one side while she donned the cloak Hannah held for her. Collecting her gloves from the table, she smiled at him uncertainly. Ethan dutifully kissed her cheek and waited until Hannah closed the door behind her. Then he stalked through the house and slammed out the back door.

Josiah looked up from the horse he was grooming, saw the expression on Ethan's face, and the greeting died on his lips. Ethan snatched the ax from its peg, threw open the back door and marched down to the woodpile where he proceeded to split logs as rapidly as he could.

It wasn't until exhaustion forced him to slow his pace that he began to think rationally. Elizabeth was just as trapped as he was. Trapped by custom and duty. He doubted she wanted to spend Christmas with her former in-laws any more than he wanted her to. All either of them could do was make the best of it. *Next year*, he told himself, *when the war's over and things are back to normal, it'll be different.* The thought stopped him as he was hoisting the ax. He let the head drop to the ground. Two days earlier, he'd been thinking of leaving; now he was thinking of staying. He shook his head, having no idea what he wanted.

Despite the coolness of the air, he was drenched with sweat by the time he finished. Drained by emotion and sustained activity, he walked to the carriage barn and replaced the ax. Josiah was cleaning one of the stalls when Ethan passed by and didn't look up.

Ethan stopped at the kitchen and asked for hot water to be brought up before retiring to his room. By the time Elizabeth returned, he had washed and changed, and was seated in the library before the fire, an open book on his lap.

25

The night before she left for Christmas, Elizabeth experienced one of Ethan's nightmares for the first time. They had made love, then fallen asleep. Hours later, Elizabeth was startled awake when the bed shuddered violently. Ethan had worked himself to the far side, and as she watched, his body jerked, and he screamed, a terrible, anguished cry. Terrified, she rolled out of bed and fumbled for the matches on the bedside table. Holding up the lamp, she looked at him. The covers on his side of the bed had been kicked aside. Ethan was lying on his back, muscles tensed, staring blindly at the ceiling. As she watched, he flung himself toward her and moaned through clenched jaws.

Mindful of what had befallen Hannah, Elizabeth set down the lamp and collected her nightgown from the floor. Slipping it over her head, she stood well out of harm's way and said his name. Ethan gave no indication he heard. He slammed his heels down hard on the bed and arched his back, flopping onto his side with a cry that froze her blood. Her voice shaking, Elizabeth repeated his name.

Ethan continued to moan, his breath coming in short, ragged gasps. Tears streamed down his face, and his body glistened with sweat. He struggled mightily against some unseen aggressor as Elizabeth continued to call his name. At last, he seemed to hear her and lay still, listening. She said his name again, and his head turned toward her.

"Ethan?"

Another moment, and his face relaxed. Slowly, the tension left his body. Elizabeth continued to repeat his name, more softly now, telling him to wake up. Before long, his eyes opened. He looked at her, blankly at first, then with mounting concern.

"Elizabeth? What's wrong?" he asked, coming fully awake. Supporting himself on one elbow, he held out a hand.

"Are you awake?" she asked, reluctant to take it.

He seemed confused by the question. "Of course I am."

He beckoned with his fingers, and she cautiously reached out a hand. He took it and pulled her onto the bed, sitting up and taking her in his arms. He was soaked with sweat, and when she pressed a hand against his chest, she could feel the frantic beating of his heart.

"What's wrong?" he asked.

"You were dreaming. A nightmare."

His stomach gave a sickening lurch. "Did I hurt you?"

She shook her head. "No."

Ethan hugged her to him. "Thank God," he murmured. And, after a moment, "I'm sorry."

"There's nothing to be sorry for, Ethan. It was a nightmare. It's over." Elizabeth hoped she sounded calmer than she felt. In truth, now that it was over, she was more frightened than ever. Whatever had happened to trigger that kind of memory scared her to death. She shivered, and he misunderstood.

"You're cold. Let's get you back under the covers." He reached around, straightening the bedclothes, and moved to make room for her. When she was settled, he tucked the blankets around her and held her close. Safe in his arms, she slept. Ethan lay awake for hours, afraid the nightmare would return.

When Elizabeth awakened the next morning, Ethan was sleeping soundly. She kissed him, and when he didn't respond, slipped out of bed. She donned a robe over her nightgown and puttered about the room, gathering things she would take with her while waiting for him to wake up. She was beginning to think she would have to wake him, when he stirred. She turned to find him watching her. He smiled, the same sweet smile that melted her heart, and she went to stand beside the bed. Eyes holding hers, he loosened the tie of her robe. As the robe slid to the floor, he folded back the covers and she slipped in beside him.

He made love to her tenderly; employing everything she'd taught him, desiring nothing more than to give her pleasure. Afterward, they lay together; Elizabeth nestled against him, her head on his chest.

It was Ethan who finally broke the silence. "It's getting late," he said softly. "I should go so you can get dressed."

At first, Elizabeth didn't respond. Then she hugged him, burying her face against him. "I don't want to go. You know that, don't you?"

Ethan raised his head from the pillow and kissed the top of hers. "I know." Lifting her arm, he slid out from under her.

She watched as he dressed, accepted the kiss he planted on her forehead. The door closed behind him, and she lay without moving. Eventually, she let out a long, unhappy sigh and rang for Hannah.

Ethan was waiting when she came downstairs. Hannah helped her with her cloak, while Isaac, laden with gifts, stood near the front door. With both servants watching, their good-byes were restrained and brief. As the buggy carrying Elizabeth vanished down the drive, Ethan turned from the window and prepared to spend the next four days alone.

* * *

The horse's hooves made splashing, sucking noises as Josh turned into the slush-covered lane that led to the farmhouse. He was tired and cold, and the pain in his shoulder was intense. Barely a month had passed since he'd been shot, and he'd been in the saddle for hours.

He had spent two and a half weeks in the hospital at Chattanooga. Upon his release, he'd been granted a furlough. He had started immediately for home, traveling much of the way by train. At Springfield, he'd been a day's ride from the farm, and decided to press on. Now he regretted it. He hoped he could stay in the saddle long enough to reach the house.

The horse passed the line of trees bordering the river, and in the hazy blue light of evening, the farmhouse came into view. Light from the kitchen window glowed a welcoming amber, and smoke wafted from the chimney. Josh's spirits lifted, even as he braced himself for what lay ahead—his first meeting with his parents since the deaths of Jamie and Duncan. It would, without a doubt, be strained and sad, and the closer he'd come to home, the more he'd found himself dreading it. *But not as much as I dread seeing Ethan.* He couldn't, for the life of him, understand why Ethan had deserted. Just thinking about it made him angry.

Relax, he told himself. *Just relax.* There was bound to be a confrontation eventually, but just now, he hadn't the strength.

One of the dogs ran down from the porch, barking. Within seconds, the others joined it. Josh exhaled, a long white cloud, and forced his mind back to the problem at hand—how to get down from the horse without falling. The matter, as it turned out, solved itself.

The horse drew to a halt beside the back porch, the kitchen door opened, and his father stepped out, shotgun in hand. He and Josh stared wordlessly at one another. Josh smiled weakly and pitched forward in the saddle. James set the gun down, yelled at the dogs to be quiet, and crossed the porch in two quick strides to grab his son before he fell. Easing him to the ground, he called to Sarah and Kate.

Kate bolted through the door, followed closely by her mother. Together, they half-carried Josh into the kitchen and lowered him onto a chair. They'd been at supper, and the warmth of the room and smell of food revived him. While James held him steady, Sarah helped Josh out of his coat. Kate rushed to the stove to pour a cup of coffee. She set it on the table before him, regarding him with wide, anxious eyes. Josh stared at her in amazement. The last time he'd seen her, she had been a gangly tomboy, tagging after Ethan, imitating his every move. Now suddenly, she was a beautiful young woman with skin the color of honey, thick-lashed hazel-green eyes and a mass of long, curling chestnut hair. She smiled, a smile identical to Ethan's, and Josh tore his gaze from her and looked around the room.

"Where's Ethan?"

His father's fingers dug into his shoulder. His mother, who had turned from hanging up his coat, stopped dead.

"What do you mean, Josh?" his father asked, his voice tight with anxiety. He moved to face his son. "He's been with you, hasn't he?"

Josh looked at his father, aware suddenly of how much he'd aged. There were lines on his face that hadn't been there before, and his hair was more gray now, than blond. The grief that Josh suspected never left his fathers' eyes was tinged with dread.

"What do you mean, Josh?" James repeated.

"Duncan wrote to you," Josh said, feeling the first wave of uncertainty hit him.

A small, strangled moan escaped his mother. Josh looked at her as Kate darted to her side. The two women held one another, Kate staring at him over her mother's shoulder, eyes wide with alarm.

His father lurched to the closest chair and sat down heavily. "Duncan wrote to us, Josh, more than the two of you ever did. Ethan, too, up until August. But we never got anything from Duncan saying Ethan was missing. What are you saying happened?"

Josh stared at his father in disbelief. "August?" he repeated. "Ethan disappeared last March. We thought... We all thought he'd deserted and come home."

James looked at him, uncomprehending. "What... ?"

Josh shook his head. He felt terribly weak. "Duncan was sure he'd come home." *Another brother gone! What happened... ?* Suddenly, he couldn't make his eyes focus. His father's face blurred, then faded as he slipped sideways off the chair.

It was dark when he woke. By the faint glow of a bedside lamp, Josh made out details of the room and remembered he was home—in the same bed he'd shared with Jamie. At the thought of his twin, a moan escaped him. One of the shadows shifted, and his mother appeared at his side, her brow creased with worry. He attempted a smile, and the lines eased. She sat on the bed next to him, a hand caressing his cheek.

"How do you feel?"

"Weak."

"You were shot," she said, and he nodded. "I made some soup. Shall I bring you some?"

He nodded again, and to his surprise, she leaned down and kissed him on the forehead before disappearing into the darkness.

She returned a short time later, carrying a steaming bowl, and propped him up so he could eat. When he finished, she sat with him, holding his hand until he slept.

The next time he opened his eyes it was morning. He stirred, and Kate appeared above him. He smiled, amazed all over again by how grown up she was. The impression lasted only until her eyes welled with tears and she snuggled next to him, the same way she had as a child. Josh wrapped his good arm around her, and she clung to him and wept. Josh felt his own eyes fill. He closed them tightly and hugged her to him.

After a time, her sobs diminished, and Kate raised her head and looked at him. Seeing where tears had run down the sides of his face, she used her fingers to wipe away all trace of them. Looking into his eyes, she smiled, a beautiful, sad smile. "I was crying for Duncan and Jamie and Seth and Ethan, but mostly I was crying because I'm so happy to see you," she explained. Tears welled up and she added, "I thought I might never see any of you again. I've missed you so much."

Josh hugged her to him. "I've missed you, too, Katie."

She snuggled against him. After a while, she said, "Does it hurt? Where you were shot?"

In truth, the pain was considerable, but he said, "A little. Not as much as right after it happened."

There was another silence before she asked, "Are you going to stay for Christmas?"

He smiled at the hopeful note in her voice. "It's tomorrow, isn't it?"

"Yes."

"In that case, I'll stay."

Her head popped up, and she smiled. "For how long?"

"A little over a month. The end of January."

"And then you have to go back," she said, gravely. "Will you have to fight again?"

"Yes. Unless the war ends before spring."

A spark of hope came into her eyes. "Do you think it will?"

Josh looked at her for a long moment, then smiled sadly. "No."

It was late in the day by the time he felt strong enough to go downstairs. Ignoring his half-hearted protests, his mother helped him dress while Kate went to the barn to fetch their father. Both parents steadied him as he made his way down the stairs. By the time they reached the bottom, Josh was grateful for their assistance. He was amazed at how much the trip had weakened him.

A comfortable chair and a footstool had been moved into the kitchen, the only heated room in winter. His parents led him to the chair and helped ease him into it. Josh leaned back, resting his head on the pillow Kate slipped in behind him.

He noted the haggard expression on his father's face as he donned his coat and headed back to the barn. His mother smiled as she set a cup of coffee on the table beside him. She moved away to begin preparations for supper, and Kate covered his legs with a blanket. Placing a chair from the table close beside him, her hand sought his. Excited at having him home, she embarked on a detailed account of everything that had happened while he was away. Half listening, Josh watched his mother move about the kitchen.

Until now, he'd never fully appreciated what a remarkable woman she was. She had left her home and family, moved to another culture, adapted to its ways and raised six children, five of them boys. Yet to look at her, she was still a young woman. Josh realized suddenly that he had no idea how old she was. He subtracted dates in his head and was amazed to discover that she had to be at least thirty-five. He shook his head in disbelief. She looked no more than twenty. Her hair, pinned in a thick, shining coil at the nape of her neck, was black as coal. Her face, aside from lines of worry that creased her brow on occasion, was smooth and youthful. Only her eyes betrayed her. Like his father's, they reflected the pain and grief of having lost three, possibly four sons.

She glanced his way, and when she saw him looking, gave him a smile of such tenderness that a lump formed in his throat. It had never occurred to him that she loved him. For as long as he'd had Jamie, he hadn't needed her love. Without being particularly aware of it, he'd held her at arm's length, preferring to think of her as Ethan and Kate's mother. Only now did he realize how much she meant to him. She held his eyes a moment longer as he responded to her smile, then turned back to the stove.

"Are you listening?"

Josh swiveled his head to look at Kate. "Sorry," he said, giving her hand a squeeze. He gave her his undivided attention until their father came in and supper was on the table.

26

Ethan leaned a shoulder against the rough bark of a southern pine and looked down the shallow slope to the cluster of tents surrounded by a spiked wooden fence. Armed guards patrolled the perimeter, and he could see prisoners moving about inside. It had taken the better part of four days, but he'd found the camp where Thomas was being held.

The first day, when he'd slipped away from the house, all he'd done was retrace the route he'd taken with Isaac. It was a long walk back to the city, and his palms were sweating, his stomach in knots, by the time he reached the pretty square he remembered. It was then his nerve failed him. He covered the three miles back to the safety of the house in record time.

On the second and third days, he'd grown more confident, wandering further afield, getting his bearings and learning the city. He was surprised by the diversity of its population. In addition to English, he overheard fragments of conversations in French and Spanish, and other languages he didn't recognize. Mixed-blood Indians, and even a few full-blooded Creeks, mingled with whites, blacks, mulattos, and quadroons on the city's streets. Ethan blended easily into the mix. No one paid him the slightest bit of attention, and he moved without fear.

The city's architecture was as diverse as its population. He wandered the streets—Dauphin, Royal, St. Francis, St. Louis, Joachim, Conti—looking and listening. He received his first clue to Thomas' whereabouts from a snippet of conversation overheard outside the Battle House. A few hours later, in the marketplace at City Hall, another comment led him to where he now stood.

He had spent time prowling the perimeter, looking for a way to get closer without being seen. This was the best vantage point he could find, but the distance to the camp was too great for him to identify Thomas amid the shifting clumps of prisoners.

Ethan blew out a long breath and squinted up at the sun. *Almost noon. Time to be getting back.* Elizabeth intended to be home by mid-afternoon, and he didn't want her to worry. More to the point, he didn't want to have to lie about where he'd been. Ethan cast a final searching look at the camp before turning back the way he'd come.

As he approached Elizabeth's property, he was seized by a sudden urge to flee. Far from the long, empty hours he'd envisioned when Elizabeth announced her intention to leave, the last three and a half days had meant freedom. Elizabeth's return would put an end to that. For her peace of mind, he would no longer be free to come and go as he pleased.

Ethan looked around, making sure he was unobserved before slipping into bushes at the edge of the property. Sinking to his haunches, he considered his options. He could go home now; he was sure of it. Any anxiety he'd harbored about getting back to Union lines was gone. All it required was a walk into town, a left on St. Joseph Street, and following the road north out of town. Excitement stirred in him as he considered it.

But then he thought of Elizabeth. He imagined her despair at finding him gone and knew he couldn't just leave her. *Not like that.* His debt to her was too great to simply vanish without a word. And when it came right down to it, he wasn't at all sure he wanted to go. *Not just yet.*

Since their first night together, he'd struggled to sort out his feelings for her. At first he'd been terrified that she would decide it was all a mistake and ask him to leave. More recently, there had been times when he felt smothered. Even so, he cared deeply for her, feelings compounded by physical desire. He envisioned the night ahead and felt a pleasant stirring in his loins. *This isn't the time to go*, he thought with a grin. *Not just yet.*

He stayed where he was, savoring his last few minutes of freedom. The road was populated by the usual Sunday afternoon traffic. A group of horsemen ambled by, followed by an open carriage carrying a family with six chattering children. When it was gone, Ethan sighed and stood up. He cast a final look along the road and headed back through the trees.

"That you, Mista Ethan?"

Hannah's voice, coming from the dining room, stopped him as he started up the back stairs.

"It good you here, Mista Ethan. Miz 'Lizbet 'spected shortly."

Ethan tilted his head toward the top of the stairs. "I was just going up to wash. Will you see that I have hot water?"

"It waitin' fo' you. Could be it cold by now, but it waitin'."

Ethan considered asking for more, but Hannah's tone warned against it. "Thanks," he told her, and started up the stairs.

Hannah wasn't about to let him off easily. "When it start gettin' late, I sent Josiah to look fo' you. He say you warn't nowhere to be found."

Ethan stopped halfway up the stairs. He threw his head back, and with an exasperated sigh, turned to face her. "I went for a walk."

"Where?"

"Around, Hannah. Just around."

"Not anywhere aroun' here, you dint." Her voice was hard, her eyes disapproving.

"I went for a walk, Hannah. Nothing more."

"Like yestaday? An' the day befo'?"

Ethan considered her before saying, simply, "Yes."

"Miz 'Lizbet ain't gonna like it when she find out you been leavin'."

"Who's going to tell her, Hannah? I'm back and nothing happened. I don't see any point in worrying her, do you?"

"You gonna get both a' you in trouble. When they catches you, you gonna bring a whole lotta sufferin' down on this house."

"No one's going to catch me, Hannah. With Elizabeth back, I swear I won't be going anywhere."

Hannah wasn't at all certain she believed him. "You promise me, Mista Ethan?"

Ethan laid his hand on his heart. "I promise."

She mistook the gesture for insolence. "Ain't nothin' you kin say to make me believe you no mo'." Turning on her heel, she swept into the dining room.

"There's no point in saying anything, is there Hannah?" Ethan took a step down the stairs. "Hannah?" The only response was the angry clank of silverware. He waited another moment before turning to climb the rest of the stairs.

He was in her sitting room, seated where he could look up from his book and see the drive, when Elizabeth's buggy appeared. Ethan walked to the window, watching as Isaac pulled the horse to a stop in front of the house. He heard Hannah's step in the foyer, heard the front door open. Elizabeth looked toward it expectantly. Ethan smiled, wondering how he could ever have thought of leaving. Isaac handed her down, and as she ran up the steps, Ethan left the window and went to meet her.

Elizabeth came into the hall and stopped in confusion at not seeing him. When he appeared in the doorway, a look of pure delight spread across her face, and she ran to him, throwing her arms around him and burying her face against his chest.

"These have been the longest four days of my life! I thought they would never end!" She leaned back to look at him. "I've missed you so much."

At her touch, Ethan's senses came alive. He held her close, inhaling her scent. He wanted to kiss her deeply, passionately, to carry her upstairs and stay with her until morning. *Or the morning after...*

The front door closed with more force than necessary, and Ethan looked up. Hannah's brow was furrowed, her lips set in a hard line.

"Let Hannah take your cloak," he said softly.

Elizabeth stepped back reluctantly, allowing Hannah to remove the cloak from her shoulders. They waited until the door beneath the staircase closed behind her, then turned to one another and kissed with the pent-up desire of long separation.

Several minutes passed before Ethan pulled back, smiling as he looked into her upturned face. "It might be best if we celebrated your return somewhere besides the front hall," he said, his voice husky with arousal.

Elizabeth smiled and nodded. He offered her his arm, and together they hurried up the stairs.

27

With Elizabeth's return, Ethan envisioned a return to their normal routine. It was not to be. Each afternoon during the week between Christmas and New Year's, he was forced to withdraw as friends and acquaintances came calling. When the first visitor arrived, Ethan retreated outdoors. Unwilling, for Elizabeth's sake, to leave the grounds, he quickly discovered it was a mistake.

He ended up standing where he could watch the front of the house and the handsome carriage drawn up before it. A liveried slave stood at the horses' heads, another sat on the seat, holding the reins. After what seemed an interminably long time, the front door opened and Hannah ushered the man out. He was well dressed, overweight, and probably well into his fifties, but his presence stirred resentment nonetheless. Not only was he calling on Elizabeth, but he was free to do so in expensive clothes and a fine carriage while he, Elizabeth's lover, was reduced to lurking in the shrubbery. Ethan's mouth tightened in anger as he waited for the man to depart. When the carriage vanished down the drive, he slipped back through the trees and walked circuits around the grounds, waiting for his mood to improve before going indoors.

After that, when callers arrived, Ethan took a book and retired to his room. Fortunately, most of the visits were brief, and unless several parties arrived in rapid succession, he was only confined for short periods at a time. Even so, when the sound of an approaching carriage reached them on the fourth afternoon, Ethan rose abruptly, glared at Elizabeth and stalked from the room. He climbed the stairs, mildly ashamed of his boorish behavior, but angry nonetheless.

And, he thought bitterly, *the worst is yet to come.*

Elizabeth had told him that, according to custom, James' family would arrive to celebrate New Year's Day. The Magraths would send over additional help, arriving at dawn, to assist Hannah and Hattie in the kitchen, and members of the family would begin arriving early in the afternoon. It would late by the time they left. Ethan was to remain locked in his room the entire time.

Elizabeth watched Ethan's departure with dismay. She had seen him try to hide his resentment each time he was forced upstairs, but this time, he hadn't bothered. His display of temper, directed at her, left her feeling wounded. It was all she could do to greet the arriving couple and make pleasant conversation until they left. They had no sooner departed, than another carriage came up the drive, and then another. It was late when Hannah showed the last of the visitors to the door.

When she returned to the parlor to collect the tea things, Elizabeth said, "I'd like to have supper in my room tonight, Hannah. If you would bring it up at seven, you can have the rest of the evening to yourself. I know you have a long day tomorrow."

Hannah added the last of the plates to the stack on the tray. "An' Mista Ethan?"

"Why, his supper, too, of course. And while you're at it, will you look in the cellar for a bottle of champagne? There should still be some. If not, send Isaac to the warehouse."

Hannah nodded grimly and picked up the tray. At the door, she turned back, looking as if she had something to say. Shaking her head, she started from the room.

"Was there something else, Hannah?"

Hannah hesitated. She turned back and set down the tray. "It Mista Ethan."

"What is it, Hannah?" Elizabeth asked coolly, certain it had to do with the impropriety of their relationship.

"While you was away at Christmas, Mista Ethan, he went away, too."

Elizabeth's insides trembled. Her reserve vanished. "What do you mean?"

"He left here every day while you was gone. Stayed away all day. The firs' day, he was back fo' dinner, so maybe he dint go nowhere, but the next day an' the next, no one seed him from breakfast until jus' befo' supper. An' the day you come home, he come in jus' befo' you did."

Seeing Elizabeth's distress, she hastened to add, "I dint mean to upset you none, Miz 'Lizbet. I warn't sho' if'n I should say sumptin'. I jus' worry that sumptin' bad gonna happen." She shook her head and picked up the tray. "I worry he gonna get you in trouble."

She looked so upset that Elizabeth forced a smile. "It's all right, Hannah. I'm sure Ethan's very careful." *But I hope you're wrong.* The thought of Ethan going into the city terrified her. She couldn't bear the thought of anything happening to him.

Eventually, she pulled herself together and stood up, determined not to let anything stand in the way of her plans for the evening. Ethan was coming down the stairs when she stepped into the foyer. He stopped on the landing and stood with both hands on the railing, looking down at her.

"All clear?" he asked, a conciliatory smile on his face.

"All clear." A mischievous twinkle came into her eyes. "I have a *very* special evening planned—just the two of us. Our own private New Year's Eve celebration."

He responded with an affectionate smile and came down the stairs to join her.

He dressed as she asked him to, in his finest evening clothes from a wardrobe that had grown considerably since he moved into the house. When he knocked on the door to her room at half past seven, Elizabeth answered immediately, dressed in the same blue gown she'd worn the first evening. She smiled, noting the appreciation on his face, and twirled slowly, giving him a full view of her.

"You're beautiful."

She laughed, a mixture of delight and excitement, and invited him in.

Ethan looked about in approval. The lamps had been turned down low, and a pair of candles burned at the center of a table set before the fire. Another table held covered plates of food.

"I'm afraid I've given the servants the evening off," Elizabeth said, closing the door and turning the key in the lock. "We'll have to serve ourselves tonight."

Their eyes met, and Elizabeth laughed in pure delight. "Come," she said, taking his arm and guiding him to the table. "I have a special treat."

She picked up a dark-colored bottle from between the candles and held it out to him. "Champagne! Probably one of the last bottles in Mobile. Maybe in all of Alabama. It's not as cold as it should be, so we'll have to drink it quickly before it gets warm."

She looked at him, expecting him to share her excitement. When all he managed was a polite smile, her face fell. "What's the matter?"

"I don't drink."

"But this is champagne, Ethan. It's New Year's Eve! Everyone drinks champagne on New Year's Eve. Or, at least, they did before the war. Tonight it's just you and me." She watched his face for some sign he was relenting. When he didn't, she asked, "Do you mean you don't drink, or you've never had a drink?"

"I had a bad experience once," he said, his discomfort growing. "I don't drink."

At that, Elizabeth's face brightened. "Just a sip, then. I promise you won't have another bad experience." When he didn't respond, she said, "Please? For me, Ethan? For tonight? I went to a great deal of trouble to get this."

He looked at the floor, then at her, and gave a slight nod. "For you."

The smile she bestowed on him was his reward. She went to work immediately, opening the bottle. When it proved too much for her, she handed it to him, coaching him until the cork came away with a resounding pop. Ethan hadn't expected it, and the startled expression on his face caused Elizabeth to laugh until she wiped away tears. Ethan laughed too, and it was all he could do to pour champagne into the wobbling glasses she held out for him.

He set the bottle down, and Elizabeth handed him a glass. "I would like to propose a toast," she said, suddenly serious. "May this be the first of many years we begin together. And may they all begin as happily as this." Looking into his eyes, she raised her glass.

Ethan raised his, and following her lead, took a cautious sip. The taste surprised him. It was sweeter than he'd expected, and fruity. Nothing at all like the fiery liquid that had been forced down his throat on the banks of the Chattahoochee. He held the glass to the light, watching the bubbles rise.

"You're right," he said with a smile. "Everyone should drink this on New Year's Eve."

She laughed and took another sip before saying, "Let's see what Hattie sent up."

They ate the meal prepared for them and finished the bottle of champagne. When they rose from the table, Ethan felt light-headed and extremely happy. He wrapped Elizabeth in a fond embrace and thanked her for the evening.

"Don't thank me yet. It isn't over." The mischievous glint he knew so well came into her eyes. "Whatever shall we do to entertain ourselves until midnight?"

JANUARY 1864

28

Midnight came and went without their notice. When Hannah rapped on the door early the next morning, they were sleeping soundly amid a sea of rumpled bedclothes. Her knock roused Ethan first. He pushed himself up on his elbows and looked sleepily at Elizabeth.

She threw an arm over her eyes and groaned. "Yes... ?"

Ethan collapsed gratefully back onto the pillows. Whatever it was, he would let Elizabeth deal with it. Then Hannah said, "Time to get up, Miz 'Lizbet. You gots folks comin' in a couple hours," and the reality of the day ahead hit him.

"You hear me, Miz 'Lizbet? If I knows Miz Magrath, she gonna be here early. I needs time to straighten you room after I gets you dressed."

"Yes, Hannah," Elizabeth responded, coming wider awake. "Give us twenty minutes, please."

Ethan could hear Hannah muttering as she walked away. He sat up and looked around. Hannah was right; the room would require a good deal of straightening. Both tables were heaped with dirty dishes, and articles of clothing were strewn everywhere. He smiled, remembering how they'd got there.

"What are you grinning at?"

Elizabeth lay on her back, one arm thrown over her head, her face pale amid a tangle of dark curls. Ethan rolled down beside her and slid a hand beneath the covers. Elizabeth sighed with pleasure and pulled him to her.

Hannah returned half an hour later. Ethan had just gotten out of bed and was searching through the room for his clothes when the doorknob rattled violently.

"Miz 'Lizbet! Time to get up!"

"In a minute, Hannah," Elizabeth called, watching Ethan's progress with amusement.

"I ain't goin' away this time, Miz 'Lizbet. I's gonna stand right here 'til this do' opens."

She continued to announce her presence every few seconds during the time it took Ethan to locate his clothes and put them on. Dressed in everything but his coat and shoes, he gave Elizabeth a harried look and tilted his head questioningly toward the door. She laughed and nodded, snuggling down and pulling the covers up under her chin.

Ethan crossed to the door and hesitated, his hand on the key. Hannah knew exactly what was going on, but this was the first time he'd had to face her coming out of Elizabeth's room in the morning. And today, she was in a foul mood. He drew a breath and turned the key. Bowing his head against Hannah's reproachful gaze, he hurried past her down the hall.

The pitcher of water awaiting him was lukewarm, a testament to Hannah's irritation. Ethan washed and changed. From habit, he headed for the door, intending to go downstairs to breakfast. His hand was on the knob when he remembered: *Not today.*

He went to the table and picked up the book he'd been reading. The page marker was very near the end, and he cursed himself for not thinking to bring up another. Setting the book aside, he removed his coat and tossed it over the back of a chair. *Might as well be comfortable.* Not knowing what else to do, he lay down on the bed, irritated and already bored.

He heard a faint sound from the hall and sat up. The tapping came again. Thinking it must be Elizabeth, he hurried to open the door.

"I's to tell you to keep you do' locked an' not open it lessen you knows who it is," Rose said, eyes on to the tray holding his breakfast. "They chilluns gonna be here t'day an' they gets into everythin'."

It was a long speech coming for someone he'd barely heard utter a word. Ethan relieved her of the tray, and she darted away. She was halfway down the hall when he remembered. "Rose! Ask Miss Elizabeth to send up another book, will you?"

She glanced back as she rounded the corner. He thought he saw her nod.

He ate, then prowled the room until noise from outside drew his attention. He looked out one of the windows as two wagons pulled into carriage yard, disgorging a small army of servants carrying food to the kitchen. Ethan watched until the activity slowed, then resumed his pacing. It wasn't long before there was another knock at his door.

"It me, Mista Ethan."

He turned the key and let Hannah in. She handed him a stack of books and looked down at his feet. "I's hearin' you down in the dinin' room. Take off them boots an' quit movin' aroun'."

The gratitude he'd felt when she handed him the books turned to irritation. "First I'm to stay locked in my room. Now I'm not to move. Anymore orders, Hannah?"

Her expression hardened. "Nosuh."

She collected the breakfast tray and departed without a word. Ethan locked the door behind her and pulled off his boots. Then he went back to bed.

He had no idea how long he'd been dozing when running footsteps and the shrill clamor of children's voices roused him. He propped himself up on one elbow and listened. Doors opened and slammed closed. He tensed as the knob on his door jiggled.

"This one's locked," a child's voice complained.

"Let me try," another voice demanded, and the knob wiggled again.

"Monique, Gerard!" a woman's voice called. "Get out of those rooms and come here!"

The order was met with a howl of protest. The knob wiggled once more before the footsteps receded. Ethan waited until he heard them descend the stairs before lying back on the bed.

He spent the day alternately dozing and reading. He could hear the murmur of voices below, and periodically, women and children at the far end of the hall. Late in the day, the voices grew loudest directly below him, and he knew they had assembled in the dining room.

There was a tap at his door and a whisper. "It Rose, suh."

Ethan took the tray from her and carried it to the writing table. He nibbled at his supper, then pushed the tray aside and picked up his book.

He read until he could no longer make out the words. Lighting a lamp, he decided, even a darkened one, would be ill advised. With a sigh, he set the book aside and went to lie on the bed.

It seemed to him that the noise downstairs went on for hours. He tossed and turned, unable to get comfortable and growing more annoyed by the moment. By the time he heard the first of the carriages moving along the drive, he had worked himself into a distinctly foul mood.

It was approaching eight o'clock by the time the last of her guests bid Elizabeth goodnight. Sighing with relief, she hurried upstairs to be with Ethan. Her heart fluttered in panic when she discovered his door ajar, his room empty.

She found him in her room, standing in the shadows beyond the bed. He was holding back the edge of one of the shades, watching the activity in the drive below.

"Ethan?" She had been walking toward him, but when he didn't reply, didn't look around, she stopped, eyeing him apprehensively. Light caught his hand where it gripped the shade, but shadow, and his hair hanging loose, obscured his face.

Below in the drive, a horse snorted. Voices were raised as Josiah and the driver bid one another good night. Oyster shells crunched as the carriage started down the drive. It wasn't until the last sounds died away that Ethan released the shade. Several seconds passed before he turned and stepped into the light. His expression gave away nothing, but his silence and the bunched muscles in his jaw warned Elizabeth he was angry.

She lifted her hands slightly, palms upturned, then let them drop. "I don't know what to say, Ethan. I'm sorry about today. I'm sorry things are the way they are. I would give anything to be able to change them..." She stopped, eyes pleading. "Please don't be angry with me," she said in a small voice.

His expression softened. With a lopsided smile, he came around the foot of the bed and pulled her to him. "I'm not angry with you. I just... I get frustrated is all." He took a step back, holding her at arms' length so he could see her face. "I can't tell you what today was like—what the past week's been like. Hiding like this..." He looked away, blowing a long breath between pursed lips before his eyes came back to her face. "I don't like it, Elizabeth. If you and I are to be together, we need to find a way to go about openly."

Elizabeth stared at him in disbelief, then slowly shook her head. "You know we can't do that. Why are you even suggesting it?" Her voice took on a hint of exasperation when she added, "You're an escaped Yankee prisoner, Ethan. You're the enemy here. Have you forgotten that?"

Ethan's dark eyes were unreadable. Releasing her, he walked to her writing table and sat down, elbows on the table, head resting on the heels of his hands. Long moments passed before he dropped his hands to the table and looked up.

"I could leave..." Seeing the beginnings of panic on her face, he quickly said, "No! I don't mean forever. Just for a few days. Give me a horse, some clothes, money, and I'll leave. When I come back, we can meet properly. I'll come to the warehouse on business. Meet you there. Before long, we'll be able to go about openly." He read resistance in her face and said, "Please, Elizabeth, I can't go on like this."

Elizabeth stared at him, wishing he'd picked any other time to begin this conversation; wishing she wasn't so tired, that she had time to organize her thoughts. But Ethan was watching her, awaiting an answer. She had to say something.

"Do you have any idea what a charade like the one you're proposing would entail, Ethan? Who would you tell people you are? What would you tell them that would make them accept you as a suitable match for me? You'd need family. Connections. You can't expect people to take kindly to your riding into town, a total stranger, and sweeping me off my feet and into your bed within a couple of weeks. It will take time, quite a bit of it, if you're proposing to do it properly and be accepted.

"And where will you live while you're courting me? Have you thought of that? You can't imagine you'd be allowed to stay here? And while you're hanging about town, what's to prevent the army from conscripting you? Or a guard from the camp from recognizing you? You're very distinctive looking, you know. If one of them..." She stopped, paralyzed by the expression on his face. "What? Ethan, what is it?"

He sat deathly still, lips compressed, eyes boring into hers. When he spoke, his voice was deceptively quiet. "Is that it, Elizabeth? You're afraid people won't think I'm a suitable match for you?" He rose, nostrils flaring, his voice harsh with anger. "Do *you* think I'm a suitable match, or am I too 'distinctive looking'?"

Elizabeth stared at him in horror. "I... Ethan, I..." Words failed her.

The look on his face turned to disgust. He kicked the chair aside and strode past her, flinging the door open so hard that it hit the wall and swung back to slam behind him.

Elizabeth stood rooted for a moment too long. By the time she crossed the room and wrenched the door open, he was halfway down the hall. Before she could catch him, he slammed his door and turned the key.

Elizabeth pounded on the door, pleading with him, tears streaming down her face. There was no response. Eventually she gave up and stumbled blindly back to her own room, every step an effort, taking her away from him.

Ethan locked the door and leaned heavily against it, breathing hard. From the guilty expression on her face, it was obvious he'd caught her in a lie. It had never been her intention that their relationship be made public. *Never!* She had lied to him from the start.

Her knock startled him. He pushed away from the door and walked across the room, silent on stockinged feet. He sat on the edge of one of the chairs, elbows on knees, staring unseeing at the carpet, waiting for her to go away.

When at last she did, a feeling of loss swept over him, slowly replaced by a mounting bitterness. His initial reaction to their first kiss had been correct; he knew that now. Instinct and experience had warned him, but he'd let physical desire override judgment. He'd convinced himself she was different, but of course she wasn't.

What did I expect? he thought, and was seized by an overwhelming need to get away. He would take a horse and go. By morning, he would be miles from Mobile, and they would be rid of one another forever.

Retrieving his boots, he pulled them on. He grabbed his coat and looked around, deciding what to take with him. He was crossing the room to collect his book when realization struck. *I can't take anything. Not in good conscience.* Everything, including the clothes he was wearing, belonged to Elizabeth. He had no money. No horse. Nothing. Despite her deception, he couldn't bring himself to steal from her.

The strength went out of him. He leaned heavily against the bed, the coat falling unheeded from his fingers. He would have to see her again. He would have to ask for what he needed.

No, he thought, *I couldn't bear that. I'd rather go with nothing.* He would wait until dawn, he decided, when a man on foot was less apt to draw unwanted attention, and go. Somehow, he'd make do. He'd done it before; he could do it again.

The grim decision made, Ethan pulled his boots off and climbed onto the bed. He lay atop the covers, staring at the ceiling, waiting for the sun to rise. As the minutes dragged by, his eyes closed.

Elizabeth threw herself on her bed and wept. How could she have been so careless? How could she have let slip the concerns that plagued her constantly? She had hoped that, in time, a solution would present itself and she would introduce Ethan to Mobile society without him ever being aware of the anxiety his acceptance had caused her. *And now this.* In a single moment, she'd betrayed her doubts and driven him away.

Remembering the look on his face when he left the room, she succumbed to a renewed spasm of weeping. Even if she found a way to win him back, she was certain their relationship would never be the same. She would never again have his complete trust.

Hannah's knock roused her. Elizabeth raised her head and found voice to send her away. As her footsteps receded, Elizabeth dragged herself into a sitting position and used her sodden handkerchief to wipe her eyes. She blew her nose into it and went in search of another. As she scooped a pile of them from the top drawer of the chifforobe, a thought stuck her: *What if I've driven him away? What if he leaves without giving me a chance to explain?*

The handkerchiefs fell from her hands, and she ran to the door. Pulling it open, she stepped into the hall. It was empty, the only sound the murmur of servants' voices below. Willing the floorboards not to squeak, Elizabeth tiptoed along the hall to Ethan's room. His door was closed, a sliver of light showing under it. She would have to assume he was still inside; that if he decided to leave, he wouldn't go until the house was quiet.

She hurried back to her room, leaving the door ajar so she would hear movement in the hall. The chair behind her writing table lay on its side. She righted it and sat down. Pulling open one of the drawers, she removed a sheet of paper, then reached for her pen and a pot of ink. Biting her lip in concentration, she decided what to write.

It took time to get the wording right, but eventually she read what she'd written and nodded. It was the best she could do. It was all she could do. As she wrote his name on the envelope, a tear dropped onto the paper, blurring the ink. Without warning, the tears she'd held at bay while concentrating on the letter overflowed.

What if I've lost him forever? What if, despite what she'd written, he left and she never saw him again? The thought was too painful to contemplate.

Elizabeth pulled herself together and collected the scattered handkerchiefs from the floor. Using one of them to wipe her tears, she picked up the envelope and stepped into the hall.

Light still showed under Ethan's door. Her spirits rose, but she needed to be sure. She turned the knob, and gave the door a gentle push, sighing with relief when she found it locked. Slipping the envelope beneath the door, she stepped back, hoping he would pick it up. Minutes passed, and the envelope remained untouched. Elizabeth's shoulders slumped, and she turned back toward her own room.

Ethan came awake slowly, feeling spent and miserable for reasons he couldn't immediately identify. He realized he was lying fully clothed on top of the covers, and the events of the previous evening came rushing back. He threw an arm across his face, feeling wretched.

When he opened his eyes again, sunlight was glowing through the shades. It was later than he'd intended. Ethan slid from the bed and pulled on his boots. He retrieved his coat from the floor, and as an afterthought, pulled a wide-brimmed hat from the wardrobe and twisted his hair up under it. Taking a last look around, he headed for the door.

He spotted the envelope as he was reaching for the key. He stared at it, then squatted to pick it up. His name, the ink blurred, was written in Elizabeth's hand.

A door slammed downstairs, startling him. Ethan rose quickly, jamming the envelope into his pocket. He opened the door a crack and looked out. Seeing no one, he slipped into the hall.

The door to Elizabeth's room was ajar. He hesitated, seized by the urge to look in on her one last time. Steeling himself, he headed for the back staircase.

It was his intention to slip out of the house and disappear before anyone saw him, but the smell of baking bread assailed him the moment he stepped onto the gallery. His stomach rumbled, reminding him he hadn't eaten supper. *A lifetime ago*, he thought miserably. Forcing his mind to the business at hand, he realized it would be foolish to leave without supplies. There was no way of knowing when he might eat again, and the search for food would only slow him down. Girding himself, he pushed open the door to the kitchen. To his relief, Hattie was the only one there.

"I need food," he told her brusquely. "Whatever you have that I can take with me."

Her welcoming smile vanished. She looked down at the bacon she was slicing.

"Now, Hattie," Ethan commanded. By some stroke of luck, Hannah hadn't arrived yet, and he was desperate to be gone before he had to face her. Striding into the scullery, he grabbed one of the gunnysacks hanging on the wall and spilled turnips onto a table. Having second thoughts, he scooped half of them back into the sack. He dug around and came up with some sweet potatoes and dried apples. They went into the bag, along with a selection of tins from the shelves and a knife he spied next to the washbasin. Back in the kitchen, he swept several fresh loaves of bread into the bag. Breaking off a chunk, he took a bite and held the sack out to Hattie. Eyeing him apprehensively, she dropped in the hunk of bacon and half a dozen cold biscuits.

Ethan thanked her, crossed to the door, and stepped out just as Hannah emerged from the carriage barn. Ducking his head, he walked rapidly toward the rear of the property, certain she'd seen him. A glance back, once he reached the cover of the trees, confirmed it. Hattie had come out of the kitchen, and both women stood staring at the spot where he'd disappeared, Hattie talking and gesturing.

Ethan walked briskly along St Joseph Street. Already the last redoubt at the northern end of the city's fortifications was in sight. A few minutes, and he would be out of Mobile, headed north along Telegraph Road.

He kept up a steady pace until he was clear of the swamps. When the last of the boggy ground was behind him, he pushed aside all thoughts of what he'd left behind and began planning for what lay ahead. On foot, he figured it would take at least three weeks to travel the length of Alabama. Far from being daunting, the prospect excited him. He was in his element once again, on his own and free to do as he pleased.

The sky overhead was powder blue; sunlight filtering through the glossy green of the pines lent a final burst of brilliance to the faded autumn colors of the tangled foliage underneath. Ethan breathed in pine-scented air and smiled. He could do it now, he was sure of it. He would go back, report to General Thomas and try to find Josh.

Midway through the afternoon, he left the road and slipped into the woods. He drank deeply from one of the many small streams that fed the Mobile River, then settled in a concealed spot and opened the gunnysack. Despite his hunger, he forced himself to eat slowly. He had no idea how long he would have to make do with what little he had.

He was on the verge of setting out again when he remembered the envelope. Pulling it from his pocket, he stared at it, considered tossing it away unread. Instead, he ran a finger under the seal and pulled out a single sheet covered in Elizabeth's finely formed hand.

Dearest Ethan,

I cannot begin to tell you how deeply I regret the misunderstanding that has caused you so much hurt tonight. You should know that ever since I became aware of the depth of my feelings for you, I have struggled to devise a plan to introduce you to my friends and family in such a way that they would accept you and accept your presence in my home. Unfortunately, circumstances being what they are, I have been unable to devise a workable solution.

Despite my ill-considered choice of words, you must know that my only concern is for your safety. My greatest fear is that an incautious word will alert the authorities and they will take you away from me. After all you have suffered, I could not bear it if you were sent back to prison.

Since I have compelled you to ask, I assure you that I consider you a more than acceptable match. More acceptable than I ever imagined anyone could be until I met you. I love you with all my heart and will do anything in my power to make you happy. If it means you must leave, I will accept your decision, hoping only that you will promise to return when this wretched war is over. Should you decide to go, and ask me to accompany you, you should know that I will leave Mobile in a heartbeat in order to be with you. In the event you decide to stay, and require a further declaration of my love, I find I have nothing left to offer but my hand. That I will gladly give. I will marry you tomorrow if that is what you wish. Somehow it can be arranged.

I am terribly sorry for what happened tonight. I cannot begin to imagine life without you. I beg you, please, do not condemn me to that.

With all my love,
Elizabeth

Ethan tilted his head back and closed his eyes. *If she means it...* A tingle of excitement ran through him. If Elizabeth meant what she'd written—and the passion behind her words implied that she did—he'd been too quick to condemn her. He opened his eyes and looked around. It would be hard to go back. Especially having made up his mind, having come this far. *But if she means it...* If what Elizabeth had written was true, he owed it to her to return.

Ethan folded the letter and placed it in his pocket. He lay back, crossed arms supporting his head, and stared up at the sky, broken now by high wisps of white cloud. A squirrel scolded, then was silent. Only the burble of the stream broke the stillness. *Three weeks back to Union lines...*

Eventually, he got to his feet and collected his belongings. In the lengthening shadows, he went to the stream and took another drink before setting out.

* * *

The crick in her neck brought Elizabeth partially awake. She shifted in an attempt to ease it, and cramped muscles protested. Pushing herself upright on the settee, she looked around in momentary confusion.

Ethan! Elizabeth scrambled to her feet and nearly fell. Leaning against the settee, she waited impatiently for the blood in her right leg to circulate. As soon as it would support her, she hobbled to the door and hurried along the hall.

His door was open, the envelope gone. Elizabeth's eyes darted around the room, looking for some sign he'd read the letter. The pile of books she'd sent up sat on a corner of his writing table. Another, a page marker halfway through it, lay near the center, but no there was no sign of the letter or the discarded envelope. She crossed to the chifforobe, pulling open a door and several drawers, sighing in relief when she found his clothes undisturbed.

Her eyes came to rest on his pitcher and basin. There was no water in either to indicate that he'd rung for Hannah. Elizabeth scanned the room again, fighting down panic. The boots he usually wore were gone. The quilt was rumpled, but the bed hadn't been slept in. Nothing indicated that he'd spent the night.

Elizabeth flew out the door and down the hall. She was at the head of the stairs when the door to the back staircase opened. Elizabeth spun around, her face eager with anticipation. It fell when she saw Hannah.

"Where's Ethan? Have you seen him?"

Hannah set the steaming pitcher she was carrying on the table next to the door. When she looked at Elizabeth, her eyes were filled with sympathy. "He lef' early this mo'nin'."

Elizabeth's face crumbled, and she swayed. Hannah grasped her arms, supporting her as she sank to the floor. Crouching beside her, she stroked her hair as she wept.

When the tears subsided, Hannah pushed herself to her feet. "Come, Miz 'Lizbet," she said, helping her to stand. "It ain't no good you cryin' here on the stairs."

Elizabeth moved in a daze. Hannah sat her at the dressing table and went to the chifforobe, returning with a nightdress over one arm.

"Come, Miz 'Lizbet. Le's get you outta them clothes."

Elizabeth's eyes focused on the nightdress, and she shook her head. "No, Hannah. Bring me my gray riding dress."

"But Miz 'Lizbet..."

"I'm going after him," Elizabeth said firmly. "The gray dress."

Hannah crossed her arms, her jaw set.

"You can't stop me, Hannah." Elizabeth made as if to stand. "I'll get it myself."

At that, Hannah relented. Elizabeth issued a string of orders, sending her to accomplish them while she dressed. By the time she appeared on the front steps, Isaac was waiting in the buggy, a basket of food on the seat beside him. Josiah held the reins of two saddled horses. He handed Elizabeth into the saddle, then swung onto the second horse. With Elizabeth in the lead, they set off.

She had no idea which route Ethan would choose, but following a brief debate with herself, she opted for Telegraph Road, the most direct route north. Once they were beyond the swamps, she told Isaac to continue along the road while she and Josiah combed woods on either side.

It was late in the day when she finally conceded defeat. She pulled to a stop, tears of exhaustion spilling down her face. Josiah helped her into the buggy, and they began the long trek home.

Hannah was waiting with a lantern. As she helped Elizabeth down from the buggy, her eyes met Isaac's over Elizabeth's head. Isaac shook his head, his face grim in the lamplight.

Hannah wrapped a protective arm around Elizabeth's shoulders and walked with her into the house. Elizabeth leaned heavily on her as they mounted the stairs, and once in her room, stood listlessly while Hannah removed her clothes and slipped a nightdress over her head. Turning back the covers, Hannah helped her into bed.

"You rest now. I's gonna bring you some supper."

Elizabeth managed a wan smile. "Thank you, Hannah."

Hannah collected her soiled clothes and left the room. Opening the door to the back stairs, she nearly collided with Ethan. They both took a startled step back, staring speechless at one another.

Relief was the first emotion Hannah experienced. Then anger. Seeing remorse on Ethan's face, she held it in check.

"You bes' go to her," she said gruffly. "But don' stay long. She need her rest."

Ethan nodded and stepped past her into the hall.

Hannah watched him walk to Elizabeth's door and stop before it, one hand on the knob. He looked back, and she inclined her head, indicating he should go in. Ethan hesitated a moment longer before stepping into the room.

Elizabeth was lying up against the pillows, her eyes closed. Ethan thought she was asleep until she murmured, "That was quick, Hannah."

He approached the bed and looked down at her, shocked by her pallor and the deep sadness etched on her face. He reached to smooth an errant strand of hair, but before he touched it, Elizabeth's eyes opened. She stared at him in disbelief. Pushing back the covers, she came to her knees and threw her arms around his neck.

"I didn't read your letter right away. I'm sorry."

Elizabeth pulled back to look at him, smiling with unrestrained joy. "Oh, Ethan, it doesn't matter. All that matters is that you came back."

Ethan smiled, then kissed her. There would be time later for all that needed to be said.

After supper the following evening, they adjourned to the library. Elizabeth settled on the sofa before the fire, expecting Ethan to join her. Instead, he walked to the fireplace and stood with his back to her, staring into the flames.

Elizabeth watched him apprehensively. Despite his attempts to conceal it, she knew something was on his mind. She wasn't at all certain she wanted to hear what it was.

Ethan turned to her, his look beseeching. "I have to go, Elizabeth."

Elizabeth stared at him, incapable of speech.

Ethan crossed to the sofa and sat down facing her. Taking her hands in his, he said, "I need to go. I can't hide here any longer."

Elizabeth shook her head mutely, her eyes filling with tears.

It was the response Ethan had been dreading. "I'll come back," he said squeezing her hands. "I promise."

Elizabeth bowed her head as the tears overflowed. "When?"

"Just as soon as the war's over."

"No. When are you leaving?"

"I don't know. We need to talk. Make plans."

Elizabeth looked at him. "So not right away?" she asked hopefully.

Ethan couldn't help but smile. "Not right away. But soon. Within the month."

"And you promise you'll come back?"

Ethan nodded.

"And when you do... ?"

He hesitated, then uttered the words he knew she'd been waiting to hear. "I love you. If you'll wait for me, if it's still what you want, we can be married."

Elizabeth laughed, brushing away tears. "Oh, Ethan, yes! Yes!" she said, falling into his arms. After a time, she said, "But you're determined to go?"

"I have to, don't you see? This week's proved I can't keep hiding here. What if the war goes on for another year or more? I just... It wouldn't be fair to either of us if I stayed." He paused before adding, "So I need your permission to go."

She sat back, searching his face. "Without it, you won't?"

Ethan hesitated, then slowly shook his head. "No."

Elizabeth looked at him for several moments, then lowered her eyes. "I suppose we'd better start figuring out what you'll need to take with you."

Ethan tried to hide his relief. "Thank you, Elizabeth. I know how hard this is. It's hard for me, too. I don't want to leave, it's just—"

"I know," she interrupted. "I know how difficult the last few weeks have been. That's why I offered you this option." She smiled sadly. "In my heart, I knew it was the one you would take."

He had no response to that. "I'll come back," he whispered, pulling her to him. "I swear it. Just as soon as I possibly can."

Two days later, Elizabeth paid Thomas a visit. The hamper she carried was opened and searched, and then, unexpectedly, she was shown to a small open tent just inside the gate. She seated herself on the bench near its center, and waited. It wasn't long before Thomas was brought in.

He grinned as he ducked under the canvas. "I guess they decided to trust us together, cousin Elizabeth." The smile broadened, and he bent over the hand she offered. "It's good to see you again."

She noted with satisfaction that he was wearing the clothes she'd brought and had put the soap to good use. "It's good to see you, Thomas. How are they treating you?"

Thomas shrugged. "The same. It's what you've done that makes the difference." He looked into her eyes and smiled. "Thank you."

"I'm happy to do it." Her face fell and she blurted, "He's leaving, Thomas."

"Ethan?"

Elizabeth nodded, averting her eyes so he wouldn't see the tears that threatened.

"When?"

"Soon."

Thomas' blue eyes narrowed. "You're in love with him, aren't you?"

Elizabeth nodded.

"And Ethan?"

"He asked me to marry him."

"I don't understand." Thomas sat down next to her, genuinely perplexed. "He's leaving, *and* he asked you to marry him?"

Elizabeth nodded again, twisting the handkerchief in her lap. "He's promised to return after the war so we can be married."

"I don't understand. Why's he leaving?"

Elizabeth explained as best she could.

Thomas nodded. He supposed it made sense. "Will you be all right?"

Elizabeth attempted a smile. "Having you nearby will help. Having someone I can talk to about him." She paused uncertainly. "If you don't mind?"

Jealousy stirred, but Thomas forced a smile. "I don't mind. If it means you'll come often."

Elizabeth laid a hand on his arm. "Thank you, Thomas. I'm not sure how I'd manage without you." Leaning down, she opened the hamper. "I've brought food and more soap. Socks, and a few other things I thought you might need. If there's anything else, tell me and I'll try get it for you."

"I'm sure you've thought of everything."

The guard leaned in, and Thomas got to his feet. "Thank you, Elizabeth. I'll look forward to seeing you soon." Under his breath, he added, "Tell him to be careful. Good luck and Godspeed."

* * *

Josh pulled the team to a halt before Harrison's General Store and jumped down from the wagon. Reaching up his good arm, he took the basket of eggs from his mother and placed it on the ground. Then he turned to help her down.

Inside the store, he set the basket on the counter, exchanging greetings with the owners before heading for the back room. It was his first trip to town, and the four men gathered around the stove greeted him enthusiastically. Two were older, friends of his father's, but Peter Ware was there, his face badly scarred, a patch where his left eye had been before Stones River. A crutch leaned against the wall next to Tom Ballinger whose empty pant leg was turned up below the knee. Josh greeted his old schoolmates warmly and pulled up a chair.

He wasn't sure how long they'd been talking when his mother spoke his name. Something in her tone sent chills along his spine. Josh turned to face her.

Sarah held out an envelope, her face stricken. Josh was at her side in an instant, taking one elbow to support her and sliding the envelope from between paralyzed fingers. Postmarked December twenty-second in Mobile, Alabama, it was heavily soiled. A portion of the address had been blurred by water, but the handwriting was unmistakable. *Ethan!*

Josh met his mother's eyes.

Looking as if she might faint, she whispered, "Read it."

Josh walked her away from the curious stares, to a wall lined with bolts of fabric.

"What does it say, Josh?"

"It's from Mobile, Alabama. It's addressed to you and Pa." He ran a finger under the flap and pulled out a folded sheet of paper, skimming the brief message before reading it aloud to his mother.

"He's alive?" she asked, her voice filled with disbelief.

Josh nodded, turning the letter and envelope over in his hands as if they would tell him more.

"He's alive," his mother said again, and Josh looked at her.

She was smiling. Tears of joy streamed down her cheeks. He smiled back, and she threw her arms around him.

217

"He's alive," she repeated, and murmured something in Lakota.

Josh's mind raced, one thought eclipsing all others: *What the devil is he doing in Alabama?*

* * *

Once she accepted that Ethan was leaving, Elizabeth committed herself to making his journey as easy as possible. A month passed before the arrangements were completed to her satisfaction. Inwardly, Ethan chafed at the delay, but he couldn't help marveling at her resourcefulness. She appropriated a Confederate corporal's coat from a local hospital, and Hannah mended the bullet holes and removed the bloodstains as best she could. And somehow—Elizabeth only smiled when he asked her how—she obtained a pass for him to travel north to Dalton, Georgia.

"It's where the Army of Tennessee is wintering," she explained in the library late one evening. "I know it's not where you want to go, but it's as far north as I could get you without arousing suspicion. You can dispose of it, and the uniform, when you get close to the Union lines."

She picked up the small journal she kept, leafing through the pages until she found what she was looking for. "This is what I was able to find out about the locations of the armies. It's not much, but perhaps it will help." After briefly considering what was written, she added, "General Johnston's army is, as I said, wintering at Dalton. The Union army is spread out and I didn't know what questions to ask..." She interrupted herself to smile at him. "Or how to ask them without arousing suspicion, so I have no idea where the 36th Illinois might be." She tore out the page and handed it to him. "Maybe this will make sense to you."

Ethan ran his eyes down the page.

Gen. Johnston, CSA - Dalton, Georgia

Gen. Thomas - XIV Corps - Chattanooga, Tennessee
also Hooker? or Howard? (perhaps both)
and Palmer?
Gen. Grant - (with IV Corps?) - Nashville, Tennessee
also Granger, Sheridan?
Gen. Sherman - XV Corps - Huntsville & Bridgeport, Alabama

"I don't know how you do it." Ethan shook his head in amazement. "Thank you, Elizabeth."

"Is it helpful?"

Ethan laid the scrap of paper on the table beside him and pulled her to him. "Very."

In the pre-dawn hours of January thirtieth, they made love for last time. After a lingering kiss, Ethan left Elizabeth's bed and went along the darkened hall to his own room. He returned to find her waiting for him, sitting on the settee in the dim glow of a single lamp. He sat beside her and they spoke briefly, holding hands, their heads close together as they said their good-byes. Ethan kissed her again before rising. He stood for a moment, gazing down at her, memorizing her face. Her hands slipped from his, and he walked from the room.

When he was gone, Elizabeth's shoulders slumped. She bowed her head, fighting back tears. Minutes later, Hannah arrived.

She had run into Ethan at the foot of the back stairs. "Thanks for everything, Hannah," he'd said, taking her hand. "Take care of her 'til I get back." Giving her quick peck on the cheek, he'd pushed through the back door onto the gallery.

Josiah was waiting in the carriage barn, a revolver in one hand, the reins of a saddled horse in the other Ethan took the revolver and pushed it into his waistband before checking the tightness of the cinch and assuring himself that the saddlebags were secure. Satisfied, he took the reins and clapped Josiah on the shoulder. "Thanks, Josiah. See you soon."

"Take care, Mista Ethan."

"I will."

He had one foot in the stirrup when he spotted movement in the shadows. Handing back the reins, he walked to the foot of the stairs.

"Thanks, Isaac. Take good care of Elizabeth, will you?"

"Yessuh." Isaac nodded solemnly.

When they heard the horse's hooves on the drive, Elizabeth and Hannah rose as one and crossed to the window. She could barely make him out in the darkness, but Elizabeth was sure he looked up, raising a hand before the horse's gait quickened and hoofbeats receded down the drive.

FEBRUARY

29

Possession of the pass made it possible for Ethan to travel quickly. The wad of Confederate currency he discovered in one of the saddlebags eased his way further, providing means for food and lodging. He headed north as directly as the roads would take him, detouring only once to give a wide berth to Cahaba.

Northeast of Birmingham, Ethan buried the pass and the Confederate uniform. He took to traveling at night, passing west of Gadsden and up the wide, forested valley between Raccoon and Lookout Mountains.

Early one morning, as he topped a ridge, he spied a double line of horsemen in an open meadow just to the north of him. He rode toward them, keeping to the trees until he made out the color of their uniforms.

The double-line of Union cavalry halted, watching his approach. Ethan identified himself, exchanged greetings with the ranking officer, and asked where he might find General Thomas' headquarters. The captain assigned a sergeant and four men to escort him to Chattanooga.

At first, the sergeant was friendly enough, and curious. He sought to engage Ethan in conversation until he realized Ethan was inclined to respond with brief, vague answers while countering with probing questions of his own. The sergeant's manner cooled perceptibly, and the six men rode in silence.

They followed the railroad tracks around the great bend in the Tennessee River, past the northernmost tip of Lookout Mountain, and through the fortifications south of town. They made their way through the jumble of white tents and crude army huts that sprawled in every direction, past depots, warehouses and foundries converted for military use, and into the wasteland that was Chattanooga.

Occupation by two armies in rapid succession had taken its toll. Churches had been converted to ordnance depots, a hospital, and a prison. Vacant lots were crowded with wagons, artillery and animals. Private homes had been commandeered for use as officers' residences and headquarters, and businesses had been turned into offices and barracks. The town had been virtually stripped of vegetation—all but a scattering of trees cut down. What remained were rocks and mud, churned by the feet of thousands of men and animals. The town looked bleak and inhospitable, even in bright sunlight.

They drew to a halt before the single-story white frame house on Houston Street that served as headquarters for the Army of the Cumberland. Ethan waited under the watchful eye of his escort while the sergeant went inside. He soon reappeared and motioned Ethan to join him.

Ethan dismounted, looped his reins over the dilapidated wood fence, and trotted up the steps to the porch. The sergeant held open the door to one of the front rooms, then stepped back, closing the door between them.

A dark-haired man with general's stars on his shoulders stood with his hands clasped behind him, gazing out the front window. He turned as the door clicked closed. His hairline had receded, leaving him with an exceedingly high forehead. He wore a closely trimmed beard, flecked with gray, but no mustache. He observed Ethan silently before speaking.

"I am General Reynolds, General Thomas' Chief of Staff. I understand you've asked to see him."

Ethan glanced at the other men in the room. There were three of them, a major and two captains, listening unabashedly to what was being said.

"Whatever you have to say can be said in front of these men. Why don't you begin by identifying yourself?"

"Private Ethan Fraser, sir. Company J, 36th Illinois. I was captured by the Rebs four months back and escaped. Since I wasn't actually with the Thirty-sixth when I was captured, I thought it best to report here. You see, I'd been working for General Thomas, serving as a courier for a man named Price."

A fleeting look of surprise crossed the general's face. He and the major exchanged glances before his eyes shifted back to Ethan.

The general figured him for a half-breed, in obvious good health, and exceptionally well dressed. The collar of a shirt that looked to be cashmere poked from beneath a finely tailored brown wool riding coat. His breeches were soft, tan buckskin, and he wore a handsome pair of brown leather riding boots. Nothing about him was consistent with the story he told. Nothing connected him to the ragged, starving men who had escaped Southern prisons and survived the long trek back to Northern lines.

Ethan shifted nervously under the intense scrutiny, catching himself as the general's eyes flicked back to his face.

Without a word, General Reynolds turned to look out the window. The bay tethered to the fence was a fine looking animal. Well-fed, in marked contrast to the poor, starving beasts that were all that remained in Chattanooga.

The general walked to the desk nearest him and sat down. "Sit, Private," he commanded, motioning for a chair to be placed opposite. "Begin at the beginning. Tell us of your dealings with Price and the details of your capture and escape."

Troubled by the general's tone, Ethan looked around, noting the hostile expressions on the other men's faces. He sat in the chair provided and told of being assigned to Price, giving a detailed account of the time he'd spent with him prior to his capture, and a brief account of his travels since. He was truthful in everything he said, but omitted details of his time at Cahaba and glossed over the months spent in Mobile.

When he finished, General Reynolds regarded him at such length without speaking that Ethan was forced to look away.

"Captain Kellogg." The general beckoned with two fingers, and the captain moved quickly to his side. Following a brief, whispered exchange, Captain Kellogg left the room.

General Reynolds turned his attention to Ethan. "Private Fraser, tell us again about the time you spent with Price."

Alarms went off in Ethan's head, but he willed himself to stay calm as he repeated his story. This time the general interrupted, forcing Ethan over the same ground again and again. When he failed to catch him in a contradiction, General Reynolds focused on several points, including the trip to Macon. Major Hawkes added his voice to the interrogation, and Ethan weathered a barrage of questions. His alarm intensified, but he did his best to hide it, concentrating on what was asked and keeping his answers consistent.

The questioning was interrupted by the return of Captain Kellogg. The captain strode past Ethan and began placing objects on the table.

General Reynolds picked up the first volume of *The Count of Monte Cristo*. He fanned the pages, then looked at the captain, his brows drawn together in a question. Captain Kellogg took the book and opened it to a page near the front. As he did, a folded slip of paper fell to the desk. General Reynolds spared it only a glance before looking where the captain pointed. He read what was written and looked at Ethan.

"Is there anything you've neglected to tell us, Private Fraser?"

Ethan's stomach rolled. Elizabeth had presented the books to him the eve of his departure. He'd set them aside without opening them, leaving them for Hannah to pack. Slowly, he shook his head. "No, sir. Not that I recall."

General Reynolds read: "'To my dearest Ethan, I hope you will keep this with you always, as I wish I could be. I will count the days until your return. With all my love, Elizabeth.' It is dated twenty-eight January, this year. A little over a week ago." He looked up, fixing Ethan with a piercing stare. "Where did this come from, Private? Who gave it to you?"

"A friend, sir."

"That much is obvious. Until you return where?"

Ethan gripped his thighs. To answer truthfully would only add to their suspicions. But lying, or refusing to answer, could also prove a mistake. He raised his eyes to the general's face. "Mobile, sir."

The general's eyebrows rose. "Mobile," he repeated.

"Yes, sir."

General Reynolds shared a look with Major Hawkes. "You're planning to return to Alabama? I see. That would help explain this, wouldn't it?" He spread the pile of notes across the desk. "Let me see... What do we have here?"

"A little over fifteen hundred dollars in Confederate scrip, sir," Captain Kellogg said helpfully.

"What's it worth these days?" General Reynolds looked inquiringly at his officers. "Five or six cents on the dollar?"

There were nods and murmurs of agreement, and Captain Kellogg said, "About eighty dollars, sir. Give or take."

General Reynolds fixed Ethan with a stony stare. "More than half a year's pay in this army, Private Fraser." He held Ethan's eyes a moment longer before picking up the folded slip of paper. His scowl deepened as he read what was written. "And what is your explanation for this?" he asked turning the paper so Ethan could see it.

Ethan looked at it in dismay. It was the list Elizabeth had given him in the library. He remembered reading it and setting it aside. Seeing it now, he could only assume Hannah had picked it up and packed it.

"It's... a list... " he began haltingly, then struggled to explain. "While I was hiding in Mobile, I... there was no news. I didn't know where the armies were wintering. When I was well enough to leave, I was given that. To help me find the Thirty-sixth."

General Reynolds' expression didn't alter. He reached for the last object Captain Kellogg had placed on the table. It was a small leather drawstring pouch that Ethan had never seen before. The general struggled briefly with the string, pulled the pouch open and looked inside. His eyebrows arched, and he looked at Ethan. "How do you explain this?" he asked, upending the pouch. A thick roll of greenbacks tumbled onto the desk.

Ethan stared at the money in stunned silence. *Elizabeth!* By trying so hard to look out for him, she'd compounded the trouble he was in. Big trouble by the look of it. There was no way he could explain so much money. *Even if I tell them the truth, they won't believe me. There's too much.*

"I'm waiting, Private Fraser. What do you have to say for yourself?"

Ethan raised his eyes to the general's face. "Why are you asking me all this?" he countered. "Ask Price. He'll confirm I was his courier."

"Price is dead, Private Fraser. As you are no doubt aware, he was supplying information to both sides in this conflict. His duplicity was discovered last October, right here in Chattanooga. He was tried, found guilty, and hanged."

Ethan could do nothing more than stare at the general in horror.

A thought occurred to General Reynolds and his eyes narrowed. "He was found out by someone with your same name, a Lieutenant Joshua Fraser. No relation, I assume."

Ethan nodded numbly. "My brother."

"Ahh." The general sat back, elbows resting on the arms of his chair, his fingers tented before him. Lieutenant Fraser, as he recalled, was white. Similar in stature perhaps, but otherwise, nothing like the young man seated before him. It was yet another aspect of Private Fraser's story that would bear investigating.

"Why did you come back, Private Fraser? It would appear, by the look of you, that you were well cared for by your friends in the South." He reached out and fingered the roll of greenbacks. "Or are you being paid by someone in the North, as well?"

Ethan swallowed hard. "No, sir. No one's paying me." He couldn't believe what was happening. Worse, he could see no way out of it.

General Reynolds inclined his head, a signal to Captain Kellogg. The captain walked past Ethan, and opened the door.

"I'm placing you under arrest, Private Fraser. I suggest you use your time in prison to think about what you've told us. Should you decide you have anything to add, we will be happy to listen."

"But, sir..." Ethan protested, then stopped. He rose with the general, looking around as two men wearing the insignia of the provost guard came into the room. Ethan took a step back, casting a furtive glance at the nearest window.

His chances of escape were virtually nonexistent, but still, he had to fight the urge to attempt it. A glance at Major Hawkes convinced him. He knew what Ethan was thinking, and his eyes challenged.

One of the guards seized Ethan roughly from behind, holding his arms while the other pulled the forgotten pistol from his waistband. Ethan held himself rigid, resisting. Tense moments passed before he relaxed, submitting to the manacles that were locked about his wrists.

As he was lead from the room, Ethan twisted around and caught the general's eye. "I *never* betrayed my country, sir. I swear it."

The General Reynolds offered him a wintry smile. "I doubt that's true. But tell me, Private, which country are you referring to?"

Ethan was taken to the three-story brick warehouse on Market Street that had been converted for use as a prison. He was led to the back corner of the ground floor, to a closet-like cell, segregated from the other prisoners. The two exterior walls were brick; the interior walls constructed with heavy wooden planks. A straw-filled tick, stained and mildewed, lay on the floor opposite the door, covered by a moth-eaten gray wool blanket. Damp cold seeped from the walls and floor. Huddled on the mattress, fully clothed, Ethan found it only barely possible to keep warm.

The sole source of illumination was a lantern that hung in the passage outside the cell. Light slanted through the fourteen-inch barred opening in the door, casting a narrow pattern onto the brick wall, and leaving the remainder of the cell in shadow. The lantern was left burning twenty-four hours a day, and it wasn't long before Ethan lost all track of time.

He was taken from his cell early the first evening and questioned far into the night. A few brief hours of sleep, and the guards came for him again. As the days passed, he was allowed fewer and fewer respites and underwent endless hours of interrogation.

Initially, the questioning was routine, if mind-numbingly repetitive, but as Ethan grew more exhausted, and his interrogators more impatient, the severity of their methods intensified. He was forced to stand for hours at a time, arms trussed behind him, held in place by a rope thrown over a beam. When the need for sleep overcame him, and he swayed against it, pain roused him instantly.

As he grew more disoriented, the sergeant in charge of the interrogation resorted to yanking the rope each time he repeated a question. Infuriated by a response, Major Hawkes delivered a savage blow to his midsection, driving the air from his lungs and doubling him over against his bonds. Pain seared through his arms and shoulders. Ethan tried to straighten, sobbed with the effort to draw breath.

After that, tension on rope was increased, forcing him onto his toes. He was held there long after the muscles in his calves spasmed, then knifed through with cramps. He begged for mercy, but the rope was pulled tighter, straining muscle and twisting joints to their limits. He screamed, losing control of his bladder. When the rope was released, he collapsed to the floor in a heap.

Through it all, he stuck to his story because it was the truth. He told them his rescuer was a woman, that she had given him the book. In the end, he acknowledged that she was the source of the money. As he'd anticipated, they refused to believe him. Through it all, he managed to convince himself that, sooner or later, they would realize he was telling the truth and let him go.

* * *

Ethan had been gone for three days when Elizabeth woke one morning feeling nauseous. When she sat up, the queasiness intensified. She lay back, waiting for it to pass.

The next day, the nausea returned. The day after, she was actually sick. Hannah fussed when she came in to find Elizabeth still in bed, damp-faced and pale, and discovered the contents of the chamber pot. It was late afternoon before Elizabeth felt well enough to dress and go downstairs. When she was sick again the following day, Hannah gave her a speculative look and shook her head.

"I don't understand, Hannah," Elizabeth said, when she finally made her way downstairs. "This has been going on for four days. What in the world is wrong with me?"

"Nuttin' eight o' nine months ain't gonna fix."

Elizabeth stared at her in silence. "What are you saying?" she asked at last.

"I's sayin' you gonna have a baby, Miz 'Lizbet."

Joy spread over Elizabeth's face. "Oh, Hannah! Are you sure?"

"I seen it plenty a' times befo'," Hannah replied. "They ain't no doubt about it."

* * *

The sun was setting when Josh rode into Nashville. His shoulder ached, and his only thought was to locate Company J amid the sprawl of tents, have something to eat, and retire to bed. When he reached his tent, he had no sooner dismounted and handed the reins to one of his men, than one of his sergeants appeared at a trot and handed him a message. Josh unfolded the slip of paper, read the single line it contained, and looked wearily at the sergeant.

"It says I'm to report to General Reynolds in Chattanooga. Any idea why?"

Sergeant Hedrick did. A number of men from the Thirty-sixth had been interviewed regarding the captured spy Ethan Fraser, and speculation was rampant. Before he could respond, Josh reacted to the expression on his face.

"What?" he demanded. "What's wrong?"

"I think it's best you hear it from Colonel Miller, Lieutenant," the sergeant said, looking faintly unnerved. "It's about your brother."

Josh looked at him in confusion. He was reaching for the reins as he asked, "Brother? What do you mean? Which brother?"

"The younger one, sir. Ethan."

Josh swung into the saddle, grimacing at the renewed spasm of pain the movement provoked. "Where can I find Colonel Miller?"

Sergeant Hedrick shouted directions as Josh spurred his horse and rode away.

It was dusk, four days later, when he crossed the Tennessee River and made his way to Army Headquarters in Chattanooga. The news he received there was devastating, the evidence damning.

Physically and emotionally spent, Josh followed one of the general's aides to the house where he was to spend the night. He dismounted stiffly and walked like an old man to his room. Lacking the strength to undress, he lay on the bed fully clothed and stared into the darkness.

He had been taken completely by surprise when informed that Ethan had volunteered to spy after Stones River. But that Ethan had used spying as an opportunity to turn traitor was impossible to believe.

And yet, he was assigned to Price. Josh had personally witnessed Price's corruption of another young man. Ethan was the same age; it stood to reason that Price had held the same sway over him. All the evidence pointed to it.

There was the money—a staggering amount of money. The shirts from Ethan's saddlebags—*three of them, no less!*—were quality-made; the trousers a fine wool weave. It appeared he'd done very well for himself in the South. The inscription in the book sealed it.

Josh let out a long sigh. Everything he'd seen and heard helped explain the cryptic note from Mobile, the existence of which he'd kept from his brother's accusers. As much as he wanted to deny it, it looked like Ethan had been tempted or coerced, and he'd changed sides. Thinking him dead had been bad enough, but this was worse. *Much worse.* Josh groaned, dreading the impending confrontation with Ethan and the letter he would have to write to their parents.

30

At the end of five days and nights of questioning, the guards dumped Ethan in his cell and left him. He didn't stir when his breakfast was delivered, was still dead to the world an hour later when a guard nudged him with his foot. He moaned in protest.

"Wake up, boy. You got comp'ny."

Ethan opened his eyes to see a lone officer standing silhouetted in the doorway to his cell. Dreading what would come next, he stiffly sat up. The officer stepped aside to let the guard out, and light from the lantern fell across his face. Grinning with relief, Ethan surged to his feet. And ran smack into Josh's fist.

The blow sent him spinning into the wall. He sagged to his knees. Before he could recover, Josh grabbed a fistful of coat and jerked him around.

"You bastard!" he hissed. Bracing himself with one hand against the wall, he pulled his brother's face within inches of his own. "You stupid little bastard! What the hell were you thinking, coming back here? If you were going to change sides, the least you could do was stay there."

Ethan stared at him, eyes wide with shock and dismay. "No, Josh! It isn't true. I swear it."

"Don't lie to me, Ethan!" Furious at his denial, Josh slammed him against the wall. "I've seen the money, I've seen the book. I heard what Private Myers had to say. And I knew Price. I watched him turn another boy in a matter of days."

"Please, Josh. It isn't true. I never changed sides. I swear it."

Josh glowered at Ethan. With a grunt of disgust, he shoved him away.

Ethan sat up slowly, his eyes never leaving his brother's face. "Please, Josh. I've been hoping you'd come. Please. Let me tell you what happened."

Josh continued to glare at him, at the same time taking in his appearance—the long, unkempt hair, the soiled and wrinkled clothing, the anxious eyes pleading from a face worn with exhaustion. Josh's shoulders sagged. He sat down on the stool the grinning guard had left for him. "All right," he said wearily. "Tell me your side of it."

Ethan began his story, telling Josh everything that had happened since they'd last seen each other. It was easy to speak of the time he'd spent with Price, and he was gratified by Josh's relief at learning Thomas was alive. He told him of the escape from the train and the trek across Georgia.

But as he went on, Ethan discovered that speaking of some things to an older brother he barely knew was more difficult than he'd imagined. Head bowed, hair falling forward to mask his face, his voice dropped to a whisper when he spoke of his time at Cahaba. Josh leaned close in order to hear; recoiling in horror when he realized what Ethan was saying.

It proved equally awkward to confide the details of his relationship with Elizabeth. This time, however, Ethan favored his older brother with an occasional self-conscious glance as he explained what had passed between them.

By the time Ethan described his reception in Chattanooga, three hours had elapsed. There was a long silence when he finished speaking.

Anxious that his brother still didn't believe him, Ethan said, "It's the truth, Josh. I swear it."

Josh looked into Ethan's eyes and knew that it was. He nodded, forcing a brief, tight-lipped smile. "I believe you, Ethan." Leaning forward, he grasped his brother's shoulder and gave it a squeeze. "I believe you," he repeated softly.

"Will you talk to General Reynolds? Explain that it's all a misunderstanding?"

Josh's hand dropped away. He sighed heavily and stood up, turning to the door and staring out through the bars. Behind him, Ethan rose uneasily.

Finding no good way to say it, Josh turned to face him. "They're going to court-martial you, Ethan."

Court-martial! Ethan's stomach gave a sickening lurch, and his knees went weak. He sat down hard. "Court-martial?" he repeated.

Josh nodded miserably. "They only agreed to let me see you because they thought I could get the truth out of you. Or what they think is the truth," he amended quickly.

"But how... ?" Ethan gestured helplessly. "I haven't done anything wrong. They don't have any proof."

"They think they have plenty to charge you with spying and desertion. They had me convinced, and I'm your brother. How do you think it looks to people who don't know you?"

"But, Josh..." Ethan shook his head, eyes glistening with tears. "I haven't done anything wrong. You have to make them believe that."

Josh's expression softened. He laid a hand on his brother's shoulder. "I know you haven't. You've been through hell and you don't deserve this. I promise I'll do what I can to convince them you're innocent."

Ethan heard the reservation in his voice. "You don't think it'll do any good, do you?"

Josh let out a long breath. "No."

Ethan's head dropped, his shoulders slumped. "When is it?"

"What?"

"The court-martial."

"It's set to begin day after tomorrow."

Ethan looked up sharply, then away. Josh sighed and sat down. A gloomy silence stretched between them.

"You can't face this alone," Josh said, after a time. "You'll need someone to act as your advocate. Someone good. I know a man who might agree to do it, if he's still in Chattanooga. He was a lawyer before the war. When I leave here, I'll see if I can find him. If I can't, or he won't, I'll find someone who will." When Ethan didn't respond, he continued, "On Monday you're going to be asked if you request counsel. Tell them yes. Unless you hear otherwise, tell them you want Captain Fredrick Johnson."

Ethan gave a slight nod, but didn't look up.

"Do you understand how serious this is, Ethan? We're talking about your life."

At that, Ethan looked at him. His eyes were old beyond his years. "I understand," he said wearily. "It's just... It seems so pointless. Even you believed them. And..." He shook his head in defeat. "I'm so tired..."

Josh stared at him, sympathy turning to anger. He grabbed Ethan by the arm and leaned in close, his voice harsh. "Don't you dare talk like that, Ethan Fraser! Ma got your letter. You weren't there to see her face, but I was. I don't care how unfair you think life is, you will not give up." His grip on Ethan's arm tightened. "Do you understand me, Ethan?"

Ethan's eyes widened. "She got the letter?"

"Yes."

Ethan nodded. "I'll do it. I'll ask for Captain Johnson."

"Good," Josh said, releasing him. He stood up, grimacing at the pain his injured shoulder caused him. "I'll go look for him. I doubt they'll let me back in, but I'll see you have clean clothes for Monday."

Ethan pushed himself to his feet. For a long moment, they considered one another. Then Josh stepped forward and embraced him.

"It's good to see you, Josh. Thanks." Ethan's voice cracked.

"Take care, Ethan," Josh responded gruffly. "Don't give up hope. I'll do what I can to get you out of here." He clapped Ethan on the back and pulled away, calling for the guard.

Turning back he said, "Take my advice, and cut off that hair. Looking like that won't help you any."

Ethan was awakened midway through the afternoon and told his advocate was waiting to meet with him. With the guard grasping him firmly by the arm, he was led to the same room with the bricked-over window where he had been interrogated. The man seated at the small wooden table near its center looked up expectantly. When Ethan stepped into the full light from the lantern, the man's expression turned from anticipation to dismissal.

"I'm afraid they've brought you to the wrong place," he said, rising and starting for the door. "I'll call the guard."

"Are you Captain Johnson, sir?"

The officer turned. "I am."

"I'm Ethan Fraser. My brother spoke to you?"

Pale eyes widened behind wire-rimmed spectacles. "*You're* Josh Fraser's brother?"

"Yes, sir."

Captain Johnson had the good grace to look embarrassed, but he continued to eye Ethan skeptically, searching for some indication that he was indeed related to fair, blue-eyed Josh Fraser. He took in the copper skin and the long, dark hair, and found he couldn't shake his first impression: The young man was, without a doubt, at least part Indian. But, the captain realized, if one ignored his coloring, his height and build were similar to Josh's, and their features were remarkably the same. He indicated the chair opposite where he'd been sitting.

"My apologies, Private Fraser. Please sit."

Ethan stepped over to the chair and waited, eyes following the captain as he walked to the far side of the table. He was tall, in his mid to late thirties, lean with angular features, short brown hair receding at the temples, and a closely trimmed beard and mustache. The captain sat, and Ethan did the same.

"Your brother has explained your circumstances," Captain Johnson said. "It is because he believes so strongly in your innocence that I agreed to meet with you. I need you to tell me exactly what happened, from beginning to end. But before you do, I want to make sure you understand what a court-martial entails and the charges against you."

Ethan nodded. "Yes, sir."

"You will be prosecuted by the United States of America, in the person of a judge advocate. Your judges will be a group of from eight to thirteen officers detailed to perform that duty. Those officers, the Court, are required to administer justice according to the Articles of War. If there is doubt, the Court is expected to vote according to its conscience. Or to the best of its understanding. Or, failing that, according to the custom of war in like cases."

"I understand, sir."

Captain Johnson raised an admonishing hand and continued. "You are being charged with Acting as a Spy and Desertion. Typically, when a man is charged with Acting as a Spy, there is evidence to support that charge. In your case, it has been decided to prosecute based entirely on circumstantial evidence. Do you understand the meaning of circumstantial, Private?"

Ethan nodded, but Captain Johnson went on. "It means—"

"I know what it means, sir."

Captain Johnson gave him a long look, reevaluating. "Right," he said with a slight nod. "You are being prosecuted based solely on circumstantial evidence. From what your brother tells me, there is quite a lot of it, and it appears fairly damning when considered all together."

Captain Johnson paused, watching Ethan to see that he understood. Satisfied that he did, he went on. "Are you aware, Private Fraser, that in addition to your acknowledged association with Price, suspicions regarding your return to Chattanooga, and the questionable items found in your possession, a man has been located who is willing to bear witness against you? There are others less willing, but I am given to understand they cannot refute what he says."

Just when he'd thought the nightmare couldn't possibly get any worse. Ethan shook his head, his mind unwilling, unable, to grasp what was happening. "Who...?"

Captain Johnson pulled a leather-bound journal from the haversack lying on the table beside him and thumbed through the pages. Finding what he was searching for, he looked up. "A Private Myers. Do you know him?"

The same name Josh mentioned. Ethan's mind reeled back over the past eleven months. He could recall no one by that name. "Who are the others?"

"Corporal Fisk and Privates Connelly and Klestil. Do you know them?"

They made it! Ethan nodded, unable to speak. *Private Myers. Frank!* Frank, who'd disliked him from the moment they met. Frank, who was free because Ethan had used every skill he possessed to lead him halfway across Georgia. Frank, who was apparently willing to lie to see him condemned. Ethan realized Captain Johnson was speaking and tried to focus.

"...with them, Private Fraser?"

Ethan looked blank, and Captain Johnson repeated his question. "How do you know these men? What was your association with them?"

"We were captured at Chickamauga Creek." Ethan forced out the words, trying to make sense of what was happening. "I knew Zach and Fergus from the Thirty-sixth. I met Frank and Horst in the stockade at Atlanta. We escaped from the Richmond train together."

"What reason would Private Myers have to testify against you? What led him to believe you were spying for the Confederacy?"

"I don't know, sir," Ethan said, the beginnings of hysteria creeping into his voice. "I... I was a courier..." He took a breath and started over. "I was a courier, never a spy. And only for the Union. I spent six months traveling through the South. I knew the country and was familiar with their ways down there, so when we escaped, it seemed logical I should lead them back."

Captain Johnson opened the journal to a blank page and took out a pen and a pot of ink. "Why don't you begin at the beginning and tell me everything that's happened since you left the Thirty-sixth in, what...?" He referred to his notes. "March of last year."

For the second time that day, Ethan began his story. He repeated what he'd told Josh, omitting the worst of his treatment at Cahaba and the exact nature of his relationship with Elizabeth. It had been hard enough speaking of them to Josh; he couldn't bring himself to repeat it to a stranger.

Captain Johnson took copious notes, interrupting frequently with questions. When Ethan reached the end of his narrative, the captain continued to write for several minutes before looking up. "Is that all? There's nothing you've neglected to tell me?"

Ethan met his gaze briefly, then lowered his eyes and shook his head. "No, sir."

The captain closed the journal and stood up. "Your court-martial is scheduled to convene at nine o'clock Monday morning. When asked if you desire counsel, give them my name. I will be there."

Ethan looked up. "Thank you, sir."

"You must understand, Private Fraser, that the army believes it has a strong case against you. From what I've heard thus far, I can't say I disagree. I would be derelict if I were to lead you to believe there is any chance of acquittal. All I can do is try to save your life. I should warn you however, that if I am successful, you will undoubtedly spend some, if not all of it, in prison."

He paused, watching Ethan's face as his words sank in. "I'm willing to believe what you've told me, but I'm not convinced it's the entire story. I need to know everything, even things you think are unimportant, if I am to represent you properly. Think about it, and we'll talk again tomorrow."

With that, he walked to the door and called for the guard.

As the key turned in the lock, Ethan blurted out the question that been nagging at him. "How did they know to talk to Frank? To Private Myers?"

Captain Johnson motioned the guard to wait. Pushing the door closed, he turned to Ethan. "You told General Reynolds that Lieutenant Fraser is your brother. The 36th Illinois is in Nashville, so a man was dispatched to fetch him. When Sergeant Heartsner arrived in Nashville, he discovered Josh was on furlough. Since he was there, he took it upon himself to ask around, see if anyone from the Thirty-sixth remembered you. He came across Private Connelly, and Private Connelly supplied him with several names, including Private Myers." The captain paused, watching Ethan. "Is there anything you wish to add, Private? Shall I send the guard away?"

Ethan shook his head. He needed to come to grips with what was happening. He needed time to think.

At first, he gave up all hope. To spend the rest of his life in prison would mean thirty, maybe even forty years behind bars. The prospect was too awful to contemplate.

Why should I make any effort to save myself? he thought. *Life like this isn't worth living.* Memories of Cahaba came rushing back, and he sank deeper into despair. *I'd rather die.* He huddled on the mattress, wallowing in misery and self-pity for the remainder of the afternoon.

The arrival of a guard with his supper roused Ethan from his lethargy. He had no stomach for food, but the interruption set his mind moving in other directions. He despaired thinking of Elizabeth, waiting and wondering, not knowing what had become of him. He would, he decided, ask for pen and paper and write to her.

Another thought struck him: When the war ended, Thomas could confirm his story. *And so can Elizabeth.* If he lived, the two of them could set him free.

Ethan paced the narrow confines of his cell, carried away by this new train of thought. After a time, he picked up the tin plate and cup and placed them on the mattress. He ate distractedly, planning what he would say to Captain Johnson. Then he was up again, filled with restless energy. Now that he had made up his mind, he wanted desperately to live.

Ethan downed his breakfast quickly, then paced his cell, waiting for a guard to fetch him. He had no way of knowing what time it was, but as the hours dragged by, he found it more and more difficult to control his anxiety. He alternated between fear that something terrible had happened, and hope that Josh or Captain Johnson had prevailed and put a stop to the court-martial. He eyed the door, pressing his face to the bars each time he heard a sound in the passageway. When a guard finally did appear, it was to deliver his supper.

"Get back," the man ordered, and Ethan retreated two steps to the mattress.

"Where's Captain Johnson?" he asked as the guard placed the tin plate and cup on the floor. "Why didn't he come?"

The man straightened and pushed the door closed. "Gone with the army 'ud be my guess."

"What do you mean?" Ethan demanded, panic rising.

"Army left first thing this morning. General Grant's orders. More 'n likely, the captain's gone with 'em." He turned the key in the lock and walked away.

Ethan crossed to the door in a single stride. "What about me?" he demanded, peering through the bars. "When will he be back?"

The man shrugged, throwing words over his shoulder. "When they drive your friends outta Dalton 'ud be my guess. Don't no one consult me." His voice trailed off as he rounded the corner.

General Thomas set out with the XIV Corps and the 1st Division, IV Corps on the fourteenth of February. His orders were to verify reports that General Johnston had weakened his forces by sending reinforcements to General Polk in Mississippi and General Longstreet at Knoxville.

Owing to the lack of sound horses, they took only eighteen pieces of artillery and a limited number of supply wagons. They angled southeast, crossing into Georgia, and passed unchallenged through Ringgold Gap. They continued toward Varnell's Station, where on February twenty-second, they routed Confederate cavalry. Two days later, they took a dozen prisoners a few miles from Dalton. But the following morning, as they approached Buzzard's Roost Gap, they ran up against a strong Confederate defense. A day of heavy skirmishing convinced General Thomas that the reports had been incorrect—the Confederate army was still present in strength in and around Dalton. Lacking adequate artillery, he determined it impossible to take Rocky Face Ridge. On February twenty-sixth, the Union Army withdrew and turned back toward Chattanooga.

* * *

Ethan was left all but forgotten in the cold, semi-darkness of his cell. No one came near him but the guards who arrived twice each day, once to bring his breakfast and exchange the encrusted wooden bucket he used as a toilet, and again to deliver his supper. Ethan tried to engage them in conversation, but they were disinclined to linger.

As time went on, he discovered that certain of them would tell him what the day was like outside. Beyond that, they refused to converse. His request for pen and paper was denied, the guard informing him that as an accused spy, he wasn't allowed to write or speak to anyone. There was no news of the army or Captain Johnson, and no word from Josh.

At first, Ethan cursed himself for leaving Mobile. "Stupid!" he muttered, slamming a balled fist against the wall. *I had everything there. Everything but my precious freedom.* If only he'd been patient. He pressed his forehead to the cold brick, fighting back tears.

Eventually, he went to sit cross-legged on the mattress. Wrapping himself in the blanket, he went back over the time spent with Price, mortified to realize how thoroughly Price had taken advantage of him. By supplementing the sketchy information Price provided, he had played directly into his hands, enhancing Price's credibility with the very army he was betraying.

He spent time rehashing the weeks he'd spent with Frank, knowing full well why Frank disliked him, but not understanding his willingness to lie. And he thought about Cahaba, deciding to tell Captain Johnson everything that had happened there—everything except the rape. It was bad enough that the nightmares persisted without it becoming a topic in open court.

But I will explain about Elizabeth, he decided. *Enough that he'll understand why she gave me the money.*

Ethan spent every waking hour formulating the list of things he would tell Captain Johnson. Even so, time seemed to stretch without end. He found the silence oppressive, the loneliness almost impossible to bear. But more than anything, he longed for a breath of fresh air, a glimpse of the sky.

On the morning of Ethan's twenty-second day in captivity, Captain Johnson returned to the prison. He found Ethan enormously relieved to see him and eager to talk.

Ethan began by telling how Price had used him. How Price must have decided, albeit incorrectly, that Ethan had grown suspicious. How on their last day in Atlanta, Price had handed him a thick packet of information, more comprehensive than any he'd sent north before, with orders to carry it directly to General Rosecrans. Then, at the last moment, Price's urgent appeal had sent him to Macon instead, guaranteeing that the documents would arrive in Union hands too late.

He told Captain Johnson of being left to die of cold in the yard at Cahaba, of the constant torment by the guards, of being beaten and isolated by Shunk, chained to his bunk and starved. He described his health and state of mind when he was rescued by Elizabeth, her circumstances, and how her care and devotion had restored not only his health, but his faith in himself.

"So you see," he said, imploring the captain to believe him, "she thought she was helping when she put the money in my saddlebags. I found the Confederate scrip right away, but the other... it must have been buried at the bottom. I had no idea it was there until the captain found it." Ethan paused, trying to gauge Captain Johnson's reaction. "Please believe me, sir. I swear everything I've told you is true."

Captain Johnson looked down at the page in front of him and discovered that, midway through Ethan's narrative, he had forgotten to take notes. He looked into Ethan's anxious eyes and nodded. "I believe you."

Ethan sagged in relief.

"There is one thing you haven't explained. Why is Private Myers so eager to testify that you are a Confederate spy?"

Ethan shook his head, obviously at a loss. "I don't know. He made it clear from the start he didn't like me, but I never thought he'd carry it this far." He paused before adding, "Maybe Zach or Fergus knows. Has anyone asked them?"

"I doubt anyone has asked questions of them that don't pertain directly to your guilt."

"Will you be able to talk to them?"

"I will. In the meantime, I would like to hear your explanation for some of the things Private Myers has said." Captain Johnson thumbed through his journal, running his finger down the pages until he found what he was looking for.

An hour later, he closed the journal and set his pen aside. Removing his eyeglasses, he placed them atop the journal and leaned his elbows on the table, massaging his temples with his thumbs. He looked up to find Ethan watching him.

"Will what I told you make a difference?"

"It's made a difference to me, Private Fraser. I believe in your innocence and will do all in my power on your behalf. But again, I must warn you against getting your hopes up."

Ethan nodded. "I understand, sir. Thank you. But, if you don't mind my asking... ?"

He hesitated, and the captain motioned him to continue.

"I've been thinking about something you said last time. About being concerned with saving my life. That can't be true, can it? I mean, taken all together the evidence looks bad, but there's an explanation for everything. What this is really about is people's perceptions and opinions. And Frank's word against mine. The Court wouldn't decide to hang me based on that, would they?"

Captain Johnson picked up his spectacles. Ethan watched in mounting apprehension as he used his handkerchief to give the lenses a thorough cleaning, then hooked the wire earpieces carefully over each ear. When they were in place, the captain looked at him.

"Article 57 of the Articles of War states that anyone providing intelligence to the enemy shall suffer death, but there is nothing to prove you guilty of having done that. On one occasion you admit failing to provide intelligence to this army, but that's hardly the same thing.

"Article 87 states that a sentence of death requires the concurrence of two-thirds of the Court. I don't see how, based on the circumstantial nature of the evidence, two-thirds of the Court could arrive at such a decision. Not in good conscience, at any rate.

"Desertion..." He shook his head. "I don't understand how they expect to prove it. Granted, it's a hanging offence, but to my way of thinking, there's nothing to support the charge." He looked steadily at Ethan. "In my opinion, the answer to your question would have to be no."

Seeing relief spread across Ethan's face, he hastened to add, "But don't fool yourself regarding the seriousness of peoples' perceptions and opinions, Private Fraser. Especially when taken together with Price's duplicity. You must know that you would have aroused suspicion, showing up as you did, well fed and well dressed, even without the money, and even with a loyal Price to vouch for you. As things now stand, your situation is precarious at best.

"Despite having absolute faith in your innocence, it would be derelict of me not reiterate that you will undoubtedly spend time in prison. Perhaps until the end of the war. Perhaps longer."

"But," Ethan protested, "when I testify, I can explain everything. The same as I explained it to you and Josh."

Captain Johnson gave him a long look before replying. "I'm not sure testifying is a good idea. It would open you up to cross-examination, and there are several points that would be better left to me to explain."

"But, sir..." Ethan started to argue, then thought better of it. "Whatever you think best. You've said you believe me. The least I can do is trust you."

"There's no need to decide just yet. We'll talk again once the judge advocate has presented his case." Captain Johnson sat back, looking at Ethan with genuine regret. "I truly believe you are a victim of circumstance, Private Fraser. I'm sorry not to be able to offer you more hope."

He gathered his belongings and pushed himself to his feet. Ethan rose with him.

"Thank you, sir," he said softly. "I understand."

* * *

Thomas looked at Elizabeth in astonishment. Just two weeks earlier, she'd announced she was pregnant with Ethan's child. Now she sat beside him, beautiful and serene, telling him she planned to leave Mobile.

"What do you mean, you're leaving?" he demanded. "Where will you go?"

"To Illinois," Elizabeth answered quietly. "I'm pregnant, Thomas. I want this baby desperately. I can't stay here with James' family so close by. I respect them too much to ask them to suffer my embarrassment. I need to leave Mobile, and it's only logical I should go to Ethan."

"But," Thomas sputtered, "you don't know where he is. If he's back with the army, they're not going to let him up and leave."

"I understand that, Thomas," Elizabeth said patiently. "But I know where his parents live. Surely, they won't turn me away. But if they do, a good deal of the money James left me is still in New York banks. I intend to set up housekeeping and send word to Ethan, letting him know where I am. When he's able, he can come to me and we'll make things right for our child." She looked imploringly at him. "Don't you see? It's the only way."

Thomas regarded her silently for several moments before trying another tack. "There's a war on, Elizabeth. How do you expect to get from southern Alabama to central Illinois?"

Elizabeth smiled. Holding up a hand, she rubbed her thumb and two fingers together. "Money, Thomas. If there's one thing I've learned during this war, it's that with money, you can buy just about anything." She laid a hand on his arm. "Don't worry. I intend to take two of the servants with me, so I won't be traveling alone, and I'll see that Josiah continues to bring whatever you need."

Thomas looked reproachfully at her. "Somehow, it won't be the same."

"I've thought this through," Elizabeth said, smiling sweetly. "Everything will be fine."

There was no sense arguing with her. Her mind was made up. *And she's right,* Thomas thought. *She can't very well stay in Mobile.* Oh, but he would miss her!

He had known from the moment they met that she was an exceptional woman. It would be so easy to fall in love. *And of course*, he realized suddenly, *I have.* He pushed the thought aside. "I'll miss you."

Elizabeth squeezed his hand. "I'll miss you, too, Thomas. I've come to rely on our time together. I don't know how I'll manage without you to talk to. But with luck, the war will end soon, and the three of us will be together."

Thomas wasn't at all sure that was what he wanted, but he nodded. "I hope you're right," was all he could think to say.

31

A pair of guards escorted Ethan from his cell to a small, windowless room where soap and a bucket of water waited. One of the guards ordered him wash and change into the clothing that had been provided. A lump rose in Ethan's throat when he saw the familiar uniform hanging over the back of the chair. He ran his fingers over the dark blue flannel sack coat, wishing the reason for wearing it was different.

"Get a move on, son. Time's a'wastin'."

Ethan did what he could with the tepid water and sliver of soap. When he finished, he lifted a hank of wet hair and looked to the guards. "Can I get some scissors... something to cut this off?"

The guards looked at one another. One of them shrugged. "I'll see what I can do."

He left, and Ethan began to dress. He saw the covetous look the remaining guard cast at his boots and pulled them on quickly, shunning the ill-fitting brogans that had been set out for him. He was dressed, all but the coat, when the guard returned.

"The lieutenant says, if you wanted your hair cut, you shoulda said something sooner. Orders are to get you dressed and outta here."

"Please," Ethan persisted. "I asked before and was told 'later'. I thought today..." He looked imploringly at the guard. "Please, it's important."

"No time. Now get a move on."

Seeing there was nothing the man could or would do, Ethan retrieved the shirt he'd been wearing and tore a strip from it. Pulling his hair back, he wound the fabric around it, tying it back from his face.

His hands were secured in front of him, and with a guard on either arm, he was hurried back past his cell and out the back door of the prison.

After weeks spent in near darkness, he was ill prepared for the brilliance of the morning. He bowed his head, screwing his eyes shut against it, and was hoisted all but blind, up the steps of the jail wagon. One of the guards followed him inside, pressing him onto one of the side benches and sitting down opposite. The other guard slammed the door and set the bar in place, locking them in.

Ethan braced himself as the wagon lurched forward, then looked toward the small, barred window in the door. Squinting into the light, he caught his first glimpse of blue sky in nearly a month. As his eyes adjusted, he looked to the guard for permission, then stood and looked out the window. Gray-brown mountains loomed west of town, and closer, sunlight glinted off the waters of the Tennessee. The morning air was fresh and clean, and he inhaled deeply, clearing his nostrils of the foul stench of his cell.

The town was every bit as shabby as he remembered, and yet the streets bustled with people. They were soldiers mostly, but a few were civilians—those who had either refused to leave, or had returned once the siege was lifted. A woman carrying a large basket with a small child in tow caught Ethan's eye. She stepped into the rutted street behind the wagon and made her way to the other side, the little boy scrambling along beside her. He was red-cheeked and tow-headed, and Ethan's chest constricted at the sight of him. He watched them until they were out of sight, aching for a return to normalcy.

The wagon drew to a halt before a large house on the outskirts of town. Knots of people, men and women, soldiers and civilians, stood scattered about. The guard pulled the door open and ordered Ethan out. Heads turned, conversations stopped, and the crowd edged forward. Ethan took a nervous step back. The guard behind him gave him a shove that sent him staggering down the steps. His arms were once again seized and he was hustled past a blur of inquisitive faces, up the steps, across the porch, and into the house.

"Prisoner in the court!"

The sergeant who'd pushed open a door leading off the foyer stood aside to let them enter. Heads turned, and the eyes of all the men assembled settled on Ethan. He caught a quick glimpse of familiar faces near the door as he was propelled past them, into the center of the room.

An American flag hung between two windows on the wall ahead of him. Seated before it, behind a row of mismatched tables, was a group of officers. There were two more tables set off to the sides, the one on the right already occupied. Ethan's guards steered him toward the table on the left. They freed his hands and pressed him into the chair before taking up positions against the wall beside him. The sergeant closed the door and stood with his back against it. Ethan waited, his heart in his throat, the unwilling center of attention.

A general seated near the center of the row of tables picked up a pistol and rapped the butt sharply on the table. "This military court is hereby convened at Chattanooga, Tennessee, at nine o'clock a.m. on February 29, 1864, by order of the Commanding General of the Army of the Cumberland, George H. Thomas."

He proceeded to read the names of the Judge Advocate—Major Blythe, seated at the table to Ethan's right, nodded in response—and the members of the court. As each officer acknowledged the reading of his name, Ethan studied the faces of the nine men assigned to judge him. One, a lieutenant, regarded him with open curiosity. A colonel looked away quickly when their eyes met. The others returned his gaze with varying degrees of interest. Ethan wasn't sure what he'd expected, but he was relieved to see no overt signs of hostility.

Lastly, the speaker introduced himself as General Starkweather. He looked at Ethan. "Has the accused any objection to any member named?"

Ethan looked again along the row of unfamiliar faces. "No, sir."

The nine officers were duly sworn by the Judge Advocate. General Starkweather, as President of the Court, swore in Major Blythe as Judge Advocate. The Official Reporter was sworn, and General Starkweather turned the floor over to Major Blythe.

The major collected a sheaf of papers from the table in front of him and rose to address the Court.

"Following are the Charges and Specifications preferred against Private Ethan Fraser, Company J, 36th Illinois.

"Charge first: Acting as a Spy.

"Specification first: In this, that he, Private Ethan Fraser, Company J, 36th Illinois, did closely associate and conspire with a known spy, a man known as Price, who was captured, tried and convicted by this army, and hanged at Chattanooga, Tennessee on the second of November, 1863.

"Specification second: In this, that he, Private Ethan Fraser, Company J, 36th Illinois, when taken into custody on the sixth of February, 1864, was found to have in his possession a document headed by the name of General Joseph E. Johnston of the Confederate Army of Tennessee at Dalton, Georgia. On that document were listed Generals Grant, Thomas, Hooker, Howard, Palmer,

Sherman, and Granger; the Fourth, Fourteenth and Fifteenth Corps, and their various locations at Nashville, Chattanooga, Bridgeport and Huntsville."

Ethan's stomach knotted as he listened. Captain Johnson had gone over the charges and specifications the day before, but hearing them read aloud in open court was far worse than he'd imagined. A trickle of sweat ran down his side. His collar, suddenly unbearably tight, threatened to cut off his breathing. He lifted a hand to loosen it, then let it drop when he realized several members of the Court were watching him.

"Specification third: In this, that he, Private Ethan Fraser, Company J, 36th Illinois, when taken into custody, was found to have in his possession over fifteen hundred dollars drawn on banks in the Confederate state of Alabama, as well as five hundred dollars in U.S. banknotes. By the accused's own admission, he was paid the money by the same citizen of Mobile, Alabama who authored the aforementioned document.

"Specification fourth: In this, that he, Private Ethan Fraser, Company J, 36th Illinois, while in the Confederate state of Georgia in October 1863, and in the company of Union soldiers captured at Chickamauga and escaped, is known to have jeopardized the safety of those soldiers through repeated fraternization with the enemy.

"Charge second: Desertion

"Specification first: In this, that he, Private Ethan Fraser, Company J, 36th Illinois, while enlisted in the army of the United States and in dereliction of duty, took up residence in Mobile, in the Confederate state of Alabama, from November 1863, until January, this year. The evidence will show that Private Fraser has formed lasting ties in the Confederacy and has expressed his intention to return."

The Judge Advocate read the name of the man who had prepared the charges before moving on to prosecution's list of witnesses.

Ethan fixed his eyes on the flag and listened to the responses. He resisted the urge to turn his head, even when the name called and the voice answering was familiar.

When it had been established that all the witnesses were present, General Starkweather turned once again to Ethan. "Does the accused request counsel?"

"Yes, sir." Ethan transferred his gaze from the stars and stripes to the general's face. "Captain Fredrick Johnson."

"Is Captain Fredrick Johnson present?"

"I am, sir." Captain Johnson came forward, and a chair was provided for him. He sat down next to Ethan, touching his arm briefly in a show of support.

"Pleading for the accused, to the first Specification, first Charge, how do you plead?" General Starkweather intoned.

"Not Guilty." Captain Johnson responded.

"To the second Specification, how do you plead?"

"Not Guilty."

"To the third Specification, how do you plead?"

"Not Guilty."

"To the fourth Specification, how do you plead?"

"Not Guilty."

"To the first Charge, how do you plead?"

"Not Guilty."

"To the first Specification, second Charge how do you plead?"

"Not Guilty."

"To the second Charge, how do you plead?"

"Not Guilty."

"Let the record show that the accused has entered pleas of 'not guilty' to all charges and specifications. This trial is set to begin. All witnesses are requested to withdraw in order that their testimony may be preserved."

During the delay while the room cleared, Captain Johnson leaned close to Ethan.

"How are you?"

"All right. Nervous." Ethan glanced along the row of officers. His eyes came back to Captain Johnson's face and he answered again, truthfully this time. "Scared. Scared to death. Until now, I didn't truly believe it would happen, but it is, isn't it?"

Captain Johnson laid a calming hand on his arm. "It is, Private Fraser, but keep in mind what I told you yesterday. Whatever is said, don't let anyone see that you're angry or upset. When the time comes, I'll see that your side gets told."

Ethan nodded, eyes straying to the members of the Court. The colonel who had avoided his gaze earlier was staring directly at him, listening to a lieutenant colonel who leaned toward him, speaking earnestly. One of the majors and a captain were also watching him. Another major looked down at the table and yawned.

"The Judge Advocate will summon his first witness," General Starkweather instructed.

All eyes turned to Major Blythe.

"On the charge of Acting as a Spy, we summon Captain Jeffrey R. Davies."

The sergeant at the door opened it and repeated the name. A man Ethan vaguely recognized crossed to the witness chair at the center of the room and was duly sworn.

"State your name, rank and regiment." the Judge Advocate instructed when the captain had been seated.

"Jeffrey R. Davies, Captain, Company L, 1st Ohio Cavalry."

"Do you recognize the accused? And if so, as whom?"

Captain Davies looked briefly at Ethan, then back at Major Blythe. "I do, sir. Private Ethan Fraser."

"State the circumstances under which you met the accused."

"We were riding south of Wauhatchie the morning of February six, this year, when he approached us and asked for directions to General Thomas' headquarters."

"He approached you?"

"Yes, sir."

"From which direction?"

"From the southeast, sir. He came out of the hills below Lookout Mountain."

"Give a full account of your meeting."

"We stopped when we spotted him and waited for him to come to us. He was smiling when he rode up and the first thing he said was how good it was to see blue uniforms again. He identified himself as Private Ethan Fraser, Company J, 36th Illinois and told us he'd been captured by the Rebs at Chickamauga Creek and escaped. I said he was looking mighty good for a man who'd spent the last four months in a Reb prison, and that's when he told me he'd escaped in late November or early December, he wasn't sure which, and someone had taken him in before he headed north. It was then he asked for directions to General Thomas' headquarters."

"What did you do then, Captain?"

"I assigned Sergeant Weldin to take four men and escort Private Fraser to Chattanooga, sir."

"You sent five men to escort the accused?"

"Yes, sir."

"Why so many?"

"His looks mainly, I guess." Once again, Captain Davies eyes flicked to Ethan. "And he was wearing fancy clothes and riding a good horse. He said he escaped in November and here it was, February. It was a feeling I had, but I thought it best to make sure he went direct to headquarters."

Major Blythe thanked the captain and returned to his seat.

Captain Johnson spoke from the table beside Ethan. "You stated that Private Fraser told you he was happy to see blue uniforms again."

"Yes, sir."

Captain Johnson rose and walked toward Captain Davies. "Did you have any reason to disbelieve him?"

"No, sir. He seemed happy enough to see us."

"Did Private Fraser indicate why he was looking for General Thomas' headquarters?"

"He said he wanted to get back to the 36th Illinois. Said he'd fought with them."

"Did you observe any change in Private Fraser's demeanor when informed that he would be escorted to General Thomas' headquarters?"

"No, sir."

"Not even when he saw the size of the escort?"

"No, sir."

"It did not appear to bother him that he had been essentially placed under guard?"

"No, sir. Not that I noticed."

"And did he go with the escort willingly?"

"Yes, sir. He did."

"Thank you, Captain."

Captain Johnson indicated that he was finished. As he returned to his seat, General Starkweather spoke.

"You stated that you assigned Sergeant Weldin and four men to see Private Fraser escorted to Chattanooga. Was it your intention that he be placed under guard?"

"Yes, sir."

"And your intention was made clear to Private Fraser?"

"Yes, sir. I told him he was to accompany them and that they had orders to shoot if he tried to run."

"And what was Private Fraser's response, if any?"

"He said he understood. Then he thanked me for my help."

The general shot a speculative glance at Ethan and leaned back in his chair.

There were no further questions. The court reporter read back Captain Davies' testimony, Captain Davies confirmed that it was correct and was dismissed. As he left the room, Ethan realized he was hunched forward nervously. He sat back, forcing himself to relax.

The second witness was Captain Davies' sergeant. After he had been duly sworn and identified himself as Sergeant Carl Weldin, Company L, 1st Ohio Cavalry, the Judge Advocate proceeded with his questions.

"You were in charge of the detail sent by Captain Davies to escort the accused to General Thomas' headquarters?"

"Yes, sir."

"During the ride to Chattanooga did you have cause to speak with the accused?"

"Yes, sir."

"Give an account of that conversation."

"I asked him what prison he escaped from and he said he hadn't escaped from a prison. He said he escaped while being moved from one Reb prison to another. I asked what it had been like, being in a Reb prison and he told me it had been... 'unpleasant' was the word he used. Then he said it was something he'd 'rather not talk about'. The way he said it made it real clear he didn't want to talk about it, so neither of us said anything for a while.

"Then he asked me was it true what he'd heard, that General Thomas had been placed in command of the Army of the Cumberland. I told him it was. He asked if I'd mind telling him about Chickamauga Creek. I couldn't see any reason not to, it being a while ago and all, so I told him what I knew. When I finished, he asked if I thought it would have made a difference if General Rosecrans had known Longstreet was coming from Virginia to reinforce Bragg."

"Was that something you had mentioned to the accused?"

After a moment's reflection, Sergeant Weldin said, "I don't think so, sir."

"What was your response to the accused's question?"

"I told him I didn't know. That's when he told me he had two brothers killed there. He said he wondered if knowing about Longstreet would have saved 'em.

Talking about it seemed to upset him, and he didn't say anything more until we were almost to Chattanooga. Then he started asking what I knew about plans for the spring campaign and wanting details about the disposition of the army. I told him he'd best get his information from headquarters. After that we didn't talk."

The Judge Advocate asked Sergeant Weldin to describe their arrival at Army Headquarters, which he did. The floor was then turned over to Captain Johnson.

"Did Private Fraser appear at all nervous or upset when he was placed under guard for the ride to headquarters?"

"No, sir."

"You stated that Private Fraser told you he was captured at Chickamauga Creek and was curious to know what happened there."

"Yes, sir."

"Did he appear to have any prior knowledge of events there or since?"

"No, sir. From the questions he asked, it sounded like it was the first he'd heard any of it."

"You stated that when Private Fraser started asking about the disposition of the army and plans for the spring campaign, you elected not to answer, even though you had answered his questions up to that point. Why did you suddenly decide to keep quiet?"

"Partly it was the way he asked. He was smarter than I figured, knew more about the chain of command. And he was asking questions I didn't know the answers to." He looked at Ethan. "And I wasn't sure why he was asking."

"Could it have been simple curiosity, not knowing? The same reason he asked about Chickamauga Creek?"

"I s'pose it coulda been. But I thought he best get his answers from headquarters."

"Thank you, Sergeant."

There were no further questions for Sergeant Weldin. After his testimony had been read back and he had been dismissed, Captain Johnson leaned over to Ethan and whispered, "Their testimony was only to establish background. Prepare yourself. It will get worse."

Feelings of dread rose in Ethan when General Reynolds' name was announced. The general's eyes sought his the moment he entered the room. Ethan forced himself to meet the man's gaze, hoping he looked calmer than he felt.

The general looked away during the preliminaries, then back when asked to identify Ethan. During the remainder of his testimony, General Reynolds' eyes rarely left Ethan's face. Ethan focused on the gold braid on the general's collar and tried to keep his expression neutral.

"State the circumstances under which you first met the accused," Major Blythe requested.

"Sergeant Weldin of the 1st Ohio Cavalry arrived at headquarters around mid-day on the sixth of February. He stated he'd brought in a half-breed they'd come across southeast of Wauhatchie that morning. He'd identified himself as Private Ethan Fraser, Company J, 36th Illinois. Private Fraser had asked Captain Davies for directions to General Thomas' headquarters. Sergeant Weldin stated that his captain had been suspicious of Private Fraser's story, so he sent him to Chattanooga under guard. I observed Private Fraser through the window and agreed with Captain Davies' assessment. I instructed Sergeant Weldin to bring him in."

"Describe what followed."

"I asked Private Fraser to identify himself, which he did, adding that he had been captured at Chickamauga Creek and escaped. Then he stated that he hadn't been with the Thirty-sixth when he was captured, but had been serving as a courier for a spy named Price."

"Explain the relevance of that statement."

"Price had been employed by General Thomas since the autumn of '62. Since before Perryville. On the twenty-fourth of October, last year, Price was detained when he attempted to leave Chattanooga and found to be carrying documents that included details of the plans to re-open the supply line to Bridgeport. Price was tried as a spy and convicted. He was hanged on the second of November."

"When the accused informed you he was Price's courier, did it appear he knew what had happened to Price?"

"He gave no indication either way. But later, when I told him Price was dead, it appeared to come as a surprise."

"Give an account of your subsequent actions regarding the accused."

"I questioned him further regarding his relationship with Price and the details of his capture and escape. I found certain aspects of his story unconvincing, so I sent Captain Kellogg to examine the contents of his saddlebags."

"State which aspects of the accused's story you found unconvincing."

"Private Fraser described documents he says he was carrying when he was captured at Chickamauga Creek. Despite being in possession of information vital to the Union, he elected to detour south from Atlanta, to Macon, Georgia, before returning to Chattanooga. He was unable to give a reason for the detour.

"In addition, I found a number of inconsistencies in Private Fraser's story regarding the month he professes to have spent in the Confederate prison at Cahaba, Alabama. Initially, Private Fraser told me most of his time at Cahaba was spent reading. Regarding the time following his escape, Private Fraser said he spent it resting and regaining his health. When I asked how it was that a month spent reading required three months to recuperate, Private Fraser amended his story, saying he'd been near starved when he arrived at Cahaba and the lack of food there left him ill. When I continued to express skepticism, Private Fraser changed his story again, claiming that one of the guards had taken a dislike to him, and as a consequence, he was starved and beaten.

"Regarding the time since his escape, Private Fraser would say only that he was taken in by a person sympathetic to the Union and kept hidden, housed with Negro servants until he was strong enough to travel. He was unwilling to supply information regarding his rescuer, other than to say it was a citizen of Mobile, Alabama. His vagueness appeared deliberate, and I was left with grave doubts regarding the truth of what he said."

The Judge Advocate produced an envelope. "Examine the contents of this envelope and state if you recognize them."

General Reynolds opened it and removed the contents. "Yes. This is the Confederate scrip brought to me by Captain Kellogg. It was found in Private Fraser's saddlebags."

"What was the accused's explanation for this money?"

"He had none."

"One thousand five hundred thirty two dollars and ten cents," Major Blythe said. "Drawn on the Confederate state of Alabama and banks in Mobile, Selma, and Birmingham among others."

He retrieved the money from General Reynolds and offered it to General Starkweather who examined it before stating, "The money may be entered in the record."

The Judge Advocate returned to his table and picked up the book. "Examine this article and state if you recognize it."

"I do," General Reynolds said, accepting the book and opening it to the inscription. "It was brought to me by Captain Kellogg who found it in Private Fraser's saddlebags."

"What was the accused's reply when you asked who had given him the book?"

"He said it was from 'a friend'. When I questioned him further, he admitted his 'friend' is a resident of Mobile, Alabama."

"*The Count of Monte Cristo*, by Alexandre Dumas," Major Blythe stated, taking the open book from General Reynolds. He read the inscription and date aloud, pausing when he finished to raise a skeptical eyebrow at Ethan. The book was offered into evidence, and he produced the drawstring pouch. "Examine the contents of this pouch and state if you recognize them."

As before, General Reynolds loosened the strings and upended the pouch. The thick roll of bills dropped into his hand. He locked eyes with Ethan as he said, "Yes. This is the remainder of the money brought to me by Captain Kellogg. It was found in Private Fraser's saddlebags."

"What did the accused say regarding this money?"

"He said nothing. He became agitated and demanded that I speak with Price, saying Price would confirm his story."

"And your reply?"

"That's when I told him Price was dead."

"What was the accused's reaction?"

"The news appeared to alarm him."

"Five hundred dollars, drawn on banks in the United States," Major Blythe announced, turning from the general and brandishing the roll of money before the Court. He paused briefly to allow for reaction before offering it into evidence.

"Give an account of what happened next."

"I placed Private Fraser under arrest. As he was about to leave the room, he told me, most emphatically, that he had never betrayed his country."

Ethan raised defiant eyes to General Reynolds' face.

"I asked him, which country he was referring to," the general concluded, eyes boring into Ethan's.

The members of the Court had become more attentive during General Reynolds' testimony, and now they stirred, glancing at one another and at Ethan as the Judge Advocate returned to his seat and Captain Johnson began his cross examination.

"You stated that Private Fraser 'elected' to detour from Atlanta to Macon before returning to Chickamauga. Were those his exact words, General?"

"Private Fraser said Price ordered him to go."

"And did Private Fraser object?"

"He said he did."

"Why, against his better judgment, did Private Fraser say he went?"

"He said Price insisted it was important."

"Important how?"

"Private Fraser didn't say."

"Private Fraser didn't say, or didn't know?"

"Private Fraser said he didn't know."

"Did Price tell Private Fraser who he was to meet?"

"Private Fraser said not. He said he was told to wait and he would be approached."

"Is that what happened?"

"Private Fraser said not. He said he waited several hours, then headed north."

"Is that what Price had instructed him to do?"

"Private Fraser said not."

"So Private Fraser disobeyed Price's orders in order to return to Chattanooga?"

"That's what Private Fraser said."

"Price was hanged for spying for the Confederacy. Knowing that, wouldn't you agree that the trip to Macon might well have been a ploy by Price to delay or prevent Private Fraser from delivering information vital to the Army of the Cumberland?"

"It's possible," General Reynolds allowed. As Captain Johnson started to turn away, he added, "It's also possible that he knew Price wanted the documents delivered too late and was a party to it."

Captain Johnson turned back, his face tight with anger. "But that is only supposition on your part. Is it not, sir?"

"Yes," the general admitted easily. "Only supposition."

As Captain Johnson returned to his seat, one of the members of the Court, a major, spoke up. "You stated that the book was given to the accused by a friend in Mobile. It appears from the inscription that this 'friend' is more than that and that theirs is a relationship of long standing. Did Private Fraser tell you how long he has known this woman or how they met?"

"He did not."

"Did you ask?"

"I did. He refused to answer."

A lieutenant spoke up. "You stated that Private Fraser was instructed to wait in Macon. What were Private Fraser's exact words?"

"He said Price ordered him to wait."

"Did Private Fraser tell you why he disobeyed orders?"

"He said he knew the documents he was carrying were vital to the Union. He said when he'd waited 'long enough', he brought them north."

Captain Kellogg was the next witness. His testimony concurred with that of General Reynolds up to the point where the Judge Advocate asked him to account for his actions when searching Ethan's belongings.

"I summoned Private Ezra Little, and we went out to Private Fraser's horse. I removed the saddlebags, and we took them to the room opposite where General Reynolds was questioning Private Fraser. With Private Little observing, I made a quick search of the saddlebags and returned to the general with the items I found of interest: a book inscribed to Private Fraser, over fifteen hundred dollars in Confederate scrip, and a pouch containing a roll of Federal banknotes."

"State your actions following the arrest of the accused."

"I returned, with Captain Willard, to the room where I had left Private Little standing guard over Private Fraser's possessions. Captain Willard and I then instituted a more thorough search of the contents. When we were done, we compared the handwriting on a note found in the book with the inscription written in the front."

Major Blythe retrieved the slip of paper and handed it to Captain Kellogg. "State if you recognize this."

"I do, sir. It fell from the pages of the book found in Private Fraser's possession."

"This piece of paper has written on it the name of General Johnston of the Confederate Army of Tennessee at Dalton followed by a listing of locations and commanders of the Army of the Cumberland, does it not?"

"Yes, sir. A good deal of what's written there is accurate."

"In addition to the information it contains, is there anything of further significance regarding this piece of paper?"

"Yes, sir. The handwriting matches the inscription in the book which has led us to believe that the woman with whom Private Fraser is romantically involved is also spying for the Confederacy."

Ethan stared at Captain Kellogg in open-mouthed disbelief. *Elizabeth? A spy?* The idea was ludicrous. He looked at the members of the Court and was brought up short by the grim expressions on their faces. It appeared they found Captain Kellogg's theory entirely plausible. The chair next to him scraped as Captain Johnson leapt to his feet.

Before Captain Johnson could object, Major Blythe diffused the situation by saying, "But that is only conjecture on your part, is it not, Captain? You have no evidence to support that statement."

Apparently contrite, Captain Kellogg agreed. "No, sir. There's no evidence. That's just how it appears."

At that, Captain Johnson sank back down. The Judge Advocate read the list aloud for the Court and entered it into evidence before yielding the floor. Captain Johnson rose quickly.

"In the testimony of Captain Kellogg this day taken, testimony has been given that is speculative in nature, and the record of the court is thereby encumbered. The accused therefore asks that all such testimony by the witness be expunged from the record."

Major Blythe, barely seated, was on his feet. "The witness has already admitted, on the record, that the portion of his testimony to which the accused objects is supposition and unsupported by the evidence at hand. As to encumbrance, there is no need to expunge the record as the witness has retracted his statement. Move to deny."

"In the interest of expediency, I would request that the defense set aside its objection and move on," General Starkweather said, casting a meaningful look at Captain Johnson.

Captain Johnson acquiesced, knowing that even with the record expunged, Captain Kellogg's words would linger in the minds of the Court. The longer he belabored the issue, the more apt they were to wonder as to their accuracy. Better to introduce another possibility. He turned to Captain Kellogg.

"You stated that the slip of paper contains a fairly accurate listing of locations and commanders for the Army of the Cumberland?"

"Yes, sir."

"And that seemingly it was written by a woman with whom Private Fraser appears to be romantically involved?"

"Yes, sir."

"It has previously been established that when Private Fraser encountered L Company on the morning of February six, he asked for directions to General Thomas' headquarters, saying he was trying to locate the 36th Illinois. It has also been established that he appeared ignorant of events that have occurred since the battle at Chickamauga Creek. Is it possible that whoever gave Private Fraser the list was simply assisting him in his search for the Thirty-sixth?"

"It's possible, I suppose."

It was the best he could hope for. Captain Johnson blew out a long, frustrated breath and sat down.

Captain Kellogg's testimony was followed by that of Major Hawkes. Major Blythe led him quickly through his recollection of events at General Thomas' headquarters and touched briefly on several moments early in the interrogation. Then he focused on the final night of questioning.

"You were present while the accused was being questioned on the tenth of February?"

"Yes, sir."

"Give an account of that evening."

"Sergeant Horace Sully was in charge of the interrogation. When I returned from supper, Sergeant Sully was asking Private Fraser about the money—the Union banknotes, not the Confederate scrip. Private Fraser had already told us that the person who sheltered him gave him the Confederate scrip. To help him get home, he said.

"Private Fraser seemed distracted that night, and he let slip that the person was a woman. Sergeant Sully kept at him, and after a while, Private Fraser admitted she was the one gave him the book. Sergeant Sully repeated the questions, and Private Fraser came back with the same answer every time. He said he'd been rescued by a widow-woman, and she was the one gave him the book and the Confederate scrip. I was about to suggest to Sergeant Sully that he move on when Private Fraser said, 'All the money. She gave me all the money.'

"Sergeant Sully and I looked at each other, wondering what he meant. The sergeant said, 'You already told us she gave you the Confederate scrip. I'm asking about the greenbacks.'

"'All the money,' is what Private Fraser told him.

"Up to that point, we'd believed him, but the thought of a white woman giving that much money to a boy like him didn't make sense. Sergeant Sully kept at him for half the night, but he stuck to his story."

"'A boy like him?'"

Major Hawkes threw Ethan a disparaging look. "A half-breed. A white woman giving that much money to a breed? It doesn't make sense."

Ethan clenched his jaw, trying to keep his anger from showing. Beside him, Captain Johnson sat forward, his body tense.

"But you've seen the inscription in the book?"

"Yes, sir."

"And Private Fraser told you the book and the money were given to him by the same woman?"

"Yes."

"Why is it so difficult to believe she gave him the money?"

"Five hundred dollars is a lot of money. It's hard to believe a white woman just up and gave it to the likes of him. More'n likely, he stole it."

Captain Johnson was on his feet. "The accused objects to the testimony of Major Hawkes this day taken. He has made statements that are solely his own opinion and highly prejudicial to the character of the accused. The record of the court is thereby encumbered. The accused objects to the testimony and requests that all suppositions by Major Hawkes relating to how the accused came to be in possession of the five hundred dollars be expunged from the record."

General Starkweather regarded Captain Johnson for a long moment. With a rap of the pistol, he ordered the room cleared for deliberation. The guards moved in and grasped Ethan by the arms. Captain Johnson indicated they should follow and led the way upstairs to a bedroom at the front of the house, empty but for three mismatched chairs.

"Leave us," Captain Johnson said, turning the guards back at the door. "I need to speak with Private Fraser alone."

He closed the door and turned to Ethan, his expression grim. "I'm sorry, Private Fraser. I should have stopped him. Now, whatever the decision, whether the record is expunged or not, the Court will remember what was said."

"What will it mean?"

Captain Johnson shook his head in frustration and turned away. He walked the length of the room and back before answering. "The Court has heard what Major Hawkes had to say. He put words to what every member has been thinking since they first laid eyes on you: That you are an Indian, and therefore, not to be trusted. Sooner or later, someone was bound to say it. Captain Davies danced around the issue, but we all knew what he meant. Now Major Hawkes added a bad connotation that will be remembered by the Court. And perhaps held against you by some." He shook his head regretfully. "I'm sorry, Ethan. I saw where his line of questioning was headed and should have stopped it. It was remiss of me not to have done so."

Ethan looked away. The anger he held inside for all the times he'd been mistreated because of his looks threatened to erupt. Not daring to reply, he turned and walked to the far end of the room. He stood with his back to Captain Johnson, staring blindly out the window, fighting for control.

When he was able, he asked, "What happens next?"

"A decision will be rendered and the court-martial will continue. When it's our turn, I will do all I can to introduce the Court to the Ethan Fraser I have come to know. To that end, I have decided to call your brother as a witness."

Ethan looked around sharply. "What good will that do? Josh only knows what I've told him."

"Think, Ethan. He was raised with you. He knows you. He can attest to your character. He's your brother *and* he's white. He will introduce the Court to the part of you they can't see by looking."

Ethan continued to stare at him, saying nothing.

"I have to call him. There's no other way."

Ethan shrugged noncommittally and turned back to the window, looking down at the people milling below. "What are they doing here?"

Captain Johnson came to stand beside him. "You must know, Ethan. People are always curious about courts-martial." Irritation lent an edge to his voice as he continued, "I'm afraid yours has drawn a good deal of attention. People who shouldn't talk do, and word spreads. You're a half-breed accused of spying. The *Gazette* is full of it. You've become a curiosity, a topic of conversation, and fair game for every wagerer in town."

"What's the consensus?" Ethan asked woodenly.

"What does it matter? Come away from the window, and forget about them." Captain Johnson took Ethan by the arm and steered him back across the room.

Ethan allowed himself to be led to one of the chairs, sitting when the captain indicated he should. His life, whether he lived or died, walked free or spent the rest of it in prison, had been reduced to a game of chance.

They sat in silence until Ethan made up his mind to ask what he'd been thinking about for weeks. He looked up, catching Captain Johnson's eye. "Could I ask a favor, sir?"

Captain Johnson reacted with mild surprise. "Certainly. What is it?"

"When this is over, will you write to Elizabeth? Tell her everything that's happened; ask if she'll agree to meet with you once the war ends. Ask her to come even if I'm dead. If she agrees, take her to see whoever she must, so she can tell them the truth and clear my name." Ethan paused, his look beseeching. "For my parents' sake."

Captain Johnson found he had to clear his throat before responding. "You're getting ahead of yourself, aren't you?"

"And tell her for me, will you, sir, that I love her."

Captain Johnson shook his head. "I'm not sure I understand. Why don't you tell her yourself? Surely it would be better coming from you?"

"I tried, sir. I asked for pen and paper, but it's not allowed." One corner of Ethan's mouth twitched. "I doubt the rules'll change once I've been convicted."

"I see."

"Will you do it, sir?"

"Yes," Captain Johnson told him. "You have my word."

Ethan nodded his thanks and looked away. A heavy silence settled over the room.

32

When they returned, General Starkweather announced that the Court had acceded to the request of the accused, and the record had been expunged.

It was a minor victory, and Captain Johnson offered Ethan a brief smile of encouragement.

The Judge Advocate indicated he had finished questioning Major Hawkes, and the floor was turned over to the defense. Captain Johnson walked to the major, stopping directly in front of him.

"You stated that you believed Private Fraser when he told you the Confederate scrip was given to him by the person who rescued him?"

"Yes."

"And you have read the inscription in the book?"

"Yes."

"Do you agree that the inscription indicates a romantic involvement between the writer and Private Fraser?"

"I do."

"But when Private Fraser told you the person who gave him the book and the money was a white woman, you no longer believed him. Is that right?"

"It is."

"You find it difficult to believe that the woman who rescued Private Fraser and became romantically involved with him would provide him with money for his safe return home?"

"It's a lot of money," Major Hawkes said, looking contemptuously at Ethan. "No decent woman would give that much money to the likes of him."

"To a half-breed?"

"Yes."

"Thank you, Major." Captain Johnson turned to face the Court, extending a hand in Ethan's direction. "Private Fraser is, as you've so helpfully pointed out, half Sioux Indian. There's no doubt about it; we can all see it. But I would ask each of you to keep in mind that that is not the reason Private Fraser is on trial here." He looked pointedly at each member before rounding on Major Hawkes. "So, what you are saying, Major, is that you decided to disbelieve Private Fraser based solely on his looks. Is that correct?"

Major Hawkes fixed him with a chilly stare. "Because of what he is. Yes."

"I have no further questions for this witness," Captain Johnson said. Turning his back on Major Hawkes, he strode back to his seat.

Major Hawkes was read his edited testimony and dismissed. The next witness was Frank Myers.

Ethan's stomach churned at the sight of him. Frank had put on weight, the limp brown hair had been trimmed and his face scraped clean of the weeks' worth of beard he'd accumulated while on the run, but the dislike that came into his eyes when they settled on Ethan was unchanged.

Frank was duly sworn and identified himself and Ethan.

"State the circumstances under which you first met the accused." Major Blythe instructed.

"It was in a Reb stockade in Atlanta, after we were captured at Chickamauga Creek. Horst, Fergus, Zach and me came in on the first train. Thomas and Ethan got there a day or two later."

"For the record, identify Horst, Fergus, and Zach."

"Horst is Private Horst Klestil, Fergus is Private Fergus Connelly, and Zach is Corporal Zachariah Fisk. We're all with the 36th Illinois."

"Identify Thomas."

"Thomas is... was... He was Sergeant Thomas Murray, 36th Illinois."

"You appear uncertain, Private Myers. Is Sergeant Murray alive or dead?"

"I don't know, sir. He didn't make it back with us." Frank looked pointedly at Ethan. "Or with him neither, so I hear."

"When you left the stockade at Atlanta, you were put on a train bound for Richmond and escaped. Give an account of that escape."

"The door didn't get bolted right so we pushed it open. Ethan said we had to get out quick. Before the next town, he said. We rolled out and hid 'til the train was gone. Then he was up and off, expecting us to follow without so much as a by yer leave."

"The accused instigated the escape from the train?"

Frank looked helplessly at him, and Major Blythe rephrased the question. "The accused was the one who decided you should escape?"

"We all wanted to escape, but Ethan was the one that said when we had to do it."

"And, once you were off the train, you say the accused appeared familiar with the countryside?"

"Knew it like the back of his hand."

"Give an account of what happened next."

"He led and we followed. Anyone questioning got his head bit off. He led us up a crick near all night, saying it was to keep the dogs off our trail. Come morning, he led us into the woods and said that was where we'd spend the day.

We slept for a while, and then he got up an' went off by himself. Thomas tried to go with him, but Ethan wouldn't have it. When he came back, he said he'd arranged fer some food. He let Thomas go with him to get it, but before they left he stood there, and nice as you please, told us how to get back to Tennessee." Frank let out a harsh laugh and shook his head. "You could a' knocked me over with a feather when he did it."

Ethan ventured a look at the Court. They were listening intently, their faces unreadable.

"Why did the accused say he was giving you directions?"

"He said it was in case he didn't come back."

"But did he come back?"

"Yeah... Yes, sir. With an old Nigra fella. He brought food an' we ate."

"State what happened next."

"We started walking again. We walked all night." Frank interrupted himself to address the Court. "We always walked at night and slept during the day."

"The Court understands, Private Myers," Major Blythe assured him. "Please go on."

"Ethan kept us moving for two nights, even though our feet were blistered so bad we could hardly walk. We came to a river and found a boat to get across. The next day, once everyone was asleep, Ethan snuck off by himself. We didn't know he was gone 'til we woke up. It was after dark when he came back, an' that's when he told us he was planning to go a different way from what he'd said, and we could either come with him or head out on our own."

"What did you do?"

Frank leveled an accusing stare at Ethan. "Everyone decided to stick with him, so I went along."

"Did the accused tell you why he had decided to alter his course?"

Frank smirked. "He said he had friends he wanted to visit."

"The accused told you he had friends in Georgia?"

"Yes, sir. McDonough, Georgia."

"And, to your knowledge, did the accused visit his friends in McDonough?"

"Yes, sir. One morning he left us in the woods outside of town and went off by himself. We didn't see hide nor hair of him 'til way after dark. That's when he came back smelling all fancy-like." Frank glowered at Ethan. "He put us in danger so he could bed some whore."

"That was the second time the accused left you and was gone all day?"

"Yes, sir."

"How often did the accused abandon you?"

"He went off by himself near every morning. Most days he was only gone an hour or two and came back with food, but there was other times when he was gone the whole day."

"Did the accused ever tell you where he went?"

"He never told us nothing." Frank threw a sidelong look the Court. "'Cept for Thomas. Thomas watched out for him. Saw that he ate, made sure he slept. Ethan only talked to Thomas."

"Give an account of what happened when you reached the Chattahoochee River."

"We were looking to get across, and Ethan went ahead to talk to the man at the ferry. He was gone so long that Thomas went to fetch him. When he came back, he was carrying Ethan."

"Why was that?"

"Ethan was passed out cold. Thomas said he found him drinking corn liquor down at the ferryman's shack." Frank looked at Ethan with disdain. "Can't hold his liquor. Must be the Injun in him."

"Give an account of what happened next."

"Next night, we all went together to the ferryman's shack. The Nigra fella there greeted Ethan real friendly-like an' said he'd take us across fer free. We were halfway to the other side when a log hit the raft, and Thomas fell in. Ethan went in after him and that's the last I seen of either of 'em." He looked pointedly at Ethan. "'Til today."

Ethan stared at him in disbelief, unable to believe how thoroughly Frank had distorted the truth. He wasn't aware that Captain Johnson had left his side until he began to speak.

"You stated that Private Fraser was in the habit of going off by himself during the day. What reason did he give?"

Frank shrugged. "Mostly he didn't say. He just left."

"Were there occasions when he did say something?"

"Ethan never told us nothing, but he an' Thomas argued. Him saying he was going, an' Thomas saying he needed sleep."

"When nothing was said, was it understood that Private Fraser was going in search of food?"

Frank offered Ethan a derisive smile. "That's what he wanted us to think."

"Are you saying you didn't believe him?"

"Some days he was gone the whole day and came back with nothing."

"Did Private Fraser say anything by way of explanation on those days?"

"Just that there wasn't any food. But I figure he ate what he found, 'stead a' sharing it with us."

"Why did you figure that?"

"We were starving. Lotsa times Ethan didn't eat when we did, but still he kept going. I figure he was getting food an' keeping it fer himself."

"Was Private Fraser putting on weight while the rest of you starved?"

Frank shrugged. "Not so's you'd notice. But we were doing a lotta walking."

"You stated that he and Sergeant Murray were close, that Sergeant Murray looked out for Private Fraser. Are you telling this Court, that in return for his kindness, Private Fraser was allowing Sergeant Murray to starve while he had plenty to eat?"

Frank looked from Captain Johnson to General Starkweather, then back to Captain Johnson. "I don't know. It's just something I thought."

"But it's not something you actually witnessed or have proof of."

Frank stared at him, the muscles in his jaw working. "No," he answered flatly.

"You stated that once, when Private Fraser left you, he came back drunk. Were there other times when Private Fraser drank?"

Frank's eyes shifted to Ethan, who had hunched forward, watching him intently.

"Would you say that Private Fraser made a habit of drinking, Private Meyers?"

"Not so's I noticed. Like I said, he can't tolerate it, him being Injun an' all."

"On the occasion when Private Fraser was at the ferryman's shack and Sergeant Murray came back carrying him, what exactly did Sergeant Murray say?"

"He didn't have to say anything. We could smell it."

"Sergeant Murray offered no explanation?"

"He said Ethan had passed out drunk."

"Is that all?"

Frank's hands tightened on the arms of his chair and he shifted uneasily. "He said Ethan and the men he was drinking with were being kinda loud."

"How loud?"

"He said they were yelling. Said he saw Ethan fall down."

"Anything else?"

"I guess one of 'em kicked him," Frank said reluctantly.

"Not exactly friendly, in other words."

Frank shrugged. "Who's to say?"

"Did Sergeant Murray tell you anything else he observed at the ferryman's shack?"

Frank's eyes met Ethan's and held. "Not that I recollect."

"He didn't tell you that Private Fraser's hands were tied behind his back and he was being forced to drink?"

Frank looked at Captain Johnson, his expression obstinate.

"Did Sergeant Murray, or did he not, tell you he had seen Private Fraser bound, kicked, and forced to drink? Yes or no, Private Myers."

Frank remained defiant for several seconds. Then, glaring at Captain Johnson, he muttered, "Yeah. I guess that's what he said."

Captain Johnson turned away, circling behind Frank, allowing his concession to sink in before coming at him from the other side. "On the day you say Private Fraser went to visit a woman, what did he say before he left?"

"He said he knew some folks he wanted to visit."

"Anything else?"

"He told us if he didn't come back to go on without him. Gave us directions."

"Is that all?"

Frank glowered at Captain Johnson before grudgingly giving him a portion of the answer he was seeking. "He said he was gonna try to get us some clothes."

"Why was that?"

"So we could get rid a' the uniforms."

"And did Private Fraser succeed in bringing you clothing?"

"Yeah... Yes, sir."

"What did he bring besides clothes?"

Frank shrugged. "Food."

"Was anyone with him when he returned with the food and clothing?"

"A darky."

"A Negro. You say it was a Negro who brought the food the night after your escape, another Negro who ferried you across the Chattahoochee, and now a third Negro bringing food and clothing?"

"Yeah," Frank agreed, uncertain where Captain Johnson was heading.

"Every time Private Fraser sought help it was from a Negro. Was there ever a time when you saw Private Fraser associate with a white man or a military man in the South?"

"No," Frank told him irritably. "But like I said, we never knew where he went off to."

"You never saw him with a white man?"

"No."

"Only with Negroes. With slaves."

"That's what he let us see."

"You stated that you became separated from Private Fraser and Sergeant Murray while crossing the Chattahoochee River. What happened after that? Did you look for them?"

"Zach and Fergus went downriver a ways while me and Horst waited with the supplies. They'd a' looked all night, but it was dangerous so close to the ferry. Me an' Horst was getting ready to head out on our own when they showed back up."

"And you followed the directions Private Fraser gave you, back to the Union lines?"

Frank shrugged. "Pert' near, I guess."

"Would you say you found the directions to be accurate?"

"We made it, didn't we?"

"Thank you, Private Myers."

As Captain Johnson returned to sit beside Ethan, General Starkweather spoke.

"You stated that when the accused went to meet with his friends in Georgia, he was gone the entire day. Until long after the time he said he'd return. When the accused came back after dark, was the Negro man with him?"

"No, sir. When Ethan came back the first time he was alone. That's when he smelled all fancy-like. He made us wait again, almost the half the night, while he went back fer the supplies."

"He was away all day, and *then* went for the supplies?"

Frank nodded. "Yes, sir. That's what happened."

The colonel who had avoided Ethan's gaze spoke up. "You stated that on several occasions, the accused told you he might not return. Did you ever fear that he might turn you over to the authorities?"

"I didn't know what to think when he went off the way he did. I wondered about it, but I figured he'd never turn in Thomas. That's the only thing that kept us safe. How friendly he was with Thomas."

"Did you ever discuss your concerns with the other men?" the lieutenant wanted to know.

"I tried a couple a' times, but none a' them 'ud hear a word against him."

"And why was that?"

"Something Thomas said to Zach and Fergus. Horst..." Frank snorted dismissively. "He don't speak much English. You never know what the likes a' him're thinking."

"I see."

Frank leaned back in his chair, smug and self-satisfied, watching Ethan as his testimony was read back. Ethan glared at him, angry and hurt.

When Frank had gone, General Starkweather announced that, as there were only twelve minutes remaining before three o'clock, court was adjourned until nine o'clock the following morning. He banged his pistol on the table, and men pushed back their chairs and began moving about.

Captain Johnson held up a hand to stop the guards and leaned close to Ethan. "I'm going to go talk to Josh and get something to eat. I'll come by later, and we'll talk about tomorrow." He laid a hand on Ethan's arm. "Today was the worst, Ethan. Tomorrow should be better. There are only two prosecution witnesses left and neither of them wants to see you convicted."

"You've talked to them?"

"I have." Captain Johnson signaled for the guards to approach. "I'll tell you about it later."

When Ethan had been taken from the room, Captain Johnson collected his belongings and went in search of Josh. He didn't have to look far.

Josh had been pacing on the other side of the street, separate from the crowd, a copy of the *Chattanooga Gazette* jammed under one arm. He saw Ethan when he was brought out, head bowed against the epithets hurled at him by some of the Union soldiers. Worse, to Josh's ears, were the shouts of encouragement from several citizens of Chattanooga. Their comments left no doubt that they considered him an ally.

The guards wasted little time getting Ethan into the wagon. The bar dropped into place, the driver slapped the reins and urged the horses into a trot. Josh watched it round the corner onto Fifth Street, then turned as Captain Johnson came up beside him.

"Have you seen this?" he demanded angrily, shaking the newspaper in the captain's face. "They're calling him a 'Godless savage and a traitor to the Union'. According to this piece of garbage he's guilty on all counts and will hang before the week's out." He threw the paper away in disgust. "How can they print that? A boy's life is at stake!"

"Calm down, Josh," Captain Johnson said, taking him by the arm. "You can't take what they say seriously. Walk with me and get some supper. I'll fill you in on what happened today, and there is something we need to discuss."

Ethan returned to his cell completely demoralized. The day had gone very badly, and to have it end with Frank's testimony was the worst blow of all. If only Fergus had been allowed to testify, maybe he would have blunted the impact of Frank words. As it was, the members of the Court would have all night to consider every damning thing Frank had said. Ethan ignored his supper when it came and sat wrapped in his blanket, hunched against the cold, waiting to be taken to Captain Johnson.

The captain was apologetic when Ethan was brought to him. "I'm sorry it's so late. First I had to calm your brother down, then we had to go over what he plans to say tomorrow."

Ethan didn't respond. He took the seat opposite the captain and stared at his hands, clasped on the table in front of him.

"What is it, Ethan?"

Ethan shook his head. "It was bad today."

"It went pretty much as I told you it would."

"But Frank... he..." Ethan gestured helplessly and shook his head.

"Forget about him. You can't see it now because his attack was so personal, but he discredited himself pretty thoroughly toward the end. Tomorrow Fisk and Connelly will dispel any lingering doubts the Court may have. Right now, we need to concentrate on your testimony."

Ethan sat without speaking for several moments, then raised his eyes to the captain's face. "What's there to talk about?"

"There are two more witnesses for the prosecution. When the prosecution finishes, I intend to call them as witnesses in your defense. After that, I'll call Josh. Right now, we need to discuss what you intend to do. Can you forget Frank long enough to do that?"

Ethan nodded without enthusiasm, and the captain continued, "You saw today how words can be turned against a witness. In my opinion, you would be taking a big risk by testifying—open yourself up to who knows what line of questioning from the Judge Advocate. As you saw, there is little I can do to repair damage once it's done. It's up to you to decide, but I strongly recommend against testifying."

"How will my side of it get told?"

"I'll tell it: In your own words, exactly as you've told it to me. If you agree that's what you want, we need to spend tonight going back over everything to make sure I have it right."

Ethan thought about it, then nodded. "All right. Let's go back over it."

MARCH

33

When the court-martial reconvened the following morning, the previous day's proceedings were read and approved. Then the Judge Advocate surprised everyone by announcing his decision not to call his remaining witnesses. The floor was turned over to the defense.

Captain Johnson summoned Zach to the stand. Ethan waited anxiously for him to appear, unsure what to expect. Once Zach had been duly sworn and identified himself and Ethan, Captain Johnson began his examination.

"State the circumstances under which you first met the accused."

"I knew Ethan... Private Fraser, when he was with the Thirty-sixth during the fall and winter of '62. I fought beside him and his brothers at Perryville and Stones River. We met up again at the prison stockade in Atlanta, a few days after we were captured at Chickamauga Creek."

Zach went on to describe the meeting at the stockade, the escape from the train, Ethan's victory in out-smarting the hounds, and the trek across Georgia.

"He kept going even though he was sick."

"What do you mean, he was sick?" Captain Johnson asked.

"From what Thomas said, Ethan got hurt pretty bad when he was captured." He looked at Ethan. "He had headaches. You could see in his eyes how much he hurt."

He went on to give an accurate account of Ethan's decision to change course and his reasons for stopping at McDonough.

"In previous testimony, Private Frank Myers described it as a visit with friends, most notably, a woman. Is it your testimony that that was not the case?"

"Yes, sir. Ethan went to see if he could get us food and clothes. When he came back, he said he'd fallen asleep. He apologized, but none of us held it against him. It was prob'ly the first decent sleep he'd had since we escaped."

"Describe what occurred while you waited for Private Fraser to return."

"Ethan was late coming back, and Frank was complaining about him. We'd heard it before, but that day he kept on, calling Ethan a 'red nigger' and saying you couldn't trust him. Thomas jumped him, and there was a fight. Later, Thomas asked why he'd said it. I told him what Frank had told me, how Frank's brother and his family had been massacred by the Sioux in Minnesota in '62. Because of that, and because Ethan's half Sioux Indian, Frank hates Ethan."

Zach described the journey from McDonough to the banks of the Chattahoochee and told the Court what Thomas had witnessed at the ferryman's shack.

"Describe Private Fraser's condition when he returned," Captain Johnson instructed.

"He was unconscious. Passed out cold. Thomas was carrying him. He'd thrown up all over himself, so we stripped him and washed him and his clothes. When we got his clothes off, we could see how bad he'd been beaten. From the bruises, and the way Thomas said he'd been kicked, I thought maybe his ribs mighta been broken."

When it was the Judge Advocate's turn to cross-examine, he peppered Zach with questions pertaining to any suspicions he might have had regarding Ethan's knowledge of the South and the times he went off on his own. Zach kept his answers simple, providing him with nothing to use against Ethan.

"You stated that the accused went to McDonough to get food and clothing from people he knew. Did he explain how he happened to know people in McDonough, Georgia, Corporal Fisk?"

"No, sir."

"Did you ask?"

"No, sir."

"Why not? Weren't you curious?"

"Ethan's a quiet one, sir. A private sort. He was close to Thomas, and it was Thomas he talked to. One night early on, I asked Thomas about him, and Thomas said there was no one he'd trust more than Ethan to get us home safe. He said he trusted him with his life. That was good enough for me."

"I see. No further questions."

Much the same ground was covered during the examination and cross-examination of Fergus. To Captain Johnson's satisfaction, and Ethan's relief, his account was similar to Zach's. When Fergus was dismissed, Captain Johnson called his final witness. The members of the Court had become bored by the repetitive nature of the questioning during the previous witness, but they looked toward the door with renewed interest when Lieutenant Joshua Fraser's name was announced and he strode into the room.

"State your name, rank and regiment," Captain Johnson instructed after Josh had been duly sworn.

"Joshua Simon Fraser, First Lieutenant, Company J, 36th Illinois."

"Do you recognize the accused? And if so, as whom?"

"I do, sir, as Ethan Fraser. He's my brother."

A murmur went up among the members of the Court, and they shifted in their seats, exchanging glances and looking between Josh and Ethan.

"Your brother," Captain Johnson repeated.

"My half-brother," Josh amended. "My mother died when I was one, and my father remarried. Ethan's mother raised me and my three brothers, Ethan and our sister, Kate." Josh paused, considering the row of officers before him. "To my mind, Ethan is my brother, and his mother is the only mother I have ever known."

At Captain Johnson's request, Josh went on to give a brief account of their Christian upbringing in rural Illinois, Ethan's character, and his conduct at the battles of Perryville and Stones River.

"You were the one who discovered the spy Price's deception and ordered him detained, were you not, Lieutenant Fraser?"

"Yes, sir."

"You testified at Price's trial, did you not, that Price had corrupted a young private, flattered him into revealing more than he should?"

"Yes, sir."

"That young man, how old was he?"

"He was seventeen."

"And how old is your brother?"

"Ethan is eighteen."

Captain Johnson nodded. "So Private Fraser was seventeen when he was first assigned to Price. When you were informed of the circumstances surrounding your brother's arrest, were you reminded of Price and that other young man?"

"Yes, sir."

"And did it occur to you that Price might have had the same influence over your brother?"

"It did, sir. But only briefly."

"Why briefly?"

"I know Ethan. I've known him all his life. He's loyal and honest. It was against our parents' wishes that he ran away to fight. It's my belief that he would never betray his country."

The Judge Advocate badgered Josh, trying to get him to concede that Ethan, in his youth and inexperience, had bent to Price's will. That he had defected for love or money, or both. Josh refused to budge. When he was dismissed, Josh looked at Ethan, offering him a smile of such affection and encouragement that Ethan's spirits soared.

After he was gone, the President of the Court instructed Captain Johnson to present his defense. Captain Johnson stood and began to read from the statement he had prepared. He was eloquent and convincing, and Ethan's hopes rose as he listened.

Captain Johnson told Ethan's story as Ethan had told it to him, enhancing the language to make it more persuasive. He addressed each of the charges and specifications individually, admitting the apparent truth in each, but pointing up the erroneous conclusions.

When he came to the first specification on the second charge, he described Ethan's treatment at Cahaba and the details of his escape, adding, "It is true that, for a brief period, I resided in Mobile, Alabama. By the time I escaped, I had been beaten and starved to the point where I thought it unlikely I would survive the months, or even years ahead, in another Confederate prison. It was my good fortune to be taken in by a woman, a widow formerly of New York City, who at great personal risk, sheltered me and nursed me back to health. Though she moved to Mobile when she married, her sympathies have remained with the Union and it was she who provided me with the means to return home.

"It was not what either of us intended, but during the months of my convalescence, we fell in love. I have asked her to be my wife and she has accepted, but not until the war has ended and Alabama is once again part of the Union.

"I deeply regret the circumstances that have made it appear I changed allegiances. I assure you that nothing could be further from the truth. It was my goal, in returning to Chattanooga, to rejoin the 36th Illinois and fight beside my countrymen to help win this war, reuniting this great county under one flag, the stars and stripes of the United States of America.

"I would like to thank you, the members of the Court, for your courtesy and attention, and would ask that, in the name of justice, you find for acquittal on both charges and all of the specifications."

When Captain Johnson resumed his seat, Ethan leaned over and murmured a heartfelt, "Thank you!"

"The floor is yours, sir," General Starkweather announced, nodding to Major Blythe. "Favor us with your reply."

The Judge Advocate took his time, completing a notation at the top of a page before rising to address the Court.

"May it please the Court. Private Ethan Fraser is, according to his half-brother, an intelligent young man. Clever, well read, observant. Not at all the type to be deceived for long by a man like Price. While there is no way to verify that Price provided the accused with documents prior to the battle at Chickamauga Creek, the accused's description of their contents leaves little doubt that such documents did exist. I would ask you to consider that someone, be it Price or Private Fraser, discovered those documents and realized the harm they would do the Rebel cause should they fall into Union hands. It fell to the accused to dispose of them. He has concocted the story of his belated attempt to deliver them to account for his capture at Chickamauga Creek. In truth, we have no idea why he was there.

"It is the accused's assertion that he was in possession of the list headed by Confederate General Joseph E. Johnston, and containing the names of Generals Grant, Thomas, Hooker, Howard, Palmer, Sherman, and Granger, together with the locations of the IV, XIV and XV Corps, because he was trying to locate the 36th Illinois, and that he returned north for the purpose of rejoining the fight on the side of the Union. While the list clearly shows the IV Corps, of which the 36th Illinois is a part, to be at Nashville, the accused chose not to go there. Instead, he came here, to Chattanooga, looking for General Thomas, the man who had employed Price. I would suggest to you, that when Price did not return, the accused took it upon himself to come looking for him. And that he, like his mentor, has continued to spy for the Union as well as the Confederacy, something the five hundred dollars in his possession would appear to substantiate.

"It has been shown that the aforementioned list was authored by the same woman who wrote the inscription in the book found in Private Fraser's possession. A woman the accused would have you believe he is in love with and intends to marry upon his return to the South. I would ask you to consider that when the accused became separated from Sergeant Murray, Corporal Fisk, and Privates Myers, Connelly, and Klestil, he took advantage of the opportunity to reunite with her, his female counterpart in the South. The same woman, perhaps, with whom he passed a day in McDonough, Georgia, thereby jeopardizing the safety of escaped Union soldiers who had given him their trust. He was never a prisoner at Cahaba, as he has maintained; nor did he escape only to be rescued by a lonely widow. Instead, the woman he is romantically involved with is a spy for the Confederacy, and the accused has spent the last several months in her company, engaged in that very activity.

"The tale Private Fraser tells is an elaborate fantasy, concocted to account for his whereabouts over the past several months and his desire to continue what, by all appearances, has become a lucrative venture—spying for both sides in this conflict. Had the accused told his story, in its entirety, when he first arrived in Chattanooga, it is possible that certain aspects of it might have been believed. But the accused was unable to do that because he made it up as he went along, feeding it piecemeal to investigating officers in response to repeated questioning.

"I would have you consider, therefore, that the accused was not a victim as he would have us believe, but joined willingly with Price when he discovered that, in the South, he was able to satisfy not only his desire for wealth, but his lust for carnal pleasures, as well. He is not only a traitor, but worse, a man with no loyalties, no allegiances. A man who cannot, should not, be trusted.

"This I respectfully submit to the Court, certain that in their wisdom, and by weighing all the evidence, a verdict will be rendered on the side of truth and justice."

With a final meaningful look at the members of the Court, Major Blythe resumed his seat.

"Thank you, gentlemen," General Starkweather said, acknowledging with a tip of his head, first Major Blythe, then Captain Johnson. "The room will now be cleared for deliberation. This Court will reconvene when a verdict has been reached." He thumped the table with the butt of his pistol.

Ethan's guards once again escorted him up the stairs to the room overlooking the street. A look from Captain Johnson kept them from entering.

The door had no sooner closed than Ethan leveled anxious eyes at Captain Johnson. "It was good today, wasn't it? Until the end."

The captain nodded. "You need to keep in mind that the Judge Advocate's closing can be difficult, especially when the testimony proceeding it has been positive." He laid a hand on Ethan's shoulder and gave him a reassuring smile. "Remember everything the Court heard in your favor today. Things have a way of balancing themselves out."

"When you told them what happened, especially after what Josh and the others said, I started thinking there might be a chance of acquittal." Ethan shook his head in resignation. "But then the Judge Advocate said his piece, and I knew it wouldn't happen."

He turned and walked slowly toward the window. Captain Johnson watched him go.

The crowd outside was larger than on the previous day, and had something of a carnival air about it. Newsboys hawked papers, and a few enterprising souls peddled baked goods. As Ethan scanned the crowd, a woman looked up, and their eyes met. She stared for a long moment before shouting and pointing. Heads turned, and Ethan stepped back out of sight.

As he did, he noticed Josh across the road. He was leaning against the blackened chimney of a burned-out house, talking to Fergus and Zach. They looked when the woman shouted, but Ethan had retreated far enough that they couldn't see him. They returned to their conversation.

Ethan watched them for a long time, grateful for what they'd said in court. Fergus and Zach's acknowledgment of all he'd tried to do eased the pain of Frank's betrayal. And Josh! Growing up, Ethan had been convinced Josh barely knew he existed. Today his brother had proved him wrong.

A rap at the door caused them both to start. Captain Johnson took a half step toward it, then stopped. "Yes," he said guardedly. "What is it?"

One of the guards poked his head in. "They're done for today. We're to take the prisoner back to his cell."

That night was the longest of Ethan's life. He paced, tossed restlessly, then paced some more. He was torn between wanting the night to end so he would know the Court's decision, and hoping it would go on forever. Breakfast came, and he couldn't eat. Time crept by. At last, a guard arrived and led him along the passage to the room where Captain Johnson sat waiting.

The captain looked up as Ethan entered, the light from a lantern accentuating the lines of exhaustion on his face. "I couldn't bear waiting alone," he said with a sheepish smile. "I thought you might like some company."

Ethan sat across the table from him. "What time is it?"

"A little after noon." After a moment, he added, "They started deliberating at ten this morning."

"How long does it usually take?"

Captain Johnson shrugged. "It varies."

They sat for a time in silence. Ethan shifted restlessly, and Captain Johnson looked up to find anxious eyes watching him.

"What do you think they'll decide?"

Captain Johnson let out a sigh. "I have to stick with what I said before. I have little doubt they'll find you guilty on one or two of the specifications on the first charge, and sentence you to time in prison. Probably until the end of the war when you will no longer be considered a threat."

Ethan swallowed and looked away. After a moment, he pushed his chair back and stood up. He walked to the edge of the room and stood for a time in the shadows, then came back and sat down, elbows on the table, forehead resting on the heals of his hands. He sat motionless until Captain Johnson took out his pocket watch, glanced at it, then snapped it shut and placed it on the table. He looked up to see the question on Ethan's face.

"Nearly one thirty."

Ethan slapped both hands on the table, his chair scraping as he stood. "Why can't they make up their minds?" he demanded angrily. "I'm either guilty or not. What's taking so long?"

He stalked across the room and resumed his position in the shadows. Before long, he began to pace. He was on his ninth circuit of the room when the door opened.

The butt of the pistol hit the table with a report that reverberated through the stillness of the room.

"This military court is hereby reconvened at two fifteen p.m. on the second of March, 1864," General Starkweather intoned. "After giving full consideration to the evidence presented in the matter of the accused, Private Ethan Fraser, the Court has found as follows:

Of the First Specification, First Charge - Guilty

Of the Second Specification, First Charge - Guilty

Of the Third Specification, First Charge - Guilty

Of the Fourth Specification, First Charge - Not Guilty

Of the First Charge - Guilty

Of the First Specification, Second Charge – Guilty

Of the Second Charge - Guilty

"In consequence, the Court sentences Private Ethan Fraser to be shot until he is dead, with musketry."

Movement slowed, and sound receded. Ethan stared at the President of the Court in horror. He felt weight on his shoulder, and from a great distance heard Captain Johnson saying something he could make no sense of. The captain's grip tightened, and with effort, Ethan turned to face him. The captain was still speaking. Ethan tried to concentrate, tried to make out what he was saying. He was just beginning to make sense of it when he was seized roughly by the arm.

"No!" he protested, pulling free of the guard's grasp. "No," he shouted, turning toward the Court. "This isn't right. I've done nothing wrong. I never spied for anyone. I never betrayed the Union. What you've done today is wrong."

The Judge Advocate and the members of the Court turned startled eyes on him as the guard reclaimed his arm. Ethan struggled to free himself, and more guards descended. He fought them wildly until the butt of a pistol sent him spinning into darkness.

The first thing he became aware of was the cold. A shiver ran through him, and he curled into a ball. A feeling of unease gripped him, and he clung stubbornly to unconsciousness, not wanting to remember, not wanting to face whatever it was. When at last the cold proved too much, Ethan opened his eyes.

At first, he had no idea where he was. Then he realized he was on the floor of his cell. Memory came rushing back. His chest constricted, and his breath caught in his throat. With a ragged gasp, he struggled to his knees and crawled to the mattress, tugging at the blanket with cold-stiffened fingers until he succeeded in pulling it over him. He huddled there, shivering, unable to believe what had happened.

It can't be true, he told himself. *It can't. Any minute now someone will walk in and say it's a mistake. It has to be a mistake...*

He was still firmly in the grip of denial when keys jangled in the passage, and the door to his cell opened. Ethan raised his head expectantly. Josh came in holding up a lantern, followed closely by Captain Johnson. One look at the stricken expression on Josh's face, and the full impact of the Court's ruling hit him. Ethan closed his eyes and turned his face into the mattress.

"Ethan," Josh said, squatting beside him and laying a hand on his shoulder. "Are you all right?"

Ethan gave a brief shake of his head.

"Are you hurt?" When Ethan didn't respond, his concern mounted. "Ethan, talk to me!"

"I'm innocent," was all Ethan could whisper before his throat constricted and tears overflowed.

"We know you are," Josh said softly. "We're going to do all we can to set things right, but first we need to know how bad you're hurt."

"Not bad," came the muffled reply. "Cold. Head hurts."

"We need to know if you require medical attention, Ethan," Captain Johnson said, speaking for the first time.

"Do you need a doctor?" Josh asked.

"No."

"In that case," Captain Johnson said, "we would like you to come with us to discuss what's to be done. Knowing what's going to happen next, how we intend to proceed, might make you feel better." When Ethan didn't respond he added, "Of course, if you aren't feeling up to it, we can leave you here alone for the night and talk in the morning."

There was a lengthy pause before his words had the desired effect.

"I'll come," Ethan said, pushing himself into a sitting position. Anything was better than lying alone in his cell, dwelling on what lay ahead.

He looked up, and Captain Johnson saw his face. Turning to the guards, he ordered them to fetch a bucket of warm water, a towel and some coffee. Josh helped Ethan to his feet, and taking him by the arm, guided him to the door. Another guard intercepted them, seizing one of Ethan's wrists and locking a manacle in place.

"Is that necessary?" Captain Johnson asked, annoyed.

"Orders. He tried to escape. He's to be chained anytime he leaves his cell."

"That's ridiculous."

The guard shrugged and gestured for Ethan's other wrist, which he offered without protest. Grasping Ethan by the arm, the guard led him back to the same room where he'd sat with Captain Johnson just a few hours earlier.

Back when I'd fooled myself into thinking they might find me innocent, Ethan thought bitterly, easing onto the chair Josh pulled out for him. Josh and Captain Johnson exchanged glances and seated themselves in silence. When the guard returned, Captain Johnson poured a cup of coffee and pushed it across the table.

Ethan accepted it without comment. He took a sip of the hot liquid, shivering as its warmth spread through him. Clutching the tin cup in both hands, he allowed Josh to push the hair from his face and wash away the blood.

Josh looked at Ethan's right eye and winced. "You've got a hell of a shiner. We'll arrange a for poultice."

"*Why?*" Ethan thought numbly. *What does it matter? Nothing matters anymore.*

Josh tossed the cloth into the bucket and sat down. Ethan looked at Captain Johnson.

"How long before they... ?" The words choked him. He drew a breath, his fingers tightening around the cup. "How long do I have left?"

"There's no need to worry about that now, Ethan. The verdict must first be approved by General Thomas. I intend to petition him personally on your behalf. Should he approve it, a transcript of the court-martial will be forwarded to President Lincoln. I intend to petition the President, as well as Secretary of War Stanton and Judge Advocate General Holt." He shared a look with Josh before adding, "Your brother, Corporal Fisk, and Private Connelly have volunteered to submit affidavits requesting that your sentence be commuted to time in prison."

Josh would have spoken, but Captain Johnson stopped him with an upraised hand. "There is something you should both know. I was late getting here this evening because I was approached by a member of the Court. He feels quite strongly that you do not deserve to die, Ethan, and has volunteered to write to President Lincoln requesting leniency. There are two others who were also opposed to the sentence, and he feels they might be persuaded to do the same. He has said he will speak with them and let me know."

"Who is he?" Ethan asked, feeling a faint stirring of hope.

"He approached me in confidence; I don't think it's my place to divulge his identity." Captain Johnson looked between Ethan and Josh, adding, "It explains why deliberations took so long. I gather it was fairly contentious."

"What do we do next?" Josh asked, leaning forward intently.

"See what action General Thomas takes. If he approves the verdict, which I have little doubt he will, you should go back to the Thirty-sixth, Josh, and speak with anyone who knew Ethan. If there are men who fought at Perryville or Stones River, and remember him favorably, urge them to write. But before you go, get word to your parents. Have both of them, and your sister, write to President Lincoln. And this is important, Josh—every one of you must make it clear that your family has lost three sons fighting for the Union. Beg him to spare this one."

* * *

Elizabeth pulled open the shutters and smiled when she saw only scattered wisps of cloud softly illuminated by the rising sun. Mobile had been beset by inclement weather for nearly a week, but today, at last, looked promising. Turning from the window, she began gathering the last of the things she would take with her. It wasn't long before nausea forced her back to bed. She lay waiting for the worst of it to pass, wondering how she would ever hide her condition from Melanie.

Family and friends had been surprised when she announced her intention to leave Mobile, but only half-hearted attempts had been made to dissuade her. Rumors of an imminent attack on the city had circulated since January, and the military commanders, along with the city's newspapers, had been persistent in urging the evacuation of all non-combatants. Elizabeth simply used their admonitions as her excuse to return to New York.

The day after she informed James' parents of her decision, one of her brothers-in-law came to call. Hiram was married to James' sister Melanie, and was preparing to send her and their two youngest children out of Mobile. They would travel by sea from Pensacola to New York City, then by rail to Boston where they would stay with one of Melanie's sisters for the duration of the war. Hiram urged Elizabeth to accompany them.

Elizabeth agreed and was instantly relieved of responsibility for planning the trip. She supplied infusions of cash upon request, but devoted her time preparing the household and the business for her absence.

She sent her parents a letter announcing her intention to visit, but had little faith it would arrive before her. Her plan was to tell them the truth when she got there, and if they wanted her to stay, spend up to a month in New York. If they turned her out, she would meet with her bankers, go by train to Chicago, from there to Peoria, and on to Lewistown, where she intended to set up housekeeping. A letter to Ethan would inform him of her whereabouts, and as soon as the war ended, they would be together again.

She smiled, remembering the warmth that came to his eyes each time he looked up and found her watching him, the feel of his hands on her skin. Elizabeth hugged a pillow to her and whispered the prayer she repeated each morning, "Please keep him safe. Please let him come home to his child."

Hannah came through the door and stopped short. "You ain't gonna get to New York City layin' in that bed, Miz 'Lizbet. Come on now, lez get you dressed."

Elizabeth sat up cautiously. The queasiness had passed. She slid off the bed and followed Hannah to the dressing table, moaning when she caught sight of her reflection. Her skin was ashen, and tiny beads of sweat glistened on her forehead and upper lip.

"Oh, Hannah," she said meeting the other woman's gaze in the mirror. "How am I going to do this? Melanie's bound to suspect."

"Miz Melanie got no reason to 'spect, so she ain't gonna 'spect," Hannah told her picking up a hairbrush. "You said yousef that lotsa folk gets sick on boats."

She arranged Elizabeth's hair while Elizabeth blotted the dampness from her face and pinched color into her cheeks. She looked doubtfully at her reflection, thinking it would have to do. Hannah helped her dress, and together they gathered the last of Elizabeth's things.

"Are you ready, Hannah?"

Fear mingled with anticipation on Hannah's face. "I's ready, Miz 'Lizbet." Picking up Elizabeth's valise, she took a last look around and followed her out of the room.

When Elizabeth had first proposed to Hannah and Isaac that they accompany her to Illinois, her suggestion had met with resistance. Both were reluctant to leave what was familiar, afraid to abandon the only real home they'd ever known for a place they'd never heard of until Ethan arrived. Elizabeth was patient, and before long, the novelty of the idea caught on. First with Hannah, who couldn't imagine being separated from Elizabeth, and eventually, with Isaac.

They emerged from the house to find Isaac standing next to a carriage stacked high with luggage. The wagon behind it was equally burdened. Josiah sat on the driver's seat holding the reins, and Hattie, Rose, Ben and Moses were assembled to see them off. One of James' managers, hired to look after the house, and his tiny, white-haired wife were there, too. Elizabeth issued a last-minute round of instructions, and there were tears and hugs all around before Isaac handed her into the carriage and helped Hannah in after her.

As the carriage rounded the circular drive, Elizabeth looked back, past the profusion of azaleas, japonicas and gardenias, to the house where she had lived for nearly nine years. She realized suddenly, that she might never see it again. Pressing her face to the isinglass, she watched until the trees blocked it from view.

34

Josh and Captain Johnson came to the prison each day to visit Ethan. Josh brought with him, for Ethan's inspection, letters he was preparing to send to their parents, to President Lincoln, to Secretary of War Stanton, and to Judge Advocate General Holt. At Ethan's request, he also began a letter to Elizabeth.

The two of them talked more during those few days than ever before. Josh tried to keep his brother's mind from straying to what lay ahead, describing the lengths he, Jamie, and Thomas had gone to to keep themselves entertained during the long months while Rosecrans dithered and his army languished following Stones River. The series of adventures had culminated in the discovery of a local whorehouse. By spring, they had virtually taken up residence in the place. By the time Duncan arrived, late one night, minutes ahead of the provost guard, life had evolved into one long, debauched party. Duncan was furious, would have seen them all busted down to private if he hadn't been instrumental in their escape. Instead, he made sure they were confined to camp, assigned no end of miserable duties, until the army finally pulled up stakes and headed south.

Josh described how they'd marched into Chattanooga without a shot being fired after Bragg abandoned the town early in September. And he told Ethan about the battle at Chickamauga Creek.

The Thirty-sixth had been held in reserve all through the first day's fighting, until late the morning of the second. The fighting in the woods south of Brotherton Field was intense; the enemy lines less than one hundred feet away, when their brigade commander, General Lytle, ordered them onto the field to the right of the 88th Illinois. The 24th Wisconsin came up on their right, and the 21st Michigan to the right of them.

They were no sooner in position than the Rebels charged from the woods, coming at them from three sides. The line faltered, and the Thirty-sixth began to give way, men screaming and falling, others turning to run. Jamie went down, blood spreading rapidly from a gaping wound to his stomach. Josh rushed to his side. Determined not to leave his twin to the enemy, he began dragging him up the shallow slope, ahead of the advancing Rebs.

Josh was nearing the top when the smoke lifted and he saw Duncan running toward him through the trees. Shouldering his way past knots of milling men, Duncan flung a hand over his head, yelling over the din of the battle, urging Josh to keep going. As he reached them, Duncan turned back, raising his rifle to fire at the advancing enemy. An instant later, his head snapped back. He took an ungainly step backwards, his rifle slipped from his grasp, and he crumpled to the ground not far from Jamie's feet, the top of his head blown away by a flying piece of shrapnel.

With a cry caught between terror and anguish, Josh grabbed Duncan's arm and tried to drag both brothers away from the advancing enemy. Their combined weight was too much for him. In the end, he chose the brother still living. Blinded by tears, he dragged Jamie over the brow of the hill, to the place where Colonel Miller was frantically trying to rally the Thirty-sixth. Josh knelt, holding Jamie who was still conscious, alternating between words of encouragement and screaming for help.

A riderless horse bore down on them, spattered with blood, its eyes rolled white in panic. Josh leapt up, waving his arms, and as the animal veered around him, recognized it as belonging to General Lytle.

As word spread that Lytle was dead, the battle lost, Jamie grabbed a fistful of his twin's coat and begged him to run. Moments later, blood welled up in his mouth, and he struggled for breath. Josh held him close, looking from his face to the last defenders atop the rise and the Union soldiers fleeing past. He held Jamie until the life went out of him, then lowered him onto a bed of leaves. Closing his twin's staring eyes, he laid a hand against his cheek for the last time. Then he ran for all he was worth, fleeing toward Chattanooga.

Josh's voice caught as he reached the end of his story. "I left them both," he said blinking back tears. "Left them to the Rebs." He turned away, burying his face in his hands.

"You did all you could, Josh." Ethan wiped away tears and laid a hand on his brother's shoulder. "There's nothing the Rebs could do to hurt them. If you'd stayed, you'd be dead too, or a prisoner. It's better that you ran."

Josh lowered his hands and shook his head. "It's the hardest thing I've ever done, leaving them like that. I never told Ma and Pa. I couldn't bring myself to tell them how it happened."

"Thanks for telling me."

During another visit, Josh told Ethan about the desperate days during the siege of Chattanooga when men stole corn meant for the horses and mules, going so far as to kill some of them for meat. He told of being with General Sheridan when his division stormed Missionary Ridge, of breaking through the enemy lines and nearly capturing Bragg himself. Of being shot by a sniper before he could join Sheridan and the rest of the division as they charged after the fleeing Rebels.

And, finally, he told him of his journey home, about their parents and Kate, and described Duncan's two children, the youngest born eight months after Duncan left. He told of the sad Christmas spent with just the seven of them, and finally, of the arrival of Ethan's letter and the joy it had brought his mother.

During the time spent with his brother, Ethan was able to distance himself from the sentence of death that hung over him. But each time Josh left, reality flooded back with suffocating force. During the long, dark hours alone in his cell, Ethan's state of mind fluctuated wildly. He contemplated everything from escape to suicide.

On the fifth of March, three days after the Court handed down its decision, General Thomas approved the verdict. Josh and Captain Johnson came together to break the news. They did all they could to bolster Ethan's spirits with talk of appeals and affidavits, but Ethan had made up his mind. He would try to escape.

It was late in the evening when Josh came to Ethan's cell, bringing with him the first volume of *The Count of Monte Cristo*.

"Captain Johnson got this back for you," he said, handing Ethan the book. "He thought you'd like to have it."

Ethan took it from him, and moving past him into the light, opened it to the inscription. For the first time, after hearing the words used against him so many times, he read what Elizabeth had written. "*...I will count the days until your return. With all my love, Elizabeth.* He stared at the words, knowing that within minutes, he would either be dead or a fugitive.

He closed the book, fingering the gold embossed lettering along the spine, and remembering the night Elizabeth had first loaned it to him. To Josh, he simply said, "Thank you."

"I've come to say good-bye, Ethan. I finished the letters today and gave them to Captain Johnson. He'll see that the ones to Ma and Pa and Elizabeth get mailed. The others'll go to Washington with his appeals. We've been given to understand that the transcript has already gone. I plan to head for Nashville at dawn, but I promise I'll be back."

"Thanks, Josh." Ethan had a hard time meeting his brother's eyes. "Whatever happens, your being here has meant a lot."

He looked so young and forlorn that Josh reached out and pulled Ethan to him. He held him for several seconds before turning away and calling for the guard.

Ethan dropped the book to the mattress, watching the guard's movements out of the corner of his eye. As the key turned in the lock, he said, "Sorry, Josh," and sprang with all his might at his brother's injured shoulder. Josh went down with a startled cry of pain. Ethan's momentum carried him into the door as the guard pulled it open. The heavy wood smashed into the guard's face and sent him reeling backwards. Ethan was on him in an instant, landing a blow that knocked him to the floor. Fumbling desperately, he grabbed the guard's revolver from its holster and pointed it at his head. The guard stared at him in horror, blood gushing from his broken nose.

"Get in the cell."

The man opened his mouth to protest; Ethan pressed the muzzle against his temple. "Any noise, and I'll kill you. Now get inside."

Ethan grabbed him by the arm, and the guard stumbled into the cell. Josh was sitting up, moaning and clutching his shoulder.

"Take off your coat and braces," Ethan ordered.

The guard complied. Ethan had him remove his boots and lie face down on the mattress. Using the braces, he tied his hands behind him. He hesitated before gagging him, but decided he had no choice. Pulling off one of the man's socks, he stuffed it into his mouth. The guard gave a muffled shriek and struggled wildly, his eyes wide with terror. Ethan saw air bubble through the blood, and turned his attention to Josh.

Josh was on his knees, clutching his injured shoulder as he attempted to get to his feet. Ethan leveled the pistol at him. "Stay put, Josh."

Josh looked up, saw the gun and the threat in his brother's eyes, and froze. "Don't do this, Ethan."

Ethan ignored him. "Take off your coat."

Josh glared at him.

"Do what I say, or I'll put a hole in your other shoulder."

Josh unfastened a single button.

"Hurry up!" Ethan stepped behind him and pressed the muzzle to his brother's shoulder.

Josh unbuttoned the greatcoat, and Ethan helped him pull it off.

"Your braces, Josh," he said, crouching to undo the buttons in back.

Ignoring Josh's protests, and his gasp of pain when his left arm was twisted behind him, Ethan used the suspenders to secure his hands. Then he removed the guard's other sock.

"Don't do this, Ethan. It'll only make things worse."

"How much worse can they be, Josh? Now, open your mouth." Ethan held the gun against Josh's shoulder and forced the sock in. He shrugged into Josh's greatcoat, belted it, then collected his brother's forage cap, with its first lieutenant's bars, from the floor and put it on. Bending to retrieve the book, he looked at the guard. The man's eyes were closed. He lay deathly still.

Fighting down panic, Ethan pulled the sock from his mouth. Unable to tell if the guard was breathing, he laid two fingers against his neck. The breath he'd been holding came out in a rush when he felt a faint pulse.

Ethan turned to crouch beside his brother. "I'm sorry, Josh," he said softly. "There's no other way. I meant what I said about how much your being here has meant. Tell Ma and Pa and Kate I love them." His voice failed him, and he stood up.

Stepping over Josh's outstretched legs, he pushed the door open a crack and looked out. The passage was empty. Stepping from the cell, he held the revolver to the light and checked the chambers. *Fully loaded.* Ethan stuffed the gun into his belt, pushed the door closed and turned the key in the lock.

The back door was only a few steps away, but it was locked and barred. Ethan removed the bar and set it aside. Somewhere behind him, a door opened and closed, and he heard voices. Ethan inserted one key, then another into the lock. His heart leapt when, at last, one turned. Willing the hinges not to squeak, he eased the door open and slipped out into the night.

The town and the mountains beyond it were bathed in the silver glow of a waning gibbous moon. Ethan made his way along the shadowed alley, stopping before he reached the street. Scattered light from windows picked out soldiers hurrying past, bundled against the cold, their breath vaporous in the moonlight. Less than twenty feet away, two horses stood tied to a rail. Ethan waited until no one was near, then started toward them. He had only gone a few steps when a door opened, spilling light. Ethan scurried back into the shadows as four men emerged.

They stopped near the horses to talk. Ethan glanced nervously over his shoulder, back the way he'd come. He had just about made up his mind to retreat, to try another route, when the men separated. Ethan pressed deeper into the shadows as three of them walked past him. When they were gone, he stuck his head out and looked up and down the street. The nearest man was fifty feet away, headed in the opposite direction.

Heart pounding, Ethan stepped from the shadows and walked to the horses. Collecting the nearest set of reins, he swung into the saddle and turned the horse east, resisting an almost overwhelming urge to kick it into a gallop. Following the rutted streets past warehouses converted to barracks, past lighted windows in the houses where officers were quartered, through the sprawl of gray-white tents, and campfires where men huddled, Ethan held the horse to a walk.

He was challenged only once, near a redoubt at the eastern edge of town. His heart rose in his throat when a picket, rifle in hand, stepped across his path. Ethan pulled the horse to a stop, his right hand seeking the revolver. The man spotted the first lieutenant's bars on the forage cap, acknowledged Ethan by rank, and waved him on with only a brief comment on the coldness of the night.

Ethan urged the horse into a trot, following the Tennessee River along its wide curve to the north. After about ten miles, he came to a bridge. Passing over it without incident, he kicked the horse into a canter and headed north along the face of the mountains, away from both armies.

Coming upon a narrow track that climbed into the mountains, Ethan abandoned the road, and giving the horse its head, allowed it to pick its way up the rugged slope. After several miles, the track petered out amid heavy undergrowth. Seeing no alternative, Ethan forged ahead. Several times, he was forced to dismount, slipping and sliding down one side of a rocky ravine before clambering up the other, leading the horse. It slid and lunged beside him, hooves fighting for purchase, the whites of its eyes glinting in the moonlight.

After hours of fighting his way over treacherous terrain, Ethan came to a road clinging to the side of the mountain. It was steep, and in places precarious, built on logs set one end against the mountain, the other extending over empty space, shored up by heavy timbers.

As he climbed, Ethan became aware of the sweet scent of death and decay. The horse began to sidestep, snorting nervously, ears twitching. Twice it shied from dark objects close beside the trail, the first time so suddenly that Ethan was nearly unseated. Ethan's fears fed on those of the horse, and he urged it forward, faster than was prudent, up the steep, winding trail.

Several times, he was certain he heard hoofbeats closing behind him. Each time, he pulled the horse to a stop and twisted in the saddle to listen. Once, he glimpsed something wild slink into the underbrush; he heard the howl of a wolf, an owl's screech. Beyond that, there was only the whisper of the breeze among bare branches, spidery webs against a cold backdrop of stars.

Dawn's first light was beginning to color the woods around him when Ethan reached the top of Walden's Ridge. Further brightening revealed that the dark lumps, the source of the smell and the horse's agitation, were the carcasses of horses and mules in various stages of decay. There were tens, hundreds, maybe even thousands of them, scattered along the trail, their remains interspersed with the wreckage of wagons and spilled and broken cargo. He was, Ethan realized, following the same road the army had used to bring supplies to Chattanooga during the siege. He pressed on, sickened by the monument to futility and despair unfolding around him.

The horse slowed, then staggered to a stop. Ethan gave it a kick that sent it racing across the top of the mountain. He was nearing the other side when the horse stumbled, and caught itself. It stumbled again and nearly fell. Ethan pulled to a halt and felt it shudder beneath him. When he dismounted, the horse's head dropped. It stood trembling, forelegs splayed, blowing hard. Ethan ran a hand over the sweat-soaked neck, and for the first time, took a good look at the animal.

The mare, a sorrel with a pale mane and tail, was little more than skin and bones. Ethan was amazed she'd kept going as long as she had. He dropped the reins and moved away from her, listening. An occasional birdcall and the soughing of the breeze among the trees were the only sounds he heard. Satisfied that no one was closing on him, he retrieved the reins, and began rubbing the white blaze between the mare's ears, talking softly to her until her breathing slowed. Then he led her off the trail, into the woods.

The forest opened onto a wide, rocky ledge overhanging the western rim of the mountain. Ethan stopped, and the mare dropped her head, greedily cropping the withered tufts of grass that sprouted from between the rocks. He loosened the cinch, and leaving her to eat, wandered out onto the precipice.

Dotted with hearty table mountain pines that had forced their way up through the cracks and survived, the rocks stepped down as they jutted into space. Ethan made his way to the outermost edge and sat feasting his eyes on the spectacular vista spread before him.

Directly below, the Sequatchie Valley was still in shadow, but the distant mountains, and the vast, wooded sprawl of the Cumberland Plateau, were bright in the early morning light. Sunlight glanced off outcroppings of rock, infusing them with gold, a brilliant contrast to the deep green of the surrounding pines and hemlocks. Leafless stands of hickory, yellow poplar, ash, and beech were tinted pink in the early light, mimicking the color of the scattered clouds overhead.

I did it! Ethan thought, a tingle of relief running through him. *I'm free!* He sat savoring the glory of the morning, watching the shadows shift and the colors change as the sun rose higher over the mountain behind him.

Sunlight had advanced halfway across the valley floor when he bestirred himself and turned his mind to what he should do next. The chances of escape had seemed so remote that he hadn't thought beyond his initial flight. The decision to head west had been for no other reason than it seemed to present the least potential for capture. Now he needed a plan.

Ethan drew the book from his coat and opened it to the inscription. He read what Elizabeth had written and allowed himself to be swayed. He looked up, gazing across the endless expanse of the Cumberland Plateau. To head south would risk capture, a return to Cahaba. Even if he made it, nothing guaranteed he'd be safe in Mobile, especially if the North won the war.

I can't go back, he told himself. *Not now. Maybe later, once the war's over and my name has been cleared.*

Unless I killed the guard… The suspicion had nagged at him for hours. By now, he was almost certain the pulse had been imagined. If the guard was dead, he could never go back. *Not to Elizabeth. Not home. Not ever.* Ethan ran moist palms down his pant legs, regretting the force with which he'd hit him, wishing he hadn't gagged him.

It's too late, he told himself. *There's nothing I can do about it now.* All he could do was hope the guard lived. And figure out what to do next.

A shadow passed over him. He looked up as a bald eagle soared overhead. Coming from the east, it swooped over the side of the cliff and turned north, gliding along the face of the mountain for a ways before doubling back. It passed in front of Ethan, so close that he could see the yellow glint of its eye as it swept south. Before long, it turned again, catching an updraft and soaring high into the sky.

Only the eagle flew high enough to view all of Mother Earth. The wisest of animals, he represented strength, agility and grace. He was the symbol of his mother's people, and it was a bad omen to kill him. His sudden appearance seemed to Ethan an omen of another kind.

The eagle passed in front of him once more, then turned and floated across the Sequatchie Valley. Ethan watched until it was only a tiny spec above the Cumberland Plateau. By the time the eagle disappeared into the western sky, he knew exactly what he would do. He would try to find his mother's people.

PART II

MAY 1864 – AUGUST 1865

MAY

1

Elizabeth was hit by a renewed wave of anxiety as Isaac pulled the hired buggy to a stop before the garden gate. Her stomach fluttered nervously, and she laid a hand on it, letting the reassuring bulge of the child calm her.

The farm was exactly as Ethan had described it. The whitewashed two-story farmhouse with the wide, covered porch and weathered picket fence stood nestled beneath a stand of newly leafed oak and hickory bordering the Spoon River. The spreading linden tree in the front yard was heavy with clusters of creamy blossoms, and a scattering of spring flowers bloomed along the fence. Elizabeth could see a chicken coop off to the side of the house, and beyond it the barn, set against a backdrop of newly green fields. Nesting birds twittered among the branches, chickens clucked as they pecked about the yard, and from somewhere nearby came the deep, contented lowing of cows. Elizabeth inhaled deeply, letting the peace of the place settle over her.

The quiet was shattered when a dog emerged from the barn and ran toward them barking. A familiar figure appeared in the open door of the hayloft, and Elizabeth's heart leapt. She waved excitedly, and he leaned forward on his pitchfork, then turned and disappeared from sight.

Isaac helped Elizabeth down from the buggy. Her feet had barely touched the ground when another dog raced around the corner of the house, followed almost immediately, by a woman. Elizabeth looked expectantly toward the barn, assuming Ethan would come running. When he didn't, she turned to the gate to greet his mother.

She had no doubt that was who the woman was. Ethan had inherited her slender build, her coal black hair and copper skin. But it surprised Elizabeth to see how little the son actually resembled the mother. They shared the same high cheekbones, but his mother's face was rounder, her nose more prominent, her mouth wider. Then Elizabeth saw her eyes. They reminded her so much of Ethan that it took her a moment to find her voice.

"Mrs. Fraser?"

Sarah nodded, her expression guarded.

"Mrs. Fraser, my name is Elizabeth Magrath. I'm a friend of Ethan's from Mobile, Alabama."

Sarah's response was a quick intake of breath. She muttered something Elizabeth didn't understand and took a step toward the gate, grasping a picket with each hand.

"Ethan?" she said. "From Mobile?"

Elizabeth nodded eagerly, and smiled. "Yes. Is he here?"

Sarah cast anxious eyes toward the barn. Elizabeth followed her gaze as a man emerged and walked toward them across the barnyard. His build was similar to Ethan's, but sunlight revealed sandy hair, heavily streaked with gray. Elizabeth's heart sank; the look of anticipation drained from her face. As he drew near, Elizabeth saw it was his father Ethan favored in all but coloring.

"She knows Ethan," Sarah said breathlessly.

An odd, pained expression crossed her husband's face, and his step faltered. Recovering himself, he came on, rubbing his hands down his britches and offering the right one to Elizabeth.

"James Fraser," he said. "Ethan's father."

"Elizabeth Magrath. I was telling your wife I'm a friend of Ethan's. We met in Mobile."

A look passed between Ethan's parents. James said, "We were never clear how Ethan came to be there. And now..." The pained expression again before he asked, "How can we help you, Mrs. Magrath?"

Elizabeth's heart gave a painful thump. She looked between them, certain something was terribly wrong. She fought the urge to ask; telling herself it would be unwise to press them as a stranger. "Please," she said. "I was hoping we might talk."

The Frasers seemed to collect themselves then, realizing it had been impolite to keep her standing at the gate. Elizabeth introduced Isaac, and they were shown into the house. Sarah settled Isaac in the kitchen while Elizabeth went with James to the parlor. He pulled aside worn burgundy drapes and opened the windows, flooding the room with light and driving away the musty smell.

Elizabeth stood just inside the door and looked around. The room was small, papered in a faded floral pattern of pinks and greens on a yellowed background. A maroon sofa faced the fireplace, flanked by a pair of worn, cushioned armchairs. There was a small, unimpressive breakfront centered on the wall at the back of the room, its shelves populated with an ill-assorted collection of plates. A large roll-top desk filled the space between front and side windows, a vase of dried flowers on its top. On the wall beside them was a framed photograph. Elizabeth walked to it, leaning in to study the faces.

Ethan was easy to spot. He stood beside his mother, both of them gazing solemnly at the camera. His hair was shorter, barely brushing his collar, and an errant lock trailed across his forehead. He looked extremely young. *Innocent,* Elizabeth amended. *So innocent, in a picture taken just three years ago.* His father stood next to them, one hand resting on the shoulder of a pretty, smiling girl. Flanking them were four young men in uniform, one holding a child, a woman close by his side. He, along with two of his brothers, was dark-haired and sturdily built. The fourth, slender and fair, bore a striking resemblance to his father.

"We paid to have that made before the four oldest went off to the fighting," James said, coming to stand beside her. "Ethan, I'm sure you recognize. The girl is his sister, Kate. That's Duncan holding Grace. He was the oldest. And that's his wife, Alice. Seth is the one with the mustache, and the other two are the twins, Jamie and Josh."

Elizabeth had assumed the twins were identical. It surprised her to see they looked nothing alike. She looked at Ethan again, then at his father. James' eyes had misted as he gazed at the photograph. When he saw Elizabeth looking, he turned away.

Elizabeth studied the photograph a moment longer, turning as Sarah came into the room. Sarah threw her husband a searching look and moved quickly to his side, murmuring something Elizabeth couldn't hear. James nodded and turned to Elizabeth, forcing a smile.

"Have a seat, Mrs. Magrath," he said, indicating one of the chairs. When she was seated, he sat on the sofa next to his wife.

"Please," Sarah said, leaning forward. "Tell us about Ethan."

Elizabeth began by describing how Ethan had come to live above the carriage barn. She went on to tell them what Ethan had told her of his life since leaving the Thirty-sixth, as well as what she'd pieced together from his nightmares and her talks with Thomas. One or the other of his parents interrupted occasionally with a question, but mostly they listened.

When she could put it off no longer, Elizabeth told them the rest. She had gone over it countless times in her head, but still she struggled to explain how she and their son had become lovers and the events leading to his departure. They listened without interruption; James' expression hardening, Sarah's unreadable.

"But what Ethan doesn't know, what I didn't know until after he'd gone..." Elizabeth looked at the knotted handkerchief in her lap. Steeling herself, she said, "What he doesn't know is that I am pregnant with his child."

Their reaction wasn't at all what she'd expected. Surprise, certainly; or perhaps, like her own parents, dismay or even outrage. Instead, Sarah's eyes brimmed with tears. She turned to James, spewing a torrent of words in Lakota. James swallowed hard, his eyes holding Elizabeth's. Responding briefly in the same language, he put an arm around his wife and pulled her to him.

Fear tightened in Elizabeth' chest. "Please," she whispered. "Please, tell me what's wrong. Is he...? Has something happened to him?"

James murmured, and Sarah nodded. Both women watched as he pushed himself to his feet and walked with painful slowness to the roll-top desk. Pushing back the lid, he reached into one of the cubbyholes and returned with a pair of envelopes.

"These are from Josh," he said. "Read the top one first."

Elizabeth took them, sick with dread. A glance showed that they had been mailed from Chattanooga. She opened the first.

> *8 March 1864*
>
> *Dear Ma, Pa and Kate,*
>
> *I have found Ethan. He is well but in terrible trouble. He has been Court Martialed and found Guilty of Spying for the Confederacy. His sentence is Death by Firing Squad.*

"It can't be true!" Elizabeth cried, looking up.

The anguish in his parents' eyes confirmed that it was.

> *Ethan swears he is Innocent and I believe him. His Advocate says you all must write to President Lincoln. Explain that you have already lost Duncan, Jamie and Seth fighting for the Union and beg him to spare Ethan. I am sorry to write with such bad news but I am to tell you from Ethan that he sends his Love. He would write himself but it is not allowed.*
>
> *Love,*
> *Josh*

Elizabeth wiped away tears that had blurred the last portion of the letter. "Did you write?" she asked.

"We did."

"Have you heard... ?"

James motioned to the envelope still on her lap. "Read the other. Then we'll talk."

> *16 March 1864*
>
> *Dear Ma, Pa and Kate,*
>
> *Friday a week ago Ethan escaped. I rode with Troops sent to hunt him down, hoping to keep them from shooting him on sight, but there was no sign of him. I blame myself for not realizing what he was up to and putting a stop to it. His escape has made him appear even more Guilty. If he comes home you had best send him away or keep folks from finding out he's there until his name can be cleared. I return to the 36ᵗʰ at Nashville tomorrow.*
>
> *Love,*
>
> *Josh*

Elizabeth knew from their expressions what the answer would be, but she had to ask. "Have you heard from him?"

Sarah shook her head.

"No," James said. "We don't know where he is. That's what we told the soldiers sent up from Springfield."

A stricken look crossed Elizabeth's face. *He's gone to Mobile!* Aloud she said, "If he hasn't come here, he must have gone to Mobile. He'll arrive to find I've gone." She stood abruptly. "I must go."

James moved quickly, laying a restraining hand on her arm. "This has been a shock, Mrs. Magrath. Best you think things through before doing anything rash. It's been two months since Ethan escaped. He could be anywhere by now."

It took Elizabeth several moments to realize he was right. If Ethan had returned to Mobile, he would already have discovered her gone. It was pointless to guess what he might have done next. For all she knew, a word from Josiah had sent him to Illinois. "You're right," she agreed. "I'm not thinking clearly. It's all..." She shook her head to clear it. "It's been a terrible shock."

"A shock to us all," James agreed. He looked to his wife, then at Elizabeth. "I don't mean to be rude, Mrs. Magrath, but it would be best if you went now. We appreciate what you've told us, but Ethan's mother and I, we need some time to ourselves."

Elizabeth nodded mutely.

"I'll fetch your man. Let him know you're ready."

Elizabeth nodded again, her limbs, her whole body leaden.

"Ethan will write," Sarah said softly.

Elizabeth looked at her, seeing her own anguish reflected in Sarah's eyes. She reached out, would have gone to her, but James and Isaac came into the room.

"He will write," Ethan's mother repeated, and for the first time, Elizabeth was aware of the unusual cadence of her speech. "Ethan is a good boy. He will write again, the same way he wrote from Mobile."

James offered Elizabeth a smile that conflicted with the sadness in his eyes. "Sarah's right. When he's able, Ethan will let us know where he is. He doesn't like his mother to worry."

Elizabeth nodded numbly. Clinging to Isaac for support, she turned toward the door.

In the privacy of her room, Elizabeth wept. For Ethan, unjustly accused, alone, and on the run. And for herself, giving in to the fear that she might never see him again. Eventually, she pulled herself together and considered what she should do.

She rose early the next morning and spent the day composing letters. She was applying the seal to the last of the envelopes when there was a knock at the door. Hannah looked up from the dress she was mending, and the two women exchanged looks before Hannah set the dress aside and went to see who was calling. She opened the door and took a startled step back.

"I'm looking for Mrs. Magrath," the girl announced boldly.

Hannah continued to stare. "You mus' be Mista Ethan's sister."

"You know my brother?" the girl asked, unable to contain her eagerness.

"I knows Mista Ethan real good," Hannah assured her. "You come on in. Miz 'Lizbet gonna be real happy to see you."

Elizabeth had risen when she heard the exchange. As Kate entered the room, she stepped forward, smiling, and offered her hand. "Hello, Kate. I'm Elizabeth. I'm delighted to meet you."

Kate wasn't at all sure how she felt. She had arrived home the previous afternoon to discover there'd been news of Ethan. Excitement quickly turned to suspicion when she'd learned that the bearer of the news was a fine Southern lady intent on marrying him.

Ever since hearing of Ethan's escape, Kate had hoped he was on his way home. She'd spent hours formulating elaborate schemes for hiding and caring for him until his name could be cleared. The woman's sudden appearance threatened all that. She had agonized late into the night over what should be done. At school she'd been reprimanded for inattention, but couldn't keep her mind on her lessons. By the time school let out, she had decided to confront her. But nothing had prepared her for such a friendly, pretty lady. Reluctantly, Kate took her hand.

"Ethan told me all about you, Kate," Elizabeth said, noting her guarded expression. "He spoke of you often. He loves you and has missed you terribly."

Kate's defenses went down a notch.

"Come," Elizabeth said, indicating the armchairs on either side of the window where she and Hannah had been sitting. "Sit with me and let's get to know one another. I've waited a long time to meet you."

Kate seated herself stiffly, poised for flight.

"Ethan described you as a little girl, Kate," Elizabeth said, resuming her own seat. "He'll be delighted to see what a beautiful young woman you've become."

Kate smiled shyly before remembering why she'd come. Her expression hardened. "I *was* a little girl when Ethan left. But that was a long time ago. When he comes home, I don't want you to take him away." Realizing she'd been rude, she added meekly, "At least I hope you won't."

So that was it! Elizabeth smiled. "Don't worry, Kate. I'm not planning to take him anywhere. All I want is to be with him again. The same as you."

It wasn't the answer Kate expected. "But... But my folks said you live in Alabama. When you marry Ethan, won't you want to go home?"

"I have a house in Mobile, Kate, but it doesn't have to be my home. It belonged to my husband, and I went there with him. Once Ethan and I are married, we'll decide where we want to live. I'm sure once he's safely home, he won't want to leave."

"So you might live here?" Kate asked, suddenly hopeful.

Elizabeth smiled. "We very well might."

Kate smiled, looking so like her brother that Elizabeth's heart ached.

"Will you tell me about him?" Kate asked shyly, settling into the chair.

Elizabeth did, dwelling on what was good, and leaving out what she thought Kate too young to hear.

"But if he was safe, and if he loves you, why did he leave?"

"It's not easy to understand, Kate, even for me. There is nothing I wanted more than to have him stay, but he had made up his mind. I had given my word, so I couldn't argue." Elizabeth was seized by the same anguish she'd experienced the night she'd made that promise. Pushing it aside, she tried to explain. "Ethan didn't feel it was right to hide while other men fought. He wanted to do his part so we could all be together again."

"But if that's what he wanted, why did they arrest him? Why did they put him on trial and say he had to die?" Kate's eyes brimmed with tears.

Elizabeth left her chair and knelt beside Kate, covering the girl's hand with her own.

"I don't know, Kate," she said gently. "There are things we don't know, things Josh didn't mention in his letters. We won't know more until we hear from him. Or from Ethan."

Kate looked sharply at her. "Do you think he's on his way home?"

"I know this is where he wants to be, Kate. You and your parents are very dear to him. But with things as they are, he may have decided it's not safe to come here." She gave Kate's hand a comforting squeeze, then rose and crossed to the desk.

"I've written three letters today. One is to President Lincoln, telling him what I told you—that Ethan had been a prisoner and was ill when I found him, explaining that he was in my care. One is to a man who served with your brothers and can vouch for Ethan's loyalty. The last is to your brother Josh, asking what I can do to help clear Ethan's name."

She turned to Kate, her voice breaking. "I love him. The same as you do, Kate. All I want is for him to come home."

2

Ethan pulled the mare to a stop, gazing across a carpet of wildflowers and new grass toward the Cheyenne camp, clusters of white, conical tipis spreading out from the line of trees that marked Ash Creek. The sun was long past its zenith, and the tipis, and the immense pony herds, threw elongated shadows across the prairie. Tendrils of smoke from hundreds of campfires wafted into the late afternoon sky.

As he watched, a section of the pony herd parted, and a group of riders made their way through, headed for the village. He could see people moving about; hear a dog's bark, a child's cry. The same mixture of dread and anticipation rose in him as had two weeks earlier when he first ventured onto the open prairie, leaving behind the last vestiges of familiar eastern forest.

Vast and treeless, rolling like an ocean, newly green and empty as far as the eye could see, the prairie was unlike anything he had ever imagined. Too immense to take in, foreign and intimidating, he'd wanted to turn from it, to close his eyes against it. He hesitated now, as he had then, wondering if the decision he'd made on Walden's Ridge had been the right one.

Ethan tore his eyes from the camp and looked up, following the endless sweep of azure sky to the western horizon where a line of pink and gold clouds marked the transition from blue to green. He shuddered, remembering the cold, dark isolation of his cell, and the agonizing moment when his sentence was pronounced.

Shot until dead, with musketry. The memory still had the power to tie his stomach in knots. Shaking it off, Ethan nudged the mare forward.

He had traveled west in much the same way he'd traveled through the South, relying on his wits and the kindness of strangers when possible, resorting to lies and thievery when necessary. As quickly as possible, he'd replaced every article of clothing identifiable as army issue. Josh's cap and greatcoat were the only exceptions. In one of the pockets, he'd found his brother's furlough and a pass allowing travel to Chattanooga. He'd stuffed them back, along with the forage cap, thinking they might come in handy. He had kept to himself, the mare he named Faria his only companion, but for two occasions when he'd found himself in the company of others.

Early on, as he made his way across the Cumberland Plateau, he came upon a boy two years his junior, a deserter headed home after a brief, unhappy stint in the Union army. The boy took him for a fellow deserter, and Ethan did nothing to dissuade him. They parted company near Manchester, and from there, Ethan followed the Duck River west and north, across the Natchez Trace, to the banks of the Tennessee. Once across, he struck west, coming upon the south fork of the Obion and following it until it curved south. Leaving the river behind, he angled northwest until his way was blocked by the waters of Reelfoot Lake.

Five miles wide and fourteen miles long, formed when the Mississippi was diverted and dammed by a massive earthquake on the New Madrid fault fifty years before, the lake was a formidable barrier. Ethan followed its shoreline north, dodging scattered patrols from both armies, and crossed into Kentucky at the lake's northern boundary. A few more miles, and he came to the Mississippi.

There his resolve weakened. The temptation to take a steamer north and home, or south to Elizabeth was so strong that he lingered on the outskirts of a small settlement for the better part of three weeks. To earn money for his passage, he spent his days working for a woman whose husband was away at war, doing repairs and helping her two young sons with the plowing and planting. Nights were spent sweeping floors, cleaning spittoons, and washing up for the local saloonkeeper in exchange for room and board and feed for the mare.

A good many of the patrons at Harlan Mallory's dingy saloon were Confederate officers. Initially, they regarded Ethan with suspicion, but he adopted the same subservient attitude he'd used in the past, and they soon came to accept his presence. They called him boy and ordered him around, and then forgot about him. As drink loosened their tongues, Ethan listened.

The three girls who worked the saloon and the rooms upstairs were another matter. They took one look at Ethan and immediately began vying for his attention. Ethan was polite, but distant, and before long, all but one lost interest. Her name was Frieda, and when he looked closely, Ethan decided she was about his age. She was pretty, in a worn sort of way, with an unruly mass of red hair and a buxom figure. She took to hanging about whenever she wasn't busy, watching him work and seeking to engage him in small talk. Ethan heard her entire life story in a single evening, but over the course of three weeks, revealed very little about himself.

On the day he made up his mind to continue west, he mentioned it to Frieda after the last patron staggered into the night. Her eyes lit up in a way that made him instantly regret it. When she came around the bar, snuggling close as he dried the last of the mismatched glasses, he knew it had been a mistake. The flowery perfume she wore mingled with the odors of sex and sweat; her breath was stale and smelled of whiskey. Ethan dried the last glass and stepped away.

"Take me with you, won'chu, Ethan?" she said, coming after him, running her hand lightly up his back and twisting his hair around her fingers.

Ethan chose to treat it lightly. He let out a short laugh as he ran a towel along the top of the bar. "Why would you want to go west, Frieda? It's dangerous out there."

"To be with you, Ethan," she replied, moving closer, pinning him against the bar with her body. Her free hand came to rest on the outstretched arm holding the towel.

Ethan looked over his shoulder and saw the desire in her eyes. And the determination. He forced a smile. "I can't take you with me, Frieda. Sorry." He tried withdrawing his arm, but her grip tightened, so he let it be.

"Why not?" She pressed tight against him, running her hand up over his shoulder and caressing his cheek. "Don'chu like me, Ethan?"

"I like you fine, Frieda," he told her, eyes on the bar. "But I don't know exactly where I'm headed. It wouldn't be a good idea for you to come with me."

"Please?" She moved her hips, rubbing suggestively against him. "Come on, Ethan. Take me back to yo' room. No charge. Afterward, you an' me kin go off t'gether."

He heard the desperation in her voice; knew any answer he gave would be wrong. "You're a nice person, Frieda," he told her, meaning it. "I've enjoyed talking to you, but I can't take you with me. Sorry."

For a long moment, Frieda said nothing. Then her hand fell away from his cheek and she took a step back. When Ethan turned, she slapped him hard across the face.

"I thought you was different," she cried, her eyes ablaze with anger. "But you ain't. Yo' nothing but a thievin', no 'count half-breed."

Ethan's eyes watered from the force of the blow. "Please, Frieda," he begged. "Keep your voice down. I swear I'd take you with me if I could. But you wouldn't be happy where I'm going. Please. You have to believe me."

"Liar!" Frieda turned on her heel and stormed away. At the foot of the stairs, she turned back, leveling a finger at him. "Wait 'til I tell Harlan how you stole from the till an' used me without payin'!"

Ethan looked after her as she ran up the stairs. When she was gone, he threw down the towel and left the bar. He went around back to the lean-to where he'd been living and gathered his meager possessions. It distressed him to leave without collecting the money the farmer's wife owed him, but there was no way of knowing who Harlan would choose to believe, him or the whore. The threat of jail or worse kept him from lingering.

Ethan rode north out of town, armed with the knowledge he'd gained from patrons at the bar that General Buford's troops had attacked and were demanding the surrender of the Union forces at Fort Halleck, fifteen miles away at Columbus, Kentucky. A whiff of cigar smoke, carried on the breeze, sent him veering away from the Mississippi long before he reached Columbus. Picking his way through dense forest, he gave wide berth to the town and the troops entrenched there. The mare sensed his unease and fidgeted under him, forcing him to keep her on a tight rein. Twice she snorted and shied at shadows, setting his heart racing. Both times he slid from the saddle, and holding her head to quiet her, peered anxiously into the darkness.

He was only a few short miles north of Columbus when the sky eased from black to gray, then quickly brightened. As the morning advanced, Ethan fought the urge to hurry, aware that one false move could lead to capture, and that capture by either side might easily prove fatal.

When he judged himself well beyond the town, he began angling back toward the Mississippi. His body ached; he was bone-tired and thirsty. He considered stopping to rest, but every instinct screamed against it. He needed to keep moving, to get back to the river and follow it north until he found a place to board a steamer.

The sun warmed him, and his grip on the reins slackened. He slouched, half-dozing, as the mare ambled along a narrow track through the woods. His thoughts drifted to Frieda, to the memory of her breasts pressing soft against him. She had presented them as an invitation from the day he arrived. Round and full, straining at the fabric of her low-cut dress, she'd leaned over the bar, giving him a clear view of all she offered. The invitation had been his to accept, but he'd chosen to ignore it.

Not for the first time, he wondered what it would have been like to lie with her. He'd never been with a whore, despite the teasing invitations from Jamie and Josh in months following Stones River. Back then, the pain of losing Maggie, the look of revulsion on her mother's face and her father's threats, had been too fresh.

He'd known Maggie Peebles since they were five or six, when they first started school together. As a child, she'd been a wisp of a thing, with long, flaxen hair and cornflower eyes too big for her face. Ethan had paid her scant attention. Then, one day when he was sixteen, in the spring following Seth's death, he looked up from his lessons to find her watching him across the schoolroom. Maggie smiled when their eyes met, and he was amazed to see how much she'd changed. Overnight, it seemed, she'd become a young woman, grown beautifully into her features and rounded in all the right places. Something in him stirred. Embarrassed, he looked away.

Maggie was persistent, and before long, he started walking her home from school, leaving her at the end of the lane that led to her parents' house. When school let out for the summer, they found ways to meet almost every day.

"My parents think I'm too young to be with boys," Maggie told him, and they sought refuge in secret places—in haylofts, among the cornrows, and in the bushes along the river. Initially, their time was spent talking. Maggie was the first person outside his family to take an interest in him, and when Ethan realized her interest was genuine, he opened up, sharing secrets he'd never told anyone. Maggie, in turn, told him of the pressures growing up her parents' only child, proceeded and followed by a succession of miscarriages and stillbirths. It wasn't long before talk turned to the future, to comparing hopes and dreams that, more and more as the summer progressed, came to include each other.

On a balmy evening in early July, as the last of the reflected light faded off the river, Maggie allowed Ethan to kiss her. Really kiss her. After that, much of their time was spent wrapped in each other's arms, kissing and touching through their clothes. Ethan desperately wanted more, but for more than a month, Maggie held him at bay.

It was on a hot, sultry Sunday afternoon, nestled in the shade of a haystack, in a field near her parents' house, that Maggie finally let Ethan slip a hand under her chemise. Excitement surged through him as he cupped her small breast, feeling the nipple pucker beneath his fingertips. Maggie moaned with pleasure.

Yes! Ethan thought. *Surely this time—*

Something crashed violently into his back.

"No!" Maggie screamed, overlapped by her mother's voice, thick with fury. "Get your filthy hands off my daughter!" She brought the broom down again.

Ethan pitched sideways, throwing up his arms to protect himself, rolling and scrambling as blows continued to rain down. Out of range, he staggered to his feet and turned back, panting.

"Don't you ever come near my daughter again," Mrs. Peebles screamed, her face distorted with loathing. "You're not fit for decent girls. Get off this property, and don't come here again!"

"Please," Maggie begged, tears streaming down her face. "Please, Ma! I love him!"

Her mother rounded on her, grabbing her by the arm and yanking her to her feet. "Don't let me hear that kind of talk from you ever again, Missy. You're not throwing yourself away on the likes of him." She turned to Ethan, gesturing angrily with the broom. "Now get!"

Ethan slowly backed away.

"No! Ethan, please!" Maggie cried, craning to look at him as her mother hauled her toward the house.

Ethan watched until they vanished around the corner of the barn. Then, half-blinded by tears, he turned and ran.

He stayed away from home until late that night. The house was dark when he crept up the stairs to the room he'd shared with his brothers, glad none of them was there to see him cry. The next morning, he went to Maggie's favorite spot along the river, hoping she would find a way to join him.

The day crept by with agonizing slowness. When Maggie failed to appear, Ethan went to the foot of the lane and stared toward the line of trees that screened her house. In the field between, her father rode the hay rake behind a pair of horses. Ethan waited until he was at the far side of the field, then darted up the lane. Selecting a hidden spot among the trees, he hunkered down to wait.

It wasn't long before Maggie and her mother came out the back door and began removing wash from the line. When the last of the clothes had been folded and stacked in the basket, Maggie's mother shepherded her daughter back inside, and that was the last Ethan saw of her.

"What're you doing sneaking around here?"

Ethan shot to his feet and whirled to face Maggie's father. Taller and a good forty pounds heavier, the older man grabbed him by the shirtfront.

"I thought it was made real clear you ain't to come poking your nose around here."

"Yes, sir," Ethan answered breathlessly.

"Then what're you doing sneaking 'round here, boy?" Mr. Peebles slammed Ethan backward against a tree. "Answer me!"

"I—"

Maggie's father cut him off, grasping him by the throat and forcing him onto his toes. His grip was so tight Ethan could scarcely breathe. The older man leaned in, his eyes ablaze with fury.

"I oughta kill you. Forcing yourself on my little girl." His grip on Ethan's throat tightened, cutting off the last of his air. "I find you planted one of your little red bastards in her, I'm gonna come looking for you. I find you, I am gonna kill you. You hear me?"

Ethan clawed at his hand, but succeeded only in causing the vise around his neck to tighten.

"It's time you learned decent girls ain't meant for the likes of you. You find one of your own kind to dally with. You hear me?"

The pain was intense. Blood roared in Ethan's ears. His vision reddened, then began to dim. He was all but unconsciousness when Maggie's father released him. He crumpled to the ground, choking and gasping for air.

He had no sooner begun to recover, than the older man hauled him to his feet.

"I never wanna lay eyes on you again. You hear me?"

To frightened to speak, Ethan nodded. Maggie's father held him a moment longer, then gave Ethan a shove that sent him staggering down the lane.

Ethan never saw Maggie again. A couple weeks later, he heard that her parents had sent her to live with relatives in Chicago. A week after that, just shy of his seventeenth birthday, he'd run away. He wondered now what had become of her.

Faria yanked at the bit. Her ears pricked forward and her pace quickened. Startled, Ethan pulled back on the reins and reached for the revolver. Close by, a horse nickered. Faria responded as a man stepped from the bushes to block his path. He was unwashed and bearded, dressed in the tattered remains of a Rebel uniform. He leveled a battered flintlock at Ethan. Four more men, armed with stones and heavy sticks, emerged from the undergrowth to array themselves before him.

The first man stepped forward, his lips twisting into a smile that revealed tobacco-stained teeth. He spat in the dirt and said, "At's a real nice horse ya got there, boy. Why don'chu toss down that there pistol, an' git down off'n 'er? Real easy-like." He took a step closer.

Death here was more certain than at the hands of either army, and beyond a doubt more brutal. Taking a chance that the deserters had no ball or powder for the musket, Ethan cocked the revolver and fired, knocking down the man with the musket and scattering the others. Wheeling the mare, he slammed his heels into her sides and squeezed off two more shots. There were angry shouts, and a rock sailed harmlessly past his head. Another smashed into his right shoulder, nearly knocking him from the saddle and sending the revolver flying. Grasping the mare's mane, Ethan barely managed to right himself. He leaned low over her neck as more missiles flew by.

When he was safely out of range, he turned Faria and guided her north, urging her on at a canter for another mile before allowing her to slow. His shoulder throbbed, and he cursed the loss of the revolver, but didn't dare go back. The deserters were bound to have found it, and it still held three bullets, while he was now unarmed.

3

He rode without stopping until he reached the Mississippi. The river was approaching flood stage; its waters muddy and swift. Ethan found a place where the water calmed in the lee off a jutting bank, and climbed down from the saddle. He lowered himself to his stomach and drank, splashed water onto his face, and drank some more. When the mare had drunk her fill, he climbed back into the saddle. His stomach rumbled hollowly, reminding him he hadn't eaten, but he pressed on, by-passing the next settlement when he saw it had no place for a steamer to dock.

It was late in the day when he reached the next town, and for once, luck was with him. He arrived at the wharf as the mail steamer, *City of Alton,* was preparing to cast off. There were blue-clad troops everywhere, so Ethan donned the forage cap and pulled out the furlough. Waiting until the dockmen moved with purpose toward the gangway, he charged forward, pulling Faria to a sliding stop before the ticket seller's window and flinging himself from the saddle. Gesturing toward the steamer, he waved the furlough and shouted, "St. Louis!" As he'd hoped, the startled clerk took in the forage cap and the coat, and barely glanced at the furlough. Scooping Ethan's money through the slot, he shoved a ticket at him and shouted, "Hurry!"

The boiler deck was jammed with wagons, horses, mules, freight and people. After a good deal of jostling, he found a place to tie the mare. Then he made his way to the starboard rail and sank down next to it, wedged next to a steel column.

Looking out at the wharf, he blinked and looked again at the sign, unable to believe his eyes. *Cairo, Illinois.* Homesickness swept through him. He could see the farm, the faces of his parents and Kate. The longer he allowed himself to dwell on it, the more tempted he was to abandon his plans and go home. Surely it would be safe...

Shot until dead, with musketry. His stomach rolled. There was no way to know what lengths the army would go to to find him. *They'd never come this far north,* he told himself, desperate to believe it. *Not with spring campaigning under way.* But if they did, they'd know from Josh exactly where to look. *Shot until dead...* The dead guard ensured there would be no reprieve. Ethan tilted his head back and sighed. He had no idea what to do.

Blasts from the steam whistle broke in on his thoughts. Black smoke billowed from the twin smokestacks, swirling down in great choking clouds as the water churned beneath the massive paddlewheel, and the steamer inched away from the wharf. The smoke cleared as the breeze off the river caught it, and Ethan watched Cairo recede before leaning back and closing his eyes.

He had no idea how long he'd slept when the whistle screeched, jarring him awake. He sat forward, peering heavy-lidded through the rail. Lamplight illuminated the wharf at Cape Girardeau. Heavy hemp lines snaked through the air, into the waiting hands of the dockmen. As the steamer bumped against the levee, Ethan pulled himself to his feet. His right shoulder had stiffened; his stomach cramped with hunger. He waited while freight and mail were unloaded, watched people and animals file off, before joining the stragglers going ashore. He bought a meat pie from a vendor and joined the passengers waiting to board.

Back at his place by the rail, he slept until the steamer docked at Chester. As the *City of Alton* set out on the final leg of its journey, the eastern sky began to lighten, daylight gradually revealing the distant green of the Illinois shore. Ethan watched it slip by, all the while wrestling with the decision he'd already made. By the time the steamer found its berth along the teeming levee in St. Louis, he had overcome emotion and desire and convinced himself to go on.

Disembarking, he took a last, lingering look across the wide expanse of brown water before pushing his way through the noisy throng along the levee. He found the city crawling with Union troops and detoured south, wending his way through unpaved back streets until he reached the far side of town. At a shop run by Germans, he used the last of his money to purchase a few necessary supplies, and impulsively, a copy of the *St. Louis Daily Union*. The lamplighters were beginning their rounds when he emerged from beneath the pall of coal smoke that hung over the city and headed west into the setting sun.

He stayed in the saddle until long after dark, pressed by an urgent need to put as much distance as possible between himself and the lure of Illinois. It was late when he bedded down in a grove of trees along the Missouri. The next morning, he was up with the sun. A few bites to eat, and he was on his way. He pushed the mare hard until dark, then collapsed, utterly exhausted. Rising at sunrise, he pressed on.

Late in the day, thunderheads began building in the west, looming until they blotted out the sun. When Ethan happened upon a spot likely to provide shelter from the storm, he made camp. Tethering Faria on a long lead, he spent the remaining hours of daylight indulging himself, eating and pouring over the newspaper.

He read with interest the account of the evacuation of women and children from Columbus, Kentucky the day before he detoured around it, and of the plan by the Army of the Potomac to take Richmond by siege. Most fascinating were the "valuable historical reports appearing in the *Union* in advance of all other papers in St. Louis"—the full text of General Thomas' official report on the battles that led to the capture of Lookout Mountain and Missionary Ridge. The account reminded him of Josh, renewed his guilt for having hit him. Ethan looked up, past the gray, leafless branches to the leaden sky above, longing for home.

The night was marked by distant flashes of lightning and the low rumble of thunder as the leading edge of the storm passed to the north of him. Day dawned gray and dreary. By the time he swung into the saddle, the first heavy drops of rain were beginning to fall.

It rained without let-up all day. Ethan was wet through, and miserable, when toward evening, he began looking for a sheltered spot to spend the night. He had almost given up when he glimpsed a flicker of firelight through the trees. Instinct warned him to keep to himself, to trust no one, but he was cold and wet and the fire beckoned seductively. He nudged the mare toward it.

As he drew near, he saw that a canvas tarp had been strung between two trees and the side of a massive freight wagon. A man sat under it, cooking his supper. When Ethan pulled Faria to a halt beyond the edge of the tarp, the man regarded him silently for several moments before calling out, "Hitch up that horse a' yourn, an' come in outta the wet."

Ethan was more than happy to comply. He pulled the saddle from the mare and stowed it under the tarp before hobbling her and setting her loose to graze.

When he ducked under the canvas, slapping water from his hat, the man was spooning the contents of the pot onto a pair of tin plates.

"Figgered someone 'uz bound to turn up wet an' hungry. Si'cherself down and have a bite."

After a week without a decent meal, Ethan needed no further encouragement. Dragging his saddle close to the fire, he sat down. The stranger handed him a hot cup of coffee and plate of bacon, beans, and biscuits. Ethan accepted the food with thanks and began to eat, surreptitiously studying his host.

He was a big man, thickset with broad shoulders and large, thick-fingered hands. A tangle of curling black hair hung well past his shoulders; a drooping mustache hid his upper lip. His nose was large and beaked, his eyes deep-set beneath heavy brows. His skin was deeply furrowed, turned brown and leathery by the sun.

The man looked up, saw Ethan looking, and grinned, dark eyes twinkling in the firelight, the wrinkles around them deepening. "Name's Henri," he said. "Henri Broulat." Laying down his spoon, he extended a hand.

"Ethan Fraser." Ethan tried not to wince as his hand was caught in a powerful grip.

Henri nodded and returned to his supper. He emptied his plate and ladled out more, nodding a question to Ethan. Ethan held out his plate and Henri refilled it, studying Ethan as he did so.

"Who're yer people?" he asked, once he'd settled back.

"Excuse me?"

"Yer people? What tribe?"

"Oh." Ethan eyed him warily, but saw only friendly interest. "My father's white." After a moment, he added, "My mother's Lakota. Sioux."

"Ahh." Henri nodded knowingly. "Mixed-blood. That explains it. You got the colorin', but not the looks. I be mixed-blood m'self. My mother 'uz Suh'-tai, squaw to a French trapper. Spent mosta my life in the Upper Country—what they's callin' Colorado Territory now'days. 'At's whar I'm headed." He tilted his head toward the wagon, and by way of explanation added, "Trader."

Not knowing what to respond, Ethan said nothing.

"Whar ya bound fer?"

Ethan shrugged, staring into the flames. "I'm not sure. I was hoping to find my mother's people."

Henri eyed him skeptically. "Ever been west a' the Mississipp' afore, son?"

"No, sir."

"It's mighty big country. You got any idee who they is, these folks yer lookin' fer? Whar to go lookin' fer 'em?"

"Some."

"Yer gonna hafter do better'n that, son. They's lotsa Injuns out thar. 'Nother month or so, they'll be man-ha-stoz spread out over hunnerds a' miles."

Ethan looked up. "I don't understand. What does that mean?"

"Man-ha-stoz? Bands. Families. Twenty, thirty people. They split up after Medicine Lodge so's to have enough graze fer their ponies."

Tiospaye, Ethan thought. The Lakota word meant the same thing.

"You'll have a devil of a time findin' 'em, less you got a durned good idea whar to look."

"My parents met at Fort Laramie. Ma always talked about the Paha Sapa, the Black Hills. In Dakota Territory." Ethan shrugged. "I was thinking I'd head there."

"You speak the language?"

"Some."

Henri shook his head. "Good luck to ya, son. I reckon you'll need it."

Ethan looked down at the fire, wondering if his decision had been the right one.

By morning the rain was gone, leaving a sea of mud, dazzling blue sky, and a scattering of puffy white clouds in its wake. At Henri's suggestion, Ethan joined him on the wagon, hitching the mare on behind. The going was arduous and slow as Henri expertly guided his team of six mules around the most treacherous of the mud holes on the rain-soaked road. They covered only eight miles that day. Ethan would have made better time on his own, but he had never met anyone quite like Henri, and he found his company fascinating. He ended up riding with him all the way to Westport, listening and learning.

Henri had lived his entire life on the hills and prairies along the Front Range of the Rocky Mountains. His father was a Frenchman who, in 1810, headed up the Missouri from St. Louis with the Spanish trapper Manuel Lisa, and never looked back. Philippe Broulat had worked for Lisa until Lisa's death in 1820, then stayed on as a free trader. He'd married a Suh'-tai woman on the upper reaches of the Missouri, and Henri had come along soon after. Before Henri was old enough to remember, they'd migrated west with the Cheyenne and Arapaho, to the high country east of the Big Horn Mountains, along the Tongue and Powder Rivers, and north of the Moonshell.

"The Moonshell," Ethan repeated. It was a name that figured often in his mother's stories.

"Whites call it the North Platte."

Ethan nodded. He'd guessed as much from poring over maps.

When a portion of the tribe moved south, Henri's parents had gone with them, roaming the vast, buffalo-covered plains between the Tallow River[1] and the Flint Arrowpoint.[2] When Henri was old enough, he'd begun trapping and trading with his father. He had countless stories to tell, filled with names of people and places: John Fremont, Jedediah Smith, Jim Bridger, Jim Beckwourth, William Sublette, Robert Campbell, Kit Carson, Ceran St. Vrain, the Bent brothers, John Smith, Cinemo, Yellow Wolf, Black Kettle, Fort Laramie, Bent's Fort, the Smoky Hill River... The list went on. Ethan recognized a few, but most he did not. Henri described in vivid detail the rendezvous he had attended with his father up along the Seeds-ke-dee in 1833, and again in 1835 and 1836, where trappers, mountain men and Indians from many tribes came together to trade, and for virtual orgies of drinking, gambling, horse racing, and boasting.

Ethan soaked it all in, intrigued not only by Henri's tales, but by his manner of speaking. When reminiscing, Henri was apt to slip into the vernacular of the mountain man, a corrupted mix of English, French and Spanish with a smattering of words from various Indian dialects. More than once, Ethan had to ask him to repeat himself in English.

Henri described the country along the Arkansas as it had been in his youth. Vast, rolling prairies ranged over by tens of thousands of buffalo, where ample rain fell, grass grew taller than a man's head, and rivers flowed full, lined with dense stands of trees—cottonwoods and willows mostly, but dogwood and sumac, as well. Some of the larger drainages supported locust, oak, hickory and other hardwoods.

"Them days're gone," Henri said with a sigh. "Warn't long ago, a man could ride fer days, months even, with nary a sign of a white man. Now they's ranches an' towns springin' up ever'whar. An' wagons bringin' more folks ever' day. Even if they're just passin' through, them iron wheels grind the prairie to dust, and the

---

1   South Platte River

2   Arkansas River

livestock eats ever' blade a' grass fer miles out from the trails. Timber's goin', too. And small game. Even the buffler ain't what they us'ta be."

Henri went for several minutes without speaking, before adding, "It ain't all the white man's doin'. A while back, things started changin' in this country. Started gettin' hit hard by drought. The first bad 'un was in forty-nine, and there were another long about fifty-five. Worst was the summers of sixty and sixty-one, an' it ain't got much better since. Now'days there's naught but cracked dirt where seeps and ponds use to be, an' creeks an' rivers run half-empty. Grass don't grow tall anymore, an' come mid-summer, it's shriveled up an' burnt.

"Drought and white men've made life hard in these parts. Injuns're hard-pressed to find summer graze fer their ponies. They go to their winterin' grounds an' find the timber's been cut down. An' the buffler..." Henri shook his head. "Makes me glad I got a house with walls now'days."

He told Ethan about the small stockade he'd built years before, along the Santa Fe Trail west of Trinidad, nestled in the foothills of the Rockies near the headwaters of the Purgatoire River. He lived there with his Cheyenne wife and some of her relatives now that his sons were grown and gone. The eldest had married a Northern Cheyenne years before and gone to live with her people up along the Powder River. The middle son had lived with his mother's people until he'd been killed in a drunken brawl.

"They's traders cheat the Injuns by bringin' whiskey into the camps to trade fer buffler robes," Henri explained. "The Cheyenne got no tolerance, an' it don't take much to get 'em drunk. Micah, my youngest, was thar, an' the way he tells it, Henry 'uz tryin' to talk sense into some a' the young bucks, explainin' how the traders was takin' advantage, tradin' a pint a' whiskey for a robe that takes a woman weeks to dress proper. It turned mean, an' Henry got stabbed. Warn't much Micah could do but hold him while he died." Henri shook his head sadly. "Left a wife and baby daughter, Henry did."

They traveled a while in silence before Ethan asked, "And Micah, where is he?"

"Still with the Wú-ta-pi-u clan, last I heared. Black Kettle's bunch. Seed him last fall when I was headin' east. They 'uz plannin' to winter down along Ash Creek." Henri glanced at Ethan and clarified. "Kansas. A ways off from Fort Larned. They got so's they take handouts from the fort to make it through the winters. If Ash Creek's whar they wound up, I aim to see him when I pass through."

Ethan said nothing, intrigued by the thought of another "mixed-blood" as Henri put it, living among Indians. *Maybe what I'm doing's not so far-fetched after all—*

"He's about yer age, I reckon."

"Excuse me?" Ethan looked up to find Henri watching him.

"Micah. About yer age. How many years ya got on ya, son? Nineteen, twenty?"

"Eighteen," Ethan told him. "Nineteen come September."

Henri nodded. "Yup, 'bout the same. Micah's just nineteen. A good boy. The two a' you'd get on jus' fine."

Long before they reached Westport, Ethan began toying with the idea of asking Henri if he could go with him as far as Ash Creek. The more he thought about it, the more the idea appealed to him. It would be good to have someone like Henri around the first time he ventured into an Indian camp. And someone like Micah. Someone who spoke the language and could teach him their ways. *Maybe*, he thought. *Maybe I'll ask...*

Henri had been observing his companion for nearly a week by the time they reached Westport. He was certain the boy was on the run. Judging from the blue coat and the "US" branded on the mare's shoulder, he figured it had to do with the war. At first he'd figured him for a deserter, but after watching him for several days, he decided Ethan was running too far for that.

Ethan had volunteered little about himself, and Henri hadn't pressed. The few times Ethan had mentioned home and family, Henri had heard the longing in his voice. And there was the book. Ethan kept it in one of his saddlebags, and each evening he pulled it out and opened it to a page near the front. Sitting cross-legged by the fire, he stared at what was written there. Sometimes, before closing it, he touched the page lightly with his fingertips. Then, without a word, he lay down with his back to Henri and pretended to sleep.

Yup, Henri thought, *he's runnin'.*

As he guided the mules along the teeming main street of Westport, Henri said, "I been thinkin'. 'Less'n you got some real pressin' need to head direct fer Dakota Territory, how 'bout you go on with me fer a ways? Least 'til we come across Black Kettle's bunch."

Ethan looked at him in surprise, but Henri was staring straight ahead. He flicked the reins over the mules' backs and added, "Them what's lookin' fer ya ain't gonna go lookin' among the Cheyenne any more'n 'ay are the Sioux."

Ethan opened his mouth to deny it, but Henri's eyes flicked over, stopping him. Ethan looked away.

"How'd you know?"

"Warn't hard to figure, son. Been watchin' you fer nigh on a week. 'At's how it adds up."

"I didn't do it. What they said I did."

Henri considered Ethan's profile. "You ain't given me cause to doubt'cha, son. You seem decent enough, or I wouldn't a' asked you to join up with me."

They rode in silence as Henri maneuvered through the throngs of people, animals and white-covered wagons that filled the streets. By the time Henri turned the big freight wagon onto a side street, Ethan had decided to tell him the truth.

"I fought for the Union. They accused me of spying for the Confederacy, and I was court-martialed. They found me guilty and sentenced me to die. I killed a man when I escaped, stole his gun and a horse." He glanced at Henri. "Knowing that, you might want to reconsider."

Henri shrugged. "None a' that means much out here, son. Even less whar we're headed." He looked at Ethan and grinned. "'Cept the part about stealin' the horse. That kinda thing's been known to git folks riled up."

When Ethan didn't respond in kind, Henri's look turned serious. "The offer stands. The Cheyenne's allies with the Sioux, and they's always some round about. Brulé and Oglala mostly. If they're the ones yer lookin' fer, so much the better. If not, I'll see yer welcome to stay with the Wú-ta-pi-u. Go with 'em when they make up their minds ta' head north, and yer bound to run across folks knows the ones yer lookin' fer."

Oglala! Ethan's heart skipped a beat. His mother's people were Oglala. Maybe finding them wouldn't be as difficult as he'd imagined. "Thank you, Henri," he said gratefully. "I'll take you up on it." He hesitated, then looking faintly embarrassed, added, "Listening to you's made me realize I don't have any idea how to find my mother's people. I appreciate the offer."

"Tain't nothin', son. Glad fer the comp'ny." He pulled on the reins and called to the lead mule. "Gee, Pat. Gee."

He maneuvered the wagon to the side of the street and pulled the team to a stop before looking at Ethan. "I got things to tend to afore we head out. Yer welcome to tag along."

"Thanks," Ethan said. "But I need to write a couple of letters and see them mailed."

***

In Illinois, Elizabeth waited. Waited for news of Ethan, for a reply from Josh, and for word from Ethan's parents. Kate had been back twice to see her. Both times she had dropped by unexpectedly after school, eager to hear more about Ethan, but reluctant to linger. When Elizabeth offered to have Isaac drive her home, Kate had looked uneasy and hastily declined.

It doesn't bode well for what's being said at home, Elizabeth thought as she set her napkin aside and prepared to rise from the breakfast table.

The day stretched before her. She would, she decided, have Isaac hitch up the buggy and drive her past the house she'd seen the day before. If it still appealed, she would arrange to see the inside. It would be a relief to leave the rented house with its cramped, dreary rooms. And the work entailed in furnishing a new home would provide a much-needed diversion.

There was a knock at the door followed by Hannah's footsteps in the hall. Elizabeth listened as she greeted the caller, then came toward the dining room.

"You gots visitors, Miz 'Lizbet," Hannah announced, her voice an excited whisper. "It Mista Ethan's folks."

Elizabeth ran nervous hands down her skirt, willing herself to be calm. "Show them to the parlor, will you, Hannah? And offer them something to drink. I'll be along in a moment."

Dashing to her bedroom, Elizabeth checked her appearance in the mirror above the bureau, smoothing hair that didn't need smoothing and replacing two hairpins that didn't need replacing. She pinched color into her cheeks, and pulled a fresh handkerchief from the drawer, tucking it into her sleeve before straightening her skirt. Casting a final, anxious look in the mirror, she resolutely squared her shoulders and walked along the hall to the greet Ethan's parents.

James turned from the window as she came into the room, hat in hand, his stance awkward. Sarah perched on the chair next to him. Neither spoke. Elizabeth used the silence to seat herself across from them.

"Won't you be seated, Mr. Fraser? Has Hannah offered you anything to drink?"

"She did," James answered stiffly, continuing to stand. "We need to talk, Mrs. Magrath. Your arrival the other day took us by surprise, and there are some things didn't get asked."

Elizabeth was certain they could hear her heart hammering in her chest. "Yes. Please. Ask whatever you like." She gestured to the empty chair next to Sarah's. When James didn't sit, her hand fell to her lap, seeking the handkerchief.

James glanced at Sarah before tossing his hat on the chair and taking a step toward Elizabeth. "What we'd like to know first, Mrs. Magrath, is how old are you?"

Elizabeth blinked, taken aback by his directness. "I'm twenty-five, Mr. Fraser."

"Do you know how old Ethan is?"

"I do. He's eighteen."

"He's a boy, Mrs. Magrath. Just a boy. You're... You're seven years older than he is. What on earth possessed you?"

At the accusation in his voice, Elizabeth grew defensive. "Ethan is not a boy, Mr. Fraser. Not anymore. He may have been when he left home, but a lot has happened since then. He has been in battle, killed men, seen and suffered unspeakable things." Her voice hardened. "I have seen him more recently than you, Mr. Fraser, and I can assure you, Ethan is *not* 'just a boy.'"

She held James eyes until he was forced to look away. He picked up his hat and sat down, hunched forward, dangling it between his knees. When he looked at her again, his face had lost some of its combativeness.

"From what you've told us, you're a wealthy woman, Mrs. Magrath. And a lot older than Ethan. It was natural for us to think you'd taken advantage in some way... Influenced him... With the trouble he's in, we were wondering if it had something to do with being in Mobile."

"What on earth are you saying, Mr. Fraser?" Incredulous, Elizabeth looked to Sarah. "Mrs. Fraser?" She looked at James, her expression hardening. "Ethan was accused of spying. Is that what you're accusing me of? Of seducing him in order to recruit him or some such nonsense? If I weren't so angry, I'd laugh.

"Ethan came to me starving, and according to Isaac, who you are more than welcome to interview, covered with bruises and open sores. He has a scar on his leg where he was shot. He has others, on his face and neck, where a guard struck him with a whip, and more on his wrist where he was chained. Those are the ones he told me about. He has other, deeper scars from things he won't talk about, but I know they happened because I've witnessed his nightmares." Elizabeth's voice trembled. She drew a steadying breath before continuing. "I love your son more than life itself. I would never have him come to harm. If I'd had my way, he would still be safe in Mobile. But because I love him, I let him go when that was what he wanted. When I found I was carrying his child, I came here to wait for him. I hoped that, once I explained everything, you would understand and possibly, *possibly*, accept me as the woman your son loves and the mother of his child. I see now I was mistaken." Elizabeth rose, angry tears welling, and pointed toward the door. "Now, if you will please leave, I have things to attend to."

James sat without moving, stunned by her outburst.

Sarah said, "Please. There are things that must be said, but not in this angry way. It would not be good for us to go while there are bad feelings between us. Can we please stay, Mrs. Magrath, and speak more quietly?"

At the first sound of raised voices, Hannah had called for Isaac, and they'd come to stand together in the doorway. Elizabeth looked at them.

"It's all right, Isaac. Hannah, would you please bring Mr. and Mrs. Fraser some coffee?" And to the Frasers: "It's important that we try to be friends. For Ethan's sake and the baby's. If you'll excuse me for a few minutes, we'll begin again."

4

As Ethan drew abreast of the lumbering freight wagon, a group of about a dozen horsemen left the village and came charging toward them across the prairie. When they drew close enough to distinguish individual riders, Henri stood up and yelled, swinging one arm in an arcing wave. One of the horsemen waved back.

"That's Micah," Henri announced proudly, standing with his hands on his hips watching them come.

The Indians surrounded the wagon, a revolving throng of men and horses, all yelling at once. Henri shouted back, calling greetings in their language and laughing, leaning down to clasp upraised hands. He grasped his son's hand, and Micah sprang from his pony's back and scrambled up to embrace his father.

"Ni-nǐi-ho-vi Ma-hi-o-nah."

Ethan turned to face the speaker, a handsome man with probing eyes, seated astride a wiry brown and white pony. His hair hung in long plaits over his scarred chest, and he wore shell earrings and a bone and bead necklace. He gazed at Ethan, awaiting a response.

Ethan gestured helplessly. "I... I'm sorry. I don't understand." He looked toward the wagon, but Henri's attention was focused on his son.

"Ni-gi-don-sshi-vi-ha-ni?" The man's words were accompanied by a series of gestures.

"He's askin' yer name," Henri called before addressing the man in Cheyenne. After a brief exchange, Henri reverted to English. "Red Hand says yer welcome here."

Ethan looked at Red Hand. "Thank him for me, will you?"

Henri relayed the message, and the corners of Red Hand's mouth turned up slightly. "Ee-tin." He dipped his head in a nod, and turned his pony toward the village.

Henri slapped the reins and called to his mules. Micah slipped onto his gray pony. As the little procession moved across the prairie, Ethan observed the Cheyenne warriors. Naked but for breechclouts and leggings, they were a magnificent looking bunch. Lean and muscular, riding as one with their ponies, they were a far cry from the last group of full-blooded Indians he'd seen, the impoverished, domesticated Kaws, a week or so back, on the reservation at Council Grove.

"Howdy."

Ethan looked around as Henri's son trotted up beside him. He was dressed like his companions in breechclout and leggings, but he had on a calico shirt that he wore untucked and unbuttoned, the sleeves rolled up to reveal a heavy silver armlet adorning one forearm. Silver and shell earrings dangled from his earlobes, and he sported a necklace fashioned from silver balls and deer teeth. His long brown hair curled like his father's, glinting red in the setting sun. He had inherited the aquiline nose, as well, but on a much smaller scale.

"I'm Micah," he said, favoring Ethan with a smile that lit up friendly gray eyes. "Pa says you'll be needing someone to show you around."

"He's right," Ethan said, eyeing their escort. "This is a lot different than I figured."

"This your first time out west?"

Ethan nodded.

"So you know what I felt like the first time I went to the States." Micah laughed at the memory. "Nearly jumped out of my clothes the first time I heard a steamboat whistle."

Ethan looked at him in surprise. "You've been east?"

"St. Louis. Pa sent us there for schooling. He didn't have any, so he figured we should get some. Philippe and Henry finished up years ago. Then the war broke out, and Pa wanted me home, so I missed my last two years." He lifted one shoulder in a shrug. "Don't matter, though. I've had more'n enough of cities and book learnin'." He waved an arm, encompassing everything around them. "This is where I belong."

"How long have you lived with the Cheyenne?"

"All my life. 'Cept when I was away at school."

"What's it like?"

Micah grinned. "Like nothing you've ever experienced 'ud be my guess. Not if your life's like mine was in St. Louis—all walls and ceilings, rules and uncomfortable clothes." The smile faded, and his eyes flashed with anger. "Not to mention a whole passel of schoolmasters and classmates, all thinking they're better an' smarter than me 'cause they're full-blood white."

He read empathy in Ethan's eyes, and his expression softened. "No question it's different from what you're used to, but there's no good way to describe it. Compared to school, life here's a whole lot freer, but at the same time, there's an order to things. All I can say is try it; see what you think. Pa's asked me help out while you're here."

They were approaching the camp, and a group of boys mounted on ponies trotted to meet them. Behind them tumbled a swarm of smaller children, all shouting greetings to Henri who appeared to be a particular favorite.

"You'll be needing a place to stay," Micah said. "I live in the lodge of one of my mother's sisters. You'll be welcome there."

"Thanks." Ethan said, grateful for the offer. "I appreciate it."

By the time they reached the lodge, Ethan was certain he knew exactly what it must be like to travel to a foreign land. Micah kept up a running commentary in two languages all through the camps, pointing out war shields set on stands outside lodges, their painted designs identifying their owners. Ethan heard his name repeated time and again as Micah introduced him. He rattled off a list of names in English, assigning them to a seemingly endless array of faces: Men and women, young and old; little boys naked, but for a strip of rawhide around their waists; older boys in breechclouts; girls, pretty and plain, dressed like their mothers and grandmothers in knee-length dresses and leggings. They returned his greetings, conversing amongst themselves and calling out to children in their strange flowing tongue, as dogs yipped and danced beneath the horses' feet.

And the smells. There was a veritable potpourri of them, some revolting; others enticing. A few were identifiable as animal or human; others were too alien for Ethan to even guess at. The pervasive smell was of wood smoke, and a variety of aromas wafted from pots over countless cooking fires in and around the lodges. Intriguing scents shifted and mingled on the evening air making him realize he was hungry.

"This is it," Micah said, pulling his gray to a stop before a glistening white lodge that, to Ethan's eye, was indistinguishable from all the others.

Three small children stopped their play and stared as Ethan dismounted. He looked around, thinking that if he left the lodge, he would never find it again.

Following Micah's lead, he unsaddled the mare. Micah removed the loop of rawhide from his pony's lower jaw and the gray ambled away. Ethan kept an uncertain hand on Faria.

"Let 'er go," Micah said, stooping to pick up the stirruped pad saddle he used. "She'll stay with the herd. The boys keep an eye on 'em."

"I don't know. I've always hobbled her."

"She'll be fine. Let 'er go."

Ethan turned the mare loose, and she headed off obediently after the gray. Micah pulled open the door flap and motioned Ethan in ahead of him. Ethan picked up his saddle and ducked through the opening, then stopped, eyes adjusting to the dim light that glowed through the upper part of the covering and filtered down through the smoke hole. Two women bending over the fire looked up, startled. Micah came in behind him, saying something as he slung his saddle onto a wooden rack.

"I told them you're a guest," he said, indicating where Ethan should hang his saddle. "The one on the right is my aunt, Plum Moon Woman. The other's my cousin, Singing Bird."

Ethan heard his name again as he was introduced. Both women eyed him curiously. Plum Moon Woman spoke, and Ethan looked to Micah, but he replied without translating. The conversation went on for several minutes before Plum Moon Woman addressed Ethan.

"Plum Moon says you're welcome in this lodge," Micah translated. "I told them what I know, that you're half-blood Sioux, raised by whites, and you plan on staying here to learn our ways before heading north to find your mother's people."

He gestured toward one of the low, fur-covered pallets that ringed the lodge. "Sit. When Pa gets here, we'll eat. Then we'll pay a visit to Feathered Bear."

He sat down cross-legged on the pallet, and Ethan sank down beside him. The fur was thick and surprisingly soft to the touch. Ethan ran a hand over it, then looked up to find Micah watching him, an amused expression on his face.

"Buffalo."

Ethan nodded, taking in his surroundings. The area inside the lodge was more oval than round, the fire set slightly toward the rear. There were two more low pallets like the one he was sitting on, one against the wall opposite, the other at the back of the lodge. Between them stood sets of slender, painted poles, tied together at the top and spread wide at the bottom, filling the gaps between the pallets. Each supported a painted mat, woven from willow and bound together by sinew. The spaces beneath the poles were hung and stacked with possessions. Near the door, opposite the racks where the saddles were stored, another wooden rack held a variety of weapons—bows, quivers of arrows, lances, clubs, tomahawks, a Sharps carbine and a rusted Enfield muzzle-loader that had seen better days.

A layer of painted hides lined the interior of the lodge, stretching from the floor to a height of about six feet. Above them, the outer cover glowed warmly translucent where the setting sun touched it, softly illuminating an assortment of items hanging from the lodge-poles: stuffed birds and bags in a variety of sizes, many of them fringed and decorated with quills and beads or paint.

A gurgling sound caught Ethan's attention and he looked around. An infant stared down at him from a backboard suspended from one of the poles.

"That's Minnow." Micah said. "He's Plum Moon's youngest. Feathered Bear has four children by her. Singing Bird is the oldest, and there are two other boys. Long Sleeper's prob'ly with Pa, and Little Crow lives in the lodge of Plum Moon's sister."

Ethan looked at Singing Bird, realizing she was little more than a girl.

"Plum Moon is Feathered Bear's second wife," Micah went on. "He's married to another of my mother's sisters and a cousin. Plum Moon's older sister, Wind

Woman, is his first wife—you'll meet her when we go to her lodge tonight, and the cousin is his third. With them, Feathered Bear has seven more children."

"Three wives," Ethan muttered, thinking Feathered Bear must be a wealthy man.

Micah confirmed it. "A Cheyenne man is allowed as many wives as he can support, and Feathered Bear has many horses." He shrugged. "It's a good arrangement. The more wives and daughters a man has, the more hides can be prepared for trade. Everyone profits."

The entrance flap lifted, admitting a boy of about four, followed by Henri. The boy, wearing only a breechclout, stopped short when he saw Ethan, then scooted around to the opposite side of the fire and crawled onto the pallet.

The two women cried out in delight when they saw Henri and hurried to accept the gifts he'd brought. Henri grinned and set down the large wooden crate he was carrying, presenting them with several lengths of trade cloth and a small painted box that, when opened, revealed a mirrored lid and an assortment of colored beads and bangles. Hoisting the crate closer to the fire, he set out a pair of tin cups, a large metal spoon, and bulging canvas bags of sugar, coffee, flour, and dried apples. The women chattered happily for several minutes before turning back to their work.

Henri looked at Ethan. "I see Micah go'chu settled."

"Yes." Ethan smiled sheepishly and added, "You were right to suggest I come with you. I'm not sure how I'd have managed on my own."

Henri grunted, acknowledging the fact, and lowered himself onto the pallet beside the boy. Leaning against one of the willow mats, he stretched his legs out before him. He saw Ethan looking, and grinned. "Backrest. Very civilized, the Cheyenne."

The women offered food, stewed rabbit and prairie turnips, supplemented with fried bread mixed with dried apples, and heavily sugared coffee. While they ate, Henri caught up on news of the camp and told them of his travels. He shifted between English and Cheyenne, making an effort to include Ethan. Micah translated when he thought of it, but as the conversation went on, becoming increasingly to do with people and places Ethan knew nothing about, his attention wandered. He watched the speakers, returning the friendly, open smile Plum Moon Woman offered when she saw him looking, and noting how her dark eyes danced when she said something that made everyone laugh. Singing

Bird smiled at him, too, then shyly averted her eyes. Watching the two of them together reminded him of his mother and Kate, and made him long for home.

He thought of his mother and sister as he'd last seen them, remembering their last evening together, when he'd known he was leaving and they'd suspected nothing. He remembered Kate, clinging like a monkey to the back of her horse, her long hair streaming behind her as they raced each other through the warm autumn twilight toward the house. How they'd come up the steps to the porch, laughing and exhilarated, and their mother had looked at them with such love that Ethan had very nearly decided not to go.

He was still with them, hundreds of miles away, when Micah shifted beside him and stood up. Henri was standing too, handing the little boy, who'd fallen asleep on his lap, to Singing Bird.

"Let's go," Micah said. "Feathered Bear's expecting us."

The air, when they stepped into the lodge, was overly warm, thick with the odor of wood smoke, tightly packed bodies, tanned leather, tobacco and rancid bear grease. Among the men seated around the fire, Ethan recognized several who'd ridden with Micah that afternoon. Red Hand acknowledged Ethan with a nod, then looked away as another man, seated further back in the lodge, began to speak.

"That's Nah'-ku-wut-un'-ivt. Feathered Bear," Micah said, speaking softly. "He welcomes you to his lodge. If you walk around the fire to your right, there's a place where he's asked us to sit."

Ethan stepped forward, and Micah grabbed his arm. "Never walk between people and the fire. It's bad manners."

Ethan led the way to the back of the lodge, then stood aside as Feathered Bear and Henri exchanged the greetings of old friends. Henri took the seat Feathered Bear indicated and motioned Ethan down beside him. Micah settled next to Ethan.

When they were seated, Feathered Bear produced a pipe and filled it from a pouch. A young boy brought a burning twig from the fire to light it. Feathered Bear drew on the pipe, and when he was satisfied, began to speak. He held the pipe before him, gesturing up, down, and in each of the four directions, honoring the spirits. He then drew on the pipe, using one hand to move the smoke over him. Holding the pipe, stem up, he passed it to Henri.

"When my father offers you the pipe, smoke it like they have," Micah whispered. "Then pass it to me the same way."

Ethan took the pipe from Henri, recalling how sick he'd been as a child when he'd sneaked one of the twins' little black cigars. He drew on the pipe as he'd seen Feathered Bear and Henri do, holding the smoke in his mouth before slowly releasing it. Holding the pipe as instructed, he passed it to Micah.

Considerable time passed while all the men smoked. The pipe continued around the circle to the left until it reached the man seated nearest the door. Then it was passed back the way it had come until it reached the man on the opposite side of the door. He drew on the pipe before handing it the man on his left.

"The pipe is smoked from right to left," Micah whispered by way of explanation. "It's bad luck to pass it in front of the door."

Eventually the pipe made its way to Feathered Bear. He drew on it, and assured that the spark was gone, emptied the ashes into a small horn cup. As he set the cup and pipe aside, one of the older men began to speak, addressing Henri.

"He is Moka-ta-va-tah, Black Kettle, one of the head chiefs of the Cheyenne," Micah whispered. "He's asking my father to tell about his travels since they last saw him. He asks if the white men still war with one another."

As Henri replied, Micah added, "Black Kettle has always been friendly with the whites, and he tries to learn as much as he can about them. Last year, he and Starving Bear, the man on his left, went to Washington and met with President Lincoln. They saw for themselves how many whites there are. Black Kettle knows the Cheyenne will never be able to drive them away, so he tries to live in peace, even though some of the other chiefs, and most of the warriors, would rather fight."

Micah sat back, listening as Henri continued to talk. Understanding none of it, Ethan studied the faces ringing the fire. They ranged in age from boys younger than himself to a wizened man with long gray hair. As each man spoke, Micah identified him by name: Lone Bear, Wolf Chief, Red Hawk, Star, Pawnee Man, Lame Wolf, Bull Hump, Buffalo Calf. Micah pointed out Black Horse, Feathered Bear's oldest son by Wind Woman, and seated back from the fire, Plum Moon Woman's ten-year-old son, Little Crow. Beyond that, he provided little translation.

Ethan listened to the rhythm of language, trying to pick out words or phrases. He found it impossible to distinguish one sound from another, other than the frequent choruses of 'hau', which signified agreement.

The man Micah had identified as Lone Bear, one of Black Kettle's sub-chiefs, caught Ethan's eye and spoke. Micah translated. "Chief Lone Bear would like to know, if your mother is Sioux, how did you come to be raised among whites?"

Ethan explained his parents' meeting at Fort Laramie, his birth in the Black Hills, and his parents' return to Illinois.

When Henri translated, a murmur went up among his listeners.

"It interests them to hear that your father took you and your mother back to the States," Micah said. "Most white men leave their Indian wives and children behind. You'll find there are lots of mixed-bloods in the camps."

A young man spoke harshly, and Red Hand responded, rising to his knees and jabbing a finger at him across the fire. Others joined in, taking sides. Before the disagreement could escalate, Black Kettle intervened.

"Some say, that though your skin is the same as ours, you have grown to be a man among the whites," he said to Ethan. "For many years you have lived according to white customs and learned to think as white men think. Some say you are more white than Sioux and cannot be trusted. They wish to know why you are here."

When Micah translated, Ethan looked to Henri for guidance.

Henri stared into the fire. *Now ain't the time to be interferin'*, he thought. *Time for him to make his own way.*

"During the war I..." Ethan began, and then had second thoughts. He started again, looking directly at the warrior who'd challenged him. "You're right when you say I've lived my whole life among whites. But because I'm part Lakota, I haven't always been accepted. I've had bad times because of it." A thought occurred to him, and he added a challenge. "I was hoping things would be different here."

Good enough. Henri nodded to himself. Ethan had got it right. Now wasn't the time to mention he'd ridden with the blue-coated soldiers, even if they had turned against him in the end.

When Micah translated, Red Hand grunted in satisfaction and settled back. The man he'd argued with addressed Ethan. Henri responded while Micah translated.

329

"Black Coyote says, if what you say is true, why have you come to the Tsi-tsí-tas, to the Cheyenne, instead of the Sioux? Pa says he invited you." He paused while Feathered Bear spoke, then added, "For as long as you're here, you're a guest in his lodge."

The man seated next to Black Kettle spoke.

"Starving Bear wants to know what you can tell them of your mother's people."

"My mother is Pine Leaf, of the Bear people, Chief Smoke's band of Oglala. Her mother is Blanket Woman, sister to Worm and Long Face. Her father is Standing Elk, brother-in-law to White Hawk, the brother of Smoke."

Comments came from around the fire.

"The old men remember Chief Smoke," Micah murmured beside him. "His people, the Smoke People, live to the north, beyond the Moonshell. They are allies of the Northern Cheyenne. Tell them what you know and word'll spread. Sooner or later, it'll reach your mother's people."

As talk continued, the entrance flap opened to admit two women and three children. The children retired quietly to a pallet at the side of the lodge while the two women came to sit behind Feathered Bear.

Micah indicated the younger of the two. "That's Wind Woman, my mother's sister. The old one is Yellow Bead Woman. She's Feathered Bear's widowed aunt and shares this lodge."

The conversation drifted to other topics, then tapered off as men filtered out into the night. Henri, Micah and Ethan remained after everyone had gone. Henri presented Feathered Bear with a gift of tobacco and spoke briefly with the women, giving them sacks of coffee and sugar. He bid them good night, was preparing to stand, when Feathered Bear motioned him to wait. Turning, he spoke to the boy who still lingered in the shadows.

The boy went quickly to the rack by the door and returned with a bow and quiver. Feathered Bear took them from him and laid them across his lap before addressing Ethan.

"Feathered Bear says you've come on a long journey from the land of the whites to search for your mother's people. He understands that you know little of our ways, and he's honored that you chose to learn among the Tsi-tsí-tas. To welcome you, he makes you a gift of this bow. He hopes it will serve you well, as it has him. He also hopes it will aid you in becoming a great warrior, if that's what you wish." Without pausing, or altering his tone, Micah added, "It would be considered bad manners to refuse, and you'd do well to thank him."

When Micah finished speaking, Feathered Bear lifted the bow and quiver, and held them out to Ethan.

Touched and a little over-awed, Ethan stared into the stern eyes of the older man. He was neither as old as some who'd assembled that evening, nor as young as others, but he was clearly a man of stature, deserving of respect.

"Tell Feathered Bear I'm grateful for his hospitality and his gift. I look forward to learning the ways of the Cheyenne and hope to master the use of this bow in a way that will make him proud."

"Well said," Micah muttered under his breath, translating as Ethan accepted the gift.

It was a fine bow, made from juniper, Micah told him later, smooth to the touch and polished to a high sheen. The quiver was fringed, and patterned with elaborate beadwork.

Henri and Micah conversed with Feathered Bear and the women a few minutes longer, then rose to leave. The camp was sleeping when they stepped outside, the air cool and fresh after the stuffiness of the lodge, the sky ablaze with millions of stars. The leading edge of the full moon, round and orange, poked above the horizon. They stopped to watch as it climbed into view, silhouetting the silent tipis and bathing the plains and the pony herds in pale yellow-white light. A wolf howled, adding its voice to the chorus of frogs that croaked and trilled along the creek.

Ethan inhaled deeply, feeling peace settle over him. In his wildest dreams, he would never have imagined being made so welcome in a place so foreign. The kindness and generosity of the Broulats and the Cheyenne, coupled with the natural beauty of the night, made it hard to believe that, far away, the war between the states still raged, and men kept an eye out to capture or kill him. As he let the breath out, Micah caught his eye and smiled.

* * *

"Mrs. Magrath! Mrs. Magraaath!!"

Elizabeth had been strolling along the tree-lined street, lost in thought. She looked around to see Kate, skirt hiked above her knees, racing toward her. She laughed as the girl came to a halt, too winded to speak.

"What is so urgent, Kate?"

"It's Ethan," Kate panted. "A letter... We have... a letter from Ethan!"

Elizabeth's heart gave a jolt. "Where is he?" she asked, grasping Kate's arm.

"Ma and Pa are at your house. They want you to come."

Elizabeth started walking before Kate finished speaking. She lifted her skirt and half ran down the street, Kate trotting beside her.

"Where is he, Kate? Is he all right?"

"He didn't say exactly, but Ma knew what he meant."

"When did the letter arrive?"

"I'm not sure. Mrs. Harrison had it when we came into the store today."

They turned the corner and the small, single-story house Elizabeth rented came into view. Pushing through the garden gate, she hurried up the steps. Hannah opened the door as she reached it and tilted her head toward the parlor, disapproval plain on her face. Elizabeth paused, nervous at seeing Ethan's parents again, despite the uneasy truce they'd forged the week before. Steeling herself, she walked into the parlor.

Sarah was seated in the same chair as before; James stood beside her, both hands clutching his hat. He stiffened when he saw Elizabeth.

"Mrs. Magrath. We're sorry to intrude, but we've had a letter from Ethan. Mrs. Fraser thought—"

"Please," Elizabeth interrupted breathlessly, "What does it say?"

James held out an envelope.

Elizabeth took it, her spirits soaring at the sight of the familiar handwriting. She sank into the chair across from Sarah and opened the letter with shaking fingers.

> *21 April*
>
> *Dear Ma, Pa, and Kate,*
>
> *I imagine by now you've heard all that has happened. It seems inadequate after all you've suffered, to say how sorry I am for the pain I've caused. I can only swear I am innocent, and hope and pray you believe me.*
>
> *Josh has no doubt told you how wrong it was for me to escape, but I had many long hours to think about it, and couldn't share his faith that things would be made right. I had no choice but to take matters into my own hands. I hope my escape has not caused you additional worry. I am safe and well. And most importantly, I am free.*
>
> *There is nothing I want more than to come home. A week ago at Chester, I nearly did, but it would be wrong to bring my troubles down on you. When the war is over, there are two people who can clear my name—*

Thomas Murray and Elizabeth Magrath. Until then, I think it best to go where I can't be found.

I love you and miss you more than I can say. I would give anything to be with you, but until that is possible, I will follow the eagle.

With all my love,

Ethan

P.S. Have faith, Kate. We'll be together again before you know it.

"I don't understand," Elizabeth said. "Where is he?"

"He goes to my people," Sarah said softly. "With them, he will be safe from the ones who would do him harm."

"Indians?" Elizabeth said, aghast. "What makes you think he'll be safe? What's to keep them from killing him?"

"Ethan knows all I have taught him. He knows the stories that will lead him to the Paha Sapa. He is Haŋhepi Wi Nupa, Two Moons. He was born Lakota. There is no need for worry."

"But..." Elizabeth looked helplessly from Sarah to James. "But there have been so many problems with the Indians. How can you tell me he'll be safe?"

James ran his fingers through his hair. His expression, when he looked at her, was strained. "All we can do is hope Ethan has the good sense to stay away from trouble. After what he's been through, I imagine he'll keep as far from the army as possible." Laying a hand on his wife's shoulder, he added, "I can't guarantee you he'll be safe, Mrs. Magrath, neither of us can, but I've spent time in the Black Hills, and if that's where he's gone, he's picked a good place to hide. You can rest easy, knowing that."

Elizabeth looked down at the letter, not knowing what to think. The idea of Ethan alone among wild Indians frightened her. He *wasn't* one of them, despite what Sarah said. He was Ethan, quiet and gentle, not some warring, painted savage. She bit her lip, fighting the dread that welled up in her, and ran her eyes over the letter.

Chester. The name popped out at her. "Where is Chester?" she asked.

"South of here," James replied. "A couple hundred miles."

Elizabeth looked up. "In Illinois?"

James nodded.

"He was almost here," Kate blurted, echoing Elizabeth's thoughts.

In Illinois. Only a month ago. When she arrived, he'd been just a few days south and coming closer. Now he was pulling away from her again, headed toward dangers she couldn't begin to imagine. Suddenly, it was all too much. Elizabeth folded into the chair, convulsed with sobs.

Hannah hurried to her side, pulling her close and stroking her hair, holding her as she had the morning Ethan raised a hand and trotted away down the drive.

Sarah took one of Elizabeth's hands in hers. Kate, tears streaming down her face, crouched at her feet. James looked at the knot of women and shifted uncomfortably, certain he was expected to say or do something, but having no idea what.

Minutes crept by. When the worst appeared to have passed, he cleared his throat and said, "Ethan'll be fine, Mrs. Magrath. Sarah's people are good folks. It's a hard life out there, but they'll see he's looked after."

At first there was no response. Then Elizabeth fumbled for her handkerchief and dabbed her eyes. Eventually, she straightened, nodding reassurances to Hannah. Seeing Kate's distraught face, she leaned forward and hugged her. "We have to listen to him, Kate," she whispered, for her own benefit as much as the girl's. "Your parents know best. We have to believe them when they say he'll be safe."

Kate nodded against her shoulder. Elizabeth held her a moment longer before letting go.

"I'm sorry," she said, addressing James and Sarah. "I'm not normally like this, but..." Her voice faltered and her eyes filled. "I'm so afraid for him."

"What my husband says is true, Mrs. Magrath," Sarah said. "Ethan will be safe. In my heart, I know he will be safe."

Elizabeth managed a watery smile. "Please. My name is Elizabeth. It would mean so much if you would call me Elizabeth."

Sarah smiled, her eyes so like Ethan's. "Elizabeth," she said. "Yes."

5

Ethan woke to a faint patch of light overhead and the hushed sounds of someone moving about. It took him a moment to realize he was looking up through the smoke hole. He pushed up on one elbow as two shadowy figures slipped through the door. Before the flap closed behind them, he recognized Plum Moon and Singing Bird in the dim predawn light.

He was still awake when they returned, burdened by the heavy water bladders they'd filled at the creek. As they moved about, hanging them from pegs around the lodge, Micah stirred beside him and rolled out of bed. He padded across the lodge and returned with the little boy.

"You awake?"

"Yes."

"Long Sleeper and I are headed to the creek to bathe. It's a custom among Cheyenne men. You're welcome to join us."

Ethan considered it, threw back his blanket and sat up.

He stepped from the lodge to find men and boys of all ages heading for the creek. A cold breeze had sprung up during the night, and Ethan shivered in his longhandles, hugging himself and rubbing his hands up and down his arms until he noticed that everyone else wore only breechclouts, and yet appeared unfazed by the cold. A few old men had blankets or buffalo robes wrapped around their shoulders, but the youngest boys, some barely old enough to walk, wore only the cords around their waists. They reached the creek and waded in. Ethan stripped off his underwear and joined them, his breath catching as the cold water hit.

Micah saw his expression and laughed. "You shoulda waited a few weeks 'til it warms up."

Ethan grinned through chattering teeth. "Any reason you didn't mention that sooner?"

They returned to the sights and smells of the women preparing food. As they neared the lodge, a group of boys on horseback trotted past.

"They're headed out to drive in the ponies," Micah said. "Soon as we're dressed, we'll see about catching your mare. We'll stake the horses near the lodge today. So they'll be here if we need them."

They donned their clothes and went out to find the pony herds driven in close to the camp. Micah spotted his gray immediately and walked toward him, talking in a soft singsong voice. The pony's ears flicked forward, and he took several steps toward Micah, allowing him to slip a looped horsehair rope over his head. Micah offered him a treat of dried apples before turning to scan the herd for Ethan.

The Indian ponies shifted skittishly as Ethan moved among them. Faria saw him and nickered. He was almost within reach when one of the ponies threw back its head, snorting in alarm, and trotted away. To Ethan's disgust, the mare and several others followed.

Micah came up to him, leading the gray. "You don't smell right. Not Indian enough. Another week, it won't be a problem." He held out a hand for the bridle. "I'll catch 'er for you."

He swung easily onto the gray and returned within minutes, leading the mare.

The sound of chanting reached them as they approached the camp. It continued without change in pitch or rhythm, growing progressively louder until an old man came into view, riding slowly among the lodges.

"The crier. News of the day, important announcements, that sorta thing." Micah listened for several seconds before adding, "Nothing important. Pa'll be trading this morning." He tilted his head toward one of the lodges. "We better get inside before he eats all the food."

They staked the horses next to the lodge and went inside to find that Henri had indeed started without them.

"They're gonna wanna trade fer a while," he said, looking up from the bowl of boiled meat he was scooping into his mouth with his fingers. "Then I'll head over to see Tall Grass, spend some time with my gran'daughter. I was thinkin' you an' me might hitch up later."

Micah nodded. "Sounds good. Ethan and me'll come watch the trading for a while, then I'll show him around. We'll meet you at Tall Grass' lodge."

They finished their meal and walked with Henri to where he'd left the freight wagon. People were already assembled, standing next to piles of buffalo robes and other items they'd brought to trade. Henri greeted them familiarly, walking among them and agreeing on prices before climbing onto the wagon and pulling back the canvas tarp to reveal the crates stacked beneath.

As Henri and the Cheyenne traded, Micah and Ethan wandered among them, examining the buffalo robes and admiring soft deerskin garments with elaborate quill and beadwork.

"These are made from cowhides taken during the winter," Micah said, fingering one of the robes. "That's why the fur's so thick. Cowhides taken during the summer get the fur stripped off and are used for other things—pouches, clothes, lodge covers, though a lot of them are made from canvas nowadays. Bull hides are thicker. They're used for shields and soles for moccasins."

"Porcupine quills," he commented a few minutes later when he saw Ethan examining an intricately quilled buckskin shirt.

"Yeah. It reminds me of some things Ma has. Her ma made them for her when she married. A buckskin dress, a pair of leggings, moccasins... I remember her wearing them when I was real young, and later she'd bring them out when she told stories." He smiled at the woman whose shirt it was. "Tell her it's beautiful."

Micah did, acknowledging greetings from a trio of men. "Arapaho," he said once they'd passed.

Ethan turned to look. "Arapaho? How can you tell?"

"There's not much difference. Same language; same customs. When you get to know us better, learn our ways and the language, you'll be able to tell us apart."

A murmur of excitement rippled through the crowd, and they turned toward the wagon. Red Hand had joined Henri atop the crates. Intrigued by the carbine he was holding, Ethan moved closer. Henri broke open a crate and took the gun from Red Hand. He slid a tube of cartridges into the buttstock, then fired off seven shots in rapid succession. A look of disbelief spread over Red Hand's face, and he motioned for the carbine. Henri laughed and said something. Reloading it, he handed it to Red Hand.

The sound of gunfire brought men and boys running, some on foot, others on horseback, all of them armed. As Red Hand raised the carbine and fired seven shots without stopping to reload, they stared in amazement and crowded around the wagon, eager voices raised.

Henri caught Ethan's eye and winked. "Spencer breech loading carbine. Ever handle one?"

"No."

"What a waste," Micah muttered.

Ethan turned to him. "What do you mean?"

"They don't take care of the guns they have. They worship them, carve and decorate the wood while letting them rust. I don't know why Pa bothers bringing more." He shook his head in disgust.

"Why doesn't someone teach them? It's not hard to keep a gun cleaned and oiled."

"Pa's showed 'em; I've showed 'em. Some pay attention; most don't."

"I'm going to take a look at one," Ethan said, grabbing hold of the wagon and climbing up. He looked to Henri for permission before lifting one of the carbines from its crate, inhaling the mixture of gun-oil, thick on the metal parts, and soap-oil rubbed into the new leather shoulder strap. He ran a hand over the smooth black walnut buttstock, peered into the tubular magazine and sighted along the barrel.

Henri broke off negotiations long enough to say, "Load 'er up, son. Give 'er a try."

Ethan took a tube of rimstock cartridges from the box and slid it into the carbine. He pushed down, then pulled up on the trigger guard-lever as he'd seen Henri do, loading a cartridge into the receiver. Then he flipped up the sight and raised the carbine, taking aim at a clump of dried brush ninety yards away. He fired, pushed down on the trigger guard-lever to eject the spent casing, pulled up to load another cartridge, and fired again, repeating the sequence rapidly five more times. When he lowered the carbine, the brush was gone, scattered to dust across the prairie.

"Not bad," Micah said, climbing up to perch beside him. "Where'd you learn to shoot?"

"Army," Ethan said ejecting the last casing.

"The army? You fought in the war?"

Ethan nodded. He ran a hand up the smooth wood of forestock, then touched the blue metal of the barrel lightly with his fingertips, testing its heat. More than anything, he wanted to own one, but he had no money and nothing to trade. He held the carbine a few moments longer before replacing it in its crate.

"Which side?" Micah said, obviously impressed.

"Union. Your Pa didn't mention it?"

"No. Was it exciting?"

Ethan let out a harsh snort of laughter. "I thought so, 'til my first battle. Mostly it was pretty awful. I'm glad I'm out of it."

A loud whoop saved him from further questioning. Red Hand jumped down from the wagon, holding his newly acquired Spencer above his head. Henri handed down boxes of cartridges and turned to the next man.

"Show me how to shoot the bow Feathered Bear gave me," Ethan said, starting down from the wagon.

"Sure," Micah said, climbing down after him. "Pa kept me out of it. He said it was none of our affair."

"He's right," Ethan told him, feeling years older and more experienced than his companion. "You're better off here." He spied two large groups of boys holding sticks, facing each other across an open expanse of prairie, and walked toward them. "What're they doing?"

One of the groups threw a set of hoops, crosshatched with rawhide, sending them speeding across the ground toward the opposing group. As the wheels approached, the boys threw sticks at them. Some stuck in the rawhide webbing, others glanced off, and a few missed entirely.

"It's called e´-u-tsuhk-nia, the wheel game. When a stick gets stuck in the netting, it's a 'kill', and the side that kills a wheel, keeps it. The others get rolled back."

"What about the ones that are just knocked down?"

Micah shook his head. "Don't count. The stick has to stick in the web. Once all the wheels are killed, they start throwing them. Hurts like the devil to get hit. A wheel can only be thrown once unless it's caught with a stick before it hits the ground. If it's caught, it can be thrown back."

They watched for a few minutes before turning toward the first circle of lodges.

The day was unseasonably warm, and some of the lodge covers had been rolled up. Women sat in the shade beneath them working and talking, while small children played in the dirt at their feet. They passed a group of girls playing what Micah said was in´-ni-tun-is-to, the finger game.

Plum Moon Woman and her daughter were rolling up the lodge cover when they arrived. Micah muttered a greeting and ducked inside.

They collected their bows, saddled their horses, and headed for the creek. A group of boys was roughhousing in the water not far from the camp. Micah and Ethan passed them by, continuing upstream until they came to a broad, shallow wash, thick with reeds, willow, plum, and a grove of ash and cottonwoods. They turned up the wash and dismounted in an open, grassy area. Micah showed Ethan how to string the bow, explaining the difference between arrows used for hunting and arrows used for fighting, and showing him the marks on the arrows that identified the owner.

"Every man has his own mark. If you get good enough, you'll want arrows with your mark on them."

He demonstrated how to hold the bow and arrow while drawing back the bowstring. As a target, he selected a patch of grayed wood where the bark had peeled off the broken trunk of a dead cottonwood. He fired half a dozen arrows, releasing them as quickly as Ethan had fired the carbine. When he lowered the bow, the arrows were clustered at the center of the target.

"You're good," Ethan said, impressed.

"Been practicing since I was four," Micah replied, and went to retrieve his arrows.

Ethan's first few arrows flew wide of the mark. By concentrating on how he drew back the string, and taking considerable care with his release, he found he could at least come close to the tree.

"Not bad," Micah said when Ethan managed to lodge three consecutive arrows in the trunk. "A few more years, and you'll be shooting from a galloping horse."

Ethan shook his head doubtfully and went to collect his arrows.

They took turns, shooting and talking. When there was more talk than shooting, they pushed through the willows to the bank of Ash Creek and settled in the dappled shade beneath the trees. Ethan lay on his back, clasped hands supporting his head, while Micah sat nearby, idly tossing pebbles into the muddy water. He described what it had been like growing up at a trading post with the attendant comings and goings of diverse groups of people: whites, Indians and Mexicans, traders, gold seekers, immigrants and military men.

"When I was little, we lived with the Cheyenne, traveled with them wherever they went. It wasn't until I got older, and Pa built his stockade, that we started living indoors. Mostly in winter. Even then, I still spent most of my time in the camps. The only thing Pa insisted on was sending us to school. He kept telling us how important it was to know both ways of life. So we could choose for ourselves." Micah caught Ethan's eye and grinned. "The minute we got back, we all three came to live in camps."

Micah tossed a pebble and watched the ripples spread. "I figure Henry's the only one who prob'ly wouldn't have lasted. He liked books and learnin'. The only reason he came back was Tall Grass. He'd been sweet on her since they were kids. If he'd lived, he prob'ly woulda taken her off someplace. California, maybe. To be a teacher." Micah flicked the last pebble into the water and looked at Ethan. "You have brothers and sisters?"

"A sister. I had four half-brothers, but three of them died in the war. The other..." Ethan felt the familiar twinge of guilt when he thought of Josh. "He was wounded at Missionary Ridge. He was all right last I saw him, but he's still in the fighting. My sister and my folks are on the farm in Illinois."

"Think you'll ever go back?"

Ethan stared at the billowing white clouds overhead. "I don't know," he said at last. "I can't imagine never seeing them again."

"I'll always live with the Cheyenne. After Henry got killed, Pa tried to convince me to move back with him, go into business. He keeps talking about how things are changing, and I know he worries, so a while back I gave it a try. We teamed up with William and Bob Bent, from over in Colorado Territory, and took a train of wagons to St. Louis. I know Pa was hoping I'd take a lesson from Bob. He grew up like me—half-Cheyenne, raised in the camps, then sent to live with relatives in the States and get his schooling. When he finished, he came back and teamed up with his Pa. Been working with him for nigh on five years now. I know that's what Pa wants for me, but I hated it. Coming back, I left before we got to Fort Larned and came looking for the Cheyenne. First thing I did, I joined the Hiṁ-o-we-yuhk-is"

Ethan rolled onto his side to look at him. "The what?"

"Hiṁ-o-we-yuhk-is. The Crooked Lances. One of the warrior societies. Feathered Bear belongs. So does Red Hand. It was something I'd always wanted to do, so as soon as I got back, I did it. Made clear to Pa that I'd made up my mind."

"He doesn't seem to hold it against you."

"No, he understands. But it's hard on him. Hard on both of them, what with Henry being dead, and Philippe..." Micah shrugged. "There's no tellin' where he is. It's been years since we had news of him."

Micah inspected the ground around him, selecting another handful of pebbles. "I haven't seen Ma in more'n a year. Come fall, I'm thinking I'll take Tall Grass and Girl Who Laughs and go for a visit." He looked at Ethan and grinned. "With any luck, I'll have me a wife to take along."

Ethan looked at him in surprise. "Really?"

Micah tossed a pebble. "I met a girl from the Issio-mé-tan-iu clan at Medicine Lodge a couple summers back. We see each other from time to time, and I've been thinking, maybe this summer..." He looked at Ethan, eyes twinkling, and held up his left hand, showing off the wide silver ring he wore on his middle finger. "I'm hoping at this year's Medicine Lodge she'll agree to trade rings. If so, I plan on marrying her in the fall." Micah rushed to describe Yellow Leaf Woman, telling Ethan how they'd met and about the times they'd been together since.

Ethan only half listened. He was thinking of the night he'd asked Elizabeth to marry him, remembering her joy when she'd realized what he was saying. He was deep in thought when he realized Micah had stopped speaking.

"She sounds wonderful," he said with a perfunctory smile. "You're lucky." *Elizabeth...* Leaving Mobile was the biggest mistake he'd ever made. Ethan blew out a long breath and sat up, aware suddenly, of how the shadows had lengthened. "Weren't you supposed to meet your pa?"

"Yeah." Micah sighed, his thoughts still on Yellow Leaf. He tossed the handful of pebbles into the creek and stood up, dusting off his hands. "We best be going."

They arrived at the lodge to find Henri seated on the single pallet, a curly-haired little girl on his lap, surrounded by a jumble of toys—painted wooden blocks, a ball, and a porcelain-faced doll in a dusty white lace dress. A young woman sat on a blanket nearby. She got to her feet when Micah and Ethan stepped inside. Micah introduced her as Ha-ssta-mo-i-i, Tall Grass Woman.

"Hello," she said, smiling at Ethan. "You are welcome."

It took Ethan a moment to realize that, though heavily accented, she'd spoken in English.

Tall Grass Woman gestured toward the blanket where she'd been sitting. "You please sit."

She was tall, nearly Ethan's height, slender, and long-limbed. Unlike other Cheyenne women he'd seen, her hair was cut short. It hung loose to her shoulders, framing a strikingly pretty face. The look she gave him was friendly and direct. He liked her immediately.

They accepted her offer of heavily sugared coffee from the supply Henri had brought, and watched as he played with his granddaughter. The little girl watched attentively as Henri stacked the blocks one on top of the other. When he finished, she wiggled off his lap and swiped at them, chattering and laughing as they tumbled around her.

"Girl Who Laughs was only a couple months old when Henry died," Micah said. "Last we heard, Philippe had three kids, but Pa never sees them, so he spoils her."

Ethan nodded, surveying the lodge, as Henri restacked the blocks. Unlike the others he'd seen, there were few personal belongings — only the single pallet with no backrest, a couple of blankets, a pair of water bladders, and the large pile of gifts from Henri.

"Why is this lodge so empty?"

"It's new," Micah replied. "When a man dies, all his property, including his lodge, is given to folks who aren't relatives. When Henry got killed, Tall Grass was left with nothing. She moved around, living with different uncles until a couple weeks ago when her relatives gave her this."

A shout from outside interrupted him. Micah and his father shared a glance and got quickly to their feet. Henri handed the little girl to her mother, and Ethan and Tall Grass trailed them as they stepped outside. People were emerging from other lodges, and Ethan looked where they were looking. He caught a glimpse of riders as they disappeared among the lodges.

"A runner's come from up north," Micah told him as they joined the crowd walking quickly through the camp. "Sounds like trouble."

They caught up with the horsemen where they'd come to a halt before one of the lodges. Ethan was surprised to see an American flag fluttering from a pole above it. He would have asked about it, but Micah motioned him to silence, listening to what one of the riders was saying. The man finished speaking, and Black Kettle turned toward the council lodge. Several men Ethan recognized, Lone Bear, Feathered Bear and Red Hand among them, pushed through the crowd and entered the lodge behind him.

"He's from the I-vis-tsi-nih´-pah clan, Chief Sand Hill's bunch, up on the Manó-iyo-he, the Bunch of Timber River,"[3] Micah explained. "He says Chief Raccoon's and Crow Chief's bands joined up with them after they were attacked by soldiers a few weeks back. The soldiers attacked Crow Chief's band after the ponies had been driven in, so the people escaped, but they had to leave everything behind, and the soldiers burned it. When the soldiers attacked Chief Raccoon's band, some of the men saw them coming, so they escaped with their

---

3   Smoky Hill River

belongings, but their lodges were burned. He says before that, soldiers attacked a group of Dog Soldiers on the Tallow River."[4]

"I got a bad feelin' about this," Henri muttered. He shared a grim look with his son before casting an anxious glance at Tall Grass Woman and his granddaughter.

Henri left for home the following morning, but not before taking Ethan aside and offering him one of the Spencer carbines.

"I seed how you was lookin' at it, son," he said when Ethan declined. "An' I see how yer lookin' at it now. It's plain to see ya want it."

"But I don't have anything to trade," Ethan protested. "It doesn't seem right for you to give one to me when everyone else has to pay."

Henri looked mildly put out. "I gave one to Micah an' didn't hear *him* complain."

"That's different. He's your son."

"Tell ya what. Teach Micah to shoot as good as you, an' that'll be payment enough. I got a bad feelin' hearin' about those soldier-boys attackin' the Cheyenne. That kinda thing al'ays spells trouble. If Micah can shoot, maybe it'll keep him alive. I reckon 'at's a more'n even trade."

Henri held out the Spencer, but still Ethan hesitated.

"Take it, son."

"Thank you, Henri," Ethan said, accepting the carbine. "I owe you. Someday, I swear I'll pay you back."

Henri chuckled. "Don't worry, son. Jus' look out fer yerself." His look turned serious. "You an' Micah watch each other's backs."

"Yes, sir. We will." Ethan raised the carbine and smiled. "Thank you, Henri."

Micah joined them, leading the gray, and they started toward Henri's wagon. Long Sleeper, mounted on a spotted pony, trailed along behind.

Micah grinned when he saw the carbine. "You took it. Good."

"You knew."

"I knew he was gonna offer it. I didn't know if you'd take it. I'm glad you did. He wanted you to have it."

People filtered out to join them as they walked through the camp. More collected while Ethan and Micah helped Henri round up and harness his mules.

4 Fremont's Orchard on the South Platte

Tall Grass Woman appeared, carrying Girl Who Laughs, and Henri spent several minutes aside with them before climbing onto the wagon. As a parting gesture, he dug out a supply of ginger candy and tossed handfuls to everyone assembled to see him off. Then he flicked the reins over the mules' backs, and the big wagon trundled away across the prairie. Micah swung onto his pony, and taking Long Sleeper with him, went to ride with his father for a ways. Ethan stood with Tall Grass, watching them go.

"You staying here now," she said when they turned back toward the first circle of lodges.

"Yes, I'm staying." More than anything, he wanted to keep her talking, but he couldn't think of anything to say.

Tall Grass shifted her daughter on her hip. Looking at him in the direct way she had, she announced, "I going now."

Ethan nodded mutely. He watched her until she disappeared among the lodges, then looked around. People were going about their business, no one paying him any attention. Getting his bearings, he started in the general direction of Plum Moon Woman's lodge, glad he'd staked Faria beside it so he could find it again. He would saddle her, he decided, take the bow, and ride upstream a ways.

Emerging from the first circle of lodges, he came upon a group of women hard at work over buffalo hides staked to the ground. Using bone and metal fleshers, they were busily engaged in scraping off the hair. He stopped to watch, and the woman nearest him looked up and smiled, murmuring a greeting. He acknowledged her and moved on, unaware that several of the young, unmarried women sat back on their heels and watched him go.

He hadn't gone far when a group of boys ran up to him, dancing in circles around him and admiring the Spencer. One of them touched his arm, asking a question. Ethan looked into a pair of disconcertingly blue eyes and stopped walking. The boy looked to be about ten years old, brown-haired, with sun-darkened skin. He spoke again and touched the buttstock. Ethan slipped the strap from his shoulder and handed him the weapon. The other boys crowded around. One after another, they took turns holding it. Then the blue-eyed boy took it back and handed it to Ethan. With smiles and a chorus of yells, they set off running, laughing and shoving one another.

Ethan heard the shrieking of a dog in pain before he saw the reason for it. Coming into the next circle of lodges, he saw two old women ruthlessly clubbing one of the mangy camp dogs with heavy sticks. The dog's back was broken, and it cried pitifully, dragging its hind legs as it attempted to crawl away. Ethan looked around in horror, expecting someone to intervene. With the exception of the few who watched without interest, no one paid any attention. One of the women brought her stick down in a savage blow to the dog's head and with final, desperate cry, it crumpled to the ground. The woman hit it again. It twitched and lay still.

The women each grabbed a pair of the dog's legs and started toward Ethan, carrying it between them. He took a step back as they went by and turned to watch as they heaved the dog's body, fur and all, into a large iron pot. One of the women squatted and stoked the fire. The other pushed down on the dog's legs, forcing it deeper into the pot.

"Dog eaters," Henri had told him, but nothing had prepared him for what he'd just seen. Choking down revulsion, Ethan fled in the direction of the mare, trying not to speculate on the source of the meat he'd been eating, and intent on putting as much distance between himself and the Cheyenne camp as possible.

6

At daybreak the next morning, the two hundred and fifty lodges under Black Kettle, Starving Bear and Wolf Chief set out to join the Cheyenne bands on the Smoky Hill River. Ethan was amazed at the speed with which the village was dismantled. Boys had been out while it was still dark to round up the ponies; women stowed household items and personal possessions, placing them in rawhide parfleches and canvas bags, or wrapping them in blankets and buffalo robes. They stripped the lodges of their covers and pulled down the poles, loading everything onto horses or strapping it to poledrags. Even dogs carried packs. Small children, too heavy to carry, but too young to walk long distances, were loaded onto the drags in cages made from willow branches. A supply of water and dried meat was placed inside, a blanket laid over the opening at the top.

The sun pushed past the clouds banding horizon as they set out, heading west along Ash Creek. Armed warriors galloped away in advance, fanning out across the prairie. The old chiefs, the ones who would select the next stopping place, led the way. Next came the old men, then the women and girls—some riding, others walking, many carrying babies on boards on their backs, all tending the pack animals that hauled their families' possessions. There was talk and laughter, and some of the women sang. Behind them came the herd boys, driving the extra ponies, and farthest back, guarding the rear, rode the Dog Soldiers.

Ethan rode with Micah, Red Hand and a group of Crooked Lances far out on the northern flank. At one point, as they topped a rise, he turned the mare and looked back. Hundreds of people, their possessions, dogs, and over a thousand ponies were spread across the prairie. Dust billowed behind them, driven by the same stiff breeze that sent great puffs of cumulus skimming across the sky.

"Impressive, isn't it?" Micah said, pulling to a stop beside him.

"I've never seen anything like it. How far will we go today?"

"Over ground like this—fifteen, twenty miles. If there aren't any problems."

Ethan tilted his head back, closing his eyes and feeling the sun warm on his face. Inhaling deeply, he let the breath drain out of him. He looked at Micah.

"I haven't felt this free in a long time. Maybe not ever. Not like this."

"You've figured out why I choose to live with the Cheyenne."

Micah whirled his pony and set off at a gallop across the prairie. Grinning broadly, Ethan wheeled the mare and raced after him.

As they angled away from the Santa Fe Trail, grass grew more abundant and game sightings more frequent. The out-riding warriors brought increasing quantities of fresh meat with them when they returned to camp each evening. Ethan hunted along with them, using the Spencer to bring down first a mule deer, then one of the speedy pronghorn antelope that were new to him. His first kill earned him the approval of his companions, and he slipped into an easy camaraderie with them, picking up a few words in Cheyenne, but learning to communicate mainly through the series of hand signals they all used when talking to him.

Late one afternoon, shouts went up from the men riding up ahead.

"Hoo-ho-mo-i-yoo," Micah said. "Sioux."

A tingle of excitement ran through Ethan. Shielding his eyes against the sun, he saw a group of riders trotting toward them across the prairie. Cheyenne warriors were already galloping to meet them. The men around Ethan urged their ponies into a canter, and he followed suit.

"Hau kola," one of the strangers called, signing as the two groups came together.

Ethan hung back, watching and listening as the Sioux and Cheyenne spoke, gesturing to one another. It pleased him to discover that he understood enough of what the Brulé were saying to follow their half of the conversation.

They were hunters. Their camp was close, a short distance up the creek. They had been following a herd of buffalo, a great herd, and would hunt again "hihaŋni ǩi, hihaŋni eciyataŋhaŋ ǩi." *On the morning side of tomorrow*, Ethan mentally translated. *Early tomorrow morning.*

"There are buffalo," Micah said, watching the hand signals. "They've invited us to hunt."

"I heard."

Micah looked at him. "You understand them?" When Ethan nodded, he grinned. "You never mentioned you spoke the language."

The Cheyenne went into camp along Ash Creek, not far from the Brulé. Over the course of the evening, Ethan spoke with a number of Sioux, explaining who he was and asking what they knew of his mother's people. The names he gave them were from twenty years before, and all the responses were similar: Everyone knew of them. They were Red Cloud's band, the Iteshicha, the Bad Faces, and they lived and hunted north of the Moonshell, in the vast land between the Ṗaha Saṗa and the Ḣeska.[5] Many had tales to tell of Red Cloud's exploits, but no one could tell him exactly where to look for them. In the end, Ethan had to be content knowing word of his presence would spread.

Early the next morning, Ethan, Micah, and Feathered Bear's oldest son, Black Horse, rode out with a large party from both tribes to hunt. As they breasted a low hill, a line of dark objects came into view, moving toward them across the prairie. Murmurs spread amongst the hunters.

"Soldiers," Micah muttered, as they drew back from the brow of the hill. "Only soldiers travel like that."

Ethan had reached the same conclusion. There were close to a hundred of them, by the look it.

Following a hurried discussion, several of the hunters broke away and galloped back to the camps. Ethan sat with the others, watching as the double column of cavalry drew closer.

More warriors joined them, Red Hand and Feathered Bear among them. One of the Cheyenne, an older man, began to speak. He wore a medal around

---

5   Big Horn Mountains

his neck and held up a folded piece of paper. Several warriors argued with him, gesturing toward the troops.

"Starving Bear's wearing the medal President Lincoln gave him when he went to Washington last year," Micah said. "He says he'll show the soldiers the paper the President gave him so they'll know we don't want to fight. Star and some of the others don't want him to go alone."

In the end, Star prevailed. They rode to the crest of the hill and stopped, watching as Star and Starving Bear descended toward the troops.

The soldiers spotted them and came to an abrupt halt. A trumpet blared and the column split, spreading in a defensive line across the prairie. A pair of horse-drawn howitzers were rushed forward and spun into place.

As Starving Bear and Star reached the base of the hill, one of the officers started toward them. When the two Indians came within range, he shouted an order, and the troops behind him opened fire. Starving Bear and Star fell from their ponies. The soldiers rode forward, shooting them again and again.

Roars of anger transformed instantly into a war cry. Warriors swooped down the hill, unleashing a hail of arrows and bullets at the soldiers. Faria bolted with them, and Ethan let her have her head. He was appalled by what he'd seen, but every instinct cried out against firing on men in blue. The soldiers raised their rifles, and one of the howitzers roared. Wounded ponies screamed, and the second big gun fired, opening a gap ahead of Ethan.

A bullet whipped past his cheek; another stung his shoulder. Instinctively, he raised the Spencer and fired. He had no experience shooting from a running horse, and the bullet flew wide of its mark. Just ahead, he saw a soldier raise his rifle and draw a bead on him. Ethan slammed another cartridge into the chamber and squeezed the trigger. This time the bullet found a target. The man cried out, dropping his rifle, and clutching his mangled hand.

Another group of Cheyenne warriors, lead by Wolf Chief, charged in on the soldiers' flank. Several soldiers fell, and the troops abandoned their line, bunching together around the howitzers. More warriors from both camps descended, sweeping over the hills until they outnumbered the soldiers by more than four to one.

The mare's momentum carried Ethan beyond the center of the fight. He wheeled her around, searching frantically for Micah. He saw the gray pony break free of the swirling mass of men and ponies and run riderless back toward the camps. Ethan looked back along its path and caught a glimpse of Micah. He was on the ground, trying to drag himself out of range of the soldiers' guns. Ethan slammed his heels into the mare's flanks, launching her in Micah's direction. When he reached him, he flung himself out of the saddle, and grabbing Micah under the arms, dragged him away from the fighting.

When they were safely out of range, Ethan lowered Micah to the ground and sat down hard. Panting with exertion, he looked toward the battle. The ground was littered with dead and wounded from both sides. A mortally wounded Indian pony screamed in pain and terror, its hooves tearing at the earth as it struggled to stand. A wounded Sioux clambered to his feet, and holding out a hand to a passing warrior, was scooped onto the back of a galloping pony. Other warriors hung off the sides of their ponies, leaving only a single foot as a target while firing at the soldiers from beneath the ponies' necks. A cavalry mount, arrows bristling from its haunch, broke from the center of the fight and streaked away across the prairie, dragging the body of its rider. Only the intermittent booms of the howitzers drowned out the inhuman shriek of the war cry. Vastly outnumbered, the soldiers were backing down.

"Thanks," Micah murmured, and Ethan looked at him. Micah's eyes were glazed with pain, but he attempted a smile. "I owe you."

"Just keeping a promise."

Ethan turned to kneel beside him. One of Micah's leggings was soaked with blood, and Ethan leaned over him, searching for the source.

"My thigh," Micah said through gritted teeth. "Pull the legging off."

Ethan fumbled with the unfamiliar ties that attached the legging to the cord around Micah's waist. He pulled the legging down to find blood oozing from a hole near the center of his thigh. Ethan ran a hand underneath and felt around, but failed to find an exit wound.

"The bullet's still in there," he said, pulling off his shirt and using it to bind the leg. "This'll slow the bleeding 'til we get back to camp."

Micah offered him a faint smile and closed his eyes. Ethan looked toward the battle. For the first time, he noticed Black Kettle. He was riding among the warriors, calling out to them. At first, no one paid him any attention. Then slowly, one by one and in small groups, they began to pull back from the fighting.

As the troops continued to retreat, and the fighting moved away across the prairie, women and boys came with horses and began to assist the wounded. Tall Grass Woman appeared with a pair of ponies and helped Ethan lift Micah onto of one of them. Ethan turned to thank her, but she was moving toward another wounded man. Climbing up behind Micah, Ethan supported him with an arm around his waist, and steered the pony back toward the camps.

At the crest of the hill, he turned for a final look. A quarter mile to the southeast, the battle continued to rage. A whoop came from close behind him, and a group of warriors thundered past. Black Kettle charged to meet them, gesturing and yelling. They ignored him, galloping past as if he wasn't there.

The village was in chaos when they reached it. The women had been packing to flee, but they dropped what they were doing and ran to the aid of the wounded. Young men, their bloodlust not yet satisfied, galloped among the lodges, whooping and brandishing their weapons. Panicked ponies milled, defying the herd boys' attempts to corral them. Dogs barked, and the smallest children wept in terror.

Ethan took Micah to Plum Moon Woman's lodge and helped him inside. Feathered Bear was already there, sitting on the robes he'd shared with Plum Moon the night before. Blood seeped from a long gash along one cheek, and his right forearm lay at an unnatural angle, shattered by a soldier's bullet. The lodge was filled with women and children—Plum Moon, Singing Bird and Sleeps a Lot, another woman who Ethan assumed must be the third wife, four girls and a boy. Plum Moon and the oldest girl helped him lower Micah onto his sleeping robe. Ethan declined the cup of too sweet coffee Singing Bird offered and left to look for Faria.

He found Micah's gray among the ponies the boys had gathered, but there was no sign of the mare. Mounting the Indian pony from the right as he'd seen Micah do, he set out to look for her.

High-pitched, keening wails reached him long before he reached the place where the battle had begun. Cresting the hill, Ethan pulled the pony to a stop and surveyed the scene before him. Starving Bear and Star lay where they had fallen, as did the scattered bodies of other warriors who had died. Women and girls gathered around them, wailing their grief. A girl ran past him, down the slope to kneel next to one of the bodies. With a start, Ethan recognized her from Plum Moon's lodge. Looking closely, he realized that the two women already there were Wind Woman and Yellow Bead Woman. He nudged the gray toward them, hoping against hope, but certain of what he would find.

Wind Woman looked up as he came close, her face ragged with grief. Ethan gazed down at the mangled body of Black Horse. "Fourteen winters," Micah had told him; killed by an exploding round of grapeshot from the soldiers' howitzer at only fourteen. Ethan tore his eyes from the boy's body and inclined his head toward Wind Woman, acknowledging her loss, before turning away.

The dead soldiers had been scalped, and warriors were busily stripping them of their clothing and possessions. One shrugged into a blue coat and jammed a forage cap on his head before leaping onto his pony and riding in circles around the others, a bloody scalp dangling from the tip of his lance.

Seeing them revived Ethan's guilt for having taken part in the attack. He looked again toward the bodies of Starving Bear and Star, reliving the horror he'd felt at seeing them shot, then murdered, as they lay helpless on the ground, and wondered what he should have done differently. His thoughts were interrupted by a loud whoop as the young man in blue charged across the flat ground toward him. He circled Ethan, yelling and shaking the scalp. Ethan knew he was expected to join in the celebration, but instead, he spun the gray, and slamming his heels into its ribs, galloped north, away from it all.

When he'd put enough distance behind him, Ethan slowed the pony to a walk and rode aimlessly across the prairie, weighing beliefs he'd held sacred against the choice he'd made in firing on the soldiers. Without warning, his unquestioning allegiance to the United States had been shaken. When Starving Bear and Star had been gunned down, the line between right and country had become suddenly, irrevocably blurred. The more he thought about it, the more convinced he became that, given the circumstances, his actions had been justified. Even so, he regretted it.

Ethan shook his head at the irony of it. *Two months ago, I was doing all I could to prove my loyalty and no one believed me. Today, if anyone asked if I'd changed sides, I'd have to tell them yes.* Reluctantly, and with regret, but yes. He pulled the Indian pony to a halt atop a low line of hills, hoping he would never again be forced to make the same decision.

The sun angled in from the west. Broken clouds scudded across the sky, racing shadows mottling the land. At each break, sunlight appeared in brilliant bursts before quickly vanishing. To the north, the sky was black, and Ethan could see rain where it slanted down. A sudden shift in the breeze brought the scent of it to him.

The clouds passed, the sun reappeared, and the smell of rain was gone as quickly as it had come. A hawk cried as it sailed overhead, and not far away, a rabbit crouched low, ears flattened, waiting for danger to pass. Ethan watched it until it hopped away, then raised his eyes to the distant horizon, feeling isolated and alone. With all his being, he longed for home.

Shot until dead, with musketry. He drew a deep breath and let it out slowly. Home was out of the question. He sat for several minutes longer before nudging the gray down the slope. Not yet ready to return to the Cheyenne camp, he resumed his half-hearted search for the mare.

The sun was low in the western sky, its light all but blotted out by the approaching storm, when Ethan came upon an Indian pony and two cavalry mounts grazing on the lush grass beside a rivulet at the bottom of a shallow draw. He urged the gray down the steep bank, gathered the three sets of reins, and turned toward the camps.

The wind picked up. Black clouds churned, pierced by jagged bolts of lightning. The first fat drops of rain were spattering into the dirt when he came in sight of the camps. A group of boys rode to meet him. He made no sense of their words, but they were obviously impressed by the soldiers' horses. One of them, the blue-eyed boy, came to ride beside him. He said something, making the signs, his eyes shining with excitement. When Ethan didn't respond, the boy pointed at the carbine and mimed shooting.

"No," Ethan said with a shake of his head. "I didn't kill any soldiers."

Disappointment flickered across the boy's face, but it brightened almost immediately. He gestured toward the horses, jabbering excitedly. His enthusiasm was infectious, and Ethan couldn't help smiling.

Activity in the camps had returned to normal. Children had resumed their play, and women went about their work. One of them, Ethan noticed, had shed her leggings, and her legs and face were streaked with blood. As he rode through the camps, he saw more bloodied women, and from several of the lodges, heard wails of grief.

As his little group approached the circled lodges of the Wu'-ta-pi-u clan, a dozen armed horsemen overtook them. Ethan and his entourage followed more slowly, but it wasn't long before angry voices reached them. They came into the circle of lodges to discover a group of warriors confronting Black Kettle and several of the chiefs. One of the newcomers jumped down from his pony and strode to where another man stood toe to toe with Black Kettle. Black Kettle's voice rose above the others, calm and reasoning. The man interrupted, punctuating his speech with angry gestures. Before Black Kettle could respond, the painted warrior turned on his heel and leapt onto his pony. Spinning it on its haunches, he set it racing from the camp. The other warriors followed, heading in the direction the soldiers had fled.

Ethan watched them go, then looked at Black Kettle and the other chiefs. Already another man had mounted his pony. Black Kettle stood at the pony's head, speaking earnestly. The man nodded, asked a question, nodded again, then turned and galloped away toward the south.

Ethan dismounted before Plum Moon Woman's lodge and pulled the pad saddle from the pony's back. The blue-eyed boy spoke to him and gestured, asking if he wanted the soldiers' horses unsaddled. Ethan nodded, and when it was done, indicated that all four horses should be driven out to the herd. Scooping up Micah's saddle, he went inside.

Plum Moon, her arms and legs smeared with blood, looked up and murmured a greeting. Ethan looked at her, puzzled, before turning to Micah who slouched against one of the backrests. The bloody shirt was gone, his wound dressed.

Micah offered Ethan a pain-glazed smile and nodded toward the saddle. "Thanks. Little Crow came in a while back with your saddle and bridle. They rounded up your mare with the rest."

"Glad to hear it." Ethan slung Micah's saddle over the rack. "I was out searching for her and came across two of the soldiers' horses. They're with the herd, but their saddles and bridles are outside. What should I do with them?"

"Whatever you want. They're yours."

"What do you mean they're mine?" Ethan asked skeptically. "Don't they belong to the tribe or something?"

Micah shook his head. "You captured them. They belong to you."

When Ethan continued to look unconvinced, Micah sighed. "You're gonna have to take my word for it. It ain't like there's others you can ask."

"What am I supposed to do with three saddles?"

"Trade them. Get whatever you need."

Ethan looked at him a moment longer before going to collect the saddles. Once they were stowed, he went to sit with Micah.

"How's the leg?"

"Hurts like the dickens. The bullet was lodged in bone. It took some doing," Micah offered him a chagrined smile, "and three men to hold me down, but it's out. I expect it'll be sore for a while, but it'll mend."

Singing Bird joined them, offering cups of coffee. This time Ethan took one.

"What happened to her?" he asked, tilting his head toward Plum Moon.

"She cut herself. When a male relative sheds blood, the women do the same."

Singing Bird said something and touched Ethan's arm.

"She says you're hurt," Micah said, noticing the bloody sleeve of Ethan's longhandles for the first time. "Were you hit?"

Ethan looked down. He'd forgotten the burn of the bullet grazing his upper arm. He winced as he pulled fabric away from the wound. The action started it bleeding again.

Singing Bird spoke, and Ethan looked into concerned eyes. "Tell her it's only a scratch. I'll get some water and it wash off. It'll be fine."

Micah spoke briefly, then said, "She'll bring water."

With Singing Bird hovering solicitously, Ethan ripped off the bloodied sleeve and used it to wash the wound. Caving in to her ardent desire to help, he allowed her to tear off the other sleeve and use it to bind his arm.

"You have another shirt?" Micah asked when she was finished.

Ethan shook his head. "I'm wearing everything I own. Except a coat."

"Figured as much." Micah inclined his head toward the foot of the pallet. "There's a canvas bag in that pile behind you. It's got two shirts in it. One's yours, if you want it. Or the women can prob'ly come up with a breechclout and a pair of leggings." He looked pointedly at Ethan. "About time you gave up on those britches."

Ethan looked down at the gray homespun trousers he'd lifted off a wash line somewhere in the backwoods of Tennessee. Micah was right. They'd been worn when he stole them; now they were threadbare. The hems were frayed, there were permanent stains where he'd run his hands down his thighs, and one knee had a new tear in it. Even so, he wasn't ready to part with them. *Not just yet.*

"I'll take the shirt."

He had it on, and Singing Bird was handing him food, when Feathered Bear returned to the lodge. His arm had been set, wrapped in green hide that would shrink as it dried, holding the arm rigid while the bone healed. He spoke a greeting as he crossed to the rear of the lodge. Plum Moon took some food and went to sit beside him. He smiled and touched a finger to her bloody cheek. She smiled back and leaned close. They sat with their heads together, speaking softly.

Ethan watched them for several moments before looking away. Seeing them together made him ache for Elizabeth, just as the muffled sounds coming from their bed the night before had. He leaned sideways and ran a hand under his sleeping robe, feeling for the book. When he had it, he leaned against the backrest, and holding it to his chest, closed his eyes.

Micah watched him, eyes narrowed in speculation. He'd seen Ethan transfer the book from his saddlebags to his sleeping robe often enough, but he'd never seen him read it; only open it to a page near the front. It would be easy enough to discover what was written there, but he'd decided against it. He sensed there was plenty Ethan hadn't told him, but he figured he'd wait until he was ready to talk.

Singing Bird watched him, too, thinking how sad he looked and wishing she knew some of the vi-hoi words to comfort him. She'd fallen in love the moment she set eyes on him, but until he let her tend his wound, he'd barely seemed to notice her. She was certain that knowing the right vi-hoi words would change that. She looked at Micah, wondering if she should ask him to teach her. She rejected the idea, afraid he would guess the reason and tease her.

Feathered Bear spoke, interrupting their thoughts. Micah listened, commenting and questioning before translating.

"Feathered Bear's been in council. Now that the soldiers know we're here, we're to leave at dawn. He says many warriors, especially ones from Starving Bear's band, ignored the chiefs and went to take revenge on the whites. Others are wounded and can't fight. Runners have been sent to tell the bands on the Smoky Hill we're coming. Another's gone to find William Bent."

"William Bent? I thought he was a trader. What's he got to do with it?"

"He and Black Kettle have been friends for years—since before we were born. Cheyenne attacking whites'll mean trouble. No matter that the soldiers attacked us first. Black Kettle wants to talk with the officers at the forts, try to make peace before things get out of hand. He thinks the best way to do it is through William Bent."

7

The sun rose, a pale orb burning through gray haze, as Cheyenne broke camp. The previous night's rain had barely dampened the earth, and the brisk wind that came with sunrise dried it quickly. Great clouds of dust billowed across the prairie, signaling their presence to any watching enemy. Every man who could ride did.

Micah's attempt to mount tore open the wound on his thigh and set it bleeding so badly that he reluctantly agreed to travel by poledrag. Ethan spent the day riding with Feathered Bear and Red Hand, far out on the southern flank.

Late in the afternoon, as the wind whipped up and dark clouds once again threatened, he made his way back, searching for Singing Bird with Micah's poledrag. He had her in sight, was headed her way, when he spotted Tall Grass Woman. She rode astride, as all Cheyenne women did, on her high-pommeled Cheyenne saddle, pulling a poledrag with her meager possessions. One arm was draped loosely about Girl Who Laughs, who leaned against her, sleeping. The rawhide reins hung slack from her other hand as she gazed absently into space, oblivious to everything around her. On impulse, Ethan rode to join her.

"Hello," he said, reining the mare in beside her.

The faraway look left her eyes. She focused on Ethan, and her face lit with a friendly smile. Once again, he was struck by how lovely she was; soft, intelligent eyes wide-set above high cheekbones, a smooth oval face and a strong, square chin. She looked to be his age, but her air of quiet assurance made him wonder if she was older.

"Hello," she replied in her strange, accented English.

"I interrupted your thoughts."

She looked questioningly at him.

Ethan pointed to his temple. "You were thinking."

She nodded and said, "My husband. Sometime I remember him."

"I was sorry to hear how he died."

Tall Grass said nothing; her eyes focused straight ahead, the wind tossing her short hair.

They rode in silence for several minutes before Ethan tried again. "You speak English well."

She looked at him. "When I am only young, I live much time near vi-hoi, learn vi-hoi words. And my husband teach me."

"Vi-hoi," Ethan repeated. "Is that the Cheyenne word for white man?"

He sensed a slight hesitation before she replied, "What Tsi-tsí-tas say. Yes."

"Vi-hoi," Ethan repeated under his breath, committing it to memory.

Tall Grass shook her head. "Not good, that word."

"What do you mean?"

"Means…" She wrinkled her forehead, trying to come up with the English equivalent. Transferring the reins to the hand supporting her daughter, she held up her hand, wriggling bent fingers.

Ethan looked confused, and she wriggled her fingers again. "Little. Having many legs."

"A spider?"

Tall Grass nodded. "Spider. Not good."

"Why do the Cheyenne call white men 'spider'?"

Tall Grass looked away, unable or unwilling to answer, and another silence ensued. This time, she was the one to break it. "Henri say you looking for Hoo-ho-mo-i-yoo."

"For what?"

"Hoo-ho-mo-i-yoo. Sioux people."

Ethan nodded. "Yes. My mother's people."

"Why you not go to Hoo-ho-mo-i-yoo after soldier fight?"

"They aren't the ones I'm looking for."

"When you finding them, you go?"

"Yes," Ethan agreed. "When I find out where they are, I plan to join them."

"Here not good with Tsi-tsi´-tas?"

"It's very good," he assured her. "Everyone has been kind, made me feel welcome."

"Why you not stay?"

He found he had no answer.

Jealousy swept through Singing Bird when she saw Ethan ride toward Tall Grass Woman. She had fastened Micah's poledrag to her pony, thinking it would ensure that Ethan stayed close. Then her father had made clear what was expected of all able-bodied men, and Ethan had gone to ride with him. Now, just when it looked like he was coming back, he'd gone to ride with Tall Grass Woman. Singing Bird was sure he only spoke to her because she knew the vi-hoi words. *If I knew them*, she told herself, *I would ride over there now and join them*. She watched them enviously, knowing it was something she would never do. It wasn't her nature to be so bold.

When Ethan finally did leave Tall Grass Woman, Singing Bird noted the lingering looks several young women gave him as he rode past. It made her more determined than ever to learn the right words to say to. Ethan smiled as he approached her, and her heart fluttered. His eyes moved past her, and as the first heavy drops of rain began to fall, he rode back to speak with Micah.

A day later, as the sun reached its high point in the sky, they wound their way out of the low hills south of Walnut Creek, onto the broad plain where the other bands were camped after moving south from the Smoky Hill. The women went to work immediately, unpacking and setting up the lodges near the trees that lined the creek. Ethan gave Micah a hand up from the drag, which was all he seemed to require, then rode the mare downstream a ways to let her drink.

The cottonwoods grew thick along the water, their leafy boughs arching over it. A number of children were splashing in the rain-swollen creek, excited voices raised, dappled sunlight glinting off wet skin. Ethan watched them as Faria drank her fill, reminded of childhood summers spent at swimming holes along the Spoon River.

When he returned to where Plum Moon and Singing Bird were tilting up the lodge poles, he saw that Micah had collected his belongings, and leaning heavily on a stick, was hobbling off in the direction of the creek. Ethan unsaddled the mare and turned her loose before setting out after him.

He found Micah seated on a downed tree limb that jutted over the water, his injured leg stretched out before him. His face and hair were wet and he was peering into a small mirror, running his fingers along his jaw.

"You never have to do this, do you?" he asked glancing up. Using a pair of tweezers, he plucked a hair from his chin.

Ethan winced and shook his head. "No. Not yet, anyway."

"Lucky."

Before joining the Cheyenne, his inability to grow facial hair had been a source of embarrassment. Now, having watched Micah and others perform this task often enough, Ethan was grateful for it. He pulled his shirt off and squatted beside the creek, rinsing the dust from his face before drinking deeply. Then he sat back, bemused, as Micah combed his hair, smearing it liberally with bear grease to make it shine, braided it, and added castoreum for fragrance. He pulled on a fancy pair of beaded leggings, added a necklace of colored glass beads to the one he customarily wore, and slipped on his silver ring and armlet. When he began applying paint to his face, Ethan felt compelled to ask what he was up to.

"Yellow Leaf's here. I aim to go see her." He grinned at Ethan. "Gotta look my best."

"You can barely walk. Can't it wait a few days?"

Micah's grin broadened. "She's worth it. A little pain ain't gonna keep me away." His look turned speculative and he added, "You're welcome to come meet her, but only if you promise to go away after."

Yellow Leaf was a shy, pretty girl, tall and slender like many of the Cheyenne women. Her face lit up when she saw Micah, then grew troubled as he limped toward her. Ethan was introduced, then left as promised, and wandered back the way he'd come, making his way past racks of drying meat and women hard at work over green hides staked to the ground. There had been a buffalo hunt the day before, and there would be another soon. When buffalo were plentiful, the Cheyenne hunted often, drying the meat and storing it against the winter.

The meat racks thinned, and Ethan crossed a strip of open ground before coming into the circle of newly erected Wu'-ta-pi-u lodges. He had no destination in mind, no plan for the afternoon, until he saw Tall Grass emerge from one of the lodges. She was carrying Girl Who Laughs on her right hip, a pair of empty water bladders dangled from her left hand. She smiled when she saw him, and having nothing better to do, he walked with her to the creek.

The shade was a relief after the sun's heat. Ethan sat with his back against a cottonwood as Tall Grass pulled her off daughter's dress, then held her hand as she waded naked in the water. After a time, Tall Grass plunked the little girl down in the shallows with a tin cup and a stick, and came to sit near Ethan.

"She's a happy little girl."

"Most time she happy. That why I calling her Ksi-ĩi-zhi-ho-ha-zi-zi. Until she having real name."

"Real name?"

"When she older, she having real name. Now she Ksi-ĩi-zhi-ho-ha-zi-zi." Tall Grass glanced sideways at Ethan, then looked at Girl Who Laughs. "You no have childs?" she asked.

"No."

"You having wife?"

Ethan looked at Tall Grass, but for once, she avoided his gaze. "No," he told her. "Maybe one day."

"When you go Hoo-ho-mo-i-yoo?"

"No. When I go home."

She looked sharply at him. "To white home?" When Ethan nodded, a look of bewilderment crossed her face. "You just come here. When you are going?"

"As soon as I can. When the war... When the white man's war, is over."

Tall Grass shook her head. "I not understand. You come Tsi-tsi-tas, not stay. You go Hoo-ho-mo-i-yoo, not stay. Why you go from white home?"

Ethan looked away. "It's hard to explain. Something happened and I had to leave. If things change, if they get better, I want to go back."

"Something bad happen?"

"Yes."

She sat silent for several moments, digesting what he'd said. Then she asked, "This bad thing. Is bad thing you do?"

"No. It was something other men said I did."

"White men?"

"Yes."

"What they say you do?"

Ethan looked at her. It was obvious Tall Grass was trying hard to understand, but it wasn't something he wanted to explain. "It had to do with the war. The white man's war. Something the soldiers said I did."

Soldiers she understood. A knowing look came into her eyes. "Because you Hoo-ho-mo-i," she said with absolute conviction.

"No," Ethan said sharply. Too sharply. He saw it in her face and softened his tone. "I don't think so. Maybe. I don't know. But it was more than that."

"What they do to you?"

"They put me in prison."

Tall Grass' brow wrinkled. "I not understand what is prison."

"A room. A tiny room. Cold. Dark. No sun."

"No sun? How long you are in this room?"

"A long time."

"Why you not go?"

"I couldn't. They locked me in."

She looked perplexed. "I not understand."

"The soldiers made it so I couldn't leave, Tall Grass. They locked the door; I couldn't open it." He crossed his arms at the wrists, the sign for prisoner, and watched her eyes register understanding.

"You are long time in room with no sun?" she asked, concerned.

"Yes."

"Soldiers open door, you come here?"

Close enough. "Yes," he told her, hoping the subject was exhausted.

But Tall Grass had more questions. "When you going white home, soldiers not putting you in room?"

"When I go back? No."

"How you know this?"

A good question. "I don't," he said. "I have to figure it out."

They sat together until Girl Who Laughs tired of playing in the water. She tottered over to her mother, eyeing Ethan curiously. Tall Grass rose and collected the two water bladders. As she began filling them, Ethan excused himself and wandered upstream.

Tall Grass had raised the very question that had nagged at him since the morning he'd watched Henri drive away, effectively severing his last tie to the white world. He'd realized then that he had no way of finding out when the war ended, much less discovering the outcome of Captain Johnson's appeals. Until then, he hadn't realized how completely joining the Cheyenne would cut him off from the rest of the world.

Well clear of the camps he came to a quiet spot, free of laughing, splashing children, where the water pooled invitingly beneath overhanging branches. He slipped out of his clothes and waded into the beaver pond before sliding onto his stomach. His breath caught at the first cold shock, but he quickly grew accustomed to it. He swam lazily for a while, then rolled onto his back and floated, torn by conflicting emotions.

A part of him longed for home, wanted more than anything to see his parents and Kate. At the same time, he realized, if news reached him that the war had ended, that all was forgiven, it would be hard to just up and leave the Cheyenne. Their way of life intrigued him, beckoned him in a way he hadn't counted on. It was in his blood, and he wanted time to experience it fully. And, more importantly, he wanted to find his mother's people. Always before, their existence had been abstract, but now, having lived with the Cheyenne, having talked with the Brulé, they had suddenly become very real. Somewhere to the north was a whole group of relatives—grandparents, aunts, uncles and cousins he'd never met.

No use worrying, he thought, stretching out naked on a sunlit patch of earth to dry. *Even if the war ends tomorrow, it could be months before I hear about it.*

In the meantime, he hoped the ubiquitous William Bent would intervene, the business with the soldiers would blow over, and he'd be able to make the most of his time with the Cheyenne.

That day and the next, councils were held. Over the bitter objections of many, mainly the Dog Soldiers who clamored for war, Black Kettle prevailed. It was decided they would remain where they were, awaiting word from William Bent.

Within days, the messenger returned. By chance, he had come across Bent, headed east with his train of wagons, not far from Fort Larned. William had already been overtaken by Lieutenant George Eayre's fleeing troops and heard how the Cheyenne had attacked them on Ash Creek; how the soldiers had managed to fight them off, killing many. Furious, the Cheyenne messenger told Bent what had really happened.

William was aware of the earlier attacks on the Cheyenne, and this latest made him even more concerned for the safety of his children in the camps. He sent word to Black Kettle that he would send his wagons on with Bob and ride to meet him. In the meantime, he warned, Black Kettle and the other chiefs must find a way to keep their warriors from further run-ins with the whites.

Black Kettle, accompanied by a small party of warriors, set out to meet him. He came together with his old friend, the man he called Schi-vi-hoi, Little White Man, on Coon Creek, assuring him that his sons were safe, hunting buffalo along Walnut Creek. Both men were deeply concerned by the events of the preceding month and worried for the future of the Cheyenne. William agreed to ride to Fort Lyon and meet with the officers there. He urged Black Kettle to send runners to all the tribes, asking them to assemble near Fort Larned where, he promised, he would meet them in twenty days' time.

* * *

Utterly exhausted, his shoulder throbbing, Josh sank down on the trampled grass and leaned against the bullet-scarred trunk of an ancient hickory, relishing the relative cool of the evening and using the last of his strength to undo the buttons at his throat. His eyes burned from lack of sleep, from sweat and dust and gunpowder. He ran a hand over his face, and it came away black. Wiping it down his pant leg, he leaned his head against the pocked trunk and closed his eyes.

Three weeks earlier, at the beginning of May, General William Tecumseh Sherman's push toward Atlanta had begun. The combined armies, General Thomas' sixty thousand-man Army of the Cumberland, the twenty-four thousand-man Army of the Tennessee under General James B. McPherson, and the fourteen thousand-man Army of the Ohio under General John M. Schofield, had begun marching and fighting their way through some of the most inhospitable terrain in the South. They had captured the critical rail tunnel at Tunnel Hill, and through a series of actions, had forced General Johnston to abandon Dalton and retreat south to Resaca.

At Resaca, Johnston's army, reinforced by the arrival of General Polk's Corps, had retrenched. For two days, heavy fighting had ensued. On the sixteenth of May, with a Union division moving against his rear, General Johnston had withdrawn from Resaca and once again retreated south. The massed armies of the North had pursued him, making their way over steep, rocky ridges, through deep valleys and dense forest, across rushing rivers and murky swamps.

Through it all, Josh had done his duty, riding tirelessly along the line of plodding men, urging them on; using encouragement, pleas, even threats when necessary—whatever it took to keep them moving, keep them from bunching up, or sitting down, or simply walking away when they were tired or hungry or had had enough. Before the assault at Rocky Face Ridge, again at Resaca, and now at Adairsville, he'd walked among them, encouraging them to do their duty and fight for victory. In the thick of the fighting he'd been with them, holding them in line and urging men forward to fill the gaps.

When the sun finally sank below the mountain ridges at the end of this day's battle, when the shooting diminished, then stopped, three of his sergeants and more than two dozen of his men lay dead. Twice that many were wounded, many of them grievously. Josh had looked around, taking in the death and destruction, and then, light-headed and dazed with exhaustion, staggered from the field. He'd done his duty, but his heart was no longer in it.

He'd had less than nine months remaining in his enlistment when he was shot, nine months he could have spent recuperating. Instead, intent on avenging Jamie and Duncan, he'd committed to rushing back. Time spent with his grieving parents had made him question that decision, but it was Ethan's treatment at the hands of the Union Army that had changed everything. His allegiance had begun to waver the day Ethan was convicted. Then Ethan escaped, and during the rabid hunt for him, Josh realized he'd had enough. All he wanted was to go home and help his father on the farm. And, more importantly, do what he could to prove Ethan innocent. He'd written to Elizabeth, enclosing his letter with the one he'd written for Ethan. He had also sent a note to Thomas. Sitting beneath the hickory, he wondered if either had been received, and if so, what the chances were of getting a response.

He touched a hand to his pocket, assuring himself the letter was still there. There was no need to read it; he knew every word. Ethan was safe and well. He was grateful for all Josh had done and deeply sorry for having hurt him. He hoped Josh would find it in his heart to forgive him. No mention was made of his whereabouts, but the envelope was marked Westport, Missouri.

Not for the first time, Josh wondered where he'd gone. *California, maybe? Or Oregon?* Beyond that, his knowledge of western geography was hazy, at best. He and Jamie had been anything but conscientious students—something he'd recently come to regret. Just as he regretted not getting to know Ethan better, sooner. *California or Oregon.* Both seemed a long way off. Especially when there was still a chance Ethan's sentence might be commuted. More remote now, certainly—Captain Johnson had made that clear after his escape—but still a chance. There was no way of knowing what action the President might take once the all facts were considered. *But if Ethan could be proved innocent...*

"Lieutenant?"

Josh opened his eyes to the concerned face of his one remaining sergeant.

"You all right, Lieutenant?"

"Tired."

Sergeant Aston held out a hand. "Let me help you to your tent, sir. You'll rest easier there."

Josh took the proffered hand, wincing as he was dragged to his feet.

"Shoulder still bothering you?"

"A bit."

"If you don't mind my saying, much as those of us that's served with you likes having you with us, I wouldn't 'a come back, if I was you."

"You're right," Josh admitted, saying it aloud for the first time. "It was a mistake."

"If it was me, I'd say something. Explain to the captain. Or Colonel Miller."

Josh didn't answer right away. His eyes were fixed on the last of the pale light rimming the western treetops. The sergeant's suggestion wasn't new to him—it was something he'd contemplated for more than a month. He turned to Sergeant Aston, offering him a brief, tight-lipped smile. "The campaign's underway, Sergeant. At this point, I reckon it'll take another bullet to get me out of here."

8

Aim for the heart. Wait for the front legs to come forward, and aim behind the shoulder. Aim for the heart. Stay clear of the horns. Wait for the front legs to come forward...

Adrenaline surged through Ethan as he struggled to maintain control of his excited mount, the buffalo-runner loaned him by Feathered Bear for his first hunt. The pony had begun to fidget long before the pungent, musky odor of the buffalo reached Ethan's nose. Now, as he waited beside Red Hand, watching the great herd of hump-backed beasts that darkened the prairie for miles, the pony danced under him, eager to be off.

A mirror flashed on a distant hill, and the hunters surged forward, converging on the herd from both sides. Ethan relaxed his hold on the rawhide reins, and the pony was off like a shot, racing down the slope toward the sea of black bodies.

"Avoid the bulls at the edge of the herd," Feathered Bear had advised. "Pick a cow and guide the pony to her. Then let him run. He will carry where you want to go. All you will need to do is wait for your shot, and make sure your aim is true."

It was important to Ethan that he succeed. Of the adult males in Feathered Bear's lodge, only he was capable of riding and wielding a weapon with the skill necessary to bring down one of the great beasts. For that, Feathered Bear had loaned him his best pony. He couldn't afford to fail.

Aim for the heart. Watch for your shot, and make sure your aim is true.

The buffalo at the edge of the herd milled in momentary confusion at the sight of the hunters. Then they began to run. Clumsy for the first few steps, they quickly gathered momentum. Panic spread through the herd, and pounding hooves shook the earth as hundreds of animals began to stampede.

Select a cow, and cut her away from the herd. A black shape crossed Ethan's line of sight, and he guided the pony toward it. The pony saw the intended target and careened after it, easing between it and another massive shape that loomed suddenly out of the swirling dust. Ethan suffered a momentary bout of panic as a large, pointed horn bobbed next to him, dangerously close to his leg. A moment later, it was gone, and Ethan was in the clear, the pony matching its stride to the cow beside it. Ethan dropped the reins and sighted along the carbine, watching the rhythm of the churning legs, waiting for a shot. As the front legs started forward, he squeezed the trigger. The buffalo kept running. Ethan stared in disbelief and quickly pumped the trigger guard lever, loading another cartridge. He was raising the Spencer when the buffalo's front legs crumpled. Ethan barely kept his seat as the pony leapt clear of the twisting rear hooves.

His mother's blood coursing through his veins, he raised the carbine over his head and yelled. Another hunter galloped past, yelling a response, and together they charged after the herd.

Exhilarated like never before, Ethan selected another cow and set the pony at her. Once again, they worked the animal into the clear, the pony keeping pace until Ethan had his shot. The carbine roared and bucked against his shoulder. The great beast faltered, then skidded along the ground. Ethan twisted in the saddle, searching for another target.

The last of the herd was charging past him now, the stragglers already pursued by hunters, many of them boys on their first hunt. Ethan spun the pony on its haunches, peering through the churning dust, searching for one last kill. Far out on the flank he spotted it, a massive black shape running all alone. Ethan slammed his heels into the pony's ribs and they were off, gaining ground quickly.

Before Ethan's eyes, another hunter appeared right on top the great beast. For several moments the other man's pony and the buffalo ran side by side as one arrow after another slammed into the cow's hide. The buffalo staggered and slowed, dropping to its knees as its forelegs buckled. The pony raced ahead, then screamed as it tumbled to the ground, its rider catapulting through the air.

Ethan slowed his pony's charge, dividing his attention between the wounded buffalo and the ground ahead of him, pocked with prairie dog holes. The other man's pony struggled to stand, a front leg broken. The hunter lay unmoving where he had landed.

The buffalo staggered to its feet, a fan of arrows protruding from its ribs, its tiny eyes wild with fury. It snorted and pawed the ground, then lumbered a few steps toward the struggling horse.

Ethan nudged the pony forward, passing between the enraged beast and the fallen hunter. The great head turned, the angry, near-sighted eyes following the movement. A moment later, the cow snorted again and charged. Ethan touched his heels to the pony's ribs and sprinted away, leading the angry animal away from the downed horse and rider.

The charge was short-lived. When the buffalo stopped, Ethan edged back to where it stood, swaying on its feet, blood streaming from its nose and mouth. The buffalo snorted again and tottered toward him. Ethan trotted out of range, and when the animal stopped, raised the Spencer and shot it squarely between the eyes. The buffalo stood unmoving for several seconds. Then the air went out of its lungs in a great groan, and it sank to the ground.

Ethan looked beyond it to the injured hunter. Already other men had arrived. The pony lay motionless on the ground; the man who'd been leaning over it straightened, wiping blood from his knife before returning it to its sheath. The injured man was sitting up, holding his head in his hands, a man on either side of him. One of them looked at Ethan. Raising a fist, he let out a yell. The others followed suit. Ethan raised the carbine over his head and echoed a response.

Beyond the next rise, a thick cloud of wind-blown dust marked the passage of the buffalo. Closer, many of the hunters had begun guiding their ponies back past the downed beasts, finishing off the wounded and collecting their arrows. Ethan turned the pony and looked back the way he'd come, amazed to discover that black lumps dotted the prairie for a distance of two, maybe three miles. He had no memory of riding that far. It had all seemed over in an instant.

He looked around as Red Hand pulled his pony to a stop beside him. "Do-do ni-nau-ho-oh i-ssi-von-ni-ho?" he asked, signing. How many buffalo did you kill?

Ethan grinned and held up two fingers.

Red Hand let out a whoop and called to his companions. They had come to know Ethan over the past few weeks, and they shouted back, acknowledging his success. One of them, a man called Two Bulls, leapt from his pony's back and pulled his arrows from a carcass. He carved out the heart and held it up to Ethan, dark red and dripping with blood. Unsure what was expected, Ethan looked to Red Hand. Red Hand grinned and gestured for the heart. He took a large bite, chewing and smacking his lips as blood ran down his face and arms. Then he handed it to Ethan.

Ethan took a small, tentative bite. It tasted good, the juices moistening his parched mouth and throat. He realized, suddenly, how thirsty the chase had left him. He took another larger bite, and the men around him hooted their approval. Ethan shouted, too, raising the dripping heart in the air before handing it to the man nearest him. They passed it among them until the last morsel was gone, then started back the way they'd come, stopping periodically to cut another delicacy from one of the scattered carcasses, boasting and reliving the hunt.

Already the women had arrived, descending on the dead buffalo with their knives and hatchets. Ethan watched in amazement as a group of them deftly pealed back a hide and began carving off long strips of meat, stacking them on the underside of the hide. By the time he and his companions reached the place where the hunt had begun, the first of the carcasses were stripped to the bone. Packhorses, heavily laden with meat wrapped in hides, were heading back toward the camps.

Flames leapt high, sparks swirling into the night sky. The pounding of drums was relentless.

"No. No more." Ethan begged off from yet another round of dancing. Shaking his head and gesturing 'no', he backed away from beckoning hands.

"I can't eat another thing and I can't dance another step," he said, dropping onto the robe next to Micah and Yellow Leaf and rolling onto his back. "What did they feed me tonight? I swear some of it was never meant to be food."

Micah laughed. Ethan's skin was flushed from dancing and the heat from the fires. His eyes were bright with excitement. He appeared to be having the time of his life.

"What're you complaining about? You killed your first buffalo today and provided for Feathered Bear's wives and children. The women made sure you got all the best parts. The nose, the tongue, the heart, the liver..."

"Stop!" Ethan protested, holding up a hand. "I don't want to know."

"Well, here comes Singing Bird with more."

Ethan groaned. "Tell her no. Tell her I can't eat another bite. Make her go away."

"I can't do that. It'd break her heart."

Something in the way he said it caught Ethan's attention. His smile faded. "What are you talking about?"

"Ever since I've been laid up, she's been coming around, asking me English words for things. She never showed any interest before, so I wondered why. I started watching her, and it didn't take long to figure it out. She's smitten."

"Smitten?"

Micah offered him a sly grin. "Smitten. With you."

Ethan sat up, staring at him in disbelief. "What do you mean? She's just a girl. What is she, twelve? Thirteen?"

"Sounds about right."

"She's younger than my sister," Ethan protested. "You can't mean it."

"I do," Micah assured him, looking past him to Singing Bird. "Shall I tell her to go away?"

Ethan looked at Singing Bird as she knelt beside him. She said his name, mumbled something, and looked shyly at him, offering the food she'd brought. Now that it had been pointed out, her infatuation was obvious. Ethan couldn't believe he hadn't noticed.

"No," he said, looking from her to Micah. "Just tell her I'm full. I can't eat another bite. And thank her." He smiled politely at Singing Bird, dismayed by the eager reaction it provoked.

Micah translated her reply. "She says she'll leave it. In case you get hungry later."

"Later." Ethan repeated, eyeing the faint lightening in the eastern sky. "You mean for breakfast?" He looked at Singing Bird, careful not to smile this time, and indicated that she should leave the food. "Ha-ho," he said. Thank you.

She smiled. When he didn't look at her again, she rocked back on her heels and stood up.

"What am I supposed to do?" Ethan asked as she walked away.

"I s'pose you could court her," Micah replied, unable to resist teasing.

Ethan shook his head. "You can't be serious. She's only a girl, and besides I... No!"

"You could court her for two or three years, the Cheyenne way," Micah said, enjoying himself. "Wait 'til she's old enough, then marry her." Seeing the horror on Ethan's face, he burst out laughing. "Ignore her. One of these days, someone'll come along and she'll forget about you."

370

"I hope you're right." Ethan lay back, flinging an arm over his eyes. "But what am I supposed to do in the meantime?"

Ethan sat with his back against a lone cottonwood, watching lazily as a rider separated himself from a group of horseman and cantered across the prairie toward him. In the two days since the buffalo hunt, while Micah courted Yellow Leaf and continued to mend, he'd taken to spending most of his time away from the camps, exploring, practicing with the bow, and thinking. He knew hiding wouldn't solve anything, but he didn't have the faintest idea how to deal with Singing Bird. For the moment, avoidance seemed the best solution.

The rider pulled his horse down to a walk. "You any good with that thing?"

The words, spoken in English, got Ethan's full attention. He studied the man as he rode closer. He looked to be about his own age, close to the same height, but heavier. He wore a breechclout, leggings and a leather vest. His long, square face was framed by jet-black shoulder length hair, parted on the left and tucked behind his ears. He sported a thin mustache.

Ethan slid the unstrung bow into his quiver and set it aside. "Not really. No."

"Heard you're good with a rifle, though. Killed three buffalo your first hunt."

"Two, actually. I just hurried the third one along."

"Could be. But the way I heard it, you kept Charley from getting killed."

"Charley?"

"My brother. You led that cow away when his horse went down." The man pulled his horse to a halt, swung a leg over its neck, and jumped to the ground. "Name's Bent," he said, coming forward. "George Bent."

That name again! Ethan eyed him curiously. "Ethan Fraser."

George looked him over appraisingly. "I hear it's your first time in this country. That you came west looking for Sioux relatives."

Ethan nodded.

"Where you from?"

"Illinois. My folks have a farm there."

George scanned the ground, looking for a place to sit. "I went to school across the river in St. Louis. 'Til the war broke out."

"Then you came here?"

"No." George selected a spot and sat down cross-legged. "Pa has a farm in Westport. I went there for summer break and ended up joining the cavalry. I fought in Missouri, Arkansas and Mississippi before I got captured."

"Captured?" Ethan repeated, his interest piqued. "Where?"

"We were retreating from Corinth, Mississippi. The Yanks cut us off and captured a few hundred of us. They took us up to St. Louis and were marching us through the streets when someone I'd gone to school with recognized me. He went to my brother Bob, and he got me released. I had to promise to come home and stay out of the war. I came back early in '63."

Ethan picked up a twig and toyed with it. "You were lucky," he said, watching it twirl between his fingers.

"How so?"

"When I was captured, the exchange was done with, so I wound up in a Confederate prison. Some of the guards there didn't like my looks. They made my life a living hell."

George's dark eyes narrowed. "You fought with the Yanks."

"Yeah." Ethan met his gaze. "And you're a Reb."

For several tense moments, they considered one another. Then one corner of George's mouth turned up reluctantly and he said, "Well the war's a long ways off from here. I don't reckon it matters much to either of us."

After a moment, Ethan nodded. "Don't reckon it does."

They sat in uneasy silence until George asked, "If the exchange was done with, how'd you get out of prison?"

"I escaped."

"And you say you have family in Illinois?"

"Yeah."

"Why didn't you go home?"

Ethan began breaking the twig into small pieces. *It doesn't matter*, he decided. *Not anymore.* He was tired of the effort it took to avoid answering questions. He tossed the pieces of the twig away. "When I got to Chattanooga, I tried rejoining my old outfit. Instead, they arrested me and charged me with spying for the Confederacy."

George eyed him intently. "Had you?"

"No. But they court-martialed me anyway. Found me guilty." The words of his sentence echoed in Ethan's head. He looked at George and said them out loud, almost with relief. "I was sentenced to die by firing squad."

George's look turned to one of horrified fascination. "But you're here. What happened? They realize they'd made a mistake?"

Ethan shook his head. "No. I escaped. Again. Killed a guard doing it, so I couldn't go home—couldn't go anywhere I knew..." He shrugged. "I didn't know what else to do, so I headed west. I met up with Henri Broulat outside Westport, and that's how I came to be here." He stared across the prairie, surprised at how much better he felt for having told someone.

George didn't respond. Ethan looked to find George watching him.

"They sentenced you to die?"

Ethan nodded. "Yeah."

George gave him a long look. "Yeah," he repeated. "It's best we're out of it."

Ethan smiled grimly, feeling the tension between them dissolve. "What about you? Why are here?"

"My ma was Cheyenne. I grew up in the camps. All of us did. Spent most of my time there until the spring of '53. That's when Pa took Bob and Mollie and me to live with our uncle in Westport so's we could get our schooling. When I came back, there were threats made against me. There's some don't like that I fought for the Confederacy." George grinned. "I figured it was as good excuse as any to come live with the Cheyenne."

"You been with them ever since?"

"I go back and forth. Pa pushes hard for me to stay with him, go into business." He inclined his head toward the sorrel where it grazed nearby. "He bought me the horse, hoping I'd stick around, but..." He shook his head. "Compared to this, it gets awful boring at home." A glint came into his eye. "You rode in the hunt the other day. You know what I mean."

Ethan's blood stirred with the memory. "I never imagined anything like it."

"Last summer, I joined one of the soldier societies and rode out with a war party. We ran across some Delaware trappers. It was a devil of a fight. We killed and scalped two of 'em and sent the rest packing. You shoulda seen it when we rode into camp, our faces blackened, leading their horses, loaded down with furs. It was the most exciting thing I've ever done. Nothing compares to it." He paused, eyes alight with the memory, then added, "Except maybe Medicine Lodge. I went to three last summer. We were camped on the Red Shield River,[6] and there were two other camps not far off, some Cheyenne Dog Soldiers and

6   Republican River

Spotted Tail's Brulé. All three bands held their Medicine Lodge and invited the others. Good times, they were."

"Medicine Lodge is the same as the Sun Dance, right?" Ethan asked, remembering his mother's face when she reminisced about the great social occasions the Sun Dance had been. It was one of the rare times when the entire tribe gathered—a time when acquaintances were renewed and important matters discussed, a time for ceremony, ritual, and gift giving, when social dances were held, and young men and women courted.

"For the Cheyenne, the Sun Dance is part of Medicine Lodge," George replied. "We call it 'the renewing of the earth'. During Medicine Lodge, everyone considers himself blessed by the spirits. Anyone who's asked favors from the spirits, or made promises, makes good on them. Men who've promised self-sacrifice swing from the pole or drag skulls."

"Yeah," Ethan said, suppressing a shudder at the thought of chests and backs pierced with sharpened skewers which, when pulled free, tore through skin and muscle. "Ma told me stories. I never understood why anyone would do it."

"It's a right of passage. Other times, a man might be carrying out instructions that came to him in a dream, or hoping his sacrifice'll bring good fortune, or keep something bad from happening. There are warriors who've done it more than once for different reasons."

Ethan thought of the scars on Red Hand's chest and the chests of many of the other men he'd come to know. He shook his head. "Sounds barbaric to me."

"Wait'll you've been to Medicine Lodge." George cocked an eyebrow at him. "Bet you change your mind. One thing's for sure, you'll never forget it." He squinted up at the pale leaves overhead, adding, "It'll be the season for it soon. Go to one, you'll see."

"Could be," Ethan agreed. Changing the subject he said, "You grew up here. You speak the language?"

"Cheyenne, Kiowa, Arapaho and Spanish. I was a little rusty when I first got back. Being away ten years, you forget things, but they come back quick."

"Cheyenne's hard," Ethan said, shaking his head. "I can't make sense of it. I've picked up a few words, but I doubt I'll ever be able to string them together."

"In Cheyenne there are..." George thought for a moment. "I don't know, close to thirty words for buffalo. If you're not planning to stick around, learn sign language. It's easier."

"I am. Working on it, anyway. It helps if I have some idea what's being talked about, or catch a word or two. If not..." Ethan gestured helplessly. "Lucky for me, Micah's usually around to translate. It's harder since he's been laid up."

George looked questioningly at him. "Laid up? What happened?"

"You know Micah?"

"All my life. Haven't seen him in years. Not since his Pa pulled him out of school at the start of the war."

"He took a bullet in the leg over on Ash Creek. Nothing serious."

"You were there when Starving Bear got killed?"

"Uh-huh."

"Tell me about it."

Ethan did, including the guilt he'd experienced afterwards.

George nodded understanding and gazed across the prairie. "It's hard to give up something you've believed in your whole life. The same thing happened when I went to the States and had it drilled into me that the people I'd grown up with—all my friends and relatives—were savages, and everything I'd grown up believing was wrong. Makes it hard to know what to think." He looked at Ethan. "I'm with you as far as soldiers are concerned. I'd rather avoid them. Keep from fighting them if I can."

"But what they did to Starving Bear and Star was wrong. Are you saying you wouldn't have fought if you'd been there?"

George shrugged. "If it happened the way you say it did, I would have. Especially since the soldiers in these parts aren't regular army anymore, just volunteers filling in 'til the war's over. Signing up gives them an excuse to kill and steal from us. Like what happened to Crow Chief and Chief Raccoon's bands a few weeks back. The likes of them, I wouldn't have any trouble taking a shot at." He looked at Ethan. "If you're clear in your head what you did was right, it prob'ly was. Still, I'd rather steer clear."

"So would I. That's one reason it won't bother me to head south. From what Henri and Micah say, there's been trouble up north for a while now. If we can stay out of it, avoid the troops 'til it blows over, that's fine by me."

"There's been trouble up north for a long time. Last summer, soldiers attacked the Sioux up on the Little Missouri. Last winter, their chiefs sent a war pipe down to the Arkansas. Our chiefs and the Arapaho chiefs refused to smoke it, but if they had, we'd have gone north to join the Sioux in their war on the whites." His eyes met Ethan's. "The way things stand, it's prob'ly best you're with the Cheyenne."

Ethan nodded, thinking that for once, fate appeared to have intervened on his behalf.

They talked companionably for the remainder of the afternoon. George was two years older, born in July 1843. He told of growing up in and around his father's forts, where the Cheyenne and Arapaho came to trade, and wagons bearing loads of brightly colored blankets, silver coins and bullion arrived from as far away as Taos and Santa Fe. In addition to Robert and Mary who were older, and Julia who was younger, he had a half-brother, Charles. His mother was Owl Woman, the daughter of Gray Thunder, keeper of the sacred Cheyenne Medicine Arrows. Her two sisters had long been part of his father's household. The youngest, Yellow Woman, was Charley's mother. When Owl Woman died giving birth to Julie, her sisters had raised them all—most of the time in Cheyenne camps.

"Mollie got wed four years back to a man she met in Westport, name a' Moore. They have a couple kids and live down on the Purgatoire. Pa built himself a stockaded ranch there after he sold his fort to the war department." George looked at Ethan. "You heard of it? They call it Fort Lyon these days."

Ethan shook his head, and George went on. "He still does some trading, but not like the old days. Bob's in it with him, married to a Cheyenne named Cedar Woman. Julie lived there off and on 'til she married Ed Guerrier. Now she spends all her time in the camps. Charley's been here about two years. Pa keeps after him to come home, but I doubt he ever will."

There was a brief silence before George asked, "What about you? You think you'll ever go home?"

"I'd like to. Once the war ends, if my name can be cleared." Ethan squinted into the setting sun. "There's someone waiting for me. Someone I promised I'd go back to."

"A woman?" George asked with a grin.

"Yeah. She took me in when I escaped the first time and we ended up..." Ethan paused awkwardly. "Before I left, I asked her to marry me. One way or another, I have to go back."

9

Over the next few days, Ethan spent a good deal of time with George and was introduced to his half-brother Charley, his sister Julie, and her husband, Ed Guerrier. Charley Bent was Ethan's age, but they quickly discovered they had nothing in common. Small and lean, dark-skinned and wild, Charley was extremely vocal in his contempt for whites. Together, he and Micah were apt to engage in such vicious diatribes that Ethan went off in search of more agreeable company.

Ed Guerrier, on the other hand, moved easily between the red and white worlds. Five years Ethan's senior, he had known the Bents all his life. Dark-complected, with wavy black shoulder-length hair and a thick mustache, he was the product of a union between a French father and a Cheyenne mother. Shortly after his mother died of cholera, his father had packed him off to the States to be educated, first at a mission school in Kansas, and later, at St. Louis University. By the time he returned to the plains ten years later, his father was dead, killed in a gunpowder explosion on the Powder River. Ed worked for a time as a bullwhacker in New Mexico before returning to the upper Arkansas, where the year before, he'd taken sixteen-year-old Julia Bent as his wife. Together, they'd come to live in the Cheyenne camps.

When he was introduced to Julie, Ethan thought her easily the most beautiful girl he had ever seen. Copper skinned and dark haired, her features combined the best of both races. She preferred her Cheyenne name, Um-ah,[7] and considered herself more Cheyenne than white. Unlike her siblings, she hadn't gone east to be educated, preferring to remain among her mother's people. She was, as Charley took great pride in pointing out, an excellent horsewoman and as skilled a hunter as any man.

From George, they all knew Ethan's story. Ed brought it up one afternoon as they rode back to camp at the end of a day's hunting. He was curious to know how the court-martial had come about and wanted to hear what evidence the army had. When Ethan explained, Ed shook his head. He'd never been in the army, he said, but he'd spent enough time around military posts to know that the vast majority of white soldiers looked down on Indians, considered them little more than animals, and weren't inclined to treat them well. Half-breeds, more often than not, fared the same.

---

7   Talking Woman

"I'm willing to bet things woulda turned different if you'd been white," he said.

Ethan shrugged, preferring to let the matter drop. Ed's suggestion wasn't new to him. The suspicion had always been there, but he refused to think about it, unwilling to accept that it might be true.

Micah was more persistent a few evenings later. He had heard the story from Charley and was incensed by it.

"What they did had nothing to do with money or books or whatever evidence they said they had," he insisted angrily. "Why can't you see it, Ethan? They wanted you dead because you're half Sioux."

"What makes you so sure?" Ethan countered, temper flaring. In his opinion, the conversation had gone on long enough. "You weren't there. Now let it drop!"

But Micah was just getting started. "How many times have white folks treated you bad because of your looks? Answer me that. When I was in the States, just about everyone thought they were better'n me. The folks I boarded with looked down their noses at me the whole time I lived with them. They only let me stay because Pa does business with them."

"My family isn't like that."

"I'm not talking about your family, Ethan, and you know it. How many times did someone call you names or pick fights when you were growing up? How many people made a point of letting you know you weren't as good as them? You can't tell me it never happened 'cause I know it did."

Ethan got up and started toward the horses. Micah heaved himself up and limped after him.

"Why don't you admit it, Ethan? That's the way white folks are."

"Not all of them," Ethan muttered.

"But you're willing to admit some are?"

Ethan turned so quickly that Micah nearly collided with him. "All right. Some of them are. I've had my share of run-ins, but that's a long way from sentencing me to die because of it."

Micah took one look at Ethan's face and raised both hands in capitulation. "Look, Ethan, I'm sorry. I wasn't trying to pick a fight, but hearing what they did made me mad."

"That's because you heard it from Charley. Knowing him, things got blown way out of proportion."

Micah grinned ruefully. "Could be you're right. We tend to get each other going." He tilted his head back the way they'd come. "Let's go back. Enjoy the sunset. I promise I won't say another word."

Ethan glared at him. When Micah continued to look contrite, Ethan dipped his head in agreement, and they returned to the fallen tree where they'd been sitting when the conversation began.

They had stopped at a bend in the river where a handful of cottonwoods grew. The sky overhead was powder blue; the sun, low in the west, etched golden halos around a scattering of pink clouds and glittered gold across the water where it pooled behind the crumbling remains of a beaver dam. They sat without speaking as the sun dropped below the horizon, the sky building to a sudden, fiery orange before slowly fading.

Lost in thought, Ethan barely noticed. It was true what Black Coyote had accused him of the night he arrived—he was more white than Indian. Raised among whites, he'd always thought of himself as one of them. *A little different, but still white.* When a classmate's taunt, or a thoughtless comment by an adult, pointed out the difference, his family, Duncan and Seth in particular, had always stood by him, reminding him when he came home bloody or in tears, that it was ignorance that made people say and do what they did.

It wasn't until he saw the loathing in Maggie's mother's eyes, heard her father's threats, that he realized, with some people, it was more than that. Even so, even with Shunk and his boys, even with Major Hawkes, he'd convinced himself they were the exception, not the rule. Now everyone was telling him he was wrong. Telling him it was hatred—there was no other word for it—hatred of who and what he was that had swung the vote at his court-martial. If they were right, everything he'd ever believed in, including his belief in who he was, was a lie.

Ethan's shoulders slumped. He drew a breath and let it out slowly.

Micah misunderstood. "I'm sorry for what I said. It made me mad when I heard what they did." He paused, glancing sidelong at Ethan before adding, "Part of it was hearing it third-hand."

Nearly a minute passed before Ethan replied. "It wasn't planned, me telling George. It just happened."

Micah nodded, eyeing the golden reflections that lingered in the still water.

They sat in silence until Ethan broke it. Raising his head, eyes fixed in the distance, he said, "It's hard for me to talk about what happened, Micah. There've been too many times in the last six months when I was convinced I wouldn't live to see another sunset." He paused, lowering his eyes to the water. "The first time the Rebs caught me, they ordered me hung as a spy. Only a miracle kept it from happening. Then, because I'm half Lakota, a guard saw to it I was starved and beaten until I nearly died in their prison. When I made it back to the Union lines, my own countrymen, men I'd fought beside, put me on trial and sentenced me to die. Now, as if all of that wasn't bad enough, you and Ed, and even Tall Grass, keep telling me they did it because of who I am, not because of what they thought I did.

"I'm to the point where I don't know what to think. If I accept what you're saying—and believe me, the thought crossed my mind long before any of you said it—if I accept it, it means the entire Court, nine men who didn't know me, hated me enough to want me dead." He looked at Micah, eyes filled with anguish. "I can't let myself believe that. If I do, I won't have anything left."

Micah sat silent for several moments. Choosing his words carefully, he said, "I understand what you're saying, Ethan, but did you ever stop to think that maybe everything that's happened was pointing you this way? That maybe this is where you belong? Where you've always belonged. Maybe you should forget going back, and stay here with us."

Ethan gave him a long, silent look, before raising his eyes to the sky. Only the undersides of the clouds were still brushed with light. The horizon glowed faintly yellow, stretching to the palest of blues overhead. Fireflies flickered across the prairie, and the banks of the stream had come alive with the trilling and croaking of frogs.

"It's a great life, Micah. It really is. But I can't stay here forever. That's why I can't let myself believe what you're saying. I've got family back home. When the war ends, if everything works out, I need to go back to them. And Elizabeth."

"Elizabeth?"

"The woman I promised to marry." Ethan looked at him. "I don't suppose Charley bothered mentioning her?"

"No."

One corner of Ethan's mouth twitched, and he shook his head. "Figures. So you see, I have to go back. Eventually."

Ethan came awake with his face pressed to the dirt floor of the lodge. He continued to struggle until it penetrated that it was Micah repeating his name. He grunted in recognition and gasped, "Stop!"

"Ethan! You awake?"

"Yes." Ethan tried to move, but his arms were pulled tight over his head, and weight on his back wouldn't allow it. "Awake," he panted. "Let go."

The grip on his wrists loosened. Micah muttered something and the leg that had been twisted up behind him was released. The weight on his back lifted. Ethan pushed himself up on his elbows.

"What happened?"

Seated on the ground in front of him Micah said, "You started thrashing in your sleep. Then you yelled. I touched you, and you hit me. That's when the fight started. Between my leg and Feathered Bear's arm, it took both of us to hold you down."

Ethan twisted around. Feathered Bear was crouched close beside him. In the dim light from the dying fire, he could make out the wide eyes of Plum Moon, Singing Bird, and Long Sleeper, staring at him from their pallets.

"Sorry," he said, sitting up. "Tell them I'm sorry. I have nightmares sometimes."

Micah did as he asked, and Plum Moon responded.

"She wants to know if you need anything. If there's anything she can do for you."

Ethan shook his head, embarrassed. "No. Tell them to go back to sleep. Sorry I woke them."

Micah translated. Feathered Bear grunted and padded back to his place beside Plum Moon. Ethan stood and offered Micah a hand.

"Did I hurt you?" he asked when Micah was on his feet.

Micah touched his jaw, flexing it. "Nothing that won't mend."

Ethan ran a hand over his face, wiping away sweat and dirt. His longhandles clung to him, drenched. "Sorry," he repeated. "I haven't had one of those in a while. I thought they were done with."

Micah waited until they were lying together on the pallet before asking, "What causes them?"

After a brief silence, Ethan replied, "Things I told you about earlier. Mostly stuff that went on in the Reb prison."

"Musta been bad."

"It was." Ethan rolled away from him, signaling the end of the conversation. He lay awake, haunted by recurring images from the dream. The water-closet. Rat-Face and the harelip. Shunk was there, flanked by Major Hawkes and Sergeant Sully. The harelip reached for him. Frank sneered and the Court watched. He turned from General Reynolds' accusing stare to find himself in a long, narrow corridor, fingers digging into his arms, resisting as he was dragged toward a line of armed men waiting in the sun.

Ethan jerked. His eyes flew open, and he realized he'd dozed off. Despite the warmth of the night, a shiver ran through him. He forced his mind to other things.

He was still awake, watching the hanging objects take shape overhead, when the women began to stir. He closed his eyes, waiting for them to leave. Instead, he heard Plum Moon whisper. Beside him, Micah muttered a reply. Plum Moon said his name, and there followed a brief, whispered conversation, then more movement, and a soft thump as the door flap fell shut. By the time the women returned, Ethan was asleep.

The lodge was stuffy and warm when he woke, the shaft of sunlight through the smoke hole nearly vertical. At first, he thought he was alone, but then, out of sight behind the backrest, he heard movement. Plum Moon Woman came to perch on the pallet beside him. She asked a question—was he awake, was he all right—he couldn't be certain, but he nodded and pushed himself up against the backrest. She got to her feet and left. Ethan leaned his head back and closed his eyes, drugged by heat and lack of sleep.

Before he knew it, Plum Moon was back. She sat down facing him, holding out a tin cup of sweetened coffee and bowl of stewed meat. The coffee was all he wanted, but he took the bowl and tried to eat. When he handed it back, she set it on the ground at her feet and began to speak. Ethan watched her hands, not understanding what she was saying until, as if to make her point, she grasped the fabric of his longhandles between her thumb and forefinger.

He looked down at the worn gray fabric, stained now with sweat and dirt. "I know," he said, looking up at her. "I wash them, but it doesn't do much good." He shrugged with upraised palms. "I don't understand what you're saying."

Plum Moon gave him a long look without replying. She understood some of the vi-hoi words, but the only one familiar in all he'd said was 'wash'. Unsure what he was trying to tell her, she pulled the gifts she'd made from underneath his backrest. She unfolded first one legging, then the other, laying them on the robe beside him. Then she rolled out a long piece of blue cloth. She lowered a hand toward him, palm up, letting him know they were for him.

Ethan looked from the breechclout and leggings to her face. A part of him longed to accept them, but he was reluctant to take yet another step away from the world he'd grown up in. He had no idea what to say.

"What is wrong?" she asked. "Do you not want them?"

Not understanding, Ethan gave a slight shake of his head. Plum Moon bit her lip in disappointment and picked up one of the leggings. She folded it, placed it on her lap, and was reaching for the second when Ethan laid a hand on hers.

"I'm sorry," he said, making the sign. "You're very kind. Very generous. I should have thanked you." He held out both hands to her, palms down and swept them downward. "Ha-ho, Plum Moon. I'd like to keep them, if it's all right." He smiled the question and held out a hand for the legging.

Plum Moon's face brightened, and she handed it to him. Though only ten years his senior, she felt a strong urge to mother him. It pleased her that he'd accepted her gift.

Eager to make up for the distress he'd caused her, Ethan sat forward, gesturing with his hands around his waist. "I'll need something to hold them up." He raised his eyebrows questioningly, and gestured again.

Still smiling, Plum Moon reached down and retrieved a pair of beaded moccasins from beneath the backrest. She placed them on top of the breechclout and went to fetch what he'd asked for, rooting around in her things and coming up with a narrow strip of buckskin. She turned back to find Ethan on his feet, holding up one of leggings. She took it from him, demonstrating how it was to be worn and how to tie it to the cord. Ethan thanked her again before she went outside, leaving him to dress.

It was strange to toss the longhandles aside and tie the thong about his waist. Ethan centered the breechclout between his legs and pulled the ends over the strip of buckskin, adjusting the fabric where it hung down front and back. He hesitated before donning the leggings, aware that as the days grew warmer, many men wore them only when riding, and often, not even then. *Well*, he thought, *this is where being raised white comes in. I'm not ready to wander about half naked. Not just yet.* He pulled on one legging, fussing until he got the ties right, and then the other. When he was dressed, he looked down at himself, wishing he had a mirror. More than that, he wished his mother was there to see him.

Singing Bird's heart leapt when she saw Ethan emerge from the lodge. She was delighted to see him wearing the leggings she'd helped her mother cut and sew. She'd wanted to spend more time on them, painting and beading them, and adding some of the shiny tin tinklers from the box Henri had brought, but her mother wouldn't allow it. Even so, to her eyes, he looked magnificent. She wanted to go to him, to tell him how wonderful he was. More than that, she wanted to ask him if he was all right after what had happened during the night. She took an impulsive step toward him and stopped. She didn't have the words, much less the courage to approach him.

Ethan saw her and turned away, heading for the creek. He'd taken Micah's advice and ignored her, but it hadn't done much good. It seemed that every time he looked up, she was watching him, waiting for some sign of encouragement. He blew out a long, exasperated breath, thinking it was high time Micah told her he was promised to someone else.

Girl Who Laughs sat dabbling in the stream, her mother crouched beside her. Tall Grass spotted Ethan and stood up, raising a hand to block the sun. He saw her and changed direction. Coming to a stop before her, he smiled self-consciously and held his hands out from his sides.

"What do you think?"

Tall Grass smiled. "Is good. You looking Tsi-tsi ́-tas now."

"I don't look... ? I don't know... silly?"

"Is good," she assured him. "You looking good now."

Not entirely convinced, Ethan shook his head. "If you say so."

He moved past her and squatted beside the creek. As he splashed water onto his face, the little girl pushed herself to her feet and tottered to him. She laid a hand on his knee and leaned forward, her eyes screwed tightly shut. Ethan considered her for a moment before dipping his fingers in the creek and flicking water onto her face. Her eyes flew open and she jumped up and down, clapping her hands and laughing in delight. Closing her eyes again, she leaned forward.

Ethan looked at Tall Grass. "Again?"

Tall Grass smiled. "Many time again."

She watched the two of them as they laughed and water flew. Ethan's hair, hanging loose as he'd taken to wearing it, glistened blue-black in the sunlight. Muscle rippled beneath the smooth skin of his back. Her eyes lingered on the newly exposed flesh along his flank, and she found herself wishing he would stay. She pushed the thought aside. He had made his intentions clear.

Ethan glanced at her, and his smile faded. "Are you all right?"

She nodded.

"Are you sure?" he asked, rising. "You looked kind of... I don't know... sad all of a sudden."

"Not sad," she told him, as Girl Who Laughs let out a wail of protest.

Ethan leaned down and picked her up. The little girl gazed at him for a moment, then twisted away, reaching for her mother. Ethan handed her to Tall Grass, his look questioning.

Tall Grass turned to retrieve her daughter's dress from the branches of a willow. She took her time pulling it over the little girl's head. When she looked again, Ethan was seated in the shade of the nearest tree, his back against its trunk, one arm resting on a bent knee. Freed from her mother's grasp, Girl Who Laughs scampered toward him, only to stop before reaching him, eyeing him uncertainly. Ethan smiled encouragement and held out a hand, wriggling his fingers in invitation. Reassured, she tottered over and crawled onto his lap. Ethan winced as a knee dug into his groin, and shifted her to a more comfortable position.

"I take her." Tall Grass said, hurrying to his rescue.

"No. She's all right." The little girl snuggled warm against him. "Let her be."

Looking doubtful, Tall Grass sat down beside him.

"It's been two years since I last held a child. My brother's little girl. She was about this age, I reckon."

His breath ruffled her dark hair where it lay feathery soft against his chest, and he could feel the gentle rise and fall of her breathing. Ethan stroked the skin along one forearm, marveling at its velvety smoothness. After the terrors of the night, he found holding her immensely comforting. He smiled as her eyelids drooped, then looked up to find Tall Grass watching him. Their eyes met briefly before Tall Grass looked away.

Ethan leaned his head against the tree, admiring her profile, thinking how beautiful she was, how much he liked her. *If it weren't for Elizabeth—*

No! He wouldn't allow himself to think that.

Tall Grass glanced in his direction. Finding him watching her, she looked quickly at her daughter. "She thinking you like Ah-nho-sso," she said. "She missing him now he spend many time with Hi-yo-vi-vi-bo-da-i."

"Who?" Ethan asked, stung by a faint stab of jealousy. He hadn't stopped to consider that there might be a man in her life.

"Ah-nho-sso," she repeated. "Micah Tsi-tsi´-tas name. He coming to see Ksi-ĩĩ-zhi-ho-ha-zi-zi many time before. Now he thinking only of Hi-yo-vi-vi-bo-da-i."

"Micah," Ethan confirmed, feeling relief. "All he thinks about is Yellow Leaf?"

Tall Grass nodded.

"What do you call him?"

She looked confused, and Ethan said, "Say Micah's Cheyenne name."

"Ah-nho-sso. It meaning..." She wrinkled her brow. "It meaning Little Hawk."

Another mystery solved. He'd heard the word many times, but it had never occurred to him that it was Micah's name. "What's George's Cheyenne name?"

"He Do-ha-eno."[8]

"And Charlie?"

"Pe-kir-ee."[9]

Ethan nodded. A few things made sense now.

"You having Hoo-ho-mo-i name?" Tall Grass asked.

Ethan looked at her. "Haŋhepi Wi Nupa. Two Moons."

"Say again. " Tall Grass leaned toward him, listening intently.

"Haŋhepi Wi Nupa."

She tried it, twisting her tongue around the unfamiliar sounds. Ethan repeated it slowly.

"Yes!" he said, grinning when she got it right. "That's it!"

Tall Grass beamed in triumph. "Haŋhepi Wi Nupa," she said, her eyes smiling into his. "Always now I remember."

She was close. Very close. And more lovely than he'd ever seen her. Ethan felt a familiar stirring in his loins and looked away, not wanting her to know what he was thinking.

---

8   Texan

9   White Hat

Elizabeth, he told himself. *Remember Elizabeth*. Her image hovered fleetingly, then was gone. He concentrated until he got it back.

JUNE

10

Within days of Black Kettle's return, following his meeting with William Bent, the Cheyenne once again headed south, all but the warriors who were still out raiding, the Dog Soldiers, and a few smaller bands who hungered for war. The five half-breeds, in the company of numerous Bent and Broulat cousins, spent their days ranging across the prairie, practicing their riding and shooting skills, taking game, telling stories and boasting. Ethan felt more at ease than he would ever have thought possible, his transition eased by the presence of so many young men his own age, half-breeds with knowledge of both worlds.

Late one afternoon, they made camp on Ash Creek, not far from Fort Larned, and very near the place where Ethan had first joined the Cheyenne. He rode out that evening with George and Micah, coming within sight of the soldiers' fort. It wasn't the destination they'd intended, but George had begun talking about his father, wondering where he might be, and the plain half a mile southeast of the fort was where they wound up.

The evening was warm, the sun lingering in a nearly cloudless sky. The stars and stripes stood out clearly where they fluttered on the flagstaff above the parade ground. Corrals and a jumble of sod and adobe buildings nestled against the scattering of trees that marked the bend in the Pawnee River. Closer, stood row upon row of white tents. Smoke rose from cooking fires, and men and horses moved about.

To Ethan, the fort looked much as it had when he'd passed through with Henri. He'd kept his distance then, too, feeling betrayed, hurt and achingly alone. This time, he gazed at it more objectively. The sense of betrayal was still there, but he was no longer alone and the raw edge of hurt had dulled considerably.

"Let's ride closer," George said, nudging the sorrel forward.

"No," Ethan replied. "This is as close as I get. Closer than I want to be."

"No," Micah agreed. "Too many soldiers. Maybe the same ones as attacked us."

George ignored them and kept going, closing the gap by half. A few of the soldiers stopped and stared, but that was the extent of it. His father didn't appear and there was no armed charge. After a while, George turned and rode slowly back.

"I thought if he was there, he might recognize the horse and come out," he said as he passed.

As Ethan and Micah turned their horses, the first notes of a bugle rent the air. They all looked back, but only Ethan stopped to watch as the flag slid swiftly to the ground. When it was gone, he turned the mare and trotted after his friends.

The following morning, the Cheyenne forded the Arkansas, passing a large camp of Santanta's Kiowa before moving into the low hills south of the river. The landscape grew harsher, the hills dotted with sage and yucca, sunlight glinting off eroded pockets of white sand. The struggling carpet of green grass was all but obscured by dense brown-black scrub.

They continued south, and when the land turned green and rolling once again, came upon Left Hand's band of Arapaho. At Medicine Lodge Creek they made camp, not far from the sprawling camps of the Comanche and Prairie Apaches. There they settled in to wait for William Bent.

* * *

"My orders are to kill hostiles, not waste time talking to them."

A bull of a man, at over six feet tall, and weighing two hundred and fifty pounds, Colonel John M. Chivington towered over William Bent. "You have the audacity to stand here and tell me the Cheyenne chiefs want to talk peace, knowing the havoc their warriors have wrought this past month. They've attacked ranches and stations all along the road from Fort Larned to Fort Riley, stealing everything they can lay their hands on and running off stock. They killed a man at Cow Creek station, ten soldiers were butchered on Boxelder Creek, and just yesterday I had a telegram from Denver City saying they'd killed and mutilated a man, his wife and two little girls up north of there. You tell your chiefs I'm on the warpath. The time for talk is over."

William stood his ground. "To hear the Cheyenne tell it, it was Lieutenant Eayre's troops started it at Ash Creek," he responded, repeating what he'd already said. "Until Starving Bear was shot, the Cheyenne had been going about their business, and every time it was soldiers attacked them. You tell me the bad things the Cheyenne have done to whites, but what about the things the whites have done to the Cheyenne? Three warriors wounded at Fremont's Orchard, women and children killed at Cedar Bluffs, lodges burned, possessions stolen or destroyed, and now Starving Bear and a dozen Sioux and Cheyenne warriors dead. In the last two months, your boys have given every Indian south of the Platte a reason to go looking for revenge."

Colonel Chivington started to respond, but William cut him off. "Like I been saying, Colonel, that group Lieutenant Eayre attacked weren't hostile. It was Starving Bear, going out to tell Eayre they were friendly and being gunned down that was the start of this latest business. Eayre and his men would be dead if Black Kettle and some of the other chiefs hadn't put a stop to it."

"Haven't you heard to a word I've said, Bent? Your so-called friendly chiefs haven't put a stop to anything. Word has it, there are over sixteen hundred of the red devils swarming north toward the Overland Road as we speak. I intend to see every last one of them dead, whenever and wherever I find them."

"You're asking for trouble with that kinda talk, Colonel," William insisted, knowing he was wasting his breath. "You keep after them, and one of these days you're gonna find the tribes have all up and banded together. They rise up like that, and there ain't enough troops in this part of the country to protect the government wagons coming up from New Mexico, much less the civilian trains and ranches. You're setting yourself up for a bloodbath, Colonel, the likes of which you ain't ever seen before. Mark my word."

"I have a job to do here, squawman. I don't have time for your Indian-friendly yammering. I intend to put a stop to the thieving and murdering once and for all. The citizens in this country are going to have to look out for themselves until it's done. I suggest you devote your energy to looking out for your own. Word is, you've got a pair of renegade sons running with the Cheyenne. Take my advice, Bent. Get them out of those camps if you want to keep them alive."

Hoping for a chance at peace, William continued to press until Colonel Chivington lost all patience and ordered him out. Frustrated, and having no idea what to say to the chiefs, he left Fort Lyon and rode back to his ranch on the Purgatoire.

He had been home less than a week when a messenger arrived, summoning him back to Fort Lyon to meet with S. G. Colley, Indian agent for the Upper Arkansas Agency. William had little use for Colley, knowing him to be less than honest in his dealings with the Indians. Reluctant, grasping at straws, he agreed to meet with him.

At Fort Lyon, Colley presented William with a copy of a proclamation from John Evans, Governor of Colorado Territory. It requested all friendly Indians to gather at designated locations: the Southern Cheyenne and Arapaho at Fort

Lyon, the Northern Cheyenne and Arapaho at Camp Collins, the Kiowa and Comanche at Fort Larned, and the Sioux at Fort Laramie. Once there, he assured them, they would be fed and protected until the hostiles who had been attacking the white trains and settlements could be hunted down and punished. Unwilling to go to the Indian camps himself, Colley had sent interpreter John Smith and his half-breed son Jack to carry copies of the proclamation north. He asked William to deliver it to the Indian bands scattered east along the Arkansas.

At about the same time, Major T. I. McKenny, inspector general of the Department of Kansas, was dispatched to Fort Larned to investigate reports of Cheyenne disturbances along the road from Fort Riley to Fort Larned. He arrived at Fort Larned in a driving rainstorm, on the evening of June fourteenth, to find Eayre's troops still ensconced there, and the commander of the fort, Captain Parmetar, drunk. McKenny's report to Army headquarters in Washington contained much the same warning Bent had given Chivington: If the Indians were not treated fairly, and the volunteers held in check, the result would be all-out war.

Several days later, on the twentieth of June, H. D. Wallen of the Seventh Infantry echoed McKenny's warning in an urgent telegram to Washington, stating that "an extensive Indian war is about to take place between the whites and the Cheyennes, Kiowas, and a band of Arapahos. It can be prevented by prompt management."

***

The child shifted, jabbing her with an elbow or knee. Elizabeth laid down her pen and pushed back from her writing table. Pressing a hand to her swollen belly, she gazed about the room, taking pleasure in it. Of all the rooms, this was her favorite. Like the others, it was spacious and well proportioned, but it had the added appeal of being exceptionally bright and airy. She'd elected to furnish it first, incorporating the same combination of blues and creams she'd used in her Mobile sitting room. It was comfortable and familiar, and it was where she spent much of her time.

She turned to look out the window nearest her, gazing across the wide expanse of mowed grass to the line of trees that masked the house of her nearest neighbor. It was the location of the house that had first appealed to her. Set on a large plot of land on the outskirts of Lewistown, it offered more privacy than a house in town. A look inside, and she'd wired her lawyers instructions to buy it.

It was large, though nothing on the scale of the house in Mobile. A formal parlor, her sitting room, the dining room, and the kitchen occupied the first floor. There were four bedrooms on the second floor, and above that, a spacious, dormered attic. She'd purchased it furnished and spent most of June separating the pieces she wanted from those she planned to get rid of.

Elizabeth sighed and picked up her pen. Furnishing a house with a war on was turning out to be more of a challenge than she'd bargained for.

"Miz 'Lizbet?" Hannah poked her head into the room. "They a lady come callin'."

Elizabeth sighed again and leaned back. Since she'd moved in, any number of inquisitive ladies had come calling. "Do you know who it is?"

"She say she Miz Fraser."

Elizabeth straightened. "Not Ethan's mother?"

Hannah wagged her head. "She a white lady. I ain't never seed her befo'."

"Show her in, Hannah," Elizabeth said, her curiosity piqued.

She pushed herself out of the chair and checked her reflection in the mirror above the mantle. Her normally milk-white skin had taken on a healthy glow in recent weeks. She smiled. With the morning sickness passed, pregnancy agreed with her.

Elizabeth turned toward the door as Hannah ushered a woman roughly her own age into the room. Pretty enough, blue-eyed with a spray of freckles across her nose, she was dressed all in black, a color that sallowed her skin. Her dress was serviceable cotton, high-necked with long sleeves, and dulled by many washings. She wore her auburn hair in a knot at the back of her head, covered with a crocheted black hair net. Something about her was familiar, but Elizabeth couldn't place her.

The woman stopped just inside the door. "Mrs. Magrath?" She took a timid step forward. "My name's Alice Fraser. I'm... Duncan was my husband."

The photograph. She had been standing with Duncan and the child. Elizabeth offered a welcoming smile and moved to her across the room. "I should have known. Please call me Elizabeth." To Hannah, she said, "Would you bring some tea, please?" And to Alice Fraser: "Or would you prefer coffee?"

Duncan's widow shook her head, flustered. "Oh, no. Please, don't go to any trouble on my account."

"Tea please, Hannah."

Elizabeth led the way to a pair of chintz-covered chairs flanking a south-facing window. Alice Fraser sat, ramrod straight, and ran calloused hands down her skirt. Her eyes flitted nervously around the room before settling on Elizabeth.

"I want to apologize," she said. "I should have called sooner. I just... I didn't know what to think when the Frasers first told me about you. Mr. Fraser was so upset... so angry. And I was shocked. Even when Kate started telling me how nice you were, I... I can't say I approved." She hesitated awkwardly. "I came here today because I promised Sarah I would."

"Sarah?" Elizabeth's face registered surprise.

Alice's eyes dropped briefly to Elizabeth's swollen stomach. "I still can't say I approve, but Kate kept telling me what a nice person you are. How much you love Ethan. She's been insisting I meet you. When Sarah told me I should get to know you, I promised her I'd come."

"Why, if you disapprove?"

Alice ran her hands down her skirt. Her fingernails were cut short, the cuticles dry and cracked. "Sarah's so honest. So sensible. When she tells me something, I believe her. She's been in shock over everything that's happened to Ethan. Over you, too. So when she told me she'd accepted you, I knew it wasn't my place to judge." She glanced shyly at Elizabeth. "You're not at all what I expected."

"What did you expect?"

Alice blushed beet-red and stared at her hands. "I don't know. Someone more..." She shook her head. "I don't know."

"I think I do," Elizabeth said stiffly. "I'm sorry to disappoint."

Alice's eyes flew to her face. "Oh no! I'm sorry. I didn't mean to offend. I just..."

"I'm not offended." Elizabeth offered her a thin smile. "After what Ethan's father accused me of, you'd be hard-pressed to offend me."

"Was he awful?" Alice asked apprehensively. "He's such a nice man, but the last two years have been hard. I think he came to accept it after Seth was killed, but when they got word about Jamie and Duncan, it was like the life went out of him. What happened to Ethan made him bitter."

"I understand. It's made me bitter, as well."

Hannah returned, placing a silver tea service on the table between them. Elizabeth thanked her and took her time pouring. She handed a cup to Alice and offered her the plate of thinly sliced cake. Alice looked longingly at it, but shook her head. Elizabeth sat back and took a sip of tea.

"What shall I call you?" she asked.

Alice looked flustered. "Oh. Alice. Please."

"How long were you and Duncan married?"

"Six years." Alice bit her lip, and her eyes watered.

Elizabeth tried to recall what Ethan had told her. Something about his father giving them land when they'd married. "Do you still live near the Frasers?"

Alice nodded. "I work the farm as best I can. Mr. Fraser helps when he can, but he's got his own place to run. There's a man, Peter Scott, a friend of Duncan's that was wounded in the war. He helps me sometimes."

"And you have two children?"

Alice's face brightened. "Oh, yes. A girl and a boy. Grace is four and little Duncan will be three in November." Almost shyly she added, "Ethan was very fond of Grace."

"I'm sure he still is."

"Oh." Alice looked mortified. "Yes. That's what I mean."

Elizabeth sipped her tea, watching Alice's eyes skip nervously around the room.

"It's very nice here," Alice said, after a few moments. "Very pretty."

"Thank you."

Alice looked at her lap, then at Elizabeth. "I'm sorry for what I said. About disapproving. I didn't know you. I had no right to judge."

"We judge other people all the time. It's to be expected. I'm sure people will judge me unkindly for my relationship with Ethan, but I refuse to apologize because I love him, and what happened between us took place under extraordinary circumstances. When he comes back, we'll be married, and in time, the irregularities concerning our child's conception will be forgotten by everyone who matters. In the meantime, I live my life quietly and take my friends as they come. I'd like it if you choose to be among them, but if not, I understand."

Alice looked at her for a long moment, then gave a slight nod. "Sarah was right. You are nice. For her sake, and Ethan's, let's try." She looked at the cake. "Would it be all right if I had a piece after all?"

***

Thomas looked again at the hawk-nosed matron who'd slipped him the envelope. Her expression warned against speaking. She turned to the next man in line and handed him a parcel. The ladies had become more organized since Elizabeth's first visit to the camp, even as the quantity and quality of the goods deteriorated.

Clutching his parcel and the envelope to him, Thomas shuffled after the man ahead of him, following the line of prisoners until he was beyond the guards. As soon as he reached the main part of the camp, he headed for the tent, hoping none of the men he shared it with would be there.

Luck was with him. He sprawled on his blanket, turning the envelope over in his hands. Curiously, there was no writing on either side, and the seal was intact. He slid a finger under it and popped it open, withdrawing a single sheet, tightly written in a neat, precise hand. He looked at the signature. *Elizabeth!* He closed his eyes for a moment, then began to read. As he read, the crease between his brows deepened. *Ethan court-martialed as a spy?* He couldn't believe it.

Thomas read the letter through twice before rolling onto his back, the letter pressed to his chest. On the steamer bound for Mobile, Ethan had been certain he wouldn't live to see the end of the war. In a way, he'd been right. Closing his eyes, Thomas thought back to what Ethan had told him. If he could remember it all, if he survived, he might be able to help.

***

"Come with me," George insisted when he heard their father was in the Arapaho camp. "What harm will it do? You haven't seen him in months."

Charley stood defiant before his older brother. "He'll start pushing me to go home. Go if you want, but I'm staying." Turning on his heel, he walked away.

George went alone to the Arapaho camp. When he returned, his father was with him.

William Bent was a small, wiry man, cheeks scarred by small pox, his graying hair ill-cut and thinning on top. Shrewd, dark eyes squinted from beneath thick brows, and his broad mouth was set in a grim line. The strain and exhaustion of the past few weeks made him appear older than his fifty-five years.

Following the two hundred and forty-mile ride he'd made alone from Fort Lyon, William had spent days riding back and forth between the various Indian camps and Fort Larned, translating, coaxing, and negotiating. Now he rode into the Cheyenne camp, bringing with him a copy of Governor Evans' proclamation.

Once again, he sat among the chiefs, endeavoring to convince them that the proclamation was in their best interest, urging a party of them to ride with him and the chiefs from the other tribes to meet with the officers at Fort Larned. Following a lengthy discussion, the Cheyenne chiefs agreed.

When William and the chiefs arrived at the fort, it was to find Captain Parmetar, and many of the men under his command, drunk. Instead of the friendly talk William had envisioned, the chiefs were subjected to rudeness and insult. They left the fort angry and returned to their camps, not at all inclined to consider the proclamation. Frustrated in his attempt to intervene, William convinced George to go with him and headed back to the Purgatoire. Before leaving, he once again warned the chiefs to keep their warriors away from the whites.

JULY

11

From atop a hill, Ethan watched them ride away, wondering how long it would be before George tired of life on the ranch. The night before, he had vacillated between staying and going; torn between duty and love for his father, and his desire to remain with the Cheyenne. William was in the saddle when George finally appeared and agreed to go with him.

Ethan watched them out of sight before turning away. As he came close to the camps, he saw that many of the lodges had already been taken down—another reason George had been reluctant to go. Little Bull, a man from the Red Shield Society, had come forward to sponsor the Medicine Lodge. A site had been selected, and today was the day of the move. It was also the day Ethan had promised Micah and Red Hand he would hunt with them. Raising a hand to shield his eyes, he scanned the prairie. In the distance, he spied a group of riders. Determined not to miss out, he rammed his heels into the mare's flanks and charged after them.

The next week was so busy that there was little time for missing George. The buffalo hunt was a success, but mounted on the mare, Ethan brought down only one of the lumbering beasts. Caught up in the excitement of the chase, he failed to ensure that there was enough room between him and the rest of the herd. He fired, and the buffalo toppled. Faria, already panicked, leapt sideways. It was all he could do to wrench her around and keep her running with the herd until he could work his way clear. When he dismounted, he found her bleeding from a jagged tear along her shoulder. Then and there, he decided to trade the two cavalry mounts for a trained buffalo runner. Or at the very least, a pony with prospects.

By the time they returned, all the Cheyenne camps had been combined into one, the circle of lodges south of Medicine Lodge Creek nearly a mile wide. The center pole of the Sun Lodge, painted, decorated and hung with offerings, had been tilted into place, and everyone was engaged in completing the lodge, raising a ring of posts around it and joining them together at the top with horizontal timbers. Notched logs radiated out from the central pole, spanning the distance to each of the outer posts. Ethan joined in, working with Micah who explained what was happening.

"While we were gone, Little Bull and his wife were with the priests in that lodge over there." He tilted his head toward a lodge Ethan hadn't noticed, standing by itself inside the circle of lodges. "It's called nu-kih-uḿ, the lone lodge. That's where the priests taught them the duties and ceremonies of the Sun Dance. There've been other ceremonies, too, most of them honoring the earth because the earth feeds the buffalo, and the buffalo provide for the Cheyenne. There was a ceremony when the center pole was chosen and cut down, another when it was raised. Tonight, the lodge'll be dedicated, and there'll be dancing."

Micah and Ethan helped lift another of the notched logs into place before Micah continued, "Tomorrow, after the altar's assembled, the Sun Dance begins. It's not dancing like you've seen before. The dancers dance for four days and nights without food or drink. Their bodies'll be painted five times, and each time they dance it's to honor a part of nature. You'll see what I mean—a red or blue spot on the chest is the sun; a black spot the moon; white spots, hail; that sort of thing. Then the warriors who've vowed to do it, swing from the pole. They stand in a circle around the center pole and go up and down on their toes, blowing eagle-bone whistles they hold in their teeth. After they pull free, a pipe is smoked and there's another dance to honor the spirits of the four directions. Then the chief priest and his wife, and Little Bull and his wife, go to the sweat lodge to be purified. Once the paint's been removed from the dancers, and they end their fast, the Sun Dance is over and the Cheyenne are reborn."

Ethan nodded. It was similar to the Lakota ceremony his mother had described. "Am I allowed to attend?"

"Allowed? It's expected. Otherwise, you chance something bad happening. No one wants that, or the risk of your bad luck spreading."

"I wasn't sure, not being Cheyenne and all."

"You're Sioux," Micah told him pointedly. "Your people are our allies."

Ethan grinned in anticipation. "Growing up, I never thought I'd get a chance like this. Tell me where to be, and when, and I'll be there."

His first Medicine Lodge was, as George had predicted, an experience he would never forget. The camp was charged with anticipation as people emerged from their lodges, resplendent in their finest clothing—quilled, beaded, painted, baubled and feathered, and sporting bits of greenery—grass, leaves, and in some cases, entire branches. Ethan felt very much the outsider, despite being similarly adorned. Red Hand had presented him with a quilled armband, and Plum Moon had made him a gift of a fine pair of painted and beaded leggings. Micah had given him a pair of hammered silver earrings, but Ethan had drawn the line at having his ears pierced. Instead, he followed Micah's lead and daubed his face with paint.

When the dancing began—drums pounding, voices chanting, painted bodies moving—Ethan forgot his initial awkwardness as tales he'd heard repeated from childhood came to life around him. His blood pulsed with the beat of the drums, and he echoed the chants, feeling them well up inside him. When the time came for the torture dance, he leaned forward, breathing with the dancers as they blew their eagle-bone whistles, their naked, painted bodies glistening with sweat as they circled the center pole, straining against the sinews that held them. Every fiber of their being was concentrated, their eyes riveted on the medicine bundle and the offerings attached to it. When at last they began to pull free, tearing the muscles in their chests, it wasn't the blood or the terrible wounds that held Ethan's attention, but the ecstacy on each man's face. Whether weeping silently or laughing out loud, it was clear that each one fervently believed he'd seen the face of his god. Ethan envied them their unshakable belief. A part of him longed to share their courage and conviction.

The days flew by, a blur of color, sound and movement. When he wasn't observing the rituals of the Medicine Lodge, Ethan joined with the other spectators in the feasting, socializing, and dancing. Added to the stimuli was a newfound awareness of the effect he had on young women. He heard the whispers and giggles, noticed the smiles even as his admirers saw him looking and averted their eyes. He approached one girl during the dancing, and before long, found himself more popular than he'd ever been in his life. It was a heady experience, and he reveled in it.

Late on the third evening, with a group of shy, giggling girls clustered before him, he looked up and locked eyes with Tall Grass. She turned away abruptly, vanishing into the crowd, but something in her expression bothered Ethan. He stayed where he was a while longer, his awkward attempts at communication the source of much hilarity among his admirers, but the feeling nagged at him. Eventually he disengaged himself and went looking for her.

He didn't find her that evening, and there was no sign of her the next day. He found himself thinking about her, wondering what she was doing. When the dancers broke their fast, and the Cheyenne celebrated their rebirth, he once again went in search of her. He found her among a group of dancers.

Tall Grass saw Ethan watching and looked away. She had spent a sleepless night trying to convince herself that she didn't care for him in a way that warranted the jealousy she'd felt when she saw him laughing with the girls. She was willing to admit she was attracted to him, not only because of his looks, but because he was good with Girl Who Laughs, and his quiet manner reminded her of Henry. *But,* she told herself, *he is only friendly to me because there are so few people he can talk to.* He had made it clear from the start that he intended to go back to his white home and marry the white woman. If it was true that her feelings went beyond friendship, the only thing to do was stop seeing him.

Tall Grass ventured a glance at Ethan. He was still watching her, waiting to talk, but she wasn't ready. She worked her way to the opposite side of the fire, intending to slip away, but when she stepped from the circle of dancers, he appeared beside her.

"Are you all right?" he asked, seeing her startled expression.

"Ksi-ïï-zhi-ho-ha-zi-zi," she said by way of explanation, and started away.

Ethan fell in beside her. "I'll come with you."

"No," Tall Grass said, shaking her head. "Now not good time."

"Why? Is something wrong? Is..." Ethan hesitated before attempting the name. "Is Ksi-ïï-zhi-ho-ha-zi-zi all right? She's not sick, is she?"

In spite of herself, Tall Grass smiled. His pronunciation was nearly perfect. She held up a hand to stop him. "No. She not sick. I going now. Bye."

Ethan watched her hurry away, knowing something was wrong, but having no idea what. He watched until darkness swallowed her, then turned back to the dancing.

Too early the next morning, the criers rode through the camps, announcing the move north for the summer hunt. Already, some of the smaller groups were packing to leave; the rest would follow within days. Ethan had retrieved the mare, was staking her next to the lodge, when the peace was shattered by shouts and pounding hooves. He straightened to see two men riding hard from the north. They splashed across the creek, reining in long enough for one of them to shout a question. The woman it was addressed to pointed, and the riders urged their lathered ponies on.

Ethan joined the crowd that surged after them, craning his neck to look for Micah. Instead, he spotted Ed and Julie. They were standing with Charley's mother, Yellow Woman, near where riders had stopped, at the lodge beneath the

American flag. An angry rumble spread through the crowd as he pushed his way to them.

"What is it?" he asked, coming up beside Ed. "Who are they?"

"Arapaho. They say the soldiers at Fort Larned shot at Left Hand and some of his warriors yesterday. He'd gone to offer help after what happened with the Kiowa."

"The Kiowa? What happened with the Kiowa?"

The angry voices were growing louder. Ed silenced Ethan with an upraised hand as he strained to hear.

"They ran off the soldiers' horses," Julie muttered.

"Every head from the fort," Ed added. "They sent women in to distract the soldiers with a dance, then ran off the herd. When the soldiers saw what was happening, they started shooting. Satanta shot one of the soldiers. When Left Hand heard what had happened, he took twenty-five men and went to offer help getting the horses back. He was carrying a white flag, but the soldiers opened fire with a howitzer. Left Hand wants Black Kettle to know he couldn't stop his warriors. They've gone out to raid."

Ed was shouting, but Ethan could barely hear him. Warriors were yelling at Black Kettle and the chiefs assembled with him. Many of them, including Lone Bear, Wolf Chief and even the old men, Yellow Wolf and White Antelope, were yelling back.

"What's happening?" Ethan hollered, as the crowd grew even more agitated.

Ed was shouting at one of the warriors and didn't answer.

"They wanna fight." The voice came from close behind him.

Ethan turned to look into the pale gray eyes of a stranger. A head shorter, he was copper-skinned, but his hair was sandy blond, cut short, curls framing a baby face. He was dressed in breechclout and leggings.

"They wanna fight," the stranger repeated, looking from Ethan to the chiefs. A wicked gleam came into his eye. "And it don't look like the chiefs are gonna stop 'em."

The veracity of his words was born out seconds later as first one group of warriors, then another, broke from the crowd and started away. Yelling and brandishing their weapons, they goaded others to join them. Some followed, but most stayed, arguing among themselves and with the chiefs.

Through it all, Black Kettle slowly raised and lowered his hands, asking for quiet. When the commotion began to die, he spoke. At first, he was interrupted by angry voices challenging him, but as he continued to talk, the dissenters gradually quieted. A low hum of agreement, initiated by the women, spread through the crowd. It took a good deal of persuading, but eventually people began to drift away, returning to what they'd been doing before the riders appeared.

"So that's it?" Ethan asked as the crowd thinned. "There won't be any trouble? We're still heading north tomorrow?"

Julie nodded, and Ed said, "Yeah. Left Hand don't want to fight the whites, and it's him was attacked. The chiefs convinced most everyone it ain't our fight. Not this time, anyhow."

Ethan nodded and looked around. He noticed Micah walking toward them and saw the light-haired man, in the company of four warriors, headed toward the pony herds.

"Who's that?"

Julie looked where he pointed. "Wo-pi-kon-ni."[10]

"Jack Smith," Ed clarified. "John Smith's son. He joined up with us right before Medicine Lodge. Long about the time George left."

Micah came up to them, grinning and holding up his left hand, the back facing them. The silver ring was gone, replaced by a narrow one carved from horn on his little finger. "Yellow Leaf traded," he announced. "All I need's a couple more horses to offer her folks, we'll be married."

They were camped a day north of the Arkansas when second group of riders bore down on them from the north. Sioux this time, they announced that raiding had begun along the Overland Road. Once again, Black Kettle and the chiefs sought to control their warriors, but the prospect of horses and plunder from the heavily traveled river route proved irresistible. The chiefs were shouted down.

"What are you doing?" Ethan demanded, as Micah gathered his belongings. "You're not going with them?"

Micah grinned, stuffing cartridge tubes for the Spencer into a buckskin pouch. "It'll be fun, Ethan. Come along. Get some horses to trade for that pony you want."

---

10   White Eyes

"*Fun?*" Ethan repeated incredulously. "You're going out to steal, maybe even kill people, and you're telling me it'll be fun?"

Micah lifted his saddle from the rack. "I don't plan on killing. Not unless I have to."

Ethan followed him as he ducked out of the lodge. "Fighting soldiers is one thing, but there's no call to go after innocent folks. Think what you're doing, Micah. You're part white for chrissake."

Micah flung the saddle onto the gray and fixed Ethan with a cold stare. "And you're half Sioux. If you had any idea what you're talking about, you'd be coming with us 'stead a' shootin' off your mouth. They're not innocent, Ethan. None of 'em. They steal our land, give us a smaller piece, and promise us it's ours—that no whites will come there. But you know what? They do. So they force us onto even less land with no buffalo and promise they'll feed us. But they don't. You talk about innocent? Babies and old folks starve to death in winter now. It didn't used to be like that. Not before the whites came. I may have some of their blood in me, but I was raised Cheyenne. I *am* Cheyenne. You'd do well to remember that."

He turned away, pulling the cinch tight. Ethan stared at his back, not knowing what to say. After a moment, he turned and walked away.

The camps were in an uproar. The women were pulling down lodges, warriors preparing to ride. Charley galloped past with a group of friends, whooping and hollering. Jack Smith vaulted onto his pony, and noticing Ethan, asked, "You coming?"

Ethan shook his head. "No."

"Too bad. There's scalps and booty to be had." Flashing a devilish grin, Jack turned his pony and trotted away.

Micah left without speaking to Ethan. Ethan saw him go, along with Feathered Bear, Red Hand and many of the Crooked Lances he'd come to know. The rest of the tribe was under way when the last of the war parties galloped past.

Still smarting from Micah's words, Ethan went looking for Tall Grass. He found her walking with two other women, leading their horses, apparently deep in conversation. He rode close, seeking to catch her eye. One of the women noticed him and spoke to Tall Grass. She looked up, offered him a perfunctory smile, and resumed her conversation. Ethan continued to ride near her, assuming that when she could, Tall Grass would break away and join him.

Minutes passed, and as it became increasingly clear that she had no intention of doing so, Ethan jammed his heels into the mare's sides and galloped away. He spent the rest of the day alone, wondering what he'd done to offend Tall Grass and missing George and Micah.

Late in the day, he startled a pair of deer out of a wash and sent them bounding across the prairie. He brought the first one down easily, had his sights on the second, when he decided against it. Without a packhorse, he had no way of transporting both animals back to camp. Heaving the gutted doe over the mare, he collected the reins, and set off on foot, following the cloud of dust.

Tendrils of smoke drifting on the evening air led him to the camps just as the sun was setting. He waved off a group of boys who rode to meet him and made his way to Tall Grass' lodge, hoping to exchange the deer for dinner and company.

He found her lodge empty. Thinking she was bound to return soon, he waited. Minutes stretched, and as darkness descended, he gave up. He hadn't gone far when he saw her walking toward him, carrying Girl Who Laughs against her shoulder. She saw him, appeared to hesitate, then came on.

"Hello," he said, waiting for her to come to him.

"Hello," she responded, not meeting his eye.

He turned to walk with her. "I was hoping to trade the deer for dinner."

She glanced at him. "Now not good time."

"What do you mean? You said the same thing four nights ago, and you've avoided me ever since. Have I done something to make you angry?"

"Not angry," she said, stopping before her lodge. "Now not good time."

"What's wrong, Tall Grass?"

"Nothing wrong." She pulled open the door flap. "Now not—"

"I know," Ethan interrupted crossly. "Now's not a good time. When will it be a good time, Tall Grass?"

He'd raised his voice; Girl Who Laughs whimpered in her sleep. Tall Grass placed a foot inside and looked at him, appearing to waiver. Then she said softly, "Never good time, I think."

Before Ethan could react, she ducked inside, pulling the flap closed behind her.

"Tall Grass!" Ethan very nearly followed her. He had the flap part way open before he stopped himself. "Ha-ssta-mo-i-i," he said, softly. "Please talk to me.

Tell me what's wrong." He listened intently, but there was no sound from inside the lodge.

Never good time. He stood there, trying to figure out what he'd done to offend her. Nothing he could think of, unless he'd inadvertently violated some Cheyenne custom he knew nothing about.

He let out a long breath and lowered the flap. Micah and George were gone. There was no one he felt comfortable asking, so it would have to wait. Frustrated and hurt, he scooped up Faria's reins and headed for Plum Moon's lodge.

Plum Moon and Singing Bird looked up, startled, when he flung open the flap and stepped into the lodge. "There's a deer outside," he told them brusquely, making the signs and pointing. "What do you want done with it?"

He stepped aside, allowing Plum Moon to go out past him. She saw the deer and called to Singing Bird. The girl sidled past, watching him from beneath lowered lids. Ethan ignored her. He dropped the mare's saddle near his sleeping robe and looked around, thinking how familiar the lodge had become. He'd begun to think of it as home. *Until now.* On the heels of the argument with Micah and rejection by Tall Grass, he once again felt out of place.

Ethan sighed and shook his head. He wanted desperately to talk to someone. *Tall Grass.* It was her company he wanted more than anything. *Out of the question. For the time being, anyway.*

His eyes settled on the iron pot beside the fire, and he realized he was hungry. Squatting next to it, he fished around with his fingers, digging out chunks of boiled meat. When he'd eaten all there was, he stripped off his leggings and flopped down on his sleeping robe. He was still awake when the women came in. In no mood to attempt conversation, he pretended to sleep.

***

"Ha-ssta-mo-i-i. Please talk to me. Tell me what's wrong." Her heart thumped painfully, and she felt the sting of tears when she heard him say her name in her own language. He was pleading with her, and she wanted desperately to respond, but she forced herself to stand silent, eyes riveted on the faint glow from the partially open door flap. If he followed her inside, she knew her resolve would crumble. She waited, scarcely breathing, hoping he would.

After what seemed a long time, the flap gently closed, and she heard the soft thud of the mare's hooves in the dirt. A few seconds, and he would be gone. Tall Grass sucked in a great breath of air, fighting the urge to go after him, to call him back. Instead, she turned from the door, and in the darkness, made her way to her sleeping robe. She lowered her daughter onto it, provoking a sleepy whimper of protest as she pulled off the little girl's dress. Tall Grass stripped off her own dress and leggings and settled next to her, feeling terribly alone.

AUGUST

12

Ambitious, a proponent of statehood, and intent on becoming one of the state's first senators, Colorado Territorial Governor John Evans had spent the winter convinced that, come spring, the plains tribes would rise in an all-out war against the whites. His goal was to see the Indians defeated, Colorado territory free of hostiles, and his political ambitions secure. That the uprising failed to materialize did little to deter him. In June, prior to his proclamation to the friendly Indians, Governor Evans sent the first of a series of requests to the War Department in Washington, requesting permission to raise a regiment of hundred-day volunteers to attack and kill hostiles.

In the weeks following the death of Starving Bear, Cheyenne warriors attacked the one hundred and fifty-mile stretch of road between Fort Larned and Fort Riley, sacking ranches and driving off stock. A man was killed at Cow Creek ranch, and at Walnut Creek station, warriors warned the station keeper to leave before departing with his Cheyenne wife. The Arapaho warriors that rode out after Left Hand was fired on at Fort Larned, traveled west along the Arkansas, running off stock from Point of Rocks, south of Fort Lyon.

As raiding began along the Overland Road, the violence spread. On the twenty-fourth of July, Indians besieged four emigrant trains near Salina, Kansas. Two weeks later, and forty miles to the west, warriors killed four buffalo hunters and attacked a ranch. Further north, wagon trains were attacked on the Little Blue River in southern Nebraska. The next day, a horse herd was driven off from Salina.

The bloodiest single day of raiding came on August eighth. Two white men were killed when wagon trains were attacked and burned east of Fort Kearny, Nebraska. Trains were attacked at Plum Creek Station, and fourteen men died; women and children were taken captive. At the Little Blue settlements in northern Kansas, more women and children were taken, and fifteen men killed.

On subsequent days, a wagon train was attacked and burned forty-five miles west of Fort Kearny. Four soldiers were slain west of Salina. A man and a boy died at Running Creek, south of Denver. Further south, emigrant trains were attacked near Cimarron Crossing, leaving ten white men dead. Telegraph wires were cut; ranches and all but one stage station burned. The last stagecoach to reach Denver arrived on August fifteenth. From then until the twenty-fourth of August, Indians controlled the Platte River Road, sealing off east from west.

On August eleventh, without bothering to notify the friendly Indians that he was voiding his earlier proclamation, Governor Evans, issued a second: "Having sent special messengers to the Indians of the plains, directing the friendly to rendezvous... for safety and protection, warning them that all hostile Indians would be pursued and destroyed... the evidence being conclusive that most of the Indian tribes of the plains are at war and hostile to the whites, and having to the utmost of my ability endeavored to induce all of the Indians of the plains to come to said places of rendezvous, promising them subsistence and protection, which, with few exceptions, they have refused to do...[I authorize] all citizens of Colorado, either individually or in such parties as they may organize, to go in pursuit of all hostile Indians... also to kill and destroy, as enemies of the county... all such hostile Indians. And further as the only reward I am authorized to offer... I hereby empower such citizens... to take captive, and hold to their own private use and benefit, all the property of said hostile Indians..."

On the day Governor Evans issued his second proclamation, he received permission from the War Department to raise a militia of one hundred-day volunteers.

* * *

"Ethan!"

Ethan pulled the mare to a stop and turned in the saddle, scanning the dusty, sun-baked sprawl of the camp for the source of the familiar voice.

"When'd you get back?" he asked, as George rode to meet him.

"A couple days ago." George tilted his head toward the two burdened packhorses. "Been hunting?"

"With Ed and Julie. We've been gone a couple weeks."

"Where 'bouts?"

"Up north. The Red Shield River."

"Lotta of buffalo up there."

"Yeah. Too bad you and Micah weren't here to go with us."

Ethan turned the mare, and George fell in beside him.

"We're here now. We'll go again."

Ethan looked around sharply. "Micah's back?"

George nodded. "The war party he was with came in yesterday." After a brief pause, he added, "He got himself a couple more horses to offer for Yellow

Leaf. Plum Moon took them to her parents' lodge this morning. If they accept them, Micah'll be getting married."

Ethan digested the news in silence. Eventually he said, "That'll change things."

"Not much, I'd think."

"For me it will. It's because of Micah I'm living in Plum Moon's lodge. Without him..." Ethan shook his head. "Things tend to get awkward when he's not around." He glanced at George. "Singing Bird, and all."

"If that's what's worrying you, come stay with us. It's just Charley and me, with Julie and my stepmothers looking out after us."

Ethan offered him a grateful smile. "I will, if you mean it."

"I do."

"It's probably a good idea anyway. Micah and I had words before he left. We didn't part on very good terms."

"Micah's hot-headed, but he gets over it quick. My guess is, he's forgotten by now."

Ethan wasn't entirely convinced. "I hope so."

Plum Moon's lodge was deserted when they reached it. The covers, rolled up against the heat, revealed the stolen goods heaped within. Noting them with disgust, Ethan swung down from the mare. He unhooked a fringed buckskin case containing the Spencer from his saddle and held it up for George to see.

"From Julie. She made me a shirt, too."

"She's handy at that sort of thing."

"I got to know her better over the last couple weeks. I like her. She loaned me a pony to hunt."

Ethan began loosening the packs on one of the horses. George dismounted and started on the second. They worked together, hauling hides and dried meat into the lodge. It was hot, sweaty work, and Ethan had no sooner finished, than he peeled off his leggings. George released the horses and stepped inside the lodge, using one arm, then the other to wipe the sweat from his face.

"I hear tell there's a white woman in one of the camps," he said. "I was headed off to find her when I spotted you. You interested in coming along?"

Ethan looked at him in surprise. "A white woman? Here?"

The camp was a sprawling one, spread for miles along the Solomon River in northwestern Kansas—bands of Cheyenne, Dog Soldiers, Arapaho, Brulé and Oglala Sioux camped close together. War parties came and went, drums pounded, bloody scalps hung from lodge poles and lances, and lodges were filled to bursting with plunder. It was no place for a white woman.

"She was taken a couple weeks back, up along the Platte. The group Micah was with."

Ethan's expression hardened. "Micah had a hand in kidnapping a woman?"

"He was with the group that took her. I don't know his part in it."

"Where is she?"

"Cut Face's lodge. White Antelope's band. You wanna come along?"

Ethan shrugged. "I guess so. Sure. What are you planning to do?"

"Find out who she is. See if she needs anything."

There were two women sitting outside the lodge, a girl and her mother. George spoke briefly with them before indicating to Ethan that they should go in. The covers were down, despite the heat, and the air inside was stifling. The woman was lying on one of two pallets. She shrank away when George and Ethan stepped through the door, her eyes wide with fear, swollen and red from crying. Her dark hair was dirty and matted, the dress she wore in tatters, stained with dirt and dried blood. She tugged at it, trying without success to attain some degree of modesty. The flesh the torn garment revealed was scraped and bruised and blistered with sunburn. Ethan gaped in horror, then quickly averted his eyes.

George stepped forward. A moan of fear escaped her, and he stopped. "My name's George Bent, ma'am," he said softly. "I'd like to talk to you."

The woman let out a sob of relief. "You're a white man?" she whispered, not daring to hope.

"Half white," George said. "Mind if I come closer?"

The woman hesitated, eyes flicking between George and Ethan. She bit her bruised bottom lip and nodded uncertainly.

"Only you!" she cried in panic as they both stepped toward her. "Not him! Keep him away from me! Please."

Ethan stared at her in disbelief.

"It's all right ma'am," George assured her. "He don't mean any harm. He's half white, same as me." He threw Ethan a meaningful look.

Ethan looked from George to the woman. "Ma'am," he said, with a slight tip of his head.

She eyed him apprehensively before her eyes swiveled back to George.

"Is it all right if we come closer, ma'am?"

Her teeth worked the bloodied lower lip. After a moment, she nodded. Her eyes moved back and forth between them as they approached.

George sank down at the foot of her pallet, and Ethan hunkered down next to him. Up close, he was surprised to see how young she was. Her face was pinched and gaunt, her complexion sallow beneath bruises and peeling sunburn. Sweat beaded her brow and upper lip, and droplets hung from the fine hairs along her temples.

"What's your name?" George asked.

"Morton," she whispered, eyes darting nervously between them. "Nancy Jane Morton." Her eyes brimmed with tears. "Please help me."

"Can you tell me what happened, Miss Morton?"

"We..." The fingers of her right hand clutched at the torn bodice of her dress and she trembled. "My husband and I... my brother... my cousin John. Our three wagons and nine others. They came on us west of Plum Creek Station. When I saw it was Indians, I jumped off our wagon, but a wheel hit me and knocked me down. I saw William and John killed down by the creek. And they shot me." Her left hand moved down the bloodied side of her dress, lingering below her ribs before moving to her left thigh. "I had two arrows in me." She choked on a sob, and tears overflowed. "The men... They scalped them right in front of me!"

Ethan looked at George in horror, but George's eyes remained fixed on Nancy Morton's face. She slowly regained her composure, wiping her eyes with her fingers.

"They plundered the wagons... ripped apart my bed... feathers all across the prairie. My trunks..." Another sob shook her. "After they set fire to the wagons, they put little Danny and me on horses. Made us ride for days. There was nothing to eat but raw meat. They..." Her voice broke. She buried her face in her hand, and her shoulders shook. "They did terrible things."

"What can we do to make you more comfortable, Mrs. Morton?"

"I..." She shook her head. Lowering her hand, she looked at him. "My ribs," she said. "I think I broke some ribs when the wagon hit me. And where the arrows were... I had to pull them out myself. Please. I've been so ill. Can you fetch a doctor?"

"Not a doctor exactly, but I'll see someone tends to you. What about the other person you mentioned—little Danny?"

Nancy Morton drew a shuddering breath and shook her head. "I don't know." Her look turned cautiously hopeful. "Please. Can you find out what happened to him? He's only eight."

"I'll do what I can, Mrs. Morton."

George got to his feet, Ethan with him, and Nancy Morton's face crumpled.

"Don't leave me," she pleaded, reaching up an imploring hand. "Please."

"I'll be back," George assured her. "In the meantime, I'll see you're looked after."

He started away, then turned back. "Try not to cry, Mrs. Morton. You'll find you're treated better if you don't cry." With a brief smile, he ducked out of the lodge.

Ethan took a last look at her stricken face and hurried after him. He caught up after a few steps and grabbed George by the arm, pulling him around. "You can't just leave her!"

"There's nothing I can do. She belongs to Cut Face."

"Belongs?" Ethan repeated incredulously. "You don't mean that?"

George's expression hardened. "Those two packhorses? You captured them; they belong to you. Cut Face captured Mrs. Morton. She belongs to him."

"But she's a person!"

"It doesn't matter, Ethan. The sooner you accept that, the better off you'll be. The only way I can take Mrs. Morton from Cut Face is to buy her. Even if I had the horses, I don't care to be saddled with a white woman."

Ethan opened his mouth to argue.

"Accept it, Ethan. It's the way it is."

"I won't accept it," Ethan told him angrily. "I've been in her position. I know what it's like."

"I'll see she's looked after," George said, making an effort to control his temper. "It's the best I can do."

"That's not good enough, George. She's a woman. Where I come from, women aren't treated like that."

"Really?" George's eyebrows arched. "You telling me you never knew any of your fine Yankee boys to steal from a Southern woman? Rape her? Burn her home? How's this different?"

"She's a prisoner, George. She's at their mercy. You wouldn't know about that because your brother rescued you. But I... They did things to me..." Ethan's voice faltered. He swallowed hard, and looked away. "Things like that shouldn't happen to a woman."

George regarded his profile before replying. "I'll see she's looked after. Let her know she's not alone. Now, if you've got the backbone for it, let's see if we can find the boy."

Ethan glared at him. George stared back. Ethan was the first to look away. "It's wrong," he insisted.

"It's the way it is."

It didn't take long to discover where young Danny Marble was being held. In the course of his questioning, George learned there were three more white captives scattered among the Cheyenne, one with a band of Sioux, and another with a band of Arapaho. Ethan went with him to the far reaches of the camps, staring into the terrified eyes of two women and a little girl, and watching the brave face Danny Marble put on as he tried to hide his fear. By the time they left the last little boy, in one of the far-flung Cheyenne camps, Ethan's initial horror had long since turned to outrage.

They made their way back along the river, tension running high between them. At one of the camps they passed, a war party had recently returned, and the women were busily picking through the shattered remnants of people's lives. Boots, shoes, dresses, coats, petticoats, canned goods, bolts of fabric, and sacks of grain, flour, sugar and coffee were scattered throughout the camp. Drunken men strutted about, their lances hung with clumps of hair, wearing everything from shirts and shawls to women's bonnets.

Ethan threw George a blazing look. George's expression challenged him to say something. Ethan bit back comment, and they rode on in silence.

Micah was standing before Plum Moon's lodge when they came in sight of it. He had released the gray, and was leaning down to pick up his saddle, when he spotted them. A grin spread over his face; he let the saddle sink to the ground and strode to meet them. The grin faded when he saw their expressions.

"What's wrong?"

"Did you have fun?" Ethan snapped. "Was it *fun* killing people and kidnapping women and children so you'd have horses to buy a bride?"

Anger flared in Micah's eyes.

George leaned over and grabbed Ethan's arm. "That's enough!"

Ethan was not about to be deterred. He shook off George's hand and jumped down from the mare. "Did you rape her, Micah, or is that where you draw the line?"

Micah let out an angry snarl and lunged at him, catching Ethan below the ribs and knocking him to the ground. They rolled in the dirt, grunting and cursing and grappling for the upper hand. Everyone in sight came running, and as the commotion grew, more people joined them, shouting encouragement and wagering on the outcome.

In strength, they were an even match, but Micah was heavier. It wasn't until they were both gasping with exhaustion that he was able to pin Ethan face down in the dirt, one arm twisted behind his back.

"Take it back," he panted. "Take it back or I break your goddamn arm."

Ethan squirmed beneath him. Micah pressed down harder.

His anger spent, fighting for breath, Ethan quit struggling. "Did you do it?" he gasped, turning his face out of the dirt.

"Do what?" Micah demanded furiously, his breath rasping in Ethan's ear. "Rape her? No."

"Any of it."

"Yes," Micah said, forcing Ethan's arm to the point where he yelped in pain. "Is that what you wanna hear? I killed a man. His scalp was mine to take, so I took it. I took what I wanted from the wagons, and mules to carry it, but I had nothing to do with the woman. Now, are you gonna take it back, or do I break your arm?"

"Take it back," Ethan gasped.

With a final upward thrust, Micah let go, pushing himself back on his heels and wiping an arm across his forehead. Shouts of approval erupted from those who'd backed him, and wagers changed hands. As quickly as they'd assembled, the spectators began to disperse.

Ethan shifted beside him, bringing his left arm around painfully before pushing himself into a sitting position.

"Damn near broke it anyway," Micah muttered. When Ethan didn't respond, he said, "What the devil set you off?" He looked at George. "What the... ?"

George motioned him to silence and held out a hand. Micah took it and was pulled to his feet.

"Ethan."

Ethan looked at George's outstretched hand. A moment later, he was standing beside them.

"I'm sorry," he said, not looking at Micah. "I was wrong to say it."

"Damn right you were. Say anything like that ever again and it'll be more than your arm gets broke." Micah turned on his heel and stalked away.

Rubbing his strained shoulder, Ethan watched him go. "I doubt he'll get over it this time."

"Can't say as I blame him. But knowing Micah, he probably will. " George turned on Ethan then, giving vent to the anger he'd held in check all afternoon. "Micah was right, Ethan! You deserved to have that arm broke. You've been spoiling for a fight ever since we left Cut Face's lodge. Whatever your problem is, you'd no call to accuse Micah."

"You're right," Ethan agreed, refusing to meet his eyes. "I was wrong. I'm sorry."

"Mrs. Morton belongs to Cut Face. If he raped her, it's his right. It's time you understood that. And you need to get out of your head it's only Indians to blame here. There's plenty of Cheyenne women been raped by whites."

"I—"

"No!" George cut him off. Eyes blazing, he leveled a finger at Ethan. "You hear me out! You made it real clear today how much you disapprove. If our ways offend you so much, get out! Go to the Sioux. See if they meet with your approval. Or go back and take your chances with the whites. After today, I don't much care what you do. But I'm telling you, if you stay, you'll find life a whole lot easier if you accept our ways. Quit holding us up to whatever glorified picture of white society you're carrying in your head. You, of all people, should know better!

"And while you're at it, keep in mind that, since spring, Cheyenne people have been shot at and killed. Their possessions have been stolen and their lodges burned. Now the tables are turned, and the same thing's happening to whites. You may not approve, but that's the way it is."

George started away, then stopped and looked back. "You wanna do good for those women and children? Come with me next time I go see them. *If* you're still around." He snatched his horse's reins, and flinging himself into the saddle, wheeled the animal and set off at a gallop.

Ethan stared after him. Everything George had said was true. For three months he'd trod the line between two worlds, embracing all that was good about the Cheyenne way of life, while condemning everything his white sensibilities perceived as bad. It had been safer than acknowledging that their actions might be justified; safer to think of the people he still considered his own as victims, not the Cheyenne.

Ethan tilted his head back and closed his eyes. To acknowledge what he knew to be true would move him a step closer to taking the Cheyenne side in an escalating war he wanted nothing to do with.

"Ee-tin?"

The voice was the last one he wanted to hear. "What?" he demanded, whirling on her.

Singing Bird's face fell. The vi-hoi words she'd planned to say flew from her head. She turned and fled.

Ethan ran a hand through his hair, regretting his rudeness. He considered going after her, but decided against it. An apology of any sort was bound to be misconstrued.

He looked at the mare, reins trailing as she pulled at clumps of dried grass. As he walked to her, her head came up, and she nickered. Ethan collected the reins and flung an arm over her neck, pressing his forehead against her smooth coat.

There was no point in talking to Micah until he'd cooled down. *Not until morning anyway*. The only other person he wanted desperately to talk to was Tall Grass, but that was out of the question. Ethan considered going to her anyway. *Maybe enough time has passed...*

The mare arched her head around, nibbling at his fingers with velvety lips. Ethan smiled in spite of himself. She was the one constant in his life, the only one he could absolutely count on. "Faria, miṫakola," he said moving to her head. Faria, my friend. He scratched between her ears, murmuring nonsense, while he thought about what he should do.

His leggings, blanket and saddlebags were on the pallet where he'd left them. Ethan collected the Spencer and stuffed some dried meat into the saddlebags. He knew Plum Moon was watching, but he avoided her gaze. She said something as he left, but he pretended not to hear.

He rode until sundown, stopping when he came to a shallow depression where the grass was lush and green, and a thicket of plum, willow and half a dozen cottonwoods grew. Near its center, along a mere trickle of a stream, water pooled invitingly before seeping into the porous rock below.

Ethan dismounted a short distance from the pond, pulled his belongings from the mare's back, and turned her loose. She drifted into the green grass and began feeding hungrily. Ethan stripped to the cord around his waist and wandered over to the pond. The water wasn't deep, reaching barely to his knees, but it was enough that he could lay back and submerge his entire body. After the unrelenting heat, the cool water closing over his head was heaven. Tomorrow he would go back and make apologies all around, but tonight he would relax and enjoy the solitude.

He built a small, smoky fire with green willow branches to ward off the black swarm of mosquitoes that rose from the grass and followed him from the pond. The handful of plums he picked whetted his appetite, and he felt around in his saddlebags for a piece of dried meat. Instead, his fingers closed around the book.

Ethan pulled it out, turning it over in his hands and gazing guiltily at the title. It had been weeks since he last opened it. Turning to the inscription, he read what Elizabeth had written. For the first time, the words failed to move him.

It's time, he told himself. *Time and distance. Things are so different here. When I go back, when we're together again, everything will be the same.* He closed the book, holding the place with his finger, and lay back on his blanket, summoning Elizabeth's image. The delicate, heart-shaped face slipped away almost immediately, replaced by the sculpted beauty of Tall Grass.

He had tried, once more, to talk to her after the night with the deer, but she'd rebuffed him. He had retreated, baffled and hurt, and made do with watching her from a distance. Just as he'd begun to think he couldn't bear it any longer, they'd arrived at Turkey Creek," and Julie had invited him to hunt. He'd leapt at the offer. With a last, lingering look at Tall Grass, he'd ridden away, determined to put her out of his mind.

It wasn't as easy as he'd hoped. No matter how busy he kept himself, thoughts of her crept in. One was no sooner banished, than another replaced it. The day they turned back toward Turkey Creek, the tingle of anticipation that ran through him confirmed that nothing had changed. Tall Grass had bewitched him from the start. He was obsessed with her. All he wanted was to be with her. Each day, as the distance between them grew less, his excitement mounted. When they finally reached the camps, he scanned faces eagerly, searching for her. He knew in his heart he would have gone to her if George hadn't intercepted him.

It's not right, he thought, mentally shaking himself. *I made a promise to Elizabeth.*

A mosquito buzzed past his face, and Ethan swatted at it. He sat up and fed more branches into the fire. Smoke swirled about him, and he settled back, rereading the inscription and reminding himself of all Elizabeth had done for him, of all he'd promised. *I owe it to her to forget Tall Grass.*

Even as he thought it, he knew it was impossible. He was in love with Tall Grass — hopelessly, desperately in love. And he was beginning to resent Elizabeth's hold on him. There'd been a time when he thought he'd loved her, but he knew now he'd been wrong. Gratitude, yes; affection, certainly; but not love. *Not like this.* For the first time, he acknowledged what he'd resisted subconsciously for weeks — he had no desire to return to Mobile.

The last of the light was fading when he returned the book to its place and pulled out a handful of dried meat. The quiet of the prairie surrendered to the symphony of night. Crickets chirped and frogs set up a chorus along the creek. A sudden breeze rustled leaves overhead, and dead branches on one of the cottonwoods clacked together. Nighthawks darted against the darkening sky, their piercing cries reverberating across the prairie. Nearby, an owl hooted. A coyote yipped, and when others joined it, Faria lifted her head, ears cocked. Ethan watched her until she went back to grazing. Then he pulled his blanket around him and rolled down onto his side, wondering how he could ever have thought the prairie an empty, desolate place.

He heard gunfire the next morning when he was still a good distance from the camps. Ethan turned toward it, urging Faria into a canter. Breasting a small rise, he reined her in sharply, looking with dismay at the scene before him.

A company of soldiers had surprised a group of Cheyenne hunters. Several had taken refuge in a dry creek bed, wedging themselves between a cutaway bank and two dead ponies. They lay on their stomachs firing arrows at the soldiers, outnumbered five to one. Three of their comrades lay unmoving on the ground. Half a mile distant, a running battle was taking place between another group of soldiers and a few hunters who'd managed to escape. The Indian ponies were pulling away from the cavalry mounts, but the chase was taking them away from the camps.

Ethan had no sooner taken it all in than the soldiers spotted him. A shout went up, and eight of them broke off their siege of the creek bed and came charging across the prairie toward him. Ethan wheeled the mare and sent her flat out in the direction of Turkey Creek. The soldiers pounded after him. Several hundred yards separated them, and Ethan maintained his lead, out of range of the soldiers' guns, but they fired at him anyway.

As he neared the camps, Ethan began firing too, emptying the Spencer in warning. Topping the last rise above the river valley, he saw mounted warriors streaming toward him. Ethan brought clenched fists together in the sign for soldier. A torrent of warriors exploded past, and he pulled the heaving mare to a stop. Micah was last among them, riding a brown and white pony bareback and leading another.

"Here!" he shouted, holding the reins out to Ethan. "For you!"

Ethan jumped down from the mare, swung onto the pony, and they were off. The soldiers who'd pursued him were fleeing back the way they'd come. Mounted on fresh ponies, the warriors were closing rapidly. First one soldier fell, then another and another until only one remained. A few warriors kept up the pursuit, but most began to turn back.

"No!" Ethan yelled. "Tell them to keep going! They have hunters surrounded!"

Micah spared him only a glance and began shouting. The warriors turned their ponies and raced after the fleeing man.

One look at the hundreds of armed warriors bearing down on them, and the soldiers fled. The howling Indians charged after them.

Ethan left them to it, pulling the pony down to a walk as he approached the embattled group in the creek bed. The rush of adrenaline was wearing off, and with it any thought of firing on soldiers. Besides, he'd emptied the Spencer, and clinging to the back of the galloping pony had given him no opportunity to reload.

He slid to the ground and walked to the body of the nearest packhorse. One of the hunters lay dead across it. Three others were standing in the creek bed, Two Bulls among them. He nodded grimly when he saw Ethan, then looked at the prone man at his feet. Ethan stepped around for a better look and realized with a jolt that the injured man was Red Hand. He lay still as death, blood pooling beneath his head.

Ethan pushed his way to Red Hand's side and laid his fingers against his neck. To his surprise, he felt a strong pulse immediately. Moving carefully, Ethan turned the left side of Red Hand's head out of the dirt. Blood was gushing from a deep groove that ran along his left temple, burying itself in his hairline. Ethan looked up, and his eyes lit on a piece of bright fabric a man called Coyote Tail wore knotted diagonally across his chest.

"Give me that," he said, gesturing.

Coyote Tail looked at him, then at the others. He took a step back.

"Give it to me," Ethan repeated.

Two Bulls muttered, and Coyote Tail untied the fabric and handed it to Ethan.

Ethan used one end to wipe away dirt and blood, then folded it over and laid it against Red Hand's temple, pressing hard with the heal of his hand. Red Hand jerked and muttered and grabbed Ethan's wrist.

"Hold him," Ethan commanded.

Two Bulls squatted and pulled away the hand. Red Hand's eyes fluttered open. They focused, and he looked from Two Bulls to Ethan. He mumbled something, and Two Bulls released his arm and sat back. Red Hand lay unresisting while Ethan kept pressure on the wound. When the bleeding slowed, he wrapped the length of fabric around Red Hand's head and helped him sit up.

Already, the other hunters, and some of their rescuers, had cut packs from the dead ponies and loaded them onto others, including the pony Ethan had been riding. He sighed when he saw it, dreading the long walk back to camp.

He was spared it when a Brulé called to him, offering a hand, and pulled Ethan up behind him. They were almost to the camps when Micah trotted up beside them.

"Were you coming back on your own, or did you get chased?" he asked by way of greeting.

"Both." Ethan touched the Sioux's shoulder. "Pilamayayelo," he said. Thank you. Sliding to the ground, he fell in step beside Micah's pony.

"So you hadn't figured on leaving for good?"

"Just overnight. Thought I'd give things a chance to cool down."

"You mean me."

"I mean both of us. I needed time to think."

Micah rode for several minutes in silence. Without looking at Ethan, he said, "You're wrong, you know. There's plenty in these camps enjoy raping women, but I ain't one of 'em."

"I know. I was angry and took it out on you."

"You sure as hell did." Micah looked down at him. "I meant what I said, Ethan. If you're dead-set on thinking you're white, that's fine by me. Just don't expect me to feel the same. I'm Cheyenne, and I intend to fight for my people. Nothin' you say's gonna change that."

"I understand. It won't happen again."

Micah's gray eyes narrowed. "You come to your senses, or just decide to keep your mouth shut?"

"A little of both, I guess. I've given it a lot of thought. If soldiers attack us, I'll fight. But that's it. You do what you think's right, and I'll keep my opinions to myself."

One corner of Micah's mouth curled up reluctantly. "'Bout time you figured that out." He slid down from the pony and removed the rawhide loop from its lower jaw.

"New horse?"

"Don't know whose it is." Micah slapped the pony on the flank and watched it trot toward the herd. "In an emergency, it's all right to take the first horse you come to, just as long as you remember anything you bring back belongs to its owner."

Ethan nodded, reminded of the question he'd been waiting to ask. He told Micah what had happened with Tall Grass.

"Doesn't sound like you did anything wrong," Micah said. "Want me to talk to her?"

Ethan hesitated, sorely tempted. "No," he said at last. "I don't think so."

Micah looked sidelong at him, but for once, refrained from comment.

SEPTEMBER

13

The key caught momentarily, then turned in the lock, the click echoing along the empty corridor. Edmund Stedman, pardon clerk to Attorney General Edward Bates, let himself into his office, stifling a yawn as his eyes lit on the papers littering his desk. They were the reason he was back at such an early hour. Through the windows, he could see trees standing dark against the faint bluing of the eastern sky. It was barely six hours since he'd left, but the papers' contents had nagged at him, keeping him from sleep. He hung his hat on the hook behind the door and moved about the room, lighting lamps, before settling behind his desk.

It was his job to sift through transcripts of courts-martial, the often wordy and occasionally scathing opinions written by commanding generals, the pleading letters from distraught parents, wives and children, and see to it that only the most deserving cases were passed on to the Attorney General and Judge Advocate General Holt. In Stedman's reading of this particular transcript, the proceedings had appeared straightforward, the verdict correct. All the evidence pointed to the private's guilt. The tersely worded missive from the headquarters of the Army of the Cumberland, alerting the Judge Advocate General to the prisoner's escape, had confirmed it.

It wasn't until he started through the letters that Stedman had begun having second thoughts. The appeal from the young man's advocate had been predictable, if more impassioned than usual. The letters from the men Private Fraser had served with were equally ardent, but offered little beyond a rehash of their testimony. The pleas from the father, brother, and sister might have tugged at his heartstrings if he hadn't read hundreds just like them over the course of the war. It wasn't until he read the letter from the lieutenant who'd served as a member of the Court that he'd begun to have doubts. The one from the illiterate Sioux mother, and the other from Mrs. Magrath, had caused him to stop and reconsider.

The mother's letter, written by another hand, with a scrawled, child-like signature at the bottom of the second page, had captured his attention in a way few such letters did. Unlike other mothers, she had not begged for mercy for her son. Instead, she described her son's upbringing, listing his faults as well as his virtues. The letter rang with her utter conviction that he would never have committed the acts of which he had been convicted. Seeing Ethan Fraser through his mother's eyes, Stedman was inclined to agree.

The letter from Mrs. Magrath convinced him. He was familiar with her parents' name; prominent in banking for more than half a century, mention of one or the other of them appeared frequently in the financial and society notices in New York's newspapers, even rating occasional mention in Washington's *National Intelligencer*. In his estimation, Elizabeth Magrath's pedigree was beyond reproach, and she corroborated every claim to innocence Private Fraser had made.

Stedman skimmed both letters again before sifting through papers; searching for notes he'd made the night before. He jotted down several more; convinced the verdict was unjust.

As he finished, he became aware of sounds from other parts of the building; footsteps echoed along corridors, voices seeped through the walls from adjoining offices. Stedman looked up to discover that morning had arrived. From his desk, he had a limited view of the Executive Mansion half a block away. The sky above it was eggshell blue, mottled by a scattering of broken clouds. It was the first day of September, and the breeze-tossed leaves would soon begin to turn. All too soon, another Washington winter would be upon them.

Stedman glanced toward the sound of voices coming from the Attorney General's office and began setting his desk in order. In doing so, he came across an unopened envelope. Leaning back in his chair, he ran a finger under the seal. His eyebrows rose when he saw who it was from. By the time he reached the bottom of the page, he was sitting forward, rigidly erect.

Taking the transcript and the four letters with him, Stedman headed for Bates' office. If the President of the Court disagreed so strongly with the verdict that he'd been moved to write, it was imperative that the Attorney General recommend disapproval of the sentence to President Lincoln. No matter that, at the moment, no one appeared to have the slightest idea where Private Ethan Fraser might be.

***

The roar that erupted from the throats of nearly seven hundred painted warriors was enough to raise the hackles of the dead. It crossed Ethan's mind that, by now, he should be used to it. The thought was swept away as the line of soldiers began to advance. The howls intensified; the warriors strained forward, a heaving mass of men and horses held in check by an invisible barrier.

The soldiers, in battle formation with their wagons circled behind them, rode to within two hundred yards of where the head chiefs waited, resplendent in their finest regalia. There they halted, insignificant in the face of so many.

Off to one side, with Micah and the Crooked Lances, Ethan did a quick count. Close to a hundred soldiers, he figured, along with the interpreter John Smith and the three hostages. Chief Lone Bear, his wife and another man were being held behind the officers near the center of the line. The fourth hostage, Eagle Head, had been released from Fort Lyon and arrived in camp the day before, bearing word that the white soldiers, lead by Major Wynkoop, the commandant from Fort Lyon, were on their way in response to the chiefs' letter.

The center of the line parted, and Chief Lone Bear rode forward. The noise level dropped. Lone Bear held his pony to a walk across the open expanse between the two groups. He reached the chiefs and disappeared from view as warriors encircled them. The two sides eyed each other, waiting.

"What do you think'll happen?" Micah shouted to be heard above the commotion.

Ethan shook his head, eyes fixed on the troopers. "I don't know. They're either real brave or real stupid to ride in here like this."

"They must want the prisoners real bad."

"Real bad," Ethan agreed.

Nearly two weeks had passed since George and Ed had been summoned to a council of the chiefs and asked to write identical letters, one to the commanding officer at Fort Lyon, the other to Indian Agent Colley. The chiefs had dictated, and afterwards George had relayed the letters' contents to Micah and Ethan:

"We have received a letter from Bent, wishing us to make peace. We held a council in regard to it; all came to the conclusion to make peace with you, providing you make peace with the Kiowas, Comanches, Arapahoes, Apaches, and Sioux. We are going to send a messenger to the Kiowas and to the other nations about our going to make peace with you. We heard that you have some prisoners at Denver; we have some prisoners of yours which we are willing to give up, providing you give up yours. There are three war parties out yet, and two of the Arapahoes; they have been out some time and expected in soon. When we held this council there were a few Arapahoes and Sioux present. We want true news from you in return. This is a letter."¹²

Lone Bear and his wife had taken George's letter, and Eagle Head had been given Ed's. Together, they had headed south toward Fort Lyon. After they had gone, the combined camps of Cheyenne, Dog Soldiers, Arapaho and Sioux had begun a slow migration toward the headwaters of the Smoky Hill.

As they moved west, the few trees dotting the Kansas prairie all but disappeared. Drought-cracked creek beds were defined by scrub willow and other low-growing shrubs, islands of dusty green in an endless sea of parched yellow grass, dotted with cactus and yucca. The terrain grew more rugged, broken by eroded bluffs and outcroppings of gray-white chalk. As the elevation increased, the nights turned crisp with the first hint of autumn.

"What's that?" Ethan asked one afternoon, squinting at a series of tiny, angular white shapes far out on the western horizon.

"Mah-kho-ho-nĩ-va," Micah told him. "The Rocky Mountains."

"The Rocky Mountains," Ethan repeated, gazing at the distant peaks in awe. "I never figured on seeing them. How far off are they? And why are they white?"

"Snow. They're so high it never melts. Not even in summer. They're a good two days' ride from here, I'd say."

"Two days' ride," Ethan repeated, trying to imagine something so high that it could be seen from such a distance. "Have you ever seen them close up?"

Micah chuckled. "Sure. Lots a' times. Pa's stockade's in the foothills down south. I've hunted 'em all my life, traveled the face all the way to Denver City."

Ethan looked from the distant peaks to Micah. "How much closer will we get?"

"Not much. My guess is, we'll make camp tonight and wait for word from Lone Bear and Eagle Head."

Micah had been right. Here they were, four days later, faced off against a troop of cavalry, waiting to see what happened next. Ethan looked to his right. Far in the distance, the tiny shapes beckoned. *One day,* he thought, *I'll go there.*

Renewed yips and howls signaled Lone Bear's emergence from his council with the chiefs. He rode back at the same leisurely pace, and this time it was

---

12   Signed "Black Kettle and the other Chieves", the letters were dated "August 29,1864, Cheyenne Village"

the troopers and John Smith who encircled him. After what seemed a very long time, the soldiers began to retreat.

A roar went up. The warriors would have surged after them, but the chiefs had anticipated their reaction. They fanned out, urging them back. The majority complied, all but a group of Dog Soldiers who followed the troopers at a distance, hooting and taunting.

"Why are they leaving? I thought they'd come to talk." Ethan looked questioningly at Micah.

Micah shrugged. "Don't know." He turned the gray in the direction of the camps. "It's over for now. You still want to hunt?"

Ethan hesitated, anxious to know the fate of the remaining white captives. Mrs. Morton had vanished, traded away by Cut Face. Another women, a Mrs. Snyder, had hanged herself. But Ethan had made a determined effort to stay in contact with the others. The two boys had been reasonably well treated and were of less concern than Laura Roper and five-year-old Isabel Eubanks. Ethan had begun the day with high hopes of seeing them released, but now the soldiers were retreating, and Black Kettle and the other chiefs were turning toward the camps.

Ethan looked from the soldiers to Micah. "I'm going to find George. See what happened."

"Suit yourself."

Micah nudged the gray and trotted off in the direction of the lodge he shared with Yellow Leaf among the Issio-mé-tan-iu. Ethan cantered past the circled lodges of War Bonnet and Black Kettle's bands, reining in when he came to the lodges of the I-vis-tsi-nih́-pah, Chief Sand Hill's band. Everywhere, women were busy unloading the animals they'd readied in case it became necessary to flee.

Julie was by herself, disassembling a drag. She lowered the poles to the ground as he drew close and smiled fondly. "The soldiers're gone?"

"They rode away. I'm not sure what happened. I was hoping George could tell me."

"He ain't here. Prob'ly with the chiefs. Try the Wú-ta-pi-u camp."

Ethan thanked her and turned back the way he'd come. He hadn't been back to Black Kettle's camp since Micah's marriage. Now he rode slowly toward the next circle of lodges, nervously hoping for a glimpse of Tall Grass. Before he reached them, George came riding toward him.

"The chiefs are meeting with Major Wynkoop tomorrow at the soldiers' camp," he announced. "I'll be going along to help translate."

Accepting the hand Ethan offered, Laura Roper stepped from the lodge. Squinting into the early morning light, she surveyed the mounted Arapaho warriors. Her grip on his hand tightened.

"Will you come with me?" she asked, turning to him with pale, anxious eyes.

Ethan shook his head. "I can't. You'll be safe with Left Hand. And when you get to the camp, the soldiers will look after you."

"But I want you with me," she whispered breathlessly, her eyes tearing for the first time since he'd known her. "Please, Ethan. I'm afraid to go without you."

Her round, baby-face made her look younger than her sixteen years, and now, fighting back tears, she appeared even younger. Ethan felt his resistance crumble. He had spent more time with her than any of the captives, and he'd grown quite fond of her, admiring her courage and resilience. Throughout her ordeal, she'd remained determinedly cheerful and optimistic, earning good treatment from her captors, even as she was traded among them.

But ride into the soldiers' camp...? He looked at George.

George shook his head. "Don't do it, Ethan."

Laura's eyes flicked from George to Ethan and back to George.

"Why not?" she asked. "Why can't he come with me?"

"It won't do for him to go to the soldiers' camp." And to Ethan: "You'd be risking too much. She'll be fine without you."

"Please, Ethan," Laura pleaded, grasping his hand with both of hers.

George saw Ethan waver. "If he's foolhardy enough to go with you, you can't say anything about him. Not his name, or that he's half-white. You do, you risk him getting shot."

Laura looked beseechingly at Ethan. "I promise I won't say a word. Please come with me."

She had been so brave through so much. Ethan wanted to do all he could for her. Even as instinct screamed at him not to go, he drew a breath and nodded. "I'll do it. I'll go with you."

When Lone Bear had returned to the line of cavalry bearing word that Black Kettle and the other chiefs would meet with him in council, Major Wynkoop had taken his men and withdrawn eight miles downriver. The next afternoon, following a protracted meeting with the chiefs, he had removed his troops another twelve miles and settled in to await the return of the captives.

When they came to the place where the council had been held, Left Hand's small band fanned out, riding cautiously. The flat, open prairie, and the dusty tangle of scrub along the creek, provided little opportunity for ambush, but the warriors held their weapons ready. The soldiers' trail was easy to see—grass trampled beneath iron-shod hooves, and the parallel tracks of heavy, iron-wheeled wagons stretched across the hard-baked earth to vanish into the distance.

"What's wrong?" Laura asked as Ethan pulled his bow from its quiver and strung it.

"This is where the soldier's camp was yesterday."

"They left without me?" she asked in a small voice.

"Don't worry. There are scouts watching. We know where they are."

The afternoon sun beat down when the huddle of white tents and wagon covers came into view. Ethan eyed the soldiers' camp with trepidation.

Laura sat forward eagerly. "It's true," she whispered. She turned to Ethan, eyes bright with excitement. "It's true! I am going home! Oh, thank you!"

"You didn't believe it?"

"Not until this moment. After all that's happened, I didn't dare hope." She reached out impulsively and touched his arm. "Thank you, Ethan! Thank you so much!"

"It's not me you should be thanking," Ethan said, eyes riveted on the double line of soldiers trotting toward them across the flat, open ground. "Left Hand bought you so he could bring you back. It's him you should thank."

Laura followed his gaze, her breath coming in quick, excited gasps. Ethan began dropping back.

Laura twisted to look at him. "Ethan... ?"

He offered her a brief smile. "Please don't talk to me again. Good-bye, Mrs. Roper. Have a good life."

He maneuvered his pony away from her, hoping she would keep her promise. He had done all he could to avoid calling attention to himself—he was riding one of Red Hand's ponies with a Cheyenne saddle, and he'd left the Spencer behind, bringing only the bow.

As the soldiers drew near, a shouted command brought them to a halt. A sergeant, accompanied by John Smith, rode forward to meet Left Hand. They conferred briefly before the old chief rode back and spoke to his warriors. His words were met by a murmur of comment. A signal from the sergeant, and the soldiers fanned out, moving to surround them.

Ethan's stomach knotted, his knuckles whitened where they gripped the reins. One of the troopers fell in beside him, another close behind. Ethan looked to his companions, wishing he knew what was going on. The Arapaho warriors were eyeing the troopers and muttering, watchful, but not overly concerned.

Ethan ventured a look at the man beside him. Blue eyes stared at him from a pale, heavily freckled face; a thick, ginger-colored mustache all but obscured the man's upper lip.

The soldier saw him looking, and one eye twitched. "Handsome beggar, ain't he?" he said to the man behind them. "Whadda ya think he'd want for that fancy knife he's wearin'?"

Ethan kept his face blank, not wanting the man to know he'd understood.

The trooper edged his mount closer, reaching out to touch the long hunting knife in the fringed and beaded sheath Ethan wore on his left hip. "Whadda ya want for the knife, Injun?"

For a panicked instant, Ethan had no idea how to respond. "Hiya!" he said in his mother's tongue, signing as he spoke. "Wope watuŋ waciŋśni yelo." No! I don't want to trade.

One of his companions, a man called White Horse, saw what was happening and spoke loudly. Heads turned, and the sergeant bellowed, "Get away from him, Harker!"

The man called Harker glowered at Ethan before yanking his horse's head and moving away. Ethan sighed in relief, but it was to prove short-lived.

Fear rose in him like bile as they entered the soldiers' camp. They were ushered through it, past circled wagons and armed soldiers, to the tent where Major Wynkoop and his officers waited. As they drew to a halt, Left Hand gestured for Laura Roper's pony to be led forward. She twisted to look over her shoulder, but Ethan avoided her eyes.

Left Hand took the reins and spoke to Major Wynkoop. John Smith translated.

"Left Hand says he's brought you the only white prisoner among the Arapaho. Black Kettle sends word to his white brother that he has arranged the purchase of the last of the prisoners in his camps. He hopes to come here with them before sundown tomorrow. There are still three captives in distant camps who have to be located. Black Kettle asks his white brother to understand that to find them, and make trades for them, will take time."

Left Hand spoke to Laura and gestured.

"He says you're free to go, ma'am."

With a sob of relief, Laura Roper leaned into the waiting arms of a lieutenant who stepped forward and lifted her to the ground. A group of officers clustered protectively about her, and she was whisked away.

When they were gone, Major Wynkoop spoke to Left Hand. "You have kept your word today, and we thank you for that. To ensure that Black Kettle also keeps his word, you and your men are to remain as hostages in this camp until he arrives with the other prisoners."

Ethan looked sharply at the major, his heart thudding in panic. He had assumed they would ride in, deliver Laura, and ride out. Confinement, even for a brief period, wasn't something he'd counted on.

Ethan's reaction wasn't lost on John Smith. His eyes narrowed speculatively as he continued to translate.

"As a show of good will, you will be allowed to keep your weapons, but you will be placed under heavy guard. Any man using a weapon against my troops or attempting escape will be shot."

Ethan looked at his companions. They showed no reaction, and it occurred to him that the sergeant had told Left Hand what to expect.

They were escorted to the open-fronted tent where Lone Bear, his wife and the other man were lodged. The two chiefs settled in companionably together, and the warriors hunkered down around them. Ethan sat off to one side, fighting down waves of panic that washed over him each time a soldier's eyes lingered on his face.

The excitement generated by their arrival gradually subsided; the camp settled into the dull routine of waiting. Not a breath of wind stirred to relieve the unseasonable warmth of the afternoon. Scattered groups of soldiers lounged in whatever shade they could find, coats and shirts discarded, the sleeves of their longhandles pushed above their elbows. Flies droned against the steady murmur of voices. A horse stomped and blew loudly. A burst of comment erupted from a group of men playing cards, then died away, replaced by the thud of hooves and the jangle of bit chains as a troop of horsemen trotted past, raising a choking cloud of dust. One man balanced a mirror on a wagon wheel, leaning it against the wagon box to shave. A few read or wrote letters, while others cleaned and oiled their weapons. Whatever his occupation, each man's eyes turned periodically to the hostages.

As the afternoon progressed, Ethan realized that the looks the soldiers gave him held the same curiosity, the same suspicion, the same fear and contempt as the looks leveled at his companions. After a lifetime of being different, it dawned on him that, for once, he didn't stand out. As the realization sank in, he relaxed.

John Smith joined them late in the day. The interpreter sat with the chiefs, and the others wandered over to join them. As they smoked and talked, the sun dipped below the horizon. The temperature dropped, and Lone Bear's wife built up the fire. Off to one side, away from its heat, Ethan pulled his blanket around his shoulders.

It was dark by the time the interpreter left the chiefs and walked to where Ethan sat. He spoke in Cheyenne, a disparaging comment, and chuckled when Ethan failed to react.

"You understand English, but not Cheyenne," he said, lowering himself to the ground. He was a short, sinewy man with a long, clean-shaven face and chiseled features. "I hear from Lone Bear that you're half-Sioux, raised white. What in tarnation're you doing here?"

Ethan eyed him silently.

"No point in not answering, son. Anything I don't know, I can find out."

"Mrs. Roper was afraid. She wanted me to come with her."

The older man nodded. "Fair enough."

"I'd appreciate it if you didn't mention my being here."

Smith's eyes narrowed. "To the major, you mean?"

"To anyone."

"You got something to hide?"

Ethan looked down. "I'd just appreciate it if you wouldn't."

The interpreter squinted at him in the dim light, waiting until Ethan looked up. "It ain't my affair, I reckon, but you'd do well to watch yourself. I saw right off that you understood what the major was saying."

"You did?" Ethan asked, his fear resurfacing.

"Saw it all over your face. Plain as day."

"You think anyone else noticed?"

Smith shrugged "Even if they did, I don't know as it'd matter much. To them you're just another half-breed."

"Even so..."

The other man waved him off. "No point worrying. If Black Kettle's true to his word—and mark you, he will be—you'll be miles from here this time tomorrow." He shifted, preparing to stand. "Say hello to my son if you run across him."

Ethan nodded as Smith got to his feet. As an afterthought, he asked, "Do you know what day it is? The date?"

John Smith ran a hand through thinning hair. "We left Fort Lyon on the sixth of September and traveled north three days. Been here another three. That 'ud make it the twelfth by my reckoning."

He'd had a birthday. He was nineteen. "And the war?" Ethan asked. "Have you had any news of war?"

"Last I heard, Sherman took Atlanta. Long about the first of September."

Atlanta! Ethan's heart leapt. Surely that would mean an end to it.

"Anything else?"

"No, sir. Thank you."

When he had gone, Ethan rolled down into his blanket, thinking about the end of the war and what it would mean, admitting for the first time that he had no intention of leaving the Cheyenne. *Not just yet. Maybe come spring...*

He drifted off to sleep listening to the well-remembered sounds of an army at rest.

* * *

In another enemy camp, hundreds of miles away, Thomas lay atop his blanket, soaked in sweat. The shaking and chills had subsided, and now, at last, the steel grip of the headache was beginning to loosen. Before long, the fever would run its course, and he'd be all right for a few days. Using what little strength he could muster, he raised one arm above his head and turned his face into it, trying to wipe it dry. When the attacks came, he was helpless as a baby, and he hated it.

He'd come down with the shakes soon after word filtered in that Atlanta had fallen. Until then, discounting hangovers, he'd never been sick a day in his life. The first attack had lasted eight hours and left him weak and shaken. It was closely followed by another, and he'd been moved to the hospital tent. His fever was treated with quiniae, the bitter white powder washed down with a shot of whiskey.

Three days had passed without an attack, and he'd hoped for the best, despite knowing what the disease did to other men. Then his fever rose, and he'd been given more quiniae. This attack hadn't been as bad, hadn't lasted as long. He wondered if it was the quiniae. *Or the whiskey?*

A mosquito buzzed past his face. The high-pitched whine stopped as it settled somewhere on his body. Thomas was too weak to raise his head and look for it, much less slap it. A plague of them had risen from the swamps during the past few weeks, and he had more bites than he could count.

What harm will one more do? he thought listlessly, as his eyes closed.

* * *

Cold fear gripped Tall Grass when she heard where Ethan had gone.

"No-da-khi vi-hoi vii-no?" she repeated in disbelief. The white soldier camp? "But it is too dangerous."

"I know." Micah shook his head. "George tried to talk him out of it, but Ethan was friendly with the white woman. She begged him, and he agreed to go."

"What will happen to him?"

"I do not know. Nothing, I hope."

"When will they return?"

Dusk was settling across the prairie. Micah stared at a distant line of gray hills. "The scouts say they are being held at the soldiers' camp. To ensure Black Kettle brings the other captives."

Tall Grass bit her lip, turning away before Micah could see the water that filled her eyes. "You will tell me when you hear he is safe?"

Micah looked at her. "You care for him."

Not trusting her voice, Tall Grass nodded.

"He has not said it, but he has feelings for you, too. Why did you drive him away?"

Tall Grass turned, and Micah saw the suffering in her eyes.

"He made a promise to a white woman. He will honor it. There is no place in his life for me."

"Have you told him how you feel?"

Tall Grass shook her head. "It is best not to."

"I do not agree. Tell him how you feel. Perhaps he will stay."

Tall Grass didn't reply. She gathered her blanket about her and stared across the darkening prairie.

"We will wait for him to return before we leave for Trinidad."

Tall Grass gave him a look of profound gratitude. "You will tell me when you hear he is safe?"

Micah nodded. "You should talk to him, Tall Grass," he repeated before walking away.

Tall Grass barely slept that night, coming awake at every sound, real or imagined. Up at dawn, she went about her work with only half a mind to what she was doing. She saw Black Kettle's small band of warriors depart with the three children, and after that, time slowed to a crawl. The sun had reached its zenith and started down the other side of the sky when she gave up all pretense of work. Delivering Girl Who Laughs into the care of an aunt, she saddled her pony and rode out to watch for riders.

It was late when she saw them coming; a stirring of dust far to the south, then riders cresting a distant rise before vanishing from view. She trained her eyes on the place where they would reappear. As the riders drew closer, the figures more distinct, she strained to catch sight of Ethan. For the longest time, she was unable to pick him out, and her chest tightened with dread, certain something had gone wrong and the soldiers had put him in their prison. Then, suddenly, there he was, riding beside Red Hand, his hair blowing loose in the breeze.

Tall Grass stood in her stirrups, her heart bursting with joy. Then, overcome with uncertainty, she settled back. She would have turned her pony, forcing herself to be content with the knowledge that he was safe, but Ethan picked that moment to break away from the others. Urging his pony into a canter, he closed the distance between them.

Ethan had been unable to believe his eyes when he recognized the lone rider; his only thought had been to go to her. As he drew near, he pulled his pony down to a walk, unsure what to expect.

"Tall Grass?" he said as he came to a stop before her. He was dismayed when she turned her pony and started away. Trotting up beside her, he grasped her by the arm. "Ha-ssta-mo-i-i?"

She looked at him, and Ethan was shocked to see tears in her eyes. "I'm sorry," he said, releasing her. "I didn't mean to hurt you."

"Not hurt," she said softly, lowering her eyes.

"Then why... ?"

A tear rolled down her cheek. She brushed it away with the heel of her hand and looked at him. "I am worry, you going to white soldier camp. I thinking they put you in room with no sun."

"There's no need for worry, Ha-ssta-mo-i-i." He smiled encouragingly. "I'm back. Nothing bad happened."

She dropped her eyes and said nothing.

Ethan watched her anxiously for several seconds before blurting, "I've missed you, Ha-ssta-mo-i-i. Can we please talk?"

"I missing you, too."

"But you... I thought I'd made you angry."

"No," she said softly. "Not angry."

"Then why did you send me away?"

She looked up, and he saw the anguish in her eyes. "Is too hard, seeing you. I liking you too much. But now I missing you too much."

Ethan could only stare at her. This wasn't at all what he'd expected.

The ponies had come to a stop of their own accord, at the edge of a steeply cut bank bordering a shallow wash. Ethan looked around. Assured they were alone, he slid to the ground and reached up a hand to Tall Grass.

"Can we talk, Ha-ssta-mo-i-i? Please?"

She dismounted, and together they slid down the bank. Tall Grass settled with her back to it, tucking her legs up beside her. Ethan sank down on one leg, the other tight against his chest. Breaking off a blade of dry grass, he toyed with it. They avoided each other's eyes, sitting in awkward silence until Tall Grass spoke.

"You telling me you go white home, to white wife. Is not good, my feeling for you."

"I have feelings for you, too, Ha-ssta-mo-i-i." Ethan looked up to find her watching him. "Very strong feelings for a long time."

"What feelings?"

Ethan took a deep breath. "I care for you very much. I want to be with you."

Tall Grass looked away. "You not go white home?"

Ethan didn't answer immediately. He concentrated on the piece of grass, breaking it into tiny pieces. The feelings she stirred in him were unlike any he'd ever experienced. All he wanted was to be with her. He dropped the bits of grass and pushed a hand through his hair before looking at her. "I'll be honest, Ha-ssta-mo-i-i. I don't know what I should do. I made a promise, and I feel honor bound to keep it. I always figured on going home if it turned out I could. I just never figured on falling in love with you."

Tall Grass looked up, hungry eyes searching his face. "You loving me?"

Ethan nodded. It was more than he'd meant to say, but now that the words were out, he had no desire to take them back.

"So you loving me and loving white wife?"

"She's not my wife, Tall Grass."

"But you promise her."

Ethan looked down, then back up at her. "Yes. I promised."

"So now you wanting Tsi-tsí-tas wife and white wife."

"No!" he said sharply. Drawing a breath, he softened his tone. "No, that's not what I want. At the moment, all I want is for you and me to be friends. I've missed being with you. I've missed Ksi-ĩĩ-zhi-ho-ha-zi-zi. I want us to be together, and then... I don't know... We'll see what happens. It could be I can never go back. If that's how it turns out, my promise won't mean a thing, and we'll be free to do what we want."

Tall Grass stared into the distance. She was silent for so long that Ethan shifted nervously. At last she said, "Is hard, only friends with this feeling."

"You mean you want it to be more?"

Tall Grass nodded.

"So do I, Ha-ssta-mo-i-i. More than anything. But can we start by being friends? See what happens? Isn't it better than not seeing each other at all?"

"Both very hard."

"Can we try? Ni-mo-mo-zi-ma-zi?" Please?

When she didn't answer, he pressed on. "If it doesn't work out, if it makes you unhappy, I swear we'll put an end to it. But how will we know unless we try?"

She looked at him in a way that wrenched his heart and said softly, "Never you making me unhappy, Haŋhepi Wi Nupa. Only too happy. But it making me too sad, you going Hoo-ho-mo-i-yoo or white home. Maybe friends not good for me."

"Please," Ethan pleaded, desperate to convince her. "Ni-mo-mo-zi-ma-zi, Ha-ssta-mo-i-i. I'm not going anywhere right now. Not until spring, at the earliest. Maybe not ever. Can't we please start by being friends again?"

"Micah saying what white soldiers do to you. Is more than you say to me."

Ethan drew back, thrown by the sudden shift in the conversation. "It's true," he admitted.

"Micah saying white soldiers wanting to kill you."

"That's right. Some of them do."

"How you can go white home if white soldiers wanting to kill you?"

"There are people trying to make it so that doesn't happen. If they succeed, I'll be able go home. If not, I'll stay here."

"You staying here with Tsi-tsí-tas?"

Ethan nodded. "Yes. If that's what you want, I'll stay here with you."

She held his gaze for a long moment, then said solemnly, "We try friends together, Haŋhepi Wi Nup̄a."

Ethan's heart leapt. More than anything, he wanted to pull her to him, to hold her and kiss her, but he forced himself to sit quietly. He looked into her eyes, and said, "Thank you. Ha-ho, Ha-ssta-mo-i-i. I've missed you so much."

"I missing you, Haŋhepi Wi Nup̄a. Many time."

14

Black Kettle, White Antelope, and Lone Bear of the Cheyenne, Bull Bear of the Dog Soldiers, and four Arapaho sent by Left Hand left the Smoky Hill to ride with Major Wynkoop and the former captives back to Fort Lyon. From there, they would proceed to Denver City and a council with Governor Evans to talk peace. Assuming it was now safe to do so, the Cheyenne and Arapaho moved east, headed for Fort Larned to spend the winter.

"I won't be going with you," Micah said on the day the criers announced the move. "I'm taking Yellow Leaf and Tall Grass to Trinidad to see my folks."

Ethan touched a finger to the newly sharpened blade of his hunting knife. Satisfied, he slid it into its sheath. "Tall Grass told me."

"You interested in coming along?"

"I'd like to. I'd like to see your Pa again, but now's not a good time."

Micah gave him a curious look. "I thought things were fixed up between you two."

"We're talking again, if that's what you mean."

Micah waited.

"She wants more than I can promise. So do I, for that matter." Ethan shrugged. "Time apart probably isn't a bad idea."

"And it's what she wants."

Ethan nodded. Tall Grass had been adamant. "How long do you expect to be away?"

"A month. Six weeks at most. Any longer, and Pa'll start thinking I'm home for good."

Their parting was stilted and brief. All around them, the camp bustled with preparations for the move. Wearing Josh's greatcoat against the early morning chill, Ethan held Girl Who Laughs while Tall Grass made final adjustments to the straps binding the poledrag and climbed into the saddle. The little girl clung to him when he handed her to her mother, and cried out in protest. Tall Grass settled the struggling child in front of her and looked down at Ethan.

"I missing you, Haŋhepi Wi Nupa," she said softly.

"I'll miss you, too." He stepped back and slapped the pony on the rump. As it started away, Girl Who Laughs craned her head around, dark eyes watching him. Ethan stood where he was and watched them go. Just when he'd decided she wouldn't, Tall Grass twisted in the saddle and looked back. Ethan held up a hand, letting it drop when she turned away. He watched until she was out of sight, then mounted the mare and turned her in the opposite direction.

The move east along Hackberry Creek was unhurried. A week passed before they came to the place where it flowed into Walnut Creek. Riding with Red Hand, Two Bulls and Coyote Tail, Ethan by-passed the first lodges being erected and headed out to hunt. They rode until dark, then made camp in a shallow draw that intersected the creek. The bank was high enough to shelter them from the wind and hide the small fire they built for warmth. After a meal of dried meat and berries, they settled into their blankets around the fire. Lying on his back, gazing up at the night sky, Ethan thought this was the part of Indian life he liked most—away from the camps, in the company of friends, sleeping under the stars on the night before a hunt. *It'll be hard to give up if— When*, he corrected. *When I go home.*

At a few minutes after sunrise, as they were saddling their mounts, gunfire erupted to east. Ethan pulled the cinch tight and flung himself into the saddle, looking to Red Hand for direction. Before they could react, six Indian ponies appeared over a rise, five of them ridden full out by warriors hunched low over their necks, and the sixth running free. Another man appeared behind them on foot, running for all he was worth. They were headed directly toward Red Hand's party, and as they drew near, more than fifty mounted cavalrymen exploded over the crest of the hill behind them.

Ethan and the others spun their horses and joined the fleeing men, headed for the camps. The Indian ponies pulled away from the mare, leaving Ethan and the man on foot further and further behind. Ethan glanced back. Two soldiers were gaining on the runner. He was twisting and turning as he ran, trying to evade them, but his strength was ebbing. Just as it appeared they would overtake him, warriors began arriving from the camps, their numbers increasing rapidly. Red Hand and the others joined them, turning back toward the soldiers. As Ethan pulled the mare to a halt and spun her around, three Cheyenne warriors surged past him, launching arrows at the two cavalrymen, killing them before they could retreat. The runner was hoisted onto the back of a galloping pony.

The soldiers, suddenly outnumbered, beat a hasty retreat, but it was too late. Warriors were spreading across the plain, intent on surrounding them. As the Indians encircled them, the soldiers clumped together on a low hill south of Walnut Creek.

Torn by conflicting loyalties, Ethan circled the perimeter, whooping and yelling with the rest, but reluctant to fire on the soldiers. With so many surrounding so few, he reasoned, a show of support was all that was required.

He spotted Charley in the midst of the melee; his face twisted in vengeful glee, and caught a distant glimpse of Ed. A flash of light-colored hair told him Jack Smith was there, too, but there was no sign of George. Ethan had only a fleeting moment to wonder where he might be before howls went up, and a group of warriors charged the hill. They were driven back by heavy gunfire. Several fell and lay still. Others were scooped onto running ponies or dragged away.

Another group charged, then another and another, each time with the same result. Ethan saw Charley with one group; Jack with another. During one such charge, he recognized White Horse, the Arapaho he'd ridden with to Wynkoop's camp. Ethan pulled the mare to a stop as a volley of shots erupted from atop the besieged hill, and the men with White Horse fell back. White Horse kept going, charging in amongst the troops, slashing wildly with his tomahawk. A bullet wrenched him from the saddle, and with a howl that could be heard above all else, the Indian scouts descended on him. One of them, a man with long, black braids, straddled him, brandishing a knife. He held up White Horse's scalp as his companions hacked him to pieces.

Ethan raised the Spencer and fired. The man with the scalp was lifted off his feet, then crumpled to the ground. The other scouts stared at him. When Ethan's second shot felled another of them, they ran, dispersing among the white troops. Ethan continued to fire until the hammer fell on an empty chamber. As he hastened to reload, the tenor of the yelling around him changed. Warriors galloped past, headed away from the hill. Ethan looked up to see a large body of cavalry bearing down on them from the south. He jammed the magazine home before spinning Faria and joining the flight.

They rode hard, the soldiers in hot pursuit. When they reached the place where the camps had been, only trampled grass and fire rings remained. They galloped north, following the signs.

Eventually, they began to overtake stragglers. When they reached the main body, they cut fresh ponies from the herd. While some warriors remained with the people, hurrying them along and providing a last line of defense, Ethan fell back with Red Hand, Feathered Bear, and the Crooked Lances of the Wu'-ta-pi-u clan to watch the soldiers' progress. He saw their dust where it billowed into the sky; caught occasional glimpses of them as they topped a distant rise.

"The Indians with the soldiers, who are they?" he asked, signing.

"Sa-va-ni." Red Hand made a sign Ethan had never seen before.

"I don't understand."

"Sa-va-ni." Red Hand made the sign again, and Ethan shook his head.

Red Hand made three signs: Cheyenne. Friend. No.

Ethan made the only sign he knew for a Cheyenne enemy: Pawnee.

"Ho-vah-hun-ni." Red Hand said. No.

They looked at one another in frustration. Much of the time they communicated without a problem, but every once in a while, they came up against something that left them both stymied.

As he usually did, Ethan said, "Di-no-ssto-vo Do-ha-eno." I'll ask George. Or Micah. Or Julie, or Ed.

Red Hand nodded, eyeing the distant soldiers. "Sa-va-ni,"[13] he said disparagingly, and spat into the dust.

Some of the warriors had hung back even further, and runners brought news that the soldiers' horses were beginning to tire. Late in the day, word came that the soldiers had gone into camp. For a second night, they bedded down on the open prairie, only this time there was no fire.

---

13   One of any number of eastern tribes, in this instance, Delaware

Gray light was streaking the sky when word came that the soldiers were preparing to march. Just after sunrise, more warriors arrived with news that the soldiers had left their camp and were heading north at a steady clip. Runners were dispatched to alert the people, while the rest stayed behind.

The soldiers moved so quickly throughout the early part of the day that Ethan was convinced they would have to turn and fight. But as the sun continued its steady march across the sky, the pace of the pursuit slowed. By mid-afternoon, as they approached the Smoky Hill River, the soldiers went into camp. Runners reported that their mounts were played out.

Ethan was among the warriors that rode back to keep watch on the soldiers' camp. They left him with the ponies, in a stand of trees beside a creek, and crept toward the camp on foot, melting into the autumn twilight without a sound. Ethan checked the ponies' tethers and sat with his back against a tree, turning up the collar of Josh's coat. As night descended, he ate the last of his dried meat, then wrapped himself in his blanket and settled in to wait.

At first, there was no moon, the darkness relieved by the great swath of the Milky Way. Aside from the usual night sounds, and the occasional snorting and shifting of ponies, the prairie was silent.

Ethan watched the moon rise, nearly full, thinking that just a year before he'd looked up at the same sky from the stockade in Atlanta. So much had happened since then, much of it relegated to distant memory. For the first time, he realized he was content. After a lifetime spent looking, he'd found a place to fit in.

The moon was long into its journey when Red Hand's voice, coming from close at hand, startled him.

"Ee-tin."

"Ma-hi-o-nah."

A moment later, the other man was squatting beside him. It was too dark to sign, so Red Hand whispered one of the English words he'd learned.

"Go!"

Ethan pushed himself to his feet, and together they led the ponies along the creek. The sky was beginning to lighten when Red Hand motioned Ethan to stop. They hunkered down to wait, their breath and the horses' hanging white in the cold pre-dawn air. As the sun broke over the horizon, the piercing notes of *Reveille* shattered the stillness. Moments later, Black Coyote and Two Bulls appeared with the news that the soldiers were preparing to march. Swinging aboard their ponies, they galloped north to spread the word.

The sun rose higher, glinting off crystals of frost that clung to the brown grass before building up enough heat to dissolve them. The bugle sounded again, *Boots and Saddles* this time, and soon after, Feathered Bear and the others filtered in with the news that the soldiers had given up the chase and were slowly heading south.

The Crooked Lances trailed them for the better part of the morning. Satisfied that the soldiers had indeed called off their pursuit, they turned their tired mounts and headed back toward the Smoky Hill.

OCTOBER

15

The mood, when they reached the camps on the Smoky Hill, was both angry and sad. Black Kettle and the other chiefs had promised there would be peace once the white prisoners were returned. Instead, only fourteen sleeps later, a dozen warriors were dead and three times that number wounded. Many were saying Black Kettle had been blinded by his friendship with the whites and that his words could no longer be trusted. Ethan understood the gist of it even before Ed explained.

He had returned to find the lodge he shared with George and Charley empty. George, Julie told him, had left before the fight on Walnut Creek, gone with a war party to hunt Pawnee. Charley had left during the flight north, headed out to raid.

With George away, Ethan was relieved to have Charley gone, as well. Tensions between them had run high since the August raids. Charley had returned with two scalps adorning the tip of his lance, one of which hung in long ringlets, the hair the same copper color as Kate's. The sight of it offended Ethan, and he'd made the mistake of asking Charley to put it where he didn't have to look at it. Instead, Charley took perverse pleasure in leaving it where Ethan couldn't help but see it. On the rare occasions when they were alone together, he made a point of toying with it, coiling its length around his fingers and describing how he'd got it. After the horror of the first telling, Ethan refused to be baited. Their relationship moved from strained to openly antagonistic.

In the constant quest to provide forage for the horses, the camps moved twice before George returned, his war party having failed to find any Pawnee. They moved again before the chiefs returned from their meeting with Governor Evans at Camp Weld.

Despite being confused by some of what had been said, the chiefs told their people they felt confident their proposals would be accepted and a lasting peace would be achieved. While Governor Evans had shown little interest in talking peace, preferring instead to point fingers and assign blame for past atrocities, they had found the words of Colonel Chivington reassuring. The colonel had spoken in a way they understood, explaining that his way of fighting was always the same—whether against white men or red, he would continue to fight until they lay down their arms and submitted to military authority. He suggested that, since the chiefs had developed a relationship with Major Wynkoop, they should go to him when they were ready to surrender. Major Wynkoop had further reassured them, repeating that they should bring their people in near Fort Lyon as spelled out in the Governor's proclamation. He assured them that, at the fort, they would be protected and provided with food until the peace went into affect.

In the aftermath of the attack on Walnut Creek, many in the Cheyenne camps were skeptical. The Dog Soldiers announced that they had no intention of surrendering to the soldiers. Other groups expressed similar sentiments. When word reached the camps that Big Wolf and his family had been attacked and killed by soldiers just a few miles from Camp Weld, the arguing escalated. As Black Kettle and the other chiefs pleaded for peace, young men headed out to raid. The Mah-sih´-ko-ta clan, along with several smaller groups, announced their intention to remain with the Dog Soldiers on the Smoky Hill River.

Ethan listened to it all, through George, and failed to be convinced. "Why should we trust them?" he asked as they rode toward the I-vis-tsi-nih´-pah camp late one blustery afternoon. "From what I've heard, no one at those talks guaranteed peace. All they want is for us to surrender, to put ourselves at their mercy, something I, for one, refuse to do!"

"So what *are* you planning to do, Ethan? Everyone you know's a member of the Wú-ta-pi-u, I-vis-tsi-nih´-pah, or Issio-mé-tan-iu clans. We're all heading south. You plan on moving in with someone else? Or going to look for the Sioux?" George waited until Ethan's eyes met his. "Now?" he asked pointedly. "With winter coming on?"

"Why can't you see it, George?" Ethan asked, incredulous. "What the chiefs are proposing is bad. It's too much of a risk. Nothing I've seen convinces me the soldiers can be trusted. It has to be a trap."

"The Cheyenne, all the tribes, have wintered near the forts for years. Nothing bad's ever happened. The only reason you don't like it is you want to stay away from soldiers."

"You're right. I do. But tell me, in all those winters, have they ever told you you had to give up your weapons?"

George shrugged. "We won't do it. If they demand it, we'll give them just enough to satisfy them."

Ethan rode in silence for several moments. With a sly glance at George, he said, "You're only going along because you have your eye on Mo-hi-hy-wah."[14]

George looked at him in surprise, then let out a snort of laughter. "What makes you say that?"

"I hear things."

"It's Julie, isn't it? She's been talking."

When Ethan didn't reply, George's look turned shrewd. "Fort Lyon puts you closer to Trinidad. The closer you are, the sooner you'll see Tall Grass."

Ethan looked away, but not before George saw him smile. "She belongs to the Wú-ta-pi-u clan. Micah and Yellow Leaf are Issio-mé-tan-iu. If you stay here, it'll be months before you see them again." He could see that Ethan was on the verge of relenting and pressed his advantage. "At Fort Lyon, we're only a few miles from Pa's stockade. If we don't like the look of things, or something bad happens, we'll head there."

Ethan blew out a long breath and shook his head. "I swore I'd never put myself at anyone's mercy ever again. If it comes to that, I'll leave."

"If it comes to that, we'll go to my father's place."

After a moment, Ethan nodded. "All right. I'll go."

While the Cheyenne argued amongst themselves, the one hundred thirteen Arapaho lodges under Left Hand and Little Raven left the Smoky Hill and headed south to Fort Lyon. Eventually, the Cheyenne bands under Black Kettle, War Bonnet, White Antelope, Bear Tongue, Lone Bear and Sand Hill set out after them.

Ethan rode with George, scanning the landscape for any sign of riders. It had been more than six weeks since Micah and the women departed, and each day he grew more convinced that something bad had happened. Only George's admonitions kept him from setting out to look for them.

"They'll be along," George assured him, not for the first time. "Could be they decided to stay a while longer. Or maybe the weather's bad in the high country and it's slowed them down."

"Or they've been attacked like Big Wolf and his family," Ethan replied, determined to think the worst.

---

14   Magpie Woman, Black Kettle's niece

"Trust Micah to take care of himself," George said, his patience wearing thin. "He's lived in this country all his life. Your riding out to look for them won't accomplish a thing." He stopped short of adding, *Except get you lost.*

NOVEMBER

16

The sky was leaden, thin flakes of snow swirling on a chill wind, when the Cheyenne went into camp where the trail crossed the big bend in the Little Dried River.[15] It wasn't long before runners arrived from Left Hand and Little Raven, warning that the Arapaho had been ill-treated by the new red-eyed chief who had replaced Major Wynkoop at Fort Lyon. The Arapaho chiefs had taken their people and moved away from the fort. Black Kettle and a delegation of sixty warriors, including Feathered Bear and Red Hand, left the camps and headed south.

Major Anthony, whose most recent encounter with Indians had been on the besieged hilltop at Walnut Creek, had no desire for peace. When he arrived to take command at Fort Lyon, he had been shocked to discover more than six hundred Arapaho camped within a mile of the fort. He was further dismayed when word reached him that another six to seven hundred Cheyenne were camped just forty miles north. He wired a series of urgent messages to headquarters, requesting troops to attack them.

When Black Kettle's contingent arrived at Fort Lyon, Major Anthony and Agent Colley met with them, offering gifts of tobacco, but explaining that they were unable to provide food or protection as promised. Major Anthony told Black Kettle he had no authority to make peace, but assured him that, should he receive such authority, he would personally ride to Sand Creek. Black Kettle replied that he had thought to move his people south to the Purgatoire. Fearing he would lose track of their whereabouts, the major did his utmost to convince Black Kettle to remain at Sand Creek where, he said, game was plentiful, and his people would be assured of food to last the winter.

Black Kettle was non-committal. He and his men spent the night at the ranch of John Prowers, son-in-law of Chief Lone Bear, before continuing west for a visit with William Bent. It wasn't until he returned to the camps that Black Kettle made his decision. He announced that they would remain on the Little Dried River for the winter.

Feathered Bear returned with word of another sort. At Bent's ranch, he had heard news from Trinidad. Micah's mother was gravely ill. It was expected she

---

15   Sand Creek

would die soon, if she hadn't already. Micah and the women were still at Henri's ranch.

Ethan listened to both announcements with relief. His concern for Tall Grass had been mounting steadily. At the same time, he'd been grappling with what to do if the Cheyenne moved closer to Fort Lyon. Now the weight of both problems lifted simultaneously. When George announced his intention to visit his father, and asked Ethan to join him, he declined. He scribbled a hasty note to his parents and asked George to see it mailed. Then he completed a trade Red Hand had proposed: buffalo robes for a young pony that showed promise as a buffalo runner. Grateful to Red Hand for giving him what he considered the better part of the bargain, and eager to test his new pony, Ethan rode out with a party of men to hunt.

* * *

Heavy white flakes drifted down, softening edges and obscuring familiar landmarks. From her vantage point at the second floor nursery window, Elizabeth watched the road in front of the house gradually disappear. As she often did, she wondered where Ethan was and what he was doing. Despite constant reassurances from Sarah and James, she had yet to accept that he was safe living among savages. She watched the snow, hating the thought of him forced to spend the winter in a tent. Heaving a sigh, she told herself it probably wasn't any worse than the winter he'd spent with the army. She winced, thoughts fleeing, as the infant at her breast jerked impatiently, demanding her full attention.

Brown eyes fixed on her mother's face, one clenched fist waving, Sarah Amelia, named for both grandmothers, pulled hard at the nipple, demanding more. Elizabeth smiled and shifted her to the other breast. The little girl settled in with a satisfied sigh as Elizabeth set the rocker in motion.

"Just wait 'til your daddy sees you," she cooed, running her finger over a silken cheek.

Emma, as she'd been dubbed by Kate, mewed softly and looked as if she understood.

Her daughter's eyes closed, and Elizabeth returned to staring out the window, watching as a lone rider materialized out of the white, the tracks left by his horse marring the pristine blanket of snow. He pulled to a stop before the gate and swung down from the saddle, tall, slender and very familiar. Elizabeth's breath caught, and she stopped rocking.

Emma whimpered in protest and released the nipple. Elizabeth looked down. Assured that her daughter slept, she leaned forward, watching the man as he came up the walk. His collar was turned up against the cold; the brim of his hat hid his face. She wished with all her heart he would look up. He stepped under the cover of the porch roof and was gone.

Her heart thudding against her ribs, Elizabeth heard his knock, followed by Hannah's footsteps in the hall below. Barely breathing, she strained to hear the murmured voices. It seemed an eternity before she heard Hannah's step on the stairs.

The door opened, and Hannah announced, "It Mista Josh. Home from the war."

The air went out of Elizabeth, and she slumped in the chair, fighting down disappointment. Hannah lifted the sleeping infant from her arms, and with shaking fingers, Elizabeth did up the buttons of her bodice. A glance in the mirror told her she looked pale and anxious. Putting on a brave face, she went downstairs to meet Ethan's brother for the first time.

Hannah had shown him to the drawing room. He stood with his back to the door, warming his hands before the fire. He turned as she stepped into the room, stopping her dead in her tracks. For a moment, neither of them spoke.

"Mrs. Magrath."

In the same instant, she blurted out, "Welcome home, Mr. Fraser."

As her initial surprise wore off, Elizabeth saw Josh's resemblance to his half-brother diminish.

Thinking her prettier than anyone had led him to believe, Josh cocked an eyebrow, favoring her with a crooked smile.

The familiar mannerism flustered Elizabeth once more. "Welcome home," she repeated, struggling to regain her composure. "When did you arrive?"

"Late yesterday." He held out a hand, slender with long, graceful fingers.

Elizabeth stared, then touched it briefly. Unable to meet his eyes, she moved past him, seating herself in one of the chairs before the fire. She watched Josh discreetly as he sat in the other. The resemblance, though difficult to pinpoint, was most certainly real.

Josh looked at her and smiled. "Strange, isn't it. We're not even full brothers, but he's more like me than my twin. Something I never noticed until his court-martial."

Elizabeth leaned toward him. "Tell me about it. Tell me everything that happened."

* * *

The wind was bitterly cold. Ethan hunched his shoulders against it, pulling the collar of Josh's coat more closely around his neck. He was wearing every article of clothing he owned, but still the cold found its way in. John Smith glanced in his direction, making eye contact briefly before turning back to the woman he was bartering with.

The trader had arrived earlier in the day, in the company of two other white men; a teamster employed by Agent Colley and a soldier from Fort Lyon. They'd brought a wagonload of goods. Most of the men from the camps were away hunting, but the women had remained clustered about Smith all afternoon, eager to trade for the coffee, flour, sugar and other supplies he'd brought. Ethan, on the other hand, was looking for information. He hadn't spoken with a white man since his last encounter with Smith and was eager for news. The trader caught his eye again, and inclined his head. Ethan turned away, assured Smith would find him when he got a chance.

He headed back through the camps, his fur-lined winter moccasins crunching on the patches of frozen snow that were all that remained once the rest had blown away to drift in gullies and along the creek. Chief Sand Hill's camp was the furthest downstream, and to reach it, Ethan made his way through the camps of White Antelope, Lone Bear and Black Kettle. Ten lodges belonging to Left Hand's newly arrived Arapaho came next. From habit, when he came to the open ground beyond, Ethan turned and looked south.

At first, he saw nothing. Then, far out beyond the pony herds, something moved in the fading afternoon light. Ethan squinted, watching as the shape grew more distinct, dividing itself into two, then three separate forms. His pulse quickened. He took several steps, then stopped, still uncertain. A portion of the pony herd moved between him and the riders, and he strode impatiently to the edge of the creek. The herd parted to let the riders through, and Ethan had his first good look at them.

He leapt the drifts lining the bank, moccasins sinking into the sandy creek bottom as he ran upstream. Leaping the scattered, ice-encrusted pools that pocked the creek bed, he raced the two hundred yards to the opposite side, angling toward the place where the trail intersected it, and the steep bank had been worn down.

Micah and the two women had seen him and quickened their pace. They were almost upon him when he dashed up the slope. Micah called a greeting and leaned down to grasp his hand. Ethan welcomed him warmly, if distractedly, and nodded a greeting to Yellow Leaf.

Tall Grass had stopped her pony several yards back, suddenly shy at seeing him again. He saw, as he walked toward her, that she had begun braiding her hair again. It flattered her, accentuating the fine bones of her face.

She smiled suddenly, her eyes alive with happiness. "Haŋhepi Wi Nupa."

"Ha-ssta-mo-i-i," he said, taking her hand. He was aware of the soft thud of hooves as Micah and Yellow Leaf departed, leaving them alone.

At the sound of his voice, the mound of blankets in front of Tall Grass stirred, and a bright pair of eyes peeked out. "Ee-tin?" the little girl said, and wriggled against her mother's hold on her.

Tall Grass handed Girl Who Laughs into Ethan's arms before climbing down from the pony. Ethan held out a hand, and when she came to him, hugged them both to him.

"I've missed you, Ha-ssta-mo-i-i," he murmured, pressing his cheek to hers.

"I missing you, Haŋhepi Wi Nupa."

They stood together until Girl Who Laughs whined in protest and began to wriggle. Parting reluctantly, they started toward the camp, as far out on the horizon, a line of clouds blocked the sun and evening drew in around them.

Ethan waited off to the side while aunts and cousins emerged to help Tall Grass erect her lodge. When it was done, they turned toward their own lodges, but not before casting knowing looks in his direction. He waited, shifting from foot to foot against the cold, watching as smoke began to drift upward, and the top of the newly erected lodge glowed warm in the winter twilight. Just as he was beginning to wonder if he'd misread her, Tall Grass pushed open the door flap and beckoned.

He sat on the robe she spread for him, opening his coat to Girl Who Laughs, who snuggled onto his lap, chattering happily. Ethan divided his attention between them, eyes following Tall Grass as she moved about the lodge, unpacking her belongings and preparing food. Neither of them spoke, but every so often their eyes met, and they smiled.

As the lodge warmed, Girl Who Laughs crawled off Ethan's lap. He set the blankets aside and removed his coat. It never ceased to amaze him how quickly the lodges warmed and how well they retained the heat.

"How was your trip?" he asked, when Tall Grass served him and sat down to eat.

Tall Grass' face clouded. "Ho-do-vi-hi[16] being sick many moons. Is good she seeing Micah. And she happy seeing Hi-yo-vi-vi-bo-da-i and knowing there is baby."

It took Ethan a moment to figure out what she'd said. "Yellow Leaf's pregnant?"

"Having baby, yes."

Ethan shook his head, smiling to himself and wishing he'd taken time to greet Micah and Yellow Leaf properly. *Tomorrow*, he told himself. *There'll be plenty of time tomorrow.*

"How is Henri?"

"Much sad. He is gone when Ho-do-vi-hi being sick."

"She got sick while he was in St. Louis last winter?"

For a moment, Tall Grass looked as if she didn't understand. Then she nodded. "When he is gone, yes."

The meal finished, they talked of things of little importance, acutely aware that whatever was going to happen couldn't be put off indefinitely. After a time, not knowing if she would invite him back inside or send him on his way, Ethan put on his coat and stepped outside to relieve himself.

The night was clear and bitterly cold. A gusting wind moaned across the prairie, rattling the leafless branches of the cottonwoods and slicing at the exposed skin of his hands and face. It was a relief to duck back inside.

Tall Grass had moved Girl Who Laughs to the robe where she'd been sitting and was settling her for the night. Ethan squatted next to the fire, holding his hands to the flames. After what seemed a very long time, Tall Grass stood and walked to him around the fire. Ethan rose to meet her. He looked into her eyes, and his chest tightened in anticipation. She came to a stop before him, slowly undoing the buttons of his coat. He waited until the coat fell open, then shrugged it off impatiently and pulled her to him.

At first, all they could do was cling to one another. Then Ethan turned his face into her hair, kissing it and her ear before her lips eagerly sought his.

Tall Grass moaned softly, holding him to her and running her hands up under his shirt. He let go of her long enough to pull it off, then watched as her dress dropped to the ground. His excitement mounted when he saw she wore only leggings underneath. Tall Grass shuddered when he cupped the soft mound between her legs, and her fingers sought the front flap of his breechclout, pulling it free. Then they were on the ground, both crying out as he entered her, their coupling frenzied and brief.

It wasn't at all what Ethan had envisioned for their first time together, and when it was over, he had no idea what to say. He moved to the robe and pulled her to him. Tall Grass wrapped her arms around him and pressed her face to his chest, her breath coming hot and quick against his skin.

Her breathing slowed, and he thought she slept until her lips began to move softly against his chest. The fingers of one hand began tracing lazy patterns down his back, working their way across his hip before sliding between his legs, their movement gently insistent. As Ethan grew aroused, Tall Grass tilted her head back and smiled at him.

"I loving you now, Haŋhepi Wi Nupa," she said softly. "Until you go white home."

I'll never leave you. To say it aloud would break a promise. Instead, he said, "I love you, Ha-ssta-mo-i-i." He saw in her eyes it was all she needed to hear.

They made love again, slowly this time, savoring the joy of being together.

The fire had burned down, a chill settled over the lodge, when Ethan woke. A shiver ran through him. Beside him, Tall Grass shifted.

"Is cold," she murmured, snuggling closer.

He held her until the cold grew too much for her. She slipped away, and selected several small sticks from the pile, placing them atop the embers. The coals glowed red when she blew on them, followed by a bright burst as the fire re-ignited. Tall Grass added larger pieces of wood, stacking them as the flames grew. Then she stood, fully exposed, the firelight flickering gold and copper across her skin. Ethan's pulse quickened. Tall Grass' eyes met his, then traveled the length of his body. She smiled at what she saw and came to lie beside to him.

As they lay together afterwards, she whispered, "You going now. For me is not good people see you."

Ethan nodded. He wanted nothing more than to stay with her, but it was one thing to have people suspect, and quite another to be seen emerging from her lodge. He kissed her once more before rising to collect his clothes. When he was dressed, he knelt beside her.

"I'll see you later," he told her. "I love you."

"I loving you," she whispered, reaching up to caress his cheek.

He took her hand and turned his face into it, kissing her palm and holding it there for several seconds before tucking it back into the warmth of the robe.

"I love you, Ha-ssta-mo-i-i." His reward was a dazzling smile as he rose to leave.

Conscience pricked him as he stepped from the lodge. Hunched against the cold, he walked rapidly through Black Kettle's camp, knowing he needed to make a decision.

A dog snarled as he passed. Further on, another barked, setting off the rest and a chorus of angry shouts from inside the lodges. By the time he reached the Arapaho camp, the dogs had quieted; the only sounds were the clack of branches and the mournful sighing of the wind.

Clear of the Arapaho lodges, Ethan broke into a trot, covering the open ground quickly before coming into the circle of I-vis-tsi-nih́-pah lodges and heading for one he shared with George and Charley. He stopped just outside, looking east and thinking that soon it would be light.

I'll talk to her first thing. Tell her I'm never going back. Tell her all I want is for us to be together. Always.

The decision made, he lifted the flap and ducked inside.

17

Shouts, and the frenzied barking of dogs, jarred Ethan from a sound sleep. There was a flurry of movement on the other side of the lodge, more shouts from outside, and the thud of feet as people ran past. The door flap slammed open, spilling light as Charley ran out. Seconds later, George followed. There was more shouting, joined by women's screams.

"No-da-ki vi-hoi!" White soldiers!

Ethan threw back his robe, grateful he'd fallen into bed fully clothed, and felt for his moccasins. He was on his feet, reaching for his coat, when the first gunfire crackled.

George burst into the lodge. "Soldiers!" he shouted. "They fired on John Smith. Get your weapons and come quick!"

Ethan grabbed the coat, thrust his arms into it, scooped up his ammunition pouch, and jammed it into one of the pockets.

George shoved the Spencer into his hands. "Go!"

George grabbed his Sharps rifle and charged after him. They collided going though the doorway, and Ethan fell. He scrambled to his feet and looked about frantically. There were mounted troops south of the creek and in the open area between the I-vis-tsi-nih´-pah and Arapaho camps. They had begun surrounding the main body of the camp, and as people poured from the lodges, the soldiers opened fire. Most were half asleep and only partially clothed. At first they stood stunned, staring in disbelief. Then, as people around them began to fall, they ran in every direction, men shouting, and women and children screaming.

South of the creek, Ethan could see soldiers driving off the pony herds. A soldier spurred his horse into the creek bed, charging after a woman who was running along the near bank, dragging a small boy with her. As the trooper raised his saber, Ethan aimed the carbine and fired. The soldier fell from his horse; the woman and child kept running.

A howitzer roared, and Ethan looked around, seeking George. He was nowhere in sight. A bullet whined past his head and smacked into the lodge cover beside him. He started to run. Ducking and weaving, he raced into the thick of it, heading through the troops toward Tall Grass' lodge. He emptied the carbine indiscriminately, not knowing if he inflicted damage, concerned only with getting through.

The carnage, when he came to the Arapaho camp, was appalling. The dead, most of them women and children, lay where they had fallen. The cries of the wounded compounded the horror. A few men stood their ground, firing at the troops with bows and arrows, but most who could run, did. Ethan knelt in the shelter of one of the lodges to reload before racing toward Black Kettle's camp.

The situation, when he reached it, was even worse. He recognized people he'd seen everyday among the dead. One of the girls he'd flirted with at the Sun Dance, her buckskin dress smeared with blood, was trying to pull an old woman to her feet. When she saw Ethan, she called out for help. As Ethan hesitated, a soldier rode from between the lodges and opened fire. The girl's knees buckled, and she fell to the ground, still reaching out to Ethan. He raised the carbine, but was too late. An arrow launched from between the lodges wedged itself between the man's shoulder blades. He slumped across his horse's withers. Ethan glanced once more at the girl's body before turning to run toward Tall Grass' lodge, pushing through a panicked stream of people surging in the opposite direction.

He cried out in despair at finding the lodge empty. Looking around in desperation, he tried to identify Tall Grass amid the chaos, but she was nowhere in sight. A hurried inspection of the closest dead assured him she wasn't among them. Not knowing what else to do, Ethan set off for Plum Moon's lodge.

The scene, when he got there, was devastating. The lodge was one of the first the soldiers had come upon. Plum Moon Woman lay sprawled in the doorway, cut down as she stepped through. Nearby lay the tangled, bloody bodies of Singing Bird and Long Sleeper. It was obvious without going closer, that all of them were dead. Ethan crouched beside the lodge, waiting as a group of soldiers spurred past on the other side. Then he ran, leaping over bodies, heading for White Antelope's camp.

The old chief, the friend of the whites, was standing at the edge of the creek bed when Ethan darted from between two lodges. His arms were folded across his chest, and he was singing his death song. Ethan had no sooner spotted him, than there was an explosion of gunfire. The old man's body jerked crazily and crumpled to the ground. Ethan leapt backward, throwing himself behind one of the lodges as soldiers thundered past. When they were gone, he scrambled to his feet and ran on.

A glance showed Micah and Yellow Leaf's lodge to be deserted. Ethan looked about wildly, not knowing which way to go. People were still running in every direction, but most appeared to be headed up the creek. Ethan started after them, and it was then that he saw Micah.

Hooves pounded directly behind him, and he spun around. A trooper was bearing down on him, pistol in hand. Ethan dove to his left, into the path of the galloping horse, as the gun discharged. The bullet tore past his ear. He rolled clear of the slashing hooves and sprang to his feet, bringing the carbine up and firing. The soldier fell from his horse and lay still. Ethan glanced around, then sprinted to where he'd seen Micah.

He lay face down on the ground between two of the lodges, one arm outstretched, still clutching the carbine his father had given him. He had been shot twice in the back. Beyond him lay Yellow Leaf. Ethan gave a hurried look around. Satisfied that none of the soldiers were near, he went down on one knee and held his fingers to Micah's neck, feeling for a pulse. There was none. A choked sob escaped him, and his eyes flooded with tears. He knelt beside Micah for several moments before giving his shoulder a final squeeze and starting to rise. As an afterthought, he slipped the heavy silver armlet from Micah's forearm and slid it onto his own.

As he got to his feet, the first thing to catch his eye was the American flag fluttering loosely in the distance, on the pole above Black Kettle's lodge. Anger boiled up inside him. At that moment, he hated the sight of it.

A renewed volley of shots sounded somewhere behind him, and a group of people rushed past, jostling him as they went. Stunned with grief, Ethan turned and ran with them. He stayed with them through the village and into the creek bed, turning with them to flee upstream—directly into an ambush.

Soldiers were firing from both sides of the creek. Bullets whipped past Ethan and slammed into people around him. Blood and bodies were everywhere. An old woman fell, and an old man turned to help her. His chest blossomed red, and he sank to his knees before tumbling over on top of her. A woman stopped running and stood stunned, staring at the bloody body of the infant in her arms. Then she, too, went down. Up ahead, another woman's head exploded in a spray of red. Her body went limp, but her legs carried her several more steps before she fell. The toddler she'd been carrying flew from her arms and skidded through the sand. The little girl came up on her hands and knees, screaming in terror.

With a cry of horror, Ethan recognized Girl Who Laughs. He veered toward her, leaping over Tall Grass' lifeless body, and scooping the child into his arms. Hatred and grief combined to propel him up the creek bed, past the few people still running; past the bodies of men, women and children, all dead or too badly wounded to flee.

A bullet hit him low on the left side, shattering a rib as it entered; another as it exited. Ethan cried out, but kept running. Seconds later, another bullet smashed into his right shoulder, throwing him off his stride. He reached out a hand to steady himself, and a third tore into his lower back, spinning him to the ground. He rolled, clutching the Spencer and the screaming child to him, and came to rest in a shallow depression. Moaning in pain and terror, he struggled frantically to get to his feet. Several panic-filled seconds passed before he realized his legs would not respond. With a frightened sob, he lowered his head to the ground and lay gasping for breath.

When the worst of his panic subsided, Ethan raised his head. Waves of agony washed through him, and he teetered on the brink of consciousness. When his vision cleared, he gritted his teeth and looked toward his legs. The right one, the only one he could see, was splayed across the ground in front of him. He tried moving it. Cold fear gripped him when nothing happened. He couldn't feel his left leg either, couldn't tell where it was, but he tried moving it. As near as he could tell, it too, was paralyzed. When he realized how badly he was hurt, Ethan wrapped himself around Henri Broulat's grandchild and lay still, shielding her with his body.

The din of the massacre slowly subsided. The little girl's screams turned to whimpers, then died away completely. The steady crack of gunfire continued somewhere further up the creek, but where Ethan lay, the only sounds were the cries and moans of the wounded. Fighting pain and nausea, he raised his head once more and looked around. He was lying on his right side, his body wedged in a narrow channel carved into the sandy bottom, separated from the dead and wounded by a barrier of sand and tall grass. He knew he should make an effort to pull himself out, afraid that when the soldiers left, and the rest of the tribe came searching for survivors, he would be overlooked.

Wait 'til the shooting stops, he thought. *Then try.*

As he lowered his head, he was hit by the full horror of what had happened. In his mind's eye, he saw the familiar figure running ahead of him, graceful even in flight, the slender hips he'd caressed just hours before swaying beneath her dress as long, bare legs bore her up the creek. Then the burst of red and a nightmare image of her crumpled form, eyes staring, seeing nothing, as he'd leapt over her. No longer graceful. No longer full of life. *Ha-ssta-mo-i-i!* He remembered her smiling up at him, and turned his face into the sand, convulsed with sobs.

He was only dimly aware that the little girl began to whine, struggling to get out from under him. He shifted his left arm, allowing her to wriggle free.

"Ee-tin?" Girl Who Laughs cried fearfully, crouching beside him.

Consumed by grief, Ethan barely heard her.

"Ee-tin?" the little girl repeated, laying a hand on his shoulder.

She persisted, her voice rising with anxiety, until Ethan turned his head to look at her. At first she was only a blur. He blinked until frightened brown eyes came into focus, peering at him from a face streaked with tears and blood. At the sight of her, grief welled up, threatening to engulf him until he noticed that the left shoulder of her dress was soaked with blood. The sight of it drove everything else from his mind.

"Ksi-ïï-zhi-ho-ha-zi-zi!" he cried, reaching for her. He slid his left hand under her dress, probing for the source of it. "Are you hurt? Ni-yo... ni-sshi... yo-zi?"

"Ho-vah-hun-ni."

When the little girl shook her head, it occurred to Ethan that the blood must be his own. He felt for his right shoulder. It was crushed beneath him, half-buried in the sand. He couldn't locate the wound itself, but his fingers found the hole in the front of his coat.

Sand clung to his fingers, sticky and wet, and his first thought was that he'd landed in water. Ethan wiped his hand down the front of Josh's coat and brought it up before his face. It was streaked bright red. Panic resurfaced, and he felt frantically for his other wounds, finding one on his side and choking back a sob when he realized how rapidly he was losing blood.

"Ee-tin," Girl Who Laughs said again, then something he could make no sense of. When he didn't respond, she said it again. A question. He forced a smile, which seemed to satisfy her, and she snuggled down next to him. He held her close, drawing comfort from her presence.

Rest a minute, he thought as a great weariness settled over him. *Then decide what to do.*

When he opened his eyes again, he still heard gunfire up the creek. The sun was high in the sky, but it had done little to dispel the cold. A gust of wind shifted sand in front of his eyes and sent an icy chill across the sweat coating his face. Ethan shivered, catching his breath against fingers of pain that clawed their way into every part of his body. He closed his eyes, forcing down vomit that rose in the back of his throat.

Slowly it dawned on him that something was amiss. The feeling intensified, and he opened his eyes. His view was limited to the ridge of sand in front of him and the grass above it. He turned his head, surprised that such a small movement took every bit of his strength. He rested, staring up at the sky, bright blue and empty. The cries of the wounded had died away; it was quieter now, just the distant pop of gunfire, and closer, the gurgle of the creek. The sound of it made Ethan realize how desperately thirsty he was. He ran the tip of his tongue over parched, gritty lips. *It's so close...* He would rest a minute, he decided as his eyes closed.

Ksi-ïi-zhi-ho-ha-zi-zi! Ethan jerked awake, feeling for her. Panic seized him when he found her missing. He thought to go looking for her, but had no strength. He lay fretting until the reason for it deserted him and consciousness faded.

Sometime later, he felt a presence. He opened his eyes to discover a woman seated next to him. Confused, he squinted up at her, trying to make out her features against the bright sky. His breath caught when he realized who it was. He tried to speak, but no sound came.

His mother turned her head, smiling when she saw he was awake. She reached out a hand and laid it cool against his forehead. She began to sing softly, one of the songs she'd sung to him as a child. Ethan closed his eyes and drifted.

His mother's voice broke off abruptly. He opened his eyes in alarm. She was looking away from him, up the creek. After listening for several moments, she turned to him, placing a finger against his lips.

"Haŋhepi Wi Nup̄a owaŋji yaŋk̄a ye," she whispered. Be very still, Two Moons. "Do not let them find you. When they have gone, I will return."

Ethan wanted to reach out to her, implore her not to leave him, but he hadn't the strength. He watched helplessly as she rose and glided silently away.

He remembered her words and lay still, listening, scarcely daring to breath. The sound of men's voices came to him from somewhere up the creek. There were shouts and raucous laughter. At intervals, he heard screams of pain or terror and the scattered pop of gunshots. The sounds grew louder as the men drew closer. Their voices were loud and harsh, and they spoke English.

"Got us a live one here, boys!" one of them yelled.

Ethan held his breath. There was an anguished scream and he heard another man ask, "You get her scalp?"

The grunt of acknowledgment was followed by the report of a pistol.

The soldiers worked their way past Ethan, making crude comments and laughing. Not far off, a woman pleaded and child's cry was silenced abruptly by a dull thud. Ethan closed his eyes, hoping with all his heart it wasn't Girl Who Laughs.

He woke to his mother shaking him.

"Let them know you are here," she whispered, and was gone.

The sun had set, and it was bitterly cold. He heard movement close by, and the low murmur of voices. He strained to hear. Deciding it wasn't soldiers, he cried out for help. As he did, something shifted beside him. He realized vaguely that the child had returned. She moved again, jamming a knee into his broken ribs. Ethan screamed in agony as darkness took him.

***

When the shooting started, a number of Cheyenne had managed to escape to a place two miles up the creek where the banks were high and steep. Clawing frantically at the sand, they dug pits and took cover in them. Few had robes or blankets, and the majority had been wounded during their flight. Cold and bleeding, they spent the day surrounded by soldiers, pinned down by constant gunfire.

Unable to drive the Indians out, and unwilling to go in after them, the soldiers eventually withdrew. They headed back downstream, in the direction of the camps, killing anyone they found alive, and scalping and mutilating the dead.

Afraid to venture out, the survivors remained in their holes long after the soldiers had gone. It wasn't until daylight began to fade, and it appeared certain the soldiers would not return, that they slowly began to emerge, stiff with cold and not knowing what to do next. Some set off down the creek to look for loved ones, but the majority turned upstream, away from the carnage.

Their progress was, of necessity, slow; those not too badly wounded aiding the ones who were, women and children wailing softly. Others who'd escaped filtered in to join them. Black Kettle appeared among them, carrying his wife on his back. She had been shot nine times.

At one point, they heard horses and hid in fear, waiting until they recognized men and boys from their own camps. During a hushed, tearful reunion, the boys explained that they had gone out before dawn to check the pony herds. Seeing hundreds of soldiers approaching, they had driven away as many ponies as they could. When gunfire erupted, some had ridden to the Cheyenne camps on the Smoky Hill for help, but the rest had waited, vastly outnumbered, listening to the screams and gunshots. Over the course of the day, they had been joined by groups of returning hunters. When the shooting stopped, they'd begun working their way downstream, hoping to discover what had happened.

The most gravely wounded were helped onto ponies. Men took others on their backs, turning with them up the creek. The rest continued downstream to hunt for survivors.

Red Hand was crouched next to the mutilated body of his wife's mother when he heard a muffled cry. His eyes darted toward the sound, probing the deepening shadows. He saw nothing. The cry came again, louder this time, and he moved toward it, hissing for others to follow. They moved quickly among the bodies, touching them, searching for one that was warm.

The dry grass ahead of them rustled. A small child emerged and scampered toward them. Red Hand squatted, and the little girl flung herself into his arms. It amazed him to feel how warm she was.

"It is Tall Grass Woman's child," Two Bulls whispered.

"Are you hurt?" Red Hand asked. She was covered in blood.

"No," the child said, shaking her head.

He examined her anyway, finding no source for it. Standing, he handed her to another man and started away. The little girl cried out in protest and began to struggle.

"Ee-tin!" she said, pointing to the tall grass. "Ee-tin."

Red Hand and Two Bulls moved quickly. Two Bulls crouched and pushed aside the grass, revealing a body lying hidden in a shallow depression.

He touched Ethan's cheek. Finding it damp and deathly cold, he leaned low over Ethan's mouth. Several seconds passed before he felt a faint stirring of breath. He looked at Red Hand, who was crouched beside him. "His spirit has gone. His body will soon follow. We should leave him and look for others who still live."

Red Hand shook his head. "No, I will take him."

The blood from Ethan's wounds had frozen to the ground. He moaned as they pulled him free, hoisting him up in front of Red Hand astride one of the ponies. Red Hand wrapped his blanket around him and turned upstream. Two Bulls walked beside him, carrying the child. Behind them, the others continued their sad search among the dead.

Considerable time passed before the faint sound of voices reached them, borne on the icy wind. It was the survivors calling out to anyone still lost and wandering on the frozen prairie. Soon the light from dozens of small fires came into view, leading them to the shallow ravine where the wounded had collapsed, unable to go further. They lay huddled together on the open ground while everyone who was able worked feverishly to keep them alive. Many had given up their own robes and blankets, and when those weren't enough, they pulled handfuls of dead grass, mounding it over the wounded and the children, and feeding it into the fitful flames of tiny fires.

When Red Hand rode among them, hands reached up to take Ethan. As they lowered him to the ground, Julie came running. She knelt beside him, taking an icy hand in hers and touching his face. For a moment, she thought him dead and looked questioningly at Red Hand. Then Ethan drew a shuddering breath and moaned. Red Hand cast a final look at him, then turned back toward the bloody creek bed to search for his wife and son.

With hours still to go before dawn, the survivors rose from the frozen prairie and started toward the Smoky Hill River. Red Hand had returned alone from his search, and once again, took Ethan up in front of him, supporting his limp form with an arm around his waist. Ethan had opened his eyes only once, Julie told him, giving no indication that he knew her, and muttering something in the language of the Sioux.

As the sun appeared above the horizon, Red Hand turned his pony and looked back the way they'd come, searching the lightening prairie for any sign of movement. Beside him, George did the same, his face tight with pain from the bullet he carried in his hip.

"Nothing," George said after several moments, shivering and hugging a single blanket to his bare chest.

Red Hand continued to scan the prairie, searching for any sign of soldiers. Satisfied there was no pursuit, he grunted, and they turned their ponies north.

"If they come, if they catch us, few will live."

George surveyed the straggling line of people spread across the prairie and nodded agreement. Most were women and children. Many of the wounded were on foot; others carried on people's backs. Few had weapons. There was no way they would be able to fight, or outrun the soldiers. George shivered again and looked at Ethan. His head was thrown back, resting against Red Hand's shoulder. It bobbed loosely with every step the pony took. His skin was a sickly gray.

"Will he live?"

"There is no way to know until we see his wounds."

"Do you know where he was shot?"

"There was a large amount of blood, but in the dark, and with the dark coat he wears, it was not possible to tell about his wounds."

George looked again at Ethan, then turned his pony away, scanning faces as he rode, searching for people he knew. It appeared that many from the I-vis-tsi-nih'-pah clan had survived. Chief Sand Hill was with them, as were many of George's own aunts, uncles and cousins. A cousin had been among those who had met them coming along the creek and loaned him the pony. Julie was safe. And so was Ed. But Charley was missing. And Micah. George realized suddenly, that no one from Micah's immediate family was with them. Not Yellow Leaf, not Feathered Bear, not any of his wives or children. He saw few faces from either the Wú-ta-pi-u or Issio-mé-tan-iu clans.

As the sun rose higher, people turned more and more often to look back the way they'd come, certain it was only a matter of time before the soldiers discovered their trail and came after them. Then, amazingly, a shout went up from the people in the lead. Horsemen appeared from out of the north, riding fast in their direction. More appeared over the horizon, and still more. The Cheyenne from the Smoky Hill camps swept down upon them, bringing food, clothing, blankets, robes and ponies. As each group arrived, more people were fed and clothed. A few at a time, they mounted the ponies and began heading north.

DECEMBER

18

Ethan hovered near death for four days after reaching the camp at the headwaters of the Smoky Hill. The afternoon of the fifth day, his fever broke. He woke to a number of confusing sensations: intense pain, a bitter taste in his mouth, and the sound of rattles and chanting. He gagged, spat and opened his eyes to find an old woman peering closely at him. Her thin lips curled into a smile, and she sat back on her heels, speaking to someone behind him. He was jostled and laid flat. The pain of it took his breath away. He closed his eyes, waiting for it to ease.

When he opened them again, it was to find Julie looking down at him. He stared at her, wondering dazedly where he was. The air was dense with pungent smoke, and when he tried to speak, it caught in his throat, making him cough. This time, the pain was more than he could stand, and he passed out.

When he woke, the smoke and rattles were gone, and it was night. Firelight cast wavering shadows over the inside of the lodge, and the soft murmur of voices came to him from somewhere beyond his sight. Pain radiated through him with every breath he took. Too weak to move, he lay as he was, half-dozing until a shadow fell across his face.

"You're awake," Julie said, when his eyes opened.

"Yes," he tried to say, but found he hadn't the strength.

"I have something for you to drink."

Ethan moved his tongue inside his mouth, realizing he was thirsty. He tried to nod, but that even that small movement was more than he could manage.

Julie seemed to understand. She was gone, then back again, holding a cup. "I need to raise up your head. Relax and let me do it, and maybe it won't hurt too bad."

Ethan couldn't have helped if he'd wanted to. Julie slipped a hand under his head and tilted it up. Pain arced through him. He moaned, a deep, guttural sound, and the edges of his vision drew in sharply.

Julie waited until his breathing steadied and his eyes drifted back to her face. "This has a real bad taste to it," she told him. "You're gonna wanna spit it out, but you can't. It's what you need to mend. You understand me, Ethan?"

Taking his silence for agreement, she raised the cup to his lips.

It was the vilest concoction he'd ever tasted. The moment it touched his tongue, Ethan spit.

"You want water, Ethan?"

He did. Desperately.

"You're gonna hafta drink this first."

She held the cup against his lips until he opened them. Taking some of the liquid into his mouth, he forced himself to swallow. He managed to drink nearly all of it before it gagged him. He looked at her, imploring her not to make him drink more.

"You did real good, Ethan," Julie said, holding the cup to the light to see how much was left. "You take it easy while I fetch some water."

She lowered his head and was gone. She returned almost immediately, but he was asleep.

When next he woke, light glowed through the upper part of the lodge telling him it was day. Once again, Julie appeared above him.

"How you feel?"

"Hurt." His voice came with effort, barely a whisper.

"Remember the medicine I gave you last night?"

He did. His expression told her so.

"You need to drink more if you wanna mend proper."

Ethan swallowed dryly and turned his eyes away. When she returned with the cup, he refused to look at her.

Julie ignored his protest. She lifted his head and held the cup to his lips. "Drink this, Ethan, or I can't bring you water."

Ethan turned accusing eyes on her.

"I know it's bad. But it's what you need if you're gonna get better."

Too feeble to resist, Ethan opened his mouth. The liquid was every bit as disgusting as he remembered, and he forced it down. When it was gone, he glared at her accusingly. Julie lowered his head and went away.

When she brought the water, Ethan sucked it down greedily.

"More?" he whispered when the cup was empty.

Julie brought it, and this time he drank more slowly. Before she could leave, he murmured, "Hurt."

"You were shot. Three times. It's gonna take time for you to mend."

Shot. The memory of it hung just beyond his reach.

"Don'chu remember? Soldiers attacked us. Down on the Little Dried River."

It came rushing back. *Tall Grass!* Ethan's breath caught before coming in great, rasping sobs. Pain tore through his insides, a mere extension of his anguish. He cried until what little strength he had was gone, then dropped into a deep, exhausted sleep.

Fire shot from his shoulder. Ethan's eyes flew open and he tried to struggle, but strong hands kept him from moving. The old woman sat back, chewing and muttering.

Julie leaned in and pressed a stick to his lips. "Here, Ethan. Bite down on this."

Ethan looked at her, then at the old woman. Eyeing her warily, he opened his mouth and bit. He realized that the weight of the robes was gone, and once again, the air inside the lodge was thick with pungent smoke.

Still chewing, the old woman leaned over him. Ethan screamed in agony and struggled against the men holding him. Then, suddenly, it was over. Trembling and gasping for breath, Ethan opened his eyes to find the old woman grinning down at him. She held up a misshapen lump of bloody lead for him to see.

"The bullet's out, Ethan."

Ethan heard the words and closed his eyes in relief. He didn't see the old woman spit into her hand and lean toward him. She pressed the glob to his shoulder, and he screamed as she worked it deep into the wound. Just when he thought it couldn't get any worse, he was manhandled onto his stomach and she began probing the wounds to his ribs.

Ethan was gasping and shaking and covered with sweat when the torture finally stopped. He lay with the stick clamped firmly between his teeth, oblivious to the conversation going on above him.

"He feels nothing," the old woman said, prodding the angry wound low on Ethan's back.

Julie looked from her to the wound. "What do you mean?"

"He has no feeling here. Or here." White Calf Woman grasped the skin of one buttock and gave it a firm pinch. Ethan gave no indication that he felt it. She pinched him several more times along the length of both legs.

"He feels nothing below his waist. It is not a good sign." She reached for her medicine bag and felt around until she found what she was looking for. Opening a small pouch, she sprinkled a tiny amount of powder on the back of one thigh and rubbed it in.

"Ask him if he feels a prickling here."

"Do you feel prickling on the back of your right leg, Ethan?"

He felt plenty. Pain radiated from his ribs and shoulder. The entire upper portion of his body throbbed with it. But he felt nothing on the back of either leg.

"Tell him to move his legs."

"Move your legs, Ethan."

He tried.

"Move your legs," Julie repeated.

Ethan heard the tension in her voice, remembered lying helpless in the creek bed. Panic seized him. He tried to look at his legs, but pain and weakness defeated him. His eyes filled with tears as the old woman ordered him rolled onto his back.

"Open your mouth, Ethan."

Deep in despair, Ethan relaxed his jaw, allowing her to remove the stick.

"I wan'chu to move your legs."

"Can't," he told her, his voice breaking. "Not since... shot."

Julie offered him a strained smile. She laid a reassuring hand on his arm before giving her full attention to White Calf Woman.

Ethan's eyes went to the old woman's face, then to Julie's. "What's she saying?"

Julie spoke, and the conversation went on without translation.

"Please, Julie. Tell me what she's saying."

Julie glanced at him. "In a minute."

The conversation ended, and the old woman pushed herself to her feet. Julie went with her, leaving Ethan's sight. When she returned, she knelt beside him, avoiding his eyes. She picked up his left hand, taking it between both of hers before speaking.

"White Calf Woman says the wounds on your back and shoulder still ooze white, but not as bad as before. She says soon the poison'll be gone, and the wounds'll heal. There's a rib or two broken, and that's why it hurts so bad."

"My legs," Ethan whispered, his eyes never leaving her face.

Julie drew a deep breath and looked at him. "She's seen this kinda thing before, Ethan. Sometimes people walk again; sometimes they don't. The bullet's still in your back. She can't see it, but she thinks if it can be removed, maybe you'll walk again."

If? Maybe? Ethan shook his head. "No," he whispered. "No." Julie's features blurred and he blinked against tears. "I can't live like this. Why didn't you let me die?"

Worn down by exhaustion and grief, Julie was in no mood for self-pity. She placed Ethan's hand beside him and leaned across, dragging the robes over him. When she spoke again, her voice was low and harsh. "People did die, Ethan. You're one of the lucky ones. The soldiers missed you when they came back down the creek, but Red Hand didn't. He found you and brought you to us. People worked all night in freezing cold to keep you alive. Even now, when there's so many wounded, White Calf Woman tends to you. Should I tell her to quit wasting her time—tell her to spend it with people that ain't afraid to live? Is that wha'chu want?"

She waited until Ethan looked at her before continuing. "You're gonna do what I say. You're gonna build up your strength, and when you're strong enough, we'll cut the bullet out and you'll walk again. You hear me?"

They stared at each other for several seconds before Ethan nodded. Without word, Julie pushed herself to her feet. He heard her moving about, and when she returned with the cup, drank its contents without protest.

"You want water?"

"Yes."

"And some broth? Are you hungry?"

He was.

She brought them both and held him while he drank. When he finished, she rose without speaking and would have left him.

"Julie?"

She gave an exhausted sigh and turned to face him.

"How many were killed?"

Her shoulders slumped, and she sank down beside him. "No one knows. More'n a hundred, but people keep turnin' up every day."

"George?"

"He's here. And Ed. But Charley's missing."

"Micah's dead. And Yellow Leaf. I saw them." His throat constricted. When he was able, he listed the dead he'd seen.

When he finished, Julie sat without speaking, her head bowed. When she looked at him, her eyes were filled with intense sadness. For the first time, Ethan noticed the dark circles under them.

"You're tired."

She pressed her hands to her face and nodded. "There's lots a' wounded. There ain't been much time for sleep."

"Sorry," he said. "Sorry to be a burden."

She lowered her hands. "You ain't a burden, Ethan. Don'chu ever think that." She offered him a wan smile and touched his cheek with her fingertips. "Rest up now. Tomorrow's gonna be rough. We're heading fer Turkey Creek to join with the Sioux and Northern Arapaho."

She pushed herself to her feet and left him. Ethan heard her moving about, heard her speaking to others, and realized she tended other wounded inside the lodge. Beyond its walls he could hear wails as the Cheyenne continued to mourn their dead.

He lay quietly for a time, agonizing over not having stayed with Tall Grass, convinced that if he'd been with her he could have saved her. Grief threatened to engulf him, and he tried once more to move his legs. Nothing happened. He couldn't feel them move against the robes, couldn't feel the weight of the robes pressing down on them. Ethan shifted his left hand, and using what little strength he possessed, pinched his thigh. He felt nothing.

A sob rose from deep within him, but he forced it down, not wanting anyone to hear. He closed his eyes, but nothing would stop the tears that overflowed and coursed down the sides of his face. He would never ride again; never hunt. The life he'd begun building for himself was over; the people he'd planned to spend it with, dead. Without Tall Grass, without his legs... Fire shot from his broken ribs as Ethan caught his breath, stifling a sob.

He had become a burden. A liability. There was no place for him among the Cheyenne. *And no way to get back to Illinois.* He thought of his parents and Kate and Josh. When Tall Grass was alive, he'd accepted that he might not see them again. Now, faced with knowing that he would never be with them, never be with Tall Grass or Micah, his sorrow was more than he could bear. Without his legs, without Tall Grass, he had no desire to live.

Chest heaving, Ethan stared blindly ahead. "You won," he whispered in his mother's tongue, addressing Sergeant Shunk, General Reynolds, Major Hawkes, the members of the Court, and most bitterly, Frank Myers. "I am Lakota. For that you hated me enough to want me dead. Now you will have your wish."

* * *

Josh closed the door, shutting out the cold. Pulling off his gloves, he looked around the store. Mr. Harrison was balanced on a step stool behind the counter, retrieving a tin from one of the upper shelves.

"Be with you in a minute, Josh," he said, glancing over his shoulder.

"No hurry, Mr. Harrison. I'm waiting for Kate to get here from school." Josh set the basket he was carrying on the counter and nodded to the woman customer. "Afternoon, Mrs. Peebles."

The woman's eyes narrowed, and her mouth tightened into a hard line. She jerked her head in curt response and looked away.

Taken aback by her rudeness, Josh shook his head and headed for the back room.

Harvey Peebles was getting to his feet when he walked in. He passed Josh without speaking.

Josh looked after him, puzzled, then spun a chair, straddled it, and held out his hands to the stove. The newspaper Maggie's father had been reading caught his eye, and he picked it up, scanning the headlines: 'SHERMAN LEAVES ATLANTA FOR MARCH TO SEA', 'LINCOLN REELECTION – FINAL VOTE TALLIES', 'CONGRESS TO FACE CONSTITUIONAL ABOLITION OF SLAVERY', 'CONFEDERATE ATTEMPT TO BURN NEW YORK CITY', "INDIAN TROUBLES – BLOODY BATTLE IN COLORADO TERRITORY." The bold letters midway down the second column grabbed his attention.

"Colonel J. M. Chivington, commanding the District of Colorado, in a letter to the editor of the *Rocky Mountain News* reports that between four and five hundred Cheyenne Indians have been killed in 'one of the most bloody Indian battles ever fought on these plains.' The battle took place on the twenty-ninth of November on the South Bend of the Big Sandy in southeastern Colorado Territory. Reported among the dead are chiefs Black Kettle, White Antelope, and Little Robe. According to Colonel Chivington, several hundred horses and mules belonging to the savages were captured. Nine soldiers were reported killed and thirty-eight wounded—"

"I'm here, Josh."

He looked up to find Kate standing in the doorway, eyes bright, her cheeks flushed with cold.

"Mr. Harrison has the things on Ma's list. We can go just as soon as you pay."

Josh tossed the newspaper aside and followed her. He paid the tally Mr. Harrison set before him and hefted the basket. They were almost to the door when the bell above it tinkled, and Mrs. Harrison burst in on a blast of cold air.

"Josh! Kate!" she exclaimed. "There's a letter for you. All the way from Washington!"

Josh and Kate exchanged looks and followed her to the counter. Mrs. Harrison bustled behind it, unwinding her scarf as she went, and disappeared into the small room that served as office and cloakroom. She re-emerged, absent her coat and hat, and clutching a stack of envelopes.

"It's here somewhere," she muttered, sorting through them. "Ah, yes! Here it is."

Josh took the envelope. The upper left-hand corner was imprinted with the words 'Executive Mansion, Washington, D. C.'; it had been addressed in a flowing hand to "The Family of Private Ethan Fraser". A combination of hope and dread surged through him.

"What is it?" Kate asked, craning to see.

Josh looked at the Harrisons. They were staring at the envelope with undisguised curiosity. "It's addressed to all of us, Kate," he said, slipping it into his pocket. "We'll open at home."

Kate and the Harrisons looked equally disappointed. Josh picked up the basket, and with Kate following, started for the door.

"Wait!" Mrs. Harrison said, holding up a small, grimy envelope. " Here's another one. In all the excitement, I forgot. This one's for you, too."

Kate went back for it. The handwriting was unfamiliar, and there was nothing to indicate where it had been mailed. Josh glanced at it briefly before slipping it into his pocket.

As soon as they were clear of the town, Josh pulled the wagon to a stop and looked at Kate. "What do you think? The letter's addressed to all of us. Shall we open it?"

Kate looked at him, caught between anticipation and dread. After a moment, she nodded.

Josh pulled out the envelope and handed it to her.

"What if it's bad news?" she asked, eyeing it apprehensively.

"We'll know one way or another soon enough. You want to find out now?"

Kate nodded again, and using her teeth, pulled off a mitten. She slid a finger under the seal and drew out the letter, glancing nervously at Josh before unfolding it.

At the top, were the words 'Executive Mansion', and below them, 'Washington' and a space for the date. It had been filled in the week before, on the thirtieth of November. Kate ran her eyes down the page. Josh leaned in close, squinting to make out the words in the fading light.

"He's been pardoned!" Kate whispered, unbelieving. "Ethan's been pardoned! Look! It's signed by the President himself!"

She flung both arms around him, forcing him to hold the letter up and read it over her shoulder. When he got to the end, Josh closed his eyes for an instant, then looked heavenward. "Thank you!" he whispered, and wrapped his arms around Kate.

The trip home was accomplished at a fast clip. Josh had no sooner pulled the snorting horse to a halt, than the two of them were down from the wagon and into the barn. Failing to find their father, they hurried to the house.

Their parents were seated together at one end of the kitchen table, hands entwined, deep in conversation. They looked up, startled, when Kate and Josh burst into the room.

"It's Ethan!" Kate announced, unable to contain herself. "He's been pardoned by President Lincoln himself! Show them, Josh!"

James had started to rise, but he sank back as Josh handed him the envelope. He held it on the table before him for several moments before pulling out the letter. He read it aloud to Sarah, his voice shaking. At the end, his eyes misted, and he groped for her hand. She took it and leaned toward him, pressing her cheek to his. James wrapped an arm about her, and for the first time in their lives, Kate and Josh saw their mother and father weep. They waited uncertainly, eyeing each other over their parents' heads. Then Sarah reached for Kate and they were all in each other's arms, laughing and talking all at once.

"We need to find him," James said, as the initial relief wore off. "Find him and bring him home."

Josh nodded. "I'll go. Just as soon as it warms up." He looked at his mother. "You can tell me where to look, can't you, Ma?

Sarah nodded. "I can draw for you. Show you places the Lakota go in the warm months. Tell you things to look for."

"We'll draw a map," James agreed. "Your mother can help mark it."

"We need to tell Elizabeth," Kate interrupted. "And Alice."

"You're right," Josh said, wondering why he hadn't thought of it himself. He folded the letter and restored it to its envelope. "Elizabeth deserves to see this. I'll take it to her."

Sarah laid a hand on his arm. "Wait," she said, her voice gentle, but firm. "It is dark now, and supper will be ready soon. Elizabeth can wait until morning."

"Your mother's right. Not knowing for a few hours won't hurt her." James took his coat from the peg and shrugged into it. "Come on, Josh. I'll help you with the horse."

With reluctance, Josh laid the envelope on the table and followed his father out to the barn.

It wasn't until she was in bed that night that Kate remembered the second envelope. She thought of it again midway through breakfast. Looking across the table at Josh, she asked, "What happened to the other letter?"

He paused with his fork halfway to his mouth. A moment passed before he remembered. "Oh. Right." He pushed back his chair and went to retrieve it.

"Here, Pa," he said, handing his father the small, stained envelope. "In all the excitement yesterday, I forgot this."

Sarah stared at the envelope, gripped by a sudden, nameless terror. It threatened to choke off her breath, but she forced out the words, "What is it? Who is it from?"

James' brow wrinkled. "Doesn't say." Turning the envelope over, he broke the seal. He unfolded the slip of paper, saw the familiar writing, and looked up smiling. "It's from Ethan."

"Where is he?" Josh and Kate asked in unison.

"What happened?" Sarah echoed, her heart filled with dread.

"Dear Ma and Pa and Kate," James read. "Much has changed since I last wrote. Since May, I've been in western Kansas with Black Kettle's Cheyenne. I have made some great friends among them and am happier now than I have ever been. This life appeals to me in ways you would understand, Ma. If things work out as I hope, I may stay with them for some time to come. We're wintering now along Big Sandy Creek in Colorado Territory. It's easy to get letters mailed from here, so I will try to write more often. I love you all and miss you. Ethan."

"He's not coming back?" Tears glistened in Kate's eyes.

Sarah shook herself, wondering what had come over her. Ethan wasn't with her people, but he was with their allies. He was safe and happy, and that was all that mattered.

Josh stared at his father in horror. "The Cheyenne?" he asked. "Ethan's with the Cheyenne? In Colorado Territory?" He reached for the letter. "Let me see that."

Black Kettle. The name from the newspaper account leapt out at him. *Big Sandy Creek. Colorado Territory.* It was all there in Ethan's hand.

"Josh?"

His mother's voice conveyed her premonition of doom. He looked up. She was sitting absolutely still, eyes fixed on his face, imploring him to tell her. He glanced at Kate and his father. They were looking at him in alarm. Josh opened his mouth, but no words came.

"The *Register*," he blurted. "Yesterday, while I was waiting for Kate. There was a report of a battle between the Cheyenne and the army at a place called Big Sandy in southeast Colorado Territory. It said this chief, this Black Kettle, was one of the ones killed. Him and four or five hundred of the men with him."

His mother didn't move, but he saw in her eyes that part of her died. Kate shook her head in disbelief.

"Are you sure, Josh?" His father's voice was raw with emotion.

Josh nodded.

"What else?"

"I don't know. Kate came in and..." Josh gestured helplessly. "I didn't know it was important."

"I want to see it!" James slammed his fist onto the table. "I won't believe it until I've seen it with my own eyes."

Josh surged to his feet, knocking over his chair. "I'll go."

He threw a saddle on his horse and rode at breakneck speed into town, trying not to think and hoping he was wrong. At Harrison's Dry Goods, he ignored the greetings of people he knew, pushing past them to grab the newspaper. "I need this," he said, waving it before a startled Mr. Harrison and tossing coins on the counter. Then he was out the door, flinging himself into the saddle and whirling the horse, spurring it past curious onlookers and ignoring angry shouts from people forced to leap out of his way.

He rode until he was almost home. Pulling the horse to a stop in a grove of winter-bare trees along the Spoon River, he opened the paper and looked again at the article midway down the third page. It was all there, exactly as he remembered. Sorrow welled up, choking him, and for several minutes all he could do was sit, the fingers of one hand pressed to his eyes. *Four to five hundred men.* With that many killed, odds were, Ethan was among them.

But maybe not. Maybe he hadn't joined in the fighting. Maybe he'd kept out of it. Or maybe being half white had saved him. Hope took hold, and Josh clung to it.

19

"No!" Elizabeth crushed the letter to her breast and turned to stare out the window. *First James; now Ethan. It isn't right!* Snow was swirling down, and she was struck by a vision of Ethan lying still on the ground, white flakes settling unheeded on his face, slowly burying him.

"No!" She said, shaking her head to rid herself of the image. She turned to Josh, her eyes bright with angry tears. "Your parents told me he'd be safe. They said it over and over again!" Elizabeth thrust the crumpled letter at him. "And now you're showing me this? Are you telling me he's dead?" A sob escaped her, and she brushed away tears with the back of her hand.

"No." Josh stepped forward and retrieved the letter. "That's not what I'm saying. I just wanted you to know what we know; that he was with the Cheyenne when this happened. Nothing tells us how many Indians survived. Chances are, Ethan was one of them. Chances are, he wasn't in the fighting. I can't see him joining a fight against soldiers, can you?"

Elizabeth said nothing. Josh waited; watching as despair slowly gave way to hope.

"Maybe you're right," she murmured. "Maybe he wasn't part of it." She looked at Josh. "We have no way of knowing, do we? It could be he's just fine, and we'll hear from him soon."

Josh nodded.

"But if we don't... ?" She bit her bottom lip, leaving the question unfinished.

"If we don't, I intend to go looking for him. I plan on going even if we do hear from him—to tell him it's safe to come home."

"What do you mean?"

"There was another letter. From Washington. Ethan's been pardoned."

Elizabeth's eyes widened. "He's free to come home? Oh, Josh..." Tears overflowed and this time she did nothing to stop them. "He can come home", she said, offering him a watery smile.

"If he's alive," Josh cautioned. "And if I can find him. It won't do to get your hopes up."

"He's alive,' Elizabeth said fiercely. "And you will find him. I know you will." She took his hand in hers. "Promise me you won't come home without him. Promise me, Josh."

Josh shook his head. "It's not a promise I can make. You know that. I'll do my best. If I find him, I promise I'll bring him home."

"When will you go?"

"Before we knew what happened in Colorado, I was thinking I'd wait for spring. But now..." Josh lifted a shoulder; let it drop.

"Go now," Elizabeth urged. "Please, Josh. Before anything else happens."

Not for the first time, Josh found himself wondering how Ethan could have left her. It occurred to him that he was dreading it himself.

"Before the week's out," he promised, gently disengaging his hand.

* * *

In the first gray light of dawn, Ethan was bundled into layers of robes, and two of the Bent cousins carried him outside. They secured him to one of the many drags that would bear the wounded north and left him. For the first time, he saw that the camp was in an area of heavy timber. It was clear and bitterly cold, the sky slowly lightening to a pale, crystalline blue above the skeletal gray branches of the cottonwoods. All around him was the usual flurry of activity that accompanied a move. Women, shapeless in their winter garments, their breath coming in white puffs, hoisted the drags into place and secured the heavy loads on pack animals. Dogs barked and horses stomped, snorting plumes into the frosty air. The only difference was the complete absence of chatter and laughter. The silence was eerie, broken only by an occasional muttered comment or wail of grief.

As Ethan lay there, an idea began to take shape. His heart beat faster, charged with a combination of anticipation and dread. Already an opportunity was presenting itself. Somewhere along the way, out of Julie's sight, he would simply roll off the drag and be left behind.

It'll be easy, he told himself. All he needed was to work free of the robes. Once the shivering stopped, he would simply fall asleep. All in all, an effective and painless way to go. Resolved to do it, he caught his breath as the drag bumped forward and the first wave of agony coursed though him.

It didn't take long to realize that, simple as his plan was, accomplishing it was beyond him. Early on, before pain dulled his senses, he tried extracting his left arm from the robes, only to discover that he barely had strength to move it, much less work it free and push himself off.

By the time the jolting stopped, midway through the afternoon, he was barely clinging to consciousness—only dimly aware of sound and movement as the drag was laid flat and lodges erected. He was no sooner deposited inside, than he was instantly asleep.

The next day was much the same—and the next. Midway through the fourth day, the Cheyenne reached the Solomon River and went into camp near Spotted Tail and Pawnee Killer's bands of Sioux and eighty lodges of Northern Arapaho. This time, as Ethan was lifted from the drag, a sharp pain spasmed through his lower back. Memory of it was gone in an instant, blending with all his other aches and pains as he succumbed to exhausted sleep.

It was dark when Julie woke him. Ethan opened his eyes to the sight of the dreaded cup. It wasn't until she went to fetch his supper that he became aware of an odd sensation in his legs. He tried wriggling his toes, certain he felt them move against the robes. He wriggled them again before calling out.

Julie heard the urgency in his voice and was at his side in an instant.

"My toes," he said breathlessly, not daring to hope. "Tell me if they move."

Julie pulled back the robes, and Ethan had a fleeting sensation of weight being lifted and cooler air moving across his legs and feet. He wriggled his toes.

"They moved!" Julie said excitedly. "Do it again."

He did.

"Can you move your foot?"

He tried, not certain anything had happened until Julie looked at him smiling, and nodded. She ran a fingernail along the top of one foot and up his leg. "Do you feel this?"

He did.

"And this?" She ran the fingernail down the other leg.

"Yes!"

Ethan closed his eyes, taking a breath and holding it before slowly letting it out. His life wasn't over, after all. He realized suddenly, that he hadn't been ready for it to end. The depression that had weighed on him every waking moment was gone. A sob of relief welled up. Ethan caught his breath, stifling it.

Julie laid the robes over him and leaned down, pressing her cheek to his. "I told you, didn't I? I told you, you'd walk again!"

Ethan nodded. "I felt something. Today, when they lifted me."

Julie sat back on her heels. "I'm gonna fetch you your dinner. Then I'll get White Calf Woman. I want her to take a look at you."

Ethan nodded, too relieved to protest. Once again, he'd been offered a reprieve, a chance at life, and he grasped it gratefully.

He was dozing when someone touched his shoulder. His first thought was that it was White Calf Woman come to torture him again.

"Ethan? You awake?"

"George?" Ethan struggled to wakefulness to find George sitting beside him.

"I hear you'll be riding again soon."

Ethan offered him a weak smile. "Soon."

"I wanted to see you before we go."

"Go? Where... ?"

"Down to the Purgatoire. Me and Ed. We got us some horses from the Sioux, and we're heading out tomorrow morning."

"Why?"

"We figure we can get weapons. Get some news. Find out what happened to Charley."

"He never showed up?"

George shook his head. "No sign of him."

"You coming back?"

"Yeah. I don't plan on being gone long. When we got to the Smoky Hill, a war pipe was sent out, and the Sioux and Northern Arapaho smoked it. We have more'n a thousand warriors. We're going to war against the whites."

"You aim to be part of it?"

"You bet." George leaned forward, his gaze intense. "You were a soldier, Ethan. You know how soldiers fight. They don't attack women and children; don't gun them down when they're begging for their lives. But that's what they did. Slaughtered them like animals." George sucked in a breath, and his voice shook with anger. "That's what we are to them, Ethan. Animals. Vermin to be exterminated. What they did..." He shook his head and looked away. "You don't know the half of it."

What they did... Ethan saw Tall Grass stagger, saw her fall. His eyes burned, and he swallowed hard.

"They mutilated the dead, Ethan. Scalped them; cut them up. The men who went back to look for survivors said some had been cut so bad there was no way of telling who they were."

"I heard them," Ethan murmured, remembering the loud voices and the laughter. "I heard the soldiers when they came back down the creek. I just... I didn't know..."

"You're lucky they didn't find you. What they did was unspeakable. Worst were the ones had their private parts cut away. Men *and* women."

Tall Grass. Ethan stared at him in horror. He opened his mouth, but no sound came.

"They've declared war on us, Ethan. They deserve to die."

Tall Grass. And Micah. Plum Moon and Singing Bird. So many people... Hatred boiled up inside him.

"Ee-tin!"

George turned as a small figure barreled across the lodge toward them. He grabbed her before she could launch herself at Ethan.

"Ksi-ii-zhi-ho-ha-zi-zi!" Julie came and took her by the arm. "Ni-hi ni-i-na-zi-hi-da-zi?" she said, kneeling and pulling the little girl to her. Remember what I told you?

Hand in mouth, Girl Who Laughs looked from Julie to Ethan. She nodded, and Julie released her. The little girl knelt beside the pallet.

"She's been asking to see you. I thought this'd be a good time."

"Ksi-ii-zhi-ho-ha-zi-zi." Ethan smiled, even as the sight of her tore at his heart.

"Ee-tin." Girl Who Laughs reached a hand toward his face, then stopped, looking to Julie for permission.

Julie nodded. "Hi-gi-zhi-ss-da-zi." Be gentle.

The little girl touched her fingers to his cheek and asked a question. Julie answered. The child said something more, and once again, Julie responded.

Ethan moved his left arm beneath the robes, trying unsuccessfully to extricate it. Julie came to his aid, and he wrapped it around the little girl, holding her close.

"Who's looking after her?"

"A family from the Mah-sih́-ko-ta clan took her in."

"Her family?"

"Two uncles and some cousins. They were hunting when the soldiers attacked."

"None of the women?"

Julie shook her head. "Not that I heard of."

"She should go to her grandfather. To Henri Broulat."

"That's up to her uncles."

"It's what her mother would want, Julie." Ethan said it with all the force he could muster. "It's what I want." His eyes shifted to George. "Take her with you tomorrow."

"It's up to her uncles," Julie repeated.

"Talk to them. Now. Tonight. She should go to Henri. She's all he has left."

"Talk to them, Julie," George urged.

Julie looked from him to Ethan. After a moment, she nodded. "All right. I'll talk to them."

"Convince them."

"Yes, Ethan. I'll convince them."

She reached for Girl Who Laughs, but Ethan gripped her tighter. "Leave her be."

"But..."

"Julie." George reverted to Cheyenne, speaking softly.

Their conversation was brief, and when it ended, Julie got to her feet and left them.

George and Ed had been gone less than a week when Ethan had another visitor. He was awake, propped against a backrest when the door flap opened.

"Ma-hi-o-nah!"

Red Hand knelt beside him, placing the butt of the Spencer on the ground between them. "Yours," he said, making the sign.

Ethan looked at the carbine in astonishment. He reached out and touched the scarred wooden stock with his fingertips. "How... ? Where find?" he asked in rudimentary Cheyenne.

Red Hand laid the carbine across Ethan's lap. "Black Coyote. He picked it up where we found you. He kept it for you."

Ethan watched Red Hand's gestures. "Ha-ho!" he said. Thank you! Making the signs as best he could with his left hand, he added, "Tell him I'm grateful."

He had thought everything he owned was lost. Now, unexpectedly, he had the Spencer back. Ethan ran his fingers over it, the mere sight of it boosting his spirits. He took the deepest breath his broken ribs would allow and looked at Red Hand. "Ha-ho! Thank you for everything. I heard how you found me and brought me back. I owe you my life."

Red Hand shook his head. "Once, when I was shot by the soldiers, you helped me. Now we are even."

It wasn't true, and they both knew it, but to argue would have been pointless. Instead Ethan said, "I heard your wife and son came to the camp on the Manó-iyo-he.[17] I was happy to hear it."

Red Hand nodded. "They escaped to the sand hills. They found other people there and dug holes to pass the night. They started walking before the sun came up; before the soldiers could find them."

"They walked all the way to the Manó-iyo-he?"

"Much of the way. Each day, men rode out to look for survivors and watch for soldiers. They were found and brought to the camps."

Ethan was beginning to tire. Making the signs was exhausting. Red Hand saw it and rose to leave. "I look forward to the day when we will ride together again."

Ethan offered him a wan smile. "It'll be a while. I can't even sit up yet. And I don't have a horse."

Red Hand grinned as he turned away, but Ethan missed it. His eyes were already closing.

Julie smiled when she came into the lodge and saw the carbine lying across Ethan's lap. She set down the wood she was carrying, and moving quietly so as not to awaken him, collected the things she'd saved from underneath his

---

17   Bunch of Timbers River, the Smoky Hill River

backrest. She set the pile on the robe beside him and looked up to find him watching her.

"My clothes!" he murmured softly.

"Some of 'em were ruined—the coat and shirt, but I kept the rest for you." She smiled, holding up his ammunition pouch. "This was in one of the coat pockets. I reckon you have a use for it now. The leggings and moccasins are in good shape, and I cleaned the blood outta the breechclout."

Ethan rubbed the blue fabric between his thumb and forefinger, remembering the day Plum Moon had given it to him. Grief welled up, and he averted his face. He felt Julie lift his left arm and work something cold over his hand, sliding it halfway up his forearm.

There was a catch in her voice when she said, "We'll be movin' again tomorrow. You want me to help you dress?"

Ethan nodded, unable to speak. When she had gone, he looked down at the heavy silver armlet. *They'll pay*, he promised Micah. *Just as soon as I'm able, I'll see that they pay.*

The drums had quieted, the war parties gone out to raid, and Ethan was on his feet again, able to walk short distances unassisted, by the time George returned to the eight hundred lodges of Sioux, Cheyenne and Arapaho massed along Cherry Creek in the northwest corner of Kansas. Charley was with him, as were Charley's mother, two other women and three children the soldiers from Fort Lyon had rescued and turned over to his father.

Charley and the women had first-hand accounts of the unspeakable brutality of the soldiers and the depredations inflicted on the bodies of dead. Much of it was already known, but the newcomers had new horrors to relate: an old woman scalped alive and left to wander, blinded by blood and a flap of skin that dangled over her eyes; fingers and ears sliced off for their jewelry, children with their skulls crushed, captive women and children shot and scalped, a baby cut from its mother's stomach and left to die in the cold, another tossed from a wagon as the soldiers departed. Nine high-ranking Cheyenne chiefs—White Antelope, Lone Bear, War Bonnet, Yellow Wolf, Spotted Crow, Standing in Water, Two Thighs, Bear Man, and Yellow Shield—along with a number of lesser standing, had been killed. Everything not stolen by the soldiers had been burned; the dead left for the animals.

"It was my own brother led them to us," George told Ethan, his face reflecting a mix of anger and guilt.

"Your brother?" Ethan's eyes met Charley's across the fire.

"Bob." Charley spat the name. "Bastard led 'em right to us. I ever see him again, he's a dead man. Him and the old man both."

The exchange had taken place in English. One of the men gathered with them in the lodge spoke, and Charley responded in Cheyenne.

Ethan turned to George. "It's true?" he asked in disbelief.

George nodded.

"How could he? He's half Cheyenne, married to a Cheyenne."

"The soldiers forced him. Threatened to kill him and his family. Pa, too."

Ethan shook his head. "But he led them to family—to you and Julie and Charley. To his own blood kin. Why didn't he lead them somewhere else? Tell them he didn't know where to find us?"

"Old Jim Beckwourth was with them. Bob said Jim had a pretty good idea where our camp was, so there wasn't much he could do. He said he'd hoped to get their ammunition wet, but they kept too close an eye on him."

Ethan looked at Charley, who was spewing a torrent of angry words, his lean face contorted with hate. "You think he'd kill his own brother?"

"He might. If he gets a chance. They held him in chains for a week at Fort Lyon. When they let him go, he went wild, threatened our father. The old man kicked him out. Told him never to come back." George shook his head. "There's no telling what he'll do."

The angry conversation around them was escalating. Ethan had to raise his voice to be heard.

"What about Ed?"

"Turned himself in. When we got close, we could see soldiers camped all around Fort Lyon. There were more tents over by my father's ranch. Ed thought we'd never make it past without getting shot, so he went and turned himself in. That was before we heard about Jack Smith." George looked at Ethan. "You hear about him?"

"No. What happened?"

"He's dead. When the worst of the shooting was over, he and Charley went back to the camp and surrendered. The soldiers kept at them, accusing them of murder and rape. Charley says Jack admitted it, boasted of it even." George eyed his brother. "I'm willing to bet he did, too. The next day, one of the soldiers stuck a pistol through the side of old man Smith's lodge and shot Jack where he sat. Murdered him. Charley says they came for him next, but he was with the Autobeas boys—from Fort Lyon. We've known them for years. They threatened to shoot anyone who came near him. When the soldiers couldn't have Charley, they spent the day dragging Jack's body behind a horse."

"Where was his father?"

"Word is, the soldiers called him outside before they shot Jack. There wasn't anything he could do to stop it."

George was speaking loudly, but there were so many angry voices raised that Ethan could barely hear him. The talk had renewed his anger and grief, and his strength was beginning to ebb. He reached for his robe. "I need to go."

George leaned in to hear him.

"I'm tired. I need to lie down."

George nodded. "I'll help you."

He helped Ethan to his feet, and they made their way behind the circle of men gathered around the fire. They had reached the door when Charley's voice rose, harsh and taunting above the rest.

"Runnin' away, E-nu-tah?"[18]

Ethan stopped, then slowly turned. George looked from Ethan to his brother. There was a cruel light in Charley's eyes as he rose to confront Ethan.

"Time to pick a side, half-white. Us or them. You pick them, you better light on outta here. Else I aim to kill you, same as every other vi-hoi I come across." Reverting to Cheyenne, he shook a fist at Ethan and shouted, "Death to the whites!"

A shout went up, cutting off any response Ethan might have made. Charley leered at him and sank back down, adding his angry voice to the others.

Furious, Ethan slapped the flap and ducked outside. He caught his breath, wincing as he straightened.

George came out behind him and took him by the arm. "You all right?"

Eyes closed, Ethan nodded. They stood without speaking until Ethan indicated he was ready to walk. "He made me mad," he said between breaths. "I can't move that fast."

"He's out of control. I'll talk to him. Get him to leave you alone."

---

18   Woman of another tribe; foreigner

Intent on making his way over the broken snow to the next lodge, Ethan didn't reply. Once he reached it, he stopped and looked at George. "Tell him I intend to kill every soldier I come across. Just as soon as I can ride."

George nodded. "Figured as much."

He stepped into the lodge ahead of Ethan, reaching back a hand to help him. Ethan leaned heavily on it, but the pain of bending and straightening was considerable. George walked him to the pallet they shared and helped lower him onto it.

Ethan collapsed against the backrest, eyes closed, waiting for the pain to subside.

"They take the bullet out of your back?"

"No."

"Why not?"

"Doesn't bother me. Can't take any more pain."

George nodded understanding. "I brought back some clothes. There's a shirt, coat and a pair of britches, if you're interested."

"Thanks." The pain was beginning to ease, but Ethan still lay with his eyes closed. All he wanted was to lose himself in sleep, to shut out the thoughts that tormented him. To try not to think what the soldiers had done to Tall Grass.

JANUARY 1865

20

Snow flurries and biting winds marked the days as the war parties returned to the camps, bearing plunder and driving cattle and horses before them. Red Hand appeared with an armload of canned goods, not understanding what they were and wanting an explanation. Ethan showed him how to open them and was rewarded with a feast of canned peaches and oysters.

When all the war parties returned, councils were held to plan revenge for Sand Creek. Leg in the Water and Little Robe spoke for the Cheyenne, replacing Black Kettle, who many blamed for the massacre and no longer trusted. It was decided that the target for retaliation would be Julesburg, a tiny settlement on the South Platte, in northeastern Colorado Territory. The Sioux knew it well; saying that, in addition to the stage station and the stock, there was a telegraph office, a store, and a large warehouse filled with the stage company's supplies. There was a fort as well, but it was of no consequence. It stood off from the town and had few soldiers.

It was agreed that everything possible would be done to preserve the element of surprise. The war party would move quickly and quietly, with soldier societies deployed to the rear and along both flanks to keep order and prevent the over-anxious from slipping away on individual raids that would betray their presence to the whites. The attack, when launched, would be made according to strict plan. The criers rode through the camps, and preparations began.

There was nothing Ethan could do but watch, consumed with envy, when the massive war party set out. He stood among the old men, the children, and the trilling women, hearing the names they called as their men rode past. It was an orderly departure, led by the chiefs of the Sioux and the Dog Soldiers, the first to smoke the war pipe, followed by the chiefs of the Arapaho and Cheyenne.

Behind the chiefs came more than a thousand warriors, flanked by the warrior societies charged with keeping order. The sight of Red Hand riding among the Crooked Lances made Ethan even more desperate to be with them. Two Bulls and Black Coyote were there, and Ethan stared in disbelief when Feathered Bear caught his eye. No one had thought to mention he was alive. He began watching closely, and caught sight of several people from the Wŭ-ta-pi-u clan he'd thought never to see again. Wind Woman and Little Crow were among them, riding with the women and boys going along to tend the extra ponies.

Julie and her stepmothers were there, too. Julie caught Ethan's eye as she rode past and mouthed, "Next time."

Ethan nodded grimly. He continued to watch until the last of the Dog Soldiers, George and Charley among them, blended into the distant prairie. Only then did he turn away, certain he'd missed out on his best opportunity for revenge. It was galling to be left behind when each day, he could feel himself growing stronger. To look at them, his wounds were all but healed. He felt certain he could ride with the broken ribs; it was his shoulder that was holding him back. There was no way he could handle a horse and a weapon with only one arm. Ethan flexed his right arm and grimaced. He couldn't tolerate the kick of the Spencer. *Not just yet.*

He blew out a long breath, swept away white on the wind, and shrugged down into the coat George had given him. It was buckskin, gray with age, and when the wind blew, as it almost always did, the cold went straight to his bones. He considered going back to the lodge for a robe, but decided against it. The indoor warmth would tempt him when what he needed was to walk and rebuild his strength. He headed for the nearest stand of trees, seeking refuge from the wind.

He was in their lee, absently eyeing the depleted pony herd, when a shock of light-colored mane caught his eye. Ethan stopped and stared. The icy wind brought tears to his eyes, and he blinked to clear them. Scarcely daring to hope, he began walking toward the distant hillside. His heart beat faster when he saw it was a horse, not one of the Indian ponies. He whistled, but the sound vanished on the wind. Another hundred yards, and he whistled again.

This time, the horse's head shot up, ears pricked. Ethan saw the distinctive white blaze and let out a whoop. He whistled, and the mare cantered toward him, slowing to a walk as she drew near, neck extended, nostrils quivering as she sought the smell of him.

Ethan spoke her name and held out a hand, wishing he had a treat to offer her. She nuzzled his palm and took the last step to him, butting him in the chest with her head. Unable to believe his good fortune, he rubbed her neck, cooing softly while he looked her over. Her winter coat had grown in thick, but not thick enough to hide the ripple of her ribs. She had lost weight, but it pleased him to see she was faring better than some of the Indian ponies. Exhilaration swept through him. A saddle, a bridle, a few more weeks to mend, and he'd be ready to ride.

* * *

The horses' hooves punched through the frozen surface of the snow drifted along the edge of a shallow gully. Gathering themselves, they lunged up the bank to the brown, wind-blown grass on the far side.

"That's it up ahead," the man in the lead said.

Josh squinted at the wide swath of creek bed a mile or so distant, but didn't reply. He was too busy dreading what he might find.

His first indication that events at Sand Creek had not occurred as initially reported had come from a short item, buried deep in the *St. Louis Daily Union* beneath the heading, "CONGRESS TO INVESTIGATE." It suggested that the Cheyenne had surrendered before they were attacked, that most of the dead were women and children. The report had been confirmed one bleak afternoon a week later, when he chanced upon a troop of cavalry on the east Kansas prairie. The officer in charge, a Major Wynkoop, was riding from Fort Riley to retake command at Fort Lyon and investigate the attack. Weeks had passed since he'd first heard of it, but he was still fuming.

"Most of them were friendlies," he said, when Josh joined the officers huddled around the fire that evening. "The old men, the chiefs, came in under my offer of protection, and Chivington attacked them."

"I'm looking for a half-breed. Half Sioux. Last I heard, he was with them."

"Half Sioux, you say?" The major accepted the bottle of whiskey being passed among them, took a healthy swig, and handed it to Josh. "The only half-breeds I know tend to run with that bunch are part Cheyenne—a couple of the Bent boys, Ed Guerrier, Jack Smith, one of Henri Broulat's sons. I never heard of a half Sioux, but that doesn't mean he wasn't there. There's too many half-breeds in the camps to keep track." He studied Josh before asking, "What's your interest in this one?"

"My brother."

"Ahh." The major looked into the fire. "I'll be conducting interviews when I get to Fort Lyon, talking to men who were there. If I hear anything, I'll let you know. Meantime, you might look up old William Bent. See what he knows. John Smith, too, if he's anywhere to be found."

Major Wynkoop had pointed the way to the Bent ranch as they approached Fort Lyon, and Josh had ridden there directly. The old man hadn't been particularly helpful, but a show of cash had persuaded his eldest son to lead Josh to the site of the massacre.

Now, as they descended the shallow incline leading to a sandy creek bed a couple hundred yards wide, Bob Bent turned in the saddle. "That's it, yonder," he said, tilting his head toward the opposite bank. "Where the camp was."

Josh wasn't looking. He had stopped his horse and was staring down at a scattered pile of bones, the remains of more than one person, with fragments of hair and flesh still attached. One skull was tiny, the side of it crushed. He looked to where Bob waited near the far bank, horror plain on his face. "This was a baby," he protested. "An infant."

The half-breed said nothing. After a moment, he turned his horse and rode on.

Josh prodded his mount toward the charred willows that lined the far bank. To his left, a mangy dog rose snarling from beside a half-eaten corpse. He turned his horse toward it, and the dog bared its teeth, growling deep in its throat before slinking off a short distance. Josh looked at what the dog had left. The face was gone, as was the hair at the top of the head, but what remained was long and gray. *Not Ethan.* As Josh moved away, the dog skirted around him and returned to its feast.

He followed the trail of scattered remains for two miles up the creek. Every corpse he came upon had been ravaged by animals, but the desecration by humans was worse. All had been scalped, and many had had ears, noses or fingers cut off. He found women with one or both breasts missing; men, women, and even children, with their sex cut away.

Fighting down bile that rose at the back of his throat, Josh forced himself to examine every male body he came to before moving on to the next. Sometimes it was impossible to tell the sex, and he had to dismount for a closer look. Occasionally, he was forced to turn a head, or pry a corpse loose from the frozen ground and roll it over.

Once, just as the light was beginning to fade, he thought he'd found Ethan, and his stomach gave a dangerous lurch. The young man had been horribly mutilated. He was tall and slender, very like Ethan, and it wasn't until Josh dismounted and turned what remained of his face out of the sand that he knew for certain it wasn't him.

It was then he was sick. He staggered away from the corpse and went down on his hands and knees, retching until there was nothing left to come up. He sat for several minutes afterward, too shaken to move. Then he pushed himself to his feet and climbed back into the saddle.

He reached the sand pits just as it was getting dark. He rode among them, appalled by what he saw. It hadn't been a battle at all. Everything pointed to a frantic flight up the creek, followed by a desperate fight to survive. Josh turned in the saddle, surveying the pocked creek bed, wondering if this was where he would find Ethan. With a heavy heart, he turned his horse and headed back to look for his guide.

Bob had set up camp next to the creek, downstream from the piles of burnt rubble that marked where the last circle of lodges had stood. Guided by the flicker of firelight, and the smell of roasting meat, Josh made his way to him.

"It was a slaughter," he said, as he came into the light. He dropped his saddle and sank down next to it. "A slaughter. They didn't stand a chance."

Bob was preparing the meal and didn't look up. "Some got away. More could of, if they'd tried."

Josh stared at him in amazement. "What do you mean? There are bodies for at least two miles up the creek. They did try."

"Not at first. At first they just stood there."

"How do you know? Were you here?"

"For a time."

"Why didn't you say so?" Josh shifted impatiently and leaned toward him. "Do you know my brother?"

"No."

"Do you know if he was here?"

"No idea."

Josh stared at him for a long moment, then sat back, frustrated by the man's reticence.

Bob pulled slabs of meat off the fire and dropped one onto each plate. He ladled liberal portions of beans onto them and piled three cold biscuits a piece on top.

"Ed would," he said, handing a plate to Josh. "George and Charley, too, but they've gone Injun. You'll have to ask Ed."

"Who's Ed? Where can I find him?"

"Brother-in-law. Prob'ly back at Fort Lyon."

"Back at Fort Lyon," Josh repeated, struggling to keep his exasperation in check. "Why didn't you tell me before we set out?"

Bob shrugged. "Figured you knew."

He began eating, shoveling food into his mouth. Josh watched him for several moments before turning to his own plate. Three bites, and he realized he wasn't hungry. He toyed with his food until Bob finished his, then set the plate aside.

Bob looked at it. "Not hungry."

It was more a statement than a question, and Josh didn't bother to respond. He was as annoyed with himself as he was with Bob. If he'd slowed down some, asked the right questions, it might have saved him a trip.

"Does Ed have a last name?"

"Guerrier."

Bob wrapped Josh's steak and biscuits, and scraped the beans back into the pot.

A frigid gust caught the bare branches above them and set them rattling. Josh shrugged deeper into his coat, thinking he could be at the fort right now, indoors with a glass of whiskey, instead of huddled on the cold prairie in the company of a man he was finding it increasingly difficult to like. In the darkness beyond the campfire, the snarling and fighting intensified.

"Wolves," Bob remarked.

"How do you know?"

Bob shrugged. "Just do."

"What about Indians? There any around here?"

"Arapaho, maybe."

Josh sat bolt upright. "Here?"

"Don't know. Maybe."

"Will they bother us?"

"Doubt it."

With that, Bob rolled into his bedroll and was soon snoring. Josh sat for a time, staring up at the stars, trying not to dwell on the reason for the escalating chorus of yips and growls. Eventually, he reached for his oilcloth and spread it on the ground. Wrapping himself in his bedroll, he snuggled down next to the fire. He closed his eyes, but sleep refused to come.

He was up with the sun and got his first good look at what remained of the Cheyenne camp. His first impression was of a frozen, desolate wasteland, charred black, and dusted gray with snow and ash. The lodges resembled the remains of giant bonfires, the ground around them scorched. As he walked through the camp, Josh began to notice bits of color: a tin trinket gleaming among the ashes, a scrap of bright fabric, a strip of leather painted red, a handful of colored beads amid trampled brown grass.

He zigzagged the entire length of the camp, searching for Ethan, before turning back. What he saw destroyed any appetite he might have had. His only thought was to check the sand pits and get away as quickly as possible.

He was striding across an open area between two groups of burnt lodges when a flutter of white amid the blackened branches of a willow caught his eye. His first thought was that it was a bird, but a gust of wind caught it, and it moved again. Curious, Josh walked toward it. His pace quickened when he saw it was a piece of paper. Not just a piece of paper, but part of a book, the charred top pages rising and falling in the wind, revealing whiter pages underneath.

Heart pounding, Josh squatted next to the willows and pulled it free. The back cover, and about a third of the pages, had burned away; the rest were badly singed. Without looking, he knew exactly what it was. Taking a deep breath, he turned it over. Most of the gold had worn off, but the title was easy to read: *The Count of Monte Cristo.* Josh's hands shook as he opened the front cover. The inscription was still there, protected from fire and weather by the thickness of the book itself.

Josh sat down hard, staring at the words. For several moments, his mind was blank. Then a feeling of doom settled over him. The presence of the book confirmed that Ethan had been in the camp when the soldiers attacked. *In the camp, but where?*

He looked up, scanning the mounds of blackened rubble nearest him. Had he been thorough enough? Had he examined every corpse? He ran a hand over his face, tired eyes burning when he closed them. Eventually, he pushed himself to his feet and began re-examining the bodies nearest where he'd found the book. Convinced that none was Ethan, he headed for his horse. Now, more than ever, he dreaded the search of the sand pits.

It went faster than he'd thought it would. Two thirds of the bodies were women and children. Many of the others were gray-haired men. Only a few could have been Ethan. None were.

Under a lowering sky, Josh left the creek and rode in ever-widening circles around the camp. He found more bodies in the sand hills and a few scattered across the prairie. None were the one he sought. It was late afternoon, dry, white flakes sifting down, when he finally gave up.

Bob was waiting, horse saddled, packhorse packed, when Josh returned. "You were a long time," he said flatly. "We won't get far before dark."

"It doesn't matter," Josh replied brusquely. "As long as we're away from here."

They covered seven miles before darkness caught them, but for Josh, it was enough. He ate his supper in silence and rolled into his bedroll. Sleep eluded him as the horrors he'd witnessed came back to haunt him. At daybreak, he was saddled up, ready to ride.

As soon as they came within sight Fort Lyon, Josh paid Bob the amount they'd agreed on and spurred away. He made arrangements for the care of his horse and headed directly to the sutler's store where he spent the evening downing glass after glass of the man's fiery, over-priced whiskey.

It was mid-morning when he stirred, opening his eyes to an unfamiliar ceiling. His head pounded, and his stomach rolled threateningly. Girding himself, he sat up, swinging his feet to the floor and staring through blurred eyes at the room. It was long and narrow, lined along its full length with identical plank beds, each made up with a pair of pillows and gray woolen blankets. Two long wooden tables, surrounded by ladder-back chairs, filled the other half of the room.

Fort Lyon, he remembered. Somehow, he'd wound up in the enlisted men's quarters.

Josh ran a hand over his face, fingering a week's worth of stubble. His stomach heaved, and he reached for his boots. He stood up cautiously, but still the room tilted. Steadying himself with a hand against the wall, he inadvertently located his coat. Josh lifted it from the peg and stumbled toward the door, noting in passing that his belongings had been placed at the foot of the bed.

He pulled the door open and staggered back, blinded by the sun. Raising a hand to shield his eyes, he stepped outside.

"I hear tell you're looking for me."

Startled, Josh turned and squinted. The man was nearly a head shorter, with a dark, pocked face, wavy black hair that reached to his shoulders and a thick black mustache. Josh was certain he'd never seen him before. He belched and swallowed.

"I'm going to..."

The man stepped aside, allowing Josh to hurry past.

When he returned, the man was waiting, chair tilted back against the wall in the sun. The front legs dropped to the ground, and he stood up.

"You're Ethan's brother."

Josh stopped short, staring at him.

"Name's Guerrier. Ed Guerrier."

A moment passed before the name registered. "I was planning to ask around about you. How did you..." Josh stopped in confusion.

"Last night you made sure everyone knew."

"I..." Josh ran fingers through tousled hair and smiled sheepishly. "I'm afraid I don't remember much." He stuck out his right hand. "Josh Fraser. You know where Ethan is?"

"Yup."

"Is he alive?"

"Last I saw, he was in a camp up on the Republican. Got himself shot up real bad when Chivington's boys attacked."

"But he's alive?"

"Last I saw."

"When was that?"

Ed's eyes focused in the distance as he calculated. "More'n a month. Long about the ninth, tenth of December. Sometime around then."

"How bad is he hurt?"

"Bad. No one thought he'd live."

"But he did?"

"Last I saw. He wasn't doing too good, but he was awake. Talking some."

Josh blew out a long breath, eyes sweeping the parade ground. "How can I find him?"

"You can't. Least not now. A pipe was sent out. The Sioux and Arapaho smoked it. We're at war."

"At war?"

"The Cheyenne people want revenge for what the soldiers did at Sand Creek. The Sioux and Arapaho joined them."

"How long is this 'war' going to last?"

Ed shrugged. "Hard telling."

"What about you? Can you take me to him?"

Ed's eyes moved to Josh's sandy hair. "That's prob'ly not a good idea right now. Not if you want to hang onto that."

"But with you... ?"

Ed shook his head. "You and I go into those camps right now, chances are only one of us rides out. That ain't gonna help Ethan."

"How do I find him?"

"Wait a few weeks. See what happens."

"Guerrier's right. You don't want to go anywhere near those camps right now, even if you could find them." Major Wynkoop rose from behind his desk and stepped over to a map tacked to the wall.

"A war party attacked Julesburg, here, on the seventh of this month," he said, pointing. "Reports say there were more than a thousand warriors, but only a few showed themselves at first. They lured a small party of soldiers and civilians out of Fort Rankin, and that's when the rest showed themselves. They surrounded Captain O'Brien's force, killing fourteen soldiers and four civilians before they made it back to the fort, along with a group of folks that had just come in on the stage. The Indians kept them pinned down all day while they looted the town, tore down telegraph wires and ran off the stock." A thought occurred to him. He smiled wryly and added, "There was a United States paymaster on that stage. He had a metal strongbox filled with pay for our troops here in Colorado. When he ran for the fort, he left the box, and the Indians broke it open. After they'd gone, the men from the garrison found bills scattered all across the valley, but they only came up with half of what the paymaster had with him." He shook his head. "Appears some of us'll be going without pay for a while."

Major Wynkoop pointed lower on the map. "Long about sunset, they vanished into these hills. No one's seen or heard from them since. When General Mitchell heard what happened, he started pulling in troops from all along the stage line." The major's finger moved east to the convergence of the North and South Platte. "They assembled here, at Camp Cottonwood. Two days ago, he marched to look for Indians, here, along the Republican."

"And if he finds them?"

"There'll be a fight. A bloody one, I'd imagine. Mitchell marched with over five hundred men, four twelve-pound howitzers and two three-inch Parrot guns."

Images of the decimated camp filled Josh's mind. If Ethan was as badly hurt as Guerrier indicated, he wouldn't be able to fight or run. *Even if I went after him now, I'd still be too late,* he thought dully. Aloud he said, "What do you suggest I do?"

"Wait." Major Wynkoop resumed his seat. "See what news comes from General Mitchell in the next week or so."

Josh shook his head in exasperation and leaned back in his chair. The thought of doing nothing chaffed at him, but it didn't appear he had much choice.

* * *

"Catch."

Something shiny, trailed by a glittering tail, arced through the air. Ethan caught it and turned it over in his hand, admiring the new gold pocket watch and chain.

"Nice," he said, preparing to toss it back.

"It's yours," George told him. "There was a whole case of them. I got that one for you."

Heavily laden ponies had been streaming into the camps all morning. Already, there was more plunder than Ethan had ever seen piled in and around the lodges. And still the ponies kept coming. For the first time since Sand Creek, voices in the Cheyenne camps were raised in something other than mourning. The drumming and scalp dances had begun.

"I got this for me," George said, holding up a blue frock coat with gold piping on the sleeves. "Brand new. Yankee blue for a Rebel half-breed. I aim to kill soldiers wearing it."

Ethan's jaw tightened, and he nodded.

"And this!"

George upended a canvas bag. Greenbacks tumbled out, fluttering onto a pallet and across the ground. Ethan went down on his knees and began gathering them up.

"There's hundreds of dollars here!" he exclaimed, dumping a fistful onto the pallet. "Where'd it come from?"

"Compliments of the U. S. Army."

"Really?" Ethan offered him a sly grin. "What else is there?"

There was a large portion of the contents of the Julesburg store and warehouse: flour, sugar, molasses, coffee, rice, dried fruit, canned goods, hams, bacon, shoes, boots, socks, gloves, hats, clothing, bolts of fabric, tools and hardware. A herd of cattle had been driven in. The drumming and feasting went on for five days before the criers rode through the camps announcing a move.

The combined tribes headed northwest, stopping at White Buttes Creek on the barren, windswept plains of northeast Colorado Territory. As the feasting and celebrating resumed, the chiefs held another council. All but a faction headed by Black Kettle favored a series of raids along the South Platte before heading north to band with the Sioux and Northern Cheyenne.

On the day the camps moved again, Black Kettle and eighty lodges of Cheyenne turned south, headed back to the Arkansas. Feathered Bear and the remnants of his family were with them, as were Red Hand, Two Bulls and several other Crooked Lances.

Ethan had gone from man to man with George the night before, shaking hands and saying good-bye. Many were good friends, and parting was hard. But hardest was saying good-bye to Red Hand.

"There are too many whites," Red Hand had said, when he told Ethan of his decision to go with Black Kettle. "We cannot win against them. You know that."

"You're right," Ethan replied. "We can't win in the long run, but they murdered our friends and families. Slaughtered them like animals. You went to Julesburg; you had your revenge. I haven't had mine yet."

"Even so, it would be better if you came with us."

"Apart from you, everyone I care about is dead or headed north. And north is where my mother's people are. If I go south, I'll never find them."

Red Hand shook his head. "I understand your search for your people, but I hope you do not regret this."

"And I hope you don't regret going back. It's taken me a while, but I've learned never to trust soldiers. Nothing says they won't lie about wanting peace and attack again. From now on, I intend to attack first."

Red Hand understood Ethan's hatred of the white soldiers. He nodded solemnly. "I hope one day our paths will cross."

"So do I. I owe you for saving my life."

Red Hand smiled, waving off any mention of a debt.

The day of their parting dawned clear and cold, sun glinting off a dusting of new-fallen snow the wind hadn't whipped away yet. Ethan watched Red Hand ride away, out along the flank with the other Crooked Lances who'd elected to go. When the last of Black Kettle's band blended into the mottled brown and white of the southern plains, he turned Faria and set out after the women, children and old men, following the warriors who'd stayed behind to protect them.

The rest, George and Charley among them, had formed war parties and headed out to raid. The plan was to attack every white settlement along the stage road from above Julesburg to within a few miles of Denver City. The Sioux had fanned out to the east, the Cheyenne to the west, and the Arapaho were headed for settlements in between.

Ethan had hoped to go with them, but his first few times aboard the mare had proved he lacked the stamina for long days of hard riding. Even now, with the stragglers mere specs on the distant prairie, he held the mare to a walk, knowing if he was to remain in the saddle all day, he would have to pace himself.

The last of the wintry light was fading when he rode in among the newly erected lodges. The long miles had taken their toll. There wasn't a part of him that didn't ache when he slid down from the mare, and he was limp with exhaustion. Even so, he waved off the woman who emerged from the lodge, preferring to tend Faria himself. He fed her a treat of dried apples and staked her beside the lodge before fetching a bucket of shelled corn from the Julesburg raid. Running a hand along her flank, he thought her ribs seemed less pronounced. Corn feeding appeared to be doing her good. Darkness had fallen by the time he collected the Cheyenne pad saddle he was using and staggered inside.

He began the next day riding near Julie and Yellow Woman. Midway through the morning, he caught himself scanning the faces of the women, searching for Tall Grass. The realization brought him up short, the certainty of never seeing her again numbing him, before he was hit by a renewed crush of grief.

"Ethan? You all right?"

Ethan glanced at Julie and nodded. Without a word, he turned and went to ride along the flank.

Being alone did nothing to diminish his grief, but it spared him trying to hide it. The pain of losing Tall Grass was, at times, more than he could bear; made worse by having lost her just as he'd committed to spending his life with her. It tormented him that she'd died not knowing.

The crackle of distant gunfire broke in on his thoughts. The warriors nearest him charged ahead, angling across the wide valley of the South Platte.

Ethan followed more slowly, seeing smoke and flames long before he reached the white settlement.

By the time he arrived, the structure was fully engulfed, the warriors rifling through the clutter of crates, barrels, and canvas sacks they'd hauled out before the building was torched. The mutilated bodies of two men lay on the ground, red blood vivid against pale skin. Ethan barely spared them a glance. He slid down from the mare as a Sioux warrior drove his tomahawk into the top of a wooden cask. Ethan smelled the fiery liquid even before men began to shout.

"Mniwakaŋ!"

Warriors rushed past him, abandoning their loot to crowd around the barrel, dipping into the whiskey with anything they could lay their hands on. Ethan turned away, tossing aside broken wood and torn sacking, hoping to discover riches similar to the ones George had described at Julesburg. He was disappointed. The store had been a small one, stocked with basic foodstuffs already in over-supply in the camps. Ethan had to content himself with salvaging sacks of shelled corn for the mare.

He was headed back to her, weighed down by two heavy canvas bags, when a portion of the lettering on a half-buried crate caught his eye. Lowering the bags to the ground, Ethan pulled away the shattered remains of another crate to reveal the rest. Excitement surged through him. Scanning the ground around him, he looked for something to pry the lid off.

"Misuŋ, le uŋ wo." Use this, brother.

An older man, a Sioux, was offering him the use of a tomahawk. Ethan accepted it, wedging the blade under the lid. It came up with a screech, rewarding him with the sight of '50 CARTRIDGES — FOR HENRY'S REPEATING RIFLE' printed in gold on multiple rows of black boxes. At forty-four caliber, they were wrong for the Spencer, but that didn't matter. Possession gave him means again.

Squatted beside him, his companion grunted approval. Ethan dug out one of the cardboard boxes and piled nine more on top. He handed them to the man, along with the tomahawk.

"For you," he said in Lakota. "Thank you."

The man accepted the cartridges readily enough, but waved away the tomahawk. Ethan hesitated briefly before accepting it. Already he'd accomplished his first trade.

All through that night and the next, the length and breadth of the Platte Valley reverberated with the sound of drums. The sky glowed in every direction as ranches and stage stations burned and war parties celebrated. Through the last days of January, supply trains bound for Denver and Salt Lake were plundered, the Overland Stage stopped running, and miles of telegraph line were destroyed, poles cut down and burned, wires dragged away or left in tangles. Any white unlucky enough to be caught was killed. By the time war parties began drifting back to the main camps, every settlement for a hundred miles had been destroyed.

George was among the first to return, the party he was with driving five hundred head of cattle before them. "We let the lean ones go," he informed Ethan, as he dismounted. "The soldiers from one of the forts came out after dark and rounded 'em up, but they were afraid to fight us for these."

Cattle were slaughtered, and the feasting and dancing continued as more war parties returned, and wagons rolled in, loaded with foodstuffs, clothing and other supplies. Ethan helped himself, adding to his wardrobe, and taking anything he thought might be of value for trade.

A returning group of Cheyenne warriors told of coming across nine of Chivington's men, released from service and heading east. They had attacked and killed them, finding in their valises two scalps they recognized as belonging to friends killed at Sand Creek. Enraged, they had hacked the bodies to pieces. There were other stories, too, and the more Ethan listened, the more certain he became that it would all be over before he was strong enough to fight.

FEBRUARY

21

On the first day of February, the criers rode through the camps announcing the move north. At the same time, a war party would stage a final raid on Julesburg.

"I figured this was coming," George said, later that evening, when they were gathered inside the lodge. "We didn't burn it last time so we'd be able to go back for more."

"You plan on joinin' us, E-nu-tah?" Charley asked insolently, eyeing Ethan across the fire. "Or ain't you got the guts for killing whites?"

"Leave him be, Charley." Julie's voice was sharp, and for once, Charley looked chastened.

Ethan spared him only a glance. "I'm going with you," he said softly to George.

"You feeling up to it?"

Ethan nodded. "I've had it with being an invalid."

It was a heady feeling riding out with a war party for the first time. Riding through the camp, past the trilling women, the children and old men, Ethan realized that everything had been pushing him toward this moment. The memory of words, uttered on a golden evening beside the still waters of a beaver pond, came back to him, and he knew Micah had been right. He was where he belonged—where he had always belonged.

Led by the Sioux, the war party slipped into the shelter of the sand hills south of the river and waited, held in check by the soldier groups. Under George's tutelage, Ethan applied paint to his face and the mare, and tied up her tail for battle. A group of men showed themselves, but failed to lure the soldiers out. Flashed signals from mirrors sent the warriors surging out of the hills, galloping across the valley floor toward the fort.

Catching his first glimpse of soldiers since Sand Creek, hatred welled up in Ethan. Combined with remembered horror and tales of atrocities, it pushed grief aside, coiling like a serpent into an all-consuming need for revenge. Ethan charged the tiny garrison with nothing on his mind but seeing every man there dead. Raising the Spencer, he drew a bead on an exposed head. He squeezed the trigger and instantly regretted it. Gasping in pain from the recoil, bullets pocking the earth around him, he drew back out of range and circled with the others, adding his voice to the taunting and curses as they attempted to draw the soldiers out.

When it became clear that the soldiers had no intention of abandoning the protection of their stockade, most of the war party turned toward Julesburg, leaving a small group to keep the soldiers occupied. Ethan rode into the abandoned cluster of log buildings determined to have his due. The store and warehouse were everything he'd hoped for, and he quickly discovered that his ability to read gave him a distinct advantage over his companions. While many of them tore open crates and boxes to see what they contained, or carried away items he deemed useless, Ethan moved methodically through first the store, then the warehouse. Pulling a large hunting knife from its sheath, he used it to slice open several bags of flour, spilling the contents onto the floor and stuffing the bags with loot. He scooped boxes of cartridges for the Spencer from shelves, snatched a holstered revolver from beneath a counter, found a worn saddle and blanket, and stumbled across a sling for the Spencer. Rummaging through the spilled contents of a draw, he discovered a pair of army-issue field glasses and stuffed them into a bag. When he had the essentials, he set about collecting a few luxuries: a pair of gloves, matches, pencils, a handful of blank journals, soap, and some favorite canned fruits.

Staggering under his load, he stepped outside just as flames shot from the roof of the telegraph office. One by one, his companions torched every building in town. As black smoke darkened the winter sky, Ethan joined the warriors riding back and forth between the town and the fort, challenging the soldiers to come out and fight. The soldiers stayed put, loosing occasional shots at anyone who strayed too close.

The last of the buildings collapsed in a roar of blackened timber and flying sparks, and the war party began making its way across the Platte. The going was treacherous, several hundred yards of solid ice dotted with sandy, brush covered islands. The women had gone ahead, scattering sand, but even so, more than one heavily laden pack animal lost its footing and went down.

Once across, they set up camp within sight of Fort Rankin. It wasn't long before two war parties set out—the Cheyenne and Arapaho heading upriver, the Sioux heading down. Ethan watched them go, exhausted and sore, and content for once, to stay put. Telegraph poles were dragged in and great fires lit. The singing, drinking and scalp dances began. Ethan helped himself to food, then wandered off and spent the better part of the evening peering through the field glasses, watching the nervous movements of the soldiers on the other side of the river.

Once, before darkness fell, he ventured onto the ice, heading for one of the willow-covered islands. He found a Sioux already there. He was squatting at the edge of the sand, idly watching the movement of the soldiers in their fort.

"Hau kola," he said, as Ethan hunkered down beside him. Looking across the river, he signed as he spoke. "It is too bad none of them were brave enough to die today."

"It is too bad," Ethan agreed, and the man looked at him in surprise.

"You speak Lakota."

Ethan nodded, eyes on the fort. "If we could get them to come out, I would have a shot at them from here."

The other man looked at the Spencer and smiled. "They will come out."

He stood up and yelled. Turning his back to the fort, he flipped up the flap of his breechclout and slapped his hands on his bare behind, wriggling it at the soldiers.

Sporadic gunfire erupted, but the bullets fell short. Ethan's companion laughed and stepped out onto the ice. "Watch for them. They will come."

He had no sooner spoken than Ethan spotted movement outside the shadowed walls of the stockade. Crouched over in a run, two men were heading for the river. Reaching its edge, one of them went down on one knee, sighted along his rifle, and fired. Ice sprayed several yards ahead of the Sioux. He laughed as Ethan raised the Spencer and opened fire. The men on the bank sprang backward, then sprinted for safety as dirt spurted from the ground around them.

Ethan lowered the Spencer and shook his head. Pain and residual weakness had interfered with his aim. His wounded shoulder throbbed.

His companion grinned. "They were lucky this time. But next time, I think not."

"You are right," Ethan agreed, his voice harsh with frustration. "Next time, I think not."

After a night spent celebrating, the war party moved north into Nebraska Territory, destroying mile after mile of the Overland Telegraph, and joining up with the main camp late in the day. Another grueling day's march across the high, desolate ridge separating the branches of the Platte, brought them to water at a place the Sioux called Muddy Springs Creek. A Sioux war party joined them there, driving a herd of cattle and twenty head of horses and mules. There was a ranch at Mud Springs, they said, the only place between the North and South Platte inhabited by whites. Early that morning, they had swooped out of the hills and run off the herd.

When the Indians attacked, the small group of soldiers and herders inhabiting the ranch had taken refuge in the log ranch buildings. The lines to the west were still intact, and the telegraph operator sent out an urgent plea for help. Fifty-five miles away, Lieutenant William Ellsworth set out from Camp Mitchell with thirty-six men from the 11th Ohio Volunteer Cavalry. Further west, Colonel William Collins and twenty-five handpicked men left Fort Laramie. Behind him came an even larger force from the 11th Ohio and 7th Iowa, escorting wagons and supplies. Colonel Collins was still more than fifty frozen, windswept miles away when Lieutenant Ellsworth's command arrived at Mud Springs Ranch in the wee hours of Sunday morning.

The day dawned bitterly cold, light from the rising sun pale along the horizon as Ethan threw the saddle on Faria's back and pulled the cinch tight. Already, the women were packing to leave, and warriors, armed and painted for battle, streamed past him, headed for the ranch.

"You ready?" George asked, his painted features grotesque in the dim light.

Ethan rammed the Spencer into its scabbard and swung onto the mare. "Ready," he replied, pulling her head around and urging her forward.

They rode quickly, the breath from a thousand men and horses issuing in plumes that swirled wraithlike around them. The country they passed through was rugged and hilly. At one point, the mare sailed over a gully, landing hard on the other side. Ethan caught his breath in a gasp. Charley, riding beside him, favored him with a mocking grin. Ethan kept his eyes straight ahead, unwilling to admit how much it hurt. Moments later, they heard gunfire.

"A fight!" Charley shouted.

His pony sprang forward, and all around him, others did the same. Gritting his teeth, Ethan urged Faria into a gallop.

They came out of the hills above the ranch to find warriors already engaged in a fierce fight with the men barricaded inside the buildings. Ethan circled, looking for a shot. A single circuit told him it was impossible. The surrounded men were firing through narrow slits in the walls, only the barrels of their guns visible.

Ethan craned around, searching for George. He spotted him as he slipped into a gully and disappeared from sight. Whirling the mare, Ethan went after him. Handing her reins to one of the boys, he crouched low, following other warriors as they crept along the gully to within a few yards of the buildings. George and Charley were there, hunkered down, exchanging fire with the whites. Ethan went down on one knee and took aim with the revolver, emptying it at a slot already bristling with arrows and scarred by bullets.

"What's the plan?" he asked, pausing to reload.

"There isn't one." George fired a round and pulled his rifle back. Turning to sit with his back against the bank, he reloaded.

"What do you mean?" Ethan broke off a hunk of frozen snow with his heel, kicked it aside, and sank to the ground beside him. "There has to be a plan. I don't know how many there are, but we've got them outnumbered. There has to be a way of getting them out of there."

Reloading complete, George shrugged and turned to lay the barrel on the lip of the ravine. "There's no plan, Ethan. That's not how Indians fight. Relax. Give it time. See what happens."

The shooting continued throughout the morning, neither side willing to show itself. Ethan fired when he thought he had a shot, but as the sun climbed higher, he grew impatient. Eventually, he crept back along the gully. Retrieving Faria, he circled through the hills, examining the ranch buildings from every angle, trying to figure a way to end the stalemate.

There was sudden shouting from the ranch, and the corral gate swung open. Horses and mules spilled out, scattering in every direction. Warriors erupted from behind every snow-drifted clump of sage, every rock, out of every gully, leaping onto their ponies and giving chase. Several of the animals charged directly at Ethan. Drawing the Spencer from its scabbard, he whirled the mare to run with them. Reaching out with the carbine, he touched one of the horses on the rump, then another, claiming them for his own before going after a mule. When it was his, he went after another horse, but a man beat him to it.

Ethan pulled the mare to a stop and looked back at the ranch. The last of the warriors were abandoning the siege and heading into the hills. Ethan stared at the buildings, frustrated by the outcome of the fight, but gratified at having gained the horses and mule. Suddenly weary, he turned Faria north, joining a group of Sioux for the ride to camp.

Another war party rode out early the following morning. Ethan placed a bucket of shelled corn before the mare, and laying a gloved hand on her withers, watched them go. In his opinion, a second attack on Mud Springs was a waste of time. He remained with the main camp as it continued north, seeking out acquaintances he'd made among Spotted Tail's Oglala. He'd discovered it was easier being with them than among the Cheyenne. Riding with them, listening to stories and asking questions, he was able to set aside grief for hours at a time.

The light that morning had a remarkable clarity to it, a brightness unusual even in the high plains. Thrown into sharp relief by the angle of the sun, rolling hills stretched without end beneath a cloudless azure sky. No wind stirred to bend the tall tufts of grayed grass or shift the snow humped beneath them. As the sun climbed higher, the temperature rose with it. For the first time in recent memory, it could reasonably be called warm.

A great day to be alive, Ethan thought, and was instantly overcome by guilt.

Midway through the morning, they emerged from the hills and dropped down onto a broad plain. Ahead, sunlight glistened off a wide swath of pale ice that wound its way, amid sand hills and gray, leafless clumps of willow, from one distant horizon to the other.

"The Moonshell," one of Ethan's companions announced. "We will go there," he added, pointing to an escarpment rising steeply from the plain beyond the river. "In half a day's ride, there is water."

"And beyond?"

Lame Wolf grimaced. "Beyond is not good. The hills are of sand, and for three sleeps there is no wood and little water. Not until the Surprise River[19] does the land become hospitable again. There are trees and water, and plenty of deer and elk for hunting." He glanced sideways at Ethan. "All the way to the Black Hills, Two Moons."

Ethan looked sharply at him. "That's where we're headed? The Black Hills?"

Lame Wolf nodded. "Soon you will join with the Bad Faces."

"No-da-khi vi-hoi!"

---

19   Niobrara River

The words came as part of a nightmare. Ethan jerked, coming partially awake. It was bright inside the lodge, and for a moment, he wondered why. Then he remembered the night spent feasting, drinking, and dancing. Buoyed by the prospect of the Black Hills, he had joined in all but the drinking. The sun had been well up by the time he tumbled into bed.

"No-da-khi vi-hoi!"

The shout came from just outside the lodge. Ethan's heart seized, and he bolted upright. All around him, people were tossing aside their robes and scrambling to their feet, women's voices rising in fear, men seizing their weapons. Ethan slid his feet into his moccasins, grabbed his ammunition pouch and the Spencer, and was second through the door.

George was outside, fully dressed, standing with a group of people who watched a Sioux lookout ride back and forth along a ridge to the south. The man rode slowly, motioning with his arms. Periodically, he stopped and held his robe up beside his head.

"Enemy south of the river," George said, glancing at Ethan. "Soldiers."

"How many?"

"Hard to say."

Men were running toward the pony herds. George joined them. Ethan started after him, then reconsidered. The day was comparatively mild, but too cold for nothing but a breechclout. He rushed back into the lodge, pushing past women who were already packing, snatched his coat from the hands of one, scooped up a pad saddle and a rawhide bridle, and dashed back outside.

Mounted warriors hurtled past him, hundreds of them, heading south. Ethan shrugged into his coat, and without pausing to button it, ran toward the milling herd, whistling for Faria. She was nowhere in sight, and it occurred to him that another man might have taken her. Grasping the mane of the pony nearest him, he slipped the loop over its lower jaw and cinched the pad onto its back. His ribs shrieked in protest as he vaulted aboard. Adrenaline pumping, he barely noticed. Jamming his heels into the pony's sides, he set off after the others.

He arrived atop of the escarpment to see that, far to the south, beyond the river, the soldiers were circling their white-topped wagons, preparing to defend themselves against the horde of warriors streaking toward them across the plain. Closer, he spotted George. He was part of a group making its way down the steep face of the bluff. Ethan urged his pony after them.

He came out on the plain among them, galloping toward the place on the far side of the river where warriors were amassing. As they drew close, a cry went up, and the warriors attacked, charging in on the soldiers. They were met by a barrage of gunfire. Ethan heard yelps and cries, saw men and ponies racing among the sand hills. Slowing his pony, he allowed it to pick its way over the ice. Once across, he galloped toward the soldiers—and directly into chaos.

The soldiers had chosen their defensive position well. Their horses and mules safely corralled within the circle of wagons, they were concealed in hastily dug rifle pits. Beaten back under withering fire, unable to see their enemy, the warriors were shouting and gesturing to one another, ponies fretting and prancing under them. Amid the confusion, Ethan lost sight of George. Spinning his pony, he cast about, trying to decide what to do. Many warriors were dropping to the ground, ducking behind dunes, raising up to exchange fire with the soldiers, and using the uneven ground for cover as they slipped closer.

Ethan spotted a low ridge of sand that angled away from the river, toward several of the rifle pits. Sliding from the pony's back, he bent double and ran to where the ridge played out a mere fifty yards from the nearest pit. Sprawling on his stomach, he took aim with the Spencer as a flight of arrows rose from the river. There was yelling in the pits, and one of the soldiers rose to his knees, looking behind him. Ethan squeezed the trigger. The man's body jerked, then toppled sideways. Hands reached up and hauled him into the pit.

For you, Micah. Ejecting the spent casing, Ethan slammed the lever home, loading another cartridge.

Half a dozen Sioux scrambled up, dropping to the ground around him. One of them spoke, but Ethan's attention was riveted on the spot where, moments before, a man with silver leaves on his shoulders had sprinted between two of the wagons. Finger on the trigger, he waited for the colonel to reappear.

Long minutes passed as the soldiers weathered a blistering assault from all sides. Then Ethan spotted the officer again. He stepped from behind a wagon, yelling and making sweeping gestures with one arm. Ethan fired just as the colonel dodged from sight. Beyond him, one of the mules went down, hooves tearing at the earth, its agonized screeches rising above the din of battle.

Minutes later, soldiers appeared through a gap between the wagons, leading their horses. Shouts went up as they were spotted. Many, Ethan among them, made a mad dash for their ponies.

The soldiers were mounted by the time he swung onto the pony's back. Forming a line, bugle blaring, they charged toward the river. Ethan dug his heels into the pony's ribs, intent on catching them in the open.

The warriors hiding along the riverbank ran for their ponies as the soldiers bore down on them. Flinging themselves aboard, they raced away, all but a boy whose mount, white-eyed with terror, circled away from him. A soldier's bullet struck the boy in the chest, and he staggered back. Only then did he manage to hurl himself onto the pony's back and gallop away.

Charging in on the soldiers flank, Ethan saw it all. Clinging to the back of his racing pony, the Spencer slung under one arm, he squeezed off a shot. It flew wide, and the soldiers continued to gain on the fleeing boy. As they started up a small hill, more than a hundred mounted warriors exploded over the top. Vastly outnumbered, the soldiers whirled their mounts and began a panicked race back to the wagons.

Pulling the pony to a sliding halt, Ethan pumped another bullet into the chamber, took aim and fired. One of the soldiers arched backward, caught himself, and slumped over his horse's neck. Ethan spun his pony and fled, following his companions back the way they'd come.

Several soldiers broke off firing at their pursuers and took aim at him. A bullet slammed into the pony's neck, spraying blood, but the pony kept running. Another tore into its heart. A more few strides, and the pony's knees buckled. It tumbled head over heels, sending Ethan flying.

He landed on his back, the wind knocked out of him. Pain from his ribs made his eyes water. Gasping for breath, he rolled onto his side. A bullet sprayed sand near his face. Another plucked at his sleeve. Panicked, he reached out, grabbed the Spencer, and pushed himself to his feet. One arm pressed to his ribs, he staggered, then began to run.

He heard a shout and saw several Sioux charging hard at him. A man he'd seen several times, a man with pale skin and hair, bent low, reaching out a hand, as the warriors with him unleashed a hail of arrows at the soldiers. Ethan grasped the outstretched hand, and with a leaping stride, was hoisted onto the pony's back. He clung to the man as the pony's muscles bunched under him and carried him to safety.

His rescuer dropped him in the cover of the sand hills and turned back to the fighting. Ethan sank to the ground, eyes closed, one arm supporting him, the other clutching his ribs. When at last the pain began to ease, he lifted his head and looked around. Pale in the winter sky, the sun hovered just above the horizon. All but the tops of the sand hills were in shadow, and the temperature was falling rapidly. Even as the fighting continued, warriors were beginning to make their way back across the ice.

Ethan sat for several minutes, then slowly pushed himself to his feet. His legs, bare from hip to ankle, were numb with cold, and the rest of him wasn't much warmer. Slinging the carbine's strap over one shoulder, he did up the buttons of his coat and began the slow walk to the river. He was halfway across when his name was called. He looked around as George rode up behind him.

"You hit?"

Ethan shook his head. "My ribs. Pony got shot out from under me."

"I saw. You plan on walking back to camp?"

"Not if I have a choice."

"Here." George reached down and hauled Ethan up behind him.

The camp was where they'd left it, the last of the light gone by the time they reached it. Warriors streamed in around them, the fight abandoned for the night. As George pulled to a halt before the lodge, a group of men trotted up.

One of them spoke rapidly, holding up a piece of paper. Ethan eased himself to the ground, making what he could of the conversation: *Soldier... horse... kill... something find.* It was a word he didn't recognize, assumed it must be the paper.

Women were crowding around them, celebrating their return. Boys ran to take their ponies. Grabbing the paper, George pushed past them and ducked into the lodge. Ethan and the other men followed.

George squatted next to the fire, unfolding the piece of paper and holding it to the light. Ethan crouched behind him, reading over his shoulder. It was from Colonel William O. Collins, Commander 11th Ohio Volunteer Cavalry, to Major Thomas L. Mackay, Post Commander at Fort Laramie, requesting immediate aid. Written at 1:00pm, from the mouth of Rush Creek, it stated that he and his men had come under attack from three thousand warriors, had corralled their wagons, and were fighting for their lives.

Ethan's brows arched. "*Three* thousand? He seeing double?"

George didn't reply. He translated the contents of the letter, and the men gathered around the fire grinned, a few of them laughing out loud when they heard the number.

"Where did you catch him?" Ethan asked, signing.

"On the Holy Road,"[20] came the reply. He had been among the soldiers that charged out from the wagons. When the others retreated, he'd kept going, riding straight through the warriors. He had been mounted on a fast horse, and it had taken a long time to catch him. After he was killed, they found the paper.

"Was he the only one?" Ethan wondered.

The men looked at one another. "The only one we saw," one of them replied.

"You think there were more?" George swiveled to look at Ethan.

Ethan shrugged. "If it were you, wouldn't you send a second man in case one didn't make it?"

George nodded. "I would. Fort Laramie's a long ways off, though. It'll take days for reinforcements to get here."

"Even so..." Ethan shook his head, leaving the statement unfinished.

The sun was not yet up, the eastern sky turning reluctantly from black to gray, when the women began packing to move. Small bands of warriors rode back to the corralled wagons, hoping to steal the soldiers' horses, and intent on delaying them. The remainder stayed to guard the camps.

An arctic wind had sprung up during the night, and when the sun pushed over the horizon, the light it cast was dimmed by thick layers of gray cloud. Pausing on a ridge above where the camps had been, Ethan turned up the collar of his coat and looked back the way they'd come. Nothing moved against the snow-specked hills to the south. Nothing but wind-tossed grass and an errant tumbleweed that bumped and skidded along the ground, took flight momentarily, then disappeared behind a ridge of sand. Ethan watched a few moments longer before turning Faria and urging her forward. Ice-encrusted snow crunched beneath her hooves as she bore him north, into the sand hills of Nebraska.

---

20   Oregon Trail

MARCH-APRIL

22

"He will never return to his white home. He no longer trusts the whites. He has told me this himself." The men gathered around the fire nodded, muttering agreement.

When Ed translated, Josh shook his head. "He has family. A daughter. Ethan would go home if he knew he could."

Red Hand looked to Ed for translation, but Ed responded directly to Josh. "It's like I been telling you, there's plenty to keep him from going back. From what Red Hand says, he's dead-set against it."

"He carries a soldier's bullet. He will have revenge for what they did. For Little Hawk and Tall Grass Woman."

"I don't believe it," Josh said when Ed translated. He shifted uncomfortably in the smoky heat, glancing around the spartan interior of the lodge. It was hard to believe Ethan would willingly choose such an existence. His eyes swept the faces of the men gathered around the fire before settling on Red Hand. "If I knew where he was, if I could find him, the things I have to tell him would convince him. He'd go back with me."

Red Hand considered Josh for a long moment before replying. "I think you do not know your brother well. Living among us, he has found his Sioux blood to be stronger than his white blood. Ours was the life he chose even before the soldiers attacked. He will never go back."

"I don't believe you. Tell me where to find him."

Ed translated. Red Hand responded, and the discussion went on for several minutes before Ed turned to Josh. "Ethan made a choice. He coulda come back here, but he decided not to. They're headed north to join up with the Sioux and Northern Cheyenne and make war on the whites."

"Tell me where to find him," Josh insisted stubbornly.

He had raised his voice, and on the other side of the lodge, a child whimpered. His mother held him close, quieting him, staring over the top of his head at Josh. The look in her eyes brought a return of the same chilling sensation he'd experienced when he first rode into the camp.

The men had watched him grim-faced. There had been fear in the eyes of the women as they gathered their children around them. It had occurred to

Josh that he was looking at the survivors, that the ravaged remains, the corpses he'd seen and touched, were people they'd known, family and friends. Unable to meet their eyes, he'd stared nonetheless, in horrified fascination.

Tearing his eyes from the woman's face, Josh addressed Red Hand. "Please. I need to know where he is. It's important that I talk to him."

"There is no way to know," Red Hand replied. "Many Sioux winter in the place they call the Black Hills, others along the river called the Powder. I have never been to these places, but I have heard tales of them. The land is big. Unless Ethan wishes it, you will not find him."

Josh held Red Hand's eyes for a moment, then shook his head and looked away.

Red Hand watched him. He felt for the fair-haired man who reminded him so much of his friend, but there was little he could do to help. "The soldier forts," he offered. "In the north, there is one they call Laramie. Many go there to trade—Cheyenne, Arapaho, Sioux. Perhaps people there will know where to find him."

Josh nodded, forcing a smile. "Thank you. I appreciate what you've told me."

He extended his hand and Red Hand took it, giving it the vigorous shake of the uninitiated, before reaching for his pipe. "You will stay," he said. "Join me in another smoke. Soon it will be night, and there is nowhere for you to go until morning."

Josh left Black Kettle's camp with no idea what to do next. He had won well at cards during his stay at Fort Lyon, and his welcome there was wearing thin. And Red Hand's words, the conviction behind them, had given rise to doubt. If it was true that Ethan was content—his letter had implied that he was—why expend more effort looking for him? A part of him was inclined to admit defeat and go home.

But there was Elizabeth to consider. And Emma. He owed it to them to keep looking. And, Josh admitted, the idea of going to Fort Laramie, of seeing it for himself, was intriguing.

Two weeks later, he was in Denver City, blown in on a storm that buried the town under a thick blanket of snow. For days, nothing moved in or out.

Josh was content to pass the time patronizing the town's numerous gambling establishments, pitting his skill against more seasoned players.

"'Ere's no doubt you got the head for it, son" a flint-eyed veteran commented three weeks later, as Josh scraped his winnings across the table. "Best take yourself on outta here afore someone accuses you of cheating."

The look in the man's eyes discouraged discussion.

On the ninth of April, angling northwest along the Great Platte River Road,[21] Josh had his first look at Fort Laramie. Huddled on a broad expanse of rugged, treeless plain, backed by distant snow-capped mountains dominated by Laramie Peak, the seemingly random scatter of buildings was anything but impressive. As he drew nearer, the fort slowly separated itself from the prairie, gaining definition and significance. Josh counted more than thirty buildings of various shapes and sizes. Two had second stories; half a dozen were long and low and appeared to be barracks. There were houses for the officers, stables and any number of outbuildings. The stars and stripes hung limp atop the flagstaff at the eastern end of the parade ground, and soldiers and horses moved about below it. Closer, along a broad stretch of bottomland dotted by willows and traced through by the Laramie River, were the conical shapes of tipis.

He was halfway across the river when shouts, and the staccato pop of gunshots, rent the late afternoon air. Pulling his rifle from its sling, he looked toward the Indian camp. A group of men had been sitting around one of the fires. They rose and looked toward the fort.

The shouting escalated. More shots were fired, and riders galloped across the parade ground, whooping and hollering. Josh glanced once more at the Indians, then spurred his horse up the shallow bluff toward the fort.

"Lee's surrendered!" A mounted soldier galloped toward him, emptying his pistol into the air.

"When?" Josh shouted, pulling his mount to a sliding stop.

The man was already past and didn't hear. Josh spurred toward the building at the center of the commotion. Looping his reins over the rail, he waded into the mass of blue uniforms.

"Is it true?" he shouted, grabbing a soldier by the arm. "Is it true Lee surrendered?"

"You bet it is!"

---

21   Oregon Trail

"When? Where?"

"Today! Some courthouse in Virginia!"

The soldier whooped and tossed his hat into the air. Josh whooped louder and sent his hat sailing. The war was over! The north had won! Somehow it seemed fitting that the news should greet him at Fort Laramie. Josh whooped again, and was swept along with the crowd to the sutler's store.

He woke in unfamiliar quarters, this time, on the floor. He had a spectacular hangover, little memory of the night before, and no idea how he'd wound up in the squad room. His only consolation was that, all around him, other men were in the same condition. There were groans and the sound of someone retching. A man staggered past, tripped over Josh's feet, and fell heavily to the floor. Holding his aching head, Josh sat up. When he was able, he dragged himself to his feet and staggered to the door, wondering what had become of his horse.

* * *

Spring arrived in fits and starts, winter only reluctantly releasing its icy grip on the northern plains. It was late April, the land just beginning to green, fat buds on the cottonwoods unfurling the first pale leaves, when a blizzard dumped three feet of wet, heavy snow, breaking branches and all but burying the lodges.

Ethan forced the door flap open wide enough to get a gloved hand out, clawing at the drifted snow and tossing handfuls aside until he was able to push his way out. Standing thigh-deep in snow, he squinted into the morning light, the rising sun glinting off a pristine blanket of white. From the lodge behind him came the quiet murmur of voices. Somewhere, a dog barked, then was quiet, leaving the world in frozen silence. Not a breath of wind stirred to shift the snow off the branches of the cottonwoods or disturb the smoke that drifted from the smoke holes and climbed straight up into piercing blue sky. They had traveled hundreds of miles during the cruelest months to come to this place, the camps of the Northern Cheyenne and Red Cloud's Oglala, on the Powder River, just below the Yellowstone.

The Niobrara, the Surprise River, had proved true to its name, appearing suddenly after three days with little water and no wood. Appearing just as Ethan had begun to think the sand hills would go on forever and they would perish among them. Another day, and he caught his first glimpse of the Ṗaha Saṗa, the Black Hills. After the distant intrigue of the Rockies, they were a disappointment, pale humps rising from frozen grassland, only barely distinguishable from crystalline winter sky.

They came to a place sheltered by heavy timber and fed by a small, sandy stream, and paused to rest the ponies and hunt. Four days later, they set out again, the mountains gaining significance as they moved closer, rugged, pine-covered slopes looming dark beneath the winter's accumulation of snow. Ethan was eager to press on, certain he was within days of finding his mother's people, but instead, they went into camp along a river the Sioux called the Bear Lodge, and settled in to await the return of runners who'd gone ahead to find the winter camps of the Sioux, Northern Arapaho and Northern Cheyenne.

When the first runners returned, Spotted Tail's band departed, heading east. The Northern Arapaho went next, moving west to join with the rest of their tribe. At last, news reached them of the Northern Cheyenne. They were wintering near Red Cloud's Oglala, in a place with good grass and heavy timber, on the northern reaches of the Powder River.

Several Northern Cheyenne arrived with the runners, wild-looking men dressed entirely in skins. Their primitive appearance was a source of great curiosity among their southern cousins, and for the first time, Ethan understood how thoroughly his life was about to change. Once the supplies from the raids were exhausted, many of the things he took for granted—basics such as coffee, sugar, flour and tobacco—would be hard to come by.

With the Northern Cheyenne to guide them, the remaining bands of Sioux and Cheyenne continued north along the eastern flank of the Black Hills. Putting the snow-covered peaks behind them, they angled west across a windswept landscape of gray-brown hills and frozen, drifted snow, hung over by slate-gray sky.

As they topped the last bluffs east of the Powder River, the camps came into view on the plain before them, smoke from the fires hanging thick among the branches of the cottonwoods. Shafts of sunlight pierced the clouds, mottling distant hills and sparkling ribbons of water where the river ran free of ice. The tribes separated, the Northern Cheyenne returning to their camps, the Southern Cheyenne aiming for a site half a mile downriver, and the Sioux moving past them, toward lodges only faintly visible to the north.

People swarmed to meet them as they approached the Sioux camp. Ethan scanned faces, unsure who he was looking for. Then, over the excited chatter, he heard a thin, wavering voice. His heart gave a jolt, and he stood in the stirrups, searching for the source of it. His eyes lit on a stooped, gray-haired woman, one gnarled hand clutching her buffalo robe to her throat, the other gripping the knobbed end of a stick. She swayed gently, in time with the chant, her eyes searching the passing faces.

"Haŋhepi Wi Nupa, Wazi Ape ciŋca hoksila." Two Moons, son of Pine Leaf.

Ethan urged the mare toward her. "Haŋhepi Wi Nupa emaciyapi yelo," he said when he drew near. I am called Two Moons.

The old woman looked up. For a moment, she simply stared. Then her expression softened, the lines of her weathered face deepening in a smile of recognition. Tears filled her eyes, and she held up a withered hand. "Two Moons. It is you. You look much like your father."

Ethan leaned down and took her hand. Frail and amazingly warm, it was like holding an injured bird. "Grandmother?" he asked tentatively.

The old woman nodded, unable to speak.

"You have made a long journey, Two Moons. You are welcome here."

The speaker was a tall woman standing next to his grandmother. Like everyone else, she was wrapped in a brightly painted buffalo robe. Long plaits of black hair hung on either side of a strong, pleasant face.

"I am called Brings the Buffalo, first wife of Black Wolf."

Suddenly, there were people all around him, women and children mostly, all talking once, jostling one another and the mare. Faria snorted nervously, throwing back her head and pulling Ethan's hand from his grandmother's.

"Haŋhepi Wi Nupa emaciyapi hwo?" You are called Two Moons?

Ethan turned as a group of horseman pulled their ponies to a halt beyond the circle of women and children. They wore painted robes drawn up over their heads like hoods, a single arm exposed to handle the reins.

Ethan inclined his head in response. "Haŋhepi Wi Nupa emaciyapi yelo."

The man who had spoken nudged his pony closer. "Šungleška emaciyapi yelo." I am called Spotted Horse. He indicated his companions. "He is called Fat Bear, he is Bone Necklace, and he is Long Face. We are your cousins."

He used the word "taŋhaŋsi", a word unfamiliar to Ethan. But Bone Necklace was the name of one of his mother's brothers, and from that, Ethan assumed cousin.

"You knew I was coming?" he asked.

"Runners came from the Red Shield River. They told us of the attack by the white soldiers. They said Two Moons, the mixed-blood son of Pine Leaf, rides with Black Kettle's Cheyenne." Spotted Horse turned his pony's head. "Come."

Ethan nudged the mare forward. His cousins, and the women and children, fell in around him. Nearby, amid a group of warriors being welcomed by friends and family, he saw the man who'd rescued him from certain death during the fight on the Moonshell.

"Who is he?" he asked. "The one with the pale skin and brown hair."

"He is called Crazy Horse," Spotted Horse replied.

Riding in among the lodges was painfully reminiscent of his initial entry into the Cheyenne camp. But instead of Micah, it was Spotted Horse reeling off names and relationships, too many to keep track of. The blur of faces was the same, the yipping dogs, the excited voices—so many people talking at once that Ethan caught only snippets of what was said.

Unlike the gleaming white lodges of the Cheyenne, the Sioux lodges were intricately painted. Quilled pendants, tipped with horsetails and feathers, hung in rows on either side of the doors. Many lodges sported quilled or beaded discs with horsetails dangling from their centers. Long red and white deerskin streamers, designed to flutter in the wind, hung from the tips of the lodgepoles.

They approached a cluster of lodges where women bent over cooking paunches; buffalo stomachs supported at the corners by sticks and filled with heated water. The smell of boiling meat reached Ethan as he swung down from the saddle.

"Come," Spotted Horse said, as women came to take their horses.

It was warm inside the lodge. The furnishings were similar to Cheyenne lodges, but the floor was carpeted with buffalo robes, fur side up. A number of men were seated to the right of the fire; the space to the left was empty. He sat where Spotted Horse indicated, to the right of the fire. Fat Bear, Long Face, and Bone Necklace joined them.

His cousins shed their robes, and Ethan got his first good look at them. They wore earrings and necklaces made from a variety of beads, stones, bones and shells. Feathers and other ornaments dangled from their hair. Spotted Horse was the tallest, good-looking and muscular. His hair was cut even with his jaw on the sides, hanging to his waist in back. Fat Bear was anything but. Sinewy, with angular features, a hooked nose and piercing black eyes, he had a dangerous air about him that reminded Ethan uncomfortably of Charley Bent. Long Face and Bone Necklace were younger, fourteen or fifteen, at most. Bone

Necklace was the taller of the two, but not by much. They looked at him with eager, curious eyes.

An even younger boy came into the lodge and sat next to them. He was slender and small-boned, saved from appearing feminine by a slight thickening along the brow. He saw Ethan looking and shyly averted his eyes.

Without preamble, the man to Ethan's left lit a pipe, offering it to the Sky, the Earth, and the Four Winds, before passing it to Ethan. Ethan took several puffs, moving the smoke over him with his hand before passing it to Spotted Horse. When all the men had smoked, conversation began, and women entered the lodge, bringing food and taking their place on the opposite side of the fire. Ethan saw them stealing glances at him, heard his name and his mother's whispered.

He looked up as Brings the Buffalo offered him boiled deer meat from a wooden bowl. She was his aunt, the wife of Black Wolf, his mother's eldest brother. His mother had been young girl when they married. Three years later, Black Wolf had taken her sister, Chasing As She Walks, as his second wife. That same summer, Bone Necklace had married a Brulé named Moccasin Woman.

Black Wolf was the man who'd offered him the pipe. Chasing As She Walks, shorter than her sister, sat next to her across the fire. His grandmother sat off one side, next to Moccasin Woman, who was Black Wolf's third wife. From that, Ethan deduced, his second uncle had died.

The shy boy was another taŋhaŋsi, male cousin, called Kicking Bird. Ethan discovered that he had two haŋkaśi, female cousins, and any number of other relatives. He remembered a few of the names, but most of the relationships, and the words to describe them, defeated him.

His mother had taught him that Lakota children call their biological mother 'mother', as well as her sisters and anyone she calls sister. 'Father' includes the biological father, his brothers, and anyone he calls brother. Anyone a father calls sister is 'aunt'; anyone a mother calls brother is 'uncle'. Children of two or more brothers are 'brother and sister', as are children of two or more sisters. Cousins, in-laws, male and female, older and younger, the relationships were complex, the terms many, and Ethan had had no reason to learn them.

They had many questions, and he did his best to answer them. Struggling for words, signing when necessary, he conveyed news of his mother, offered the same simple explanation he'd given Tall Grass for joining the Cheyenne, and briefly described what had occurred at Sand Creek. He could tell there were things they didn't understand, but his command of the language didn't allow for detailed explanations.

It was dark by the time people began returning to their lodges. Ethan accompanied Spotted Horse and Fat Bear to one of the lodges at the edge of the camp where the unmarried men resided.

Two days later, the camps had been dismantled, and they had moved north in search of better grazing for the horses. They had come to this place, where the Powder River flowed into the Yellowstone, where timber was thick and grass plentiful. The three tribes had set up their camps close together, clusters of lodges spread for three miles along the river.

Ethan gazed across the snow-covered Lakota camp, basking in the quiet beauty of the morning. Eventually, he blew out a plumed breath and began plowing his way toward the river. There were other paths broken through the snow, and as he neared the water, he heard voices and knew others were there before him.

Turning upstream, he made his way toward the Southern Cheyenne camp, half-hoping he'd run into George. He'd seen little of him during the last month, and missed his company. Two men emerged dripping from the water and greeted him as he passed. He spotted Charley in the distance, but there was no sign of George. Ethan stopped at a hole that had been broken in the ice and stripped to the waist. Squatting, he dipped a piece of softened deer hide into the frigid water. Repressing the urge to shiver, he scrubbed his face, arms, and chest.

"Hau, E-nu-tah́."

The mocking voice startled him. Ethan looked up. Charley was standing a few feet away, his face twisted in its familiar sneer.

Ethan pushed himself to his feet. "Mornin', Charley."

The man with Charley shifted, eyeing Ethan intently. Ethan glanced at him and felt the blood drain from his face.

Micah!

In the instant it took his heart to resume beating, Ethan knew it wasn't. Philippe Broulat looked more like his father than Micah. He had Henri's bulk, thick through the chest and arms, and Henri's prominent beaked nose. His hair hung over his scarred chest in long brown plaits, water dripping from the curling tips.

"Something scare you, E-nu-tah́?"

Ethan tore his gaze from Philippe. Charley's eyes glittered with malice.

"You scare easy, don't you? I hear you stayed safe with the women and children while we went after the Crow."

Ethan said nothing, refusing to let Charley bait him.

"Coward." Charley spat the word.

Philippe's dark eyes narrowed, the same way Micah's had when he didn't understand.

"Ni-vi-ni?" Ethan heard him ask as they turned away. Who is he? He didn't hear Charley's reply, but was sure it was less than flattering.

Still watching them, he bent to pick up his shirt. Philippe turned his head once, and looked back. Ethan reached for his coat, and as he straightened, felt a sharp twinge in his lower back. The length of his right leg tingled. It was gone in an instant, but that it had happened at all was disturbing. Ethan reached back and fingered the lump of scar tissue next to his spine. He twisted from side to side, then bent at the waist and straightened. When it didn't happen again, he donned his coat and started back toward the lodge, wishing Charley hadn't felt it necessary to call him a coward in front of Philippe.

The Crow war party had slipped in close to the camps shortly after the move north. The valuable horses had been corralled among the lodges for the night, so they'd rounded up the loose stock and driven them off. When the theft was discovered, a number of warriors, George, Charley, and Ethan's cousins among them, had ridden out to hunt them down. None of Ethan's horses had been taken, and he'd figured he had no fight with the Crow. Besides, he had more pressing things to attend to.

There had been plenty he hadn't understood living with the Cheyenne, but it took only a few days among the Lakota for him to realize just how much he needed to learn. He needed not only a better command of the language; he needed to learn basic skills—things his cousins had been practicing since childhood. He knew that courage, stamina and the ability to endure pain were essential to being a warrior, but now he began to understand that it required skill at more things than he'd thought possible—skill as a horseman and marksman, certainly, but also as a tracker and observer of nature. He couldn't tell the tracks of a raccoon from those of a badger, or differentiate between the scat of a mule deer, antelope, or elk. It wasn't until Fat Bear placed his foot in a sprinkling of new-fallen snow and told Ethan to place his beside it, that he realized moccasin prints differed between tribes. He was told he needed to recognize birdcalls, and not only learn to mimic them, but understand what the signals meant. And he needed to learn how animals moved and birds flew so he could recognize signs of danger and find his way to water.

He could tell from the looks his cousins exchanged that they were amazed by the gaping holes in his education, but it wasn't long before the give and take achieved a sort of balance. Ethan had things they'd rarely, if ever, seen—the repeating rifle, field glasses, matches and canned food. And more important, he had firsthand knowledge of whites.

Spotted Horse was his age, inclined towards vanity, and occasionally arrogant. Fat Bear was a year younger. The aggressiveness Ethan had detected on the first day turned out to be a combination of doggedness and fierce loyalty. Ethan decided early on that if he were ever in a fight, he wanted Fat Bear beside him. Fat Bear's older brother, Standing Elk, was twenty-two and recently married. The brothers looked nothing alike, but were of similar temperament. Standing Elk was the other person Ethan knew he could always count on.

Long Face and Bone Necklace were the same age, not yet warriors, but fiercely competitive, engaging wholeheartedly in games and competitions. Twelve-year-old Kicking Bird was the opposite. He could track, and was skilled with a bow, bringing down small game with ease, but he wasn't competitive, and avoided danger and roughness. Ethan had never met an Indian boy quite like him. He thought him more suited to becoming a clerk or a shop assistant than a Lakota warrior.

But, of course, he reminded himself, *I never pictured myself a Lakota warrior. And here I am, doing everything I can to become one.*

MAY

23

"I don't know what to do. I'm afraid Peter's going to ask me to marry him."

Elizabeth looked at her companion with knitted brows. "I don't understand. I thought that was what you wanted. That's why I invited him to Sunday dinner."

"I know." Alice sighed, kneading the fabric of her skirt. "I keep telling myself I should say yes if he asks. He's been good to me. So much help with the farm, and the children dote on him, but..." She bit her lip, and gave a slight shake of her head. "My feelings don't go beyond friendship."

"I see," Elizabeth muttered, distracted by Emma who set off at a fast crawl toward the steps. Setting aside the lace she was crocheting, she started to rise, but five-year-old Grace was quicker. Dashing across the porch, she fell to her knees in front of Emma, coaxing her from danger. Elizabeth smiled. "Thank you, Grace."

She settled back in her rocker, sighing contentedly in the lazy warmth of the afternoon. Birds twittered among the branches, bees hummed, and the air was rich with the smell of freshly cut grass. She closed her eyes briefly, and when she opened them, noticed a man walking along the road from town. His steps were halting, and he stopped periodically, appearing to sway before coming on.

"I'm afraid if I say no, he'll go away. I don't want that. I just want things to keep on as they are."

Elizabeth was barely listening. Something about the man was familiar. He was tall, dressed in brown homespun, a knapsack slung over one shoulder. She stopped rocking and sat forward. "I wonder who that could be."

Alice looked at her, then out at the road. "Another man home from the war, I reckon."

Elizabeth continued to stare. As the man drew closer, she saw that he was bone-thin, his clothes hanging loosely on his large frame.

He stumbled, caught himself, and came on. He was only a few yards from the gate when he stumbled and fell to his knees. Hands in the dirt kept him from pitching onto his face.

Both women were on their feet in an instant.

"Stay here, children," Alice directed.

"Hannah!" Elizabeth called through the open door. "Come watch Emma."

Together, the two women hastened down the steps and through the gate. The man didn't move as they rushed to him along the road. Alice slowed as they came near, but Elizabeth kept going. She'd glimpsed yellow curls beneath the brim of his hat.

"Thomas?" she said, crouching next to him.

He was shivering, despite the heat, and several moments passed before he was able to push himself back on his heels and look at her. Elizabeth gasped. His skin was ashen, his sunken eyes bright with fever. There was a brief glint of recognition in them, and he half-smiled before another bout of shaking took him. Elizabeth held out her arms, and he sagged into them.

"Elizabeth?" Alice's voice was filled with uncertainty. "Who is he? What's wrong with him?"

Elizabeth twisted to look at her. "Fetch Isaac." When Alice hesitated: "Now, Alice! Quickly!"

Alice fled back along the road, returning shortly with Isaac. They got Thomas to his feet, and supporting him between them, staggered toward the gate. Alice rushed ahead to open it. Hannah was waiting on the porch, Emma in her arms, Grace and Duncan clinging to her skirt.

"The back bedroom," Elizabeth panted, straining to help Thomas up the steps. "Is the bed made up?"

"Miz 'Lizbet?" Hannah's expression was curious and disapproving all at once.

Elizabeth's tone booked no argument. "Now, Hannah!"

Hannah handed Emma to Alice and hurried up the stairs. Getting Thomas to the top was an ordeal. Isaac bore most of his weight, but Elizabeth was trembling by the time they lowered him onto the bed. When she bent to pull off his boots, Hannah took charge.

"That's enough," she said, shooing Elizabeth and Isaac from the room. "This ain't no job fo' a lady."

"Fetch Doctor Benson," Elizabeth instructed, as Hannah closed the door behind them. Isaac looked from her to the door, then headed down the stairs. Elizabeth steadied herself with a hand on the newel post.

"Who is he?" Alice asked, looking up from the floor below. "What's wrong with him?"

"His name is Thomas Murray. He's a friend of Ethan's." She saw the frown of doubt and disapproval begin to form, and added, "And Josh and Duncan's.

They were in the same company. He and Ethan were in the Confederate prison together."

Alice only heard part of it. "A friend of Duncan's?" Her brow lifted, and she took an eager step toward the stairs. "He's a friend of Duncan's?" She stopped, doubt once again clouding her face. "But Elizabeth, he can't stay here. What will people think? What will James and Sarah think? They'll be here on Sunday."

"We'll worry about that when the time comes. Meanwhile, let's see what the doctor has to say."

Doctor Benson was a tall, lanky man, shoulders stooped in apparent apology for his height. His beard and mustache were gray, but the shaggy hair that hung over his forehead and brushed the collar of his coat still retained some of its original brown.

"Malaria," he announced half an hour later when he appeared in the doorway to sitting room. "Complicated by dysentery and malnutrition."

"Malaria?" Alice asked, nervously. "Is it contagious?"

"It's a Southern disease, Mrs. Fraser, spread by pus corpuscles that float in the air like dust. They settle in a wound, a scrape or a cut, and cause infection. I've never heard of anyone catching it this far north."

"What about the children?"

Doctor Benson favored her with an indulgent smile. "I find it rarely hurts to take precautions." To Elizabeth, he said, "He's extremely weak. I'll bring some quiniae to treat the fever, but what he needs is proper food and rest. If you find yourself sharing Mrs. Fraser's concern, you might open a few windows. The best prevention for malaria is good ventilation." He started to leave, then turned back to them. "I recommend washing your hands with soap after dealing with him. Have your woman do the same. Wash anything he uses—utensils, bowls, cups, plates, chamber pot. Folks scoff, but I firmly believe good hygiene is essential to good health."

Elizabeth saw him to the door and turned to find Alice shepherding Grace and Duncan into the hallway.

"I can't take a chance of them getting sick," she said, with an apologetic smile. "I'd never forgive myself if something bad happened to them."

Elizabeth nodded and watched them down the steps. Then she went to the kitchen and washed her hands thoroughly before climbing the stairs to the second floor. She stood in the doorway to her bedroom, watching Emma nap in her cradle, wondering if she'd jeopardized her child's health by bringing Thomas into the house.

I had no choice, she told herself. *I couldn't just leave him in the road.*

She crossed the room, pushed the sashes of both windows open wide, and turned to look at Emma. *I should have taken him to the barn when I saw he was sick.* She bit her lip. It was too late for that. All she could do was take every precaution and pray for the best.

She went through the house, opening windows. Twice she went to the door of Thomas' room; twice she went away without going in. When Hannah emerged to say the fever had broken and he was asleep, Elizabeth insisted she wash her hands, going so far as to stand next to her while she did it.

Doctor Benson returned at dusk. Elizabeth met him at the door, wrapped in a shawl.

"No need to open every window in the house, Mrs. Magrath."

"But you said... Emma."

"Does Emma have any open cuts or scratches?"

"I don't think so."

"Do you?"

"No."

"Then no need to worry. You'll be fine. Crack the windows in the patient's room tonight, and open them wide again tomorrow."

He showed her how to measure the white powder and produced a bottle of whiskey. "Have him wash it down with a shot of this. And remember—use it sparingly. The cure lies in rebuilding his strength, not the quiniae."

It was late, the rest of the house sleeping, when Elizabeth went to the door of Thomas' room. This time she went in. She stood at the foot of his bed, holding up the candle she'd brought with her, noting the deep lines on his face and the gray in his hair and beard. In a little over a year, he'd aged ten.

Standing there in the middle of the night, she realized she barely knew him. He was little more than a stranger; a stranger who'd brought sickness into her home. For that, she resented him.

As she thought it, Thomas' eyes opened. "You're a sight for sore eyes," he murmured, offering her a poor imitation of the grin she knew so well.

She smiled back, feeling her resentment fade as his eyes closed.

Thomas stirred, coming slowly awake. He lay for a time without moving, reveling in the downy plumpness of the pillows and the feel of smooth bed linens against his skin. Eventually, he pushed himself up against the pillows and surveyed the room. Sunlight slanted through gaps beneath the window shades, reflecting off the polished wood floor. A breath of spring air lifted the chintz curtains and ruffled the crocheted lace edging the bureau cloth. His clothes, he noticed, were neatly folded on the seat of the chair beside it.

He got out of bed, stomach rumbling, and picked up the pitcher next to the washbasin. It was empty. Supporting himself with one hand on the bureau, he leaned into the mirror. There was no denying it; disease, and a year and a half in prison, had aged him.

Well, he thought, *I'm a whole lot luckier than some.* He shuddered, recalling the tales he'd heard when he passed through Cairo the week before.

Freed prisoners from Cahaba, and a few from Andersonville, had boarded a side-wheeler called the *Sultana* at Vicksburg, bound for home. The steamer was overloaded, and word had it that there'd been a problem with the boilers at Vicksburg. The Mississippi was at flood stage, and the *Sultana* was running upstream against it. Seven miles north of Memphis, the boilers exploded. Men not killed outright by the explosion had either burned to death or drowned. Of the more than two thousand on board, only a couple hundred had survived.

Thomas shook his head and turned from the mirror. If not for the weeks spent hospitalized in Mobile, he might easily have been onboard. He crossed to one of the windows and raised the shade. His eyes drifted past the barn, to the trees and the turned fields beyond, unseeing.

Eventually, he turned back into the room. He put on his clothes, which had been washed and ironed, and opened the door.

Elizabeth's voice came to him from the front of the house, intermingled with the unintelligible chatter of a small child. Seized by curiosity, Thomas walked toward a door that stood slightly ajar.

Elizabeth stood with her back to him, facing a chest of drawers in what was obviously the nursery. Her body masked his view of the child, all but one hand, then the other, as Elizabeth held them up and pulled them through sleeves.

"Good morning."

She jumped, startled, and looked around. "Thomas! What are you doing out of bed?"

Thomas shrugged. "I'm hungry."

"Hannah should be up soon with your breakfast. I've no doubt she's preparing it now."

"I wouldn't mind eating at a table, if it's all right with you."

Elizabeth didn't know what to say. Thomas in the house as an invalid was one thing, but Thomas up and around was quite another. Alice was right, what would James and Sarah think? "All right," she said. "Let me get Emma dressed, and I'll tell Hannah."

She leaned to her right, reaching for a pair of shoes, and Thomas got his first look at the child. He wasn't sure what he was expecting, but what he saw wasn't it. Her hair was like spun gold, her skin the color of honey. She saw him, and brown eyes opened wide with alarm as she reached for her mother.

"She's *Ethan's* child?" The words came without thinking. Thomas flushed in embarrassment. "I'm sorry. I didn't mean..."

Elizabeth's lips compressed as she worked a shoe onto a tiny foot. "You're not the first, Thomas, believe me. I had to suggest to Ethan's father that he look in a mirror. My mother is fair as well, so Emma comes by it honestly."

Elizabeth finished tying the laces of the second shoe and straightened, transferring Emma from the bureau to one hip and motioning toward the door. "Shall we?"

Thomas was weak, and he leaned heavily on the banister as he made his way down the stairs. Elizabeth showed him to the dining room and went to speak with Hannah.

Hannah said nothing, merely grunted in disapproval, collected a place setting, and followed Elizabeth to the dining room. She returned a few minutes later, and set Thomas' plate on the table in front of him. At the door, she caught Elizabeth's eye and shook her head.

Thomas failed to notice. He was too busy inhaling his food. Elizabeth bounced Emma on her knees, watching him. He broke one of Hannah's biscuits in half, used it to wipe the plate clean, popped one half, then the other into his mouth, and pushed the plate aside.

"Sorry," he said, when he looked up and found Elizabeth watching. He chewed and swallowed. "I can't seem to get enough to eat."

She could think of no polite way to ask, so she simply said it. "Why are you here, Thomas?"

"Ethan," he said, sounding like she should have known.

"Ethan?"

"You sent me a letter after his court-martial, remember? Asking for my help."

Her expression softened, and she reached a hand across the table.

Thomas took it, eyeing her with trepidation. "They didn't...? I'm not too late, am I?"

Elizabeth shook her head. "You're not too late. What you are, Thomas, is a good friend. Thank you." She gave his hand a quick squeeze and pulled away, hugging Emma to her. Thumb in mouth, the little girl stared at Thomas.

"Where is he? What happened?"

Elizabeth sighed. "I'm not sure. He escaped from prison, and Josh went looking for him. In five months, we've only had two telegrams." She shifted her hold on Emma and stood up. "It's a pretty day. If you're feeling up to it, let's sit outside, and I'll tell you what I know."

Peter Scott settled one hip on the porch rail and knocked the bowl of his pipe against the wood, watching the group assembled around Thomas. Watching Alice, to be exact. She sat at the top of the steps, angled so she faced Thomas, hanging on his every word. James Fraser was there, too, along with his Indian wife, his half-breed daughter, and of course, Mrs. Magrath.

Peter had been puzzled when Alice first mentioned that his former comrade from the Thirty-sixth had shown up on Mrs. Magrath's doorstep. He couldn't for the life of him figure out how they knew each other. Curious, he'd stopped by the house and ended up passing several pleasant evenings in Thomas' company. He understood now how they'd met in Mobile, but he still hadn't figured out the connection between the Frasers and Mrs. Magrath.

She had been a source of gossip and speculation since she first arrived in town, widowed, but not recently enough to still be in mourning, and so obviously pregnant. It was rumored that she was related to James Fraser, but no one knew for certain. Alice, who probably did know, remained irritatingly vague.

The pipe packed to his satisfaction, Peter struck a match along the rail and touched it to the tobacco. As smoke curled into the afternoon air, he studied Mrs. Magrath. She sat apart from the others, head resting against the back of her rocking chair, watching the children play on the lawn. Peter wondered if she was listening until a remark from Thomas made everyone laugh—Alice, he thought, a bit too loudly. Mrs. Magrath smiled, but didn't look around, didn't see the way Thomas looked at her.

It wasn't the first time he'd seen Thomas look at her like that. Early on, he'd wondered if Thomas was the baby's father, but he'd seen no sign of intimacy, and Thomas' story didn't allow for it. He was nearing the end of it now, looking pale and drawn. Peter figured it wouldn't be long before he excused himself.

"You're saying the fighting kept on in Mobile after Lee surrendered?" James asked.

Thomas nodded. "There hadn't been any fighting the whole time I was there. None that got that close. It lasted a little over a week, got all our hopes up, then stopped. The guards were jumpy, wouldn't tell us what was going on. We woke up one morning, and they were gone. Some of the boys, the ones still strong enough, walked to Mobile. A few hours later, some Kentucky boys from Granger's XIII Corps showed up and told us the war was over, had been for three days."

"What happened next?" Alice asked, even though she knew the answer.

"They brought wagons and took us into town. Two weeks later I was on a ship to New Orleans, and from there, a side-wheeler up the Mississippi." Thomas grasped the arms of his chair, preparing to stand. "If you'll excuse me, I need to lie down."

Alice was disappointed that he'd left out the part about hearing the band playing *Yankee Doodle* and *The Star Spangled Banner* as he was carried into the city; how he'd wept for joy when he realized the war was truly over. She stood, eager to assist him, but James was there ahead of her, shaking Thomas' hand.

"Good to meet you, Thomas. Thanks for telling us about our boys." His voice caught, and he cleared his throat before adding, "I hope you and me'll have another chance to talk before you go."

"Yes, sir. I'm sure we will." Thomas bowed his head in Sarah's direction. "Pleasure, ma'am." And to Kate: "You, too, miss."

The door closed behind him, and Elizabeth stifled a sigh of relief. The meeting with James had gone better than she'd expected. Blinded by her own concerns, she hadn't stopped to consider all Thomas could tell him about his sons.

"A good man," James remarked, seating himself in the rocker Thomas had vacated. "And loyal." He turned to Elizabeth, fixing her with a look that added meaning to his words. "How much longer will he be staying?"

Elizabeth looked at Alice. She was staring at the door. It had taken three days for her desire to hear about Duncan to outweigh her fear of disease. Over the past few days, Elizabeth had watched curiosity turn to fascination, then infatuation. She doubted Alice understood what she was feeling, but one look at Peter, sitting at the far end of the porch, told her he did.

"I don't know," she said, looking at James. "He's still weak, still has occasional bouts of fever. It wouldn't be right to ask him to leave. Not just yet."

Alice flashed her a look of gratitude, and Peter stood up abruptly.

"It's time we were going."

Alice considered him for a long moment, then sank down onto the step. "I'm not ready just yet, Peter. But go ahead if you like."

Peter flushed angrily, stared at her for several seconds, then bowed stiffly to Elizabeth.

"Mrs. Magrath. Thank you for the fine meal." A nod to James. "Mr. Fraser." Without another word, he turned and limped down the steps.

"How rude!" Kate exclaimed, as he rounded the corner toward the barn. She realized what she'd said and turned to Alice, mortified. "I'm sorry."

"No, Kate, you're right." Alice realized he hadn't spoken so much as a word to Sarah or Kate all afternoon. "He was rude."

"But aren't you... ?"

"I am *not* going to marry him."

Sarah, who had said very little, smiled "Good. You need a man, but he is not the one."

They watched Peter's wagon trundle down the drive. He turned onto the road, urged the horse into a trot, and drove away without looking back.

James shook his head. Surrounded by women, they remained a mystery. He settled back, closing his eyes for a nap. Sarah went to sit on the lawn with her granddaughters. Emma shrieked with joy, and was lifted onto her lap.

"*Now* will you come see the kittens?" Grace asked, turning to her Aunt Kate.

"I'll go, too," Alice offered, and the three of them headed for the barn. Little Duncan, who had been digging in one of the flowerbeds, scrambled to his feet and trotted after them.

Elizabeth picked up the book she'd been reading, but didn't open it. She sat with it in her lap, watching Sarah play with Emma. There was a special bond between them that had everything to do with Sarah's love for Ethan. Elizabeth wondered where he was, whether Josh had found him, and when he would be coming home.

* * *

The North Platte River was running high and fast, tumbling over itself in its haste to reach the Missouri. Ethan watched as the first warriors plunged their horses in and began swimming them across. He looked around, saw Spotted Horse watching him, and he knew he was once again being tested.

Ethan twisted a hand into the mare's mane and urged her into the river, gasping as the current caught them, and icy water surged above his waist. He held the Spencer and his ammunition pouch high, keeping them dry as they hurtled downstream. All around him bodies thrashed in the water—men, boys and horses straining for the opposite bank. At last, the mare's hooves dug in, and she lunged out of the churning water, trailing great streams of it behind her.

When the entire war party was across, when the boys had gathered the loose horses, they left the river behind and climbed into the sage and juniper-dotted foothills, intent on distancing themselves from the Holy Road before night. Humped layers of blue mountain rose ahead of them, sunlight glancing off pockets of snow that still clung to the north face of Laramie Peak. As they climbed higher, limber pine sprouted from the rocky hillsides, bent and twisted by wind and weather.

At one point, Ethan looked back. The Platte spread wide below them, raging brown waters buffeting the half-submerged willows at the edges of the flood plain. The low angle of the setting sun cast streaks of golden light and purple shadow across the hills and gullies on either side, adding brilliance to the new green of sage and grass and bestowing the harsh land with deceptive beauty.

They made camp in a stand of lodgepole and aspen, next to a clear, rushing mountain stream, its waters as cold as the melting snow that fed it. The scouts arrived, saying there were soldiers and horses at the camp, and it was close. There were no fires that night, and dinner was papapuze, dried jerked meat.

They were up with the sun, preparing for the raid. Ethan applied paint to his face, a single slash of red along the scar left by Shunk's whip. Despite his cousins' protests, it was the only paint he wore. He tied up the tail of the big gray gelding he'd acquired in an earlier raid, threw a pad saddle on his back, and pulled the cinch tight.

Leaving the boys to watch the spare ponies, they angled up a long slope, littered with rocks and small boulders. The pines thinned, giving way to grass, sage and a profusion of wildflowers. As they neared the top, a high-pitched screeching sound reached them, borne on the crisp, dry mountain air. Ethan's heart quickened as he recognized the mechanical whine of a saw.

They crested the ridge, dropped into a shallow drainage, then started up the long slope of the next, higher ridge. They stopped just shy of the top, and several warriors, Spotted Horse and Fat Bear among them, dropped to the ground. Crouching low, they trotted to the brow of the ridge. Ethan took his field glasses and joined them.

A wide canyon spread below them, dropping away to foothills to the east. To the west, near the base of the next ridge, stood the sawmill—three log buildings, a corral, and a couple of small sheds. Smoke spewed from a tall smokestack at the back of the largest building; a wooden carriage rolled through it on tracks, guiding logs through the saw. Piles of logs and rough-cut lumber littered the ground around the mill, and wagon tracks snaked away from it in several directions, winding through fields of stumps and debris until they reached the edge of the trees. Through the field glasses, Ethan could identify three men dressed as soldiers, and five civilians near the mill. Closer, halfway up the near slope, men with axes worked among the pines. And straight ahead, grazing in a green meadow beside the stream, was what they'd come for.

"Šuŋkawakaŋ ake sakowiŋ," Ethan muttered. "Nahaŋ šunšuŋla šagloğanpi yelo." Seventeen horses and eight mules. He scanned the land around them. "No guard."

They raced to their ponies and leapt aboard. As one, they surged over the top of the ridge.

Josh drove the ax deep and pulled it back. The tall pine trembled, then slowly began to topple. It twisted as it fell, picking up speed, and crashed to the ground in an explosion of dirt and broken branches. Out of the crash came the most ungodly sound he had ever heard. It pierced the morning air and sent chills racing up and down his spine.

"God help us!" Private Ed Wilkerson blanched, staring past him.

Josh spun around.

Indians, at least twenty of them, were sweeping down the ridge less than two hundred yards away. Josh dropped the ax, grabbed his Henry rifle, and looked toward the mill. The men there were running for cover. Alfred Hynes, handling the team of mules hauling logs to the mill, was caught in the open. He slapped the reins over the mules' backs, but the heavy wagon couldn't go any faster. Alf grabbed his rifle and leapt to the ground, running toward the shelter of the trees.

The Indians were racing toward the herd, but five of them broke away and galloped after the man on foot. Josh raised the Henry and took aim at the leader. The shot reverberated through the canyon, and the Indian tumbled from his horse. Two warriors veered off, charging toward Josh.

"C'mon, Lieutenant! Run!"

Private Wilkerson was scrambling up the steep slope toward a fortress-like outcropping of boulders. Josh took a step after him, then stopped as an arrow embedded itself Alf's thigh. Alf fell, then scrambled to his feet and hopped toward a slash pile, tumbling over the mound of debris and disappearing from sight. Josh loosed eight more shots at the warriors pursuing him. They veered toward Josh, and he turned and ran.

Hooves pounded behind him. An arrow whirred past his ear. Another thudded into a tree trunk as he weaved around it. He stumbled, caught himself with his hands, and a bullet tore into the earth ahead of him. Another plucked the hat from his head; a third ricocheted off the rocks. Gunfire erupted from above as Private Wilkerson returned fire.

Josh reached the rocks and threw himself over.

"They're turning back!" Private Wilkerson shouted, loosing a parting volley.

Josh drew himself up, panting, and looked down through the trees. The Indians were indeed retreating. Two of them had cut the mules loose from the wagon and were driving them after the rest of the herd, heading into the foothills below the canyon.

The man Josh had shot was on his feet. A warrior, mounted on a dappled gray with black mane and tail, raced toward him, leaning low and reaching out a hand. The man on the ground grasped it, and with a running leap, landed behind him. Another warrior raced after the loose Indian pony, setting it running, and the three of them galloped after the others.

"Damn!" Josh turned and sat down, wiping the sheen of sweat from his face.

"First time ever attacked by Indians, Lieutenant?"

Private Wilkerson was seventeen and irritatingly cheerful.

"Yes. And like I keep saying; I'm *not* a lieutenant. Not anymore."

"Yes, sir."

Josh pushed himself to his feet. "Alf got himself shot. Let's see if he's all right."

"Yes, sir. Looks like we'll be walking back to Fort Laramie, doesn't it, sir?"

JUNE

24

The leather ball hurtled along the ground, caroming off a rock and heading directly for Ethan. He charged it, bringing back the curved stick he held in his right hand and swinging it with all his might. Before it made contact, one of his opponents raced in from another angle and kicked the ball away. They collided hard, bouncing apart and crashing to the ground. Ethan grunted as the fall jarred still-tender ribs. Gritting his teeth, he scrambled to his feet. The other man was already up. Together they sprinted after the ball.

There were two teams and two designated lodges, one at either end of the camp. The object was to hit the lodge the other team protected. The team that scored two out of three hits was the winner, and at the moment, the score was tied at two. There were no boundaries, and the game ranged far from the camp, spectators, as well as players, following the ball across the prairie.

The ball reversed direction suddenly, bumping over uneven ground. Ethan and his opponent raced to meet it, attempting to shoulder one another out of the way. Two men from the other team joined them, and their sticks cracked together as they scrabbled for control of the ball. Ethan's stick connected, and the ball skidded towards Standing Elk. He hit it neatly, sending it toward the camp. Another man, running in at an angle, kicked the ball to Fat Bear, who ranged ahead of him. Fat Bear prodded the ball with his stick, keeping it in front of him as he trotted toward the lodge.

Both teams took off after him, running more slowly than at the beginning of the game. Jostling his opponents, Ethan ran with them. The first few times he'd played, it had been all he could do to keep up, to keep from crying out or limping when he was hurt. But he'd kept at it, determined not only to rebuild strength and stamina, but to fit in. Six and a half months after being shot, he was more fit than he'd ever been. To prove it, he forced a burst of speed.

Spotted Horse, Standing Elk and several others sprinted ahead of Fat Bear. Before he could hit the ball to them, an opponent knocked it away. Ethan swooped in on his right and knocked it back to Fat Bear. Fat Bear kicked it, and sent it sailing toward Spotted Horse. Spotted Horse hit it toward the first of the men lining up near the goal. They passed it along until the last man lifted it with his stick, and slapped it into the side of the lodge.

A cheer went up among the players. Fat Bear turned to Ethan and clapped him on the shoulder.

"Did you wager?"

"Yes. Did you?"

"Of course." Fat Bear rolled his head to one side, stretching the muscles at the base of his neck. The wound from the sawmill was well on its way to healing; the bullet had grazed the collarbone and passed through cleanly. Stretching was the only indication Fat Bear gave that it still bothered him.

For his part, Ethan felt bruised and battered. He knew some of the scrapes on his arms, legs and back were bleeding, but it wouldn't do to look. He smiled inwardly; fantasizing about an afternoon spent relaxing with a good book. *Not likely*, he thought, and realized Fat Bear was watching him.

"You have a strange look in your eyes, Two Moons. Sometimes I wonder what you are thinking."

"I am thinking about what I won. Come. I will show you."

They joined the other wagerers streaming toward the meeting lodge. Before the game, men from their team had gone to the other team and collected bets, bringing them back to be looked over. Ethan had seen what he'd wanted and tied his wager to it. Now he picked up the silver bracelet he'd appropriated after the first Julesburg raid, and untied his prize from it.

Holding up a pair of earrings made from pounded brass and white shells, he said, "What do you think? I have decided to have my ears pierced."

* * *

"Why not?" Colonel Thomas Moonlight demanded. "Bastards've been stealing and murdering up and down the Platte Road for two months. Able-bodied man like you, it's your duty to help put a stop to it."

"Like I told you, Colonel, I'm finished with the army. I didn't come here to fight Indians."

The colonel grasped the porch railing and leaned down, fixing Josh with a bloodshot stare. Josh could smell the whiskey on his breath.

"They're animals, Fraser. Thieves and murderers and defilers of women. Hell, they tried to kill you; stole your horse. Didn't that make you angry?"

"Yes, sir. It did. But I don't plan on doing anything more for the army than swinging an ax."

A knowing look came into the colonel's eyes, and his head bobbed. "You're an Indian lover. Think I've forgotten about your brother being one of them? No, sir. I remember." He let go of the railing, swaying slightly before pulling himself to his full height and staring down at Josh. "Maybe it's time you were on you way, Mr. Fraser. Wherever it is you're headed."

"Yes, sir. I'll certainly consider it."

Josh watched the colonel along the length of the porch and down the steps at the far end. Then he turned and walked to the sutler's store.

The sutler, W. G. Bullock, was standing in the open doorway. "Man's a drunk," he muttered, stepping aside for Josh to enter. "He was drunk when he ordered them Indians strung up, and according to the boys from California that was just here, he was drunk when the Sioux stole their horses."

"That right?"

"So they say." Bullock headed toward the bottles he kept at the far end of the counter. "Whiskey?"

"Thanks."

There had been close to two thousand friendly Oglala and Brulé camped in the vicinity of the fort all spring. Josh had spent time among them, initially seeking news of Ethan, and later, because he found them interesting. Eight days ago, Secretary of War Stanton had ordered them rounded up and marched east to Fort Kearny. Fort Kearny was in Pawnee territory, and the Sioux had not been happy. No one had thought to disarm them, and three days out, they'd attacked their escort, killing five and fleeing. When word reached Fort Laramie, Colonel Moonlight had assembled a force of two hundred thirty-four Ohio, Kansas, and California cavalry and gone after them. He and his troops had returned a few hours earlier, most of them on foot, after the Sioux ran off their horses.

In Josh's opinion, it wasn't the first time Colonel Moonlight had proved incompetent in his dealings with the Indians—inflaming tensions rather than soothing them. Back in May, a couple weeks before the attack on the sawmill, two friendly Oglala chiefs, men he'd talked to, had come to the fort with a captured white woman and her eighteen-month-old son. Josh had been among the spectators who'd witnessed their arrival. Mrs. Eubanks was horrifying to look at, half-naked, a mass of open sores and bruises from head to foot. Despite their claims, in sign language and broken English, that they had purchased the woman in order to return her, the post commander ordered them locked in the guardhouse. A week later, when Colonel Moonlight returned from an unsuccessful attempt to hunt down hostiles, he had ordered both chiefs hung in trace chains, ignoring protests from his own officers, Bullock, and even Mrs. Eubanks. Since then, Indian attacks along the Platte River Road had intensified.

Josh accepted the glass of whiskey, nodded his thanks to the sutler, and walked to the door. Stepping outside, he looked toward the bluffs northeast of the fort. There, in the slanting light of late afternoon, the remains of the two Indians still hung from the gallows. Seeing them reminded him of the other Indian he'd seen hung shortly after his arrival. Turning back into the store, he asked, "What was the name of that woman, the one they hung Old Crow for kidnapping?"

"Mrs. Morton," Bullock replied. "Nancy Jane Morton."

Josh nodded and took a sip of whiskey. He wished he'd had an opportunity to talk to her, but she was safely back in the states by the time he arrived. According to Mrs. Bullock, who had befriended her and accompanied her east, Mrs. Morton had had nothing good to say about her captors or their treatment of her. But at one point, she'd mentioned an encounter with a pair of half-breeds. One of them, she said, had spoken kindly to her, seemed concerned for her welfare. His name, she recalled, was Bent. Josh had always wondered who the other one was.

Leaning back, bracing a foot against the wall, he took another sip of whiskey. There had been a thunderstorm earlier in the day, gusting winds and blowing dirt preceding it, then towering black clouds lanced through with bolts of lightning, thunder booming across the prairie, and a deluge so intense that the land was awash within seconds. An hour later, it was over, the sun radiant in a vault of blue sky, the line of black vanishing toward the east. There was nothing to show for it now but a few drying patches of mud where the deepest puddles had been.

It's an incredible land, he thought, staring past the scattered buildings to the river and the green hills beyond. *Incredible and cruel. If the Indians don't kill you, the weather will.* Even so, it intrigued him. For more than a month, he'd considered heading west to Fort Bridger; only the escalation of the Indian attacks had stopped him. Now, after the latest run-in with Moonlight, he figured he'd wait until the end of the month, draw his pay from the sawmill, and join a wagon train or a detachment of cavalry headed west. *One last shot at finding Ethan, see a little more of the country, then home.*

JULY

25

Throughout May and June, as war parties rode to the Platte and returned bearing plunder, the camps followed the buffalo. They moved south to the Little Powder, then angled northwest, across the broad basin of the Powder, to the Tongue River. From there, they turned southwest, following the Tongue to the foothills of the Big Horn Mountains. They moved at the same pace as the buffalo, hunting, drying meat, and dressing hides as they went.

In early July, they migrated east along Clear Creek, back to the Powder River. There the tribes gathered; the Oglala, Miniconjou, Brulé, and Sans Arc Sioux, the Northern and Southern Cheyenne, and the Northern Arapaho, more than a thousand lodges spread for miles along the river. The Sioux held their Sun Dance, the Cheyenne their Medicine Lodge, and then the chiefs held councils, selecting Platte Bridge Station as the site for a concerted attack against the whites, and charging the soldier groups with seeing that no more small war parties left the camps.

Then began a slow move south along the Powder, the old men and the medicine men teaching the young men the traditional ways of preparing weapons, shields, war bonnets and war shirts, all the things that would aid and protect them in battle. At Crazy Woman Creek, they stopped to make final preparations.

"If you are to be a warrior, you must wear a scalp lock," Spotted Horse said, assuming the superior attitude, chin in the air, feet apart that never failed to irritate Ethan.

Fat Bear scowled at Spotted Horse. "A scalp lock is your challenge to the enemy," he said to Ethan. "You decorate it so he cannot help but see it; you challenge him to take it."

Ethan nodded. He had traded for a hair ornament, a quilled rawhide disk with down feathers dangling from four soft strips of leather, and had every intention of wearing it.

"It will be a good fight," Fat Bear said, winding a new bowstring around the lower end of his bow and making it fast. "We will return with many scalps, boasting of the coups we have counted. There will be much celebrating." He grinned, imagining it, then looked at Ethan. "You understand that to touch a living enemy is a greater honor than to kill him?"

"I understand. But in this fight, I intend to kill."

The announcement was met with silence. Fat Bear pulled the bowstring taut, fitting the looped end into the notch at the upper end of the bow. Spotted Horse coiled extra bowstrings, watching Two Moons out of the corner of his eye as he placed them at the bottom of his quiver and replaced the arrows. After the first night, Two Moons had never again spoken of the soldier attack at Sand Creek, but it was known that he carried a great sadness with him—and an even greater hatred of the white soldiers.

Ethan stuffed the last tube of cartridges into his ammunition pouch and tied it closed. Stooping beneath the rolled up lodge cover, he placed the ammunition pouch on top of the other things he would take with him: a rawhide case containing a shirt, an extra pair of moccasins and his match safe, a pouch with war paint and a small horn bowl for mixing it, a rolled blanket, a length of rope, his tomahawk, the pistol in its holster, a sheathed knife, and the Spencer in a new fringed and beaded case. He would ride Faria, taking the gray for battle and one of the bays from Mud Springs Ranch as a backup. He was ready. With nothing left to do, he stepped outside.

The lodges threw long shadows across the golden prairie grass, still in bright sunlight against the blue shadow of the Big Horns. High up, beneath towering blue sky, only bare granite peaks still caught the light. Already, a fresh coolness had come to the dry air, a welcome relief after the intense heat of the day.

Throughout the camps, women were preparing food. Chasing As She Walks crouched next to a fire, using a pair of forked sticks to lift hot stones and drop them into the cooking paunch. As the water boiled, her sister added sausages, freshly made from buffalo intestines stuffed with meat. Moccasin Woman knelt nearby, grinding dried meat between stones. Her youngest daughter sat next to her, pulling stems and leaves from the fresh berries that would be mixed with the meat to make pemmican. Walks Alone, Standing Elk's pretty young wife, emerged from between the lodges and dropped an armload of wood next to the fire. Straightening, she saw Ethan watching her. A shy smile touched her lips, and she turned away.

The familiar ache tightened in Ethan's chest. He turned and headed for the creek. Lately, he'd begun to wonder if he would ever feel whole again. He filled each day, driving himself to exhaustion so he wouldn't dream at night, but all it took was a woman's laugh, a smile, a familiar gesture, and grief came rushing back.

Revenge, he thought. *When I've had it, when I've done to them what they did to Tall Grass and Micah, maybe then it'll ease.*

He was starting down the steep bank to the water when he heard his name called.

"Come," Black Wolf said, when Ethan looked around. He and Standing Elk turned their ponies in among the lodges, trailed by three strangers.

They were seated beneath the rolled up covers of the lodge, along with Spotted Horse and Fat Bear, when Ethan arrived. Long Face and Bone Necklace joined them. Black Wolf lit his pipe, offering it to the Sky, the Earth, and the Four Winds, before handing it to the man seated next to him. Ethan studied the strangers while they smoked. One was Black Wolf's age; the other two, closer to his own—father and sons, by the look of them. The older man wore a stained vest of red silk brocade; their breechclouts and leggings were made of cloth.

"These men are from Bad Wound's band of Oglala," Black Wolf said, when the last of the fire had gone from the pipe. "They are wagluĥe[22] from the fort called Laramie. There is one there who seeks a mixed-blood called Ethan Fraser."

Ethan didn't know what wagluĥe meant, but he understood the rest. A chill went through him. Somehow, they'd discovered where he was and come looking for him. "Who..." he began in English, then switched to Lakota. "This man, he is white?"

"He is white," the older man agreed.

"A soldier?"

"No."

Ethan glanced at his sons. Their expressions told him nothing. His eyes narrowed as he looked at the older man. "What does he want?"

"He looks for one he calls brother."

"Brother," Ethan repeated. "What is his name?"

"He is called Josh Fraser."

---

22   Followers, loafers; given the name for their custom of loafing around forts, taking handouts from soldiers, and begging from emigrant trains

Ethan couldn't hide his astonishment. He leaned forward eagerly. "When was he at the fort?"

The man studied him, dark eyes appraising. "You are his brother?"

"Yes. When did you talk to him?"

"He came to my lodge the first time in the Moon of the Birth of Calves.[23] He came again many times, to smoke and to talk."

"Why does he look for me?"

"Now that the whites no longer war with one another, he has much to say to you."

The war was over. Hearing it, on top of the news that Josh was alive and looking for him, left Ethan momentarily speechless. He looked at Fat Bear and Spotted Horse. They watched him curiously.

"Who won?"

The man's brow wrinkled in confusion. He looked at his sons.

"The war. Did the blue coats win the white man's war?"

"The blue coats," the man agreed, nodding. "Josh Fraser rode with the blue coats, but no more."

"Is he still at the fort?"

"When the white chief sent us away, he was there."

"How long ago?"

"One moon." The man moved his hand in a vague gesture. "Perhaps a little more."

One moon. A little over a month ago, Josh had been at Fort Laramie. Ethan's first impulse was to go there. Then he realized how foolhardy that would be.

The women came, bringing food, and talk turned to other things, much of it already known in the camps: How Two Face and Blackfoot had been hung by the drunken soldier chief and deprived of a proper burial, their bodies still hanging on the bluff when the same soldier chief had ordered the Lakota marched to Pawnee territory. How, during the march, soldiers had come to the lodges at night and taken young girls for their own use. How warriors from the north had slipped in among the marchers, and the Lakota had struck back, killing the little white chief who spoke to them in loud, angry words, and escaped into the sand hills where others from the north, led by Crazy Horse and He Dog waited. How the drunken chief had gathered many soldiers and come after them, stopping at a place where only a fool would camp and turning his horses loose to graze. The

---

23   April

story had been told many times, but still there was laughter at the description of the soldiers burning their saddles, or carrying them the long, dusty miles back to Fort Laramie.

Ethan paid scant attention to the conversation. He was preoccupied with how to find Josh—and how talk to him without getting killed.

The next day, warriors from all the tribes, painted and dressed for battle, their horses painted and feathered with tails tied up, formed a great line and paraded through the camps. Standing before the circled lodges, the old men, the women and the children joined in singing each band's war songs as they rode past. All that night, there was dancing, and as the sun rose, the war party, two thousand warriors led by the war chiefs bearing the war pipes, started south. Roman Nose, Dull Knife, and White Bull were prominent among the leaders of the Cheyenne; Red Cloud, Young Man Afraid Of His Horses, Pawnee Killer, and High Back Bone among the Lakota. An advance guard of Dog Soldiers followed the chiefs, then the long columns of warriors, more than two hundred women, the herd boys with the extra horses, and Dog Soldiers guarding the rear.

Spotted Horse, Standing Elk, Fat Bear, Long Face, and Bone Necklace were there, along with George, Charley, Philippe, Julie, Yellow Woman, Walks Alone and Kicking Bird. Riding among them, singing the songs, Ethan felt a pride in belonging that he'd never experienced before. He envisioned the battle ahead, the deaths of the soldiers and what he would do to them, until anticipation grew almost suffocating.

Very soon, he promised Micah and Tall Grass. *Very soon they will pay for Sand Creek.*

* * *

"I'm out." Lieutenant Jim Hanna tossed his cards on the table and tipped his chair back, stretching mightily and yawning.

Josh tapped his cards on the table and considered his opponent.

Caspar Collins grinned. "You know I got you beat, Josh. Quit before you lose it all."

Josh was almost positive he was bluffing. "Call," he said, tossing the last of his money into the pot.

Caspar beamed, fanning his cards on the table. "Four of a kind. Jacks."

Josh's eyebrows arched in surprise. They'd known each other a little more than a week, and he'd thought he had the young lieutenant figured out.

Caspar was reaching for the pot when Josh tossed down his cards. "Straight flush. Diamonds. Six high."

Caspar stopped in mid-reach, his expression turning from glee to disbelief.

A sly grin slid over Josh's face. "You know I never walk away empty-handed."

Caspar sat back, shaking his head. His lips curled into a reluctant smile. "A man has a right to dream, doesn't he?"

"He does," Josh agreed, pulling the pot to him. "But you've won the evening. I can't let you have it all."

Jim pushed his chair back, and stood up. "I don't know about you gents, but I'm calling it a night."

"Yeah." Josh set both hands on the table and pushed himself up.

"I'll walk out with you," Caspar said. "At this hour, it's probably safe to get a breath of air."

Second Lieutenant Caspar Collins, Company G, 11th Ohio Volunteer Cavalry, commanded the four upper posts guarding the telegraph line along the North Platte—Sweetwater Bridge, Three Crossings, Rocky Ridge, and South Pass. Jim Hanna had introduced them shortly after Caspar arrived with a detail of ten men to pick up new mounts. The men and horses had returned to Sweetwater Station, but Caspar had remained behind, ostensibly waiting for a new uniform to be made, but enjoying the company of his good friend Jim Hanna and hours spent at his favorite pastime, playing poker. It was a favorite of Josh's, too, and they'd taken an instant liking to one another.

Smart, friendly and perceptive, Casper had been in the region three years, two as an unpaid civilian clerk, engineer and draftsman during his father's tenure at Fort Laramie, and one as an officer. He had traveled extensively during that time, coming to know the land and its inhabitants. By his own admission, he found the Indians at once intriguing and infuriating. He had spent a good deal of time among the Sioux, learning their language and their ways, but recently, men he'd come to think of as friends had destroyed endless miles of telegraph line, stolen stock, burned the post at Rocky Ridge, and attacked and killed his men.

The summer night, when he and Josh stepped onto the covered wooden porch of the bachelor officers' quarters, had a welcome coolness to it. Josh pulled a pair of cigars from his vest pocket and offered one to Caspar. He accepted, and Josh struck a match, cupping his hands around the flame. When the tip of Caspar's cigar glowed red, Josh flicked the match over the rail and lit another.

Once his own cigar was going properly, he leaned a shoulder against a post and looked up at the night sky. The number and brightness of the stars at this high elevation never ceased to amaze him.

"How much longer you plan on staying?"

Caspar walked from the shadows to the edge of the porch and looked up. He was a few inches shorter than Josh, slender with light brown hair, and clean-shaven. Fine-boned features made him appear younger than his twenty-one years.

"Not long. My last encounter with General Connor was bad enough. I hate to think what he'd do if he found out I'm still here."

"He was wrong to say what he did."

"I know. Only a fool bent on suicide would travel alone right now, but letting Jim convince me to hide in his quarters makes me feel Connor was right in calling me a coward." Caspar ran a hand through short-cropped hair and shook his head. "I don't know why, but this time I dread going back."

"I've been thinking," Josh said, tilting his head back and releasing a long stream of smoke. "If you decide to go, I'll go with you."

Caspar looked sideways at him. A smile played at the edges of his mouth, and he shook his head. "You've been here what, three months? And now, when the hills are infested with hostile Indians, you decide to head west? You're out of your mind."

"You're going. I figure two guns are better than one."

"Two guns will see us both killed."

"It's settled, then." Josh grinned and started away down the length of the porch. "Let me know when you decide to go."

He was shaken awake before it was light.

"There's a mail ambulance leaving for Platte Bridge in half an hour," Jim Hanna said. "Caspar's going with it. He said you'd want to know."

Josh mumbled his thanks, rolled onto his back and closed his eyes. Several minutes later, he blew out a breath and sat up. It didn't take him long to pack. As he swung into the saddle, he could see the escort for the mail ambulance assembling near the stables.

There were fourteen of them: the driver, Caspar in back with the mail, Corporal Henry Grimm with ten men from 11th Kansas Volunteer Cavalry, and Josh. He looked back once before hills blocked his view of the fort, thinking how insignificant it looked, buildings clustered on an empty plain.

If they're insignificant, he thought with a shake of his head, *what are we?*

26

The Powder River narrowed until it was little more than a trickle. The war party left it, angling southwest across an arid landscape of alkali flats, sage and dried grass, cut through by gullies and dotted with prickly pear. A dark line of mountains appeared to the south, and as they drew closer, they held their horses to a walk so as not to throw up dust and reveal their presence to the soldiers. They came to another stream winding its way south to the Platte, and set up camp. There were no trees, only a few straggly willows too small to offer protection from the sun. The women began assembling shelters made from branches and hides, while the chiefs sent scouts ahead to see how things were at the bridge.

The sun had sunk low over the western mountains by the time the scouts returned. The breeze had cooled, but the dry earth continued to radiate heat. The chiefs sent three criers through the camps, one Cheyenne, one Sioux and one Arapaho, to announce the plan for the following day. There was to be no loud talking that night, and no singing, nothing that would alert the soldiers.

At dawn, ten men selected by the chiefs headed for the bridge. Behind them rode the war chiefs, followed by the rest of the war party, hemmed in on all sides by Dog Soldiers. When they reached the hills north of the river, they stopped to prepare. Men with war bonnets and war shields removed them from their cases and began the ceremonies that would aid and protect them in battle.

Ethan was with his cousins, squatting in the shade of their horses, when he saw George start up the low bluffs, wearing his blue uniform and carrying field glasses. Grabbing his own glasses, he followed. A pair of Dog Soldiers moved to intercept him, saw the glasses, and let him go. Red Cloud, Roman Nose and Young Man Afraid were already at the top, along with half a dozen men with field glasses. George glanced at Ethan when he dropped to his stomach beside him, then looked again when he realized who it was.

"Mornin'," Ethan said. "Been a while."

"It has," George agreed, a smile tugging at his lips as he raised his glasses. "See you got your ears pierced."

"Uh-huh."

The Lakota pierced their children's ears as part of the ritual of the Sun Dance. For the price of a horse, Black Wolf had agreed to pierce Ethan's. Using a sharp knife and a block of wood, he'd done it amid a group of screaming babies. Ethan had had no choice but to endure it in silence.

"How big's the garrison?" he asked.

"Don't know. Still counting."

Ethan took in the scene without raising his glasses. The Platte, running high, and the thousand-foot bridge that spanned it, dominated the foreground. The emigrant trail and telegraph line came from the east, winding down from the bluffs on the far side of the river, across a broad expanse of bottomland dotted with sage, grass and sand hills, past the huddle of buildings that comprised the station, crossed the bridge, then ran along bottomland for a couple of miles before climbing into the hills to the west and disappearing toward the Sweetwater. The Platte looped around the station in a wide arc, its waters glinting in the distance before vanishing among sage and grass-covered foothills that began a rapid, irregular ascent toward a humped line of mountains that stretched as far as he could see to the east, and terminated abruptly a couple miles west.

Ethan raised his field glasses and studied Platte Bridge Station. A building of freshly peeled logs stood just beyond the bridge, a spur of the telegraph line terminating at its near end. There was a smaller, weathered, log building east of it, and further back from the river, a group of adobe buildings that formed three sides of a square, a flagstaff at the center. The buildings were surrounded by a stockade made of logs driven into the ground. In the area that served as a corral, Ethan could see horses moving about. The rest of the stock, about twenty horses and mules, were at pasture just east of the post. Closer, between the herd and the river, were several rows of white tents. To the west stood a pair of Indian lodges.

"Who are they?" Ethan asked. "The Indians."

"Not sure."

Ethan asked again in Lakota.

"Snake," came the muttered reply.

It was just after noon, and the soldiers were eating their mid-day meal. Many of them sat outside, clustered in what little shade they could find. Ethan had counted to forty, when suddenly, the soldiers grew agitated, standing and pointing downriver and seizing their weapons.

Ethan lowered his glasses and watched the ten warriors ride leisurely toward them along the broad stretch of land between the bluffs and the river. At the station, men were shouting and running toward the corral. Within minutes, a mounted group appeared, galloping toward the bridge. Others rode to the grazing herd and began rounding it up. Ethan waited until the soldiers crossed the bridge, and the warriors began their retreat, before scrambling back down the hill.

Dog Soldiers still surrounded the waiting warriors, but as gunshots cracked beyond the ridge, the mass of mounted men began to heave, attempting to break free. The soldiers beat them back, using quirts and war clubs. Ethan ran for the gray and flung himself aboard. His cousins were all around him, but for several minutes they went nowhere, ponies snorting and jostling as the Dog Soldiers struggled to hold them. Then a group of Lakota broke through. Ethan, his cousins, and several others surged after them.

They came to a deep ravine, running perpendicular to the river, about half a mile east of the bridge. A number of Cheyenne were already turning down it, intent on cutting the soldiers off once they'd been lured past. The Lakota urged their ponies up the far side and continued downstream at a gallop. When the river curved north, they plunged in and swam their ponies across.

"We need a plan," Ethan said to the men nearest him, as they loped into the low hills south of the river. "Before we come in sight of the station, we should leave our horses and slip in close, leaving only a few to show themselves. That way, when the soldiers give chase, they will be in our trap before they expect it."

Fat Bear looked at him, weighing what he'd said, even as others around him muttered disagreement.

"We use the same trick every time," Ethan persisted. "The soldiers have learned what to expect. They know not to follow us too far."

"There is truth in what Two Moons says," Fat Bear put in, knowing his cousin had ridden with the white soldiers and understood their ways.

"They have been fooled many times," a warrior said, a man with a war shield and many scalps on his shirt. "They will be fooled again." His pony leapt forward, and others followed.

"There is truth in what you say," Fat Bear repeated. Riding next to him, Standing Elk nodded.

Ethan blew out a breath in disgust and urged the gray faster. He hadn't expected his suggestion to be acted upon—he was a newcomer, younger than the proven warriors and yet to make a name for himself. But he hadn't figured on being so summarily dismissed.

They showed themselves south of the station, a few at first, to lure the soldiers out, then more as they led them further away. Four warriors fell, wounded by the soldiers' guns, but not a single soldier died before they turned and raced back to the safety of their stockade.

North of the river, the soldiers had already retreated. Ethan could see the chiefs atop the bluffs. There were warriors with them, mounted on their war ponies, and more along the river, about fifty in all. He was bitterly disappointed by the outcome of the fight, but as they headed back to the crossing, he took some satisfaction from knowing he'd been right.

***

"Indians!"

"Where?"

Corporal Grimm pointed. "There."

The cattle herd from Platte Bridge Station dotted the hillsides half a mile southwest of the road. Beyond the cattle, atop a line of hills fronting the mountains, Josh made out thirteen mounted Indians. The ambulance driver urged his team faster, and around him, the men of the 11th Kansas broke into a canter. The Platte was dead ahead, winding away to the south, and next to it, across bottomland dotted with sand hills, dried grass and sage, was the station.

A scream split the afternoon air, the same unholy cry Josh remembered from the sawmill, and the Indians charged toward the herd. Josh looked back as the herders began bunching the cattle. Then hills came between them, and they were lost from sight.

The station was in an uproar when they reached it.

"Injuns! More'n a hundred of 'em!" a private yelled, grasping the lead horse's bridle as the ambulance rolled to a stop. "We run 'em off about an hour ago. You see any?"

"They're attacking the herders about two miles back, trying to steal the cattle!" Corporal Grimm responded, addressing a major who stepped from a doorway to his left.

"Captain Greer!" the major shouted.

"Yes, sir!"

"Form a detail and go to their aid."

"Yes, sir!" The captain headed for the corral, pointing to men and calling out names.

"We'll go with them, sir," Henry Grimm announced, his excited horse circling under him.

"As will I," Caspar said, jumping down from the ambulance. "If someone will loan me a horse."

"Take mine," Josh said, swinging down from the saddle.

"You're not coming?"

"Nope." Josh pulled the Henry from its sling and removed his saddlebags. "Here," he said, handing Caspar the reins. "See I get him back."

Josh stood among the remaining company, watching the twenty-nine men ride away. When they disappeared atop the bluffs, the major, a tall man with deep-set eyes, a receding hairline, long black beard and a full mustache, turned to him.

"Major Martin Anderson, 11ᵗʰ Kansas Volunteer Cavalry." He looked at the Henry. "You have ammunition for that thing?"

"Josh Fraser. Yes, sir. I do."

"Had any experience fighting Indians?"

"No, sir."

The major looked at Josh appraisingly. "But you *do* know how to use it?"

"Killed my share of Rebs with it."

"Good. I expect we'll be needing another gun tomorrow."

"You think they'll be back?"

"I'd bet on it, Mr. Fraser." Major Anderson started away, then turned back. "My men have been sleeping in tents due to the heat, but I've ordered them inside tonight. They'll make room for you."

"Thank you. And sir," Josh added, as the major turned away. "The Indians. What tribe are they?"

"Sioux and Cheyenne. A few Arapaho, according to our Shoshone scouts. Anything else?"

"No, sir. Thank you."

* * *

Like many of the warriors who had broken away, Ethan felt the sting of the soldiers' quirts when he returned to the main war party. The Dog Soldiers forced everyone into a dense column and marched them back to the camp. The sun beat down mercilessly from a pale, cloudless sky, and heat rose in shimmering waves from the earth.

Ethan was furious at having been whipped. Riding packed close together, amid choking dust, with flies settling on his lips and at the corners of his eyes, wherever there was moisture, only made it worse. The quirts had raised welts on his back and shoulders, and the memories it stirred, combined with the heat and the failure of the attack, kept him fuming all the way to camp. He watered the gray, then shunned the shelter where his cousins gathered, and set off by himself.

The soldiers kept him from going beyond the camp, so he walked for a time along the perimeter, until the heat drove him back to the creek. It wound down the middle of a broad wash, carved by years of springtime flooding. Deposits left by the floods were scattered and heaped along it, rocks worn smooth over time, branches and bits of wood, and one scrawny tree with a flat web of roots protruding skyward. Ethan squatted on the hard mud and splashed water over his face. It was warmer than the Platte, but served to cool the last of his anger. A shadow fell across him and he looked up, squinting into bright sky.

"Julie!" He stood, wiping water from his face and shaking it from his hands.

"Hi, Ethan," she said, smiling. "You been avoiding me?"

He had, but he denied it. "I've been busy, is all."

Her smile faded. "I know. Bad memories. I been busy, too."

Ethan gave a faint nod and looked away. It was partly true. Seeing her did trigger a flood of memories, but it also made him uncomfortable. She was young and beautiful, and she'd done everything for him when he was wounded, knew him in ways he would never know her. He wasn't quite sure what to say.

"I... I'm sorry," he said, avoiding her eyes. "I've had to work to get my strength back."

"I understand. But I've been giving a lotta thought to something, and now I see you, seems like the time to say it.

"I know how you feel about Tall Grass Woman dying; how you weigh yourself down thinking you're to blame. But there's something you forget, Ethan. You saved the only life you could. Because of you, that little girl will grow up safe with her gran'pa." She paused before adding, "I was wrong to try and stop it. I'm sorry. I wanted you to know that."

Ethan looked at her as she spoke. Now he shook his head. "Julie. You, of all people, don't need to apologize to me. Without you... Without everything you did, making me drink that awful stuff..." He grimaced, pleased to see the smile return to her face.

"It was you, Ethan. Once you decided to live, it was you, not me."

"You're wrong. I owe you, same as I owe Red Hand." He moved a step closer, taking her hand. "I mean it, Julie. Thank you."

She looked away, self-conscious, and took a step back, pulling her hand free. "You look real good, Ethan," she said as she turned away.

"Thanks," he said, feeling a rush of affection for her. "I promise I'll come visit soon."

She waved without looking back. Still smiling, Ethan watched her disappear among the shelters.

The sun was setting, the last rays stretching across the prairie, when the criers rode through the camps, announcing the plan for the following day. When Ethan heard it, he decided it was time to talk to George.

He found him upstream, one of a group that included several Bent cousins. They greeted him familiarly, inviting him to join them. Ethan returned their greetings in Cheyenne, then asked George, in English, if they could talk. They walked along the creek, stopping at the edge of the wash as dusk settled across the prairie.

"You heard what the criers said, that the chiefs' plan for tomorrow is basically the same as today?"

George shrugged. "Split into groups, but basically the same, yes."

"We came here to kill soldiers, George, to have our revenge for Sand Creek. Doesn't it bother you that the chiefs intend to go back there tomorrow and repeat a strategy that's already failed? Why don't they try something different?"

"I hadn't given it much thought."

"There has to be a better way." Ethan paced a few restless steps away before looking back. "We could surround the place, set it on fire, force the soldiers out."

George grinned. "You look Sioux, Ethan, but you still think white."

"Thinking white to fight against whites doesn't seem like such a bad thing to me." He came to stand before George. "What better way to beat them than knowing how they think?"

"You're right," George agreed. "Up to a point. You can think white, I can think white, but how do you get them to think white?" He swung his arm in a wide arc. "No matter what you or I say, no matter how good a scheme it is, they're going to fight the way they've always fought."

Ethan started to speak, but George silenced him with raised a hand. "Did you follow the chiefs' plan today? Stay back like they wanted us to, or did you race off first chance you got?"

Ethan looked away, saying nothing.

"They had a plan, and you didn't follow it. Why should they listen to yours?"

"Their plan's the same every time, George. How dumb do they think the soldiers are?"

"It's worked before."

"Did it work today? Did it work a second time at Julesburg? It didn't work with the war parties I rode with last month. Chances are, it's not going to work tomorrow. There are what, seventy, eighty men at that station? There are over two thousand of us. We can overwhelm them by sheer numbers if nothing else."

"Like at Mud Springs?"

Ethan thought for a moment, then shook his head. "There was no plan there."

"You think it would have made a difference?"

"Probably. Maybe." Ethan raised both hands; let them drop. "I don't, George, but you and me, between us we can come up with something to take to the chiefs."

George gave a quiet laugh. "What makes you think they'll listen?"

"They'll listen to you. The Cheyenne will, at least. They know you. To them, I'm nothing."

"You're not nothing, Ethan. You're half-white, and you carry scars from Sand Creek. People know who you are."

Ethan eyed him intently for several seconds, then shook his head. "That's not the point, and you know it."

"I know what your point is, Ethan, and I'm not saying I disagree. But now isn't the time. Since before we left the camps, things have been done in the old way. You know that. The rituals, the soldiers keeping everyone together, our greatest war chiefs leading us and planning the attack. Maybe there'll be other times when men'll listen. But not tomorrow. Tomorrow, I intend to do what the chiefs say." When Ethan looked unconvinced, he added, "You were lucky today. They coulda shot your horse and quirted you 'til you couldn't stand."

Ethan blinked in disbelief. "They'd do that?"

"They would. Do what they say tomorrow. And after that..." George grasped Ethan's arm, and his eyes lit up as he smiled. "After that, you and me, Ethan, we'll see if we can't teach them a thing or two."

***

"They saw us coming, and turned and ran," one of the Kansas men said.

"They saw us coming and tried to lead us into a trap," Caspar corrected. Turning to Josh, he added, "They headed back toward the river, and we went after them. More kept appearing, and when we saw what they were up to, we turned back."

"But not before we shot the chief."

Caspar nodded agreement. "Not before we shot the chief. They came at us like demons after that, trying to get him back. If reinforcements hadn't showed up, I hate to think what would have happened. But they did, and we drove them back to the river."

"He rode into the brush and fell off his horse," Private Lord persisted. "We thought he was dead when we went in after him, but we stabbed him just to make sure. We went to scalp him, and he came alive and started pleading. That's when Jim here shot him through the brain."

"Then we scalped him," Private Porter put in. "Cut him up, too. Cut off his fingers. Same as they did to Bill Bonwell[24] last month."

Josh looked at Caspar. "He was Cheyenne? You're sure about that?"

"He wasn't Sioux."

Josh pushed himself to his feet, arching his back and pressing bent elbows back in a stretch. They'd gathered outdoors because it was too hot inside, and he was stiff from sitting on the ground. *Tense, too*, he thought, taking several steps toward the river and staring at the dark hills beyond. There had been Indians there earlier, just before sundown. They'd ridden up and down, shouted insults, fired a few shots into the air, then disappeared. Now, in the darkness, Josh wondered if they were watching.

"They're out there," Sergeant Hervey Merwin said, coming to stand beside him. He was with the 11th Ohio, in charge of the howitzer, and unlike the

---

24   Private William T. Bonwell, Company E, 11th Kansas Cavalry, killed by Indians near Platte Bridge on June 3, he was found scalped and mutilated

Kansas troops, had been in Indian country long enough to know what he was talking about.

"How do you know?"

"The horses. Listen."

Josh listened. He could hear them back in the stockade, snorting and pacing restlessly. "How do they know it's Indians?"

"They smell 'em. Been pacing like that for two days. My guess is there's a lot of 'em and they're close."

A chill of dread ran along Josh's spine. He'd never been in a fight like this, and the sergeant's words confirmed what he'd already begun to suspect—that out here, miles from anywhere, they were hopelessly outnumbered and out-gunned. Over the course of the evening, he'd discovered that a quarter of the men at the post had no weapon at all. Of the rest, three quarters had single-shot, breech-loading Smith carbines, the remainder, only revolvers. To make matters worse, there were less than twenty rounds per man for the Smiths, and little more for the other arms. All evening, men had been running bullets and making Smith cartridges, but there was a limit to what they could produce in a single night.

Josh tilted his head back and looked up. With only a waning sliver of moon, the stars were more numerous than ever. He wondered if this would be the last night he ever saw them.

It was after midnight when he finally went inside. Even with the doors open, the crowded room was airless and over-warm. Josh lay atop his bedroll fully clothed. Like most of the men, he was too jittery to take off his boots. He shifted, knowing he would never get comfortable enough to sleep, and was seriously considering taking his chances outdoors when a sentry shouted an alarm.

"Riders coming!"

Josh was on his feet in an instant, Caspar beside him.

Hooves clattered onto the wooden bridge, and the sentry shouted a challenge.

"Lieutenant Bretney, 11th Ohio," came the response. "Captain Lybe, 6th U.S. Infantry. Hold your fire."

"What the..." Caspar said. "Henry?"

They stepped outside as the riders pulled their horses to a stop. More men emerged, a few holding up lanterns, exclaiming in surprise and relief when they saw reinforcements had arrived.

"Henry," Caspar said, stepping forward as the tired men climbed down from their mounts.

"Caspar!" Henry Bretney exclaimed. He was tall and good-looking, with a thick shock of dark hair and a closely trimmed beard and mustache. "Didn't expect to see you here!"

"I could say the same."

"Had a telegram this morning ordering me to Fort Laramie to draw pay for the company. We left Sweetwater about two o'clock."

"See any Indians along the way?"

Lieutenant Bretney looked surprised by the question. "No," he said, with a slow shake of his head. "Not a one. Why do you ask?"

"We fought off a least fifty, two miles east of here. The Kansas boys chased a hundred more away from the station." Caspar looked toward the river, and Henry's gaze followed. "We figure there are a lot more out there. Figure they'll attack again tomorrow."

"Today," Josh muttered. He'd checked his pocket watch in the light from one of the lanterns. "It's two a.m."

Henry looked at Caspar in consternation. "There's a supply train out there. Sergeant Custard with twenty-four men. We left them at Willow Springs about nine o'clock." Scanning the faces of the gathered men, he said. "I need to talk to Major Anderson."

"In his quarters," a man volunteered.

"You men, put your horses in the corral and bed down here," Bretney commanded, indicating the area directly in front of the buildings. Turning away, he hastened toward the major's quarters.

He returned a short time later, rigid with anger. "His own men out there, and he refuses to send help. You know what he said before he went back to bed? 'They're well-armed.'" Henry snorted in disgust and turned to glare at the closed door of Anderson's quarters. "Fool! Been in this country a couple of months and thinks he knows better than us." He looked at Caspar and shook his head. "He'll see us all killed. Mark my word."

"Let's hope you're wrong about that, Henry."

Bretney had brought ten men with him, Lybe another fourteen. Josh and Caspar joined them outside for what remained of the night. Josh slept fitfully, waking at every sound, real or imagined. He was dozing off yet again, when a sentry began to shout.

"Indians! Indians north of the river!"

In the strengthening light, Josh counted ninety Indians riding among the hills beyond the bridge.

27

I've been given orders. I have to go."

"No you don't," Josh insisted. "Your orders came from General Connor, and he told you to return to your post. Last I heard a general outranks a major."

Josh and the men from the 11th Ohio were gathered around Caspar as he checked the cinch on a borrowed gray gelding. He flipped the stirrup down, and the nervous horse danced sideways, nearly pulling the reins from the man holding them.

"There are Indians all through those hills," Henry said. "You know as well as I do that for every one you see, there are ten more hiding. It's certain death out there."

"I'm no coward, Henry."

"No one's saying you are, Caspar," Private John Friend put in. "But it's wrong. They're Kansas men. Their own officers should be leading them."

"I have my orders, John. I have to try to rescue the men with the train." Casper took the reins from him and swung into the saddle.

"At least take our Spencers," Henry insisted. "If something happens, you won't stand a chance with the Smiths."

"The major wants the Spencers at the station, Henry. You know that. But you could do me the favor of lending me your pistols."

For a moment, Henry looked as if he would continue to argue. Instead, he blew a burst of air out through his nose and handed over the pistols.

Casper stuffed one into the top of each boot, then leaned down and stuck out his hand.

"Thanks, Henry."

Henry shook. "Good luck. If things get bad, if you have to turn back, we'll be waiting for you on the other side of the bridge."

"Good luck, Caspar" Josh said, offering Caspar his hand. "Get back here so I can win back the money you took from me."

The horse sidestepped, tossing its head as Caspar turned it. He offered Josh a brave smile. "It's with my old uniform. No need to count it. I promise it's all there." He took the cap from his head and tossed it to one of his men. "Something to remember me by." Touching his heels to the horse's sides, he trotted to where Corporal Grimm waited with twenty-three men from the 11th Kansas.

Josh watched him go, then pulled out his watch. *Seven-twenty.*

Lieutenant Bretney turned on his heel and stalked to where Major Anderson stood in the company of several of his officers, watching the now empty bluffs. At first, their words were muted, but as Bretney's face grew red and his voice louder, Josh heard him repeat the same arguments he'd used with Caspar.

The discussion broke off as the twenty-five men, riding double-file with Caspar in the lead, set off across the bridge. Bretney motioned to his men, and they followed on foot, Captain Lybe and his men close behind. Captain Greer climbed onto the roof of the telegraph office, and Josh followed, tossing his rifle up ahead of him. As the captain scanned the bluffs to the north and west with his spyglass, Josh watched Caspar's party arrive at the far end of the bridge. Their orders were to proceed straight ahead to the top of the bluffs, then turn west. By following the brow of the ridge, they would remain in sight of the station for two miles before rejoining the road.

"Indians west along the river!"

Josh looked where the captain pointed. He could make out two groups, about half a mile distant, walking their horses along the road. Some of the Kansas men began moving across the bridge. The major yelled for twenty more to saddle up. Sergeant Merwin and his men rolled their howitzer to the edge of the river.

Josh jumped down from the roof as Caspar's detail reached the top of the bluffs. He sprinted across the bridge, looking upriver. The Indians had urged their ponies into a lope, angling toward the hills.

Captain Lybe's men, armed with Springfield muskets, were forming a line on the far side of the bridge. Josh ran past them, loosing sight of Caspar as he reached the base of the hill and scrambled up. Chest heaving, he arrived among Bretney's men to discover that the detail had turned north, moving fast to avoid the Indians.

For several moments, it appeared everything would be all right. In the next, a band of Dog Soldiers broke from cover. All around Caspar's detail, mounted Indians emerged from behind hills and out of gullies. Screams rent the air as several hundred Cheyenne charged from a stand of willows a quarter mile upriver. Josh and the men from the 11th Ohio shouted warnings, but their words were lost beneath the war cries.

Caspar saw what was happening and ordered a retreat. Whirling their horses, the detail began a mad gallop back toward the bridge, Caspar bringing up the rear. Indians closed in around them, more appearing every second. Caspar ordered a volley with the Smith carbines that cut a swathe through the front ranks, but there was no time to reload before the next wave was upon them.

A bullet caught Caspar in the hip. "Revolvers!" he shouted, dropping the Smith into its sling and pulling Bretney's pistols from his boots.

The Indians were packed so close together that they had to abandon their bows or risk shooting each other. They attacked with clubs, tomahawks, spears and sabers. Caspar and his men opened fire at point blank range, at times pressing the barrels directly against the bodies of warriors galloping next to them.

One soldier fell, then another. A horse tumbled to the ground, sending its rider flying. Sprawled on the ground, the terrified man screamed for help.

As the Indians came within range, the Josh and the men around him opened fire, then watched in horror as Casper turned from certain safety and galloped back toward the man on the ground. A group of Sioux parted, letting him pass unharmed, but as he approached the downed man, an arrow struck him in the forehead. Caspar arched backward, but remained in the saddle. His panicked horse bolted. Cheyenne warriors surrounded him, and he vanished in a whirl of bodies and dust.

The first men from the detail were upon them. Josh and Bretney exchanged looks of horror, then turned and began leaping and sliding down the hill. The Indians separated at the top, veering left and right, to create an opening through which the Cheyenne riflemen behind them opened fire. A bullet grazed Josh's neck, but most flew high, slamming into the ranks of several hundred Sioux who had burst from a ravine east of the bridge, intent on taking it. Warriors tumbled from their ponies, the charge faltered, then came on.

The howitzer roared, and men poured across the bridge from the station, adding their guns to those already firing on the Sioux. The survivors from the detail galloped across the bridge to safety. Still firing, the men on foot raced over the uneven ground after them.

In the face of heavy gunfire, many of the Sioux began to retreat. Others came on, charging the men on foot, swinging clubs and tomahawks. Josh emptied the Henry at four warriors bearing down on him. One fell, another veered away, and one slumped over his pony's neck. The fourth kept coming. Pausing in his flight, Josh grasped the Henry by its barrel. He had a fleeting impression of bared teeth—of lips pulled back in a grimace of pure hatred—as he swung the rifle at the tomahawk slicing through the air toward him.

In a horrified instant, Ethan recognized Josh. It was too late to stop his swing, so he let the tomahawk go. It flew harmlessly away as the butt of the rifle glanced off his forearm. Flattening himself against the gray's neck, Ethan raced toward the bluffs.

Safely at the top, he turned to look back. All around him, warriors charged back and forth along the hilltops, loosing occasional shots in the direction of the soldiers, and shouting threats and curses. The Sioux were rescuing their wounded, retrieving the dead and pulling back out of range of the soldiers' guns. The howitzer bucked and roared, and the Sioux retreated even further. Soldiers crouched along the length of the bridge, providing covering fire for three men who ran out, bent at the waist, to retrieve a soldier's body.

Ethan slid down from the gray and squatted on the ground, appalled by what he'd almost done. He ran a hand over his face and realized it was trembling. Clenching it into a fist, he crossed his arms on his knees and squinted at the bridge, trying to pick out Josh. At first, he didn't see him, but then, as the soldiers carried the dead man's body past, he spotted him among the last of the men retreating toward the station.

The soldiers cleared the bridge, leaving twenty men and the howitzer to guard it, while they tended their wounded. On the bluffs, things gradually quieted. A few warriors still taunted the soldiers, but most retired behind the hills to talk about the battle and argue heatedly over the killing of Sioux by the Cheyenne. A group of Cheyenne appeared on the far side of the river, but pulled back when a man was shot from his horse at long range. Soldiers appeared with shovels and began heaping dirt into mounds, erecting fortifications around the station. Eighteen others appeared on horseback and headed east along the road.

Ethan could still make out Josh—he was one of the few men not in uniform, and easy to pick out, even from a distance. *If he hadn't looked up when he did...* Ethan shuddered and pressed the heels of his hands against his forehead.

When you start to hate, you start to destroy your own soul. He understood now what Hannah had meant. For seven months, he'd allowed hatred and grief to consume him, one feeding off the other until his entire reason for being had been revenge. And what had it come to? Spotted Horse, Standing Elk and Bone Necklace were wounded, and he'd nearly killed Josh.

Ethan drew his hands down his face and looked toward the fort. Talking with Julie the night before had felt good. He hadn't realized it at the time, but for a few minutes, he'd felt like his old self again. *How did I let it get this far?* he wondered. *I left the 36ᵗʰ to avoid killing, but it's all I've thought about for months.* He would always grieve for Tall Grass, for Micah and the rest of his Cheyenne family, but killing soldiers wouldn't bring them back. What he needed was to spend time with his grandmother, who he'd barely seen, and get to know Black Wolf. They both had much to teach him, if only he would ask.

But first I need to figure a way to talk to Josh. He doubted Josh had recognized him. He would have been focused on the tomahawk, not the man swinging it. *Somehow, I need to make him realize who I am.*

Ethan pushed himself to his feet and swung onto the gray. Turning him downhill, he rode as close to the bridge as he dared. He could see Josh standing with one of the soldiers in the shade of the building east of the bridge. One of the men near the howitzer raised his Spencer and followed him, but they both knew he was out of range. Eventually, the man lowered the rifle.

***

"I wonder what he's up to," Sergeant Merwin mused, watching the lone Indian ride back and forth below the bluffs.

"No idea," Josh replied. Now that the adrenaline had worn off, he was feeling the aftereffects of battle and grief at Caspar's death. To add insult to injury, an Indian had appeared on the bluffs a short time earlier, leading Caspar's horse.

Three others from the detail were presumed dead. Another, Private Camp, had fallen near the bridge, and his body had been recovered. Corporal Henry Grimm had an arrow in his back and wasn't expected to live. In all, fifteen men, including one with an arrow through his neck, were wounded seriously enough to require immediate attention. Just about everyone else suffered from minor injuries.

"How many do you think there are?" he asked, pressing his handkerchief to the bleeding gash on his neck.

Merwin considered the question. "Two, maybe three thousand. It's hard to say."

"Any chance they'll get the wire fixed and we'll get reinforcements?"

"That, too, is hard to say."

The telegraph line to the east had been cut the previous evening; the line west, at about the time Caspar was crossing the bridge. Once the Indians had been driven back, Lieutenant George Walker had taken seventeen Kansas men and headed east to try to repair it. Until that happened, they were completely cut off.

"Good thing they don't know we're low on ammunition," the sergeant commented. "If they did, and those Sioux had kept coming..." He gave a low whistle and shook his head.

"There's nothing to keep them from attacking again, is there?"

"Not a thing."

The sound of raised voices reached them. They stepped out of the shade thrown by the trader's store and looked toward the stockade. Major Anderson had called a meeting of his officers, and the voices were easily recognizable as his and Lieutenant Bretney's. It wasn't long before another voice joined in.

"Captain Greer," Merwin commented. "There's bad blood between him and Bretney."

There was a crash, and Bretney screamed something unintelligible.

"Henry and Caspar were best friends, and it's the major's fault he's dead," the sergeant said bitterly, summing up the feelings of all the Ohio men. "He had no right to send him."

"We did all we could to talk him out of it." Josh took off his hat, which he'd somehow managed to hang onto, and wiped his forehead on his sleeve. It wasn't quite ten o'clock, and already the sun was blazing hot.

"Indians fording the river!"

All eyes turned east. Half a mile downstream, a large number of Indians were in the water.

The shout brought the officers out of the stockade, all but Bretney. Sergeant Merwin left Josh and trotted toward the howitzer.

After peering intently along the river for several moments, Major Anderson said, "Give the signal, Private." The man on the roof began waving a flag, a signal to the wire crew that Indians were moving toward them.

Taking several steps toward the bridge, the major shouted, "Fire the howitzer."

Merwin turned to his men. "Let 'er rip, boys."

The man on the lanyard pulled it. The howitzer leapt back, belching smoke. Seconds later, the shell exploded above the river. In the hills to the southeast, several of Lieutenant Walker's lookouts could be seen mounting their horses. Captain Lybe and his men, who'd gone out on foot to cover Walker's retreat, turned back toward the station, leaving behind the Kansas men who'd followed them. The last of the Indians emerged from the river and galloped through the sand hills toward the road. North of the river, hundreds more, alerted by the howitzer, appeared on the bluffs.

Walker's detail appeared at a gallop. They descended the bluffs and kept coming until they reached the men on foot. Sliding to a halt, they turned to cover the retreat of four men riding flat out behind them, all but Walker himself, who continued to race toward the station. As the four reached the base of the bluffs, Indians rose from a gully ahead of them. The men beat them back with gunfire, but more emerged behind them. As the detail galloped to their rescue, one of the four fell from his horse. Another slumped forward. The detail rode within range and opened fire. The Indians drew back, fleeing into the hills.

Josh watched them go, wondering where Ethan was in all this. He'd tried, and failed, to picture him among the warriors, but he figured he had to be out there somewhere. Turning toward the river, he scanned the figures gathered along the bluffs. They were too far away to distinguish features, but a blue coat caught his eye.

"Give me your glasses," he said, walking to where Merwin and his men squatted in the shrinking patch of shade thrown by the bridge. Locating the blue coat, he raised the field glasses. The man had dark skin and hair and a thin mustache, a half-breed most likely, or Mexican, but definitely not Ethan. Something about him was vaguely familiar, but Josh couldn't put a finger on it. He was handing the glasses back when one of the lookouts shouted.

"Here comes the train!"

Men ran to where they could see. Five white dots, the canvas tops of wagons, had appeared over a ridge a mile to the west. A chorus of shouts indicated the Indians had seen them, too. Hundreds emerged from the hills on both sides of the river and galloped to intercept them.

Without waiting for orders, Sergeant Merwin and his men pulled the howitzer around and aimed it at the nearest warriors. The shell exploded halfway across the river.

"Longer fuse next time, boys."

The second shell exploded closer to the far bank, but the Indians were moving away quickly, and none of the shot found its mark.

Some of the Ohio men were climbing onto the roofs, and Josh joined them. Warned by the twin booms of the howitzer, the wagons picked up speed. They were on level ground, coming across a little plateau dotted with sand hills above the river. Five riders, little more than specs to the naked eye, were pulling away from them. No one spoke as the Indians bore down. Shoulders slumped, and faces registered frustration and despair. Short of a miracle, the men with the train were doomed.

Josh had never felt so powerless. He wiped the sweat from his eyes and looked back along the ridge. A few Indians remained, women and boys, all looking toward the train. Then his eyes lit on the man on the gray horse. He had stopped moving, but instead of looking west, he was watching the station. Distant gunfire crackled, and Josh looked toward the train.

The five riders had reached the edge of the plateau, seen the Indians, and opened fire. They turned back toward the wagons, but Indians swarmed from a ravine, cutting them off. Vastly outnumbered, they turned their horses and raced toward the river. The Indians let them go, turning to join others who were emerging on top of the plateau.

The wagons came on, vanishing one by one as a hill between the plateau and the station blocked them from view. There was a series of gunshots, and one of the wagons reappeared, moving south, away from the road. It bumped across a shallow depression and rolled to a stop on higher ground. Two more wagons followed, but stopped short of the first. Another wagon appeared atop a low ridge behind them, traveled a short distance and stopped.

"Where's the fifth wagon?" John Friend asked.

"Don't see it," Lieutenant Drew said, peering through his spyglass.

Men leapt from the wagon on the ridge and ran toward the two in the depression.

"There they are!"

"Who?"

"The men from the last wagon."

"Where?"

"There." The lieutenant pointed. "On foot. Coming from the road."

The men from the three outlying wagons ran toward the middle two. The mule teams, released from the traces, scattered. The men at the station heard howls as the Indians charged. Gunfire erupted in continuous volleys, and a cloud of white smoke blossomed above the center pair of wagons. Ponies and warriors fell, and amid swirling clouds of dust, the Indians withdrew.

The five riders reached the river and plunged their horses in. From where they were standing, the men on the roofs could see several bands of Indians riding toward them through the hills and gullies south of the river. Josh looked away, thinking he couldn't bear to watch.

Many of the Kansas men and their officers were standing on the bridge, some with field glasses, all looking west. One man sidled toward the far end and raised his pistol, taking aim at the man on the gray horse. Well out of range, the Indian continued to gaze at the station.

"Lord have mercy," John Friend muttered.

The first of the horsemen were urging their horses out of the water and up the bank about half a mile upriver. Two of them turned toward the station, but the third hesitated, then spurred his horse southwest into the foothills. With a shriek, fifteen Indians burst from cover and gave chase.

As the last two men neared the bank, the man in the lead jumped from his horse into the water. A gunshot rang out. The second man's horse pitched sideways into the river. Its rider floundered and stood up. Another gunshot, and he fell with a splash. Abandoning his horse, the remaining man scrambled up the bank and ran after his companions. They were on foot by the time he reached them, huddled next to a clump of sage. Bent at the waist, they scampered across a patch of open ground and dropped into a gully.

For a time, nothing happened. A faint breeze lifted the cloud of gunsmoke above the wagons on the plateau and cooled the sweat on the faces of the men watching. A white pelican floated past on the river. A pair of ravens swooped low, calling raucously. A jackrabbit hopped cautiously along a shallow wash west of the station, then sprinted up the side and vanished into the sage as a trio of Indians appeared on foot, searching for the soldiers.

The midday sun was beating down when gunfire once again erupted from the plateau. This time, the Indians attacked the wagons from all sides. The soldiers' gunfire was unrelenting, but amid dust and gunsmoke, it was impossible to see what was happening.

Close at hand, a pair of gunshots sounded in rapid succession. An Indian tumbled from behind an anthill and lay still. Sunlight glinted off a rifle barrel as it withdrew into the gully. Upriver, Indians appeared on foot, near the sagebrush where the soldiers had first entered the gully. More appeared, leading the soldiers' horses.

On the plateau, the Indians began pulling back. Gunfire from the wagons turned sporadic, then stopped.

The men at the station shifted restlessly, wiping sweat from their faces and drinking lukewarm water from canteens. Josh watched the plateau, wondering if the men there had field glasses trained on the station, waiting for reinforcements and wondering why none came.

The three soldiers burst into view a couple hundred yards from the station and dashed toward it. There were yells as the Indians spotted them, and dozens rose from the far end of the gully. Arrows took flight, and the men at the station returned fire, forcing the Indians to take cover.

"The gully!" men on the roof shouted, waving their arms and pointing. "Run for the gully!"

The three men sprinted to a shallow gully that ran to within yards of the station. Bending low, they ran along it as men from the station rode to meet them. Under covering fire, three of the rescuers jumped to the ground and helped the exhausted men to mount.

The jubilation surrounding their arrival was short-lived as the Indians charged the wagons yet again. They were beaten back under a withering barrage of gunfire.

After that, time slowed to a crawl. The Indians charged twice more, then leery of the soldiers' guns, began circling at a distance. The gunfire from the wagons came in scattered pops, punctuated by occasional longer bursts.

"Someone has to help them." Lieutenant Drew handed his spyglass to another Kansas man and jumped down from the roof. As he reached Major Anderson, the other officers, and many of the men, pressed in around them.

"Where's Bretney?" Josh asked, realizing he wasn't among them.

"Didn't you hear?" John Friend's voice was thick with outrage. "The major placed him under arrest."

"Under arrest? Why?"

"He punched Captain Greer."

Josh snorted in disgust and rolled his eyes. Outnumbered by more than twenty to one, and the major had robbed them of a man and rifle. Josh looked at him where he stood among his officers. The major shook his head as they sought to persuade him. At last they broke away, angry and disappointed. Josh was relieved that he hadn't made odds worse by letting them go.

Gunfire on the plateau ceased. Men shaded their eyes against the slanting the sun. Indians could be seen circling amid a haze of heat, dust and smoke. As the silence lengthened, men began shifting uneasily, exchanging nervous glances. Josh looked toward the bluffs. The Indian on the gray horse was still there, but now, he too watched the plateau.

A cry went up that raised the hairs on Josh's neck. The circling Indians changed course, charging in on the wagons. They were met by a tremendous burst of gunfire. Minutes crept by as fierce fighting continued. Then, gradually, the gunfire began to subside. It slowed to a few scattered pops, then died away completely. Dust was beginning to settle when the first twist of black smoke rose into the sky. Moments later, flames appeared, engulfing the two center wagons.

The watching men sagged with a collective groan of despair. Unable to look away, they watched as the flames climbed higher. More flames erupted as the other wagons were torched. The Indians, a few at first, then a steady stream of them, began heading north as the sun continued its steady march toward the western mountains.

28

Josh laid a hand against the adobe wall, still faintly warm at midnight, and lowered himself to the ground. The air outside was blessedly cool after the closeness of the squad room turned infirmary. He'd spent the last few hours sitting with Henry Grimm, pressing wet cloths to his fevered brow, and listening as he moaned in delirium. The arrow had been removed, pushed through once the feathers had been broken off, but it was doubtful the corporal would survive.

Doubtful any of us will, Josh thought, tilting his head back and closing tired eyes. They were low on food, had few serviceable horses, and little ammunition. Josh was down to six rounds for the Henry, just ninety shots, and the Ohio men were in even worse shape with their Spencers. Their cartridges couldn't be reloaded, but the men who'd worked all night the night before were at it again, making cartridges for the Smiths. Despite their efforts, there was no way the station could withstand the type of sustained assault that had destroyed the train. Their only hope lay in the two half-breed Shoshone scouts Major Anderson had paid to ride to Deer Creek Station.

Josh's eyes flew open as gunshots erupted from the roof above him. He grabbed the Henry and was on his feet, moving out from the building, when an arrow whirred past his face in the darkness. Another thudded into the ground near him, and he ran back to the cover of the building. Two more shots, and the firing ceased.

"Bastards!" he heard a man mutter.

Wide-awake, heart pounding, Josh climbed onto the roof and squinted into the blackness. There was no moon, nothing to see, not even Henry Bretney and the men from the 11th Ohio who stood picket behind the newly erected breastworks.

Bretney had been released an hour after the wagons burned. Josh had ridden with him and a detachment to look for Caspar and the men who'd died with him. They'd found the mangled remains of Private Moses Brown almost immediately and loaded him onto a horse. A second body had been located, but a large number of Indians had emerged from the hills east of the station, intent on cutting them off from the bridge, and forced them to retreat.

More Indians had gathered along the bluffs, but as the sun went down, they began to disperse, heading north in groups of two and three. By the time darkness fell, the plains, in all directions, were empty.

But now they're back. Josh sighed and settled on his stomach, the Henry at his side. He had considered writing to his folks, but knowing the station would burn, had decided there was no point. All he could do now was wait—for death or morning, whichever came first.

The Indians reappeared with the sunrise, arriving the same way they'd departed the previous evening, until thousands were assembled along the hills north of the river. Some ventured close to the bridge, shouting in Sioux, Cheyenne and English, telling the men gathered on the other side how they'd killed soldiers the day before and would do the same to them. The men at the station clutched their weapons apprehensively, the shortage of ammunition the only thing keeping them from firing.

There were more blue coats today, Josh observed, hit by a renewed surge of grief and anger. He looked at Bretney and saw from the tightness around his mouth and the unnatural brightness of his eyes, that he'd noticed, too.

The taunts continued for some time, the ranks of Indians swelling and ebbing, warriors racing their ponies along the bluffs, firing their weapons into the air, and making short, abortive charges toward the bridge. And then, so subtly that no one noticed at first, they began to withdraw. A cloud of dust rose to the north, and more horsemen turned from the ridge.

"They're leaving," Bretney murmured in disbelief.

"They're leaving," another man said, and it was repeated.

The cloud of dust grew larger, the Indians on the bluffs fewer. Several groups were spotted crossing the river, but they continued south, vanishing into the foothills below the mountains. By midday, only four Indians remained. After a time, three of them turned their ponies and loped away. The lone Indian, mounted on a dark bay, sat without moving, much as the man on the gray had done the day before.

Josh, like most of the men, had withdrawn to the shade of the stockade wall when it appeared no attack was immanent. There was little talk, just a smattering of speculation, as they watched the Indians depart. As the shade receded, men began moving about, eyeing the surrounding countryside, not yet willing to believe the threat had passed. Squinting at the man on the bluffs, Josh headed toward the river. He was squatting beside it, splashing water onto his face, when realization stuck. He hurried to where Bretney was standing and demanded his field glasses.

Startled, Henry obliged. Josh strode to the edge of the river and raised the glasses.

Ethan inclined his head, the barest of nods. Josh lowered the glasses and stared at him, then raised them again. Ethan arched an eyebrow. One corner of his mouth turned up.

Wondering what took me so long...

"What's going on, Fraser?" Henry had come to stand beside him.

"Nothing," Josh said, lowering the glasses. "Just curious."

"Mighty curious, I'd say."

"He's been watching us for two days," Josh said, handing him the glasses. "I was wondering what he's up to."

For the next half hour, Josh prowled the station, stopping often to look at Ethan, trying to figure a way to talk to him. When Lieutenant Walker called for volunteers to help recover the remaining bodies, Josh was first among them.

As the soldiers started across the bridge, Ethan turned the bay and loped into the hills. He watched from a distance as they charged the carrion birds clustered around the nearest body and set them wheeling overhead. The remains were wrapped in blankets and loaded into a wagon. When the detail fanned out, he moved ahead of Josh, hoping he would distance himself from the soldiers. Within minutes, more vultures took flight from beyond a hill, indicating that another body had been found.

They had ridden nearly a mile, halfway to the place where Ethan knew the body of the young officer lay, before Josh managed to separate himself from the soldiers nearest him. He was headed toward a ravine, the same one Ethan was making his way along, when the boom of the howitzer shattered the afternoon stillness. Josh turned and looked toward the station. The soldiers called to one another and began moving away. Josh hesitated.

"Don't go," Ethan muttered.

Josh turned in the saddle, eyes searching, and Ethan urged the bay out of the gully. Over a distance of fifty yards, they looked at one another. Before either could do more, there was a shout.

They looked to see a soldier galloping toward them. Others were turning their mounts. Ethan shared a look with Josh and did the only thing he could. Whirling the bay, he fled.

Fat Bear and Long Face joined him as he crested the hill. They rode in a wide arc back to the river, arriving on the bluffs downstream from the bridge as the wagon and the last of the detail crossed over. To the east, dust rose on the stiffening breeze, providing the reason for the recall.

"Soldiers," Fat Bear said, as a double line of horsemen and a pair of wagons came into view.

Ethan nodded.

The soldiers at the station were arrayed defensively, as yet unaware that reinforcements had arrived. A cheer went up when they saw who it was.

"They are many now, and we are few." Fat Bear looked at Ethan. "We must go."

"No," Ethan said, watching the new arrivals through his field glasses. *At least fifty.* "No," he repeated, lowering the glasses and looking at his cousins. "We will go were they will not think to look for us. There." He inclined his head toward the mountains. "We will watch, and when my brother leaves, we will follow him, wait until he is alone."

Fat Bear considered his cousin's words as the line of soldiers descended the bluffs, then grunted agreement. They watched the newcomers' arrival at the station before turning their horses and starting back toward the camp.

Buzzards, and a scattering of ravens and magpies, were clustered around the body of the young officer when they passed. Stripped naked and bound with telegraph wire, he had been dragged north and abandoned at the edge of the creek, a few hundred yards downstream from the camp.

Ethan had come across him the previous evening and stopped to look. Already, the heat, flies and ants had begun their work on the mangled remains the Cheyenne had left. Dozens of arrows protruded from his torso, his hands and feet had been cut off, his heart and bowels cut out, his mouth packed with gunpowder and exploded. He had not been scalped, ensuring he would be tormented for all eternity, suffering the same agony he would have endured had the wounds had been inflicted prior to death.

Looking down at the mutilated body of the young man had confirmed what Ethan already knew: He was incapable of such violence. The admission forced him to confront another truth he'd resisted—that no matter where he went, he would always be different. Less so among the Sioux than among whites, but different just the same.

The breeze had shifted, bringing the scent of death to him, and he had moved on, thinking as he stared across the darkening prairie that it was high time he accepted who he was. *Time to figure out what I want from life and take it. Quit trying to make myself over to fit in.*

Standing Elk rode to meet them as they approached the camp. He had taken a Cheyenne bullet through the upper arm; a soldier's bullet had deeply scored one thigh. Neither wound was serious, and he'd been first to join Ethan when he'd announced he was staying.

Walks Alone began packing when she heard they were moving; Kicking Bird rounded up the extra horses. They crossed the river out of sight of the bridge and angled east. Coming to a creek, they followed it south into the foothills, riding until they came to a long valley near the foot of the mountains, still green and thick with box elder and cottonwoods. The surrounding hills gave a panoramic view of the road, the bridge, the river and the plains for miles in every direction. When Standing Elk pronounced it acceptable, Walks Alone began to make camp.

Ethan was up before the sun, riding with Standing Elk, Fat Bear and Long Face back to the river. They reached the bluffs east of the bridge in time to see sixteen mounted men and a wagon start north into the hills. Through his field glasses, Ethan confirmed that Josh was among them. A second, larger party was assembling behind them. Ethan waited until the second party turned west, toward the plateau where the wagons had burned, before setting out after Josh. Weaving through hills and gullies east of the creek, keeping out of sight of the soldiers spread across the prairie, they came even with him, then passed him as he neared the body.

They watched a young private came upon it first, firing a signal with his Spencer that sent the scavenger birds soaring. His final approach was cautious, and several turkey vultures landed, sidling back toward the corpse.

Josh was the first of the converging men to arrive. He rode past the private, scattering the birds, and pulled his horse to a stop. For several moments, he looked at the body, then tilted his head back and looked at the sky.

More soldiers arrived, until they were all assembled. Josh rode off a short distance and dismounted. The young private followed, and they stood together with their backs to the others, heads bowed, while they waited for the wagon.

It arrived, bumping over the uneven ground, and the men nearest the body moved aside to make room for it. As it pulled to a stop, four men jumped down from the back, pulled out a box, and lowered it to the ground. Josh turned to watch as the remains of the officer were wrapped in blankets and gently lifted into the coffin. The lid was nailed on, the coffin lifted into the wagon, and the driver turned the team of mules downhill toward the bridge.

Most of the soldiers followed, but Josh remained, the private and a lieutenant standing with him. After a time, they mounted their horses and rode slowly back toward the station. As they rounded the base of a hill, Josh turned and surveyed the prairie behind him.

"Cover me."

Ethan handed the Spencer to Fat Bear and swung onto the bay. He crested the hill at a canter and dropped toward the creek. On the prairie below, Josh glanced in the direction his companions had gone, then started toward him. Ethan was on the near side, beyond where the body had been, when the two soldiers reappeared. One of them shouted. Josh turned in the saddle as both men spurred their horses and opened fire.

Ethan spun the bay and raced back toward the creek. He was within easy range of the Spencers, and he leaned low over the horse's neck as dirt spurted around him. The bay leapt the creek, then faltered as a bullet ripped into its heart. It fell, hindquarters arcing over its head as it hit the ground. Ethan twisted, landing on his feet, and felt a sharp spasm in his lower back. His numbed right leg buckled. Getting his left foot under him, he struggled to stand.

"*Ethan!!!*"

Josh spurred after Bretney and Friend, screaming at them to stop. Two Indians appeared on a hilltop. One opened fire with a repeating rifle; the other pressed himself against his pony's back and raced toward Ethan. Bretney and Friend pulled their horses to a skidding stop as a third Indian rose from a gully to their left, loosing a deadly stream of arrows. Fearing they were about to be surrounded, they began to retreat.

Ethan was on his feet. As Josh watched, he grasped the hand held down to him, and with a running leap, landed astride the galloping pony.

The pony raced away; the Indian in the gully vanished. Behind Josh, the remainder of the detail appeared around the base of the hill. There was shouting and confusion. Shots were fired in the direction of the fleeing pony with its double load.

Henry appeared beside Josh, eyes blazing, his face flushed with fury. "What the...? Friends of yours, Fraser?"

Josh watched Ethan out of sight before looking at Henry. "My brother."

Henry's face, if anything, grew redder. His cheeks puffed out, and he stared disbelieving at Josh. "Your brother?" he managed at last. "One of those savages is your brother?"

"Half-brother," Josh confirmed, and turned his horse away.

Caspar was buried in the small cemetery near the station. Josh stood to one side, ostracized by his grieving men, as Henry delivered a brief eulogy. The box was lowered into the ground, dry earth thudded against the lid, and minutes later, it was done. He caught Henry's reproachful gaze and turned away, sick with grief and horror, and grappling with his feelings for Ethan. On one hand, he despised him for being a party, however incidental, to Caspar's death; on the other, he worried that he'd been shot and would once again vanish.

The detail returned grim-faced from the train with more atrocities to relate, including tales of torture. Over the course of the afternoon, word spread of Josh's ties to the Indians. He distanced himself from the caustic comments and accusing stares, and watched the hills for Ethan. Night fell with no sign of him.

Early the next morning, Bretney and Lytle departed for Fort Laramie. A detachment left to bury the dead from the train, and a search party was dispatched to find and bury Private Summers, last seen being pursued into the foothills. Josh toyed with the idea of setting out on his own, going so far at one point, as to saddle his horse. Had Ethan shown himself, he would have done it, but the day waned with no sign of him. When he heard that Lieutenant Hubbard and his men would be returning to Deer Creek Station the following morning, he requested permission join them.

The sun slanted steeply as they set out. Josh scanned the empty bluffs north of the bridge one last time before turning east. There was no sign of Ethan, nothing to indicate he was anywhere near during the twenty-five mile ride to Deer Creek Station, a scattering of log buildings south of the Platte.

Josh spent the evening sipping from the canteen he'd had the sutler at Platte Bridge fill with whiskey, and deciding what to do. He could wait for an escort to Fort Laramie, or he could head east on his own. After the failure of the last two attempts, he figured Ethan was more apt to approach him if he was alone. *Assuming he's anywhere around.* Josh took another sip from the canteen, surprised at how light it had become, and decided to give Ethan one last chance. Come daybreak, he would ride alone as far as the next station.

The day was well advanced when he woke; past noon by the time he set out. Nervous at traveling alone, he rode quickly, not slowing until he came within sight of La Prele Station, some twenty miles east of Deer Creek. Relieved at arriving safely, and disappointed that he hadn't encountered Ethan, he forded the rocky creek, bypassed the small garrison, and turned south into the hills. From atop the nearest summit, he surveyed his surroundings.

Arid, dun-colored hills, eroded through with dry washes, and mottled with sage, rabbitbrush, and clumps of yellowed grass, spread away from him in every direction, giving way to the south to pine-dotted hills fronting the blue humps of the Laramies. To the north, beyond the road, straggly patches of willow dotted the edge of the flood plain where the grass still grew green and the waters of the Platte glistened. Beyond the river, the scorched hills resumed, extending yellow-gray to meet the sky.

There was no sign of Ethan, nothing to indicate he'd been followed. Shaking his head in frustration, Josh urged his horse down the slope to the creek. Selecting a broad expanse of open ground, he pulled his rifle from its scabbard and swung down from the saddle. The moment he let loose the reins, the gelding's head dropped, and he began to guzzle thirstily. Josh walked several paces upstream, and surveying the landscape once more, leaned the rifle against a low outcropping of sandstone.

He had no sooner stepped away than the horse's head shot up, ears pricked. Josh swung around, scooped up the rifle, and looked where the horse was looking. An errant breeze skipped across the prairie, ruffling dry grass. A magpie burst from a clump of sage, a flutter of black and white. Sudden clacking combined with a blur of yellow as a grasshopper took flight, then dropped silent to the ground. At the edge of the creek, a horned toad skittered to the top of a flat rock and paused, warming itself in the sun. The gelding's ears flicked back, then forward. Long seconds passed as Josh strained to see what it sensed. Then the horse shook himself, bridle jangling, and with a snort, lowered his head to the water.

Josh remained where he was, rifle ready. The horse finished drinking and moved to graze in the green grass along the creek. Insects buzzed, and water gurgled over rocks. A pair of turkey vultures wheeled overhead, and from somewhere beyond the creek, came the harsh, repetitive call of a shrike. The horned toad skittered into the grass. Josh strained, but could detect nothing out of the ordinary. Assuming he was alone, he placed the rifle against the rock, and with a final look around, squatted beside the creek.

Cold water splashed onto his face came as welcome relief in the dry summer heat. Josh lowered himself to his stomach and drank deeply. He had his hands under him, preparing to push himself up, when a pebble splashed into the water near his face. He looked up and froze.

Indians!

The sun at their backs, there were four of them on horseback, silhouetted against searing blue sky on the opposite bank. Josh looked to where his rifle leaned against the rock.

"Don't do it, Josh."

Ethan? Josh squinted into the light, looking from one man to the next, unsure which had spoken. He heard brief words in Lakota, and one man separated himself from the others and rode forward. As the pony splashed into the creek, Josh moved to stand.

"Stay where you are, Josh. Wait 'til I'm across."

Josh settled on his haunches, watching as Ethan allowed the horse to pick its way across the creek. It *was* a horse, he saw, now that the light was no longer directly behind it. Anger tightened in his chest when he saw the 'US' branded on its shoulder.

Ethan guided Faria out of the creek, bringing her to a stop between Josh and his rifle. "You can stand up now."

Jaw clenched, Josh got to his feet, eyeing the stranger that was his brother. Ethan's skin had darkened under the western sun, all but a pale mass of puckered skin below his right collarbone. His hair, hanging loose, reached halfway to his waist. Downy feathers at the back of his head shifted in the breeze. Earrings made from pounded brass and white shells dangled from his ears, and a wide silver armband adorned his left forearm.

Ethan swung a leg over the mare's neck and slid to the ground. On foot, he seemed taller than Josh remembered, no longer a skinny boy, but a man—broad shouldered, lean, and extremely fit. His face, in many ways familiar, was the most changed.

It's the eyes, Josh decided, unnerved by the cool assurance in them. Ethan was so changed that when he spoke, the familiar voice came as a shock.

"What are you doing here, Josh?"

"Looking for you."

Ethan's expression didn't alter. "I meant, what are you doing here alone? It isn't safe."

"I do a lot of traveling on my own. There's not always someone going my way when I want to go. It's friends like yours that make it—" Josh glanced across the creek, and the words died on his lips. "What the... ?" Ethan's companions had vanished.

"They're around. Keeping an eye out." Ethan's lips twitched in a brief smile. "Like I said, it's not safe."

Josh's eyes narrowed, and he nodded agreement. "I thought you were shot back at the bridge."

"A good horse. I was sorry to lose him." Ethan's stance altered slightly. "Why are you here Josh? Has something happened? Are Ma and Pa all right?"

"They're fine. I brought you something." Josh took another look around. "All right if I go get it?"

"I don't see why not."

Josh walked to his horse, opened the flap on one of his saddlebags, and pulled out the charred remains of the book. Opening it, he extracted a folded sheet of paper from between the pages.

"Pa made a copy. He and Ma have the original." He held the letter out to Ethan.

For several seconds, Ethan simply stared at it. Josh saw his composure slip.

Ethan recovered himself, and took it. Without looking at Josh, he moved several steps away, unfolding the paper as he went.

Executive Mansion. Washington. Verdict set aside. Sentence disapproved. The words jumped out as he skimmed rapidly down the page. Reaching the end, his eyebrows rose. If the copy was exact, the original had been signed by President Lincoln himself.

Ethan sank down on one knee and read the letter through thoroughly. There was no mention of murder; his escape would not be held against him. Ethan tilted his head back and closed his eyes. He had been fully exonerated, exactly what he'd once prayed for. He knew he should feel something—joy, vindication, relief—but the news meant nothing. It was as if it were meant for someone else.

"Ethan?"

Ethan folded the letter and stood up. His expression wasn't what Josh expected.

"What's the matter? It's good news, isn't it? You're free to come home."

"I am home, Josh."

Indignation burned color into Josh's cheeks, lent harshness to his voice. "What are you talking about?" He waved an arm. "Home? Here? I've been riding for months looking for you. Ma and Pa are waiting. And what about Kate? And Elizabeth? You promised you'd come home."

Ethan stiffened. "Elizabeth? What does she have to do with it?"

"You made her a promise, Ethan. So did I. I promised I'd bring you back."

"Back where? Mobile?"

"Lewistown."

Ethan's brows drew together. "I don't understand. Elizabeth's in Illinois?"

"Yes."

"What's she doing there?"

"She came looking for you."

Ethan stared at him in disbelief. "Why?"

"To marry you. Hoping you'd give your daughter a name."

Daughter? The word struck Ethan like a blow. Shocked eyes opened wide, and he fell back a step.

"Sarah Amelia. Born last September. We call her Emma."

Ethan shook his head. "No."

"No what, Ethan? You're telling me you didn't expect it? After what you said went on in Mobile?"

"No!" Ethan turned and walked away.

"Ethan!" Josh took several steps after him.

A daughter! He had made peace with never seeing his family again; justified breaking his promise to Elizabeth. *But a daughter?* A daughter changed everything. Ethan came to a stop several yards upstream, staring unseeing at the distant hills.

Josh watched him for nearly a minute before turning away. Ethan's mare had raised her head when he walked away, but now both horses grazed, the lazy swish of tails and the tearing of grass mingling with the gurgle of the creek. Josh ran his eyes over the nearest hills, then walked to his rifle. Another look around, and he picked it up. As he'd anticipated, nothing happened. He sat down on the rock, the Henry across his knees, and waited.

He heard the distant cry of a hawk and thought nothing of it. Moments later, it came again, this time from just beyond the creek. Josh twisted, squinting into the sun, trying to spot the bird.

"I'll be back."

Ethan spoke directly behind him, causing him to start. Scooping up his horse's reins, he vaulted into the saddle. "Wait for me."

Josh sprang to his feet. "Where are you going?"

"I'll be back." Ethan urged the mare into the creek. "Tomorrow morning. Wait for me."

As he splashed out on the other side, another rider rose, as if from the earth, to join him. Side by side, they urged their mounts into a canter. Moments later, they topped a ridge and were gone.

Josh looked around, wondering what had driven them off. His answer came from the smudge of dust rising to the east above the Platte Road. *Cavalry*, he thought. *Or wagons.* He looked back the way Ethan had gone. Only settling dust proved he'd been there. Josh mounted his horse and guided it across the creek, locating the gully he'd overlooked. Not seeing it had been a mistake—a big one that, under other circumstances, might have proved fatal. Josh drew the back of his hand across his mouth, wondering how long they'd watched him, unnerved by how close they'd come without his knowing.

AUGUST

29

"Two Moons is not himself," Fat Bear said, and his companions, gathered around the tiny fire, nodded agreement. "The words of his white brother trouble him."

The wagons had been miles distant, hours from La Prele Creek, but Ethan had seized them as an excuse to get away. Josh's news had rocked him to his core; he needed time to think.

Now he followed the curve of the creek, walking away from the concealed place near the base of the red cliff where they'd made camp for the night. Millions of stars, and the faint glow of a new moon, were all that distinguished sky from earth as he picked his way to the top of the soaring arc of rock that formed a natural bridge over the water. Not far off, a coyote howled. Others joined it, an eerie chorus of yips and shrieks that echoed off the steep walls of the little canyon.

As abruptly as it had begun, the howling stopped. An owl hooted, then was silent. A faint breeze stirred the prairie grasses, and the moon dipped toward the distant horizon. Sitting cross-legged on his robe, Ethan barely noticed.

A faint lightening in the east had begun separating sky from the inky crest of the canyon wall when he finally reached a decision. Gathering his blanket against the early morning chill, Ethan sat where he was, tired but at peace, watching light spread across the land.

The tops of the hills shed darkness first, ridges gaining definition as light spread across their face. Red outcroppings of rock caught fire next, separating from humps of blue-gray sage and yellow grass. Closer, the sandstone cliff glowed crimson, traced through with the shadowy veins of green scrub sprouting from the cracks. In the canyon below, the highest leaves on the elms and cottonwoods caught the light next. It wasn't until sunlight sparkled across water, glinting off white sand at the broad bend in the creek, that Ethan pushed himself to his feet and made his way down the rocky slope.

* * *

Josh spent the night within the circle of wagons. More than two hours had elapsed between Ethan's departure and the time he first set eyes on them, a faint line of dirty white beneath a great cloud of dust that gradually separated itself into a train of sixteen wagons. Another hour, and as the sun sank low, he rode to meet them. In response to their nervous questions, he told them the only Indians he'd seen that day were friendly. Reassured, the emigrants circled their wagons on level ground between the station and the river and invited Josh to share their meal. He spent the evening among them, swapping tales and catching up on news from the States.

He was preparing to ride the next morning, back up La Prele Creek to meet Ethan, when one of the men called to him, asking him to lend a hand jacking up a wagon. Most of the train was already heading out, wagons, loose stock, and people on foot spread in a diminishing line along the river. The occupants of the remaining wagons were nervous about staying, afraid of being left too far behind.

Josh led his horse toward the wagon where a Negro man, his wife and daughter were hurriedly unloading their possessions onto the ground. One of the rear wheels leaned at a crazy angle. As Josh approached, another wagon pulled away.

The three remaining men strained, raising the empty wagon box so the women could wedge rocks under the axle. The Negro was still making repairs when the last two wagons rumbled past.

"Hey!" Josh shouted taking several steps after them. "We still need your help."

The eyes of the man handling the reins of the nearest wagon remained fixed firmly ahead. On the seat beside him, the woman looked around guiltily. A sharp word, and she turned away.

"They was kind to help."

Josh turned. The Negro woman, holding her daughter close, was staring after the wagons.

"It was good of them to stay fo' as long as they did."

Josh stared at the daughter, seeing her clearly for the first time. The man's skin was dark, the woman's lighter, but the girl was, to all appearances, white.

"I ain't her pappy," the man said, noting Josh's expression. "He 'uz white man, a slave owner. Same as Hattie's pappy. Rose is three-quarter white. What they calls a quadroon." He extended a hand. "Name's Josiah. Much obliged fo' you help."

Josh tore his eyes from the girl. "Let's get your things back in the wagon."

He helped them reload and was preparing to mount, one foot in the stirrup, when the girl gasped.

"They's Injuns!"

The three adults looked where she pointed. Atop a ridge several hundred yards to the southeast, were four Indians, the breeze gently shifting feathers and the ponies' tails. Josh made out Ethan among them, recognized his mare's pale mane and tail.

"It's all right," he said, swinging into the saddle and motioning Josiah to lower the ancient muzzle-loader he'd pulled from beneath the seat. "They don't mean any harm." Swinging an arm toward the train, he said, "Catch up while you still can. I'll go talk to them."

Josiah looked from Josh to the hilltop.

"Go!" Josh commanded, and Josiah snapped the reins over the mules' backs. He waited until they were underway before turning into the hills to talk to Ethan.

He looked tired. There were lines of strain around his eyes that hadn't been there before.

"I can't do it, Josh," Ethan said, staring across the broken hills in the direction his companions had gone. "I can't go back to Illinois."

"What the devil do you mean? You made a promise, Ethan. You have obligations."

"I know." Ethan ran a hand over his face. It fell to his side, and he looked at Josh. "It's all I've thought about since yesterday, but I can't do it. My life is here."

"Your life is *here*?" Josh repeated incredulously. "You have a daughter, Ethan. A little girl. Your life is with her and her mother."

"No, Josh. It isn't." Ethan held up a hand. "Wait. Before you start yelling, let me explain."

"Explain? What is there to explain? Nothing you say's gonna change things. You have responsibilities, and I made a promise. Unlike you, I intend to honor mine."

"A promise to Elizabeth."

"Yes. You're going back."

Ethan drew breath to argue, but instead shook his head. "There's no point, Josh. I don't love her."

"You bastard..."

"I thought I did, but I was wrong. After you told me about..." Ethan stumbled over his daughter's name. "...about Emma. After you told me about her, I considered going back. I swear I did. Turning my back on her's the hardest thing I've ever done, but I can't." He turned imploring eyes on his brother. "Too much has changed, Josh. I don't belong there."

"What the hell are you saying? Why not?"

"I'm not white."

"Not white?" Josh couldn't believe his ears. "Not *white?* Not now you're not. Look at you!" He waved a hand in disgust. "Take that stuff off, cut your hair, get dressed and come home."

"This is my home. I have a life here. Family."

"Family?"

"Ma's folks. Her mother. Aunts, uncles, cousins. I'm not going back, Josh. Nothing you say's going to change that."

Josh glowered at him, then turned and took several steps away. He came storming back, spewing angry words. "I lied at your court-martial, Ethan. You know that? I lied when I told them I knew you. I didn't, but I figured being raised in our parents' home, you must have turned out decent enough. Honorable, even. That's what I told them, but I was wrong. The man who was decent and honorable is dead. Killed at Platte Bridge. He was a friend of mine, and you and your kind murdered him. Tortured him. Desecrated his body. If I'd known then what I know now, I'd have walked out of that prison and left you to rot. Hell, I might even have volunteered for the firing squad."

Ethan flinched, but said nothing, not trusting his voice.

Mistaking his silence for obstinacy, Josh pressed on. "I've wasted seven months of my life looking for you. As far as I'm concerned, when I ride away from here, you're dead. That's what I intend to tell Elizabeth."

"No! Please." Ethan's voice rose in alarm. "Don't let Ma think that!"

"So you do think of someone besides yourself."

"Think what you want of me, Josh. But please don't tell Ma I'm dead."

Josh snorted, an ugly sound. "Don't worry, Ethan. I wouldn't hurt her like that. I leave that to you."

"She understands. I know she does."

"She wants you to come home."

"She understands."

Knowing Ethan was right, and having no ready retort, Josh turned and stalked away. As he did, he saw they were being watched. A boy stood on the other side of the creek, bow in hand, arrow notched.

Ethan saw him, too. He shouted, and their rapid exchange ended with the boy walking away.

"Cousin," Ethan muttered as Kicking Bird disappeared behind the bushes clumped along the creek. "He's supposed to be minding the ponies."

Still fuming, Josh stood with his back to him, not bothering to reply. Ethan eyed him for several moments before walking to the mare and removing a small rawhide case from behind his saddle.

"She loves you," Josh muttered.

"I know. I love her, too. But she understands."

Josh spun around. "I'm talking about Elizabeth. How do I tell her you're never coming back? Convince her she needs to move on with her life, marry someone who cares for her."

"Someone like you, Josh?"

The words, softly spoken, shocked Josh from his anger. Ethan watched as realization dawned.

"If you love her, you should marry her."

"She loves you."

"Give her this." Ethan drew two folded pieces of paper from the case. "If nothing else, maybe this'll convince her." He held the letters out, then quickly pulled them back. "The other's for Ma," he said, suddenly uncertain. "You'll give it to Pa to read it to her?"

Josh walked to him and took the letters, eyes never leaving his brother's face. "I don't understand you, Ethan."

"I thought maybe you would. You of all people, Josh. You're the only one I ever told it all to."

"You're wrong. I don't understand. I never will."

The smile Ethan offered him was fleeting and sad. He turned away, stuffing the case into the rolled buffalo robe behind his saddle. Josh's eyes lit on the scars on his back, registering them for the first time.

"Those from Sand Creek?"

Ethan glanced over his shoulder, saw where he was looking, and nodded.

"They shot you in the back?"

"Yes."

"I didn't know."

Ethan placed a foot in the stirrup and swung aboard the mare. "Go back to Illinois, Josh. Make Elizabeth happy." He pulled Faria's head around, turning her in a tight circle, and looked down at his brother. "Take good care of my daughter." His voice cracked, and the mare sprang forward, plunging into the creek. On the far side, Ethan was joined by the boy and a woman driving half a dozen ponies.

"I didn't mean it," Josh yelled. "Ethan!"

Ethan didn't pause, didn't look back. Three more riders emerged from the surrounding hills to join him.

"I'm sorry."

Josh stood for a long time, watching the place where they'd disappeared. At last, he looked at the letters, sorely tempted to read them. Instead, he placed them carefully between the burnt pages of the book and slid them into his saddlebag. Mounting his horse, he rode slowly down to the road.

A train of white-covered wagons rumbled across the plain west of Fort Laramie. The dry earth, long since turned to powder by iron wheels and tromping feet, sent up great choking clouds of dust. Whipped by a steady wind, it virtually obscured all but the lead wagons.

Distant from the broad stretch of trampled earth that was the emigrant road, prairie dogs, made curious by sound and vibration, stood upright beside their holes. A warning whistle sent them diving for the safety as the hooves of loose stock tore into virgin earth, trampling brittle grasses, breaking off clumps of dirt and sending them cascading into the holes.

A lot of wagons, Josh thought when he saw them. *At least thirty.*

He urged his horse into a canter, swinging in a wide arc to avoid them, worried that any form of contact would delay him. It had taken a while for it to sink in, but now that it had, he was in a hurry—headed home to Illinois and Elizabeth with Ethan's blessing.

Atop a distant pine-dotted ridge, Ethan watched him go.

"There are many this time," Fat Bear commented, gazing at the white-topped wagons.

Long Face nodded. "When will they stop coming?" he asked, turning to his cousin who knew so many things.

"Never." Ethan's eyes followed Josh as he disappeared into the dust. He'd seen him safe to Fort Laramie; there was nothing more he could do. "He will find his own way now," he said turning Faria's head. *Time to go home.*

I have tried to keep the facts as accurate as possible while inserting fictional characters into historical events. Where accounts vary, I have taken the liberty of choosing what best fit the story.

The Thirty-sixth Illinois did indeed exist, mustered in on September 23, 1861, and fought in every important battle in the West, including Pea Ridge, Perryville, Stones River, Chickamauga, Missionary Ridge, Resaca and Adairsville. The 36th was comprised of companies A through H and K, drawn from Kane, McHenry, Warren, Kendall, Grundy and DuPage Counties, Illinois. Company J from Fulton County is entirely fictional.

Cahaba Federal Prison, described by some as an unfinished warehouse for agricultural products, by others as a former warehouse fallen into disrepair, may have housed a small number of Union prisoners as early as 1862. However, former prisoner Jesse Hawes states that he found no mention of the prison in the official papers of the Confederate Government prior to the fall of 1863. According to Hawes, the stockade walls and the first few bunks were added early in 1864, but those dates vary by historian, and I have taken the liberty of including them in the autumn of 1863.

Conditions at Cahaba were much as described, growing progressively worse as the war continued and the number of men incarcerated there increased. Prisoners co-existed with hoards of large rats and were infested with fleas and lice. They slept packed close together on hard bunks, or on the ground, with blankets estimated at two for every five men. The water supply was sulphurous and polluted, as much a contributor to sickness and diarrhea as the decayed beef distributed as rations. And though Captain Henderson was a kind-hearted, compassionate man, the commandant in later years was a brutal drunk, as hated and feared by his captives as the fictional Sergeant Shunk.

Courts-martial during the Civil War were commonplace. For minor offences, such as poor discipline at parade or losing part of a uniform, enlisted men were tried by regimental or garrison court-martial, informal tribunals that were often held during active combat and rarely recorded. Major offences such as desertion, robbery, rape and murder were tried by general court-martial, the highest form of military tribunal, and though recorded, many files are missing or incomplete. What is apparent, according to recent statistics compiled by James M. McPherson, is that ethnicity and race were indeed factors in executions. While only 26% of white soldiers in the Union Army were foreign-born, and 9% black, these two groups accounted for 54% of the men sentenced to death during the war. The number of foreign-born whites executed was 28% higher than the average for the entire army, the number of blacks, 133%.

I have endeavored to keep the court-martial proceedings as accurate as possible while enhancing what was no doubt a very dry process with a touch of courtroom theatrics, including the presence Josh and the other men from the Thirty-sixth who most certainly would not have been summoned from Nashville.

Nancy Jane Morton was nineteen when she was captured by the Cheyenne. Her manuscripts, one written shortly after her release, the other a few years prior to her death in 1912, offer vastly different accounts of her capture and captivity. The first contains an emotional account of her capture, portions of which I have paraphrased in her dialogue with George and Ethan, but it is only in the later manuscript, which was no doubt influenced by intervening events, that she makes mention of intervention by George Bent.

The Cheyenne and Lakota, need it be said, did not have written histories. The Lakota had their winter counts, symbols used to signify a memorable event by which each winter (year) would be remembered. Beyond that, the record was oral, a recounting of significant events in a man's life, the earliest of which may have occurred in young adulthood. Rarely was there mention of childhood, family or aspects of daily life.

Written records, relayed to historians by aged warriors, dredged from fading memories, and no doubt influenced by more recent events, were subject to error not only in translation, but by historians themselves as they attempted to affix dates and reconcile white place names with locations that may have had any number of Indian names. Thus, it is to George Bent who, in his correspondence with George Hyde, supplied the Cheyenne perspective on historical events, that I owe a tremendous debt of gratitude.

ABOUT THE AUTHOR

Born and raised in Casper, Wyoming, Paulie Jenkins has been honored as an exemplary alum by the University of Wyoming and by the Los Angeles Drama Critics Circle for career achievement in lighting design. During a successful career in the theatre, she has designed the lighting for productions at regional theatres across the country, as well as theme park attractions at Disneyland, Tokyo DisneySea, Lotte World Korea, and Universal Studios/Hollywood. She and her husband reside in Long Beach, California.

Made in the USA